Moonlit Gardens

She stood on the bedchamber balcony welcoming the soft night air on her skin. Then she turned and saw him standing across the room, gazing longingly at her. He held out his arms, and suddenly she was shy. His hand slowly caressed her silken hair, and a tremor ran through her. "Tis been a long, long time, my darling," he whispered.

Pleasures Yet Untasted

"Francis! Kiss me!" And she raised her head up.

For a moment he gazed lovingly at the face turned expectantly to him. His slender fingers explored it, gently touching her cheeks, her closed eyelids, her nose, her mouth. Then he bent, his arms circling her waist, pressing her against him, his mouth tenderly touching hers.

Eternal Desire

Deep within her a flame of passion flickered, and she shuddered. He had always made love to her with incredible gentleness, yet she felt tonight a fierceness lurking beneath the calm. The mouth on hers suddenly became more demanding. His hands caressed her long back, and she moaned softly, her body beginning to tremble weakly against his. . . .

Other Avon Books by
Bertrice Small

THE KADIN

BERTRICE SMALL

Love Wild And Fair

AVON BOOKS ◆ NEW YORK

LOVE WILD AND FAIR is an original publication of Avon Books. The
work has never before appeared in book form.

AVON BOOKS
A division of
The Hearst Corporation
1350 Avenue of the Americas
New York, New York 10019

Copyright © 1978 by Bertrice Small
Inside cover author photograph by Roger Thurber
Published by arrangement with the author
Library of Congress Catalog Card Number: 78-59085
ISBN: 0-380-40030-8

First Avon Books Printing: February 1978

AVON TRADEMARK REG. U.S. PAT. OFF. AND IN OTHER COUNTRIES, MARCA
REGISTRADA, HECHO IN CANADA.

Printed in Canada

UNV 20 19

To Susan Chilton and Terry Kenneally
with love—
May they each some day find their own
love wild and fair.

BOOK I

BOOK II

BOOK I

BOOK I

Part I

❧ § ❧

The Earl of Glenkirk

Chapter 1

❧ ❧ ❧

"I WISH," said Ellen More-Leslie severely, "that ye would not wear breeches when ye ride, Mistress Catriona. It is ever so unladylike."

"But ever so practical," said the beautiful young girl. "Dinna scold me, Ellie, or I'll send ye home to marry that nice farmer yer mother's had such hopes of!"

"God's toenail, ye wouldn't!"

"Nay. Not really," giggled Ellen's mistress. "Unless, of course, ye want to, Ellie. He is a fine, upstanding man. Why won't ye?"

"There's only one thing 'upstanding' I want from a man, and the farmer's nae got it! Come now, off wi yer riding clothes. Whew! Ye smell like the stables! Ye know the earl is coming to dinner this night to help celebrate yer birthday. I canna believe ye are fifteen. I can remember that stormy December night ye were born."

Catriona stripped off her clothes. She had heard this story many, many times before.

"The snow swirled about Greyhaven, and oh, how the winds howled and roared," continued Ellen. "The old countess, yer great-grandmam, insisted on being wi yer mother. I had just had my seventeenth birthday. I was the youngest of my family, and been spoilt something fierce, but as I showed no signs of wedding and

5

settling down, my old granny spoke to her mistress, yer great-grandmam, and they decided I should look after the new baby. Old Lady Leslie took one look at ye, and said, 'This one's for my laddie Glenkirk.' Sure enough ye were barely out of nappies when she was arranging yer betrothal. If only she could have lived to see ye grown and wed, but she died the following spring, and me old granny followed her but a few weeks later."

While Ellen talked she worked, setting up a bath for her young mistress in a great oak tub placed before the fire. Pouring scented oil into the steaming water, she called out, "Come now, my lady. 'Tis ready."

The girl sat dreaming while her shoulders and back were scrubbed. Then she took the soap from Ellen and finished up the job while Ellen fetched a small jar of shampoo from the cupboard. She poured a thin stream of golden liquid into Catriona's hair, added water, and, building up a sweet-smelling lather, washed and rinsed the girl's hair twice.

Seated by the fire, swaddled in a large towel, Catriona let Ellen dry her hair. The excess water removed, the tiring woman brushed and brushed the thick, heavy hair until it gleamed. Pinning up the dark-golden mass, she motioned her young mistress to stretch out and then massaged her with the pale-green cream her mother, Ruth, made up. The girl stood up, and Ellen handed her her silken undergarments. She was standing in her petticoat and blouse when her mother entered.

At thirty-six, Heather Leslie Hay was at the height of her beauty. She was radiant in a dark-blue velvet gown trimmed in gold lace, and a marvelous rope of pearls that Catriona knew had belonged to her great-grandmother. Her lovely dark hair was mostly hidden beneath a blue-and-gold cap.

"Your father and I wish to speak wi ye before our

guests arrive. Please come directly to our apartments when you are dressed."

"Yes, mama," said Catriona demurely as the door closed behind her mother.

Automatically she let Ellen dress her, all the while wondering what her parents wanted. She was their only daughter, having an older brother, Jemmie, eighteen, and three younger brothers. Colin was twelve, and the twins, Charlie and Hughy, were ten. Her parents had always been so involved with each other that the raising of their children had been left mostly to nursemaids and tutors. She had had to plan her own life from practically the very beginning.

It would have been different had her great-grandmother lived. She knew that. Tutors had been hired for Jemmie, but no one thought to teach Catriona how to read and write until she forced herself into Jemmie's lessons. When the startled tutor told her parents that their daughter learned faster than their heir, she was allowed to stay. Consequently she had been educated as a boy was, but only until Jemmie went away to school. After that it had been up to her.

She had insisted that her parents hire a tutor who was fluent in French so she might command that language. And she saw to it that the young man employed by her family also spoke Italian, Spanish, and German. Considering how thoroughly educated both her parents had been, there was no excuse for their neglect.

Twenty years after their marriage, Heather and James Hay were more in love than ever. The neglect of their offspring was innocent, a matter of thoughtlessness. The children were well fed, well clothed, and well housed. It did not occur to the young Master of Greyhaven or his wife that their children needed more than these essentials. The boys had felt secure in the

warm love of their nurses, but their daughter had
needed more. Ellen More-Leslie knew it, and did her
best. But Cat Hay grew up spoiled and willful, with
nobody to check her.

Standing in front of her pier glass, the girl studied
herself. Tonight she would meet her betrothed for the
first time in several years. He was twenty-four, and had
been to the University in Aberdeen. He had also been
to Paris, traveled extensively in Europe, and spent time
at Queen Bess' court in England. He was handsome,
assured, and well-spoken, she knew. He was also about
to sustain what she hoped was a severe shock to his ego.
She smoothed the forest-green velvet of her gown, and,
smiling, went off to see her parents. To her surprise her
oldest brother was there too.

Her father cleared his throat. "It was," he said
gravely, "always planned that ye marry Glenkirk sometime after yer sixteenth birthday. However, wi the un-
timely death of the third earl last summer, and young
Patrick's investiture as fourth Earl of Glenkirk, it has
been decided that yer marriage will be celebrated at
Twelfth Night."

Astounded, she looked at him. "Who decided,
father?"

"The earl and I."

"Wi'out asking me?" Her voice was angry.

"Asking you? Why daughter, ye were betrothed
eleven years ago. The marriage has always been a fact."
James Hay sounded annoyed. His daughter irritated
him. She always had. She was not the soft, gentle
creature his wife was.

"Ye might hae told me the new circumstances, and
then asked if I minded being wed a full year in advance!" she shouted at him. "I don't want to be married
now, and ye've wasted yer time entirely, for I hae no
intention of wedding Patrick Leslie at all!"

"Why ever not, dearest?" asked Heather. "He's such a fine young man. And ye'll be a countess!"

"He's a rutting bull, dearest mama! Since Uncle Patrick was thrown from his horse and broke his neck and the new earl came home, a day doesn't go by I dinna hear of his conquests! The countryside rings wi tales of his prowess in the bed, in the hay, under a hedge! I will nae wed wi the dirty lecher!"

The Master of Greyhaven was stunned by his daughter's furious outburst. Jemmie began to laugh, only to be silenced by a look from his mother. Heather realized, too late, that she had neglected a very important part of her daughter's education.

"Leave us," Heather commanded her husband and son. "Sit down, Catriona," she said to her daughter when the men had gone. "Do ye know anything of what goes on between a man and a woman in the marriage bed?"

"Aye," said the girl harshly. "He pushes his cock up the hole between her legs, and a couple of months later the baby comes out the same hole."

Heather closed her eyes a moment. Oh my child, she thought! In my great and consuming love for yer father I forgot ye were a woman too. Ye know nothing of the delights shared between lovers, and I dinna know if I hae the words to tell ye.

Opening her violet eyes, she took a deep breath.

"Ye are partly correct," Heather said calmly. "But the act of love between a man and a woman need not result each time in a baby. There are ways of preventing conception while still enjoying the delights of love. I shall be pleased to teach these things to ye before yer marriage."

The girl looked interested.

"Lovemaking is quite nice, Catriona."

"Is it? How, mama?" She sounded scornful.

Dear God, thought Heather, how do I explain? "Hae ye ever been kissed, my child? Perhaps some of yer boy cousins hae tried stealing kisses at parties?"

"Aye, they've tried, and I hae hit them hard! They dinna try any more."

Heather wanted to shriek her frustration. "Kissing is very pleasurable, Catriona. So is fondling. Deliciously so, I might say."

Cat looked at her mother as if she had lost her mind. "I canna imagine, mama, anything pleasurable at all about a man and a woman squeezing each other's bodies."

She was so damned superior that Heather lost her temper.

"Well, it is, daughter! I should know! Jesu, Cat, ye are woefully ignorant! Ye hae no idea what it means to be a woman, and that's my fault. In the next four and a half weeks ye shall learn. Ye will marry yer cousin of Glenkirk on Twelfth Night as we hae planned. It is a wonderful match, and ye are fortunate to hae gotten so good a one!"

"I will not marry him, mama!"

Heather took another tack. "Then what will ye do if ye dinna marry wi Glenkirk?"

"There are other men, mama. My dowry is quite large."

"Only to Glenkirk, my dear."

Cat's eyebrows rose in surprise. At last I have her attention, thought Heather, relieved. "Catriona. Your very large dowry is for Glenkirk only. Mam arranged it that way. Should ye marry anyone else, your dowry becomes quite modest."

"Did Grandmam not consider that Glenkirk might die, or even cry off?" demanded Catriona, outraged.

"If Patrick had died ye would hae married James. Mam meant for ye to be Countess of Glenkirk, and there was certainly no question of yer bridegroom's crying off. Come, child. Patrick Leslie is an educated, charming man. He will love ye, and be good to ye."

"I will not marry him!"

"The choice is not yers to make, my dear. Now, take that frown off yer face. By this time our guests will be arriving. Your cousins will all be here to wish you happy."

Her cousins! Oh, God! Fortunately, her uncles Colin and Ewan lived in Edinburgh, so she'd not have to contend with their broods. But the rest! The boys weren't so bad, but those six simpering girls!

Fiona Leslie was a widow at nineteen. Poor Owen Stewart had not withstood the rigors of the marriage bed. Lush, auburn-haired Fiona with her storm-gray eyes, her red pouting mouth, and her low-cut gowns. Next came sixteen-year-old Janet Leslie, who was to marry Fiona's brother, Cousin Charles, in the spring. Jan could scarcely contain her delight at being the future Countess of Sithean—the silly cow! Ailis Hay was already fifteen, and slated to marry James Leslie, Glenkirk's next brother. That marriage was at least two years off. Beth Leslie was sixteen, but adoring of her Uncle Charles, was to enter a convent in France soon. So she might have close family nearby, her fourteen-year-old sister, Emily, was betrothed to Uncle Donald's son, Jacques de Valois-Leslie. Last was little Mary Leslie, who, at thirteen, would wait three or four years before marrying Cat's brother, Jemmie. Cat hoped that by that time Mary would stop giggling at everything Jemmie said, though Jemmie didn't seem to mind.

Catriona entered the hall with her mother. At once she was surrounded by the cousins, and their good wishes. This was her birthday celebration, and she found it impossible to remain angry.

Suddenly Fiona was saying in her husky, feline voice,

"Cat, darling, here is your betrothed. Hasn't she grown, Patrick? She's almost a woman."

Catriona shot her older cousin a black look and, raising angry eyes, met the amused stare of Patrick, Earl of Glenkirk. His large, warm hand raised her little one to his lips. "Cousin." His voice was deeper than she remembered. "Ye were always lovely, Catriona, but tonight ye surpass every woman in this hall." Drawing her hand through his arm, he led her to the dais. Left alone, Fiona was surprised, and laughed. The earl seated his affianced at the main table. "Why are ye angry wi me?" he asked her.

"I'm nae angry wi you."

"Then gie me a smile, sweetheart."

She pointedly ignored him, and the Earl became irritated. When the meal had been cleared away and the dancing began, he found his aunt and, seeking the quiet of Greyhaven's library, demanded to know what ailed the girl.

"It's all my fault, Patrick," wailed Heather. "I am so sorry. I hae, wi'out meaning to, ignored a most important part of Catriona's education. The result is that she is void of emotion, and cold as ice."

"In other words, my beautiful, thoughtless aunt, ye hae been so wrapped up in yer Jamie that ye forgot to love Cat."

"But of course I love Cat!"

"Did ye ever say so? Did ye cuddle and cosset her as a baby? A child? A young girl? Nay, aunt. Ye had no time for it. Ye were too busy putting into practice wi the Master of Greyhaven all the delicious things Mam taught you!"

Heather blushed to the roots of her hair. "Patrick! What could ye possibly know of that?"

"What my mother told me," he grinned wickedly at her. "My mother assured me that my bride would be warm, and educated. Instead, aunt, I must thaw this ice maiden ye plan for me to wed."

"She says she will nae wed ye," said Heather in a little voice.

"God's bones!" swore Glenkirk. "Perhaps ye would enlighten me as to why not."

"I dinna know, Patrick," lied his aunt. "When her father told her this evening that the wedding had been moved up from next year to Twelfth Night, she became furious. She said no one had asked her opinion, but it didn't matter as she'd nae have ye."

"Have ye spoken to anyone of an earlier wedding?"

"We planned to announce it tonight."

"Aunt. Go discreetly, and bring my uncle to me."

Poor little Cat, he thought, when his aunt had gone. Left alone from babyhood to run yer own life. Then, suddenly, the largest moment in yer life is abruptly decided for ye. No wonder yer angry.

As to the other thing, he gave but the briefest thought. Leslie women were by nature hot-blooded, and once awakened to the world of sensual pleasures he knew Cat would bloom. It would take time and patience. But he was bored with easy conquests, and he had the luxury of time.

James Hay entered the library with his wife. "Well, nephew! What is so important that I must sneak away from my guests?"

"I think we should hold off an announcement of my wedding date, uncle. Catriona is obviously angry and frightened, and I would nae distress her."

"Girlish nonsense!"

"Was my Aunt Heather like that before ye were wed?"

"Nay." James Hay's voice became soft with remembrance. "She was all sweet eagerness."

"I congratulate ye on yer good fortune. Would ye deny me the same luck?"

"Heather and I were fairly well acquainted," mused James Hay.

"Precisely!" said the earl. "I hae been away for six years, studying and traveling. Cat wasn't even nine when I left. She doesna know me. I am foreign to her, and yet within four weeks' time she faces the terrifying prospect of being wedded and bedded wi a total stranger. Come, uncle! Ye've led a life of conjugal bliss. Gie me the time to win yer prickly daughter so I may hae the same pleasure."

"Well," reasoned the Master of Greyhaven, "the wedding was not scheduled until this time next year . . . but if she's not won over by then, willing or not, she goes to the altar!"

"Agreed," said Patrick. "But, uncle. You and my aunt must agree to something else. There will be times when my methods of wooing may seem strange, and perhaps even cruel. But no matter what happens in the courting, I plan to make Catriona my wife. Remember that."

"Aye, aye," assented the Master of Greyhaven, but his wife felt a little shudder at her nephew's words. Why, he loves her already, she thought, surprised. He has probably felt this way towards her since childhood. First he will woo her gently, but if that does not work, he will woo her harshly, for he means to have her. Oh, my innocent daughter! I hae best teach ye what I know before your impatient lover loses his patience and fills your belly wi his bairn.

She heard her nephew speak again.

"I will tell her myself of this change. She must not know that we ever discussed it."

When Patrick reentered the hall, Catriona was dancing with his brother, Adam. Taking his younger sibling's place, Patrick finished the dance with her. She was flushed, and laughing. It was all he could do not to tumble her there and then, so strong was his desire. He caught her hand and, drawing her away from their families into the privacy of a little alcove, told her, "I hae been thinking that perhaps we should nae wed until sometime next year. When I left Glenkirk ye were a little girl. I return to find ye a lovely woman. I am anxious to make ye my wife, sweetheart. But I realize ye don't really know me. Would ye mind if we took the time to know each other?"

For the first time that evening she smiled at him. "Nay, my lord. I would like that. But what if we find we don't like each other?"

He cocked an eyebrow. "Do ye snore, Catriona? Or perhaps chew the betel nut of the East?"

Laughingly she shook her head in the negative.

"Do ye like music, and poetry, and the melodious sounds of foreign tongues? Do ye like riding out in the misty quiet of a spring morning, or beneath a border moon on an autumn's evening? Does the first snow of winter delight ye? Do ye like bathing naked in a hidden stream on a hot summer's day?"

"Aye," she whispered softly, and for some reason her heart beat quickly. "I love all those things, my lord."

"Then, my dear, ye should love me, for I love those things also."

Catriona's thick dark-golden lashes brushed against her flushed cheeks and the little pulse in her throat quickened. My first breach in the ice, Patrick thought, and pressed his luck further. "Will ye seal our bargain wi a kiss?" he asked.

She raised her head, and her leaf-green eyes gazed at him a moment. Closing her eyes, she pursed her rosebud mouth at him. Gravely he touched her lips with his.

"Thank ye, Catriona," he said gently. "Thank ye for yer first kiss."

"How did ye know?"

"Innocence has a beauty all of its own, my love." He stood. "Let me escort you back to your guests."

When they appeared in the hall, Heather noted with relief that her daughter no longer looked sulky and her nephew looked content. He'll win her over, she thought. And looking on Glenkirk with a woman's eye, she said softly to herself, "Oh, my Cat! What a lovely adventure awaits ye!"

Chapter 2

❦ ❧

FIONA Leslie lay on her bed, musing about her cousin Patrick, the Earl of Glenkirk. She thought how very much she would like to be his countess. Instead, that milk-and-water virgin Catriona Hay was to be his wife! Ridiculous!

Fiona knew that there had once been talk of a match between her and Glenkirk. Then Grandmam had interfered, and she'd ended up married to that weak fool Owen Stewart. How she had hated the old lady for that. Grandmam had known it.

Owen had been sickly and, though eager for his lush, seventeen-year-old-bride, unable to consummate the marriage. It didn't matter at all to Fiona, who hadn't been a virgin since thirteen. She'd quickly found what she sought on her husband's estate.

His name was Fionn, and he was a huntsman. He was big and brutal with no sexual refinements, but when he pushed himself into her, she thought she'd go mad with delight. Then the impossible happened, and she miscalculated. She wouldn't believe she was pregnant, and by the time she'd accepted the fact, it was too late to rid herself of the brat.

She told her husband of her condition, expecting the weakling to accept it and keep his mouth shut. But again, she had miscalculated. Crawling from his sick-bed, he called her all the things she was, and told her

that come morning he would expose her to the world
for a whore. Here, however, Owen Stewart had miscalculated. While he slept, his wife smothered him with a
pillow. His death was put down to an asthmatic attack,
and much attention was lavished on his pregnant
widow.

When the child was born, only Fiona's maid, Flora
More-Leslie, attended her. The lusty boy was smuggled
out and given to a peasant couple who had recently lost
their own child. Fiona wanted no children cluttering
her life. A dead infant was substituted for her own,
and buried with much mourning in the Stewart family
vault. Fiona had not escaped unharmed, either. It had
been a hard birth. The doctor and midwife summoned
afterwards had agreed that Lady Stewart would never
bear another child. But her secret was safe. Only Flora
knew the truth, and Flora had cared for her since she
was a baby.

Fiona was gleeful this night, for she knew someone
else's secret. She had slipped into the library at Greyhaven to escape the attentions of her cousin, Adam
Leslie. Adam had been lusting after her since they were
twelve. Hidden behind the drapes drawn across the
window seat, she had heard the entire conversation
between Heather, Patrick, and the Master of Greyhaven.

She could not have been more delighted. Virgin Cat
was afraid of sex! Glenkirk would not put up with that
for long, and in the meantime Fiona intended to
dangle her ripe charms before him as often as she
possibly could without seeming indiscreet. She'd also
see that Cat continued to harbor fears.

"When ye smile like that, Mistress Fiona, I know it
bodes nae good. What mischief are ye about?"

"No mischief, Flora. I am just thinking what dresses
I'll wear to Glenkirk for Christmas."

Flora sighed delightedly. "Christmas at Glenkirk,"

she breathed. "Leslies of Sithean. Leslies of Glenkirk. Hays of Greyhaven. More-Leslies of Crannog. We haven't had a Christmas at Glenkirk wi all the family since yer grandmam died. I'm glad the new earl's put off mourning. The old Lord Patrick wouldna hae liked it. I imagine that since the earl's to be wed next year to Mistress Catriona they'll be celebrations regular at the castle again."

"Yes," purred Fiona. "Christmas should be lots of fun!"

But Cat unwittingly stole a march on her cousin Fiona. Ten days before everyone else was due, she arrived at Glenkirk by special invitation of her Aunt Meg, the dowager Countess of Glenkirk. Meg Stewart Leslie had been apprised of her niece's attitude by both her son and Heather, and she willingly supplied her eldest the opportunity to court his bride-to-be. She, too, had once arrived at Glenkirk a frightened bride, and Mam had welcomed her warmly with love and understanding. Mam was long gone, but Meg intended to pay her debt by helping Mam's favorite great-granddaughter, who was her own lovely niece.

The weather was perfect—cold and sunny. Patrick won his first victory when he presented Catriona with a snow-white mare. "She's a descendant of Mam's Devil-wind," he said. "Ye'll find her fast, surefooted, and loyal. What will ye call her?"

"Bana. It means 'fair' in the Gaelic."

"I know. I, too, speak the Gaelic."

"Oh, Patrick!" She flung her arms around his neck. "Thank you for Bana! Will ye and yer Dubh ride wi us?"

So they rode the hills about Glenkirk during the day, and in the evenings Catriona sat with her aunt and cousins in the family hall of the castle. The fire blazed merrily while Catriona and the young Leslies played at charades and danced with each other. The dowager countess smiled indulgently, and the earl swallowed his frustration, for he was never alone in the evenings with his betrothed.

Suddenly his luck changed. The night before the entire family was to descend upon them, he found her alone. It was late. His mother had retired early and, expecting the others to seek their beds, he had gone to the library to do some estate work. Returning late through the family hall he saw a figure seated alone on the floor before the fire.

"Cat! I thought ye sought yer bed." He sat down beside her.

"I like sitting alone before a fire in the dark of night," she said.

"Do ye like Glenkirk, my love?"

"Aye," she said slowly. "I wasna sure I would. I remember it to be bigger, but I suppose I saw it wi a child's eyes. It's really a lovely little castle."

"Then ye will be happy living here?"

"Yes." Her voice was a whisper.

They sat quietly for several minutes, then Catriona spoke.

"My lord, would ye kiss me? Not like before, but a *real* kiss. I hae spoken wi both Mama and my Ellen. They say the kiss ye gave me to seal our bargain was quite proper, but—" she paused, and bit her lower lip—"but a real kiss has more substance."

She lay back, her leaf-green eyes glittering in the firelight. Slowly he bent and touched her lips with his. Gently, gradually, he increased the pressure, and then her arms were around him.

"Ohh, my lord," she said breathlessly when his mouth released hers. "That was ever so much better! Again, please."

He willingly complied and, with astonishment, felt her little tongue flick along his lips. A moment later she spoke again.

"Did ye like that, my lord? Mama said the sensation is quite pleasurable."

It suddenly came to him that she was experimenting with the things Heather had told her about, but was feeling nothing herself. Chancing her anger, he caught her in his arms and, running his hand from the nape of her neck to the base of her spine, molded her to his body. Fiercely, his mouth took possession of hers. Using all his expertise, he gently but insistently forced her lips apart. Plunging deep within her mouth, he caressed her tongue with his, and rejoiced silently when a great shudder tore through her. He could feel her rising panic as she tried to struggle, but he held her firmly until it pleased him to release her.

"Patrick," she gasped, and burst into tears.

He gathered her up and soothed her. "There, hinny. There," he murmured at her while his big hand stroked her lovely hair. "Dinna greet, my love."

"Why did ye do *that*?" she demanded through her tears.

"Because, my precious little bride-to-be, ye were experimenting wi me the things yer lovely, feather-headed mother has told you. Ye did them without feeling anything yourself. Never, my sweet Cat, never make love unless ye feel it yourself."

"I did feel it."

"What did ye feel?" he asked.

"I felt—I felt—Oh, God's foot! I dinna know what I felt then. I simply didn't want ye to stop, but then I did. I was all churned up inside, and . . ." She stopped, confused.

He stood and helped her up. Putting his hands on her shoulders, he looked gravely down into her face. "When I was a lad of thirteen years I was formally betrothed to a wee maid of but four. After the religious ceremony was over, we were seated in a place of honor, and a servant brought refreshments. The wench's blouse was low, and I was just beginning an interest in the female form. I could not take my eyes from those fat white bouncing boobs. Suddenly, the child by my side poured her wine into the girl's cleavage, and scolded me roundly. I fell in love in that moment, and I have stayed in love all these years."

She looked up at him. "I am forever hearing of your conquests. How can ye claim to love me when yer life is so full wi other women?"

"A man has special needs, Cat. If he is unmarried and has no wife to satisfy those needs, then he must seek elsewhere."

"Do ye seek elsewhere now?" she asked.

"Especially now. Damnit, Cat! I want you! Naked in my bed wi your lovely hair in disarray crying out for love of me!"

She felt a little thrill run through her at his words, and looking up at him said, "If ye will gie up yer other women, Patrick, I will wed wi ye on St. Valentine's Day of the new year. If ye would say good morning and good night to yer true love, then it must be adieu to all your other women."

"Would ye dictate to me, sweetheart?"

"I will nae share ye, Patrick. I will come to ye a virgin, and ye may make of me what ye will for yer pleasure. But I must be yer only love."

"When we are wed I will consider it," he laughed. "Now off to yer cold bed, you nagging little minx, before I lose my self-control and take away yer right to wear yer beautiful hair unbound on our wedding day."

Giving him a pouting look, she left the room. Patrick chuckled. What a wench she was, his Cat Hay! Not yet married to him, and already trying to run his life. Well, he knew two things now. His bride was not the ice maiden he thought she might be, and life with her was certainly not going to be dull!

Chapter 3

❧§❧

BY the following afternoon, Glenkirk Castle bulged with Leslies and Hays. Because she was to marry the earl, Catriona was spared the ordeal of the dormitory with her cousins. Fiona also escaped that fate because of her age, and because she was a widow.

Upon learning that Catriona had been at the castle for the past ten days she hurried to find her and do what mischief she could. Cat was embroidering in the family hall, and was alone. Fiona settled herself.

"Well, little cousin. How do ye like Glenkirk Castle?"

"Very much," said Cat. "I'll enjoy being mistress here." She shot Fiona a wicked look.

Fiona gritted her teeth. "Yer a brave lass to go into the wolf's maw as calmly as ye do."

"What on earth do ye mean?"

"Lord, child! Ye must know Glenkirk's reputation."

"His women." Cat feigned boredom. "God's toenail, Fiona! Everyone knows Glenkirk's a devil wi the lasses. Tell me something I don't know."

"All right, my dear, I shall." She lowered her voice, and leaned forward. "They say that Glenkirk's cock is too big. They say he's built like a bull. Having been married I know, and I must pass this on to ye. We Leslie women are very tiny. A big cock can tear us asunder. Why my late husband, Lord Stewart, was of

23

an average size, yet when he planted himself in me on our wedding night . . ." She paused for effect, gleefully noting Catriona's white face. "Well, cousin! The pain was terrible, and it got worse each time. God assoil him! It was a mercy to me when Owen died!"

"But I'm a Hay, Fiona. It canna be the same wi me!"

"Yer mother was a Leslie, cousin. Daughters are fashioned after their mothers. I certainly dinna envy ye."

Terrified, Cat repeated the conversation to Ellen. "Not so," said Ellen firmly. "That Fiona Stewart is just trying to scare ye. There's but a moment's pain the first time when the virgin shield is broken. After that it's just fine. Yer cousin is hot for the earl herself, the wicked hussy! She's trying to frighten ye off. Little silly." She ruffled the girl's hair. "All yer mother does is moon after yer father. Is that the act of a woman who suffers constant pain?"

Annoyed at having been so easily spooked by her feline cousin, Cat watched Fiona to see if Ellen was right. Fiona grasped every opportunity to be near Patrick, to wear her lowest-cut gowns, to display her ample charms. The bitch, Cat thought! The red-haired bitch! She looked for her brother. Finding him, she said,

"Jemmie, tell me what ye know about Cousin Fiona."

Jemmie snickered. "It's said she's overgenerous wi her favors, but I hae never gotten her into bed. They say the bairn she bore Stewart was not his. He was such a weakling it's doubtful he ever stuck it in her." He looked at his sister. "Ye like Glenkirk now, don't ye, Cat?"

"Aye."

"Then beware Cousin Fiona, for it's plain to see she's stalking him, though I doubt poor Glenkirk realizes it."

But Patrick was quite well aware of Fiona's interest,

and had Cat not been staying in the castle, he might
even have amused himself for a bit with his hot-
blooded, red-haired cousin. He knew the whispers about
her were probably true, but it might be fun to confirm
them.

One night just after Christmas, Fiona attempted to
force the earl. With everyone else long in bed, the earl
remained talking before the fire with his brother, Adam.
He wanted a match between the Forbes heiress and
Adam. Adam, however, convinced him that their
youngest brother, seventeen-year-old Michael, would be
far better suited to thirteen-year-old Isabella Forbes
than he.

"I want to marry soon, and not a child. Michael
willna be ready to wed for three or four more years
yet. By that time the Forbes lass will be ripe. Make the
match between them. She'll go mad for his handsome
baby face."

Patrick laughed. "All right, brother, but who's the
maid yer saving yerself for?"

Adam smiled, and his eyes narrowed. "I've nae
opened my suit wi her, but I will soon."

The brothers sat awhile longer, drinking the mulled
wine special to the holiday season. Both were tall, as
their father had been, but where Patrick had his
mother's dark hair and the Leslies' green-gold eyes,
Adam had the Leslies' red hair—his was a warm russet
shade—and the amber eyes of the Stewarts.

Now, warm with brotherly camaraderie and rich
red wine, they climbed the stairs to their apartments.
"I've some good whisky from old MacBean's still,"
said the earl. "Come in, lad, and hae a drop wi me.
'Twill help ye to sleep." He opened the door to his
bedroom and walked in, his brother close behind him.

"*Jesu,*" Adam gasped. On his brother's bed, the
firelight playing across her naked white body, lay

Fiona Stewart. "Why, bless me, coz! Yer the sweetest sight I've seen tonight!"

"What the hell do ye do here?" demanded the earl, suddenly very sober and icy with rage.

"Ye wouldna come to me, Patrick," she said softly, "so I hae come to you."

He could smell the warm musk of her perfumed body. "I pay for my whores, Fiona. How much do ye charge?"

"Patrick!" she pleaded huskily with him. "Please! I'm mad for ye, cousin! Marry yer milksop virgin if ye must, but take me! Be my lover. Ye'll nae regret it, Patrick!"

"By God," said Adam dryly. "What's yer secret, brother? I've yet to receive such a marvelous invitation from any woman."

Patrick turned to his younger brother. "Ye want that?"

Adam looked back at him. "Aye. For some time now."

"Then take it! I'll sleep in your room tonight."

"No!" screamed Fiona angrily. "I want you, not that boy coxcomb!"

"My dear cousin," said the earl calmly, "from all the rumors I hear, ye hae certainly had much experience. Ye must know that making love to someone ye don't want is not only aesthetically distasteful, but damned boring to boot." Turning his back on her, he walked from the room.

Adam closed the door behind his brother and shot the iron bolt home with a loud thunk. "Well, Fiona luv," he drawled lazily, "I hae been wanting to get ye in this position for some time now."

"Go to hell," she spat furiously at him, and standing up she tried to walk to the door.

Adam reached out and, grasping an arm, pulled her

back. "Nay, hinny," he said cruelly, crushing a pointed breast in his hand. "Nay! Tonight ye'll spread yer legs for me!" He pushed her back onto the bed, and Fiona suddenly felt afraid.

Since she'd first been tumbled in the straw of a darkened stable at thirteen by her father's head groom, she'd always held the upper hand in these situations. Helplessly she lay on the bed, and watched her cousin slowly strip off his clothes. The back and shoulders that faced her were broad and well-muscled. They ran into a narrow waist. Off came his trunk hose. His hips were slim, his buttocks nicely rounded. Adam Leslie turned around, and Fiona gasped in shock. Once she'd seen her father's prized stud stallion mounting a mare in a field. She'd hoped then she would find a man with one as big. Now suddenly he stood laughing before her.

"Aye, sweetheart! For five years ye've been running away from the very thing ye wanted."

"Jesu," she whispered. "Ye'll kill me wi that!" But the moist, secret place between her legs was throbbing hungrily. Practically crying, she held out her arms to him. His body quickly covered hers, and he felt her warm hand eagerly reach to guide him. Carefully he pushed into her, and having ascertained that she could easily receive his bulk, he began a slow, sensuous movement. Her body writhed wildly beneath him, her nails raking his back. As his movements became faster and fiercer, she began a low moaning that a few minutes later culminated in a shriek of pure joy.

He rolled off her and lay quietly catching his breath. Then, raising himself on one elbow, he looked down at her and said, "For a wench who's been whoring since she was barely pubescent, ye know damned little, and it's yer own fault! Ye've confined yer activities to amateurish lowlifes." Bending his head, he thoughtfully nibbled for a minute at a pointed breast while his fingers played between her legs. "Now I, sweetheart," he continued, "have been educated by the finest whores in Paris, London, and Aberdeen. I shall happily teach ye everything I know."

Still resisting him somewhat, Fiona said, "I've nae said I'd be yer mistress, you vain boy!"

"I dinna ask ye, my dear."

She looked puzzled.

"I am sure that by now," he said, "the church is used to giving Leslie cousins dispensations to wed."

Fiona was stunned. "I'm older than you," she protested feebly.

"By five whole weeks," he chuckled. "I'll be twenty next week, luv." He pulled her under him again, and she could feel his hardness against her leg.

"I dinna want ye!" she raged at him. "I want Glenkirk!"

"Ye can't have him, hinny. He doesn't want you." He forced her legs apart.

"Ye hae no money!" said Fiona. "Besides, I'll nae live in someone else's house!"

"I have quite a good income from investments Grandmam made for me, as do you. Alone I am worth more than many a belted earl. I also hae a share in the family shipping, and the sheep businesses. Ye have a house in Edinburgh that belonged to yer grandmother, Fiona Abernethy. We'll travel for several years, and when wee King Jamie is grown, we'll return, live in Edinburgh, and go to court." He pushed deep into her, then lay quiet.

Fiona never understood why she spoke, but she said, "I canna have any bairns. Stewart's brat ruined me."

"I know," he replied with irritating calm. "The midwife ye called afterwards has delivered at least three of my bastards. It cost me two gold pieces to get that information. And sweetheart, I know it wasna Stewart's babe." He laughed as she swore a string of oaths. "Let Patrick, Jamie, and Michael carry on the family name wi a pack of babies," he said. "I want just you. BUT if I ever catch ye wi another man, I'll beat ye black and blue, and deny ye this—" he thrust viciously in her— "for a month!" His amber eyes narrowed, and glowed down at her.

The thought of losing what she'd been seeking so long made a shudder run through her. Wrapping her legs around him, she whispered in a frightened voice, "I'll be good, Adam! I swear it!"

The following day, to everyone's surprise, Adam Leslie announced to his assembled family that he was marrying his cousin, Lady Stewart. Since neither his mother, nor Fiona's parents had been informed, pandemonium broke loose.

Patrick spoke up in his brother's defense. "They asked my permission," he lied smoothly, "but, uncle, I must apologize to you for not consulting wi you beforehand. My own upcoming nuptials have addled my brain." He turned to his younger brother and said sternly. "It was nae yer place to announce yer intentions until I had spoken to our uncle."

Adam looked properly contrite.

"Come, my uncle of Sithean," said the Earl of Glenkirk. "Let us speak privately. Even a beautiful widow must have a dowry."

Before he could protest, the Lord of Sithean found himself borne off to the library, where Adam apprised him of the fact that his daughter would always be barren, and that he was lucky to get any son-in-law at all considering that fact.

"Then why do ye want her?" asked Sithean.

"Because, uncle, I love the minx."

Sithean said no more. He had never found his daughter particularly lovable, and he knew her reputation.

Considering himself lucky to be rid of her again, he named a very generous figure for her dowry and was accepted. The wedding was set for the spring.

When their uncle had left, Glenkirk turned to his brother. "Why?" he asked. "Ye could have had pretty Isabella Forbes, and legitimate sons."

"Because, Patrick, I really do love Fiona. I have since I was a boy."

"She's a whore! Forgie me, Adam, but she'll lie wi any man."

"Not now she won't. Dinna look so skeptical, Patrick. Remember Nelly Baird?"

"Aye," said Glenkirk ruefully, recalling a particularly lovely wench he'd been keeping in Edinburgh. She'd been all his until he let his brother spend a night with her.

Adam laughed and then, becoming serious again, said, "Fiona will whore no longer. It's just that her capacity for love is great, and until last night no man was big enough to fill it. I am, and she's content now."

"But ye could hae had legitimate sons wi the Forbes girl."

"You and James and Michael will all have sons to carry on our branch of the family. I'd rather hae my little red-haired bitch."

"I'll not say ye nay, brother," said the earl, "for young Mistress Catriona Hay has me dancing a merry tune."

"Take my advice, Patrick, and tame the wench, or ye'll hae no peace in yer house."

"Aye, but how?"

Adam shrugged his shoulders. "That," he said, "is yer problem, brother. I've got my own, and her name is Fiona."

Margaret Leslie stormed into the library.

"How could ye!" she raged at her oldest son. "How

could ye allow your brother to wed wi that . . . harlot? Sithean is chortling wi glee at having rid himself of the bitch a second time. Fiona may be my niece, but I will nae allow one of my boys to mate wi that she-wolf!"

Patrick drew himself up and looked down at his mother. "I would remind ye, madame, that I am the head of this family, not you. I make the decisions here. Adam is in love wi Fiona, and she wi him. Sithean has consented, and supplied a generous dowry. They wed in the spring. Ye will welcome her as ye have welcomed Catriona, and Ailis Hay, and as ye will welcome Isbella Forbes."

Margaret Leslie turned to her younger son. He took his mother's hands in his. "I do love her, mother," he said. "Ye had yer happy years wi father. Now I would hae mine wi Fiona."

Meg Leslie burst into tears, and her two sons put their arms about her.

"Ye were always willful. All of you boys!"

"Madame, we would be happy. You and our father set us the example," said Adam.

She sniffed delicately. Wiping her eyes, she smiled at them. "Very well, my lord earl, and my foolish younger son. I shall welcome Fiona, though I still believe it to be wrong. The lass has a streak of mischief in her. She can be wicked when she chooses. I dinna like it."

Chapter 4

ﻦﺒﻳﻦ

THE Earl of Glenkirk wooed his bride-to-be with the elegance and grace of a French courtier. When Ellen brought Cat breakfast each morning, there was always something on the tray from Patrick. It might be simple, perhaps a sprig of pine and a gilded cone tied with red velvet ribbons. Or it might be as valuable as a carved ivory box holding a dozen diamond buttons. Cat and Patrick became better acquainted on short rides through the December snows, and long walks in the sleeping gardens.

Patrick Leslie was a well-educated man, and his young betrothed, who had struggled so hard for her own education, listened to him eagerly. It amused the earl to find this serious mind housed in such a lush young body. But it worried him that she was so innocent. Raised in the insular world of Greyhaven, she understood almost none of the facts of life.

She had grown secure enough in his company to suggest they be married on St. Valentine's Day. After Easter, Adam and his Fiona would be quietly wed—though all the family knew that wedding would be a mere formality. They were already living together as husband and wife. And Fiona, who had always run to the lean, was growing as plump and sleek as a cream-fed cat.

"She almost purrs," giggled Ailis Hay. "I only hope

my Jamie's as good as the lasses say Cousin Patrick and Adam are."

"As good at what?" asked Cat.

Ailis' large blue eyes opened wide, then she giggled again. "Oh, Cat! Yer such a tease!"

"I dinna know what ye are talking about, Ailis. Ye hope Jamie's as good as Patrick and Adam in what?"

"In bed, you goose!" said Ailis, exasperated. "They say the Glenkirk men drive the lasses mad wi delight! I canna wait till I'm wed in June!"

"God, Ailis! Yer as big a whore as Fiona!"

Ailis' eyes filled with tears, and her blond curls quivered with outrage. "I am," she said with great dignity, "as virgin as ye are, Catriona Hay! But there the similarity ends! I look forward to my nights in the marriage bed, and I shall do my best to please Jamie. Yer as cold as ice. And if ye dinna change yer ways, the earl will seek solace in a warmer bed. Who would blame him?"

Cat stalked away from her cousin. Since the family had arrived for Christmas, Glenkirk's behavior had been quite correct. There had been no repeat of that night before the fire when he'd unleashed emotions in her she had never felt before, and still wasn't sure she could handle. She wanted to feel those feelings again.

That night, clad only in a soft linen shift, she crept from her apartments and hid in an alcove by the earl's rooms. It was cold, and he didn't come till quite late. She slipped from her hiding place and followed him into his room.

He turned. "Why, Cat, sweet. What is it?"

She shivered, and he quickly dropped his fur-lined cloak over her shoulders.

"Now, love, what is so important that ye come to my rooms in the middle of the night?"

Shyness overcame her. He picked her up in his arms

and, cradling her, sat down in the chair by the fire. "Tell me, my sweet."

Her voice was low. "I want—I want ye to make love to me."

"Nay, hinny. If I believed that I should have ye stripped, and in my bed in an instant."

"Please, Patrick! I really do! Oh, my lord, I am so woefully ignorant! My mother has tried to remedy this, but she makes love sound so lofty and spiritual. Then Ailis chortles and giggles about the reputation of the Glenkirk men, and Fiona is sleeping openly wi Adam, and looks so damned superior and content. *That's* not at all spiritual. So . . . I dinna know what to expect. Please teach me! Even a little!"

"Very well," he said, and there was a hint of laughter in his voice, "but if ye become frightened, or want me to stop, dinna be afraid to ask me."

"All right, Patrick."

The room grew very quiet, the crackling of the fire the only sound. His one arm cradled her, the other was free. Slowly he pushed one side of her shift down, exposing a lovely globe-shaped ivory breast, its nipple colored deep rose. For a moment he gazed at the perfection of it. His hand cupped it tenderly, and squeezed. He felt her quiver ever so slightly, and his thumb reached out to rub the tantalizing pink point into hardness. He heard her gasp softly, and a smile spread across his lips.

He bent to kiss her, and heard his cloak fall to the floor as she wound her arms about his neck. Carefully he pulled the shift off her lovely body and dropped it on the cloak. He stroked her satiny skin. Though she trembled, she murmured contentedly and clung to him. Suddenly he stopped, and she protested.

"Please, my lord! More! I am not afraid."

But the earl was afraid, for his own desires were fast

mounting. He knew he would soon have to stop, or he would take her there and then.

"Cat! Sweetheart! Listen to me. I am beginning to want you very much. If I dinna send ye away now, I may not be able to deny myself the pleasure of yer sweet body."

"Please, my lord, I want ye too. Take me now!"

Had she been anyone else he would have eagerly complied, but this was Cat, his innocent betrothed, who was just awakening to the joys of love. "Nay, hinny. In the light of morning things will look different. If I stole yer virginity now ye'd hate me for it later on."

Sighing, he slipped the shift back over her head. He carried her back to her own bed and tenderly tucked her in. "Good night, love," he whispered as he closed the door behind him.

Cat Hay lay still in the warmth of her bed and listened to the winter night. The fire burned with soft sounds. An owl hooted and was answered by a wolf. She now understood what her mother meant. But she also understood Ailis, and had more sympathy for cousin Fiona. She let her mind wander back over the last half-hour. Her breasts grew taut, and she flushed. For the rest of the night, Cat Hay alternated between restless sleep and restless wakefulness. He young body ached for Patrick's touch.

When they met to ride in the morning he greeted her in his accustomed manner. She followed his example until they were safely away from the castle. Then, turning slowly to him, she said. "I regret nothing of last night."

He smiled at her intensity. "There is nothing to regret, Cat. We but kissed and fondled . . . the innocent pastime of lovers since time began."

"I will come to ye again," she said.

He chuckled. "You will stay in yer own bed like a

good girl," he commanded, "or I'll nae be responsible
for my actions."

She pouted at him. "I willna stay away."

He stared at her and realized, to his utter amazement, that she meant it. My God, he thought! She's a
tigress! He said sternly, "If ye disobey me, I shall take
a hazel switch, and beat your pretty bottom. I mean it!"

She appeared in his room again that night. Handing
him a hazel switch, she shrugged her cloak off. She was
naked. He threw the switch in the fire and, catching her
to him, kissed her deeply. He allowed his fingers to
stray between her legs. She moaned softly, and did not
stop him.

The Twelfth Night festivities ended and the cousins
departed for their own homes. The earl insisted that
Catriona return to Greyhaven for a few weeks before
coming back to Glenkirk for their wedding. Cat had not
wanted to go. But she had been coming to Patrick's
room each night, and he felt that if he didn't get some
respite from the torture she was inflicting on him, he
would do something they would both be sorry for.

Two weeks before the wedding she returned, bringing
her dowry of clothing, jewels, linens, and furnishings.
To Patrick's dismay she was moved into the apartments
of the Earl and Countess of Glenkirk, of which his bedroom was a part. There had never been a lock on the
door between the bedrooms. For him to put one on
now would cause much talk. The first night of her return he stayed up late talking with Adam, hoping she
would be asleep when he retired.

Finally he bid his brother good night and went to
his room. The door between the rooms stood open. He
listened, but there was no sound. Quickly and quietly
he stripped his clothing off.

"Patrick." Her voice was sweet.

He turned to find her standing in the door between

the rooms. She was as naked as he was. She held out a hand to him, and he groaned.

"Come, love. My bed is already warm."

He couldn't take his eyes off her lovely, generous breasts and sensuous long legs. Her honey-colored hair fell heavy and thick to below her tiny waist. Her eyes glittered as he'd never seen them do.

"If I get into yer bed tonight, Cat, there's no turning back. I'll play no more games wi ye. If I come to yer bed this night, sweetheart, I'll take yer virginity. Make no mistake about it! What I start, I'll finish!"

"Come, Patrick." She walked back into her bedroom.

He followed her. "Are ye certain, hinny?"

She turned and put her hand on his chest, sending a wave of shock through him. "I canna wait longer, my lord. Please dinna make me beg ye." She climbed into the big bed and held out her arms. Quickly he joined her and, catching her to him, kissed her strongly. He felt her tremble against him and shifted to look down at her.

"Yer sure?"

"Aye, my lord."

She quivered like a captive wild creature as his lips began to explore her body. His kisses burned deeply into her fair skin, and when his mouth closed over a hard little nipple, she felt a delicious mixture of pleasure and fear. His hand explored the moist secret place between her legs—teasing, stroking, caressing. Gently he moved a finger into her and she arched to meet it. She was tight, and her virgin shield intact. He would have to be very gentle in order to cause her the least possible pain.

There was time, though. He had the whole night before him. He wanted her excited to a peak. She was not his first virgin, and he had found that a maiden excited to her limit felt less pain than one who was tense. He took her hand and placed it on his swelling organ. She didn't pull her hand away, but shyly and gently caressed him, and suddenly bent and kissed its throbbing head.

A great shudder tore through him. Forcing her back beneath him, he kissed her deeply. Their tongues were spears of fire, exploring, scorching. Her body began to writhe beneath him, and Patrick smiled. Bending over her, he let his mouth travel to the tiny mole that perched at the top of the cleft between her legs. Then he ran his tongue down that appealing little cleft. She gasped in shock.

Now he was atop her, lovingly but insistently, moving her thighs apart. Gently he pushed into her and was delighted when, once again, she rose to meet him. It took all his self-control not to press too hard. He stopped and looked down at her. A fine, damp sheen covered her body, and he could tell she was a little frightened.

"Easy, love, easy, sweetheart," he crooned, and caressed her trembling body.

"It hurts, Patrick! It hurts!"

"Only a moment longer, love. One bad pain, then it will quickly get better," he promised. And before she could protest further, he drew back and thrust quickly through the barrier. Her eyes widened and she screamed once in pain—a cry he half-stifled with his kisses. But he had not lied. The pain began to subside at once. He moved softly within her, and, slipping into a brilliant new world, Cat moved her body in time with his. Waves of pleasure washed over her, and as the intensity increased she felt herself drawn down into a whirling, golden vortex. She heard a girl's voice cry out, and did not know the voice was her own. Then as suddenly as it had begun, it ended. She found herself cradled in Patrick's arms, weeping.

He was stricken with remorse and self-loathing.

Covering her wet face with kisses, he pleaded with her to forgive him for being such a terrible brute. Cat caught him in mid-sentence, laughing through her tears.

"You great fool!" she said, giving him a weak chuckle. "What am I to forgive ye for? Making me a woman two weeks before our wedding?" She took his face in her hands. "I love ye, hinny! Do ye hear me? I am mad for ye, my lord! I couldna bear not having all of ye, for I am a willful wench, Patrick!"

Glenkirk looked down into her face and suddenly smiled. "I'll beat ye if you ever defy me, brat! I love ye wi all my heart, but I'll be the master of my own house."

"As long as I'm yer only mistress, m'lord!" she shot back.

He laughed. "What a minx you are, madame!" And he tumbled her back amid the pillows. "Go to sleep, or come morning everyone in the castle will know what we've been about." She cocked an eyebrow at him. He chuckled. "No more tonight, my greedy little lass. Yer too newly opened. If ye would walk in the morning, once is enough for this night. But come other nights, I'll love ye wi'out stopping the whole night long. No man with any fire in him could ever get enough of you, my bride."

In the morning, Ellen saw the bloodstains on Cat's bedsheets. But she kept silent, for 'twas no one's business that the bride and groom had celebrated their wedding night before they celebrated their wedding. She had been worried that perhaps her young mistress was marrying a man she did not love. Now she knew all was well. Cat would not have surrendered herself to Glenkirk unless she loved him.

Unfortunately, Fiona knew, too. No one had confided in her, but with alleycat instinct, she knew. Three days before the wedding she found Catriona alone and, with deliberate intention, said, "So ye finally let him stick it in ye, cousin. And before the wedding too," she said wickedly. "My, but yer brave!"

Cat blushed at having her secret discovered. But she was unwilling to let Fiona get the upper hand. "Jealous, coz?"

Fiona laughed. "Listen, my wee Cat. I've been fucking since I was thirteen. There's never been a man I couldn't have if I wanted him, and that includes yer precious Glenkirk."

"Liar!" spat Catriona.

"Nay," smiled Fiona sweetly. "I've had both Patrick and Adam. I'll stick wi my Adam. However, so there's no mistake about it . . ." And Fiona proceeded to describe Patrick's bedroom in detail.

Cat left her cousin without a word. Going to her apartments, she put on a pair of warm doeskin riding breeches, a silk shirt, fur-lined boots, and a heavy fur-lined cloak. She had sent a confused Ellen ahead to the stables to have Bana saddled. "But where are ye going at this time o' day?" she protested.

"I dinna know," said Cat, mounting Bana. "But when the great Earl of Glenkirk returns from Forbes Manor, tell him that I'd sooner marry the devil himself!"

Yanking Bana's head about, she kicked the mare and cantered across the drawbridge into the darkening winter afternoon.

Chapter 5

❧❧❧

ELLEN picked up her skirts and ran, stumbling, back into the castle to seek the Master of Greyhaven. Finding him, she gasped out, "She's gone, Lord Hay! Mistress Cat has gone!"

Greyhaven did not quickly comprehend, but his wife did. "What happened?" she demanded of Ellen.

"I dinna know, my lady. She's been so happy to be back at Glenkirk, and looking forward to her wedding."

"I wonder," said Heather thoughtfully, "if it has all been a pretense."

"Nay! Nay, my lady! She's in love wi the earl, 'tis plain. They've been——" Ellen stopped, horrorstruck, and clapped her hand over her mouth, but Heather understood.

"How long?"

"Oh, my lady!"

"How long, Ellen?"

"The first night we were back. I found the stains the next morning, but something had been going on at Christmastime. He dinna force her! Of that, I'm sure, my lady."

"Are ye saying that Glenkirk's been lying wi my lass?" said James Hay indignantly.

"Oh, Greyhaven," snapped Heather, "be quiet! It's nae important that they've been sleeping together. They're being married in three days' time. Ellen—what did Cat do this afternoon? Where did she go?"

"She slept for an hour after the meal as she always does. Then she went to the Family Hall wi her embroidery. The earl hasna been here all day, so they canna have had a fight."

Checking, they found several people who had talked to Catriona that afternoon. But Meg Leslie, her daughters, Ailis Hay, and two of the servants all remembered that she was happy and excited.

"What can have frightened her?" wondered Meg.

"She wasna frightened, my lady," corrected Ellen. "She was in a blazing temper."

There was a clatter of horses in the courtyard and the barking of dogs as the earl and his brothers returned from Forbes Manor. The four of them had just concluded the betrothal agreement for Isabella Forbes. Laughing and joking, they entered the Family Hall, then stopped at the scene that greeted them.

"What is it?" demanded the earl.

"It's Cat," spoke his mother unthinkingly.

Patrick went white.

"Nay, she's all right!" said Heather quickly.

"Then what is it?"

"She's gone off in a temper, nephew. Probably a fit of bridal nerves," replied Heather, intending to soothe.

"When?"

"About an hour ago. She spent the afternoon in here. Then suddenly she went to her room, put on her riding clothes, and rode off."

"Who spoke wi her? How do you know when she went?"

Heather told him, and then turned to Ellen to tell her story.

"She came storming into her bedroom, my lord. 'Ellie,' she shouts, 'go to the stable, and tell them to saddle Bana!' 'My lady,' I says to her, ' 'tis late, and the sun is close to setting.' 'Do as ye are bid!' she says to me.

Oh, my lord! I've raised her since she was a baby, and never has she spoken to me thus. She was in her old riding clothes when she mounted the horse. 'Ellie,' she says, 'tell the great Earl of Glenkirk that I'd as soon marry the devil himself!' Then she rode off. I came right to my lady Hay, and told her."

Patrick Leslie's mouth was tight, and white around the lips. His eyes narrowed. "Someone must have upset her."

"Upset whom?" asked Fiona, coming into the hall. "What on earth is going on?"

Patrick kept his voice level. "Did ye see Cat this afternoon?"

"Aye. She was embroidering here."

The earl looked to his brother. Adam took his wife-to-be firmly by the arm and escorted her into the library. Frightened, Fiona faced the two brothers.

"What did ye say to Cat, dear cousin?" His voice was icy.

"Nothing, Patrick. I said nothing! I swear it! We talked of girlish things."

Reaching out, Adam caught his betrothed and, flinging her across a chair, laid his riding crop across her back. She screamed in pain and tried to escape him, but Patrick held her down by her slender white neck.

"Now, cousin," he said through gritted teeth, "love ye or not, Adam will, on my order, beat you to death if necessary. What did ye say to Catriona?"

"I told her that ye slept wi me." Fiona sobbed out the entire conversation.

"You bitch!" swore Patrick. "It took me weeks to win Cat's confidence, and ye hae destroyed it in three minutes!" He slammed out of the room.

Adam looked down at Fiona. "I warned ye, my love, that if ye caused trouble I would punish you." His arm

rose, and she heard the whistle of the crop a second
before it touched her back again.

"No, Adam." She cried out, but he was merciless.
He beat her until she fainted a few moments later.

Glenkirk was organizing as quickly as he could. His
favorite stallion was winded, so he ordered his second
favorite, Dearg, to be saddled. He would allow only
Ellen's brother, Conall More-Leslie, to accompany him.
Before he left he spoke with his mother, his Aunt
Heather, and Adam.

"God knows where she's gone. It may even take me
weeks to trace her. She knows the countryside as well
as any man. It's too late to stop the wedding, so Adam,
ye and Fiona are to wed in our place." He looked closely
at his brother. "Do ye still want the bitch?"

"Aye, brother. She's a naughty puss, but I think she'll
behave now."

"Good! Tell the guests that the bride caught the
measles and gave them to the groom. That should stop
a scandal."

"Patrick, my son! Be gentle wi Catriona," begged
Meg. "She's young and innocent, and Fiona has hurt
her terribly wi her wicked lies."

"Madame," said Patrick coldly, "Catriona has been
sharing my bed for almost two weeks now. I have
treated her wi gentleness, and never forced her. She
wouldna even face me wi her accusations, but assumed
me guilty, and fled. I will nae forgie her lack of trust.
I shall find her and bring her back, and wed wi her as
planned. But before I do that I shall take a leaf from
Adam's book, and beat her bottom so she may not sit
for a week!"

Several minutes later he galloped across the drawbridge with More-Leslie. It was a cold night, but the
moon lit their way. They rode first to Greyhaven, for
Patrick suspected that Cat had fled home. She was not

there. They turned their horses to Sithean, but there, too, they met with disappointment. They stayed the night, and the following morning began to comb the district.

But Cat had apparently vanished from the earth. No one had seen her.

St. Valentine's Day came, and Adam Leslie wed his widowed cousin, Lady Stewart. The guests chuckled when they heard the earl and his bride-to-be were suffering from the measles. Wasn't it lucky, they laughed, that the Leslies had another betrothed couple ready and waiting so the festivities would not go to waste.

It was a wonderful party, but the new Lady Leslie looked tired and subdued. Fiona, looking out at her guests from the head table, wondered what they would think if she told them the reason for her pallor. For the last three nights she had been tied to a chair and forced to watch Adam making love to a very pretty and obviously insatiable peasant wench. She had tried closing her eyes, but the sounds from the bed were too tantalizing. She watched fascinated, as Adam's enormous cock plunged in and out of the writhing girl. As her own desire grew, she suffered severe pain of both a mental and physical nature, and by last night she thought she would go mad.

This morning, however, he had told her that her punishment was over. Fiona swore never to cause her cousin hurt again, and promised that when Cat was found she would apologize and tell her the truth. Adam smiled, satisfied. He knew how to handle his wench.

But Cat couldn't be found. February gave way to March and March to April before word came. Ellen, home in Crannog to see her parents, discovered her mistress living with them! Cat, fleeing Glenkirk, had gone directly to Ruth and Hugh More-Leslie. Ruth, now in her sixties, had immediately agreed to hide the girl. Hugh, retired and in his seventies, hadn't been sure. But Ruth convinced him that her long dead mistress would have approved. Ellen was amazed.

"Surely the neighbors are suspicious," she said.

"Why should they be?" said Ruth. "They never see her. She rides her Bana an hour each night for exercise, but other than that she never leaves the house."

"She canna stay here forever, mother. Did she tell ye why she ran away?"

"Aye! That wicked Fiona! I knew when she was a child she would grow up bad."

"She did, mother. Very bad. So bad that she sent Mistress Cat off in this rage. What Fiona said, however, was a lie, and Mistress Cat was wrong to run off before asking my lord of Glenkirk to defend himself. He is hurt that she thought so little of him. Yet he loves her, and still wants to make her his wife."

"Well," said Ruth, with the wisdom of her late mistress, "then we must arrange for him to find her. But not here."

"There's A-Cuil, mother. Her grandmother, Jean Gordon, had it as part of her dowry, and now it belongs to Mistress Cat. It is small and secluded, set in the hills above Loch Sithean."

"How big, and in what condition?"

"Stone wi a slate roof, and put back into shape because of the wedding. There's a kitchen, and a parlor downstairs, and a bedroom on the second floor. There's also a small stable wi two loft rooms. That's about all there is to A-Cuil."

"It'll do," said Ruth. "How long a ride?"

"A good hour up into the hills," replied Ellen.

Ruth smiled. "I shall convince Mistress Cat to go there, and then I will go to Glenkirk, and tell the earl.

In a quiet place, away from the rest of the family, they'll settle their differences."

Ruth was as good as her word. Persuading Cat that she would be happier if she could get outdoors more, now that summer was coming, and assuring her that A-Cuil was a good distance from Glenkirk, she sent the girl off. Ellen had been sent on to air the house and bring in food supplies. She had begged her young mistress to allow her to accompany her. Lonely, Cat had agreed.

A-Cuil was set high in a pine forest on a cliff that gave a view of Glenkirk, Sithean, and Greyhaven far below. It was hidden and quiet. For several days Cat prowled, restless, through the woods around her. At night she slept deeply in the big bedroom. Ellen, in the trundle, slept by her side. They had been there ten days, and Cat was beginning to feel safe.

With a bad storm about them that night they retired to the bedroom. Building up the fire, they ate a supper of toasted bread and cheese, and drank slightly hardened cider. Neither minded the lightning that crackled ominously about them, or the rolling peals of thunder. Suddenly the door flew open. Ellen gave a shriek of terror. The earl strode in.

"Yer brother's in the kitchen, Ellen. Is there a place ye both can sleep?"

"The lofts over the stable, m'lord."

"Run along, then."

"No! Dinna leave me wi him, Ellen."

Ellen looked helplessly at her young mistress. Gently, the earl took the serving woman by the arm and escorted her to the door. "Dinna come near this room unless I call you. Do ye understand?"

"Aye, my lord."

The door closed firmly behind her, and she heard the bolt slam home. Padding down the stairs, she found her brother and led him off to the loft rooms in the stable. "Is he very angry wi her, Conall?"

"Aye," said her brother calmly. "He's going to beat her."

"Never!" gasped Ellen. "He's mad for her!"

"Still," replied Conall, "he's going to beat her, and a good thing too. She's a wayward lass to have run from him like that. If he's nae the master in his own house from the first, he'll always have trouble wi her. That's no marriage for a man."

"If mother and I had known that he'd hurt her, we'd nae have let him find her."

"Sister," said Conall patiently as if explaining to a child, "he's not going to hurt her. He's just going to gie her a wee beating to help her mend her manners."

Ellen shook her head. She knew Cat Hay better than all of them. After all, she'd raised her. The earl was about to find out that beating his bride would never tame her.

Chapter 6

❦§❦

CAT Hay angrily faced the Earl of Glenkirk. Carefully he spread his wet cloak over the back of the fireplace chair and removed his damp linen shirt. He sat down. "My boots, Cat!" They were the first words he'd spoken to her.

"Go to hell!" she spat at him.

"My boots!" His green-gold eyes narrowed and glittered dangerously.

Her heart pounding wildly, she knelt and drew his boots off. I'm not afraid of him, she thought. But why was her heart beating so quickly? Standing up, he caught her by her long hair. Wrapping it around his hand, he drew her face to his. Grasping the top of her shift with his other hand, he ripped it from neck to hem and pulled it off her. "I warned ye once that if ye ever defied me I'd beat ye!"

And before she could protest, he'd pushed her onto the bed and brought his riding crop down cruelly on her buttocks. She screamed her pain and outrage at him and tried to escape. But, holding her down, he raised several angry red wheals on her bottom before stopping. Tossing the crop away, he raged at her. "Ye've led me a fine chase these last months, madame! Had Adam not been willing to wed immediately we would hae been embarrassed before every family in the district. Does it please ye to know that Fiona held the place of honor at *our* wedding?"

Turning over, she gingerly sat up and faced him with a defiant, tear-stained face. "You bastard!" she shrieked at him. "What ye put between my legs, ye put between hers also! I'll nae forgie ye that! Never!"

"Little bitch!" he shouted back. "How could ye believe her? Never did I lie wi Fiona. Once she waited in my room, but Adam was wi me. He'd been hot for her for years, so I slept in his room that night while he took his pleasure of her. Never have I slept wi that she-devil!"

"Why should I believe you? Yer bastards are scattered from one end of the district to the other! Fiona said she could have any man she wanted, and then proceeded to describe your bedroom accurately. What was I to think?"

"Why did ye believe her over me?" he demanded. "How *could* ye lie wi me, and not believe that I love ye and would do nothing to harm ye?"

"Liar! I hate ye! Get out of my house!"

"Yer house? Yers? Nay, Cat. This house is part of the dowry your father gave me along wi ye. It belongs to me now, as ye belong to me." He pushed her back onto the pillows and bent over her. "Yer my possession, Cat, as is Glenkirk, as are my horses, and my dogs. Ye are something for my pleasure. A thing on which to breed my sons. Do ye understand me?"

She raised her arm. Catching a glitter, Patrick twisted aside as the arm moved down. He wrenched the little knife from her hand and slapped her face. "A whore's trick, sweetheart! Is that what ye want? To be treated like a whore?"

"I'd be a whore before I'd be yer wife, Glenkirk! No man owns me! No man!"

He laughed. "Brave words, lass. However, since ye've expressed an interest, I'll teach ye some whores' tricks.

Ye've not begun to be facile in bed yet. Not enough practice. But I'll remedy that in the next few weeks."

"What do ye mean?" Her heart was pounding uncontrollably.

"Why, my dear. Until I put my bairn in yer belly, ye'll nae go home to Glenkirk. I obviously canna trust ye to wed me till then. When ye ripen wi my son ye'll hae no other choice, will you?"

Standing, he swiftly pulled his trunk hose off, and then flung himself back on top of her. He found her angry mouth and kissed her cruelly. Sliding down between her legs, he pulled them over his shoulders and buried his head between her legs. Her cries of terror quickly became sounds of shamed desire as his velvet tongue stroked and probed her.

"Patrick! Patrick!" she cried. "No! Please. Oh, my God. No."

Desperately, she tried to escape the demanding mouth that sucked her, the insistent tongue that tortured her. His big hands held her round hips in an iron grip while he pleasured himself by sending waves of fire and pain through her. Sobbing, she tried to deny him the victory of her climax, but he forced her twice. Then, laughing, he mounted her and pushed deep within her to find his own release. She felt herself writhing eagerly beneath him. Finished, he rolled off her and said coldly, "That my dear, was lesson number one."

Crawling into a corner of the bed, she wept silently, her shoulders shaking with great sobs. He wanted to take her in his arms and comfort her, but Patrick Leslie was certain that the least sign of softening on his part would ruin everything. He didn't want to break her spirit, but he would be master of his own home.

For her part, Cat was too inexperienced to understand the subtle ways in which a woman can control her men without them knowing it. Patrick would have been surprised to know that her tears were not for what he had done to her, but for the fact that he had bested her.

He pulled her into his arms again and began to play with her breasts.

"No!" she protested.

He paid no attention to her, but instead crushed the softness in his hand. "God," he murmured against her, "God, but ye've got the sweetest little tits I've ever known." His lips caressed her fluttering belly, but when he went to move farther down she cried out.

"No! Not again!"

Laughing softly, he raised himself on one elbow and looked down at her. His hand forced itself between her legs, and his fingers played. "Didn't ye like lesson one, sweetheart?"

She tried to squirm away. "When I tell my father how ye've raped me, he'll kill ye!"

"Nay, hinny. He gave me his blessing to do wi ye as I pleased. He knows that in the end I will honor our betrothal agreement, and wed wi ye. That's all he wants."

Cat knew Patrick was right, and it infuriated her.

He pulled her under him and kissed her bruised mouth until she cried with hurt. His lips turned soft, the touch of his swollen penis against her thighs spread them as her hips arched hungrily to meet his downward thrust.

Patrick Leslie laughed softly. "By God, Cat, yer a hungry little bitch! I wonder if Fiona's as hot as ye are."

Her fists beat against his smooth chest. He laughed again, and then slowly went about the task of reducing her resistance to compliance. At last he fell into a deep sleep. Since there was no way she could escape him at that point, she fell into a sleep of her own.

In the early hours of the morning he woke her and took her again. Her young body ached from the unaccustomed activity. Understanding this, he lugged a tall oak-and-iron tub into the bedroom and placed it before the fire. While she watched, astonished, he carried up caldrons of hot water until the tub was full. From somewhere he produced a cake of sweet-scented soap. Picking her up, he put her into the water.

"Ye smell like a brothel," he commented.

"Then ye should be right at home!" she shot back.

He stripped the bed, threw the sheets out into the hallway, and remade the bed with fresh lavender-scented linens. Then he disappeared and returned a few minutes later bearing a goblet. She was out of the tub, sitting before the fire wrapped in a towel.

"Drink this."

"What is it?"

"Sweet red wine, a beaten egg, and some herbs."

It was delicious. Taking the damp towel from her, he picked her up, carried her to the bed, and tucked her naked body into the cool sheets and down coverlet.

"Go to sleep, hinny. It's been a long night for ye." He bent and dropped a kiss on her forehead.

"Where are ye going?" she asked. Before he could answer, she was asleep.

Patrick Leslie gazed down at the sleeping girl and thought how much he loved her, and how frightened he had been—imagining all sorts of terrible things happening to her—when she fled him. He wasn't going to give her another chance to run, and he certainly would not tell her of his feelings towards her. Women were better off unsure. Too, he couldn't bear it again if she said she hated him.

He bathed, dressed himself, and went down to the kitchen. Conall rose from the trestle.

"Sit down, man," commanded the earl. "Ellen love, gie me a bowl of that oatmeal your brother's enjoying so." She placed one before him. "Conall, I want ye to ride down to Glenkirk today, and fetch some clothes for Mistress Cat and myself. We'll be staying here for several weeks. Ellen, ye'll tell me what she needs, and I'll write it down."

"I can both read and write, my lord," said Ellen frostily. "If ye dinna mind, I'd prefer to write to Lady Hay myself."

"Very well, Ellen." He smiled at her. "Dinna disapprove, chuck. I do love her, ye know."

"Did ye beat her, my lord?"

"Ten strokes on her saucy bottom. I'll be master in my own house, Ellen."

"Only ten?"

"Only ten," he replied. "She deserved more, but I am a merciful man."

"Aye," agreed Ellen. "She did deserve more. When she was a child, however, beating her did no good. She was always twice as defiant afterwards." Ellen hoped he was paying attention.

"She's nae changed," he chuckled.

Ellen wrote her message to Lady Hay and asked that she send several changes of undergarments, two soft linen shirts, half a dozen gossamer silk night garments from Cat's trousseau, a velvet dressing gown, slippers, and some cakes of sweet soap. Cat, fleeing Glenkirk, had thought to bring her comb and brush and the brush for cleaning teeth that her great-grandmother had taught them to use. She gave the list to the earl.

"It's not a great deal, but I'll be here to wash for her. This is easy to carry, and will nae weigh Conall down."

"Good girl," he said, and turned to Conall. "Take Bana back to Glenkirk, and yer sister's mare also. The only horses I want here are our two."

"Oh, my lord," pleaded Ellen. "Dinna take Bana from her. She loves so to ride."

"She'll have her horse back when we return to Glenkirk. The more horses I leave here, the greater her chances of escaping me. I'll nae gie her that chance again. We stay here until she swells wi my child. Then I'll take her home, and wed her."

Ellen sighed. "She's going to be very angry, my lord."

"Since I shall be out hunting us a deer when she wakes, I'll be spared the brunt of her anger," he replied dryly.

It wasn't until early afternoon that Cat woke. Conall had just returned from his errand, and Cat opened her eyes to see Ellen kneeling by the little clothes chest. "What are ye doing?" she asked sleepily.

"Putting away yer clean clothes, luv. Conall has just brought them up from Glenkirk."

Cat was suddenly wide awake. "Where is Patrick?"

"He's been gone since dawn. Hunting a deer for us, he said."

"Gie me a clean shirt, and my breeches, Ellie. I shall take my morning ride though it be afternoon." She swung her legs over the edge of the bed.

Ellen took a deep breath. "I canna do it, Mistress Cat, and dinna bother being angry wi me. His lordship has sent yer Bana and my Brownie home to Glenkirk."

Cat swore fiercely. "The horny bastard! Then I'll walk out of here if I must, but I'll nae spend another night in this house while he's here."

"He has also ordered," continued Ellen, "that ye not leave the house for the next few days. Ye may go naked, he says, or ye may wear one of yer sleeping gowns. I am to gie ye no other clothes."

Cat felt a terrible rage within her, but she swallowed it, for her faithful Ellie was not responsible. "Gie me something to wear," she said wearily, "and dinna bother fussing, for it makes no difference. He'll have it off me soon enough, for there's only one thing he wants from his whore."

"Mistress Cat," scolded Ellen. "He is yer betrothed, and ye'll soon be wed. Ye would hae already been had ye not misjudged him, and run away."

"God's foot, Ellie! Has he won ye over then?"

Ellen said nothing else, but handed Cat a pale turquoise-colored silk nightgown. "I'll get ye something to eat," she said, and left the room.

Cat let the gown slide down over her lush form. Picking up her brush, she sat back down on the bed and slowly brushed the tangles from her honey-colored hair. So he thought that by taking her horse and clothes away from her he would keep her a prisoner. Well, perhaps for a while he would. She would bide her time. But eventually, a way would open, and then she'd run from him again. It no longer mattered that he had or had not slept with Fiona—though Cat was glad he had not. What mattered was that she could not and would not allow him possession of Catriona Hay. Nobody owned her. Until Patrick Leslie understood that she was a person, not an extension of him, she would fight him with all the strength in her.

Ellen came back into the room bearing a tray. "Fresh bread new from the oven! Half a broiled rabbit, a honeycomb, and some brown ale."

Cat found she was hungry.

"Yer all right if ye can eat like that," observed Ellen.

"Only a moonstruck idiot stops eating in a bad situation," said Cat. "If I'm going to think of a way to escape his high lordship, I've got to keep up my strength."

"Mistress Cat! I dinna know why the earl puts up wi ye except he loves ye!"

"He loves me? Nonsense, Ellie! He thinks he owns me, and it pleases him to show his superiority over me by abusing my body."

Ellen shrugged. She didn't understand Catriona when

she spoke like that. Taking up the empty tray, she left the room, shaking her head.

Cat began to prowl the room. Until last night it had simply been a place to sleep. Now she looked on it as her prison. It could be entered only by a door from the stairway. There was a small fireplace on the door wall, and to the left was a bank of casement windows. There was one small, round window to the right. It was not a large room, and held only four pieces of furniture—a large canopied and curtained bed opposite the door, a low clothes chest at its foot, a small table on the single-windowed wall, and a chair by the fireplace. A pier glass hung on the bit of wall to the left of the door.

She stood by the windows looking out. From her vantage point she could see part of the valley below, and into the forest that surrounded the house. She saw Patrick coming out of the woods now. He was riding Dearg, and a buck was flung across his saddle. Conall ran to meet him and, taking the buck across his shoulders, went off in the direction of the stables. The earl followed.

Opening the bedroom door, Cat called down to Ellen. "Prepare a tub in the kitchen for the earl, Ellie. He's just brought in a buck, and he and Conall have gone to butcher it. I'll nae have him dripping blood all over my bedroom."

When he entered the bedroom an hour later clad only in a rough towel, she couldn't help but laugh. He grinned back at her.

"You see, madame. I've done as I've been told. Come now, and gie me a kiss."

Shyly she walked to him, and putting her arms about his neck kissed him.

"Jesu, yer sweet," he muttered, running his big hands over her silk-sheathed body and burying his face for a moment in her neck.

"Please, Patrick," she whispered.

"Please, Patrick, what?" he demanded thickly. He drew her over in front of the pier glass, and standing behind her gently slid her gown off. His big hands cupped her lovely breasts, and instantly the nipples sprang erect. "Look at yerself, Cat! I hae but to touch ye, and yer hungry for me!"

"No! No!" she protested, closing her eyes tightly.

He laughed softly, and turning her to him began to kiss her throat, her lips, her eyelids, with tiny, soft little kisses. His mouth began to move downward to her breasts. He knelt and, holding her firm but gently by the waist, kissed her shrinking belly, his kisses becoming more intense as they traveled lower. His lips found the tiny mole, and kissed it tenderly. Cat began to weep softly.

"Don't, sweetheart," he said gently. "There's nae shame in being a woman, and enjoying it."

"Ye knew?"

"Aye," he said, drawing her down on the floor in front of the cracking fire. "I knew. I've made love to enough women in my life to know when one is enjoying it, even when she struggles like a demon, and vows she hates me."

"I do hate ye," she insisted.

He chuckled. "Then in the next few weeks I'll gie ye cause each day to hate me more." Swiftly he slid between her legs and thrust his aching manhood into her softness. She tried to squirm away. "Nay, hinny! I told ye last night that ye belong to me. And what I hold, my sweet Cat, I keep!"

Chapter 7

≈§§≈

THE spring sped by, and Midsummer Eve came and went. Still the Earl of Glenkirk held his beautiful betrothed a prisoner at A-Cuil. Often he rode the almost two hours down to Glenkirk so he might attend to his estate's business. Many days he hunted to provide game for his small household. But never did he spend a night away from Cat.

Though she would never have told him so, Cat now looked forward to the nights she spent in Patrick's arms. She was young, and healthy, and more than half in love with her handsome husband-to-be. As for the earl, he was passionately in love with her, and would have killed any man who dared to look upon her with even the slightest interest.

As the days grew warmer and longer, he took her upon his horse and rode with her through the forest and the high meadows. Several times they made love beneath the sun in fields of new heather. She was as warm as wine, and as sweet as honey. Patrick marveled that he, who had never been faithful to one woman for more than a week or two at a time, dreaded the thought of returning to Glenkirk and sharing her with even his family.

The return would be soon. Cat had not yet connected her loss of a show of blood with impending motherhood. Ellen had, and she sought a way to bring the matter to her young mistress's attention. One morning opportunity presented itself.

The earl had risen early and gone to Glenkirk. Ellen cheerfully entered the bedchamber bearing a tray that held a small pigeon pie, fresh from the oven. "Yer favorite," she chortled. "Doesn't it smell wonderful," she enthused, waving the tray beneath her lady's nose.

Cat went white. Scrambling from the bed, she grabbed the basin from the table and retched into it.

"Och," sympathized Ellen, putting down the tray and wiping the girl's damp forehead with the linen chamber cloth. "Back into bed wi you, my dearie." She tucked Cat in. "The naughty laddie, to make his mama so sick," she said coyly.

Cat stared at her tiring woman as if she had lost her mind. "What are ye babbling about, Ellie? And take that damned pie away, or I'll be sick again! Get me some brown ale to drink, and some oat cakes."

Ellen removed the offending pie and returned a few minutes later with the requested meal. She watched as Cat cautiously sipped the ale, and then, apparently satisfied, wolfed down the oat cakes.

"How do ye feel now?" she asked.

"Better. I canna think what made me so sick. It's the third time it's happened in the last week. Do ye think that perhaps something has gone rotten in the larder?"

"Mistress Cat!" Ellen was exasperated beyond all. "Ye be wi child! He's put his bairn in yer belly, and now we can go home!"

Cat's leaf-green eyes widened. "No," she whispered. "No! No! No!"

"Aye! Yer ripening! There's no doubt about it. The earl will be so happy!"

Catriona turned angrily on Ellen. "If ye dare to tell him, I'll cut yer tongue out! Do ye understand me?"

"My lady!"

Cat closed her eyes for a moment. Opening them again, she spoke calmly and quietly. "I will tell my lord of my condition, Ellie, but not yet. The moment he knows, he'll rush me down to Glenkirk. I dinna want to leave A-Cuil yet. Please. I canna be very far along. There is time."

Ellen was soft-hearted by nature. The thought that her young mistress wanted a little more time alone with the earl appealed to her sense of romance. "When was yer last show?" she asked.

Cat thought a moment. "Early May," she said.

"Ah, sweeting, yer a good three months along," said Ellen, "but we can wait a week or so before his lordship must know. The wee laddie will be a winter child."

"No hints, Ellie. No arch looks. I would surprise the earl."

And she might have told him, and gone meekly home to Glenkirk, had not Patrick himself spoiled it. Kept at Glenkirk for three days and nights by a foolish problem, he arrived back at A-Cuil as randy as a young stallion in first heat.

Cat had decided to tell him, and she ran joyfully to greet him only to have him sweep her up in his arms and carry her to their bedroom. Swiftly, without preliminaries, he tore his clothing off, shoved her down on the bed, pushed her nightgown up, and thrust into her. Cat was outraged.

Satisfied for the moment, he sat up against the pillows and pulled her back against him. He had always loved her breasts, and now he fondled them hungrily. Beginning to swell with her pregnancy, they were sore, and his touch irritated her. He further annoyed her by chuckling, "I think these sweet little titties of mine are growing bigger, Cat." He squeezed them playfully. "A man's loving care can work wonders, eh, love?"

He should have been warned by the ominous silence,

but his mind was on other things, and his body was hungry for her again. He took her once more. Then, pushing her from their bed, he patted her buttock and asked for his dinner.

She descended to the kitchen. Ellen was long since in her bed, so Cat loaded a tray with half a roasted bird, a small cold game pie from the larder, bread, butter, a honeycomb, and a foaming pitcher of brown ale, to which she added a pinch of dried herbs. The earl was going to have an excellent night's sleep.

She served him sweetly, and almost felt guilty when he said, "You are going to be the most beautiful countess Glenkirk's ever had. Lord, sweetheart! How I love you!" The drugged ale was beginning to work on him. Climbing into their bed, he fell asleep.

From childhood Cat Hay had been able to wake herself on command. It was still dark when she rose and dressed herself in riding pants and a linen shirt. She packed a small bundle and, picking up Glenkirk's warm cloak, slipped out of the room and down the stairs. It was fully three hours till dawn. Cat crept softly into the stable. Above, in the loft, Ellen was snoring. Conall, she knew, was sleeping with his mistress of the moment, about half a mile away. Quietly she saddled Dearg. Putting a lead rein on Conall's Fyne, she led both horses from the stable.

She walked them a good quarter-mile from the house. Then, mounting Dearg and leading Fyne, she galloped off in the direction of Greyhaven. She planned to get there before even the servants were awake. Once in the house she would gather a few more clothes, her jewelry, and some gold from her father's cache.

Achieving her objective, she headed for the high road, but not before first releasing Fyne with a swat on his rump. He'd go straight to his stables at Glenkirk. Munching oatcakes, she rode along, chuckling to herself. She had outwitted Patrick! He had been so kind and loving in the last weeks that she had almost believed he accepted her as an equal. Last night, however, had told her the truth of the matter. It was as he had said. She was his possession, something for him to breed sons on. Well, she would soon teach him the folly of taking her for granted. She was nobody's slave.

She kicked Dearg into a gallop. Had Patrick really believed that by taking Bana from her she couldn't escape? If he had taken the time to learn as much about Catriona Hay the woman as he had taken learning about Catriona Hay's body, he would have known that there wasn't a horse bred she couldn't ride. It would have given her great pleasure to know that, at that very moment, Patrick Leslie was learning just that.

He had awakened with a headache and a funny taste in his mouth. Reaching out, he discovered that Cat was gone. A frantic knocking on the door tortured his head. "Come in, damnit!" he shouted. Both Ellen and Conall tumbled into the room, talking at once. "Silence!" he roared. "One of ye at a time. Ellen, you first."

"She's gone, my lord. Mistress Catriona has gone. She's taken both horses, and run away."

"When?"

"Sometime in the night. I am sorry, my lord. I sleep like the dead till six each morning. I never heard a thing."

"Where were ye?" said the earl, turning to Conall. "Nay. Dinna tell me. Ye were off sticking it in yer little shepherdess. Jesu!" he swore. "When I catch her this time she'll not sit down for a month!"

Ellen rounded on him. "Ye'll nae lay a hand on her. My little lambie! She's more than three months gone wi yer bairn. She planned to tell ye when ye returned from Glenkirk. What did ye *do* to her to make her flee ye, my poor Cat? Ye must hae done something."

Patrick flushed.

"So!" pounced Ellen. "Ye did do something!"

"I only made love to her," Patrick protested. "I'd been wi'out her for three days!"

"If only you Leslie men thought more wi yer heads and less wi yer cocks! So ye 'made love' to her? I can see it now." Her scornful glance swept the room. "Having come home, and wi'out so much as a by-yer-leave, ye fucked her. Was it once or was it twice? Then I'll wager ye demanded yer dinner." The earl looked shamefaced, and Ellen snorted. "God, mon! Where's yer sense? If ye'd been an Englishman or a Frenchie I'd expect stupidity, but a Scotsman knows that a Scotswoman is the most independent of creatures! Well, she's got a good start on ye now, and ye'll nae find her easily this time."

"She canna have gone far," said Patrick. "She's run home to her mother, mark my words on it."

Ellen shook her head sadly at him. "Nay, my lord. If she's run home to Greyhaven, 'twill only be to get her jewels, and perhaps steal some gold from her father. But where she'll go to hide, my lord, I dinna know. She's never traveled out of the district before."

"I thought her jewels were at Glenkirk."

"Nay, my lord. When Mistress Cat fled ye in February I brought them back to Greyhaven, and she knew it."

For a second Patrick Leslie looked stricken. Then, swinging his legs over the bed, he stood up. Without another word, Ellen handed him his breeches and left the room.

He spoke to Conall. "The nearest horses?"

"In the valley. Gavin Shaw has the nearest farm."

"Get going," said the earl. "I'll meet ye there."

Conall nodded and left. Patrick finished dressing and went down to the kitchen. Ellen handed him a large sandwich of bread and ham. "Ye can eat as ye walk," she said.

He nodded his thanks. "Pack everything up here for for me, Ellie. I'll send someone up for ye by afternoon at the latest. Will ye stay at Glenkirk until I find her? She's going to need ye more than ever now."

"I'll stay. Her apartments have never been properly refurbished, and there's the nursery to prepare."

Flashing her a smile, he left A-Cuil and began his walk down to the Shaw farm.

Several hours later Patrick Leslie knew that Ellen had been right. Cat was not at Greyhaven, and a check revealed that her jewelry and a generous portion of her father's household gold was missing.

He rode to Sithean, and stopped at Ruth's house in Crannog. Cat was not in either place. At Glenkirk his lovely mother berated him for a fool and demanded, in a voice he had never heard her use before, that he find Cat, and *her* expected grandson.

"James," she said, "can run the estate for ye while yer gone. Adam and Fiona are, unfortunately, in Edinburgh. They are going to France to visit our cousins."

"Mother, I dinna even know where to look for Cat."

She looked at him pityingly. "Ye hae a bit less than six months to find her, my son. Else the next rightful Glenkirk will be born a bastard."

Groaning with despair, he left the room. Cat Hay would have been terribly happy to see the desperate look on the earl's face.

Chapter 8

꧁ ❦ ꧂

FIONA Leslie pulled her hood over her beautiful face. Looking around to be sure she wasn't followed, she slipped into the Rose and Thistle Inn. "I seek Mistress Abernethy," she told the landlord.

"Up the stairs, to the right," came the answer.

Fiona mounted the stairs. She had no idea who this Abernethy woman was, but when the urchin had shoved the note into her hand, curiosity had overcome good sense. She knocked on the door. Hearing a voice bid her enter, she did. The woman by the window turned. "Cat!" she gasped.

"Shut the door, Fiona, and come sit down."

Fiona settled her black velvet skirts and looked at her beautiful cousin. "I thought Glenkirk held ye captive at A-Cuil? What do ye here?"

"I escaped him again, and I want yer help, Fiona."

"God's toenail, yer a fool, Cat!" she sighed. "I promised Adam that when we met again I would tell ye the truth. I never slept wi Glenkirk, though until his brother took me I was hot to." She grinned ruefully. "As a matter of fact, he wouldna have me! There I lay—mother-naked on his bed—and he wouldna have me! All he wanted was ye. And that's the truth!"

Cat smiled. "Thank you, Fiona. Thank ye for telling me. Patrick already told me he had not slept wi ye, and though I was inclined to believe him, I really do now."

"Then what are ye doing here in Edinburgh? I'll wager poor Glenkirk doesna know where ye are."

"Nay, he doesn't. He's probably looking for me now, but I'll nae go back to him! Nae until he acknowledges me as a human being and nae a brood mare! Help me, Fiona! I know we've nae been close, cousin, but I hoped ye'd understand. Ellen said that ye and Adam leave for France soon. Let me stay in yer house. No one has to know, not even Adam. I'm safer there than anywhere else. Patrick will nae think to look for me in Edinburgh, let alone in yer house."

Fiona chewed on her lip for a moment. Cat would soon be the Countess of Glenkirk, and a good friend to have. Still, if Adam learned she was helping Cat in her feud with his brother he would punish her again in that terrible way he'd twice used on her. Forcing her to watch him love another woman was the worst hell she had ever known, and she didn't owe her cousin a damned thing now that she had told her the truth.

Cat stood up, and held her hands out, pleading. "Please, Fiona."

Fiona's glance caught a little swell of belly that Cat had certainly never had before. Comprehension dawned. "My God, coz! Yer carrying his bairn!"

"Aye," said Cat bitterly. "Do ye know what he said to me, Fiona? That I was a 'thing' to get his sons on. I hate him!"

Fiona didn't think Cat really hated Patrick, but she understood how she felt. These Leslie men were so damned proud. All Cat wanted from Glenkirk was acknowledgment of her status as a person. In a few months' time he'd be frantic, and willing to agree to anything just so his son would be born legitimate.

Fiona felt the wait would do them both good. Besides, she thought, I really do owe my dear brother-in-law for slighting me. She turned to Cat and said, "The house is yers, sweeting, but I've already let the servants go."

"I need no one."

"Dinna be foolish, chuck. Ye need someone. I'll send a note to Mrs. Kerr. She usually keeps an eye on the house for me when I am not here. I'll tell her my poor widowed cousin, Mistress Kate Abernethy, is coming to stay, and would she please look after her. Have ye enough money?"

"I think so, and I've my jewels too."

"If ye run short, or need to pawn something, go to the House of Kira in Goldsmith's Lane. And Cat, go at once to see Dr. Robert Ramsey. He's but a few doors from my house, around the corner on High Street. Remember 'tis the heir to Glenkirk ye carry in yer belly."

"Thank you, Fiona," said Cat softly. Suddenly she leaned over and kissed her cousin's cheek.

"We leave tomorrow morning," said Fiona gruffly. "Come in the afternoon. Mrs. Kerr will let ye in and gie you the key." She stood up. Pulling the hood over her face, she said, "Make peace wi Patrick soon, Cat. The Leslies may be arrogant, but by God, they're men!"

Late the following day, Cat moved from the Rose and Thistle Inn to Fiona's house. The house had originally belonged to Cat's and Fiona's grandmother, Fiona Abernethy, wife to the first Earl of Sithean. The cousins' mutual great-grandmother, the legendary Janet Leslie, had felt it fitting that the house go to Fiona Abernethy's namesake, and so Fiona Leslie had inherited it.

It was not a large house. Built about seventy years before, it was a mellowed red brick, well covered with ivy on three sides. The basement held a good kitchen, a pantry, a still room, and a wash room with several large tubs for doing laundry. The main floor held a charming dining room, a formal parlor, a small family parlor that opened into the garden, and a full library. On the second floor were four bedrooms, each with its own dressing room. And in the attic were rooms for the maids.

The house had a small stable where Cat housed Dearg, and the garden was filled with flowers, herbs, and fruit trees. Set off fashionable High Street, it was quiet, and little traffic passed by.

Mrs. Kerr, a cozy, plump widow of middle years, was sympathetic. She had, she confided to Cat, once been in the same position. Her husband had been killed in a border skirmish with the English when she was six months pregnant. She had raised her boy alone, and a fine lad he'd turned out to be, too! He was apprenticed to a butcher now.

"Did my cousin, Lady Leslie, tell ye how my husband died?" asked Cat.

Mrs. Kerr shook her head.

"A border skirmish also," said Cat sadly. "In the Cheviot, only two months ago."

"Aye," said the other woman, nodding in sympathy. "I remember it. But they lost more lads than we did."

Alone once again, Cat chuckled to herself. "Kate Abernethy" would soon be established. She had recognized Mrs. Kerr as a gossip—a kindly soul, but a gossip.

The following day, she took Fiona's advice and visited Dr. Ramsey.

He examined her and then advised, "Unless there's an emergency, ye'll not likely need me, my dear. That's a fine, healthy laddie yer growing there, and yer Mrs. Kerr should be able to deliver him with no trouble. But if ye should need me, dinna hesitate to send around."

Settled into Fiona's house now, Cat found she was enjoying herself. She was no longer sick in the morn-

ings, and her appetite was picking up. Never in her
entire life had she been so far from home. No mother.
No father. No Glenkirk. No Ellen. No one to answer
to except herself. Mrs. Kerr came each morning to tidy
the house and see that she was properly fed, but she left
before dark each evening.

As autumn advanced, Cat walked the more respectable streets of Edinburgh, exploring the town. Her
dress was simple though expensive, her pregnancy
obvious, and her manner modest. No one bothered her.
As the days grew colder she confined her walks to the
garden or to short trips to market with Mrs. Kerr.

These outings fascinated her. At Greyhaven, food
had simply been there. In accompanying her housekeeper, a whole world opened up to Cat. Mrs. Kerr
expanded this new world when she took Cat shopping
for cloth to make garments for the baby. It was not
long before Cat was saying, "Mrs. Kerr, I must go to
the ribbon shop. I seem to be out of that lovely blue
silk for the baby's bonnets. Do we need anything at
the butcher, since I'll pass it on my way?"

Mrs. Kerr did not think it strange at all that her
young mistress was so innocent of everyday matters.
Cat had explained to the good woman that she had been
orphaned early, and raised in a country convent. It
was a common story.

As the days grew shorter, Mrs. Kerr decided that
young Mistress Abernethy should not be alone in the
evenings. Her niece, Sally, was brought into the house
to look after Cat. Sally was twenty, and as plump and
cheerful as her aunt. Her presence made the evenings
less lonely for Cat. The two young women sewed, or
Cat read to them before the fire. Cat liked her enough
to ask her if she would stay on and help look after the
baby. Sally was delighted.

Fiona and Adam celebrated Christmas in Paris with

their Leslie cousins. The New Year brought greetings from Glenkirk. Adam shook his head. "He's not yet found her. It's as if the wench had disappeared off the face of the earth." He looked at his wife. "Would ye ever do that to me, love?"

"Nay," said Fiona, glancing quickly away.

Adam looked at her more closely. "My God!" he shouted. "*Ye* know where she is! Ye do! Don't ye?" The look in his eyes was terrible, and Fiona panicked.

"She's in our house in Edinburgh! She made me promise not to tell! I thought she would be home, and safely wed wi him by now!" Then Fiona laughed. "She's got courage, has Cat! Good for her!"

"Ye know," said Adam ominously, "how I'm going to punish you, Fiona, don't ye?"

Fiona's temper snapped. If Patrick could be brought to heel, then so could Adam. It wouldn't hurt to try. "Ye do, Leslie," she shouted back at him, "and I'll spread my legs for the first man that comes through that door! I'll nae be treated like a naughty child any longer!"

For a moment they glowered at each other, and then Adam laughed. "I dinna think ye and Cat were friends."

"We weren't, but we are now. We must both contend with Leslie arrogance. Your ass-eared brother called her a 'thing on which to breed his sons.' Do ye blame her for fleeing him? I don't!"

"I've got to tell him, Fiona, else the innocent bairn will be born on the wrong side of the blanket."

"I know," she agreed. "The Glenkirk courier is still here. Send your message back wi him. And Adam—tell Patrick to use Cat gently. She does love him, you know, but she wants him to love her for herself and not just for the children she can gie him. He must treat her wi *respect*. This was all his own fault."

"I think," he said teasingly, "that being married to me is good for ye, sweetheart. Yer gaining in wisdom." He ducked as a pillow flew by his head.

"Write yer letter, Leslie, and come to bed," she answered him. "Cousin Louise showed me some fascinating pictures today, and I'm dying to see if we can do the same things." She looked provocatively over her shoulder at him.

Adam Leslie gazed back at his lovely wife. "I shall be your most willing and eager pupil, madame," he said, raising a rakish eyebrow.

Chapter 9

❧❦❧

THE Leslie courier had no difficulty in reaching the French coast from Paris, but once there he was forced to cool his heels. A nasty winter storm was brewing, and no captain was willing to set off across the North Sea. It wasn't that the fellow minded holing up in the cozy little French inn. He enjoyed the hearty food and excellent wine. But he knew the news he carried was of great importance to the earl. Lord Adam had given him a gold piece, and told him the earl would give him another.

Finally one windy but sunny morning, the courier stood in the center of the taproom, holding the gold piece high. He announced, "This to the man who gets me safely to Aberdeen! And another from my master, the Earl of Glenkirk, when we get there!"

The coin was plucked from his hand by a black-bearded man. "If this wind holds, laddie," he said, "I'll hae ye there in no time!"

The courier reached Glenkirk on the morning of February 2. Not only did the earl replace the gold piece he'd been forced to spend, he gave his messenger two more. The seacaptain was rewarded as had been promised.

Patrick Leslie left Glenkirk on the afternoon of February 2. He stopped at the abbey and asked Cat's uncle, Abbot Charles Leslie, to accompany him to Edinburgh.

73

"We'll have to ride hard, uncle. Ellen says she's nae due for at least two more weeks, but ye canna tell wi a first bairn."

Charles Leslie nodded, went to his apartments and returned a few minutes later. The monk's robe was gone. Abbot Charles had become a tall, hard man of forty-five, booted and ready to ride. "I'll do better in Edinburgh," he said, "if I dinna look like a priest in that heretic town."

Several days later they stood in front of Fiona's house in Edinburgh. Sally opened the door. Her eyes widened in approval of the two imposing figures.

"Is yer mistress at home?" asked the earl.

"She's sleeping, my lord." Sally wasn't sure who this handsome stranger was, but there was no doubt in her mind that he was a lord.

"We will wait then," said Charles Leslie, moving into the house. "I am her uncle."

Sally put them in the formal parlor and went to get Mrs. Kerr. The housekeeper arrived a few moments later bearing a tray with wine and biscuits. "I am Mrs. Kerr. Might I know the nature of your business, gentlemen? My mistress is in a very delicate condition at this time."

"She's nae had the bairn?" Patrick's voice was anxious.

"No, sir. Not yet, but within the next few days for sure."

"Tell me, Mrs. Kerr," asked the abbot, "are ye of the new kirk, or the old kirk?"

Years of religious feuding had made the townspeople wary. But for some reason, Mrs. Kerr trusted this man. Looking quickly around, she answered without hesitation, "The old kirk, sir."

"I am the Abbot of Glenkirk Abbey," the older man said. "This is my nephew, the Earl of Glenkirk."

Mrs. Kerr bobbed a curtsy.

"And," continued the abbot, "the young woman who calls herself Mistress Abernethy is in fact the Lady Catriona Hay, the earl's betrothed wife. For reasons I'll nae go into, my wayward niece has twice fled her marriage. Now, however, the time for foolishness is over. Within a few days' time the earl's son will be born. He must, of course, be legitimate. If ye would be so good as to show me to my niece's bedchamber, we will see her now."

Mrs. Kerr said not a word, but moved quickly out of the formal parlor and up the stairs, the earl and the abbot following her. On the second floor she pointed to a door. "That is my lady's room. Let me waken her, my lord." A few minutes later she stuck her head through the door and beckoned the men inside. Then she turned and hurried back down the stairs to tell Sally this extraordinary turn of events.

Cat Hay, wearing a dark-green velvet dressing gown, stood with her back to the blazing fireplace. "Well, uncle. What brings ye here?" she asked calmly.

For the briefest moment Charles Leslie was reminded of his grandmother, Janet. "I've come to hear ye exchange yer wedding vows wi Patrick," he said.

"Such a long ride for nothing," she said.

"Niece! Yer time is very near. Ye carry wi'in yer belly the next rightful heir of Glenkirk. Would ye deny him his birthright?"

"Save yer breath, uncle. I will nae wed wi Patrick. He does not want a wife. He wants a brood mare—a thing on which to breed his sons. He believes he owns me. He told me so himself."

Patrick winced. "Please, Cat. I love ye, hinny. I've been crazy wi worry over ye and the bairn. Please, sweetheart! 'Tis my son you carry."

"Nay, my lord. Not yer son. Yer bastard!"

The earl staggered as if she'd struck him, and for a moment Charles Leslie felt sorry for his nephew. It was going to be no easy task getting Cat to speak her vows, but he had not risen to the office of abbot by meekness.

"Leave us, nephew." When Patrick had left, and the door closed behind him, Charles Leslie turned to his niece. "All right, Catriona, let us talk. I want the whole story. A year ago ye were willing to marry Patrick. What happened to cause this breach between ye?"

Sighing, she eased herself into a chair. "At first it was but a misunderstanding. Fiona claimed to be sleeping wi him, and I was furious, and why not? He claimed to love me, and yet appeared to be sleeping wi another woman."

"You might have asked him, child," said the abbot.

"Uncle! His reputation preceded him, and I was a very young girl. When he found me at my house, A-Cuil, he beat and raped me, uncle! He said I was 'a thing on which to breed his sons,' and I'd nae go home till I was carrying his child, because then I would have to wed him. I would hae no other choice."

The abbot silently thanked God that he had chosen the religious life. Women, particularly those born into his family, could be such damned nuisances.

Cat continued. "He called me his 'possession.' I am no man's possession! When Patrick acknowledges me as an individual, and not as a part of himself, then I will consider the matter of marriage."

Charles Leslie sighed. It was worse than he had thought. However, and he chuckled at the realization, his niece was a remarkable strategist. She had the Earl of Glenkirk by the throat. If he wanted his son—the abbot never considered that the baby might be a daughter—then he must agree to her demands. The abbot decided to appeal to Cat's maternal instinct.

"Have ye no feeling for the bairn, niece?"

"No," she answered. "Should I?"

Charles Leslie exploded. "God's nightshirt, girl! Ye are the most unnatural mother I hae ever known! To have no feeling for yer child?"

Cat laughed. "Dinna be silly, uncle. Why should I hae any feeling for my child yet? I dinna know him. I hae never seen him. What is there for me to get soft about? A dream? Foolishness! If I dream the lad a blue-eyed redhead, and he arrives wi brown eyes, and black hair . . ." She stopped a moment, and then said in a solemn voice, ". . . or worse yet, a blond lassie! Why, uncle, I should be very disappointed then. And that's overlooking the fact that the bairn's father and I are not exactly on the best of terms."

Charles Leslie pursed his lips. "Ye are being deliberately difficult," he said.

"Aye," she rejoined sweetly. "It comes from being tired. I bear a heavy load, uncle. Ye and Patrick are welcome to stay the night. If ye'll send Mrs. Kerr to me on yer way out, I'll gie her instructions for yer comfort."

He retreated as gracefully as he could to the library on the main floor. Patrick was waiting. The abbot shook his head. "It's going to take time, lad. She's got the upper hand, and is in no mood to settle easily wi you."

"She must!"

"Nay, lad. Be careful, now. That's where ye made yer first mistake. Ye assume ye can bring Cat to heel, and ye cannot. She is proud, and has a wide streak of independence that I've seen before. My grandmother, Janet Leslie, was very much like that. But she had wisdom to go with her willfulness."

"I wonder if she had it when she was Cat's age," mused Patrick.

"She must have to have survived all she did," replied the abbot. "However, nephew, our problem is Catriona. She is very angry with you because of the things ye have said and done to her. She feels yer interest in her is not for herself, but for her breeding ability. Ye must humor her. Women about to gie birth have strange notions."

"I dinna understand what she wants," complained the earl. "I love her. Isn't that enough?"

"Nay, nephew, 'tis not. You are considering only yerself. I am not sure I understand entirely what it is she wants, but I think she wants ye to take an interest in her as a person. To talk wi her, to consult wi her on matters affecting yer life together—not simply to make demands. Catriona is, after all, a well-bred and an educated young woman. I think, Patrick, that yer problem stems from consorting wi so many low women, that ye dinna know how to treat a well-born one. Catriona is nae a plaything. And until ye realize that, she willna hae ye."

The earl flushed. But before he could defend himself, Mrs. Kerr was at the door asking them to dinner.

"Will yer mistress be joining us?" the abbot inquired.

"No, my lord. She'll sleep till late afternoon."

They ate in silence. The abbot noted with pleasure that Cat kept a good table. There was a hearty soup filled with carrots, barley, and thick chunks of mutton. Next came large bowls of fresh-caught oysters, a joint of rare beef, a fat capon, artichokes in vinegar, and some pastries of rabbit and of venison. There was bread, hot from the oven, and sweet butter. A tart of pears, apples, nuts, and spices and a fine cheese finished off the meal. Their goblets had been filled repeatedly with a good red wine.

Belching delicately, the abbot commented, "Ye'll nae go hungry wi Catriona in yer house, nephew. She sets a good table."

"Provided I can get her into my house to start with," the earl said ruefully.

The afternoon was long, and the abbot retired to his room to sleep and to make his devotions. Restless, Patrick found his cloak and went out into the city. The gray February cold was bitter, and he could smell on the wind the snow that would begin falling by evening. He walked without thinking. He walked to calm the feelings that raged through him. Suddenly he caught sight of a small jewelry shop and went inside. The owner, recognizing wealth when he saw it, came forward.

"Do ye hae any rings for sale?"

"Yes, my lord. If my lord would be seated." He signaled an apprentice, who hurried forward with a chair.

Patrick sat down. "A lady's ring," he clarified.

"Ahhhh," smiled the jeweler. "His lordship wishes something for a good friend." He snapped his fingers at a second apprentice, who came forward with a tray.

Patrick scornfully eyed the contents. "Lord, mon! Is this the best ye can do? I'm buying a ring for my wife, not for my whore." A second tray was presented. Patrick smiled. "This is more like it, mon!"

Four rings nestled on the pale-blue velvet; a diamond teardrop, a ruby heart, a round sapphire, and a square-cut emerald. Each was set in heavy gold. Carefully he examined each, asking its price. At last, picking up the heart-shaped ruby ring, he said, "I'll take this one, but only on one condition."

"And that is, my lord?"

"Send one of yer apprentices to the Kiras in Goldsmith's Lane. Tell them the Earl of Glenkirk wishes an appraisal immediately."

The jeweler bowed and bade one of his lads go. His prices were honest, and for that he thanked God. Getting a customer like the Earl of Glenkirk was a feather in his cap. If the earl took the ring, the jeweler thought, his wife could have the new cloak she'd been hounding him for all winter, and his mistress would get the lace cap she wanted. The apprentice reappeared soon, bringing a man with him.

"Benjamin!" The earl stood and grasped the newcomer's hand warmly.

"My lord, it is good to see you. When did you arrive in Edinburgh?"

"Just today. My Uncle Charles has accompanied me. We stay at my brother's house off High Street."

"Yes," said Benjamin Kira. "I know the house. I spoke with Lord Adam and his wife before they left for France." He smiled at the earl. "So you're buying jewelry?"

"For my lady Catriona."

"Ahh," said Benjamin Kira. He knew most of the story, but was far too polite to say so. "The ring, master jeweler." Slipping a small loop on his eye, he held up the ruby. "Ahhhhh. Yes. Hummm. Yes. Good. Very good!" He handed the ring to Patrick, and turned to the merchant. "Well, Master Adie, it's a beautiful stone. Well cut, nicely set. Your price?" The jeweler named it. "Very fair," pronounced Benjamin Kira. "In fact, you're getting a bargain, my lord. Let me see the other rings you showed the earl." He turned back to the jeweler. He examined the diamond, the sapphire, and the emerald, and then asked the price of each. "Too low, Master Adie," he told the surprised jeweler. "Raise the price on the emerald by twenty percent, and on the diamond and sapphire by ten percent."

Patrick directed Benjamin Kira to see that the jeweler was paid. Thanking him for his appraisal, the earl bid him and the jeweler good day. A blue-gray dusk lit the city, and snow was beginning to drift down in large, fat, sticky flakes. Briskly he walked back to his brother's house. Sally opened the door for him and, taking his cloak and cap, shooed him down the hall into the family parlor. "There's a good fire going, m'lord, and I'll bring ye some hot spiced wine."

He found his uncle and Cat engrossed in a game of chess before the fire. He said nothing, but sat down. Sally came in and set the goblet by his hand. He drank slowly, savoring the sweetness of the wine, the pungency of the spices, and the lovely warmth that began to seep through his chilled body.

"Check, and mate," he heard his uncle say.

"Yer far too skilled a chess player for an abbot," Cat complained.

"I generally win what I set out to win," came the reply.

"There speaks the Leslie in ye," Cat laughed. "I believe yer trying to tell me something, uncle."

"Yes, my child, I am. Whatever your misunderstanding wi Patrick, the bairn is the innocent party. Dinna let him be born nameless."

"Oh, he won't be nameless. I intend calling him James, after the king. I saw the lad out riding one day. Such a solemn boy, but verra bonnie."

Glenkirk bit his lip to keep from laughing. The minx was deliberately baiting the abbot, and she had succeeded admirably. Charles Leslie exploded in a rash of very unabbotlike Gaelic oaths. Cat stood up and curtsied. "Good night, uncle. I find I am once again fatigued," she said, leaving the room. She had never, even once, acknowledged Patrick's presence.

"Someone ought to beat the wench on her backside!" growled the abbot.

"I already have," replied the earl. "It did no good."

The abbot snorted. "Tomorrow I will speak wi her again. Now, I am for my bed. I'll need a good night's rest if I'm to contend with Catriona Hay."

Patrick stood by the window watching the snow. It was falling quite thickly now, and the deserted street outside was already well covered. The parlor door opened to admit Sally, carrying a tray. "Mistress thought ye might be hungry after yer walk, m'lord. She and yer uncle ate earlier." She put the tray on the table by the fireplace. "I'll come back in a bit, sir. Ye eat up now!"

The tray contained a steaming bowl of boiled shrimp, a plate with two thick slices of cold ham, a small, hot loaf of bread, a dish of sweet butter, and a pitcher of brown ale. Patrick devoured it all. When Sally returned she brought a plate of warm shortbread and a bowl of highly polished red apples. He ate all the shortbread and two of the apples. Sally, clearing away the tray, smiled warmly at him. "It does me good to see you eat, m'lord! It's like watching me brother, Ian. Now, sir, if you'll look in the cabinet there," she pointed across the room, "you'll find some good whisky. Will there be anything else before I go to bed?"

"Nay, lass. Thank ye kindly. Run along now."

Alone again, he poured himself a whisky and drank it slowly, enjoying its smoky bite. Trust Cat to find a man with a good still, he thought. Cat! Ah, sweetheart, I've hurt ye, and now I am going to have the devil's own time wi ye. My uncle may do all the diplomacy he chooses tomorrow, but I must talk wi ye tonight.

He put down his glass and exited the family parlor. Sally had left him a nightstick burning on the table by the stairwell. Slowly he climbed the stairs, dreading the moment he'd have to face her. Standing in front of her door, he knocked. For a moment, he hoped she was asleep. Then the door opened, and there she was in her green velvet dressing gown, her heavy, honey-colored hair loose about her shoulders. He stared tongue-tied, feeling like a fool.

"Patrick." Her voice was soft. "Either come in, or go away." She turned and walked back into the room.

He followed her, closing the door behind him. A fire
burned in the grate, lighting the room. She had been in
bed. Paying him no heed, she climbed back into the
warmth of her quilts. Two huge pillows propped her
up. He drew a chair up next to the bed and sat down.

"Well, my lord," she said, folding her hands over her
enormous belly, "I think I am safe in assuming ye've
nae come to rape me this night. What is it then ye
want?"

"I want to talk. We'll leave the diplomacy and tact
to our uncle the abbot. Ye and I can speak the truth
to each other. I am a fool, Cat!"

"Aye," she agreed.

"I love ye, lass! What is done is done. If ye canna
forgie me, can ye at least forget my boorishness? I'll
do anything to win ye back."

"Can ye change the way ye think, Patrick? Because
that is my price. I will nae be yer possession. Yers, or
anyone else's! I canna be just Glenkirk's wife. I must
be Catriona Hay Leslie, and only if ye think of me in
that way, and treat me in that way, will others follow."
She smiled gently at him. "Ah, hinny! I dinna think ye
really understand, do ye? Perhaps ye canna."

"I am trying to, Cat. Would it help if I set aside a
certain portion of yer dowry for you alone?"

"That's not quite what I mean, Patrick, but if yer
willing I'll tell ye exactly what I want from a financial
point of view. The investments that Grandmam left
me were included in my dowry. They should not have
been. They are mine alone, and I want them back.
A-Cuil also belongs to me. It was my paternal grandmother's, and Grandmam saw that it was put in my
name, as this house is in Fiona's name. Lord, Patrick!
Ye knew Grandmam better than I did, and ye know
how strongly she felt about a woman having something
of her own."

"Of course ye may have A-Cuil back," he said, "but as to the investments, love, ye dinna know finance, and I canno allow ye to waste what Grandmam left ye just to satisfy a whim."

"Then we canna proceed any further in our discussions, Patrick. Good night." She turned away from him. She would not tell him that for two years now she had been handling the investments Grandmam left her. She had the brilliant guidance of Benjamin Kira. Of all Janet Leslie's great-grandchildren, Catriona Hay's investments were the richest because she listened and learned from the Kiras, that family whose help had meant so much to Janet Leslie. Cat had a flair for investment banking, and an almost psychic sense about decisions. But she would not tell Patrick these things. The decision to return to her what was rightfully hers must be his decision. She did not care what his reasons would be, for she didn't really expect him to understand how she felt. However, he must act without knowledge of her financial talent, or it would be no good.

She heard the door close quietly. Rolling over onto her back, her eyes swept the room. He was gone. She felt the tears—hot and salty—pouring down her face. Despite her calm demeanor she was frightened. The babe she carried was the next Glenkirk and she wanted him born with both his names, but she'd not give in to Patrick before he met her conditions. The child in her womb kicked, and she protectively placed her hands on her belly.

"Dinna fret, Jamie. Yer father will see it our way soon," she whispered. And it would have to be very soon, she knew, for her son should be making his appearance any time now. She wondered if Patrick was as restless as she was, and whether he was lying awake in his bed now as she lay awake in hers.

Chapter 10

❧❧

THE snow fell all through the night, and Edinburgh woke to a sparkling silver-white city. Cat rose, relieved herself in the chamberpot, and climbed back into the warm bed. A few minutes later Sally arrived to start a fresh fire. She brought hot milk with a beaten egg and spices, and a plate of hot scones dripping butter and strawberry jam.

"Bless you," said Cat, sitting forward as Sally plumped her pillows. "I'm ravenous this morning. Is there any bacon?"

"There could be, my lady," smiled Sally. "Start wi what ye have, and I'll tell Mrs. Kerr."

Cat sipped her milk and greedily ate the scones.

"You look like something ten years old instead of a woman about to gie birth," laughed Patrick, entering the room. "There's jam all over yer face. Yer bacon, madame." He gracefully swept the plate under her nose and set it down in front of her.

"Thank you, my lord." She grabbed a piece of the bacon and chewed it with relish.

"May I breakfast wi you, Cat?"

"If ye wish."

"Sally lass! Bring it in!"

Cat waited until Sally had departed before speaking. "Rather sure of yerself, aren't ye, Patrick?"

"Damnit, Cat! Is this the way it's going to be? Always sniping?"

"Until ye gie me back what is mine, it is not going to be at all!" She took another bite of scone, and the butter ran down her little chin.

"Yer going to call my bluff, aren't ye, Cat?" He could barely keep the amusement out of his voice.

"Aye," she drawled, looking straight at him. "Would ye like to wager I'll win too?"

"What stakes, madame?"

"A-Cuil against a house in Edinburgh, but I get to choose it."

"If ye win, sweetheart."

"I will," she said, swooping up the last piece of bacon.

He laughed, enjoying her outrageous confidence. It was a side of her he hadn't seen before, and he liked it. "If," he said, "I can find a conveyance of some sort, will ye come out wi me today?"

"Yes! My size has hindered me, and I've been indoors all the last few weeks."

Benjamin Kira owned a sleigh imported from Norway. It was red, with a black-and-gold design, and pulled by two black horses. The earl settled Cat comfortably, tucking several fur robes about her, took the reins, and set off through the city.

Catriona Hay was a beautiful woman. There were enough admiring glances directed at the sleigh to annoy Patrick considerably, but his glowering looks were enough to discourage any gallants.

Cat was wrapped in a brown velvet cloak. The hood, trimmed in a wide band of soft dark sable, framed beautifully her creamy, heart-shaped face. Several tendrils of honey-colored hair escaped from beneath the hood, their rich dark gold lying in delicious contrast to the dark fur. Patrick cursed to himself. He was going to have to give in to her demands! It wasn't merely the question of his son's name. He loved this headstrong vixen, and if he allowed her to escape him again, he'd never get her back.

"I'm hungry, Glenkirk," she announced, breaking in on his thoughts.

"There's an excellent tavern on the edge of town, sweetheart. I thought we'd stop there."

He drove the sleigh smartly into the courtyard of the Royal Scot and, leaping down, tossed the reins to a young fellow. Cat flung back the fur robes and allowed Patrick to lift her out. Because of the snow, he carried her into the inn before setting her on her feet.

"A private room, sir?" asked the landlord.

"Nay, mon. The common room will do us fine if it isna too crowded."

They were seated at a window table by the large fireplace. Patrick took her cloak. Beneath it she wore a deceptively modest loose brown velvet gown with a creamy lace ruff collar, and cuffs. A heavy gold and topaz chain relieved the severity of the gown. Her hair was loose.

The landlord brought them goblets of hot spiced wine without waiting to be asked.

"We'll eat," said the earl. "Bring us yer best."

They had drunk two goblets of the wine before the waiter arrived, staggering beneath his tray. The first course consisted of a bowl of shrimp, prawns, and oysters, boiled in a delicate herb sauce. There was fresh bread and butter, a dish of artichokes in vinegar and oil, and a salad of cabbage. Next came roast duck, crisp and brown with a sweet-and-sour lemon sauce, three standing ribs of rare beef, thin pink slices of lamb on a shallow platter with red wine and rosemary, a whole broiled trout, and flaky little pastries filled with minced venison, rabbit, and fruit. The third course was a large bowl of stewed pears and apples in clotted cream, sprinkled with colored sugar. This was accompanied by jellies, sugared nuts, and a large cheese. Lastly came wafers, and little glasses of hippocras. Cat, who had never been shy at the table, ate with a particular gusto that amused the earl. At last she said, "I'm sleepy, Glenkirk! Take me home."

He paid the bill and complimented the landlord on the excellence of the food and the service. Having tipped everyone, he tucked Cat again into the sleigh and drove home. When he had returned the sleigh to Benjamin Kira and come back, Sally informed him that her mistress had retired to her room. He climbed the stairs and knocked. She bade him enter. She had exchanged the brown velvet dress for a pale blue silk chamber robe. She lay on her bed.

"I am feeling very fat and full," she told him. "I intend sleeping the whole afternoon away." She reached up, drawing him down to the bed. "Thank ye, Patrick. I did enjoy our outing so!"

"So did I, love," he answered. He bent and kissed her gently.

She took his hand and placed it on her swollen belly. A look of incredulous delight lit up his face as he felt the child in her belly kick. She laughed.

"Aye, hinny! My Jamie's a strong and healthy bairn!"

She had said "my," not "our." Patrick was hurt, but he tried hiding it, and instead said lightly, *"Our* Jamie, Cat. He's my son too."

"Nay, my lord of Glenkirk. I told ye yesterday. The bairn is my son. Your bastard."

Patrick stood. "I'll let ye sleep," he said quietly, and left the room.

He was close to giving in, Cat knew, and she was using every trick to weaken him. She knew he wanted her, and not just for the child. She didn't mind his desiring her body, for she also desired his. But until he gave her back her rightful property and saw the error of his ways, there could be no living with him. She fell asleep wondering how long it would be before he conceded defeat.

While she slept, Patrick was learning a very interesting fact from his uncle. The abbot had spent the morning in the library awaiting the return of his niece and nephew. He was feeling quite pleased with himself. He thought his talks with Catriona had begun to bear fruit. When Patrick entered the library he asked, "Well, nephew! When do I perform the wedding?"

"Not yet, uncle. She's still not ready to have me."

"God's foot, mon! What does she want? Do ye understand her? For I am nae sure I do."

Patrick laughed. "I think I am beginning to understand her quite well. She does nae wish to be treated as a chattel."

"Nonsense!" snapped the abbot. "Of course women are chattel. Why, even the Protestant heretics agree wi *that*."

"Nevertheless," continued Patrick, "she wants to be treated as an equal, and she says that both A-Cuil and the investments that Grandmam left her should not have been included in her dowry. She wants them legally returned to her. She says she'll nae wed wi me until she gets them."

The abbot thought a minute, then spoke. "Mam believed that women needed a little something of their own, and she did see that all of her granddaughters, and the great-granddaughters born before she died, had both a bit of property and some financial investments. A mad idea! No judge would uphold such nonsense. If Greyhaven included A-Cuil and the investments in Cat's dowry, then they are, of course, yours."

Hearing his uncle's reasoning, Patrick suddenly saw the unfairness of it all. In a flash he understood Cat's anger. "I have promised," he said, "to return A-Cuil to her. Has she ever done anything wi her investments other than collect the dividends?"

"Greyhaven mentioned something about it to me once, but I'm nae sure what he was talking about. You would have to ask the Kiras."

"I hae full intention of doing so," replied Patrick, "but uncle, if ye wish my son born legitimate, say nothing to Cat of this conversation. I am going to see Benjamin Kira. If she asks for me when she wakes, say I've gone out walking."

But when Cat Hay awoke she wasn't thinking of Patrick. She was thinking of the pains sweeping over her. She struggled to gain her feet, but no sooner had she done so than a flood of water poured down her legs. She screamed. Within seconds, both Mrs. Kerr and Sally burst into the room. It took but a moment for Mrs. Kerr to sum up the situation. She put a comforting arm about Cat.

"Dinna fret, my lady. 'Tis just the laddie deciding it's his time to be born. Sally, lass! Get some towels. Are ye in pain, my lady?"

"A little. The pains come and go."

"Rightly so," said Mrs. Kerr. "Sally! Go tell the abbot we'll need his help wi the table. Now, my lady, back into bed for the moment." She helped Cat back into the big bed.

Sally hurried downstairs to the library, where Charles Leslie dozed peacefully before the fire. Gently she shook his shoulder. "Sir! Sir!" Charles sleepily opened his eyes. "Mistress has gone into labor, sir. Mrs. Kerr and I will need yer help in carrying the birthing table."

The abbot was wide awake now. "Has the earl returned?"

"No, sir."

"Damnation!" swore the abbot. "I'll hae to run and fetch him."

Sally put a hand on his arm. "My lord, my little brother's in the kitchen. He'll go fetch the earl. There is plenty of time. First babies are always slow in coming."

"Gie the lad this," said Charles, handing Sally a copper. "There's a silver piece when he returns."

"Thank ye, m'lord. If ye'll wait here I'll send the boy now."

She ran to the kitchen, where her ten-year-old brother sat spooning lamb stew into his mouth. "Here, Robbie. Run to Banker Kira's house in Goldsmith's Lane. Ask for the Earl of Glenkirk, and speak to no one else. Tell him his son is about to be born. If they dinna want to disturb the earl, tell them 'tis life and death." She gave him the copper. "And there's silver when ye come back!"

Clutching the copper, the boy grabbed his cloak, and ran.

At Benjamin Kira's home the Earl of Glenkirk sat sipping Turkish coffee and listening with growing amazement as the current head of the Edinburgh Kira family told him of Catriona Hay's financial acumen. "She's almost tripled her investment in the last two years," said Benjamin Kira.

"Surely ye tell her what to do," said Patrick.

"Not for the last two years, my lord. When she was twelve, she wrote and asked if I would instruct her in financial matters. I began simply, for I was not sure either that she was serious or that she had the intellect for it. The more I taught her, the more she wanted to know. She absorbed all I told her, and comprehended everything. Two years ago she began handling her own affairs. For about six months she would consult me before she made a move, but since then she has taken full charge. She's clever, my lord, very clever. I don't mind telling you in confidence that I have been following her lead myself, and a pretty penny I have made!"

Patrick Leslie swallowed hard. "Are ye telling me, Benjamin, that when Lady Catriona has instructed ye regarding her investments, ye hae followed her advice regarding yer own?"

"Yes, my lord."

"Did ye know that the Master of Greyhaven turned over Lady Catriona's investments to me last year when the wedding date was set?"

"I did not know, my lord. We were not notified here in Edinburgh. Lady Hay has been continuing to handle her own funds, especially since she has been here in town."

"And she will continue to do so, Benjamin. Your brother, Abner, is a lawyer, is he not?"

"Yes, my lord."

"If he is here, I want to immediately draw up a paper legally returning Lady Hay's possessions to her. And Benjamin, she is *never* to know that I questioned you about her handling of the funds. I will be frank wi ye my friend. Lady Hay will shortly bear my child, and she refuses to wed wi me as was arranged years ago, unless I return her property. Naturally I'd nae hae the next Glenkirk born a bastard, but she is a stubborn lass, and neither my uncle the abbot nor I can move her."

"I'll send for my brother and his clerk immediately, my lord. You may trust my discretion. Women, at best, are unpredictable. Women about to give birth, however, are downright dangerous. It is best to just give in gracefully."

While they waited for the lawyer, young Robbie was shown into the room. "This boy," said the servant, "claims he must see the earl on a matter of life and death."

"Well, lad," said the earl kindly.

"I'm Robbie Kerr, Sally's brother. Her ladyship is having the bairn now."

"Jesu!" swore Patrick. "Is it born yet?"

"Nay, sir," said the boy calmly. "She's just begun her labor."

"Yer remarkably well informed for a lad of nine? Ten?" The earl was amused.

"Ten, sir. And I should be well informed. There's six after me."

"Your mother's to be commended, young Robbie," said Benjamin Kira.

"Nay, sir. Me mum died birthin' me. 'Tis my stepmother who had the six after me."

The earl paled and, noting it, Benjamin Kira said to him, "I'll send my wife back with the boy. She's a mother three times. She'll find out how far along your lady is. Don't worry, my lord. These first births are always long. You have plenty of time."

As Abner Kira and his clerk entered the room, Benjamin and the boy went to find Benjamin's wife. Husband and wife conferred in a language unfamiliar to Robbie. It sounded a bit like the Gaelic he'd heard spoken occasionally. Mistress Kira turned her lovely brown eyes on Robbie. "Well, laddie. Come along, and lead me to his lordship's house," she said.

Sally let them in, for Robbie took Mistress Kira to the front door. "I am Master Benjamin Kira's wife. His lordship sent me to see how his lady does."

Sally curtsied. "If you'll pray be seated, ma'am, I'll go fetch my aunt. She is wi her ladyship now."

When Mrs. Kerr came down the stairs she fussed, "Och, Sally has left you in the hallway. Come into the back parlor, and have a glass of cordial."

"Thank you, Mrs. Kerr," smiled Anna Kira, "but I must hurry back. His lordship, like most first-time fathers, is frantic. How does his lady?"

"He need not worry. Everything is proceeding normally. She'll nae deliver for hours yet."

"I think he'll be home long before," said Mistress Kira gently.

The two women looked at each other, their faces registering their understanding of the ways of men. They laughed. Returning quickly to her own home, Anna Kira reassured the earl that Cat was fine.

By this time, Abner Kira had composed the document which made Catriona Mairi Hay Leslie, Countess of Glenkirk, sole owner in her own right of A-Cuil, and of the investments left to her by Janet Leslie. The document, written in duplicate, was signed by Patrick Leslie, Earl of Glenkirk, and witnessed by both Benjamin and Abner Kira. One copy was to be kept permanently in the Kira vaults. The earl took the other with him.

He hurried through the snowy twilight, the document clutched beneath his cloak. She would wed him now. She had to!

"Not yet," smiled Sally as she let him in and took his cloak.

"My uncle?"

"In the library, sir."

He moved swiftly down the hall and into the library. "Come, Uncle Charles, get what ever ye need to marry us. I've done what Cat asked, and I'm going up to her now." He was out the door before the abbot could speak. He ran up the stairs, two at a time, and burst into Cat's bedroom.

A long table, slanted to one end, stood before the fireplace. It was covered in muslin sheets. Cat sat upon it, propped up with pillows. The earl looked around, astounded.

"Birthing is a bloody business, my lord. I dinna believe in ruining a perfectly good mattress and feather bed," said Mrs. Kerr.

Patrick walked over to Cat and stood before her. Without a word, he handed her the rolled parchment. She broke the seal, unrolled it, and read it through. Her eyes closed for a moment as pain swept through her. Then, raising tear-filled eyes to him, she said softly, "Thank ye, Patrick."

"Catriona Hay, we've been pledged for over twelve years. Our child is being born at this very minute. Say ye'll wed me now." He stopped, and grinned. "Besides, this document is made out to Catriona Mairi Hay Leslie, the Countess of Glenkirk. Ye *must* wed me to get yer property back!"

"Patrick," she asked. "Ye hae returned my property, 'tis true. But has yer attitude changed? How do ye see me?"

It was a tricky question, and he knew that their fates and that of their child depended on his careful answer. "I see ye," he said slowly, "first, as Cat Hay—a competent and lovely woman. I hope to see ye also as my wife, as my mistress, as my friend, and as the mother of our children. Ye are nae one woman, sweetheart, yer many! Some of whom I've yet to meet."

"Patrick." She smiled at him through her pain. "I do believe ye are beginning to understand me. It canna hae been easy for ye. Thank ye."

She was going to accept. He was sure of it, and felt relief sweeping over him.

"Yes, my lord . . . my love . . . my dear friend, and dearer enemy!" She squeezed his hand. "I will honor the contract between us, and wed wi ye."

On cue, the abbot bustled in, carrying his portable altar. "Well, niece! No more foolishness! If ye'll nae speak yer vows yerself, I'll be forced to speak them for ye. I should hae thought of that months ago. I dinna suppose ye can stand at this point?"

"There is no need to threaten me, uncle. I will marry Patrick, but not for another five minutes. If ye'll both leave, I wish to dress for my wedding." She winced, and said to Sally, "The ruby-red velvet dressing gown. Ohhhh, Jesu!" The men left quickly.

Sally was worried. "The pains are much closer now, my lady. I dinna think ye can stand."

"Just for a few minutes. I will not be married lying down on a birthing table!" Another spasm shot through her.

Sally helped Cat out of her chamber robe and into the heavy velvet dressing gown, as Mrs. Kerr slipped out into the hall. "Say the words quickly, my lord abbot. Her labor has increased suddenly. The next Glenkirk will be born in a very short time."

Charles nodded. Sally stuck her head out the door and called, "Mistress wants the ceremony in the parlor by the fireplace."

While Mrs. Kerr and the abbot blustered disapproval, Patrick strode back into the bedroom. Cat stood shakily in her ruby-red velvet dressing gown. Her long, heavy hair was plaited and pinned up, held fast with gold and pearl pins. He did not miss the pain in her eyes. His arms were around her. Neither said a word. Picking Cat up, he walked into the hall and carefully down the stairs to the main parlor. The abbot, Mrs. Kerr, and Sally followed.

Charles Leslie opened his prayer book and began. Patrick and Cat stood before him, Cat holding Glenkirk's hand very tightly. He knew each time she experienced a contraction, for her grip tightened. He marveled at her strength.

The abbot, having noted his niece's pallor, went quickly through the ceremony. "The ring," he hissed at Patrick. Patrick handed him the ruby. Charles Leslie blessed it, returned it to the earl and watched him slip it on Cat's finger. Her eyes widened appreciatively at the heart-shaped stone, and she smiled up at him. He smiled reassuringly at her. After a few more words,

Charles Leslie pronounced his niece and nephew husband and wife.

Patrick didn't wait for congratulations. He lifted Cat and carried her quickly back upstairs to the bedroom. Sally ran ahead, opening the door, as Mrs. Kerr followed close behind. The two women helped Cat out of the heavy gown and onto the birthing table. When he was sure she was as comfortably settled as she could be, Patrick drew up a chair and sat by her side.

"My lord, this is no place for a man," remonstrated Mrs. Kerr.

"Unless my wife objects I will remain to see my son born." He looked at Cat.

She held out her hand to him. "Stay, my lord," she smiled at him. "Ye've already missed so much."

The pains were coming faster and harder. Her entire body was bathed in perspiration. She gritted her teeth and breathed deeply.

"Don't hold back, my lady," said Mrs. Kerr. "You must cry out, or it will go the worse for you."

"I dinna want my son entering the world to the sound of his mother's pain," she insisted.

"Nonsense!" snapped back Mrs. Kerr. "He'll nae remember it, so busy he'll be with his own howling." Her eyes twinkled. "Why don't you swear—in the Gaelic—for he'll nae understand that."

The abbot of Glenkirk, waiting outside in the hallway, listened in amazement to the stream of colorful Gaelic issuing from his niece's chamber. It was followed some ten minutes later by a triumphant shout from Glenkirk, and the outraged howl of an infant. Unable to restrain himself any longer, Charles Leslie rushed into the bedroom. Mrs. Kerr was tending Cat while Sally wiped the birthing blood from the wailing child.

"I've a son, uncle! A son! The fifth Earl of Glenkirk," shouted Patrick. "James Patrick Charles Adam Leslie!"

"Aye, uncle," spoke up a tired but amused voice.

"He has a son. The fourth earl has given birth to the fifth earl. And just fancy, he did it all by himself."

"I couldna hae done it wi'out ye, sweetheart," grinned Patrick.

"No, ye couldn't have," she laughed weakly. "When do I get to see the marvel I hae produced?"

" 'Twill be a minute, dearie," said Mrs. Kerr. "Yer all cleaned up, and—" she slipped a clean, sweetly scented nightgown of soft pale-lavender wool over her lady's head—"ready to be put back into your bed. My lord, would you be so kind as to carry the countess to her bed."

Gently, Patrick lifted Cat and placed her between the warmed sheets. Then he drew the down coverlet over her. Sally placed the sleeping, swaddled infant in Cat's arms. "God's nightshirt! He's so tiny! I've seen bigger Christmas capons." But there was pride in her voice. "He's got your hair, Patrick," she said, noting the damp tuft of black that Sally had brushed into a curl.

Mrs. Kerr took the baby back and handed him to Sally.

"She'll put him in his cradle, and sit wi him until he wakes. Do ye still wish to nurse him, or shall I hire a wet nurse?"

"I'll nurse him myself, Mrs. Kerr. At least for now. I do think, however, that Sally's sister, Lucy, should come and be her assistant in the nursery. Sally cannot watch the child all day and all night."

"Yes, my lady, but now you must get some sleep."

"In a few minutes, Mrs. Kerr. You'll see that his lordship and my uncle are well taken care of at supper?"

"Of course, madam," smiled Mrs. Kerr. "I'll see to it at once." She turned to go.

"Mrs. Kerr?"

"Yes, my lady?"

"Thank ye, Mrs. Kerr. For everything."

The housekeeper bridled with pleasure. " 'Twas an honor, my lady, to deliver the future Glenkirk." She turned to the abbot. "Come, sir. I'll wager all this excitement has raised an appetite in you." Together they left the room.

Patrick came and sat gingerly on the edge of his wife's bed. Taking her hand, he raised it to his lips. "Yer overproud, Cat Leslie, and stubborn beyond belief. But, by God, I love you. I am proud and lucky to hae ye for my wife . . . and my friend!"

She lifted her leaf-green eyes to him and they twinkled mischievously. "Ye owe me a house in town, Glenkirk, and as soon as I am able, I intend to get it!"

Patrick Leslie's deep laughter sounded throughout the entire house.

Chapter 11

≈§§≈

JAMES Patrick Charles Adam Leslie had appeared on the twenty-fourth of February, 1578. Four weeks after his birth, Adam and Fiona Leslie arrived home from France. The earl had sent his messenger with news of his son's birth, and the younger Leslies returned in haste so as to be godparents to the child.

Charles Leslie performed the ceremony without delay. He had been away from his abbey for about two months now. Hiring a swift coastal cutter, he sailed north to Peterhead. He would be able to continue overland easily from there, and looked forward to spending his first night back on dry land enjoying the hospitality of Deer Abbey.

Fiona was amused to find Cat enjoying her maternity. "I didna think ye were the goo-ga type," she chuckled.

Cat grinned back. "Neither did I. It creeps up on ye wi'out yer knowing it. However, I dinna intend to hae another for several years."

"If Glenkirk's the rutting stallion Leslie is, ye'll hae no choice."

"I'll be careful," said Cat meaningfully.

"Why, cousin," remarked Fiona, raising an elegantly plucked eyebrow, "how different ye are from a year ago."

"It's been a rather busy year, Fiona."

And it got busier for Cat. She was looking for a house, for with Adam and Fiona back home, the little Edinburgh dwelling was too crowded. Adam had promised his wife they would travel, but that had changed now.

The second Glenkirk son, James, was married to Ailis Hay, and Ailis Hay's only brother, Francis, had died of a winter flux. Gilbert Hay had no other legitimate sons, and therefore James Leslie had become his father-in-law's heir. James and Ailis were moving to Hay House to learn the management of a small estate.

Michael Leslie would be marrying Isabella Forbes in less than two years, and taking over her estate. It was therefore up to Adam Leslie to learn the management of Glenkirk in the event that Patrick died before his son, James, reached his majority.

"Spend a year at Glenkirk, and ye can hae a year to travel," promised Patrick, seeing Fiona's disappointment.

Cat, meanwhile, had found a house to suit her. Like Leslie House it was on a quiet side street. But her choice was off Canongate, which ran towards the Palace of Holyrood rather than towards High Street. Built of brick, it contained a large and sunny kitchen, a pantry, a washroom, a still room, a storage room, a servant's hall, a comfortable room off the garden for the cook, and several cubicles for the kitchen help. The main floor held a wide reception hall, a bright formal parlor, a library, a dining room, a family dining room, and family parlor. The second floor was made up almost entirely of one great hall. Off it were several private anterooms. On the third floor were six bedrooms, each with its own dressing room, and indoor sanitary facilities. On the fourth floor was the nursery, and on the fifth, the servants' quarters.

The property had a flower garden, kitchen garden, and orchard. It also had a fine large stable. When the earl complained of the size of the house, he was reminded of the size of their families. Glenkirk House would serve for all the Leslies when they visited Edinburgh, and would be useful later on when the little king came into his own, and held court. Cat had hired Mrs. Kerr on a permanent basis to run her new house. She wanted to stay in Edinburgh at least till the end of June so she might attend to the ordering of the furnishings. Glenkirk gave her till mid-May.

"Why can't you and Adam go home alone?" she protested. "Fiona and I will stay in town to finish this business, and then join ye later."

Patrick laughed. "Madame," he said looking down at her, "I hae no intention of letting ye out of my sight ever again. Yer an impossible wench to catch up with, my dear. We'll return to Glenkirk together in mid-May. Ye'll hae to have yer business finished by then. Besides, what difference does it make if the house is finished now, or not?"

"Because, my lord, I hae no intention of spending the entire winter snowed in at Glenkirk. After Christmas, or before if it be possible, we will return to town for the winter."

The earl was amused. So she had plans to come to town each winter? He chuckled to himself. What a handful she was going to be. Best to keep her little belly filled with his children. A full nursery would keep her busy.

During the next few weeks Cat spoke with numerous craftsmen and, approving hundreds of sketches, ordered the furnishings. She arranged with Benjamin Kira that the craftsmen be paid, upon Mrs. Kerr's approval, after delivery had been made. She did not tell Patrick about this. The earl might have forgotten, but Glenkirk House belonged to Cat.

Before they left Edinburgh they were visited by George Leslie, the Earl of Rothes, who was the head of the Leslie clan. Both Patrick and Adam were pleased by the honor done their minor branch of the family. Cat, however, was not impressed.

"We're richer," she said. "He has decided to keep on good terms wi us in case he has to borrow money."

Though the men were shocked at this lack of respect, Fiona laughed. "Ye really are a bitch, Cat, but I happen to agree wi you. Besides, George Leslie is of the new kirk, and his family was implicated in the murder of Cardinal Beaton years ago. I dinna trust him."

They left Edinburgh for Glenkirk in mid-May. The earl, his countess, Adam, and Fiona all rode. Sally, Lucy, and the baby were comfortably settled in a wagon. A troop of Glenkirk soldiers under Conall More-Leslie escorted the party, for the roads were not safe. Many small merchants, hearing they planned to travel by way of Aberdeen, asked leave to travel with them. The larger the group, the safer everyone was.

They reached Glenkirk two weeks later. Fiona chuckled wickedly at the reception awaiting them. Lined up were the dowager countess Margaret Leslie, Cat's parents and brothers, Fiona's parents and brothers, all the Leslies of Glenkirk, and the More-Leslies of Crannog.

"Jesu," swore Cat under her breath. "They've dragged the whole clan out! The only one missing seems to be our uncle, the abbot."

"No, he's there. He just stooped to pick up Aunt Meg's glove." Fiona sounded as if she were going to laugh.

"Christ's toenail!"

"It's nae us, Cat. 'Tis his next Earlship of Glenkirk they've come to welcome," returned Fiona as the mob descended upon them.

She was right. Poor Jamie was snatched from Sally and passed, howling his outrage, among the delighted relations. Cat angrily retrieved her son, soothed him, and quelled the protest from the group. Ellen called, "I'll take him, my lady."

"Ye most certainly will not," snapped Cat. "Yer far too good a maid, and I have missed ye," she told the crestfallen woman, who immediately brightened. "Sally," called Cat. "Take yer wet master."

She endured the welcoming banquet arranged by Patrick's mother before being allowed to escape to her apartments. Her mother cornered her long enough to ask whether all was well between her daughter and the earl. Assured that everything was fine, Heather breathed a sigh of relief and returned to her husband. As evening drew in, Cat yawned hugely. Meg Leslie smothered a laugh.

"I think," she whispered to her daughter-in-law, "that it would be perfectly permissible for ye to end this banquet."

Cat leaned over to Patrick. "Glenkirk! Must I fall asleep in the jellies before ye'll end the evening?"

"All right, sweetheart, but I'll stay awhile. Let us stand up now, and put the others who also wish to retire out of their misery."

They stood, giving the signal for those who wanted to leave. Cat politely bid her guests good night and hurried to the nursery. Jamie, his eyes bright, lay on his stomach sucking his tiny fist.

"He's such a good bairn," said the doting Lucy.

Cat picked up her son and cradled him for a moment. His tiny nose twitched.

"Och," crowed Sally proudly. "The smart laddie smells the milk!"

Jamie began to cry. Lucy took the baby from Cat while Sally hurried to help her mistress remove her bodice. Cat sat down. Taking her son again, she gave him her breast. When the child had sated himself and lay drowsily in her lap, she smiled down on him. "He's growing so big," she noted, her voice soft.

"Aye, madame," answered Sally, "and bright he is, too, our little lad."

Cat lay her son back in the cradle on his stomach and drew the coverlet over him. "When I see him so helpless, so tiny," she said, "it's hard to believe he'll be a great impossible man like his father some day."

The two nursemaids giggled, and the countess, rising, buttoned her bodice and bid them good night. She hurried to her own apartments, where Ellen had a steaming tub waiting. Stripping her clothes off, Cat climbed in and luxuriated in the warm fragrant water. She, who was used to bathing daily, had not had a bath since leaving Edinburgh two weeks before. "Ellen, tell the earl's man, Angus, to hae a bath ready for his lordship. I won't hae him climb stinking into my bed this night."

And while Ellen was gone, Cat lathered up her hair, rinsed it, lathered it, and rinsed it again. She climbed from the tub and sat naked before the fire while Ellen rubbed her hair dry and then brushed it till it gleamed. Finally, Cat stood and held her hair up while Ellen powered her body.

"Perfection! You are pure perfection!" Her husband stood in the doorway.

"Angus has prepared you a bath, my lord," she told him.

Lazily his eyes traveled the length of her body. She boldly returned his glance.

"Ye smell like sunshine, love."

"And you stink of horses and two weeks on the dusty road."

He laughed. "I'll nae be long. Good night, Ellen."

Ellen chuckled. "Which nightgown, my lady?"

"Dinna bother, Ellie. Just gie me a shawl."

Cat got into the big bed and, sitting up, drew a lacy wool shawl about her shoulders. "Good night, Ellie."

"Good night, madame."

Cat sat in her bed listening with amusement to the

sounds coming from Patrick's bedroom. He splashed.
He sang off-key. He made noises like a duck, and she
laughed. A few minutes later he came naked through
the doorway connecting the two rooms, and made
straight for the bed. For a moment they just looked at
each other. Then he enfolded her in a bear hug, and she
snuggled contentedly into his arms.

"Are ye glad to be home, Cat?"

"For now, but I meant it, Patrick, when I said I
wanted to spend part of each year in Edinburgh. Soon
the little king will come into his own. He'll marry, and
there will be a real court again. I dinna want to be a
stranger in Edinburgh when that happens."

"Nay, hinny! We'll be no part of James' court.
Grandmam always said the key to survival was to stay
out of politics, and out of court. We're but a minor
branch of our clan, but we are the richest. We have
always avoided trouble by not allowing ourselves to be
noticed. We will continue to do so." He shifted his
position and slowly began stroking her lovely round
breasts.

"Then why," she demanded, "did ye buy me a house
in town?" The nipples on her breasts were pinkly
pointed, and she was furious at her body's quick response to him.

"Because I always pay my debts, madame." He bent
and nibbled teasingly on the tip of her breast.

Angrily she pulled away. "I have furnished that house
wi my own money! Am I not even to spend part of each
year there?"

"Of course ye may. We'll go to town each year, I
promise you. You can shop, see plays, and visit our
friends. But there will be no getting involved with any
Stewart court. Stewarts are always notoriously short of
funds, and one can hardly refuse the king a loan. One
can also not ask a king to return a loan. We'd be impoverished in a year!"

He pulled her underneath him and bent over her. "I'll talk no more of this tonight, madame, Countess of Glenkirk." His green-gold eyes glittered dangerously. "Are ye ready to be an obedient and dutiful wife, you impossible minx?"

Her slender fingers wound into his dark hair, and pulling his head down she kissed him slowly and expertly, her ripe body moving subtly beneath him.

"By God," he swore when she released him, "I never taught you that!"

"Didn't ye, my lord?" Her voice was honeyed.

"No!"

Her soft laughter teased him.

"You little bitch," he said. His hand wrapped itself around her heavy hair. "If I thought that any other man even considered sampling your ample charms . . ."

She laughed again, but her eyes and mouth were defiant. Suddenly, with a savagery that left her gasping, he took her.

"I'll never possess all of you, Cat, for yer quicksilver! But, by God, my dear, I'll spoil you for any other man!"

She began to struggle, but he laughed and began kissing tiny kisses over her face, throat, and breasts. He could feel her heart beating wildly beneath his lips. His big hands began caressing her hips and thighs, slowly stroking the silken flesh.

"Patrick! Patrick!" Her voice was frantic. "Please, Patrick!" She could feel her control going, and couldn't understand why she still fought him. Perhaps it was because she instinctively understood that at these times she and he both lost individual identity. It frightened her yet.

"Nay, sweetheart. Dinna fear what's happening. Go along wi it, hinny. Go along wi it!"

It was easier to surrender, and she did, allowing herself to be swept away into the whirling rainbow vortex that always gave such pleasure. She lost track of everything except the wave upon wave of exquisite sensation that followed one upon the other until the final rending climax.

Later that night she awoke to find the moon shining through the window and across the bed. Patrick lay sprawled on his back, snoring gently. Carefully, she pulled her leg from underneath his. Turning on her side, she leaned on an elbow and gazed down at him.

She took pride in his good looks as he took pride in hers. His fair skin was tanned in places from their two-week ride. Thick dark lashes spread fanlike on his high cheekbones. His straight nose broadened at the nostrils, and his mouth was wide and generous. Her eyes wandered to his broad, hairless chest. She blushed furiously as her eyes caressed the tangled mat of black hair between his long, muscular legs.

He was a strange man. On the one hand he treated her as an equal, and truly seemed to understand the conflicting feelings that raged through her. On the other hand he treated her like a slave. He was tender, thoughtful, wise, cruel, and didactic. He was hardly the average man, she knew. But then, she was hardly the average woman. In her early teens, she had resented Grandmam for forcing a match on her when she was too young to understand the importance of it. However, and she chuckled softly to herself, somehow that incredibly beautiful white-haired old lady had *known*. We are well suited, my lord, and I, thought Cat. We are damnably well suited! Satisfied, she turned over on her stomach and fell into a deep, contented sleep.

Chapter 12

❧❧❧

THE picture was a charming domestic one. The dowager Countess of Glenkirk sat at her tapestry frame embroidering the wings on an angel. Her two-year-old grandson, Jamie, played before the fire under the watchful eye of Sally Kerr. Her son Adam sat going over the estate accounts. The earl was engaged in deep conversation with Master Benjamin Kira, his banker up from Edinburgh. Her two daughters, twenty-year-old Janet, who was married to the Sithean heir, and seventeen-year-old Mary, who would soon be wed to Greyhaven's eldest boy, sat sewing clothes for Janet's expected baby. Their men, Charles Leslie, and James Hay were all dicing in the corner.

Missing was the young Countess of Glenkirk and her cousin Fiona. They were, Meg knew, in Cat's apartment trying on the latest fashions Fiona had brought back from Paris. The younger Leslies had recently returned from a year of travel. They had been in Italy visiting Rome, and to the courts of Florence, and to Naples. They had been to Spain, to King Henri III's court in Paris, and had spent a few weeks in England. Fiona could not stop talking about it all, and the more she talked, the more discontent grew in Cat.

Fiona, having seen all manner of wonderful things, couldn't resist bragging a bit. And, too, Cat had been penned at Glenkirk for over two years now with only a month's stay in Edinburgh late last winter.

Meg would not have told her son, but she knew that her beautiful daughter-in-law was using a method of birth control passed down from Mam. Cat wanted to see some of the world before she devoted herself to the raising of Leslies. Having raised six herself, Meg could not help but admire Cat.

Cat caressed the exquisitely scented lilac leather gloves Fiona had brought her from Italy. Her leaf-green eyes were narrow as she watched her husband get ready for bed. "I want to make a trip," she said.

"Yes, love," he replied absently. "We'll go to town again this winter if I can find the time." He looked up, startled as the gloves whizzed by his head.

"I do not want to go to Edinburgh, Patrick! Fiona has had a real trip to Italy, to Spain, to Paris, to England! She! The wife of a mere third son! I am the Countess of Glenkirk, and I've never been farther south than Edinburgh. I wouldn't have gotten even that far but for my own initiative."

"There is no need for ye to travel."

"There is every need! I want to!"

"I want sons, madame! So far ye've given me but one child."

"I'll bear no more bairns until ye gie me a trip!" she raged at him.

"That decision is not in yer hands, my dear," he said smugly.

"Isn't it?" she countered. "Ask yer mother, Patrick. Ask and see."

Curious, he spoke to Meg, who laughed softly and said, "So she's declared war on ye, eh, Patrick?"

"She canna stop the babes coming, can she?" His voice was anxious.

"She can and she has, my son."

"That's witchcraft!"

"Meg laughed again. "Oh, Patrick! Dinna be such a

fool! There isn't a woman in this family who doesn't know certain secrets of beauty and health brought back from the East by Mam. I dinna blame Catriona. I was wed to yer father—may God keep him—when I was fifteen. You were born a year later, James and Adam at three-year intervals, Michael a year after Adam, and Janet the next year. I would never tell her, and you must not either, but your youngest sister, Mary, was an accident. I intended no more bairns after Janie. Do ye know that in the twenty-nine years I've been at Glenkirk I've never left it except to go to Sithean, or to Greyhaven? How I would have loved to have a trip somewhere . . . anywhere!"

It gave him pause. His own mother, who had so lovingly raised them, was discontented! Mary—an accident! And Cat was able to prevent children if she chose! He thought further. The little king was fourteen, and despite all the nonsense about a match between England's Queen Elizabeth and the French king's brother, Patrick was sure there would be no such marriage. Even if there were, a woman of forty-six was hardly apt to deliver a healthy child. In all likelihood, their own little king would one day rule both England and Scotland.

He wondered how long it would be before the two countries were one. When it happened, the capital would be in London, and Edinburgh would be left behind—a second-class city in the realm of the royal Stewarts, who were notoriously short of memory. It might even be necessary to live part of each year in England if his family, and their businesses, were to survive. He had talked that very evening to Benjamin Kira about the wisdom of moving some of their ships and a warehouse or two into London. Perhaps he would go to London to check it out. He could take Cat *and* his mother!

Before Patrick had come home to marry, he had paid

a visit to Elizabeth's court and met the queen. She was a handsome female, but beneath the playful exterior was a cold, determined woman. She would have no man in her bed, for she would not share her power with anyone. Still, having made this choice, she resented women who threw themselves into their lover's arms.

Though he kept his feelings to himself, and would never allow his family to involve themselves, he resented the imprisonment of Mary Stewart. He had twice visited the court in Edinburgh while Mary reigned. She had been some years his senior. He had fallen in love, at ten, with the glorious Mary. Once she had spoken to him, acknowledging their distant cousinship through his mother. She was a charming and educated woman, and her choice of Darnley for a husband had been ludicrous. Though Lord Bothwell had been Mary's downfall, and Glenkirk didn't particularly like him, he would have been a far more suitable mate.

That Elizabeth envied Mary was obvious. The imprisonment of the Scots queen was cruel, and had been done, Patrick believed, on a whim. Therefore, he would only visit the English court. He could never live there, for he could not respect the Tudor queen.

He would put enough of his wealth in England so that when the time came that a Stewart king ruled the whole great land, from Lands End to the Highlands, he would be financially established. Then his family might go wherever they wished.

He said nothing to his wife or his mother, but closeted himself the next morning in his library with Benjamin Kira, and planned the purchase of two warehouses in London to house goods from half a dozen of his ships. It wouldn't be a great deal, but would be a start. Benjamin's London cousin, Eli Kira, would arrange everything.

Then he made arrangements with the Kiras for a trip

to England. He debated the route and finally decided that the sea route was both quicker and safer at this time of year. A rider was dispatched immediately to Leith to arrange for the flagship of his fleet to sit off Peterhead awaiting them. Another rider was dispatched to Edinburgh to Master Kira's bank with instructions that a letter of unlimited credit be sent to their London branch for the earl. Conall More-Leslie and a troop of fifty men-at-arms were sent into England, and headed south to London to await their lord. Eli Kira rented a house for the earl in the most fashionable part of the city.

Adam Leslie was put in charge of both the Glenkirk estate and the Glenkirk heir. Patrick had no intention of exposing his only child to the dangers of travel. The boy would be safer with his doting nursemaids, in familiar surroundings. His arrangements completed, the earl announced one night at supper to his wife and his mother that they were going to England.

Cat's silver goblet crashed to the table. "What? Oh, my dear lord! Are we really going? When? God's nightshirt! I've nothing to wear!"

Meg Leslie smiled at her daughter-in-law and turned to her son. "Thank you, my dear, but I am much too old to travel," she said.

"Nay, madame. We want ye wi us."

"Yes! Yes! Belle-mère," begged Cat. "Ye must come! Yer hardly past forty, and that's nae too old to travel. Please say ye'll come!"

"I *hae* always wanted to see London," mused Meg.

"Then come!" Cat caught Meg's hands, and kneeling down, looked up into her mother-in-law's hazel eyes. "Come! Oh, what fun we'll have! The Globe Theatre! The Bear Gardens! Masques at court!" She turned anxiously to her husband. "We will go to court, Patrick?"

"Yes, my dear. I imagine I still hae a few friends

there, and though I doubt her majesty will be wildly
delighted to see two beautiful women arrive on her
doorstep, the gentlemen of the court should be enchanted."

"Patrick!" Cat looked thoughtful. "What of Jamie?"

"We must leave him behind, sweetheart. I'll nae have
him endangered."

Her face fell. "I canna leave my bairn behind, Patrick."

"He stays behind, Cat. Travel is dangerous." He
looked at her. "And Jamie is our only child. Sally and
Lucy are here to care for him, and Adam and Fiona
will act as parents for us. We'll be gone but a few
months."

It was too irresistible. "Jamie stays. I go," she said.
She flung her arms about him. "Thank ye, Patrick!"

Despite her claims of a poor wardrobe, her trunks
would have filled a wagon. Patrick put his foot down.
"One trunk apiece. We'll buy what ye need in London.
A new wardrobe for each of you." Cat and Meg looked
gleefully at each other.

They reached Peterhead on an unusually balmy day.
The *Gallant James* rode jauntily offshore. They were
rowed out to the ship. Even being swung aboard in a
boatswain's chair didn't faze Cat, though Meg was not
delighted.

The journey south was surprisingly swift and smooth,
and they suffered no seasickness. They didn't even encounter another vessel until they were about to enter the
Thames and sail upriver to London. There they were
hailed by another ship with a distinctly piratical look
about it. Upon its quarterdeck stood a handsome young
man with a beautifully kept mustache and beard.

Patrick laughed, excited. "Raleigh!" he shouted.
"Raleigh! You pirate!"

The elegant on the quarterdeck peered across the

small gulf separating their ships. "God's foot! Can it be? Glenkirk! Is it you?"

"Aye, you rebel! Come across, and have a glass of wine wi me."

A few minutes later the Englishman stood on the deck of the *Gallant James* wringing Patrick's hand.

"Have ye been to court yet?" asked the earl.

"Nay. I've not the money for it. I've been doing a bit of swashbuckling. The French ships are easy pickings. I'll be on my way to Ireland soon. Then perhaps, when I've some gold in my pocket and some decent accomplishments to my credit, I can present myself to the queen. I'm a simple West Country boy, Patrick. My only claim to fame thus far is to be the great-nephew of the queen's old governess, Kate Ashley, and the great-nephew also of Lady Denny. It's not really much to recommend one."

Patrick grinned. "Come on, you ambitious devil! I want you to meet my wife and my mother." He led the way to the great cabin in the stern of the ship. Knocking first, they walked into a beautifully furnished room with large windows looking out over the sea. Meg came forward. "Mother, this is Master Walter Raleigh." His eyes twinkled mischievously. "Lady Denny's great-nephew."

Raleigh shot him a black look, then smiled brightly at Meg and bowed over her hand. "Your servant, ma'am."

"And," continued Patrick, bringing Cat forward, "this is my wife, Catriona, the Countess of Glenkirk."

Raleigh dropped Meg's hand, and stared. "Christ, man!" he exploded. "No one's wife looks like that! A mistress perhaps, but only if you're a king *and* very lucky. But never a wife!"

The Leslies laughed, and Cat, without so much as a blush, replied, "Alas, I must disillusion ye, Master

Raleigh. I am indeed the Countess of Glenkirk, a wife—and a mother also."

Lingering over her hand, Raleigh sighed. "Having seen perfection, and being unable to attain it, I shall be forced to remain a bachelor, madame."

"Raleigh, yer a most charming rogue. I fear for the virtue of all the lasses in yer West Country." She gently freed her hand.

Both Cat and Meg listened eagerly to all Raleigh said. Although he had not yet been to court, he was full of its gossip, passed on to him by friends. He was able to fill them in on the latest fashions, for Raleigh was a bit of a fop, and quite vain.

After a pleasant interval, the captain advised that the tide would be turning shortly. Unless they got into the river now, they would be forced to ride at anchor for twelve hours. Raleigh immediately stood up. Kissing the ladies' hands, he bid them all adieu. The earl escorted him onto the deck. He said he hoped to see him at court before they returned to Scotland. Soon, with the help of a good wind, the *Gallant James* slipped into the River Thames and headed upstream.

Chapter 13

꧁§꧂

THAT Elizabeth Tudor had observed her forty-seventh birthday was confirmed by her mirror. Still, she *was* queen. And although it was an open secret that she had no intention of marrying, suitors continued to arrive. She was perpetually surrounded by gallants whose clever tongues spun lovely compliments.

This is partly what made the Scots Earl of Glenkirk so enticing. He was handsome beyond decency. Most of her courtiers were mustached, and bearded, and scented. The earl was smooth-shaven, leaving bare his elegant jawline, and there was about him a clean, masculine scent that bespoke regular washing. He was tall, topping most men by several inches, well proportioned, with good skin and dark, wavy hair. Those green-gold eyes were fascinating. Above all, he was well educated. The queen detested ignorance. And he did not curry favor as the others did. He would never become one of her favorites, but his courteous coldness fascinated her. She had never forgotten him, though several years had passed since he had been to court.

He had been only Lord Patrick then, but now he was back, a full earl. He knelt and took the hand she graciously extended. But the green-gold eyes with a hint of amusement deep within them never left her face. "Majesty," he murmured. He rose to his feet.

Elizabeth was grateful she was seated on a raised

117

dais, but even so they were almost at equal eye level. It was a distinct disadvantage to the queen, who preferred gazing down from lofty heights upon her adoring court. Her amber eyes narrowed, and she spoke.

"So, Scots rogue, you have finally returned."

"Yes, yer majesty."

"And what naughty things have you been doing while you were away from us?" Elizabeth smiled archly.

"I hae gotten married and fathered a son, madame."

Several of the younger courtiers snickered, assuming the earl had ruined himself.

"And how long have you been married, my lord?"

"Two years, yer majesty."

"And how old is your son?"

"Two years, yer majesty."

Elizabeth's eyes widened, and the corners of her mouth twitched. "God's foot, Glenkirk! Don't tell me you were caught by an outraged father?"

"No, madame. I had been betrothed to my wife since she was a child."

There was a story here, thought Elizabeth, but not for the ears of her gossipy court. Let them wonder. She stood up. "Come along, Glenkirk. I want to hear about this in private." Leaving the assembled court, the queen led the way into a small anteroom. "No ceremony, man! Sit down!" She seated herself and poured out two glasses of wine. "Now, Glenkirk," she said, handing him one of the glasses, "explain."

"Cat was four and I thirteen when the match was made. We were betrothed for eleven years."

"Cat?" said the queen.

Patrick smiled. "Catriona, yer majesty. 'Tis the Gaelic for Katherine."

"So," said Elizabeth impatiently, "but how is it that both your son and your marriage are two years of age?"

"There was a misunderstanding, and she ran away three days before the wedding."

The queen's eyes widened again. They began to twinkle. "You have yourself a headstrong wench, eh, my lord?"

"Aye, madame, I do. It took me almost a year to pin her down."

"You must have pinned her down sometime before that, Glenkirk, if she was carrying your babe."

Patrick laughed. "She hid first wi some devoted, pensioned servants, then up in the hills at a small house that had been her grandmother's. I found her there, and all might have been well, but—"

The queen cut in. "You committed some great blunder, I'll wager."

"Aye," he admitted, "and she was off again. She fled to Edinburgh, where my brother and his wife were about to set off to France. She cajoled Fiona into letting her stay in their house, unknown to Adam. Fiona agreed, thinking Cat would think things out and return shortly to me. When, at New Year's, she discovered Cat was still hiding in Edinburgh and the bairn was less than two months away, she informed me. My uncle and I went immediately to Edinburgh. After some discussion, Cat and I were reconciled and married by my uncle, the Abbot of Glenkirk Abbey."

"I'll wager she made it hard for you, Glenkirk," the queen chuckled.

"She did," he said.

"And when was your son born?"

"Approximately an hour after the wedding ceremony."

Elizabeth, sipping her wine, began to laugh. She laughed until the tears ran. Gasping, she choked on the wine and began to cough. Without thinking, Glenkirk stood up, leaned over, and clapped her on the back.

When the queen had finally caught her breath she said, "I hope you have brought your wild wench with you, my lord, for I should like to meet her."

"I have brought her, yer majesty, and I've also brought my mother, Lady Margaret Stewart Leslie. I hope ye'll receive them both."

"I will, Glenkirk. Bring them anytime. Tell me, is your wife beautiful?"

"Aye, madame, she is."

"As beautiful as I am?" said the queen coyly.

"One can hardly compare the beauty of a child with that of a mature woman, yer majesty."

Elizabeth chuckled. "God's foot, Glenkirk! I do believe there's hope for you. That's the first real compliment I have ever heard you utter at my court."

Two days later Patrick brought his wife to court. As Cat advanced towards the queen the younger women thought how plain her gown was, and the more experienced ones envied her her cleverness. The Queen of England stood in a stiffly brocaded, beribboned, bejeweled red velvet gown that glittered and gleamed beneath a huge gold lace ruff. The Countess of Glenkirk wore a full-skirted black velvet gown. The wide sleeves were edged in lace and slashed to reveal white silk scattered with gold-embroidered stars. The neckline was low, and framed in a high, well-starched, sheer lace collar. Around her neck were four long ropes of magnificent pale-pink pearls. She wore only one ring, a large, heart-shaped ruby. Her hair, uncrimped, was parted in the center and drawn over her ears into a knot at the nape of her neck. A delicate little lace cap sat on the back of her head, and two fat pink pearls bobbed from her ears.

The maids of honor thought the countess' raiment too simple, but Leicester leaned over to Lettice Knollys, his wife, and whispered, "What a beauty!" to which Lettice whispered back, "Aye! I hope she'll not stay long at court."

The handsome couple had reached the queen. Gracefully sweeping off his cap, Glenkirk bowed low. His countess dropped into a graceful curtsy. They rose and faced the English queen proudly. For just a moment, Elizabeth Tudor wondered what she had missed by not following her heart.

"You are welcome at court, countess."

"I am most grateful for yer majesty's welcome," replied Cat carefully.

The queen turned to Patrick. "Your child is indeed most beautiful, Glenkirk," she said dryly. "Next time bring your mother with you. I should also enjoy meeting her." She turned back to Cat. "I hope your stay here will be a pleasant one."

Dismissed, Cat curtsied prettily. Thanking the queen, she backed off. Later she asked her husband what the queen had meant when she called her a child. He told her, and Cat laughed. A few days later they took Meg to court, and the queen received her politely, though not without pursing her lips and saying, "I don't suppose your sisters are ill-favored either, Glenkirk." Meg's warmth, however, won Elizabeth over.

Eli Kira had rented the Leslies a magnificent house on the Strand. It had a large garden ending in a terrace overlooking the river, and its own waterman to row them. They also had a house some fifteen miles from London in case they wanted to get away from the city.

Cat was in her glory. She cajoled Patrick into escorting her and Meg to one of Master Shakespeare's plays at the Globe Theatre. Afterwards she said she thought the young boys who played the female roles were quite sweet, but she really didn't see why they wouldn't allow women to act women's roles. They went to a bearbaiting, for she had wanted to see one. But the sight of a half-starved, moth-eaten bear being attacked by a dozen or more half-starved and brutalized dogs revolted her.

They entertained heavily both in London and at their

country house, near Waltham Abbey. They were quite
popular. The queen had put her stamp of approval upon
them at their third visit to court. Elizabeth, scornful of
decorative, frivolous women, had remarked to the young
countess, "I understand you have been educated."

"Yes, yer majesty. My great-grandmother believed
women should be. All her female descendants are offered a chance at learning. It takes wi some, wi others
it doesn't. I have not, however, had yer majesty's great
advantages."

"Do you know mathematics?"

"Some, majesty."

"Music?"

Cat nodded.

"Languages?"

"Aye, madame."

"What languages?"

"French, Gaelic, and Latin well. Some Flemish,
Italian, German, Spanish, and Greek."

The queen nodded, and suddenly phrased a question
in Flemish, switching to Latin in mid-sentence. Cat
replied in French, switched to Greek, and then to Spanish. The queen laughed delightedly and pinched Cat's
cheek. The Glenkirks popularity was assured. "You are
a pert minx, my dear," said Elizabeth. "I don't know
why, but I like you!"

Cat made one good friend in England, the first she
had ever had outside her own family. Lettice Knollys,
the beautiful Countess of Leicester, older than Cat, had
secretly married the queen's precious "Robin" two years
prior. Six months later their secret was discovered and
Lettice, Elizabeth's cousin, was just now being permitted back at court. She had been in deep disgrace for
all that time.

Even now she trod very carefully. The Leslies' townhouse was one of the few places Lettice and her husband

could meet without offending the queen. Cat generously gave them a suite of rooms for privacy. The queen, in jealous spite, had offered them none.

There was a delay in Patrick's business, as there were no warehouses for sale along the waterfront. There was, however, a fine piece of property along the river that Eli Kira bought for them. Bidding was opened to the builders of London for the construction of two warehouses and adjoining docks to serve them. It became necessary for Patrick to remain in London and see the plans completed.

Meg chose to return home to Glenkirk. She had seen enough of London.

Patrick delegated half of his men-at-arms, under the faithful Conall, to take his mother home. Cat wanted them to bring Jamie back with them. It would be summer before she and Patrick could go home. Patrick overruled her and said she might return home with his mother if she chose.

"And leave ye to play the honeybee among all these English roses? I think not, my lord!"

"Jealous, sweetheart?" he inquired infuriatingly.

"Of yer admirers?" she replied sweetly. "I am no more jealous of yer admirers, my lord, than ye are of mine." Her lovely eyes and mouth mocked him, and Patrick thought how lucky he was to have her. He caught her in his arms and kissed her deeply. Molding herself to him, she returned the kiss with equal passion, thinking that if she ever caught him loving another woman she would kill him. If he had known her thoughts he would have been flattered. He hated the court gallants who looked at her with lust. Well, just a few more months, and they would be on their way home.

But it was not to be that way. After Christmas, Cat miscarried the baby she had so recently conceived. Devastated by this tragedy, she fell into a decline. She wept continuously, ate almost nothing, and slept fitfully. She saw no one. Even Lettice was not received. Finally, Ellen approached Patrick.

"There is only one thing for it. Ye must bring Jamie to her."

"Christ, woman!" exploded the earl. "It's mid-January, and the snow will be heavy in the north. Conall's just back!"

"Send Conall alone. He'll get there faster without the others, and he'll bring Sally and the child back safely. Lord, mon! Sally was raised on the borders. She can ride like a trooper, even wi the bairn. Send a messenger today ahead of Conall. Hugh can bring Sally and the child as far south as Edinburgh."

He didn't like it, but Patrick did as Ellen suggested. Once Conall was on his way, he told his wife of the mission. Cat brightened immediately. She began to eat. When her son arrived, three-and-a-half weeks later, she was almost her old self. She covered the surprised little boy with kisses until he squirmed away, protesting, "Mama, no more!"

Then the winter suddenly became harsh, and snow followed upon snow. Work was halted on the warehouses and docks until the spring thaw. Then in early summer, the plague visited London and the Leslies and their household fled to the country. By the time it was safe to return to the city, it was autumn again, and they were forced to spend another winter in England.

With the spring of 1582, Cat knew she was pregnant. They remained in England until the child was born, on September 7. Elizabeth Leslie, named for the queen, had managed to be born on her majesty's forty-ninth birthday. The queen insisted on serving as the baby's godmother when she was christened, four days later. The frightened Roman Catholic priest dared not say no to the queen. The baby received from her godmother a dozen silver goblets encrusted with aquamarines and engraved with the Leslie coat of arms.

Little Bess had been born in the country house. A month later, without ever seeing London, she set off home to Scotland with her parents and her four-and-a-half-year-old brother, who rode north on his own pony.

They crossed the border in a month. It was early November, but the day was mild and lovely. Cat and Patrick rode on ahead of their train, stopping on the crest of a hill. The birches seemed more golden and the pines greener than anywhere else on earth. Below them the valley shimmered in the faint purple haze of late afternoon. To the west was Hermitage, home to the Earls of Bothwell. Ahead of them lay Jedburgh, where they would shelter tonight.

"My God!" said Patrick. "Is it my imagination, or does even the air smell sweeter?"

Cat nodded and smiled up at him. She had enjoyed the trip, but her face radiated joy at coming home to Scotland.

"Almost home, sweetheart," he said. "If the weather holds we'll be in Glenkirk in another ten days." He held out a hand. She smiled again, and took it. My God, he thought! How she has changed! I took a girl to England, and I brought back a woman—a beautiful woman! "Will ye be sorry to be away from London, and court?" he asked her.

"Nay, Patrick. I'm too glad to be home."

"Glenkirk will nae be as exciting after London."

"But, Patrick! There's Edinburgh, and the king will be seventeen next year, and surely be coming into his own soon. Once he weds we'll hae our own court."

"Madame!" he roared. "I hae told ye we'll nae involve ourselves wi the Stewarts! They are nae to be trusted and forever in debt! We dinna need them. Ye'll not wheedle me in this matter."

Her lovely mouth was turning up at the corners in a very mischievous smile. "When the king comes into his own, Patrick, I am going to court! Whether ye come wi me or not is yer concern. I will remind ye, my dearest lord, that Glenkirk House belongs to me. I have nae furnished it at great personal expense to visit it for a month once every year or two, as pleases you. Nor did I furnish it for our relations to use while I sit home at Glenkirk. Adam has promised Fiona that she'll go to Jamie's court, and ye can do no less for me!"

So saying, she kicked Bana and cantered down into the purple valley.

The Earl of Glenkirk kicked his own horse and galloped off after his beautiful, wayward wife.

Part II

❧

The King

Chapter 14

❦§⸆❧

JAMES Stewart, sixth of his name and King of Scotland, lounged on his throne, watching the dancers. He followed one lady in particular, Catriona Leslie, Countess of Glenkirk. She was partnered by the king's distant cousin, Patrick Leslie, the Earl of Glenkirk. Catriona Leslie was the most beautiful woman at James' court. She was also reputed to be the most virtuous. This was unfortunate, because the king lusted for her. And what James Stewart wanted, he got. One way or another.

James Stewart had not known his mother, having been left behind when she fled to England. He had been raised by a series of warring Protestant nobles who used him as a pawn to further their own ambitions. They believed they had taught him to hate his mother. But here they had been outwitted by his old nurse.

Nanny had adored Mary Stewart, and when James' tutor spoke vitriol against the unfortunate captive queen, Nanny had countered with her own version of the truth. For the child's peace of mind, it was fortunate that her stories had been more plausible than his tutor's. The little boy asked the old lady about the references to his mother's affairs, and was told only that women were weak when it came to men. He did not understand that until he was fourteen.

Though he had long outgrown Nanny, she remained

with him and saw to his comfort. James' guardians discovered it was cheaper to keep the old nurse than employ a bevy of housemaids.

Nanny saw the young boy's affections moving in a dangerous direction with the arrival of Esmé Stewart, Sieur D'Aubigney, from France. Fortunately, Esmé Stewart was merely ambitious, and Nanny saw her laddie safely embarked upon his sexual career by introducing him to a pretty, skilled, disease-free young whore. The whore's name was Betty, and she was honored to initiate her young king in the arts of lovemaking. He proved an excellent pupil.

Betty was a member of the old kirk, and it amused her to outwit the pious hypocrites of the stern, cold new kirk. These men preached about the sins of the flesh on Sunday morning and came masked to her door on Sunday afternoon.

James, too, enjoyed outwitting his guardians. James was a Stewart on both his dead parents' sides, and Stewarts were quite sensual. He discovered a world of delights, and understood Nanny's comment about women being weak over men. James liked women.

James Stewart was twenty-three, and king. Tomorrow he would be married by proxy to a beautiful blond blue-eyed Danish princess named Anna. It would, however, be some weeks before he saw his sixteen-year-old bride and consummated that marriage. If he was to be married by proxy, James reasoned, then he must have his wedding night by proxy also.

The idea pleased him, but no whore could substitute for his royal virgin bride. It would not be fitting. Nor would it be kind to begin an affair with an impressionable young girl. His gaze strayed again to Catriona Leslie, who was laughing up at her husband. Yes! The most virtuous woman at court would be a fitting proxy.

There were problems, however. He had twice approached Catriona. The first time she had thought him joking, and teasingly reminded him that she was older than he was. The second time she realized his serious intent, and gently reminded him of her marriage vows. She would not, she told him firmly, break them. She loved her husband, and would bring no shame to his name.

Another man might have bowed and withdrawn gracefully. But James Stewart was not such a man. He knew, of course, that he could go to Patrick Leslie and tell him he wanted his wife. His cousin, head of the smallest yet wealthiest branch of the Leslies, could be counted upon to do the correct thing and turn a blind eye while the king dallied with his wife. James, however, liked his older cousin, and saw no reason to hurt him. The Earl of Glenkirk was a fiercely proud man. If the king wanted his wife he would have to acquiese, but he would never really be happy with Cat again.

But if Patrick Leslie were out of the way, then Catriona could be made to comply. It would be done secretly, so as not to harm the lady's reputation or her husband's ego. But it would be done. James wanted a taste of that which had held Patrick Leslie's unwavering interest for nine years. He was going to have it.

The dancing ended and the courtiers, hot with their efforts, drank eagerly from the goblets of chilled wine passed by the servants. James moved easily among them, talking and laughing. Eventually he came to the Leslies.

"Cousins!" He kissed Cat on both cheeks.

"So, Jamie, tomorrow ye take a wife," said the Earl of Glenkirk.

"Aye, Patrick. Though I do wish she were here rather than in Denmark."

"Patience, lad. She will be here before ye know it, and then will come times ye'll wish her back in Denmark!"

They all laughed, and James said, "Will ye and Cat

be my guests, and stay here during the festivities? I know ye've a house in town, but I'd like to hae my family about me. Even Bothwell is back in my good graces."

"Why thank ye, Jamie," smiled Patrick. "We'd be honored, wouldn't we, sweetheart?"

"Aye, sire," said Cat. "We are most honored by yer kindness."

James moved on, secretly exulting. Now he had her under his roof!

The following day the king's marriage to Princess Anna of Denmark was celebrated with much joy. That night the Earl of Glenkirk left for Melrose Abbey on urgent business. His countess, after a delightful evening of feasting and dancing, retired to her rooms.

Ellen helped her undress, and she then stepped into a small tub, where the woman sponged her down with warm, scented water. Dried and powdered, she held up her arms so Ellen could slip a sea-green silk nightgown over her. Climbing into bed, she ordered Ellen to bank the fire, and bid her good night.

Cat lay back on the plump pillows. It was a big bed, made bigger by Glenkirk's absence. They had rarely been apart in the nine years of their marriage, and she did not like being separated. Suddenly, as she began to doze, she heard a creaking noise. She sat up just in time to see a hidden door by the fireplace swing open. James Stewart walked through it.

"What are ye doing here?" she hissed at him.

"I should think, my dear, that the answer to that would be obvious."

"I'll scream the castle down!"

"No, my dear, ye won't. The scandal wouldna touch me. I am the king. Ye, nonetheless, are a different proposition. Yer family would suffer badly if ye publicly refuse me."

"I told ye I would nae be yer mistress, Jamie." She

strove to hide her fright. She had not expected such persistence from him.

"I dinna accept yer decision, madame. Besides it is nae yers to make. Today I was wed by proxy. Tonight I intend consummating my marriage the same way, and I have chosen ye to be my bride."

"*Never*! I'll never yield to ye!"

"Ye hae no choice, my dear," he said triumphantly, and stripped off his robe. "Stand up, and come here to me!" he commanded her.

"*No*! And if ye force me I'll tell Glenkirk!"

Her eyes were bright with unshed tears, and her lovely mouth sulky in defiance. She was the most beautiful creature he had ever seen, and her anger with him excited him more than any other woman ever had.

"Tell Glenkirk?" He was amused. "If ye want, Cat, I'll tell him myself. But remember one thing, my dear. Patrick will forgie me. I am his king. He'll nae forgie ye. Now, come here to me!"

The truth of his words horrified her. If her proud lord knew that another man had lain with her, he'd cast her off. The king had trapped her as neatly as a rabbit. "You bastard!" she swore at him.

Laughing, James replied, "Nay, love, that rumor was settled before my birth." He held out his hand. Forced, she came to him. Her leaf-green eyes were blazing furiously. James laughed softly again. Oh, now she was going to fight him with her stubborn mind. Her body, however, would yield eventually. There was plenty of time, and he intended to go easily with her tonight.

"Remove the gown," he said quietly, and was pleased when she obeyed him without question.

Standing back, he viewed her with pleasure. She had a wide, well-padded chest that moved downward into the most beautiful breasts he had ever seen, lovely ivory globes with large dark-pink nipples. Her waist was slen-

der and long, her full hips nicely rounded, her legs long
and shapely. Her tawny hair fell to her hips. He could
feel desire beginning to pound.

"God's bones, cousin! Yer beautiful!"

To his surprise she blushed pink, and James was
frankly delighted. It was true then. She really had never
known another man except Patrick. She really was the
most virtuous woman at court. He would see she was
rewarded by making her a lady of his wife's bedchamber. She would be an excellent influence.

Taking her hand again, he led her across the room to
their bed. Picking her up, he placed her on it. The
tempting triangle between her legs was plucked and
pink, as befitted a lady, and at the top of the cleft sat
a little black mole. "The mark of Venus," he murmured,
touching it. He bent over and kissed the mole.

A great shudder ran through her, and James smiled
to himself. He was going to take her quickly, for once
the deed was done her foolish resistance would crumble.
Gently but firmly, he parted her trembling thighs. Her
eyes widened, and she gasped in surprise when he gently
pushed into her. Like most male Stewarts, James was
overly endowed. The suddenness of his attack made it
impossible for Cat to struggle, so she decided to lie
quietly while he satisfied his lust.

James, however, was too skilled a lover to allow
passivity from his partner. Teasingly, voluptuously, he
moved within her, deliberately rousing Cat's passion and
making it nearly impossible for her to resist him. Only
a supreme effort on Cat's part helped her to lie still
beneath him. Her hands were balled into fists by her
sides. By concentrating on the sharpness of her nails
digging into her palms, she could blot out enough of
what he was doing to her to remain a nonparticipant.

Discovering this, the king said, "Oh, no, my love,"
and, laughing, drew her arms up over her head. He held
them there with one hand. Now his sensuous mouth

found her fragrant but unresponsive lips. His insistent tongue forced first those lips and then her teeth apart, thrusting with skill. She sobbed, and another shudder shook her. She was close to yielding, for he had breached her defenses. Her lovely body, used to regular lovemaking, was simply not conditioned to resist pleasure. He increased the tempo of his movement. "Yield to me, love!" he whispered insistently.

"Never." But her voice was shaking.

"The deed is done, my love. Yield, and take yer pleasure of me as I take my pleasure of ye."

She would not answer him, but he could feel her fighting down the movement in her hips. Then it occurred to him what he must do. Loosing his hold on her hands, he said, "Put yer arms around me, my love." And he looked down into her leaf-green eyes. They were glistening with tears. "If Patrick walked into this room right now, Cat, and found me planted in ye, he'd nae stop to ask if ye were resisting me, or enjoying me. Dinna fight me any longer, my love. Yer beautiful body aches for me! Nothing can change the fact that I already possess ye! Yield!"

She still said nothing to him, but her eyes closed, and hot tears rolled silently down the sides of her face. Then her arms tightened around him, and her hips arched to meet his every thrust. Victorious, James Stewart lost himself in the deliciousness of her surrender.

Afterwards, propped on one elbow, he looked down on her, but she closed her eyes and would not look back at him. "This is how I've always imagined ye," he said to her, his voice low. "Yer eyelids purple wi exhaustion, the lashes wet on yer cheeks, yer body weak from love, and yer mouth bruised wi my kisses." He bent and kissed the nipples of her breasts.

Her eyes flew open. "I'll nae forgie ye this, Jamie Stewart!"

He smiled charmingly at her. "Why, of course ye will,

my sweet love. Of course ye will!" Cradling her in the curve of one arm, he began to fondle her soft breasts. She tried to squirm away.

"Please, sire! Ye've had yer pleasure wi me. Now, find yer own bed!"

"Why, Cat, sweet." His voice held genuine surprise. "Surely ye dinna think that one taste was all I wanted? Nay, my darling! We hae the whole night ahead of us."

"Oh, no, Jamie! Please no!" She began to struggle against him.

He held her fast, and said regretfully, "My dear, I had hoped ye would see reason now that our preliminary bout is over. It will make no difference to Patrick whether I hae ye once or a dozen times. The simple fact that I've fucked ye will be enough. I know yer no wanton, my love, but ye canna deny yer body responds to mine. Why do ye insist on fighting me? I am gentle wi ye, and I know I am a good lover. Why do ye continue to resist?"

"Oh, Jamie," she said softly. "I really believe ye dinna understand. I hae never known any man but Patrick. Before we were wed, I resisted him, but I loved him. Of course my body responds to ye. He taught it to respond. But now ye come and claim the *droit du seigneur* of me. In bed my mind and body have always worked as one because I lay wi the man I love. But I dinna love ye, my lord. I cannot help but resist ye."

"Yer very fortunate, my lovely cousin," said James Stewart. "I hae never loved anyone. I dinna ken what it really means. I was raised by those who fed, clothed, disciplined, and educated me. I canna remember a kind word or a caress when I was a child. The only person who ever showed me any tenderness was my old nurse."

"Then I'm truely sorry for ye, Jamie, for to really love is to live life to its fullest. Yer problem is that ye've never had anyone of yer own. When the little queen

comes home to Scotland, she will be yers alone. And
when the bairns come—why, Jamie! Before ye know it
ye'll hae a whole big family to love, and be loved by."

"Thank ye, Cat. Ye gie me hope." He smiled at her.
"Ye really do belong at court, my love. Ye know what
to say to yer king. I do look forward to the arrival of
my queen, but now . . ." Gently he pushed Cat back
against the pillows and, finding her mouth, kissed her
with a practiced skill. Her first reaction was to struggle
from his clutches. Then suddenly she realized the king
was right. If Patrick arrived home now his reaction to
her predicament, whether she resisted or cooperated,
would be the same. Anger at her!

Her body was in real pain from resisting. I dinna love
this man, she thought, but I can stand no more of this!

He stopped kissing her, and was looking down at her.
Her eyes met his. "I'll never love ye, Jamie, and I am
ashamed of what ye are making me do, but I yield to ye,
my liege."

"Until the queen comes," he countered quickly.

"My lord! Ye'll destroy my marriage! Ye canna hide
from Patrick the fact that yer laying wi me."

"I can if he isna here. No man in his right mind could
taste of yer sweetness and stay but one night. I will send
Patrick to Denmark wi a group of nobles to escort the
queen home. Our liaison will be kept secret from the
court. Yer reputation will remain intact. Yer husband's
pride willna suffer."

She knew she must be satisfied with that. She could
argue no more with him. "Thank ye, my lord," she
whispered.

In answer the king bent his head and began kissing
her quivering body, starting with the pounding pulse in
her slender throat. He moved his lips to her chest, her
taut breasts with their sharp, pointed tips, her rounded
belly, the mole at the top of her cleft. Suddenly, he

turned her over and took her in a way that Patrick
Leslie never had. She gasped in shock and heard the
king mutter thickly, "Here's one place Glenkirk's nae
been before me." His hands cruelly crushed her breasts.
To her amazement he brought them to a quick climax.
They lay quietly side by side as their breathing returned
to normal.

"I hope," said James Stewart, "that the queen does
nae arrive too quickly. My love! Ye are magnificent!
No wonder Patrick hasna strayed all these years!"

Her voice was trembling. "Patrick never did what ye
just did to me."

"I know," he said. "Ye were a virgin there, but ye
liked it, didn't ye, Cat?"

"*No!*"

He laughed. "Aye! Ye did! Glenkirk's used ye gently,
my love. I'll teach ye many things, including how to
please me." He rose and poured them each a goblet of
wine, and added more wood to the fire. "Soon yer
Patrick should return from Melrose Abbey. Within the
week he'll be on his way with some others to meet my
bride and escort her home. Dinna look so sad, my love.
We hae a lovely month or two ahead of us."

Chapter 15

❦

THE Countess of Glenkirk sat quietly before her mirror while Ellen brushed her thick honey-colored hair. She wore only her white silk petticoat and a low-necked underblouse. Cat Leslie was frightened, and she did not know what to do. Patrick was, she knew, within the palace giving his report to the king. When he finally came to their apartment, would he notice anything different? She prayed he wouldn't.

Since the twentieth of August—a week ago—James Stewart had been sleeping with her. God knew she hadn't encouraged him! In fact, after the first night, she had fled the palace for her townhouse. He had quietly but firmly ordered her return. Desperate, she had confided in her favorite brother-in-law. Adam Leslie listened. Shaking his head, he said, "There's no help for it, Cat. What the king wants, he takes, and he happens to want ye."

"If I went home to Glenkirk, Adam? Surely he wouldn't pursue me there."

Adam Leslie was truly sorry for Cat. She was willful and stubborn, but she loved Patrick. The agony she was enduring was unfair. Nevertheless, there was no help for it. "Ye canna leave court wi'out Jamie's permission, Cat. Ye know that."

For a brief moment she looked defiant, and Adam spoke cruelly. "Ye canna endanger the Leslies, Cat, because it doesna suit ye to be the king's mistress. He's chosen ye, and he's even been kind enough to agree to keep yer liaison secret. If ye defy him, he'll ruin us! God, woman! Yer no virgin, bargaining a good price for yer maidenhead! What Jamie wants has already been well used by Glenkirk!"

Briefly Cat hated Adam. "Ye'll not tell Patrick?"

"Nay, Cat. Dinna fear," he said more kindly. He hesitated. "Cat, thank ye for confiding in me. I'm truly sorry, lass, that I canna help ye, but I'm here should ye need to talk again."

She nodded. "Does anyone else know?"

"Only Ellen," she answered him.

Faithful Ellen vacillated between her mistress's agony and her own pride that Cat was exquisite enough to attract the king. "If ye dinna put a smile on yer face, he will wonder what's wrong," the woman said sharply.

Cat jumped. "Oh God, Ellie! I feel so dirty!"

Ellen put down the brush. Kneeling before her lady, she looked up and spoke. "What is done is done, madame. Stop being so selfish! Yer thinking only of yerself. Think of the earl instead, my baby. Think of the family. Of yer own bairns. If ye want peace in yer life, this episode must be secret. And unless ye pull yerself together it won't be!"

Two tears slipped down the countess' face. Ellen reached up and brushed them away. "The king may touch yer body, my lady, but he can nae touch yer soul," she said quietly.

"How did ye get so wise?" Cat asked. But before Ellen could answer the door burst open and Patrick Leslie entered. Cat leaped to her feet and flung herself into his arms. Ellen discreetly withdrew as the earl found his wife's mouth. Kissing her deeply, his arms tightened about her until she cried out, "Patrick! I canna breathe!" He swept her up and deposited her on the bed.

She watched as he drew off his boots and outer clothing, and then stretched out next to her on their bed. He pulled her into his arms, pushed her blouse down, and kissed her lovely breasts. "I missed ye terribly, sweetheart," he murmured from the warmth of her. She cradled him against her, grateful he was back, and hoping he might save her from the further attentions of the king.

He raised his head up. "What were ye dressing for?" he asked.

"Another damned masque in honor of the Danish match," she answered.

"I think, considering I've been away, that Jamie might not miss us." He pushed her petticoats up past her thighs.

A smile lit her face, and she held out her arms to him.

But James Stewart did miss them. "I dinna see Glenkirk and his wife," he said casually to his cousin the Earl of Bothwell. "He came back from Melrose today."

"I'm nae surprised, Jamie," said Bothwell. "I imagine that Glenkirk has taken his wife to bed. If she were mine, and I had been away from her a week, that's what I would do." He grinned wickedly at the king. "The most virtuous woman at court! A pity, eh, majesty?"

"Considering the morals of most of the women at this court," said the king sharply, "I think Lady Leslie is refreshing. I intend making her a lady of my wife's bedchamber."

Oh ho, thought Bothwell. Cousin Jamie is interested in our beautiful countess. But he hides his lust nicely. I'll wager that only I, who know him so well, have spotted it.

The earl chuckled to himself. Because James was affectionate with those about him, and these were mostly males, he was thought to be homosexual. The plain truth of the matter was that the king, having been surrounded by men since his infancy, gave his affections where he could. Stewarts were loving creatures. Until recently there had been no suitable women for the king to fix his attentions on.

James had, in a burst of romanticism, willed himself half in love with his blond bride. But Bothwell knew that the king needed someone right now. If that someone was the Countess of Glenkirk, then well and good. She was neither ambitious nor a schemer. However, the earl did not think the king stood a chance. The lady seemed quite content with her dull but loving lord. A pity, really. Cat Leslie was a gorgeous creature, obviously made for love. Bothwell couldn't help but wonder if Glenkirk had awakened her completely.

James endured the evening. When he could leave without causing undue comment he did so, and suffered himself to be put ceremoniously to bed. He then called his chamberboy to him. The lad was invaluable, being mute but not deaf. His name was Barra, and he was privy to all the king's secrets.

"I'll be in the secret passageway," said the king. "I am locking the bedroom door from my side. Have ye yer key?"

Barra held his up.

"Good," said the king. "Dinna let anyone disturb me. If there's an emergency, you come after me alone."

The boy nodded wisely, and left the room to keep watch outside James' door.

Locking the door from inside, James walked to the fireplace and touched a small carving on its side. He took a lighted candle from the mantel sconce, counted off six paces, pushed the wall, and walked through the opening into the passage. He waited until the door had swung shut behind him and then moved quickly through the secret passageway until he came to his destination. He placed his candle in a holder high on the wall. Lifting a small flap, he peered into the room beyond.

Patrick Leslie stood naked by the table pouring out two goblets of wine. God, thought James, he *is* handsome, and well hung too—though not quite as well as I am.

The king watched as the earl moved back to the rumpled bed. Cat lay naked. Lazily she reached up for the goblet. Patrick sprawled next to her.

"Jesu, sweetheart, I hate being away from ye," the earl said.

"Then let's go home, Patrick! Ye were right when ye said we should nae involve ourselves wi the Stewarts."

"Why, hinny, I thought ye were enjoying yerself."

"I was, but these people who live at court and feed off it frighten me. I want to go home wi ye now!"

"We canna, sweetheart. I didna tell ye because I didna want our reunion spoiled, but Jamie has asked me to go to Denmark wi a group of nobles to escort the little queen home. I could nae refuse him, and we leave in a week."

Cat swore. She knew the king had planned to send her husband off, but she had not expected him to act so quickly and had hoped she could foil the royal plans. "Yer sending me home, Patrick, aren't ye?"

"I wanted to, hinny, but the king has asked that ye remain at court. He wants ye to be a lady of his wife's bedchamber. He has a high regard for ye, sweetheart."

Trapped! She was again trapped by James Stewart! The earl put down his goblet and, pulling Cat under him, kissed her hungrily. "I hae only a few days, madame," he said, "before I must leave ye. It will be two months or more before we see each other again." His big hands caressed her breasts, her hips, her thighs.

Cat needed no encouragement. She yielded eagerly to her husband, unaware that the king himself was watching them.

James could not tear his eyes away from the scene below him. When the figures reached their simultaneous climax James felt the hardness in his own groin break, and the sticky fluid spurt down his leg.

I'll nae put up wi this for a week, he thought. The delegation to Denmark will leave as soon as I can arrange it.

Using the pose of an eager bridegroom, James waved his nobles off three days later. Cat knew why her husband had been torn from her early and was furious. The Eral of Bothwell suspected, and laughed to himself over the king's eagerness.

Suspecting that she would be angry with him, James stayed away from his reluctant mistress for two days. On the third day, however, Barra shyly pressed a rose on the countess' tiring woman. It was the signal for James to come that night. Ellen told her mistress.

"I'll nae receive him!" shouted Cat furiously.

"Be silent!" Ellen snapped. "Do ye want the whole world to know?"

Cat began to weep uncontrollably, and Ellen, sensing disaster, sent a Leslie servant running to fetch Adam. By the time he arrived, Ellen had already poured several drams of whisky into her mistress to calm her down.

"I am going to kill myself," the countess announced dramatically.

"Fine," said Adam Leslie. " 'Twill be far less of a scandal than if ye openly refuse the king's attentions."

"Ye'd let me do it, wouldn't ye, Adam? Have ye no feelings for Patrick, who loves ye?"

" 'Tis because I love my brother I've come. How do ye think he'd feel to return from Denmark to discover all he possesses forfeit to the crown, including the wife he adores? Christ, Cat! The king's already had ye! Why this sudden attack of nerves?"

"I dinna want to be any man's whore," she said. " 'Tis my body, and I should hae some rights over it!"

"Well, ye don't," said Adam, angrily slamming his hand against the side of the chair. "Ye belong to the Leslies, and it is up to ye to do what is best for the family! Damnit, Cat! I am nae wi'out feeling! I hate the thought of Jamie Stewart lying wi my brother's wife, but ye know that if the king had gone straight to Patrick and asked for ye, Patrick would hae said yea. This way at least he need not know. Do yer duty by the Leslies, Cat."

He did not understand at all. The whisky had calmed Cat somewhat, and she knew she had no choice. The king would use her as he wished. "I'm all right now, Adam," she reassured him. "I dinna know what came over me. I suppose it is because I miss Patrick. We've never been separated, ye know."

He nodded, relieved. "Then I'll be on my way home." He smiled at her. Thank God she wasn't going to cause any further fuss.

"Gie my love to Fiona," Cat said softly. Then, unable to resist, she added, "And best ye keep from court, Adam, lest Jamie decides to change his luck. Yer wife would have to do her duty by the family, ye know."

Adam hastily left his sister-in-law, her mocking laughter ringing in his ears.

Chapter 16

≈§§≈

THE whisky had made her slightly drunk. "What time is it?" she asked Ellen.

"Past one," came the reply.

"I shall sleep till just before the evening meal. Wake me then. I'll be back here at ten. Have a bath ready for me. Put fresh linens on the bed, and be sure there is plenty of wood for the fire. I want wine, both red and white, and fruit and cheese in the cabinet. And marchpane. The king is mad for marchpane."

At eleven that evening the king entered the Countess of Glenkirk's bedroom through the secret passage. She rose from the bed and walked slowly across the room to him.

"Stand still!"

She stopped, and James feasted his eyes on his unwilling mistress. Her nightgown was exquisite, and had obviously been designed with seduction in mind. Of pale-green silk, it had long, flowing sleeves and a deep V neckline. The bodice appeared to have been painted on, molding her glorious breasts and tiny waist. The skirt rippled with hundreds of tiny pleats, and he could see the pearly sheen of her hips and legs shimmering through the silk.

Her tawny hair was piled at the top of her head and secured with several small gilt and pearl pins. She stared back at him proudly. She was so beautiful that he was almost afraid to touch her, but then desire overcame awe and he drew Cat into his arms.

His amber eyes never left her leaf-green ones, and when his arms closed tightly around her he could feel her trembling slightly, and was pleased by what he believed was her awe of him. He held her thus imprisoned for what seemed a lifetime, and then he bent and his mouth captured hers. Reaching up, he pulled the gilt pins from her hair, and it tumbled down over her shoulders in a perfumed cloud.

He pulled at the thin silk ribbon at her waist, and the gown opened easily. He watched as it slid to the floor. She turned without speaking, walked to the bed, and got into it. James forced himself to disrobe slowly, but once in bed with her he did not think he could wait. She knew it, yet she held him off.

"I am nae a whore to be quickly fucked, Jamie."

"So ye can talk! I thought ye were angry wi me."

"I am! 'Twas nae kind of ye to send Patrick away so quickly!"

"My dear Cat, for three nights I stood in that damned passage and watched ye and yer husband make love. I could stand it no longer. Would ye rather I came through the door and asked yer husband to move over?"

Stunned, she could not answer. That anyone else had partaken of her private moments with Patrick infuriated her.

I hae a large score to settle wi ye, James Stewart, and I intend to settle it one day, she thought bitterly.

The king's mouth closed over the nipple of her breast, and sucked hungrily. His hand was between her legs, seeking her soft, sensitive secret flesh. With exquisite expertise he caressed her, his fingers teasing with unbearable gentleness. Within minutes he had reduced her to a writhing passion.

She had wanted to punish him with coldness, but as

her own desire grew she suddenly realized that the
greatest harm she could inflict on James was to be the
most voluptuous female he would ever encounter. She
would ruin him for other women! She knew that once
young Anna of Denmark arrived in Scotland, James
would devote himself to her. Above all, he wanted a
wife who belonged to him alone, and he wanted a
family. He was the kind of man who couldn't jeopardize
all that.

However, a teenaged virgin would hardly compare
favorably with a woman as experienced as Cat was. She
was no wanton, but Patrick had taught her well, and Cat
was by nature a sensuous woman. She would now use
her experience to revenge herself on James Stewart.
Shifting her lovely body, she slid under the king and
wound her arms about his neck. "Jamie," she whispered
huskily. "Love me, Jamie hinny!"

He could scarcely believe his ears, but when he
looked down at her he saw shining eyes and an inviting
mouth. The king didn't question his good fortune. He
took possession of the lips offered him. They were soft
and yielding, and they drove him to a frenzy.

Her thighs opened and she arched her body to meet
his downward thrust. Her legs wrapped tightly about
him, and each time he drove within her, her little
tongue darted within his mouth. His excitement was
fierce and he was unable to control himself. Yet, within
minutes, as she moved voluptuously beneath him, he
grew hard again with lust for her. She whispered his
name over and over again like a litany. He was mad
with passion for her, but this time he held himself in
check until she could find her heaven too.

Exhausted, they lay panting on the bed. Finally, he
spoke. "Ye frighten me, Cat! Ye canna be human, for
no woman can love like ye have just loved me!"

"But I can, my lord. Did I not please ye?"

"Aye, love, ye pleased me verra much. Did ye use witchcraft?"

Cat remembered that James was terribly superstitious. She bit back her laughter. "Nay, my lord. I used only the sorcery of my body." Standing, she stretched tall, and then walked over to the cabinet.

"Red or white, my lord?"

"Red," he said, and she poured out two crystal goblets of the ruby wine. Carrying them back to the bed, she handed him one. Sipping it thoughtfully, he asked her, "Did Patrick teach ye to make love like that?"

"Aye," she answered him quietly.

"Ye've never known any other men, have ye?"

"Nay, Jamie, none. I am by birth a Hay of Greyhaven. Our home is quite isolated, and other than my brothers and my Hay and Leslie cousins, I had no contact with the world. I came to Patrick a virgin."

"Is yer family large?"

"I hae four brothers—one older, three younger—and my parents are both living."

"Yer fortunate, my sweet," sighed the king.

"They are but part of my family," she reminded him. "Dinna forget I have a husband and six children." She looked directly at James. "When the queen arrives from Denmark, your majesty, I am going home to Glenkirk and to my children. Ye may be the king, but I'll nae allow ye to destroy my marriage! I love Patrick Leslie, and I love our bairns. If I did not I would hae sooner killed myself than submit to another man's lust!"

He caught a handful of her hair and pulled her down to him. "Yet, madame, ye respond to my lovemaking, and ye will continue to respond as long as it pleases me."

"I respond," she answered defiantly, "because Patrick taught my body to respond."

"Are all the Leslies such paragons in bed?" he asked sarcastically.

"According to their wives, and the lasses in our district, they are. My cousin Fiona was an extremely restless woman until she married my lord's brother, Adam Leslie. Since then she has nae strayed once."

"Fiona Leslie," mused the king. "Aye! Sultry, wi auburn hair, gray eyes, and skin like ivory satin. I've seen the wench, but I didna realize she was yer relative. Perhaps some evening I may entertain the two of ye."

"Am I not woman enough for ye, Jamie?" Pushing him back onto the pillows, she kissed him expertly, and her hand slid between his legs. He quickly grew hard in the silky warmth of her skilled caresses, but before he could move to mount her, she took the initiative and mounted him instead. Triumphantly, she looked down into his surprised face. And before he could stop her she began to ride him as one would ride a horse, her round knees digging into him. No woman had ever done this to James Stewart. Shocked, he struggled beneath her.

She laughed, mocking him. "How do *ye* like being forced, my lord king?"

He could not escape the iron grip of the warm thighs that gripped him. To his shame and horror he felt himself pouring his seed in furious spurts into her. She collapsed on top of him. Angrily, he rolled over, forcing her underneath him. Her eyes were sparkling wickedly, and her mouth was laughing. Slapping her several times, he was amazed to feel his desire quickening again, so he thrust brutally into her, making her cry out in pain. The knowledge that he was hurting her seemed to soothe him.

Afterwards he spoke quietly to her. "Yer the most exciting woman I hae ever lain wi, Catriona Leslie, but if ye ever do to me again what ye did this evening, I'll beat ye black and blue. I am nae a maid to be used in such a fashion!"

"I ask yer majesty's pardon," she said softly, but somehow he felt her voice wasn't contrite enough. "Sometimes," she continued, "Patrick likes me to love him in that fashion. He says it excites him to play wi my breasts while we—"

"If I want to fuck ye and play wi yer tits I can love ye in the Greek fashion," he interrupted her. "In fact, I hae a mind to do it now!"

"No, Jamie! Damn! Not that, please! I hate it! Noooo!"

Now it was the king's turn to laugh. He wanted to punish her further, and this was the way. She would feel the shame he had felt. Forcing her over onto her stomach, he took her quickly, cruelly bruising the lovely breasts. He was pleased as she wept and struggled to escape him. She was much subdued when he had finished with her, and James felt he had gained mastery over her again.

They slept for a few hours. Then, roused by the sight of his naked, tousled and sleepy mistress, the king took her again. This time he was gentle. He smiled down at her afterwards and said, "I'll be late this evening, my pet. Closer to midnight." After taking a piece of marchpane from the plate on the nightstand, he put on his dressing gown and disappeared through the passage door.

Cat fell back onto the pillows. She was exhausted. Her body felt battered and bruised, and she wasn't sure she would be able to walk. But—and she smiled as she fell asleep—if she could keep up the pace, James would soon have memories to burn his brain forever. No other woman would ever satisfy him. *That* was to be her revenge. It did not occur to her that James simply might not let her go.

Several hours later, Ellen looked in on her mistress. What she saw decided her course of action. "The countess is unwell this morning," she told the two under-maids. "Here is a silver piece between ye. There's a fair just outside the city. Ye may go, but be back by early afternoon. Ellen locked the doors of the apartment and, returning to Cat's bedroom, sat down with her knitting.

Cat awoke several hours after noon. "What time is it?" she demanded.

"Past two. Good God, my lady! What did he do to ye?"

"Everything," said Cat wearily. "Where are Silis and Una?"

"I sent them off when I saw the condition ye were in. They'll be back soon."

"I want a tub. A hot, hot tub!"

"Ye canna go on like this each night," scolded Ellen.

Cat laughed ruefully. "Nay. I can't. Dinna fear, Ellie. Last night the king and I were but gauging each other. Now he has my measure, and I hae his!"

An hour and a half later the Countess of Glenkirk was seen riding outside the city accompanied by six of her men-at-arms. She was vastly admired by the common folk, who, knowing her reputation as the Virtuous Countess, pointed her out to their daughters as an example.

Throughout the late summer and early autumn Catriona adorned James' court. There was not a noble-man, young or old, who did not desire her. Lady Leslie did not succumb. She remained warm, charming, gracious, witty—and unobtainable.

Adam Leslie was frank in admiration. "No one," he said to her, "no one would ever know yer sleeping wi the king. Patrick would be proud of ye."

"I doubt it," she answered him dryly. "By the way,

best to keep an eye on Fiona. Jamie referred to her as
a sultry wench. I think he rather fancies her." Cat enjoyed Adam's discomfiture.

"How long until the little queen arrives?" he asked.

Cat grew serious. "She set out once, but the storms
hae been unusually fierce. I understand her ship was
forced into Oslo, and there she waits until the sea
calms." Cat lowered her voice. "There is talk of witchcraft. Already several women hae been questioned.
Jamie grows anxious. I would nae be surprised to see
him go to fetch her himself."

"Leave Scotland?" asked Adam incredulously. "Why?
Let him send the high admiral for her."

"Bothwell will nae go. He says that all the fines Jamie
has imposed on him during their last quarrel hae impoverished him, and he has nae the money for such an
expedition."

Adam laughed. "He has nerve, the border lord, to
brave his royal cousin's anger again. Do ye really think
James will go?"

"Aye. After all, he wants his wife, not someone
else's."

Cat smiled. She was responsible for the King's mood.
For ten weeks now he had been sharing her bed. For
the first time in his sad life his nights were filled with
warmth and even a kind of security. The woman who
slept with him was kind and tender and generous. His
marriage bed would be just as delightful, she assured
him. Too, there would be the pleasant duty of siring
children. The Danish royal family was large, and surely
Queen Anna would prove fruitful. Why, by this time
next year, James could be a father!

The more Cat talked, the more eager James Stewart
became to be with his bride. When he could stand it no
longer, the king arranged his government to run
smoothly in his absence. Leaving as regent his cousin,

Francis Stewart-Hepburn, the Earl of Bothwell, James departed Leith for Oslo on October 22, 1589. Luck was with him. The breezes were fresh, the skies bright blue, and the seas easy. He reached Norway quickly.

With the king away there was no point in her staying at court, so the Countess of Glenkirk made plans to go home. James had, however, exacted a promise from her that she would return when he brought his queen home. She had agreed, believing she would be safe from his attentions with the queen in residence. She longed for Patrick, and wondered if he were as lonely as she.

Chapter 17

❧❧

WHEN King James reached Oslo in early November he was met by the nobles he had sent to accompany the queen home. They escorted their impatient king to the house where the Danish princess was staying. A startled servant answered the thundering knocks, and James Stewart swept in demanding to see his bride.

Directed to a second-floor salon, the King of Scotland ran lightly up the stairs. Bursting in, he cried out, "Annie luv! 'Tis yer Jamie! Gie us a kiss, lass! I hae coom to take ye hame to Scotland!"

The startled princess, who had worked very hard to learn English, could hardly understand the wild man before her. A look of obvious distaste on her face, she backed away. Then the Earl of Glenkirk stepped forward and, in slow, unaccented English, said to her, "Your royal highness, may I have the honor to present his gracious majesty, King James of Scotland."

The princess curtsied prettily. James Stewart was immediately enchanted. She was even prettier than her portrait. Anna of Denmark was slightly shorter than the king, with silky yellow hair, sky-blue eyes, and a pink-and-white complexion. She had a little cleft in her chin, and when she smiled, two fetching dimples peeped out from either side of her rosebud mouth. She was all youth and innocence, and James instantly remembered all the things Cat had promised him marriage would be.

"His majesty would like to give you a kiss of welcome, your highness," continued the earl.

Anna of Denmark did not even look at the king. Instead, she spoke directly to Glenkirk. "Please tell his majesty that Danish ladies of good breeding do not kiss gentlemen before they are married to them." Curtsying again to the assembled group, the princess signaled to her ladies and left the salon.

Open-mouthed, the king watched her go. Then he swore. "Jesu! What manner of ice maiden hae I been contracted to wed?"

His courtiers, many of whom had already learned about the promiscuity of Danish ladies, dared not say a word. Finally Patrick Leslie spoke up. "She's really a nice little lass, cousin, but ye took her unawares. I think she was probably embarrassed, and maiden-shy. Undoubtedly she wished to meet ye in fine array rather than the simple gown she was wearing. As a married man of many years I can tell ye women put great store by their appearance, especially at a first meeting."

The other courtiers murmured their agreement. Somewhat mollified, James said, "Cat sends ye her love, Patrick. I hae given her permission to go home to Glenkirk until we return to Scotland."

James was escorted away by Danish court officials, to be housed in another building until after his wedding. The Earl of Glenkirk meanwhile sought one of the princess's ladies, and told her to dress her mistress elegantly for her next meeting with the king.

They had been married by proxy on August 20. They were now formally and officially married by a Presbyterian minister who had come with the king from Scotland. The wedding took place on November 29, in a local church. A feast was held for Scots and Danish nobles. The new Queen of Scotland loved dancing and parties above all things. The evening was gay, and so were the queen's ladies.

One of them, a Mistress Christina Anders, had singled out the Earl of Glenkirk. From the first she had seen of him in early September, she had determined to have him. That he was married made no difference to her. So was she, and to her third husband, a boy of twelve.

Christina Anders was seventeen. She was petite, with silver-gilt hair and dark sapphire eyes. She was a sea goddess in miniature. She had been married at ten to an old count who liked little girls. Widowed at thirteen, she was wed to a middle-aged man who enjoyed deflowering virgins. Christina was still a virgin. When her second husband was murdered by an angry peasant, Christina quickly married herself to his heir, an eleven-year-old boy. This left her free to pursue her own life, financially secure. She had left her husband alone on his estate with his tutor, and come to Copenhagen to renew her friendship with Princess Anna, a childhood playmate. Naturally when Anna was betrothed to the King of Scotland she asked her old friend to be one of her ladies. It would have been unthinkable for Christina to refuse.

Though several men had sought Christina as a mistress, she refused any permanent liaison. She enjoyed her freedom. Then, too, her sexual preferences were sophisticated.

The Earl of Glenkirk was not unaware of Mistress Anders' interest. Since his marriage he had not strayed from his lovely wife's bed. Now, however, he faced a long cold winter without her. Patrick Leslie loved his wife, but he was no saint, and the woman who was so obviously offering herself was very tempting.

Christina had gone out of her way to look charming at the royal wedding. She wore midnight-blue velvet, so her hair looked as silver as possible and her skin its whitest. The more she danced, the pinker her cheeks became. She pointedly ignored the Earl of Glenkirk,

much to his amusement. He might have played a harder
game with her, but he had decided to bed her that night.
If she proved a disappointment he could easily dismiss
her without any hard feelings, blaming the wedding excitement for his lapse. On the other hand, it could be
the beginning of a delightful affair.

Calculating carefully, he moved into the figure, and
when the dance stopped several minutes later, Christina
Anders found herself opposite Patrick Leslie. Clamping
an arm about her waist, he looked down, and asked,
"Wine, madame?"

She nodded, and he brought it.

"Tonight?" he asked bluntly.

Caught unawares, she nodded mutely.

"What time?"

"Eleven," she said softly.

Smiling, he bowed and walked away.

Christina sat sipping her wine. It had been so easy.
She was sorry that she had no rooms of her own in
which to entertain him. The queen's maids of honor
slept dormitory-fashion near their mistress. Once the
queen had been put to bed she would be free to go to
him. Her heart beat faster. His manner told her that he
would be a masterful lover.

Margaret Olson approached her. "The Scots stallion
grows impatient to mount his mare," she said softly.
"It's time to put the queen to bed."

Christina laughed. "You are such a bitch, Mag! All
right, but let's hurry! I have a rendezvous with Lord
Leslie tonight." She smiled proudly.

"He's a big, handsome thing," said Margaret. "I
cannot decide who to sleep with. Both Lord Home and
Lord Grey have asked me."

"Try one this week, and the other next. Soon they'll
all be going back to Scotland, and we'll be left to
return home."

"I won't," said Margaret Olson. "I am going with the queen. She asked me a few minutes ago, and she is going to ask you too. Be nice to your lover if you want to keep him when we go to Scotland."

"He has a wife there, Margaret."

"I know. I have heard the men speak of her. They say she is beautiful and headstrong. They call her the Virtuous Countess. That information should be of some help to you, my dear."

Giggling, the two maids of honor hurried to their mistress's side. With a flurry of flying skirts, Queen Anna and her ladies fled the hall, pursued by a group of shouting young men. Gaining the safety of the royal apartments, they collapsed, laughing madly. Countess Olafson, who was, at twenty-four, the oldest of the queen's ladies, tried to bring about some order.

"Ladies! Ladies! His majesty will soon be here, and there is much to do. Karen, you keep watch outside the door, and tell us when the king is coming. Inge and Olga, see to the bed. Margaret and Christina, you two help me undress her majesty."

They hurried to prepare the room and the young queen for her eager bridegroom. The scented sheets were warmed, the queen undressed and wrapped in a lovely white silk nightgown embroidered in silver and gold thread. While Margaret and Christina put the queen's wedding gown away, Countess Olafson sat the girl down and brushed her long yellow-blond hair.

Suddenly Mistress Karen burst into the room. "They're coming, your majesty! The king and his men are coming!"

The queen was hurried into the bed. She sat, plump pillows at her back, her blond hair unbound, looking flushed and a bit afraid. The door flew open and the king was half-shoved, half-carried into the room by the boisterous Scots and Danish noblemen.

"Yer majesty, his majesty," said drunk Lord Grey.

"Look, gentlemen," said James Stewart triumphantly, "my sweet Annie awaits me in our bed as a good wife should! Does this not portend a happy marriage for us?"

The queen's ladies giggled, and the king's gentlemen gently hustled him behind a screen, where they undressed him and put a silk nightshirt on him. They helped him into the bed, and he sat next to his young queen while a servant passed wine to the assembled, and health was drunk to their majesties from silver goblets. At last, with much good-natured joking and laughing, the courtiers left James and Anna to their pleasure.

In the silence that followed, the king turned to his wife and said, "Now, madame, I should like that kiss I asked ye for three and a half weeks ago."

Shyly Anna lifted her chaste lips to her husband. Touching them with his own, he gradually increased the pressure, forcing her back onto the pillows. He opened her nightgown and gazed with pleasure at the fresh, virgin body that belonged to him alone. She murmured a faint protest as he kissed and caressed her. As his desire mounted, Anna lay quietly acquiescent, her blue eyes closed.

Actually she liked what James was doing to her, and she liked the delicious tingly feelings that were racing up and down her spine and fluttering inside her. She wondered if there was something she could do that would make James feel as good as she felt. She would ask him later on when she knew him better.

Sitting her up, he pulled her nightgown over head and tossed it on the floor. He stood and yanked his own nightshirt off. Anna's eyes widened in shock. Between her husband's legs was a mass of reddish fur, and sticking out from the middle of that fur a great live thing that bobbed up and down, and pointed straight at her. Shrieking, she shrank back, covering her eyes with her hands.

James looked surprised. "I've nae stuck it in ye yet, Annie luv."

"Stick it in me?" she quavered. "Why?"

James looked faintly annoyed. "Did no one speak to ye about a wife's duties, Annie?"

"I was told I must submit to my lord in all things," she whispered.

He looked relieved. "That's right, luv. Ye must submit to me in all things. Now this," he said grasping his maleness, "is my manroot, and between yer legs is a sweet little hole where I shall put it. Ye'll like it, Annie, I promise. 'Twill feel so good." The king had never had a virgin, but his lust was hot, and he had no intention of allowing this foolish girl to deny him.

"Will it hurt me?" she asked him, for somewhere in the dim recesses of her mind she remembered her older sisters talking, and there was something she couldn't quite put her finger on now.

"Aye," he answered her matter-of-factly, "but only the first time, luvie."

"No," she said. "I don't like to hurt, and I don't want you to stick me with that ugly thing." She pointed at him and shuddered.

James was stymied. "'Tis a husband's right!" he protested.

Her rosebud mouth pouted. "No," she repeated firmly.

James Stewart's eyes grew crafty. "Very well, my sweet," he said, getting back into the bed. "We'll just kiss and cuddle a bit then."

"Yes, I like that," the little queen answered him happily.

James drew his wife into his arms. Kissing her deeply, he began to caress her expertly, until she was squirming with uncontrolled excitement. Before she realized what was happening, he mounted her and, guiding himself, pushed into her. Gasping, she struggled beneath him.

Bucking her body so as to throw him off, she succeeded only in driving him further into her. Suddenly he drew back and plunged deep. Anna screamed in genuine pain, but James covered her mouth with his and kept up the rhythmic movement, ignoring the warm trickle that flowed down the insides of her thighs.

As the pain eased, Anna felt herself begin to enjoy what was happening to her. She was still angry with her husband for deceiving her. Then, suddenly, the body laboring over her stiffened, jerked several times, and collapsed. Anna felt strangely unhappy. In the silence that followed, the clock on the mantel struck eleven.

At the other end of the house, in the apartments of the Earl of Glenkirk, there were fires in both the anteroom and the bedroom. Patrick Leslie stood before the anteroom fireplace wondering if he had done the right thing in encouraging Mistress Anders. Guiltily, he realized that a good whore would have served his purposes. But when he heard the door open behind him and turned to see her, he was glad he had asked her.

"Come in, Mistress Anders."

She was wearing the same dress she had worn earlier. And she was even lovelier by firelight.

"Will ye join me in a goblet of wine, my dear? I hae a lovely white—delicate and sweet." His eyes caressed her warmly.

"Thank you, my lord," she said in a soft voice, and stood by his chair looking into the fire.

He poured the wine. Handing the goblet to her, he watched as she drained it. The earl sat down in his chair and, reaching up, pulled Christina into his lap and kissed her. "Dinna be shy wi me, little Cairi," he said.

"What is it you call me, my lord?" she asked him.

"Cairi. The Gaelic for Christina is Cairistiona. 'Cairi' simply means 'wee Christina,' and yer a wee bit of a thing."

She snuggled into his lap.

"How old are ye?" he asked her.

"Seventeen, my lord."

"Jesu, I am thirty-seven! I could be yer father."

"But you are not, Patrick," she said, pressing herself against him. Pulling his head down, she kissed him passionately. "I came to have you make love to me." Standing up, she slowly undid her dark velvet dress. Next came her snowy petticoats, silk underblouse, and beribboned busk. She stepped out of them wearing only dark silk stockings upon which were embroidered tiny gold butterflies.

She was unbelievably exciting. Smiling slowly, he stood up and followed her lead until he stood tall and naked above her.

She looked up at him and ordered, "Take off my stockings."

Kneeling, he slowly rolled them down, one at a time, and then slipped each one off its small, slim foot. The perfume of her body drove him nearly mad. She had anticipated this when, earlier, she had stroked musk on her freshly washed skin. Still kneeling, he pulled her down to the floor in front of the fireplace. Christina spread her legs wide and held out her arms to receive him.

She was warm, and sweet, and experienced, and he was immensely pleased. The woman beneath him moved smoothly, and he allowed her release twice before taking his own. He rolled off her, and they lay relaxed before the fire.

"You think I am overbold," she said quietly in her low, husky voice, "but I wanted you, Patrick Leslie. I have never been any man's mistress, but I want to be yours."

"Why me?" He was flattered, but he was also no fool.

"Because I want you, and because for once in my life

I should like to have a normal relationship with a man. My first husband was an old man who could not perform in a normal manner. My second husband, having deflowered me, was no longer interested. My third is a child, and I am free to do as I choose. I choose to become your mistress."

"Only while I am here," said the earl. "When I return home, my dear, ye'll cease to exist for me. I may sleep wi ye now, but make no mistake, little Cairi, I love my wife."

"I agree to those terms, Patrick. And now, as it is damnably cold on this floor, may we please get into bed?"

He stood and, scooping her up, walked into the bedroom and put her into the bed. "I feared a long, cold winter, Cairi. Now, though it will still be long, it will nae be cold," he said. He climbed into bed with her.

Chapter 18

❦

FOR the first time in her married life Catriona Leslie was really on her own. She closed her Edinburgh house, telling Mrs. Kerr that she would return when the court reconvened. To the horror of Glenkirk's captain-at-arms, she planned on riding home immediately, without a proper escort.

"We'll all be murdered on the road, sure as hell," grumbled Conall More-Leslie.

"Five gold pieces we make it safely," she laughed.

"Jesu, madame, the earl will skin me if anything happens to ye!"

"Leave her be!" snapped his sister, Ellen. "She needs to go home, for whether or not she realizes it she gains strength from Glenkirk. There is little likelihood of the earl returning before spring, and she will be less lonely among her bairns."

They did not, however, travel poorly escorted. Learning of her plans, Francis Stewart-Hepburn, the Earl of Bothwell, offered to escort her himself. She could hardly turn down James Stewart's favorite cousin, and regent of Scotland.

Francis Stewart-Hepburn was a tall, handsome man with dark auburn hair, an elegantly barbered short beard, and piercing blue eyes. He was an educated man, unfortunately born in advance of his proper time. His amazing fund of knowledge and his many scientific ex-

periments terrified the superstitious—educated and uneducated alike. Though he alternated between new and
old kirk, he was not a particularly religious man. Too,
sad women trying to bring excitement into their lives
by playing at witchcraft, had sometimes named Lord
Bothwell as their leader. Francis Hepburn was therefore
whispered to be a warlock. He was not, but rumors
often persist.

Cat knew the rumor to be nonsense, but it amused
Francis Hepburn's macabre sense of humor not to deny
it. Besides, it terrified his cousin James, who alternated
between love and hate for Francis. For some reason the
king brought out the devil in Bothwell. Although Francis was fond of his cousin, as one might be fond of a
clumsy hunting dog, there were times when he simply
could not resist playing on the king's absurd fears.

James admired Francis and would have given anything to be like his tall, assured cousin. Consequently,
in an attempt to impress the Earl of Bothwell, James
had told him of his affair with the Countess of Glenkirk.

Though he congratulated his cousin on his good fortune, Francis was shocked. He himself had loved many
women, married and unmarried, but he had never forced
one as the king was forcing Glenkirk's wife. That she
was being forced he knew instinctively, for he was sensitive to people, and though she tried to appear her old
self, he saw the faint darkness beneath her eyes and
heard the hollow tone in her laughter.

Gallantly, he set out to become her friend and confidant. And he did. But something else happened that
Francis Hepburn had not planned on. He fell in love
with the Countess of Glenkirk, a state he was forced to
hide from her and from his jealous royal cousin as well.

Cat had never had a man for a friend, but she enjoyed
Francis Hepburn's companionship greatly. He was a
font of knowledge, and Cat rarely found anyone learned

to talk with. Since everyone assumed their relations were chaste, the court thought the relationship eccentric. All laughed to see the greatest rake at court and the most beautiful woman enjoying intellectual discussions.

The Earl of Bothwell's lineage was an interesting one. His father had been John Stewart, Prior of Coldingham, an illegitimate son of James V—whose daughter, Mary Queen of Scots, began spelling her surname "Stuart," a spelling that eventually prevailed in the royal line. Francis and James Stewart shared the same grandfather. The earl's mother had been Lady Janet Hepburn, only sister to the last Earl of Bothwell, James Hepburn, who was Mary Stewart's third husband. James Hepburn left no legitimate issue, and his title and estates had gone to his nephew, Francis, who added his uncle's last name to his own as a gesture of respect.

Francis Hepburn's father had died when he was scarcely more than a baby. Francis had only an illegitimate brother and sister. His mother remarried, and he was ignored in early childhood and then shipped off to be educated in France and Italy.

He had returned home to Scotland in his teens, an elegant, self-assured, educated man. He was quickly married to Lady Margaret Douglas, daughter of the powerful Earl of Angus. Lady Margaret was a widow with a son, and slightly older than Francis Stewart-Hepburn. She did not like her second husband, and he did not like her. Theirs was a marriage of convenience and they dutifully sired children to maintain the line, but between them there was not a bit of warmth. Margaret Douglas was relieved that her sensuous, over-sexed husband sought other beds. She did not want him in hers.

The Earl of Bothwell, with a troop of fifty wild borderers, escorted the Countess of Glenkirk home. Conall was not sure he approved, but his lady's safe journey was what mattered. Cat insisted that Bothwell stay at

Glenkirk a few days, and though he meant to stay but
three or four, he ended up staying through Twelfth
Night. Since the dowager countess had been a cousin to
his father, he was considered a cousin himself, and
treated as a member of the family. The Glenkirk children called him Uncle Francis, the boys following at his
heels like admiring puppies and the little girls flirting
outrageously with him. Bothwell adored it. His own children had been taught by their mother to give their
loyalty and obedience to her alone, and he felt no kin-
ship with them. Even Glenkirk's younger brothers
treated him with a rough camaraderie and called him
cousin. The men hunted, wenched, diced, and drank
with him. It was the closest thing he had ever had to a
real family, and he loved it.

When he finally left, on the day after Colin Leslie's
sixth birthday, it was with great regret. But he had been
left in charge of Scotland, and the time for self-indul-
gence was over. Bothwell was above all things a disciplined man. He left with Cat a small Damascus-steel
sword with an exquisite openwork handle of Florentine
gold scattered with tiny semiprecious stones.

"For your eldest boy's birthday next month," he said.

"Oh, Francis! It's marvelous! Jamie will love it—
though I know he'd rather ye were here."

"I wish I could be, but I've indulged myself long
enough, Cat. Cheer up, my darling! The winter will go
quickly, and Patrick will soon be home."

"James has insisted that I come back to court when
he brings the queen home," she said, frowning. "I told
Glenkirk I would hae no more bairns, but Francis, I
swear I am going to do my damnedest to get wi child
when my lord comes home! The only way I'll escape
James Stewart's attentions is to be safe at Glenkirk, but
I'll nae get permission unless I am big in the belly."

Francis Hepburn kissed her lightly and rode away to
a long and lonely winter. And it was a snowy, gray,

cold, depressing winter. Had Cat not loved her children she would have gone mad, but she did, and their company saved her.

James Leslie celebrated his twelfth birthday, and if he was disappointed that his father seemed to have forgotten him, Francis Hepburn's gift made up for it. They had had no word from Patrick in months, and though Cat knew he was safe, she missed him terribly. The nights were the worst. It was now seven months since she had seen him. Alone in their big bed she wept bitterly, and swore to herself that when he came home she would obey him, and not ever return to court. He had been right not to want to involve them with the royal Stewarts. What had it gained them. Separation and shame!

Spring came, a lovely, early, warm spring. The hawthorn and pussy willow were in bloom. The hillsides around Glenkirk sprouted in yellow and white, and Easter Sunday was sunny. The Glenkirk courier who had been with the earl in Denmark arrived bearing a pouchful of messages. There was even one with the royal seal that, opened, revealed her official appointment as a lady of the queen's bedchamber. A small personally scrawled note enclosed with it from James himself stated that he expected to see her back at court when he got there. She tossed it aside impatiently and reached for the letter from her husband. It was short, almost impersonal, and she was disappointed.

"Beloved," he wrote. "By the time this reaches ye we should be under sail and on our way home. It has been a long, hard winter here, and I have missed ye. The king's wedding was performed in Oslo, but we returned to Denmark for Christmas, and have been here ever since. Tell Jamie that I am bringing him a surprise for the birthday I missed. I send my love to ye, and to all our bairns. Your devoted husband, Patrick Leslie."

It was not the letter of a man hungry for his woman,

and Cat was furious. The bastard, she thought angrily, and wondered if he had taken a mistress or was simply tumbling an occasional doxy. If he did have a mistress, then she must be part of the court. Would she be left behind, or would she be coming with them? "I'll soon find out," she muttered aloud. Damn! Here was a fine situation.

She wanted to get pregnant to escape the attentions of the king. Yet, if she did, she would have to return home to Glenkirk, leaving Patrick at court to entertain his mistress. There was only one thing to do. She would have to get rid of the whore.

On May 1, 1590, James and his queen arrived at Leith in the lead ship of a convoy of thirteen. The road to the capital was lined with a cheering populace. Their pretty young queen sat comfortably ensconced in a gilded chariot drawn by eight white horses, each dressed in red velvet blankets embroidered in gold and silver thread.

In Edinburgh the nobility were assembled to greet Anna. Catriona Leslie stood with Francis Stewart-Hepburn as the royal progress arrived at Holyrood House. She immediately spotted Patrick lifting a petite woman down from her horse. The woman had silvery hair, and was dressed in pale-pink velvet trimmed with some kind of gray fur, probably rabbit.

"Ye were in Leith, Francis. Who is the wench Glenkirk is lifting down?"

Francis Hepburn smiled wolfishly and wondered how Cat had found out so quickly. "She is Mistress Christina Anders," he said. "A childhood friend of the queen's, and a lady of the bedchamber."

"Who's bedchamber?" snapped Cat. "She's at least four months gone wi child. Damn Glenkirk! I'll roast him for this!"

Bothwell chuckled. "I am sure ye'll find a way to get even wi him."

"I will," she replied grimly. Then, "Oh, Francis! I missed him so much! It's been months since I last laid eyes on him. How could he?"

The Earl of Bothwell put a comforting arm about Cat. "Probably because he was lonely, and needed ye. So he took a woman to cheer him. 'Tis no great thing."

"I was lonely too, Francis. I burned for him every night he was away—even when the king was wi me."

"Dinna feel sorry for yerself, my darling," said Lord Bothwell. "She may have had the fire to keep Patrick warm this winter, but she doesna hae the fire to keep him permanently. See how his eyes are scanning the crowd? He's looking for ye."

"I am sure he is," she answered. "Looking to see if I've caught him wi his whore! God, Bothwell! Look how she clings to his arm! I'll scratch her face to ribbons!"

Francis Hepburn chuckled deep in his throat. "If ye make a scene in public all the sympathy will be to *poor* Mistress Anders. However, if ye greet Glenkirk in good wifely fashion, the sympathy will lie wi ye. My wife always plays that game when she ventures out of Crichton. Everyone knows yer called the Virtuous Countess because of yer faithfulness and devotion to yer lord. If ye really want to get even wi him, play the part to the hilt!"

"Bothwell, I adore ye! Yer so wonderfully diabolic!" said Cat gleefully. "How do I look?"

His blue eyes swept over her with obvious approval. She was dressed on this cool spring day in a very simple mulberry velvet gown. It had long, fitted sleeves with ecru lace cuffs, and a small stiff ecru lace collar. She wore her famous pink pearls. Though she had four ropes of them, she wore only two. She had removed her matching cape, which was trimmed in sable. Her dark honey-colored hair was caught up in a gold mesh net, and held with pearl and gilt pins.

"Dinna bat yer wicked green eyes at me, my darling," said Bothwell in a low voice. "I need no encouragement to ravish ye. If Patrick doesn't rush ye home to bed, he's a bigger fool than I think."

They had reached the reception room. Francis Hepburn squeezed Cat's hand and then gave her a little shove toward the door. Giving her skirts a small shake and her hair a final pat, she nodded at the major-domo.

She walked through the door and down the center of the room to the foot of the two thrones. Her head was high, and she could hear the faint whispers around her. Gracefully she sank into a curtsy, her head bowing for just a second.

"Welcome home, my lord king, and to ye, dearest madame, a gracious welcome to Scotland from all the Leslies of Glenkirk."

James Stewart beamed on her. "Cat! Yer as lovely as ever! Annie luv, this is Glenkirk's wife, Cat Leslie. I hae made her a lady of yer bedchamber, so she'll be serving ye now."

Anna Stewart looked down at the countess and felt sorry for her friend Christina. Not only was the countess beautiful, but her expression was sweet and kind. "Thank you for your welcome, Lady Leslie," said the queen.

"I will do my best to serve ye well, my queen," said Cat. Then before she could be dismissed she turned again to the king. "A boon, cousin!"

"Name it, my dear."

"It has been almost nine months since I have seen my husband, sire. Now that ye are so happy in yer own marriage, perhaps ye can understand how I feel. I hae not yet even seen my husband except from a distance. May I please take him to Glenkirk House for just this

.night?" She cocked her head appealingly and smiled sweetly.

"Oh, James," said the queen, "say yes! I give Lady Leslie my permission. Please give her yours."

"Glenkirk! Where are ye?" roared the king.

The earl stepped forward, and as he did Cat saw the little hand that tried to hold him back. For a brief moment they looked at each other, then Cat flung herself into his arms and kissed him passionately. Unable to help himself, he kissed her back.

"God's foot, Glenkirk! Take her home to bed," chortled the king.

They turned and, bowing to their majesties of Scotland, walked from the chamber. Just before exiting, Cat turned her head ever so slightly and looked directly at Christina Anders. Passing Francis Hepburn, she winked.

"Why," asked the queen of her husband, "do they call Lady Leslie the Virtuous Countess? I thought it was because she was cold, and only did her duty by her husband."

The king laughed. "Lord, no, my innocent Annie! Cat Leslie is deeply in love wi her husband, and always has been. She is called the Virtuous Countess because, unlike so many women at this court, she will nae sleep wi any other man. She is a most faithful wife. They hae six bairns. The reason I chose her to serve ye is that I thought she would be a good influence on ye."

"Oh," said the queen, feeling even sorrier for Christina Anders.

"Francis Stewart-Hepburn, the Earl of Bothwell," called out the major-domo. The queen turned to greet the new arrival.

Chapter 19

❦❧

SAFELY in their coach, the Earl of Glenkirk turned to his wife. "I have never seen ye gie a better performance, Cat."

"Would ya rather I had caused a scene and attacked yer mistress in public?" she asked him quietly.

"I am sorry, hinny. I dinna mean to hurt ye. Who told ye?"

"Ye did. The letter ye sent me was hardly that of a man longing for his wife. Ye hae put more warmth into yer correspondence wi the Kiras. One letter in all that time! Was she selling her wares on the dock when yer ship came into port that ye couldna find time to write to me? Jamie was devastated ye forgot his birthday! If Francis hadna left him the sword—"

"Francis?"

"Bothwell," she said. "He escorted us home to Glenkirk after the king left Edinburgh last year. His father and yer mother are cousins, so that makes him our cousin. He stayed till just after Twelfth Night. The children," she said with malice, "adore him, and yer brothers had a fine time wi him. He's a good friend, Patrick, I like him."

"Perhaps, madame, I should inquire what ye were doing while I was away on king's business. Francis Hepburn is a notorious rake."

"Dinna try to cloud the issue, Patrick! Francis is my friend, nothing more, and ye should not even have to ask. Besides, he is married. Can ye tell me that Mistress Anders is naught but a friend to ye? And the child she carries is nae yer bairn?"

He had the grace to flush, and she laughed. "Patrick! Patrick! Only the Leslie women know the secret of preventing conception. Yer so used to me that ye got careless wi yer whore."

Realizing that she wasn't too angry with him was a great relief. He would not tell her that Christina Anders had tricked him, hoping to have a greater hold on him. He had been tiring of the Danish girl and, knowing it, she had become pregnant. He had tried to make her stay behind in Denmark, but she refused to give up her post as lady of the royal bedchamber and threatened to cause a scandal if he told the queen. These things, however, Patrick Leslie would not tell his wife.

"Do ye love this girl?" asked Cat.

"God, no!" he burst out. "Damn, Cat! I am no courtier, and there I was alone in Norway and Denmark wi the Stewart court. Do ye know what they do all day? They dice. They drink. They play at games. They change clothes. Aye! Clothes are very important to them! They wench. It is still a source of amazement to me how frequently they change partners. They are the most *useless* people alive! Had I not found a Kira in Copenhagen, I would hae gone mad!"

"A Kira?"

"Aye, sweetheart! They've a bank in Copenhagen, and I was able to keep track of our business through them. It gave me something to do."

Picturing poor Christina Anders waiting patiently while Patrick kept track of his ships and cargoes made the Countess of Glenkirk laugh. Then she asked, "Ye are sure the bairn is yers?"

"Aye. Cairi is many things, but she's nae a wanton. The child is mine."

"What will ye do about it, Glenkirk?"

"I will acknowledge it, and see to its support."

"And its mother? What will ye do about her?"

"I told her from the first that I love my wife, and that our liaison was only a temporary thing. I meant it then and I mean it now."

They had reached Glenkirk House, which was located just off the Cannongate, near Holyrood House. Cat swept in and up the stairs, bidding Mrs. Kerr a good day. The earl remained below while the servants fussed over him.

Ellen was waiting for her mistress. "Is it true?" she asked. "Has the earl come home wi another woman? Well! Ye certainly need not feel so guilty now!"

Cat whirled around. "If ye ever even hint at *that* again ye'll end yer days alone at Crannog! Do ye understand me, Ellie?"

The bond of love between mistress and servant was strong. Realizing how deep the hurt done Cat really was, Ellen apologized. "I must be getting old and foolish, my baby."

The countess caught her tiring woman's hand and squeezed it. Then her eyes twinkled. "Yer gossip is partly correct, ye nosy old woman! His Danish mistress is part of the queen's entourage, and quite an embarrassment to poor Glenkirk. She went and got herself wi child to try and hold him. Poor Patrick! He's been married to me for so long he's forgotten how treacherous women can be."

"Will ye forgie him?"

"Of course. He's come home to me, and he's quite ashamed at having been caught. As long as he discards her, I will be content. Now, Ellie, see to my bath. I think that wicked new black silk nightgown will do. Glenkirk's about to receive a welcome he'll nae forget!"

Ellen laughed. "The Danish girl may deliver three

sons to the earl and she'd still nae have a chance wi
him against ye, my lady."

When Patrick Leslie entered his own apartments a
short while later he found that his valet had prepared
a steaming oak tub in front of the blazing fireplace.
Stripping off his clothing, he said, "Burn them, Angus,"
and then climbed into the tub. The water was faintly
perfumed and slightly oily. His winter-dry skin soaked
it up. He sniffed appreciatively.

"Oil of musk," Cat said, and he looked up to see her
standing in the doorway that connected their bedroom.
She walked across the room and, flinging off her black
silk robe, mounted the steps and joined him in his
tub. Putting her arms about his neck, she molded herself to him and kissed him hungrily. As her little tongue
darted back and forth exploring his mouth, her hands
fondled him beneath the warm water.

He had needed little encouragement. The mere sight
of her had roused him. Loosening his grip on her, he
reached down and, cupping her buttocks in his hands,
raised her. As her slim legs tightened about his waist
he thrust deep within her. He heard her catch her
breath. "Damn ye, Patrick! Did ye have to be away
so long?"

Much later they lay in their big bed, happy and
content with each other. Cat slept naked, safe within
the curve of Patrick's arm. He lay awake wondering
what had ever possessed him to get involved with
Christina Anders when a clean whore would have
served his purposes and given him no trouble.

At Holyrood House, Christina Anders cursed the fact
that it was too late to get rid of the bastard growing
within her. To try at this stage of the game might kill
her. One look at the Countess of Glenkirk had told her
the battle was lost. And the fantastic act that the
countess had put on for just her benefit! How she had

known so quickly was a mystery to Christina, but that she had known was patently obvious. The Danish girl sighed and wondered what would happen to her, and to the child she carried.

She did not have long to wonder. The following day the Countess of Glenkirk reported for duty as a lady of the queen's bedchamber. Anna took immediately to Catriona Leslie as to a charming and warm older cousin. No help there, thought Christina. Her aid, however, came from the most unexpected quarter. At the first opportunity, the Countess of Glenkirk separated Mistress Anders from the others. They walked in the park surrounding Holyrood House.

"How far gone are ye?" asked Cat with her usual directness.

Christina was frightened, but she stopped and looked up at the tall, beautiful woman. "Madame, I do not know what you mean."

Cat took the girl's arm. "Listen, my dear, I hae been wed to Patrick Leslie for twelve years. We hae six children, and what I guessed at, Patrick has confirmed. Now, when is the bairn due?"

Christina's composure crumbled. "Autumn," she whispered.

"Dinna fret, my dear," she heard the countess say to her. "Leslies take care of their own, and yer bairn is a Leslie."

"The child is a bastard, my lady."

"Pish!" said Cat impatiently. "Patrick's great-grandfather, the second earl, fathered a bastard son, the first of the More-Leslies. They have always served us since then. The More-Leslies are respected, and respectable. Your child will be taken care of, and ye need not worry. Yer lucky in that respect. Good God, girl! Why did ye nae pick an unmarried man who would possibly have married ye? Yer of good family."

"I am married, madame. To my third husband, a boy of twelve. Even if my lover had been free to wed me, it would have taken too long to get an annulment, and I can scarcely claim a boy not yet potent as this child's father. I appreciate and will accept your aid, but my child will not be raised as a servant! He is of good blood on both sides even if he is not legitimate."

Cat smiled. Christina Anders had given the countess the weapon she needed in order to control the situation. "Ye will be a good mother, my dear, and the Leslies will see yer bairn is raised as befits a noble bastard. However, if ye attempt to ensnare my husband again, I will see ye sent back to Denmark in disgrace and yer child will be sold East into slavery." So saying, the Countess of Glenkirk patted the girl's arm kindly and walked away.

Christina shuddered. She had no doubt that Catriona Leslie meant exactly what she said, and could do exactly what she threatened. Christina did not love Patrick Leslie. He had merely been a refreshing change. She was not about to get into a fight with his countess over him. Just as long as the baby was taken care of, she would be satisfied. The earl may have confessed his infidelity to his wife, but Christina would wager he had not confessed to all the presents he had lavished on her. She chuckled. She had done quite well.

That evening Cat managed a few minutes alone in their rooms with her husband. "I have had a talk wi Mistress Anders," she said calmly. The earl looked uncomfortable. "I told her," continued his wife, "that the Leslies take care of their own, so we will see the child is taken care of, but she's nae to see ye again."

"Cat! Ye had no right to tell her that!"

She flew at him. "Damn ye, Patrick! I have been patient wi ye, and kind to yer highborn doxy, but I've nae intention of sharing ye wi yer whore!" She turned her back to him.

Putting an arm about her, he pulled her back against him and pushing her tawny hair aside, kissed the nape of her neck. "I've never intended spreading myself between two women," he said gently, "and I hae no thought to involve myself wi Cairi again. But she is bearing my child. 'Tis a lonely time for her, sweetheart. Dinna be unkind. 'Tis nae like ye."

"I was alone when I carried Jamie," she answered him.

"Aye. But ye were safe in Fiona's house wi Mrs. Kerr, and Sally. Ye were in yer own land, and anytime ye chose ye could have called on half a dozen people for aid. Cairi has none of these advantages. She is alone in a strange land, and in imminent danger of disgrace should her condition become known. I only mean to offer the hand of friendship should she need it. Nothing more." He kissed the fetching little nape of his wife's neck again, and one hand gently fondled a soft, round breast.

"Damn ye, Glenkirk," she said through gritted teeth, but she turned and raised her face to him. His mouth found hers, and she felt her legs weaken. Bending, he scooped her up and deposited her on their bed. "No," she sighed reluctantly at him. "We canna now. I am due back wi the queen."

It was his turn to mutter, "Damn!" and she couldn't resist a giggle. Struggling to her feet, she smoothed her skirts down and, smiling wickedly at him over her shoulder, left him to cool off.

Patrick Leslie chuckled deeply to himself. What a wench she was! She had kept him ensnared for twelve years. Though she was stubborn, independent, willful, and perhaps too intelligent for a woman, she had never bored him. She was still the most fascinating woman he had ever known. It never occurred to Patrick that the very qualities in her that distressed him were the ones that made her so interesting.

Thinking over the last few days, he realized how lucky he was. Cairi Anders had been a lovely diversion, though he was sorry she was pregnant. At least she had made no scenes, and he was grateful to her for that. As to his wife, he sighed with relief. She could have made it very difficult for him, but she had not. She had been unbelievably generous.

While Patrick Leslie thought about his wife, Cat was in the queen's anteroom fending off the king. Struggling furiously, the Countess of Glenkirk yanked James Stewart's hand out of her bodice. "Damnit, Jamie! Behave yerself!"

" 'Tis hardly a warm welcome home ye gie me, Cat luv," protested James.

Cat swept him a curtsy. "Welcome home, yer majesty," she said coolly. "Now please allow me to pass, sire. I am already late for the queen."

"When may I see ye?"

"Publicly at any time, sire. Privately, never! I would remind yer majesty that ye are a married man now, and I have always been a married woman."

"Annie does nae pleasure me as ye do," he said.

"Her majesty is still hardly more than a maid, Jamie. It is up to ye to teach her what pleases ye."

"I am no schoolmaster," he replied sulkily. "Now, madame, let us fix a time that we may be together."

Catriona Leslie looked steadily at her king and her eyes were green ice. "In yer mother's day the word of a Stewart was good," she said cruelly.

Before he could reply the door to the queen's bedroom opened, and Countess Olafson called, "Ah, Lady Leslie! There you are! The queen has been asking for you."

Cat again curtsied to the king, but as she swept by she heard him say softly, "Ye'll pay dearly for that remark, madame."

Chapter 20

❧§ ₹❧

THE Countess of Glenkirk had no time to ponder
the king's threatening remark. She was far too
busy. The queen was to be crowned almost immediately.
Her coronation robes, requiring many tiresome fittings,
were all to be Scots-made. And then, too, Anna had to
be taught the ceremony. Unfortunately, Anna of Denmark was not very bright. Beautiful, innocent, charming,
and generous she was. But she was also extravagant,
empty-headed, silly, and hot-tempered.

Fortunately, Catriona Leslie had the patience needed
to drill the queen. She also had wisdom enough to make
a game of it so Anna would not become bored.

"If," the young queen told Cat, "I had had a school-
mistress like you, perhaps I should have been more inclined to learn."

Cat laughed. "Nonsense, madame. Ye dinna fool me
a bit. Ye know that ye will not only look magnificent at
the coronation, but by knowing yer part well ye'll truly
be magnificent. Yer subjects will be enchanted."

It was a clever compliment, and the teenaged queen
preening herself before the mirror thought again how
much she liked the lovely Countess of Glenkirk. Such an
agreeable lady.

Anna of Denmark was crowned Queen of Scotland
at Scone on May 17, 1590. She played her part with a
charming, youthful dignity that touched the hearts of

the crustiest old highland lairds assembled to see the
next mother of the Stewart line. The evening was spent
in the merriest of revels with a magnificent feast that
featured roast boars, red deer, sheep, and sides of beef
all basted by red-faced and perspiring kitchen boys.
There were fowls of every kind—swans, larded ducks,
capons in sweet lemon-ginger sauce, stuffed roast geese,
partridges, grouse, quail, and pigeons. There were great
bowls of raw oysters, and boiled shrimp, mussels, and
clams with herbs. Broiled sea trout and flounders were
served whole on great gold platters. There were also
flaky pastries of minced meat, rabbit, fruits, and nuts.
Smoked hams, eels, and potted hare were also offered.
Young spring lettuces, scallions, and artichokes in vinegar filled silver bowls. Great crocks of butter were
placed at intervals on the tables along with large tren-
chers of fresh breads. For the last course the guests were
offered custards, jellies of every color and shape, oranges from Spain, early cherries from the south of
France, and fruit tarts made with the dried fruits of last
year's harvest. Silver bowls of sugared almonds and
filberts were passed with the cheeses, the wafers, and
the tiny goblets of spiced hippocras.

Wines and ales had flowed generously, and the entertainment had been continuous. There were minstrels, of
course, and jugglers, dancing dogs and acrobats.
Pipers had traversed the dining hall several times. Cat,
who had eaten sparingly, was brewing a headache when
her husband came to claim her for the dancing.

"Take me for some air instead," she begged him.

They walked about the gardens in the cool May night.

"I never get to see ye, hinny, now that yer a lady of
the queen's bedchamber," the earl complained to his
wife.

"I know," she sighed back. "Patrick, I want to go
home! Ye were right! We should nae have involved our-

selves with the court." Suddenly she was clinging to him. "Please take me home, my love. Now!"

He held her close and smelled the seductive sweetness of the scent she always wore. He stroked her lovely hair, and wondered about this passionate, almost desperate outburst. Then he smiled to himself. Though he had been back less than a month, it was possible that she was breeding. She had, of course, threatened him after Morag's birth that there would be no more children, but women were apt to change their minds. He hugged her indulgently. "Ye know we canna just go home, sweetheart. We are part of the court now, and must get permission from their majesties. To do that we need a good excuse. I dinna have one, do ye?"

"No," she replied sadly.

"Yer sure," he asked her searchingly. "Ye could be wi child."

"It's too soon for even me to tell, Patrick." Arms around his neck, she gazed up at him. "Shall I gie ye another son, my lord? Are six bairns not enough to assure yer immortality?"

"Only three of them are sons," he teased her. "Besides, we hae such fun making them." He bent and kissed her eager lips. "Damn me, Cat! I am tired of sharing ye wi the Stewarts. Let's make another bairn, and go home to Glenkirk!" Finding her mouth, he kissed her again, and would have gone on doing so had not an insolent voice drawled, "Shocking! And wi yer own wife, too, Glenkirk!"

Startled, the Leslies pulled apart to face the amused gaze of the Earl of Bothwell.

"Who the hell—" began Patrick, but Cat had already launched herself at Bothwell. "Francis! You beast! How could ye?"

Catching her angry little fists, he laughed down at her. "I wish a woman would kiss me like that." Turning to Patrick, Francis Hepburn held out his hand. "Glenkirk, I'm Bothwell! We're distant cousins of a sort, and not only do I envy ye yer beautiful wife, sir, ye've a fine brood of bairns also!"

Patrick Leslie shook the hand offered him. "So yer the Wizard Earl. I'm pleased to meet ye, man! I owe ye my thanks for escorting Cat home last autumn."

" 'Twas my pleasure," replied Bothwell, "but I've disturbed yer tryst for a reason. The queen seeks ye, Cat. Best to hurry, my darling. Some farradiddle over a torn hem or such, and only Lady Leslie can make it right."

Sighing, Cat quickly kissed her husband. Impudently thumbing her nose at Bothwell, she gathered up her skirts and ran off. Both men laughed, and then Francis Hepburn said seriously to the Earl of Glenkirk, "If she were my wife, Leslie, I would get her away from the Stewarts, and their damned court. She is too much of a temptation."

"Aye," said Patrick, "and she wants to go. Last year I couldn't force her home, but suddenly she *must* go. I dinna understand it, Bothwell, but I am glad."

"Then take her home, man! As soon as possible."

Glenkirk had no time to think about Francis' words, for the court was on the move again. Two days after the queen's coronation, Anna of Denmark officially entered her Edinburgh capital to be greeted by the nine Muses and the four Virtues. The royal procession moved along High Street, stopping at St. Giles Church, where the queen and her court listened to a long, dull sermon.

That evening the court faced another gargantuan feast, and to Anna's delight there was a masque extolling Spring. The ladies of the court were each assigned parts. They were flowers, birds, trees, animals, elements, and all things pertaining to the season of spring. The only man in the entire production was the Earl of Bothwell, magnificently attired in silver and white, who played a

very amused North Wind. Educated in Europe, and
having spent a good deal of time at both the French and
English courts, Bothwell was quite used to these
masques and saw nothing unmanly in them.

As the North Wind it was his delightful duty to attempt to chase off Springtime, played by the queen herself wearing flowing robes of pink and pale green.
Springtime's coterie of tender creatures followed their
majesty. This lead to much scampering about and giggling. North Wind was finally vanquished by South Wind,
who wore diaphanous robes of pale blue and silver, and
who was portrayed by the Countess of Glenkirk.

The king was bored to tears by the entertainment,
though he did remark that the South Wind had the
prettiest pair of tits he'd ever seen. James thought these
amusements silly. The queen, however, was enchanted,
and extremely pleased by the success of her own efforts.
The younger members of the nobility were happy to see
an end to the dull, psalm-singing court of the king's
regency and bachelorhood.

That night Cat and Patrick slept together in their
own apartments. They worked happily at conceiving
another child, but did not do so. As the weeks went by
Cat became more distraught. It was obvious to her, as
the newness of young love wore off, that the serious
young king and his feather-headed wife had nothing in
common other than a passion for hunting. Increasingly
Cat caught James Stewart's eyes upon her, and was
frightened. She might hate him, but she could not refuse
him! He was king.

Then Patrick announced that the king had delegated
him to go to Hermitage Castle with Francis Hepburn, its
master, and make arrangements for Twelfth Night
Revels. The queen had expressed a desire to see Bothwell's famous border home. Hearing her husband's
news, Cat hurried to her mistress.

"May I go wi them, yer majesty?" she pleaded prettily. "What do men know of women's comforts? As Lady Bothwell never leaves Crichton, she will be no help."

The queen laughed. "It is a scandal how much you love your husband, my dear Cat. Yes, yes! Go along with the handsome Glenkirk. I do not blame you for wanting to be with him. Now that Christina is well again, I can get along without you for a few days."

"Thank ye, madame," said Cat, kissing the queen's hand.

"Thank you for taking such good care of my childhood friend in her illness," said the queen meaningfully.

Cat curtsied and exited. Safe outside, she chuckled to herself. Mistress Anders' predicament had been kept a discreet scandal. The Danish noblewoman had been delivered of a daughter in October. The child, Anne Fitz-Leslie, was being boarded with a healthy young farming family, near the city. The queen repaid the Countess of Glenkirk's generosity by letting her go with her husband on king's business.

Catriona and Patrick rode with Francis Hepburn at the head of Bothwell's borderers. The evening was clear and cold, with a heaven full of stars and a bright moon. They had left in late afternoon and they rode the entire night, breaking their journey several times to warm themselves with dreams of potent, smoky whisky in nameless inns. Wherever they stopped, the welcome was always a warm one for the Earl of Bothwell and his men.

Back at Holyrood, James Stewart hummed a little tune to himself as he slipped through the secret passageway that connected his bedroom with Cat Leslie's. The queen would be unavailable to him for a few days, her womanly time being upon her. He had sent Patrick Leslie off with Bothwell. And now the king looked forward to rediscovering the Countess of Glenkirk.

Opening the door at the end of the passage, he stepped into the room and was confronted by a startled Ellen, who curtsied low.

"Where is your mistress?" demanded James.

"Gone to Hermitage, your majesty," stammered Ellen.

"I dinna gie her permission to leave court! She'll be punished for this disobedience!"

"The queen sent her, sire," said Ellen desperately.

"What?"

"The queen sent my lady to Hermitage wi my lord of Glenkirk, and my lord of Bothwell," repeated Ellen. "Her majesty felt a woman's touch would be needed in the preparations for Twelfth Night."

James managed to master the anger growing within him. Reaching into the pocket of his dressing gown, he grudgingly drew out a gold piece. Handing it to Ellen, he said quietly, "Tell yer beautiful mistress that I will nae gie her up." Then he reentered the secret passage, which closed behind him.

Ellen sat down on the bed with a relieved sigh. Now she understood Cat's hasty departure. Ellen disliked the king's hypocrisy intensely. He played the moral man and the devoted husband while lusting after another woman. If only they could go home.

It was not, however, to be so simple. Like a cat at a mousehole, the king watched and waited for his opportunity. It made no difference to James that what he had already done to Cat was wrong according to the laws of the very church he was sworn to uphold. There was one thing which all the dour churchmen who had raised him couldn't erase from the royal Stewart's mind, and that was the absolute fact of the divine right of kings. Like the five Jameses before him, this James upheld the laws of the land and the church only after his own wants had been satisfied.

In attempting to punish the king by being the most exciting woman he would ever encounter, Cat had unwittingly infected him with a sexual hunger that only she could now satisfy. Her coldness enraged him. He would have her if he had to ask her husband for her. That he might destroy her marriage and perhaps even her whole life made no difference to the king. The Countess of Glenkirk was his subject. She belonged to him. She would obey him.

Like the good hunter he was, the king stalked his prey and smelled its fear. While the court stayed at Hermitage Castle he did manage, for a few minutes, to separate her from the rest of the crowd. Finding herself alone with the king, Cat looked frantically around.

James laughed. "Would I could take ye here in just the few minutes we have, my dear, but alas, I canna."

She said nothing.

" 'Twas neatly done, madame," the king continued, "but why did ye run away from me, Catriona? I sent Patrick away before I came to ye. And what did I find? Yer tiring woman packing yer clothes, and a cold, empty bed."

Cat's heart was pounding violently, and she was icy with a mixture of fear and anger. Gathering her courage, she looked up at him and spoke. "Jamie, I can say it no plainer. I dinna want to be yer mistress. Please, sire! Ye promised me that when ye brought the queen home ye would free me. I love my husband, and he is nae a man to share his wife wi another—even his king. Why do ye *do* this to me, Jamie? Yer wife is a fresh and lovely girl open to yer instruction in the arts of love. Why must ye hae me?"

He didn't answer her question. Instead he said quietly, "When we return to Edinburgh I expect ye to receive me, madame, without any further argument. If ye will not, I will be forced to ask Patrick's permission, which ye know he will gie me. If, however, ye come freely we will continue to keep our liaison secret from the rest of the world—including yer husband."

Her lovely eyes shone with tears. "Why, sire? Why?"

"Because, madame, I wish it, and I am the king," he said coldly, and walked away from her.

For several minutes she stood very still gazing with unseeing eyes out of the window at the Cheviot Hills. Then, sensing she was no longer alone, she whirled about to see the Earl of Bothwell standing there. Wordlessly they looked at each other, and then Francis Hepburn held out his arms to her. Flinging herself into them, she wept against his velvet-covered chest. A spasm crossed Bothwell's face as his arms tenderly held her. When she had regained her control he loosed her. Tipping her heart-shaped face up, he asked, "What happened wi Cousin Jamie?"

"I yield, or he asks Patrick," she answered softly.

"The little bastard!" snarled Bothwell. "What a pity the queen dinna miscarry of him."

"Francis, hush!" She covered his mouth with her hand. "To even think such a thing is treason."

He tore her hand away and swore softly. "I wish to God I was the warlock they accuse me of being! I'd like to send Cousin Jamie to the seven devils! Ah, my darling, I canna help ye, and I hae never felt so helpless in my whole life." He took her by the shoulders and looked down at her. "If I can ever help ye, come to me. Ye will remember that?" Then he took a large silk square from his doublet and wiped the tears from her face.

Her slender hand reached up and gently touched his face.

"Bothwell," she said softly, "yer the best friend I've ever had." Then she turned and left him standing in the little windowed alcove.

Francis Hepburn gazed out at the familiar Cheviot and sighed. For the first time in his life he had found a woman he could love, and not only was he married but she was also married. To add a further complication, she was lusted after by the king. The irony of the situation struck him, and he laughed sharply. Once again life had dealt him a bad hand.

Chapter 21

❦

THE court had settled comfortably back into Edinburgh. It was dull January. The Leslies' two oldest sons were also at court, having joined the household of Andrew Leslie, the Earl of Rothes, head of Clan Leslie. It was a relief to Cat to be able to see at least two of her children.

At this time Patrick Leslie decided to go home to check on his estates, and to see his other children. Unlike his wife, he had no official duties to keep him at court. Cat could not, however, be spared from service with the queen. Desperately she tried to forestall her husband's departure, but he laughed indulgently at her and teased, "Two years ago ye would hae rather died than go home to Glenkirk in winter. Now I believe ye would walk home!" Kissing her goodbye, he reassured her, "I'll be back in a few weeks, hinny. Would it cheer ye if I brought Bess wi me?"

"Nay, my lord! This court is no place for a young girl." She looked up at him astride Dubh. "Go carefully, Patrick, and come quickly back to me!"

There was something in her eyes that, for a moment, made him wonder if he should leave her. Then, laughing at himself for being a fool, he bent, kissed her again, and rode off.

It was not her night to serve the queen so, gaining permission, she went to Glenkirk House. The king would not dare chance seeking her out when the queen was available. She slept safe in her own home for the next few days. Soon it was her turn to sleep in the royal antechamber, on call in the event Anna required something, and she was again safe from the king.

At the end of her duty period the queen took her aside. "I would prefer, my dear Cat, that you not leave the palace at night when you are not on duty. Are your apartments not comfortable?"

"Aye, madame. They are most comfortable. I go home so that my sons may see me easily when their duties allow."

The queen smiled indulgently. "You are a good mother, Cat, but you are also a lady of my bedchamber. We will arrange for you to see your sons, but please remain near me at night. I awoke once with a terrible pain in my temple, and you were not there to rub it away."

"As your majesty wishes," replied Cat, curtsying. She knew full well where the idea that she remain in the palace had really come from.

Several days later the queen's monthly indisposition occurred, and that same evening the king appeared in the Countess of Glenkirk's bedchamber. First she tried to hold him off with reason, but he refused to listen. He came at her and she fought him physically, her little fists beating at him. It amused him to master her and he did so, cruelly, ravaging her body. She recoiled from his touch and hated him with a frustrated fury she could not satisfy. She was forced to endure his attentions for the next four nights.

Every morning and every evening Cat prayed for her husband's speedy return. Not a day went by that the king didn't steal a few minutes to be alone with her. That she detested him seemed to add to his pleasure.

One night as she undressed after the evening's entertainment, he appeared through the secret door. She wore only her white silk petticoats, and stood before her pier glass brushing her long dark-gold hair. Slipping up behind her, James slid an arm around her waist, and with his other hand cupped a globe-shaped breast.

Cat closed her eyes wearily, patiently enduring his unwelcome attentions. She had learned by now that to struggle was useless. As the king buried his lips in the soft flesh of her neck, a faint sound caught Cat's ear. Opening her eyes she saw her husband reflected in the pier glass, his face stiff with shock and hurt.

She would never remember in later years if she spoke his name aloud or merely mouthed it silently. It was enough, however, to rouse him, and his voice was icy. "I beg yer pardon, madame. I had nae idea ye were entertaining."

"Patrick!" she cried. "Patrick, please!" She tore herself from the king's grasp and took several steps toward him.

Behind her James Stewart looked at the Earl of Glenkirk. "I find yer wife charming, cousin, and I have been doing so for some time now. Do ye object?"

"Aye, sire," replied the earl, "I do object. Though little good it would do me, especially since the lady is so acquiescent." He turned to his wife. "I hope, my dear, ye have gotten a good price for yer virtue?"

"Come, cousin," soothed the king. "Dinna be angry wi Cat. She has done her duty by the crown admirably." He smiled winningly at the earl and, taking him by the arm, led him into the antechamber. "Let us hae a wee drink, Patrick. Yer wife keeps some remarkably fine whisky."

Numbly Cat continued the business of getting ready for bed. She was grateful she had dismissed Ellie for the evening. The tiring woman would only have tried to help her, and made matters worse. Kicking her petticoats off, she pulled a silk nightgown over her head and lay down on top of her bed. She could hear the low murmur of voices in the next room as well as the clink of crystal glasses.

She didn't remember falling asleep, but suddenly she felt a slap on her hip, and Patrick's voice—slurred with drink—said, "Wake up, madame whore! Here's two customers for ye!"

Angrily she scrambled to her feet. "Yer drunk! Both of ye! Get out of my bedroom! I canna stand the sight of either of ye!"

"Not so drunk we canna fuck! Right, cousin Jamie?" Grasping the bodice of her nightgown, Patrick ripped it to the hem, tore the two pieces off her, and flung them across the room. "Get into bed, my dear, virtuous wife, and open yer legs for the king. Ye've done it before, and very well, according to our royal cousin." He pushed her back onto the bed and before she could protest, the king was on top of her, driving into her unwilling body.

She was neither ready nor willing for the assault, and its effect was that of forcible rape. She struggled wildly beneath James, which merely increased his desire. He came quickly. Rolling off her, he said, "Yer turn, Patrick," and before a shocked Cat realized what was happening her husband had mounted her and pushed deep within her.

She could hear her own screaming.

Her thighs were sticky with another man's seed, and yet he took her. Outraged, she fought him violently, and was slapped into unconsciousness for her pains. Throughout the night they took turns raping her and drinking her whisky, until at last, in that darkest part of the night before dawn, a drunken James Stewart returned to his room via the secret passage and the very drunk Earl of Glenkirk fell into a deep sleep.

Fearful at first of awaking him, Cat lay quietly. Then, sure he was really asleep, she crawled slowly from the bed. Moving quietly and painfully across the room to the fireplace, she stirred up the fire and added some kindling, then heated the hanging kettle over it. Pouring some water into a small ewer, she took a cake of soap and a rough linen cloth and scrubbed herself until her skin was raw. Next she went to the trunk at the foot of the bed and, lifting out her woolen trunk hose, silk riding shirt, and plaid doublet, put them on. She pulled on her boots, picked up her fur-lined cloak, and silently left the apartment.

It was not yet dawn when she entered the stables. The boy on duty was fast asleep, half-buried in a pile of straw. Quickly Cat saddled Iolaire. She dared not take Bana, as she would have been spotted easily on the white mare. Leading the gelding from the stable stealthily, she mounted it and, muffling herself in her cloak, rode boldly up to the main exit of the palace.

"Messenger for Leslie of Glenkirk," she croaked in a husky voice.

"Pass," said the soldier, thinking how glad he was not to have to ride out at this early hour.

She rode south and slightly east, keeping away from the main roads. She was aware of neither the bitter cold nor approaching daylight. She felt neither hunger nor thirst. Several times she stopped to water and rest her horse, and when evening came she sought her bearings. Finding them, she headed for a small religious house, where she begged a night's shelter. Up at first light, she left a gold piece with the startled nun who kept the gate. Mounting Iolaire, she continued on her journey.

At midday she was spotted by two riders. Cat put her horse into a gallop but, unsure of the countryside, was quickly run down. She found herself facing two bearded young borderers, who grinned delightedly at her.

"I dinna know which is better," said the taller of the two. "The horse or the woman."

"The horse is yers, man," answered his companion. "I'll take the woman!"

"Touch me at yer peril," she snarled at them. "I am for Hermitage, and Lord Bothwell!"

"Ye'll nae find the earl at Hermitage," said the tall borderer. "He's at his lodge in the Cheviot."

"How far from here?"

"Two hours' ride, sweetheart. But if ye've a mind to bed a Hepburn, my father was one, and I'd be happy to oblige."

Cat drew herself up tall and, looking levelly at the two men, said coldly, "Take me to Lord Bothwell, or suffer the consequences when he finds out ye've not only detained me but refused me aid as well."

Something in her voice told them she was not bluffing. "Follow us," said the tall man. Whirling their horses around, they galloped off. Two hours later, as promised, they arrived at a small lodge, well hidden within the hills. At the sound of hoofbeats the door opened and the Earl of Bothwell himself stepped out. The taller fellow spoke out.

"We found this lady some two hours from here, my lord, riding for Hermitage. When she told us she sought ye, we brought her here. I hope we did the right thing."

Bothwell walked over to Iolaire and, reaching up, pushed away the hood of the all-concealing cape. "Cat!" he breathed.

Two large tears rolled down her cheeks. "Help me, Francis," she begged, holding out her arms to him. "Please help me!" Then she crumbled out of the saddle into his arms, fainting.

Cradling her tenderly, he turned to the two startled men. "Ye did right to bring this lady to me. But remember, lads, ye hae never seen her. When I can be of help to ye, I will be." He walked swiftly back into the house with his precious burden.

Part III

❧❧

The Uncrowned King

Chapter 22

❦

FRANCIS Hepburn had been alone at his hunting lodge. He occasionally shunned the company of his fellow humans and fled to some isolated spot, renewing himself spiritually and physically. It was his way of retaining sanity in a world that alternately admired and feared him. He liked the winter months, and he had been enjoying himself alone for several weeks.

Now his peace had been broken, and in a most disturbing way. He carried the unconscious Catriona Leslie into his house, upstairs to his bedroom, and gently laid her on his bed. He drew off her boots and, wrapping her cloak around her, pulled up a blanket and tucked it around her. Stirring up the fire, he put a brick in the ashes to warm. Then he drew the draperies shut on all the windows and lit a small Moorish oil lamp so she could see where she was when she regained consciousness. Taking the brick from the ashes with a pair of tongs, he wrapped it in a flannel and put it at her feet. Then, pouring a dram of potent whisky made in his own still, he sat on the edge of the bed and began to rub her wrists. Shortly she stirred, and he gently raised her up and put the dram to her lips. "Sip it slowly, my darling," he said.

She did as he bid her, and the color began to seep back into her cheeks. "Dinna tell Patrick I am here," she begged him.

"I won't," he promised. "Now, my darling, yer fair exhausted and chilled to the bone. I want ye to close yer eyes and go to sleep. I'll be downstairs, and there are no servants to worry about."

He was talking to himself, for she was already fast asleep. Dropping a kiss on her forehead, he left her and descended the stairs. The lower level of his house was a large open room with a huge stone fireplace. It was furnished in a rough manner with animal skins, hangings, and heavy, old-fashioned furniture. Pulling a chair up by the fireplace, he poured himself a glass from a decanter of wine before sitting down.

He wondered what had driven the Countess of Glenkirk out of Edinburgh. She was suffering from shock. Having learned some medicine from a Moorish physician, Bothwell understood her symptoms. "Poor lass," he said softly. "What in hell happened to ye?"

When Catriona awoke several hours later it took her a moment or two to realize where she was. She climbed from the big bed and padded downstairs in her stockinged feet.

"Francis? Are ye awake?"

"Aye, lass. Come over by the fire, and sit wi me."

She settled into his lap. For a time, neither of them spoke. He held her lightly, yet protectively, and she nestled against him, breathing the leather and tobacco scent of him. His heart was pounding wildly. He had always treated her casually, teasingly, in an effort to hide his feelings, and it had been fairly easy because he had never gotten too close. Now Francis Hepburn fought down his feelings lest he frighten her further. Finally, in desperation, he asked, "Are ye hungry? When did ye last eat?"

"Two nights ago. I stopped at a nunnery last night, but I could not eat then, or this morning."

"Ye should be hungry by now, my darling." He

tipped her out of his lap gently. "Can ye set a table, Cat Leslie?"

"The word is 'countess,' my lord Bothwell, not 'helpless.' Of course I can set a table."

"We'll eat by the fire," he said cheerfully. "The cloth's in that chest, and ye'll find dishes and utensils in the larder over there."

She was surprised to see him bring out from the pantry, a few minutes later, a steaming tureen and a basket of hot bread. "Sit down," he commanded her. "Eat it while it's hot."

She was going to refuse him, but the soup smelled so good. It was a thick lamb broth with barley, onions, and carrots. She discovered it was flavored with peppercorns and white wine. He shoved a thick, crusty slice of hot bread dripping with butter in front of her and watched, amused, as she devoured it. When she had spooned up all the soup he took her bowl and returned to the pantry-kitchen. Soon he came back bearing two plates. "I caught a salmon this morning before ye arrived, and I found some early cress," he announced proudly. She ate the thin-sliced fish more slowly than she had eaten the soup. He was worried by her silence, and by the fact that she had already consumed three goblets of burgundy.

Sated at last, she sat back. "Where did ye learn to cook?" she asked him.

"My Uncle James believed a man needed knowledge of that kind."

She smiled a half-smile at him, and lapsed into silence again.

"What happened, Cat? Can ye tell me, my darling?"

After a time, she looked up. The pain in her eyes stunned him. Rising, he moved around the table and knelt at her side. "Dinna tell me if it's too painful."

"If I tell ye now, Francis, I'll nae have to speak of it

again, and maybe I can forget in time." She began to weep softly. "Damn James Stewart! Oh, Francis! He has deliberately destroyed my life! I would kill him if I could. Patrick went home to Glenkirk, and I was alone. There was no one I could turn to at all. I tried to keep out of the king's way, but the lecherous hypocrite stalked me like a rabbit. Patrick came back from Glenkirk to find Jamie wi his hands all over me. The king could have saved me if he had wanted to do so, but instead he told Patrick what a marvelous mistress I was, and made it sound worse than it was. He dinna tell Patrick I was unwilling. Then the two of them got quite companionably drunk on my whisky and raped me. Oh, God, Francis! The king and my own husband! Not once, but time and time again—all night long! They wouldn't let me go, and they made me do things—" She shuddered. "Oh, Francis! Yer my friend. Please let me stay wi ye for now."

He was stunned by what she had told him. Stunned, and horrified. That James Stewart could have been that vengeful he fully believed, but that Patrick Leslie, an educated and enlightened man like himself, could have brutalized his own blameless wife astounded him. "My poor darling," he said gently. "Ye can stay wi me forever." Standing, he drew her from the chair. "Who saw ye go, Cat?"

"No one, though they will connect the rider who left the palace for Glenkirk wi me. The nuns who sheltered me last night live in an out-of-the-way place. In any event, only the gatekeeper and the mistress of travelers saw me, and not for long. There were no other visitors at the convent. Patrick will think I hae gone to A-Cuil."

He put his arms about her. "Ah, my darling! I am so sorry. So very sorry. Dinna fear. Yer safe wi me. The men who brought ye in will nae admit to having ever seen ye."

She stood quietly within the comforting circle of his arms, and then slowly she lifted her face to him. "Make love to me, Francis!" Her voice was urgent. "Here! Now! Make love to me!"

Wordlessly he shook his head at her. He understood the reasons behind her outburst. She needed reassurance, needed to be the one to do the choosing. But he was not sure if compliance with her desperate request would make matters better or worse. He loved her, and he wanted her, but dear God, not like this!

Angrily she pulled away from him. "Come on, Bothwell! Yer reputed to be the best lover in Scotland!" She tore her shirt open, and off. Her beautiful breasts tumbled out in all their glory. Pushing her riding breeches down and off, she moved seductively towards him. She was naked as the creator had made her and he fought down his rising desire. "Come on, Bothwell!" she taunted him. "Love me, or are ye not man enough? If I'm worthy of a king, then I'm good enough for ye!" Her eyes glistened with angry, unshed tears.

If she had been a man he would have hit her, but he understood. Like a child fallen from its pony who must immediately ride again, Cat Leslie needed to make love with a man who would not abuse her. If not him, who? Francis Hepburn didn't wait to find another answer. Scooping the woman before him up into his arms, he carried her up to his bedroom and deposited her on his bed. Swiftly he stripped his own clothing off and joined her.

He was in her before she realized it, taking her with a gentleness she had never dreamed any man could. Tenderly he kissed and caressed her, striving to bring her the greatest pleasure. No man had ever loved her in such a fashion. Finally he could hold back his desire no longer, and released his boiling passion.

She began to weep great, gulping sobs. "I feel

nothing! Dear God, Francis! I feel nothing! What hae
they done to me that I feel nothing?" And she began
to tremble uncontrollably.

Bothwell gathered her into his arms and held her
tightly. The hurt done her was even deeper than he had
feared. It was going to take time to bring her back, but
he would do it. "Dinna cry, my precious darling," he
said softly. "Dinna cry. They hae hurt ye terribly, and
'twill take time for ye to recover. Go to sleep now, my
sweet love. Go to sleep. Yer safe wi me, my love."

Within minutes she slept deeply, breathing lightly and
evenly. But Francis Hepburn lay awake, his anger growing with each minute. Once again he wished the role
of warlock, often attributed to him, were true. Had it
been he would cheerfully have disposed of both his
cousins.

However, he knew that the woman sleeping within
his arms was even now still emotionally bound to her
husband, and he would not grieve her further by hurting
Glenkirk. James was a different matter, though, and
Francis Hepburn was going to think long and hard on
the vengeance he'd wreak on his cousin. In the meantime, he would offer his house and his heart to the
beautiful Countess of Glenkirk.

In the weeks that followed, Cat stayed hidden within
Bothwell's lodge. There were no servants to gossip
about them, and they were content to do for themselves.
Sometimes Francis Hepburn would go on a border raid
with his men, leaving her alone for a day or more. She
never minded, enjoying the solitude of the late winter
and needing the time to heal. He had not used her physically since that first night, and she had not asked him to.
But each night he was with her she slept content in the
safety of his arms.

The Earl of Bothwell was deeply in love for the first
time in his life. Though he realized this love might come
to an end, he intended enjoying whatever time they

shared. He adored her beauty, but had Catriona Leslie been the ugliest woman alive he would still have loved her. She was an educated woman who, unlike his estranged wife, could converse with a man on a great many subjects. More important, she was a good listener, and had the charming knack of letting a man believe that whatever he said—no matter how banal—was interesting. She was warm, and she had an outrageous sense of humor that matched his. Her beauty was merely a bonus.

In early spring Bothwell returned from a raid into England bringing with him a long, delicately worked gold chain set with tiny topazes ranging from palest gold to deepest taupe. He slipped it over her head. "Now yer a true border wench," he said softly. "Yer man has brought ye back some booty."

She smiled teasingly up at him. "Whose pretty neck did ye take it from?"

He grinned back at her. "If ye must know, I liberated it from an overstocked jeweler who made the mistake of getting caught in our raid." He looked down at her and, suddenly unable to help himself, caught her to him and kissed her hungrily. She trembled but grasped his head and kissed him strongly in return.

Francis Hepburn's blue eyes looked gravely into Cat's leaf-green ones. She stood barefooted, on tiptoe, her arms about his neck. His hands moved gently to undo her dressing gown, unwinding her arms, and sliding the robe off to reveal her nakedness. Taking her face in his hands, he bent and kissed her deeply. Then his mouth gently touched her eyelids, her face, her throat.

His slim hands tangled in her honey-colored hair and then moved down to her shoulders. His mouth moved to her chest and then to her soft breasts. He slid to his knees and his lips traveled to her navel and then to the tiny mole.

Cat's whole body was quivering, and as her legs gave

way she slipped to her knees too, and their lips met.
Bothwell was deeply shaken. "Tell me yea, or tell me
nay, my darling! But tell me now," he whispered
hoarsely, "for I'll tell ye true, my sweet Cat. I want ye
as I have never wanted any woman! But 'tis you I want,
not a shadow!"

"Bothwell," she whispered softly, and he saw her face
was radiant. "Bothwell! I feel! I feel! Oh, my lord!
I want ye very much.

He drew her down to the fur rug. The crackling fire
cast shadows over them as he stood tall above her to
pull off his clothing. She smiled reassuringly up at him.
He was the first man she had chosen in her whole life.
Her husband had been picked for her by her great-
grandmother, and the king had forced her. But *she* had
chosen Francis Hepburn. And desired him very much.

Kneeling, he gently turned her over and kissed the
nape of her neck. His lips moved down across her
shoulders and traveled the length of her spine. He was
gentle beyond belief, and she shivered deliciously.

Placing her on her back, he caressed her lovely
breasts. They grew taut beneath his delicate touch, the
rosy nipples becoming hard and pointed. He buried his
face in the valley between them, his lips burning into
her skin. She moaned softly. He smiled with relief. Her
head was thrown back, her eyes closed. Her breath came
in quick little gasps.

In his travels Francis Hepburn had made love a great
deal and had learned from many women. He now used
his skill on the only woman he had ever truly loved, his
desire being to prolong her pleasure.

Kissing the soft flesh of her breasts, he felt her heart
pound wildly beneath his lips. He caught a tantalizing
nipple in his teeth and bit it gently. She moaned again,
and her hips began to move with the rhythm of love.
His lips began to wander.

"Francis!" she cried out. "Dear God, Francis! Ye'll drive me mad!"

"Do ye really want me to stop, my darling?" His eyes were laughing. Silence was his answer. He gauged how far he might drive her.

He opened her legs and, drawing them over his shoulders, gently pulled her nether lips apart and tenderly kissed the soft coral flesh. She shuddered violently once, but forbade him not. His tongue caressed and probed, and she cried out in pleasure, her body arching. Her response fired him, and when he could bear it no longer, he pulled himself up and over her, and drove his throbbing manroot deep into her softness.

She received him joyfully, wrapping her long legs and her arms about him. Once within her he was able again to restrain himself. Their bodies moved in rhythm together, seeking to pleasure each other. Then she whispered urgently to him, "Francis! I can hold back no longer!" But he forced her to ease off, and then increased her desire to a higher peak. She was buffeted by the force of his passion, and frankly amazed that anyone could give such pleasure. She had never been loved like this, and when he at last allowed her release she cried out in delighted wonder to feel him coming too.

Still coupled, they lay breathing deeply, damp with their exertion. Then suddenly she cried out with genuine surprise. "My God, Francis! Yer growing hard again wi'in me! Oh yes, my lover! Yes! Yes! Yes!"

And it began again. He was himself amazed at his body's response, for he could not seem to get enough of her. Cat was insatiable tonight. She matched him passion for passion until they were both so exhausted that they slept where they lay, unaware that the fire had gone out and the room had grown chill.

He awoke to find her dropping a blanket over him.

He pulled her down and kissed her. "Good morning, my darling."

The radiance of her smile reassured him. "Good morning, my lover," she answered him. Her mind was clear. She felt no shame. She gently disentangled herself from his grasp. "I'm fair frozen, Francis. Let me go, and I'll light the fire."

He watched her with a mixture of affection and admiration as she rekindled the fire. Within minutes the flames were leaping, and she turned her back to the fire. He sighed. "Ah, my darling! To be the flames that warm yer pretty bottom."

"Oh, Bothwell," she laughed, coloring becomingly. "Yer a wicked man!"

"Aye, my darling. I am." He cocked an eyebrow at her. "Come, warm me, my pet. 'Tis chill and lonely beneath this blanket."

She slid underneath the plaid wool and drew him into her arms and against her body. "Warmer now, my lord?"

His eyes sparkled with amusement. "Ye could bring heat into a stone statue, and ye know it, my sweet love!" Tenderly he kissed her. "Where were ye, Cat? Where were ye all these years?" He fell silent then, thinking of the night just past. "I love ye, Catriona Mairi," he said, and she was startled that he knew her baptismal name. "I hae never said that to a woman and meant it," he continued, "but as God is my witness, I love ye!"

Her eyes were bright with tears. "Bothwell! Oh, Bothwell! Dinna love me! How can ye love me? A woman who lay wi the king, and then ran away from her husband's honest wrath into the arms of yet another man. How can ye love me?"

"Ye didna lay willingly wi Jamie, Cat. There is no refusing the king. I could kill him for forcing ye!"

"And Patrick?" she asked. "What of my husband?"

"I would kill him too if I didna know it would grieve ye. He had the right to be angry, but not wi ye. And to do to ye what he did . . ."

"What would ye hae done to me if I had been yer wife, Francis?"

"If ye had been my wife, Jamie would nae have dared to force ye, but," he continued, seeing her urgency, "if he had dared, I would hae killed him wi'out a second thought. Ye, I would hae beaten for being so lovely."

"Poor Patrick," she said softly. "The look on his face when he saw Jamie fondling me. . . . God, Francis! He was so terribly hurt."

Bothwell's lip curled. "So he eased his hurt by getting drunk wi Jamie and taking turns wi the king in raping his own wife!" The earl exploded. "Be quit of them both, Cat! I have been meaning to divorce Margaret for some time. Now, I'll do it, and ye must divorce Glenkirk and marry me! I love ye! I want ye! And, by God, I'll keep ye safe from the royal Stewart."

Stunned, she could only stare at him. "My children?" she finally managed.

"I'll gie ye all the bairns ye want, and if ye must hae yer wee Leslies, I'll take them gladly."

"I think Patrick might hae something to say about that," she said wryly.

Bothwell's blue eyes looked into her green eyes. "I dinna want to talk about Patrick," he said softly, and his mouth found hers. She yielded easily. Though her conscience troubled her slightly, her feelings for Francis Hepburn were deeper even than she knew.

His mouth gently touched her forehead, her closed eyelids, the tip of her little nose. She murmured contentedly, and he laughed in spite of himself. "A fine thing," he teased. "I seek to rouse yer deepest passions, and instead ye make contented noises like a well-fed bairn."

She giggled. "But ye make me feel content, my lord."

"Good," he said, "because I intend keeping ye here all day. There's never been a woman yet, madame, that I've wanted to keep in bed all day!"

"But we're not in bed," she pointed out. "We're on the floor, under a plaid, and if one of yer great borderers should come clumping in—" she paused and her eyes twinkled mischievously—"well, my lord, yer already grand reputation will become legendary!"

Roaring with laughter, Francis Hepburn stood up and, pulling her after him, carried her upstairs, where he unceremoniously dumped her on the bed. "I'll build the fire this time," he said, bending to light the kindling.

"Will ye indeed, my lord," she asked provocatively. Francis Hepburn, turning to look at the beautiful Countess of Glenkirk, knew that if the night just past had been sweet, the day would be sweeter yet.

Chapter 23

❧❧❧

PATRICK Leslie had awakened late the morning after his return to Holyrood Palace with an ache in his head and a mouth that tasted of old flannel. Reaching for Cat brought back with tremendous shock the events of the previous evening. For a moment he lay perfectly still, unable to absorb the memories tumbling in on him. James and Catriona. Then he, and the king, and Cat.

"Oh, my God!" he whispered. Stumbling to his feet, he crossed the room to the fireplace wall, touched a piece of carving on the mantel, and watched miserably as the secret door swung open. Shutting it again, he returned to the bed and felt the place where she had lain. The sheets were icy, and he knew she had been gone for hours. He checked the trunk at the foot of the bed and found her riding clothes gone. The mantel clock chimed ten.

Dressing quickly, Patrick Leslie sought the captain of the guard. "I want to speak wi all the men on duty last night. When was the guard last changed?"

"At six this morning, my lord."

"And before that?"

"Midnight, sir."

"Those are the men I want, captain, the ones who took duty at midnight. How many were on gate duty?"

"Six men. Two at the main gate, two at the back gate, and two at the servant's postern."

Patrick thought a moment. The average person would have gone out through the back, or the servant's gate. "Send me the men who were on the main gate," he said.

Despite the violent emotions tearing through him, he could not help but chuckle wryly at discovering that he was right. A "messenger" for Glenkirk had passed through the main gate a few minutes before five that morning.

He sought his interview with the king through Barra, the chamberboy. He made it very clear that if James would not grant him immediate audience he would go to the queen. Within the hour Barra was guiding him through the secret passage. The king was still abed, having awakened with as big a hangover as Glenkirk's. Patrick wasted no time. "Ye remember what we did last night?"

The king flushed. "I was drunk," he muttered.

"So was I," replied his cousin, "but 'tis still no excuse for rape. She's gone, ye know—on horseback out the main gate, before five this morning. I intend making her excuses to the queen, and then I am going after her. When I find her I shall get down on my knees and beg her forgiveness. I only pray she will gie it me, though I am not at all sure she will do so. Remembering what we did to her, I couldna blame her if she refused. We shall remain at home at Glenkirk from now on, Cousin James, ever loyal to the Stewarts, but absent from this cesspool ye call a court."

James Stewart nodded. "Ye hae my permission," he said.

The Earl of Glenkirk returned him a look that plainly said he didn't care whether the king gave him permission or not. Then he found the question torn from him. "Was she willing, Jamie? Was my wife willing to whore for ye?"

There was a long silence, and then the king lowered his eyes and whispered, "Nay."

"You bastard!" said Patrick Leslie softly. "If ye were anyone else, I'd kill ye!" Turning, he reentered the secert passageway and closed it behind him. Dashing into his own bedroom, he found Ellen, startled by his abrupt entrance from the passage. "Pack everything that belongs to us. We're returning to Glenkirk, and we'll nae be back!"

"My lady—" began Ellen.

"Left early this morning," he said. "Now, hurry! I want to be out of here by afternoon."

He went next to the queen, and told her that he had returned late last night to fetch his wife. Their eldest daughter was seriously ill. Cat had left early this morning, begging him to make her excuses. Since it might be some months until she could return, the Earl of Glenkirk offered to sell his wife's position to whichever lady the queen chose. He would then buy the position for that lady, thus enriching the queen's private coffers. Anna always needed money. It was a very generous offer, and though she regretted losing the lovely Countess of Glenkirk, Anna Stewart had been worried lately that there were so many lovely ladies about her.

It wasn't her husband who concerned her, for, she thought smugly, he was quite unaffected by other beautiful women. But beautiful young girls attracted too many men, and invariably complications arose. She decided to give the open position to the widowed daughter of old Lord Kerr. The lady was a good woman, past thirty, and not particularly pretty.

Protocol satisfied, Patrick Leslie gave orders to his people to return to Glenkirk immediately. Then he set out alone for his castle. Cat already had a seven-hour start on him, and when he caught up with her, he wanted to settle their differences away from prying eyes.

As he rode he relived the previous night, seeing clearly now all the things his injured pride had refused to acknowledge then. Cat had begged him to take her

from court, but he had begun to enjoy it himself, and
had put her off. Ashamed of being forced into an intimate relationship with the king, yet equally fearful of
his discovering that relationship, she had been helplessly
caught in a trap. When he had walked into their bedroom to find the king fondling his wife's naked breasts,
his reaction had been shock, followed by fury at his
wife. How could he have misjudged her so? In all these
years she had never given him reason to doubt her.

Now, looking back, he saw again her frightened white
face staring out at him from the pier glass. Later, when
they were taking turns raping her, he saw her leaf-green
eyes mirroring shock, anguish, disbelief, and finally a
blankness that was the most terrible of all.

Patrick Leslie rode steadily north and east, and as he
rode he prayed that his wife would be waiting at Glenkirk. Another problem facing him was what to tell his
mother and the children. They were all old enough to
know something was wrong. He was grateful that his
two oldest boys were in service. The younger children
were easy, but he did not want to face his eldest son
and heir. Thirteen-year-old Jamie Leslie adored his
beautiful mother, and between them existed a special
closeness. Cat loved all her children, but Jamie had
always been *her* bairn.

When the towers of Glenkirk came into sight several
days later the Earl kicked Dubh into a gallop, and the
great black stallion, scenting home, responded eagerly.
Patrick quickly sought out his mother. Margaret, the
dowager Countess of Glenkirk, was still one of the most
beautiful women in Scotland. Rising to her feet at the
sight of her eldest son, she held out her arms.

"My darling! I didn't expect ye back so soon. Is
aught amiss?"

He entered the security of that embrace and then,
leading her over to the privacy of a windowseat, sat
down with her. "I hae done a terrible thing, mother.

A terrible thing to Cat. And I hae probably lost her."
Kneeling, he put his head into her lap and wept. The
sound he made was terrible—great, tearing sobs
wrenched up from deep within him. His broad shoulders shook, and Meg Leslie, stunned, touched his head
gently and said, "Tell me, Patrick. Tell me what ye hae
done to Catriona."

Mastering his emotions, he slowly and carefully told
his mother what had happened. Meg closed her eyes
when he reached the part about the rape. "She must
still have some feeling for ye, Patrick," said his mother,
"for had it been me, I would hae stuck a knife into ye
before I fled! And to answer yer unasked question—no,
she is not here. What made ye think she would be?"

"Where else could she go, mother? Greyhaven?
A-Cuil?"

"Nay. Heather was here yesterday, and said nothing.
Ye may be sure that if Cat had gone home to Greyhaven her mother would have been all atwitter with
worry, and told me. And she is not at A-Cuil. Cat's
brothers have been up there hunting wolves, and came
yesterday with Heather to bring me some skins."

"Then where is she?" he asked. "Christ in his heaven!
Where has she hidden herself?"

"Ye want her back?" said Meg. "Why, Patrick? So
ye may punish her further for not killing herself at
James Stewart's first advance. Would ye hae preferred
a dead and pure wife to a live, albeit slightly used one?
God's toenail, my idiot son! It's nae as if James took
the *droit du seigneur* of yer virgin bride! And why in
heaven's name did ye assume her the guilty party? Undoubtedly because she is but a weak woman! Fool! Has
she ever given ye cause for doubt? Never! She has been
a loving wife since the day she married ye . . . though
now I think perhaps she must have had a premonition
of disaster when she tried to escape yer marriage. She's
been a good wife and a good mother to yer six bairns."

Meg stood up and paced furiously back and forth. "Ye dinna deserve her, Patrick! Now, get the hell out of my sight, my lord earl! I detest fools, and ye are a great fool! Ye disgust me!" Pulling her skirts back so as not to touch him, the dowager countess swept angrily from the room.

He stood where she had left him, thinking that he also disgusted himself.

"So ye found out," came his brother Adam's voice.

The earl turned. "I didna know ye were here," he said dully.

"Just arrived. I was on yer trail the whole way. Ellen came to see me before she left Edinburgh. How did ye find out?"

"I came back to Holyrood to find the king's hands all over my wife's naked tits. Did ye know? And Ellen too? Am I the only one at court who didn't know that the king was fucking my wife?"

"No one knew, Patrick, except Ellen because she is Cat's tiring woman and me because when James first delivered his ultimatum to Cat she came to me for help. I told no one, not even Fiona."

"My wife came to ye for help, and ye sent her into the King's bed? Was that yer idea of helping us?" Leaping the distance between them, Patrick Leslie hit his younger brother square on the jaw.

Adam staggered back. His hand came up to rub his injured chin. The earl advanced on him. "I'll kill ye for this, brother!" The younger Leslie's hand went to his dirk and, whipping it out, he held it before him. "For God's sake, Patrick! Listen to me for a minute!" The earl stopped. "James threatened to confiscate our estates and put us to the horn. He was all ready wi trumped-up charges, for he was determined to have Cat, and knew she would protect her family at whatever cost to herself. She was terrified. She didna want to lie wi the king, but neither did she want everything lost that was yers . . . or ours. It is not permitted for a woman to refuse the king, ye know that! And even if she had refused, Jamie would have taken everything. Then what would have happened to all of us? To Mother, and the bairns. Yes! I told Cat to yield! There was no other way. If ye had been in my position what would ye have done?"

Patrick's hands fell to his side. "Do ye know what I did to her, Adam, when I found her wi Jamie? I got drunk wi the king, and then we took turns wi her. All night, brother. Drink and fuck! Drink and fuck! She's run away from me, brother. I would gie my life to find her and beg her forgiveness!"

"Christ, man!" said Adam Leslie in shocked disbelief. "What a fool ye are! I dinna think she'll ever forgie ye for that, but I'll help ye to find her. God knows ye dinna deserve her. Where hae ye looked?"

"Our house in Edinburgh. Here. Mother tells me she's nae at Greyhaven, or at A-Cuil. She's obviously not in yer house, or ye'd hae told me. Could she hae gone to Sithean?"

"I'll ride over," said Adam, "ostensibly to bring Fiona's greetings to her parents. If there's been any word, our sister Janet will know and tell us."

But they soon knew that Cat was not at Sithean. Nor was she hiding in Crannog village with old Ruth. They had exhausted all the logical possibilities, and in the days that followed they checked back in Edinburgh with the Kiras. Cat had not withdrawn any of her vast funds, either in person or through an intermediary. The Earl of Glenkirk was becoming genuinely frightened. His wife has disappeared over a month ago, without a trace and without funds to sustain her. There were only two answers. Either someone was hiding Cat—and they could think of no one with whom she was that friendly —or else she was dead.

Chapter 24

❧§❧

FRANCIS Hepburn awoke at first light and lay quietly for a few minutes enjoying the silence before the birdsong. Turning carefully, he looked at Cat. She lay curled into a tight ball like a small child. In sleep she looked so innocent.

Suddenly she awoke, opened her green eyes, and stretched. "Good morrow, my lord," she smiled up at him.

He smiled back, thinking how very much he wanted to make love to her now. "I hae a surprise for ye today, Cat. I'm taking ye riding."

A frightened look come into her eyes. "Patrick," she said.

"Patrick will eventually find ye, my darling, but 'twill be a long time before word gets to him, and then I promise to protect ye. Only someone who knows ye could tell him anyhow, and my people are loyal to me. They could see ye ride naked the length of the shire, and would nae admit to it."

She laughed. "All right, my lover, but I will need fresh clothes. Mine are worn, and I'd nae shame ye."

"Look in the trunk by the door, Cat. I brought some things back from my last raid."

She admired the silk underclothes, several pairs of green trunk hose in finely spun sheer wool, and a half-dozen cream-colored silk shirts with pearl buttons.

220

There was a soft brown leather jerkin with small buttons of polished staghorn banded in silver, and a wide brown leather belt with a silver-and-topaz buckle. It didn't take Cat more than a minute to realize that he had had the clothes made for her. She rose from the trunk and turned. "Yer so good to me, Bothwell," she said softly. "Thank ye."

He got up from the bed. "I'll get ye some water to bathe," he answered gruffly.

She blocked his way. Standing on tiptoe, she wrapped her arms about his neck and kissed him. His hands stroked her long back, and her soft, silken buttocks. "Christ, you witch! Dinna tempt me now!" But he was already hard, hungry for her. Sweeping her up, he lay her back on their bed. His lips found hers again, and his body gently possessed her body. She sighed happily, and Francis Hepburn laughed low. "Little witch! Why can I never get enough of ye?"

"Or I of you, my lover," she murmured.

Afterwards they fell asleep, and it was not until the sun was well up that they awoke again. He brought water, and they washed. Going to the little trunk, she chose a set of lace-trimmed underwear, a shirt, trunk hose, the jerkin and belt. When she had finished dressing she found he wore a matching costume. Cat bound her hair back with a green velvet ribbon and, with a smile, Bothwell placed a small bonnet of Hepburn plaid on her golden head.

"Ye'll need new boots, lass." He dug deep into her trunk, and pulled out a pair. They were as soft as butter. "Ye'll find some silk and lace nightgowns in there too."

"How did ye do it, Francis? How?" She pulled the boots on.

"I'm the Wizard Earl, remember?"

Laughing, they descended the stairs and left the lodge. Cat's bay gelding, Iolaire, and Bothwell's great dark-red stallion, Valentine, awaited them. They spent the day riding the Northumbrian hills that separated Scotland from England. When hunger overtook them they stopped at a small cottage. The welcome was warm for Bothwell and his lady. Dark bread warm from the oven with fresh sweet butter, a broiled rabbit, and brown October ale satisfied them.

"Ye eat well here on the borders," Cat remarked to the woman of the house. She had a disturbingly familiar look.

"My father was the last earl, James Hepburn," laughed the woman, whom Bothwell called Maggie. "Cousin Francis sees we're well taken care of, don't ye, lovey?"

The earl smiled at Maggie. "I do, though keeping up wi Uncle James' obligations is a mighty task."

"Made greater," she shot back at him, "by yer desire to better his record."

They laughed. Francis kissed Maggie's cheek. Then he helped Cat into her saddle and, mounting Valentine, led the way back over the hills. He did not, however, take her back to the lodge. "I want to go to Hermitage," he said quietly. " 'Tis my home, and I want ye there. Will ye come wi me?"

"Yes," she answered him. "I am nae ashamed to be yer woman, Francis."

"I dinna think of ye as my woman, Cat. I think of ye as my wife . . . perhaps not in the eyes of your church, or the kirk, or even in the eyes of our fellow men. But as God created us, he meant us to be together. I intend that we shall be, my darling."

They rode proudly into Hermitage together, and Cat discovered that he had prepared for her, hoping she would come with him. The rooms of the Countess of Bothwell with its bedroom adjoining the earl's awaited her. They were newly refurbished with deep-blue velvet draperies and bed hangings, and a bedspread embroidered with the Hepburn lions in gold.

"These rooms hae nae been used since the earl's mother, Lady Janet, died," said the little maid. "And," continued the girl, "before that Queen Mary stayed here! What a to-do the earl created, my lady, to get these rooms ready for ye! He told the housekeeper he was nae sure if ye'd even come, but if ye did he wanted the rooms fresh and inviting. It took a dozen women ten days to sew the bedspread alone!"

"What of Lady Margaret?" asked Cat. "Does she not stay here when she is at Hermitage?"

"Nay," replied Nell. "Her ladyship doesna come to Hermitage at all. She doesna like it. It frightens her, being so close to the border. Her first husband was Scott of Buccleuch from near here. She was caught in several raids, and it terrified her. She told the earl when they married that she'd nae come here ever. She loves Crichton best." Then, embarrassed by her talkativeness, she said hurriedly, "Ye'll be wanting a bath after yer long ride. I'll have it brought right up!"

Bustling out, she left the Countess of Glenkirk to look about her bedroom in amazement. It was a square, paneled room with two great leaded windows to her left, each with a built-in window seat. Each seat held a tufted pale-blue velvet cushion. Directly in front of her was a large stone fireplace with a carved marble mantel. Behind her was the door from the antechamber. To her right was the door to Francis' bedroom.

The polished oak floors were covered in thick Turkish carpets, mostly blues and golds with a touch of rose. The furniture was sparse, as was usual in a Scots house. On the wall near the antechamber door was a tall wardrobe. On the wall facing the windows was the huge bed and a nightstand. Between the windows, a round, highly polished table held a large, oval-shaped silver bowl filled

with coral-pink winter roses. By the fireplace was a
settle and a large comfortable chair. Scattered about
the room were other simple chairs.

Burying her face in the roses, she inhaled their heady
fragrance. "From my greenhouses," he said proudly.
She turned to face him. Her eyes were wet, the dark-
gold lashes separated. "I am always saying thank you to
ye, Francis. Somehow it doesna ever seem enough."

"Ye hae brought me the first real happiness I have
ever known, my precious love." He gathered her into
his arms, and she felt the depth of his love in the heart
beating wildly beneath her cheek.

No longer could Catriona Leslie deny her emotions.
They swept over her in a great tide. Looking up into the
rugged, handsome face of Francis Hepburn, she said,
"I love ye, Bothwell! May God hae mercy on us both,
but I love ye, and I would sooner die than be parted
from ye, my lord!"

A great sigh of relief escaped the big earl and, bending, he took possession of the sweet mouth offered him.
"Cat! Oh, Cat," he murmured against her lips. His arms
tightened about her.

At that moment, the maid returned with a coterie of
servants. They carried a tall oak tub and several
caldrons of hot water. Bothwell released Cat. "I thought
we might eat by the fire in the antechamber. Until then,
madame."

Her eyes followed him as he returned to his own
room. Ordering the other servants away, Nell went
about the business of preparing the countess' bath.
Climbing the steps to the tub, she poured a thin stream
of clear liquid into the steaming water. Almost immediately the room was scented with the smell of lilacs.
She left Cat to soak while she chose a simple gown from
Cat's wardrobe. It was pale lavender silk with long
flowing sleeves and a deep V neckline. Having done

this, she returned to Cat, washed her lovely hair, and scrubbed her back. Wrapping Cat in a large towel, she sat her by the fire and dried the long hair, using first a rough towel, then a hairbrush, and finally a piece of silk to give it shine. Last, Nell pared Cat's fingernails and toenails and plucked her free of extraneous body hair.

Cat remained silent through all of this. She loved Bothwell, and he loved her. What would happen to them she did not know. There were so many other lives involved, but for now it was all right. Nell helped her into the silk gown, fastened the pearl buttons beneath her full breasts, and slid a pair of kid slippers on her feet.

"Where are my riding clothes?" she asked the servant.

"I've sent yer shirt and hose to the laundress, madame. Everything else is in the wardrobe, and Will has gone to the lodge for yer trunk."

"Thank ye, Nell. Ye may go now. I'll nae need ye again this evening."

"Thank ye, my lady, but let me see to the removal of the tub before I go, and I'll take the spread from the bed also."

Cat smiled her thanks at the girl, and then went into the antechamber to await her lover. A decanter and two goblets sat on a silver tray on a table, and she poured herself some pale gold wine to still her pounding heart. There were so many problems, but she did not want to think of them tonight. All she wanted now was him, his strong arms about her and his mouth on hers. She wanted his laughter and sharp wit.

Two hefty servants lugged the tub from her bedroom and then returned for the tub from the earl's bedroom. Nell left, bidding Cat good night. The earl's man, Albert, finished up and left. Cat waited expectantly.

He came through the door wearing dark trunk hose,

a white silk shirt buttoned up to the neck, a wide leather belt with a gold-and-ruby buckle, and soft leather slippers.

She flew to him. Holding her away from him, he asked, "Is it true? What ye said to me before?"

A smile lit her face. "I love ye, Bothwell! I love ye! I love ye! Now, my lord! Do ye believe me?"

"Aye, I believe ye, my darling! I was only afraid that in my passion, I had fooled myself into imagining you said those words." He drew her against him and gently kissed the tip of her nose. "The gown becomes ye, as I knew it would."

"Another something ye picked up on one of yer raids?" she teased him. " 'Tis a surprisingly good fit."

He chuckled and lightly brushed his fingers across her chest. "It lacks one thing. Turn around."

She turned, and he clasped a necklace of pale golden pearls about her neck. Moving her around again, he put a matching pearl teardrop on each of her ears. "There," he said quietly. "Perfection made better, if possible. These belong to ye, come what may. Patrick Hepburn, the first Earl of Bothwell, gave them to his bride." He gazed at her with open admiration. "Christ! Ye hae flawless skin, Cat. I've never seen pearls look so beautiful."

Servants entered, bearing silver trays of food. The earl led Cat to the table and seated her. He had ordered an excellent supper, in superb taste. They began with cold raw oysters, which Cat adored, and finished with a flaky tart of early strawberries from the Hermitage greenhouses.

Cat ate with gusto. Amused, he encouraged her, handing over to her the last piece of tart. When she had finished and bathed her hands, he spoke in a mock-serious voice. "Now, madame. Ye must pay for yer meal." Leading her over to the settle by the fireplace, he sat her down. "I want to sketch ye, my love. Perhaps I'll do a wax model later, and then sculpt ye."

"My God," she laughed, "ye sculpt! That's what that wax-image nonsense was about. That's why they say ye practice the black arts! Oh, the fools! The ignorant fools!"

Bothwell grimaced. "Oh, yes," he said. "My enemies would have poor gullible cousin Jamie believe that I make wax images of him to stick pins into." He picked up a lap easel and, fastening a piece of paper on it, began.

Cat sat perfectly still, thinking how lucky she was to be with him. She had never known such happiness existed, and if he had asked her to accompany him into the fires of hell she would have gone without question. Her eyes caressed him. She blushed, thinking she would rather be in bed with him than sitting here posing. At last he put down his work. His eyes caught hers.

"Ye are reading my thoughts," she exclaimed.

He smiled lazily. "It isna hard to read yer thoughts when ye blush like that. Besides, mine are similar. Come, my sweet love, let us to bed." He stood and offered her his hand.

She rose. "Why, Francis? For thirteen years I lived a contented, healthy life wi Patrick. But wi ye . . ." She paused seeking the right words. "Wi ye 'tis different. 'Tis complete."

"Did ye always love Patrick?" he asked.

"He was the only man I ever knew. Greyhaven is very isolated. My great-grandmother betrothed me to Patrick when I was just four. He is nine years my senior. We were wed when I was sixteen. I wasna sure I even wanted to marry him then. He had a reputation as a terrible rake, and he was so arrogant!"

Bothwell chuckled to himself, imagining his stubborn Cat coming up against an equally stubborn Glenkirk.

"Still," continued Cat, "we dealt well together. He is a kind man, and I love our bairns."

"But ye do not really love him," said Francis Hepburn. "Yet yer lot has been better than mine. Yer a healthy woman, Cat, who enjoys her bedsport wi'out being lewd. My dear countess detests the physical aspects of marriage. Had she been able to get her hands on my fortune by means other than bearing me children, she would have done so."

"But yer bairns? Surely ye love them, Francis."

"In a way, but Margaret has raised them to be cold and correct. They dinna have the Hepburn or the Stewart charm. They tolerate me. It doesna make for a warm relationship."

"I am so sorry, my love," she said.

"Why?" He smiled down at her. "For the first time in my life I am in love. I am in love wi ye, my precious Cat! God help me! How I love ye! And ye, my darling. Ye too are in love for the first time in yer life. And I am the fortunate man!"

"Oh, Bothwell," she whispered, "what are we to do?"

"I dinna know, Cat. I hae no easy answers, but I will find a solution to our dilemma, I promise ye that."

Putting an arm about her shoulders, he led the way into her bedroom. Gently he removed her pearls and placed them on the table. Next he opened the lavender gown, took it from her, and placed it over a chair. She pulled the pins from her hair, and it tumbled down her back. He caught his breath in delight at the perfection of her lovely breasts, glowing golden in the candlelight. Having kicked her slippers off, she walked barefooted over to him, and her slender fingers tremblingly unbuttoned his shirt and removed it. Then, turning, she walked over to the bed while he finished undressing and got into it.

Trembling, she awaited him. And then he was with

her beneath the feather coverlet. He drew her lush body against his slender length and held her close. They stayed that way for what seemed an eternity, allowing the warmth of their bodies to mingle. Cat wondered if Francis felt the same desperate hunger that she did. She could not call it lust. The feelings she had ran too deep. Even the supreme act of possession did not entirely satisfy her.

He entered her, pushing deep within her pulsing warmth, and straining to go further, he cried out, "Ah, God! 'Tis not enough!" Cat wept with joy at the knowledge that his love for her was as deep as hers for him.

Chapter 25

ক্ষু৯০

WINTER deepened into early spring, the traditional time for raiding the borders. Bothwell
had not gone along on many of these ventures, prefer-
ring to stay with Cat. His men missed him greatly, and,
finally, Bothwell's bastard half-brother, Hercules
Stewart, spoke to the countess about the problem.

"Could I go too, Hercules?" she asked him.

He grinned at her. "To be sure, my lady! If Francis
will permit ye."

"Can ye use a sword or a pistol?" Bothwell asked
when he was confronted by his half-brother and Cat.

"Well enough," she replied. "My eldest brother
taught me."

He tested her and, satisfied, said, "Ye'll do." But he
instructed Hercules not to leave Cat's side.

So she rode out with Bothwell and his borderers, first
at night, and then on daylight raids. Unafraid, she
fought the English with a gusto that delighted the earl's
men. Yet she was kind to those of her own sex, and
tender with the children. Soon stories began to filter out
of the borders, stories about the beautiful lady who rode
with Bothwell and his men.

South from Edinburgh rode Bothwell's sometime
friend, Lord Home. He was curious about these stories,
and wanted to see for himself. Home rode alone. He
wanted no gossiping servants along. It was late after-

noon as he neared Hermitage, stopping for a minute to gaze at the great castle in the distance. Hearing hoof-beats behind him, he drew into a strand of trees and waited. He recognized Bothwell's stallion, Valentine, but the sleek golden bay beside him was unfamiliar. The two horses raced straight towards him, then pulled up in the grass just short of his hiding place. He could see Bothwell's face easily, and heard him exclaim, "I win, madame! Pay yer forfeit!"

The laughter that greeted Bothwell's words was soft, and Home leaned eagerly forward, but the woman turned and he could not see her face clearly. "Name your forfeit, my Lord!" she called in a clear voice. Bothwell cocked a wicked eyebrow. Reaching up, he lifted the woman down from her horse.

"Oh, Francis!" The woman laughed again. Hepburn's arms closed about her. Lord Home could see only her profile, which told him little. Home was struck by the look of tenderness and love on his friend's face. After gazing rapturously at his love for some time, Bothwell said, "Christ, my darling. How much I love ye! Come. Let us go home. Will ye race me again?"

He lifted her back onto her horse. Again Home was frustrated in his attempt to see the woman's face, for her back was to him. "If I win, Francis, I shall claim a larger forfeit than one kiss!" Her meaning was obvious, and Home almost choked. Jesu! What a wench this woman was! Bothwell laughed low and replied, "*If* ye beat me, madame." Smacking the golden bay on the rump to give Cat a head start, he mounted Valentine and galloped off after her.

Lord Home remained hidden for some minutes. What he had just witnessed had shaken him somewhat. He had known Francis Hepburn for many years. At one time they had even been enemies. But, youthful vanities soothed, they later became friends. Home had never seen Bothwell look so relaxed, or so peaceful. He had wenched enough with the man to know that Hepburn never took any woman seriously, not even his cold, correct Countess. Yet Home was sure the lord of Hermitage took this woman absolutely seriously. Mounting his own horse, Home headed down the hills to the great castle. His curiosity was truly aroused now.

In the courtyard he was met by Hercules Stewart, who offered greetings and took his horse. "I'll go get Francis. He's just ridden in, and will be glad to see ye."

Lord Home waited in an antechamber, grinning to himself, wondering who had won the horse race. Suddenly the door burst open, and Bothwell strode in. He grasped Home's hand warmly.

"By God, Sandy! 'Tis good to see ye! What brings ye to Hermitage?" The big earl busied himself with a decanter and two heavy glasses.

"Curiosity, Francis. Curiosity is what brings me. There are stories in Edinburgh that ye ride the borders wi a beautiful woman by yer side. The court is fascinated. Shall I go back and tell them that Lord Bothwell has mocked them again? 'Tis but a lad in a wig, is it not?"

Bothwell handed Alexander Home a glass of his smoky whisky and smiled lazily. "Do ye want to meet her, Sandy? Do ye want to meet my lady? I have, by the way, asked Margaret for a divorce."

Home's eyebrows shot up.

"I have told Margaret that I will sign over to the children everything except Hermitage," Bothwell continued. "What is yer news, Sandy?"

Alexander Home thoughtfully sniffed his whisky and then sipped at it. "Am I to understand that Francis Stewart-Hepburn, the man who is called the uncrowned King of Scotland, has finally fallen in love?"

Bothwell did not answer him directly. He pulled the

bellcord, and said to the servant answering it, "Ask my lady if she will join us." The two men sat in companionable silence for the next few minutes, until the door opened.

Bothwell leaped forward, putting a protective arm about the beautiful young woman. "Sandy, may I present Catriona, Lady Leslie. Cat, this is my old friend Sandy Home."

Lord Home bowed over the slender hand offered him, and then looked up into the most beautiful eyes he had ever seen. His mind reeled over the announcement of her identity.

She smiled and gently disengaged her hand from his grasp. "Yes, Lord Home. I am the same Catriona Leslie who is the Countess of Glenkirk. And yes, Lord Home, I am she who is called the Virtuous Countess."

He flushed. "Madame, I . . ." He fought for the words.

She helped him out. "Yer surprised to see me here, my lord. Francis is free to tell ye the truth of the matter if he so chooses. Now, I must go speak to the housekeeper about seeing to yer comfort." She turned to Bothwell. "I'll have dinner served in the small dining room."

"Will ye join us, Cat?"

"Aye." She smiled again at Lord Home, then turned and left.

"Good Lord, Bothwell!" swore Alexander Home. "Catriona Leslie! Does Glenkirk know where she is? He explained that she went home to nurse a sickly bairn, and he sold her position at court."

"Good," said Bothwell. "I'll nae allow her back at court. And to answer yer question, Sandy—no, Glenkirk doesna know where she is. She has written to her uncle, the Abbot of Glenkirk Abbey, asking him to arrange for a divorce."

"How did this start?" asked Home. "Glenkirk and his wife were considered happy. Damn me, Francis! Ye've fooled them again! All that time ye claimed not to be sleeping wi her! How they laughed at court at yer claims of friendship! Hepburn's met his match, they said, for she will nae spread her legs for him or for any man other than her husband. And all that time ye were sleeping wi her!" Home slapped his thigh and roared.

Then he heard Bothwell say quietly, "No, Sandy. That is nae the way it began. Fill yer glass again, man, and I'll tell ye the truth of the matter."

Lord Home needed no encouragement, for Francis Hepburn made the best whisky on the border, possibly even in all of Scotland. Settling himself back in his chair he listened, first with amazement, then with growing horror, and finally with outrage.

"God help me," finished the earl. "I've loved her from the first, but I nae expected to win her away from Glenkirk. The damned fool, to throw away anything so precious!"

"Even if ye both gain yer freedom," said Lord Home quietly, "James Stewart will never let ye wed. Damn me, Francis! Ye grew up a bit wi the royal bairn. Ye know how vindictive he can be, and ye can hardly keep it a secret that yer divorcing Angus' daughter. And what of Glenkirk? When he learns his wife seeks her freedom and where she is, he'll come roaring out of the north like a storm. He may hae lost his head in a moment of anger, but I'll wager he still loves his wife and wants her back."

"She'll nae go," said Bothwell firmly, "and I'd nae let her. Look, Sandy. Ye know they call me the uncrowned King of Scotland. I dinna seek my cousin's throne, but ye canna convince Jamie of that. When Cat and I are safely wed we intend spending most of our time in Italy. I will only retain Hermitage for the son she will someday gie me. That is the price Cat and I will pay to the king for our happiness—exile from our beloved land. As to the Earl of Glenkirk, he'll cooperate or Cat will threaten to tell the whole story. Jamie will nae allow that. He has his position as king, and as head of the kirk. Ah, Sandy! I've waited all my life for happiness, and at last I have it! I never thought it possible."

Lord Home shook his head. It was all too simple. Much, much too simple. He hoped for Francis' sake that it could be made to work. Bothwell had always been restless. A great mind, educated far beyond his time, he was constantly defending his actions to lesser men. Love had calmed him. He was quieter, less formidable.

Alexander Home did not know Catriona Leslie beyond court gossip, but any woman who could exert such a strong emotional influence over the Earl of Bothwell had to be quite a woman. He chuckled. And damned if Hepburn dinna have all the luck. She was a beauty to boot! Home decided to stay at Hermitage and learn more about the Countess of Glenkirk.

He remained during the late part of the spring—a rare spring of unparalleled good weather continuing into the summer. He rode with them on border raids, and felt the same pride in the lovely highland countess as did Bothwell and his men. Home was touched by the charming ritual the lovers performed before each venture. Bothwell would turn to Cat and say, "A Bothwell!" To which she would reply softly, "A Leslie!" They dared not utter clan warcries aloud on the English side of the border.

Returning safely over the border to their own land, Francis Hepburn would more often than not take Cat from the back of her own horse and place her in front

of him on Valentine. One strong hand holding the reins
and the other arm wrapped about his mistress's slim
waist, they rode together talking intimately.

Lord Home's boyhood nanny had spoken of true
love, but as he had grown and matured, Home had
learned that in matters between men and women of
rank there were only two paths. There was the dynastic
path in which marriages were arranged to the best possible advantage of both families with no real considera-
tion for the people involved. And there was lust.
Neither of these cases explained what had happened between the Earl of Bothwell and the Countess of Glenkirk. Alexander Home realized that he was witnessing
true love at first hand.

Satisfied that Cat Leslie was no adventuress, out to
take advantage of his friend, Sandy Home finally took
his leave of the couple and returned to his home at
Hirsel.

Chapter 26

❧❧❧

DAVID Douglas, the Earl of Angus, was a quiet man. He avoided trouble. He disliked scenes. He was at present in his daughter's house at Crichton, and had just finished reading the letter sent her by her estranged husband.

"Well, father? What shall I do?"

David Douglas winced slightly. Margaret's voice was harsh. It annoyed him and always had. "What do ye wish to do, my dear? I dinna believe ye hae not already made up yer mind. Do ye love him, Margaret?"

"Nay," she answered.

"Then what is it? He has asked ye for a divorce offering ye everything he owns except Hermitage. Do ye want Hermitage too?"

"Nay! I hate the place!"

"Then gie him what he wants, daughter."

"But why does he ask me for a divorce now? He's always been happy enough living apart from me. Divorce was not mentioned before."

"Surely ye've heard the rumors, Margaret? 'Tis said a woman rides wi him now when he raids into England. It may be he wishes to wed this mysterious amazon."

"A fit mate for him!" sneered Margaret.

"Come, daughter," said Angus, "be quit of Bothwell. Sooner or later he will clash openly wi the king. He and James have always rubbed against each other. I dinna want ye and yer bairns caught in that fight."

"Ye are right, father," said the Countess of Bothwell. "And it is better that I take all I can get now. Will ye see to the arrangements?"

"Of course, my dear." David Douglas patted her hand. He was pleased. He could always count on Margaret to be cool and sensible.

At Glenkirk Abbey, Abbot Charles Leslie pondered a letter from his niece, the Countess of Glenkirk, in which she requested that he obtain her a divorce from Patrick Leslie. Divorce was not unusual in Scotland among the nobility of either church, but Charles was shocked that Catriona wanted her release. That it should come to this, after all the fuss to wed them! And they had seemed so happy all these years! He knew his nephew was in residence at the castle, and he sent one of the monks to fetch him.

The first thing Charles Leslie noticed when his nephew arrived was that Glenkirk looked tired and worn. Something was very wrong, and Charles Leslie wondered why he had not been told sooner. Without saying a word he handed the earl the letter, and while pretending to busy himself pouring the elderberry wine, he covertly watched Patrick's face.

Intense pain and sorrow creased Glenkirk's face. "She has not told ye why she seeks to divorce me. She is justified in her actions, ye know. But God help me, uncle, I dinna want to lose her!"

"Come, come, Patrick," said the abbot, further startled to see this breakdown in his usually assured nephew. "It canna be so bad. Is it that little Danish girl ye lay wi? Surely Cat doesna hold that against ye?"

"Nay, uncle. She forgave me that, and that is why what I did to Cat is doubly terrible."

Charles Leslie demanded an explanation. Upon hearing it he roared a string of oaths at his nephew. "Fool! Stupid, arrogant fool! How could ye? Tell me no more. I'll nae let my sister's only daughter return to ye!"

The earl protested nervously. "I will nae gie my consent until I have spoken wi her. Who delivered the letter?"

"A Kira servant."

"Then I shall go to Edinburgh to see the Kiras," said Patrick Leslie, "and I shall find Cat. If, after she has spoken wi me, she would still divorce me . . . then I'll gie my consent."

The Earl of Glenkirk rode secretly into Edinburgh. He did not want the king to learn of his visit. James had been very wary of the Leslies of Glenkirk since that fatal night in February. The earl explained to his Edinburgh housekeeper that his visit must not be public knowledge. Used to dealing with the eccentricities of the Leslies, Mrs. Kerr smiled cheerfully and nodded.

Patrick's next stop was the house of the Kiras in Goldsmith's Lane. Both brothers greeted him, and he could tell from the wary look of sympathy in Benjamin's eyes that the elder Kira guessed the reason for his visit. The amenities over, and Abner Kira gone, Benjamin and the earl sat before the fire.

"Well, Benjamin," asked Glenkirk, "where has she hidden herself now?"

"My lord," replied Kira, "my house has served yours since the days of your great-grandmother, but I cannot divulge that information. I cannot even tell you if I know where her ladyship is. I could no more break faith with her than I would with you."

Patrick had expected such an answer. "Then can ye get a message to her ladyship, Benjamin?"

"I think so, my lord. Shall I have parchment and ink brought?"

"Thank ye, my friend."

The writing materials were brought and Benjamin Kira left the earl alone. Patrick sat thinking for several minutes. Finally, he composed the following message. "Cat—I will nae gie ye yer freedom until ye hae

spoken wi me face to face. If ye still wish to divorce me
afterwards, I will nae stand in yer way. I hae wronged
ye, but I beg of ye to hear me out. I still love ye.
Glenkirk."

He sanded the parchment, rolled it, dripped wax on
it, and sealed it with his signet. Leaving the room, he
handed the roll to the waiting servant. "Gie it to yer
master, lad. He'll know what to do wi it. Tell him I
will be at my house here in town."

A few minutes later, Benjamin Kira handed the
parchment to a messenger. "Take this to Lady Leslie at
Hermitage Castle," he said. "And be sure you are not
followed."

Cat did not want to see her husband, but Bothwell
insisted. "Ye canna be certain in yer own mind that ye
no longer love him unless ye can look him in the eye
and tell him so. Ye can meet him at Kira's house. Stay
wi yer cousin, Fiona. I shall go to Edinburgh too. I
hae been meaning to do something about these stupid
charges that I practice witchcraft against the king.
Now is a good time. Too, since Margaret has agreed to
gie me a divorce, there must be papers to sign."

"Do ye think Jamie knows about us?" she asked
him.

"Nay. No one does except Home. We will ride to
town secretly. Hercules can go wi us, and when we
reach Edinburgh he will escort ye as far as yer cousin's
house."

"What if I need ye, Francis?"

"I'll know if ye do, my darling. Dinna fear. We will
complete our separate business quickly, and be safe
back at Hermitage before ye know it."

So they rode to Edinburgh and parted. Fiona Leslie
was delighted to see her cousin, and consumed with
curiosity.

"Promise me," said Cat. "Promise me, Fiona, that

ye'll nae tell Patrick I am here. He stays at Glenkirk House, and I hae nowhere else to go if ye will not shelter me."

"I would promise ye, Cat, but Adam is sure to tell him."

When her brother-in-law arrived home, Cat confronted him. "If ye tell Patrick I am here, I'll tell him ye advised me to sleep wi the king," she threatened.

"I hae already told him," said Adam, rubbing his jaw in remembrance.

"And did ye tell him ye offered me to Jamie when Jamie actually sought yer own wife?"

"That's nae true!" roared Adam.

"No, 'tis not, but I will tell Glenkirk that it is, and Fiona will back me up, won't ye, cousin?"

"Aye," said Fiona blandly, her smoky-gray eyes twinkling at her husband.

Adam Leslie flung up his hands. "All right, ye two bitches! Ye win. Ye hae yer refuge, Cat. When Glenkirk hears, I likely as not will receive another crack on my jaw."

Cat put her hand on her brother-in-law's arm. "Sit down, Adam. Ye too, Fiona. I would speak seriously wi ye both." They sat. Looking at Fiona, Cat said, "By now Adam has probably told ye that James forced me into his bed for a time." Fiona nodded, and Cat continued. "When Glenkirk found the king wi me, he was furious. What he did to me I will never speak of again. I hae now asked him for a divorce, and he will nae gie his consent unless I speak wi him face to face. I hae come to Edinburgh to do just that."

"Where hae ye been these last months?" asked Fiona.

Cat smiled. "I'll nae tell ye that, cousin."

Adam Leslie grunted and got up to pour himself some wine. If she wouldn't tell, she wouldn't tell. But

Fiona had understood the softness in her cousin's voice, and thought with amazement, My God! She's in love! She is in love wi another man!

Fiona was desperate to learn the identity of Cat's lover, but she could think of no man that Cat had ever been friendly with outside the family. She was determined to find out somehow, however. Seeing Fiona's grim look, Cat laughed. "I'll tell ye eventually, Fiona, but not now." Caught, Fiona laughed back. "Ye always were the deep one," she returned.

On the following day a messenger was sent to the Kiras. The Countess of Glenkirk would arrive at their house to meet with her husband at one o'clock in the afternoon if the Kiras would send word to the earl informing him of the meeting.

Glenkirk arrived promptly. He was anxious to see Cat, sure that when he explained and apologized, their estrangement would be over. He had taken great pains with his appearance. A young maidservant ushered him into the room where Cat waited and then left, closing the door behind her.

The Countess of Glenkirk wore a high-necked deep-blue silk dress with ecru-colored lace cuffs. Her dark-honey-colored hair was braided and twisted into a severe knot on the nape of her neck. It was Cat, and yet somehow she looked different. "Patrick." Her voice was cool, and there was no welcome in it.

He rushed forward, stopping suddenly at the sight of the jeweled dirk in her hand.

"Touch me, and I use it," she said. "On you!"

"Sweetheart, please!" he pleaded. "Yer my wife, and I love ye." This was not going right.

She laughed bitterly. "Ye didna feel so strongly two and a half months ago when ye and the king spent the night raping me! My God, Glenkirk! I was yer good and faithful wife for thirteen years! I never once gave ye cause for doubt. Yet the moment ye found me in the king's arms ye assumed me the guilty one, simply because I was a woman. Are men never the guilty ones?"

His voice shaking, he slipped to his knees and caught at the hem of her dress. "Cat! Cat! Will ye ever forgie me? When I awoke the next morning and remembered all that had past—Christ! Ye couldna have hated me any more than I hated myself. Can ye nae forgive me, hinny?"

"No, Patrick! I will never forgie ye for what ye did to me! Do ye know what it was like for me? Do ye know what it was like having to allow another man possession of my body? For a man, lovemaking is a physical thing. He hungers for a woman, but once he has had her the feeling dies. But for a woman, love-making is an emotional experience. Her passion for a man is alive before, during, and even after the act of love. James made me feel like a whore. He used my body, and it responded because ye had taught me to respond, but I felt nothing for him but hate. Every time he pushed himself into me I hated him, and I prayed ye would never know my shame, for I couldna bear to hurt ye. If only ye had felt the same tenderness for me, Patrick, I could forgie ye now. But when ye caught me wi the king, ye punished me when ye should have defended me. No, my lord of Glenkirk! I will nae forgie ye!"

He stood, and looked down on her. "What of the children?"

"I want my girls," she said. "Jamie and Colin are already wi Rothes, and Robbie will go next year. Ye may keep the children until the divorce is settled. After that—I want them. Ye may see them at any time ye want. They are all Leslies of Glenkirk and I would nae have them forget it. Nor would I have them hate their father, Patrick. What has happened between us is not the concern of our bairns."

"Ye are generous, madame," he said sardonically. "And now that we hae settled that perhaps ye would satisfy my curiosity, and tell me where ye hae been hiding all this time?"

"Nay. I will not tell ye, Patrick. Ye forfeited yer right to any control of my life on that night in February." Reaching for the bellpull on the wall, she yanked it and told the little maid, "Please see my horse is brought around." Cat turned once again to Patrick Leslie. "Farewell, my lord," she nodded coldly, and left him.

He was stunned. He could hardly believe what had taken place. He had lost her. There had been no love at all in the beautiful leaf-green eyes that had always lit with joy at the sight of him. He had willfully destroyed that Catriona Leslie, and the woman who had risen phoenixlike from the wreckage was not his woman, nor was she ever likely to be. Sitting down, he put his head in his hands and wept. Several minutes later he left the Kira household and spent the rest of the day and the night that followed it getting very drunk.

Chapter 27

⌘⌘

WHEN Francis Stewart Hepburn surrendered himself to his cousin, James panicked. Quickly he imprisoned the earl in Edinburgh Castle. The king, an overly superstitious man, was terribly frightened of witchcraft. Chancellor Maitland knew this and, in an attempt to break the back of Scotland's nobility, had fabricated the charges against Bothwell. Breaking the border lord, he thought, would crush all resistance to James. Unfortunately, the earl's fellow nobles were most irritated by Maitland's attempt to destroy their power. They refused to meet to try Hepburn. Until they did, justice was at a standstill because no one else could try him.

Cat was terrified by the news that Bothwell was locked in Edinburgh Castle. There was nothing she could do. She could not even communicate with her lover for fear of the king, and she had no idea how to reach Hercules. So she remained quietly with Fiona, awaiting word. She would not leave Edinburgh without Francis.

It was not long before she received a message from the loyal Hercules. She was to come, masked, to the Oak and Thistle Tavern the following afternoon, and ask for Mr. Prior. Cat was in a fever of impatience.

At two the next afternoon she slipped from the house and walked quickly through the June afternoon. It was raining slightly, which was to the good as few people were on the streets to see her. Entering the tavern, she inquired for Mr. Prior, and was shown a private parlor in the back of the building on the ground floor. There was Hercules.

She barely allowed time for the maidservant's exit before asking, "Francis?"

"Enormously comfortable in a large, well-furnished two-room apartment," said Bothwell's half-brother. "Eating and drinking the best that money can buy. A favorite with his captors, but beginning to be bored by Jamie's shilly-shallying."

"What do ye want me to do?" she cried.

"Francis has decided that too much more of the king's hospitality could kill him," chuckled Hercules. "So he'll be leaving Edinburgh shortly. Can ye hide him for a few hours? A day at most?"

"Aye! At my cousin Fiona's. Ye know the house. My brother-in-law, Adam, leaves tomorrow for Glenkirk. He'll be gone about two weeks, but no more. Can Francis escape within that time?"

Hercules Stewart nodded. "Within the week, my lady."

"I'll be ready. Is there some signal ye can gie me so I'll know when?"

"A boy will deliver a bunch of wild red roses and white heather to ye. 'Twill be that night." He poured out some red wine and handed her a goblet. "Drink it, madame. Ye look worn."

She smiled at him and accepted the wine. "I hae been so worried," she admitted. "I knew nothing but what the gossips in the marketplace said, and I didna dare inquire too closely."

Hercules looked at her. "How did that rogue of a brother of mine do it? How did he get the loveliest and bravest woman in this wild land to fall in love wi him?" He gave her a grin so like Bothwell's that her heart turned over. "He's always been lucky, the devil!"

She couldn't help but laugh. "I am the one who's lucky, Hercules. He is a great man, my Francis." She picked up her cloak from the settle. "I had best go now. I'll be waiting for yer signal."

The following day, Adam Leslie left Edinburgh, leaving his wife and Cat alone in the house. Almost immediately Fiona was at her younger cousin, demanding to know the name of Cat's lover. Cat laughed. "Not yet, Ona, but in a few days ye will not only know his name, but ye'll meet him." Fiona gnashed her teeth in frustration.

Two afternoons later an urchin knocked at the door of Fiona's house. Handing the maid a bouquet of white heather and wild red roses, he said, "Fer the lady o' Glenkirk." Exclaiming her delight, the little maid put the bouquet in a silver bowl and brought it to the Countess. Fiona raised an elegant eyebrow. "Charming," she said. "Does this mean I am to meet the gentleman soon?"

"Tonight," replied Cat. "Can ye get rid of the servants?"

"It's been done. Darling Cat, 'tis Midsummer Eve, and everyone will be celebrating."

"Damn!" swore Cat. "I should hae guessed! Fiona, tell yer servants that they may hae tomorrow off as well. Please do this for me. My lord will nae wish to be seen by other than you and me."

Fiona agreed. "They'll all be suffering the effects of too much ale, wine, and lovemaking, and be no use to me anyway. Oh, cousin! I am fascinated! Who is this man?"

"Bothwell," said Cat softly.

"But he's in prison!" said Fiona, and then her smoky-gray eyes widened and she clapped her hands over her mouth.

Cat had to laugh, but Fiona recovered quickly. "Ye *really* are the deep one! Are ye telling me that Francis

Hepburn is the man? Ye hae been wi him since ye ran away from Glenkirk? He is yer lover?" Cat nodded. "Damn me!" said Fiona. "Ye really hae all the luck! First Glenkirk, and then the border lord himself!" Her eyes glittered. "What is he like?" she begged. "Is he really a warlock? Does he make love like mortal men?"

Cat choked back a fit of giggles, for she could see that Fiona was quite serious. "Nay, cousin. Francis is no warlock or wizard, and he makes love very nicely, thank ye."

"How did ye meet him, Cat?"

"At court. He was my friend then, not my lover."

"He has a wife, Cat."

"He is divorcing her as I am divorcing Glenkirk. We'll be wed by year's end, Fiona."

"Does Glenkirk know about Bothwell? Does the King?"

"Nay. Neither of them does. Say nothing, Fiona. I would rather no one know until Francis and I are safely wed."

"What should we do to prepare?" asked Fiona.

"Food, cousin! Francis eats ravenously when he's elated, and outfoxing both Jamie and Maitland will make him jubilant."

That evening, the servants gone, Catriona Leslie and her cousin Fiona waited. Cat assumed that Bothwell would not escape until late, when festivities were well underway. She was right. It was close to midnight when there came a knock at the kitchen door. Cat flew to open it, and two muffled figures slipped quickly into the room.

Flinging his cloak off, Francis Hepburn grinned impudently at Cat. "Good evening, my darling," he said.

Tears glistened in her eyes as Cat stepped forward. "Oh, Bothwell!" Suddenly she stopped. "Christ in heaven! *What* is that stink?"

He grinned sheepishly. "I'm afraid my mode of conveyance from the castle was not at all elegant."

"What was it?" she demanded.

He hesitated. "A dung cart."

She stared at him. "A dung cart?"

"It had a false bottom," he explained. "I hid there, while above me rested the contents of the entire castle stables."

Cat looked directly at Hercules Stewart. "There's a tub in the closet there," she said. "Please get it out and fill it with hot water for his lordship." She instructed the wide-eyed Fiona, "Get some of Adam's clothes and put them in my room. Bring a dressing gown here."

Hercules pulled out the hip bath while Cat began to heat water. When the tub was filled she took Bothwell's clothes from him and flung them into the fire. Before she would allow him to climb into his bath she led him naked into the scullery and sluiced him down. Once he was in the tub she scrubbed him down with a stiff brush and washed his hair. "Thank God, no lice," was her only comment. Bothwell chuckled as he climbed from the tub at last and wrapped himself in a large towel.

She sat him by the fire to dry his hair. Fiona returned with a long, soft robe of lightweight wool, which Bothwell quickly slipped on. Then he caught Fiona's hand and brought it to his lips. "Lady Leslie." He spoke in a low, intimate voice that brought a blush to her cheek and caused her heart to beat fast. "I thank ye for yer hospitality. I hope I'll not inconvenience ye in any way."

" 'T-'tis an honor to hae ye in my house," stammered Fiona. "When yer ready we've a supper in the small dining room."

"Ye'll join us, of course," said Bothwell, offering his arm to Fiona.

They had set on the sideboard a small meal of boiled shrimp, ham, ribs of nearly raw beef, roasted capon, a salad of cress and dandelion greens, hot bread, sweet butter, and fresh fruit. There were brown ale, red and white wines, and whisky. Cat watched indulgently, barely nibbling as the earl stuffed himself. Sated at last, he sat back and sipped a glass of whisky.

She had sat next to him so she might serve him. Fiona was at the opposite end of the table with Hercules. Pushing back his chair, Bothwell said softly to her, "Come sit on my lap, my darling." Cat settled herself comfortably. "Did ye miss me?" he asked gently.

"Aye," she whispered. "I was so frightened."

His mouth found her eager one and he kissed her passionately, feeling her lovely body come alive beneath his caresses. "Christ, I've missed ye," he muttered into her neck. "I had the money for whores, but I took nae a single one. I stayed true to ye, my darling, and I have nae done that before for any woman." Her hands caught his and pressed them against her taut breasts. He felt the little nipples hard against his palms. He rose, cradling her in his arms. "I am sorry, my darling, but I canna wait tonight," he said.

"Neither can I, Bothwell," she answered him softly. "Take me to bed. I burn for ye!" He complied willingly, walking from the room with his beautiful burden.

Fiona had watched the entire scene, fascinated. She could not hear what they said, but the open desire between her cousin and Francis Hepburn was stunning. Her own breath quickened, her lovely breasts became swollen, her full lips were moist. Guiltily, she looked up to see Hercules smiling a slow lazy smile at her. She blushed to the roots of her auburn hair, thinking, He's going to seduce me, and dear heaven, I am going to let him!

She tried to think of Adam and found to her horror that she could not even recall his face. Fiona stood up quickly and fled to the windows that opened on her gardens. She could smell the heady perfume of the damask roses, and silently cursed the fact that everything in the world seemed to be conspiring against her own sensuality. The air was charged with the passion created by Bothwell and Cat. Fiona was terrified by her mood, but at the same time she was elated.

Hercules was behind her now, putting an arm about her waist and drawing her back against him. He kissed her soft, bare shoulder, and then his fingers began to undo the bodice of her gown. Turning her about to face him, he pushed the gown from her shoulders and bent to kiss her lush, red mouth. Forcing her lips apart, his tongue ravished her mouth. For all her experience, Fiona nearly swooned. She made a token resistance, freeing herself to look up at him. "Sir," she protested weakly, "I hae never been unfaithful to Leslie before."

"How very admirable of ye, madame," he drawled. "Where is yer bedchamber?"

"Upstairs to the left." Fiona realized suddenly that the time for protest was long past. He picked her up as if she were a child, and carried her to her bed. As they moved up the stairs she suppressed a giggle. Why? thought Fiona Leslie. Why do I always end up wi the brother?

In the gray half-light of Midsummer Eve, Francis Hepburn made passionate love to Catriona Leslie until they fell asleep, exhausted. She woke at dawn to find him awake, watching her. Reaching up, she drew his head down to her breasts and cradled it there. "Ye'll incinerate me wi that look, my love," she whispered.

"I did not sleep well away from ye, Cat. I need ye,

my darling. I'll nae leave ye again," he murmured
contentedly. Raising himself up slightly, he leaned over
her and looked down into her face. It was wet with
silent tears. Gently he touched her cheek. "Dinna
weep, my sweetest love. We are safe together."

"For how long, Bothwell? For how long? I am
afraid! They will nae let us be happy."

"Don't, love. Don't. I am taking ye home to Hermitage today. Here ye are too close to James Stewart. I
think it frightens ye."

She clung to him, pressing her slender body against
him until his desire for her overcame everything else.
He saw that she hungered for him as strongly as he
hungered for her. Her green eyes glittered. Her soft,
round breasts hardened. He could feel the trembling in
her thighs. His laughter was soft. "Dear Christ, yer my
wench! There is no mistaking it! I never met a woman
before who could keep up wi me—but ye do."

She pulled his head down to hers. "Come into me,
my lover," she begged him, and then his mouth captured hers.

He was deep in the warm softness of her, straining
to go further, feeling her strain beneath him as he released his boiling seed within her. As always—and it
had never been this way with any other woman—he
grew hard again inside her. He strove to pleasure this
woman whom he knew loved him, and whom he loved
above all others. His own delight was greatest when she
cried out in joy.

Later, he cradled her in his arms, murmuring soft
words and placing little kisses on her face, her hair, her
throat. He had missed her terribly. He had discovered
that he needed her as he had never needed anyone before. He had always been a lone wolf. But now he had
found a mate. And he was going to have to fight the
king himself in order to keep her.

With the coming of the beautiful June dawn sounded
the frantic tolling of the alarm bell at Edinburgh Castle.
Bothwell sat up, instantly awake. "It took them long
enough to discover me missing," he chuckled. "Ah,
this is going to spoil Jamie's day." He gently swatted
Cat's pretty backside. "Come on, Cat! Wake up! If
we're riding home to Hermitage, I want a good breakfast first!"

"I am nae awake yet," she murmured, curling into
a tight little ball.

He pulled the coverlet from her and began kissing
her body. She stood it for a few minutes, then protested, "Damn ye, Bothwell! Ye could raise a corpse
with those lips of yers," and she climbed from their
bed. He watched with pleasure as she washed and then
pulled on her riding clothes. It pleased him to note that
she wore the gold-and-topaz chain he had given her.

"We'll eat in the kitchen, my lord. Shall I wake
Hercules, or will ye do it? I'll wager a gold piece he's
in Fiona's bed. I know for a fact that she's been faithful to Adam all their married life, but if she could
resist that brother of yers and his passionate looks last
night, I'll make a pilgrimage to Iona!"

Bothwell's laughter rang loudly. "No wager, Cat! If
he's not in her bed, I'll go to Iona wi ye! Hercules is
a winning rascal."

They opened their bedroom door and walked quietly
across the hallway to the opposite room. They heard
nothing. Cat gently opened the door and peered into
the chamber. Hercules awoke at once and grinned
wickedly at them. Fiona was curled naked in a corner
of the bed, sleeping soundly and looking very tousled.

Closing the door again, Cat's mouth twitched with
silent laughter. "I'll be in the kitchen," she whispered,
and ran lightly down the stairs.

The earl went back to their bedroom, where he

shaved and bathed as best he could using the china basin. Finished, he went downstairs and discovered that Cat had ready a tempting breakfast of oatmeal, cold ham, and bread. Hercules was already seated at the trestle eating heartily and washing it all down with brown October ale. Bothwell joined his half-brother. After Cat had served the men she sat down with them and ate with her usual enthusiasm.

When he had finished the earl pushed back his chair. "Hercules, I want ye to take Cat to the edge of the city by the Lion Tavern. Wait there for me."

"Where are ye going?" demanded Cat.

"I hae a wee bit of unfinished business. Dinna fret, my darling."

"Ye should nae allow yerself to be seen, Francis. Ye deliberately bait Jamie."

"No one will harm me, my love." He drew his brother from the kitchen. Cat could hear only the murmur of their voices, and then laughter.

Sighing, she collected the dishes from the night before and this morning, and washed them all in the scullery. There must be nothing misplaced, nothing to give servants cause for gossip. When she returned to the kitchen, Bothwell was putting on his cloak. "Come kiss me, my darling," he said.

"Ye promise me ye'll be safe?"

"Aye, wench! I'll be safe. Now ye must leave wi Hercules in ten minutes. Be sure Fiona knows to keep silent."

Cat laughed. "Fiona will nae admit to even having met ye, let alone sheltering ye. Adam would beat her black and blue! I'll wager he knows yer brother's reputation."

Bothwell grinned at her. "I'll be wi ye soon, my love." And in a second he was out the back door into the stableyard, where Hercules was holding a prancing Valentine.

Cat left the kitchen and hurried up the two flights of stairs to Fiona's bedroom, carrying a tray with wine, bread, and a small honeycomb. "Wake up, sleepyhead," she called to her cousin. Fiona mumbled and snuggled down into the feather bed. "I'm leaving, Fiona. Bothwell and I must go home to Hermitage this morning." She put the tray on the bedside table. Fiona sat up. "My God!" said Cat. "Ye look like a castle surrendered after a great battle."

"I feel like it," answered Fiona. "Hercules lives up to his name." Suddenly she blushed. "Christ, Cat! Dinna tell Leslie! I've nae been unfaithful to him ever before. I dinna know what came over me."

"I do," returned Cat, laughing. "I'll nae tell on ye, cousin, if ye'll nae tell on me." She bent down and hugged Fiona. "Be good, and if ye need to get in touch wi me, the landlord at the Oak and Thistle can get a message to Bothwell."

"God go wi ye, Cat," Fiona said.

Bothwell, meantime, was riding through the city making sure he was plainly seen by the populace. A crowd began to follow him. He heard their excited voices behind him.

" 'Tis Bothwell!"

" 'Tis the border lord himself!"

"Francis Hepburn!"

"He's escaped the king!"

"Did Jamie really think he could hold Bothwell?"

"Bless me, Mary, he's as bonnie as they say!"

The earl rode to Nether Bow, where he brought his horse to a stop. The crowd kept a respectful distance, wary of Valentine's sharp hooves. "A good morrow, good people of Edinburgh," his deep voice boomed.

The crowd shifted, the spectators punching at each other genially and grinning.

"Is there a man here," said Bothwell, "who would earn an honest gold crown? A crown to him who'll fetch Chancellor John Maitland here to me. If he'll but come to get me I will willingly return to prison this instant!"

The crowd broke into delighted guffaws, and several men ran off in the direction of the chancellor's house to return a few minutes later saying that the chancellor's servants claimed he was not at home. The crowd hooted with derision. Then Francis Hepburn flung a purse of crowns to them. When they had quieted, Bothwell said, "Tell Maitland I'll be waiting for him if he's brave enough to come after me! I'll be in the borders! And to my cousin, Jamie the king, I send my deepest loyalty."

Valentine reared up on his back legs as Hepburn shouted, *"A Bothwell! A Bothwell!"* and galloped unmolested from the Nether Bow, the approval of the crowd reverberating in his ears.

Chapter 28

❧§❧

WHILE Bothwell and his party galloped off to the borders, John Maitland set to work to undermine him further with the king. Maitland was a brilliant statesman. Like other statesmen of his time he was, by necessity, ruthless. He wanted only one power in Scotland—the monarchy—for then he, Maitland, could rule through the king.

For years the royal Stewarts had been plagued by their earls. They ruled only by the cooperation of their nobility. They scattered their bastards generously among the daughters of the upper class, and then married those valuable bastards to the best families in hopes of joining themselves solidly to the powerful clans. They needed their great lords' support in order to rule unchallenged.

Maitland intended putting a stop to all this. He would break the power of these troublemakers. Beginning first with Bothwell on the borders, he would proceed to Huntley, the Cock of the North. If only, he sighed to himself, the great chiefs could be more like some of the smaller clan branches. He thought in particular of the Earl of Glenkirk, and his cousin of Sithean, a minor branch of Clan Leslie who had built up great wealth. They sought no political power, kept the peace on their lands, and rallied to the Stewarts in time of war.

The chancellor called for his coach and hurried off to Holyrood Palace to see the king. He found James in a panic, and the queen trying to calm him.

"How did he escape?" shrieked the king. "How? How? How? Edinburgh Castle is impregnable. Someone had to help him! I want to know who!"

"Sire, sire! Calm yourself," said Maitland. "Though no one saw Lord Bothwell leave, there is, I am sure, a logical explanation for his escape."

"No one saw him go?" whispered the king. "Witchcraft! Again he resorts to witchcraft!"

The chancellor hid a smile, pleased that his subtle inference had not escaped the king. But he had not reckoned with the queen.

"Nonsense!" she snapped. "I am sure the chancellor means nothing of the sort, do ye, sir? La, James! Do ye think Francis really flew out of his cell on a broomstick? More likely as not he bribed the watch! Men will do anything for money."

"His men won't," said the king sourly. "I've tried to buy information from them."

"Well," allowed the queen, smiling, "Francis is a rather special person."

"Is he?" asked Maitland, hardly surprised to find the queen in Bothwell's camp. Women were quite susceptible to the man's charm. Maitland did not understand it.

"Yes," answered Anna of Denmark, looking straight at the chancellor. "Francis Hepburn could charm a duck out of water."

"I want him found!" yelled the king. "I want him found, and brought back!"

"It will be done, your majesty. It will not be easy, but it will be done."

"If ye had gone to the Nether Bow this morning ye could have had him back in prison already," said the queen blandly. Her ladies giggled, and Maitland shot the queen a venomous look which she chose not to see.

"What's this?" demanded the king.

"Lord Bothwell rode to the Nether Bow earlier this morning, James, and offered to return to prison if our chancellor would but come and fetch him. The servants claimed he was not at home, but I understand he was at home, cowering in a cabinet."

The king began to chuckle, and the chuckle grew to laughter. "He outfoxed ye, Maitland!" chortled the king. "Trust Francis! He's a good fisherman, and he played ye like a salmon! He knew damned well ye'd nae dare venture out of yer house after him. He's made ye look a fool!"

"His behavior is an affront to the crown," snapped Maitland. "It undermines your majesty's dignity. He should be severely punished!"

"It undermines *yer* dignity, Maitland," said the king, but the chancellor's words had stung him. "How would ye punish him?" he asked.

"Forfeiture," said John Maitland promptly. "His offices. His estates."

"No! No!" cried the queen. "Francis is our cousin, James. I know he is reckless, and at times arrogant, but he is the kindest man I know—and he has always been your majesty's good friend. He has never conspired against ye, or lied to ye as others have."

"There are the charges of witchcraft, Annie."

"Ridiculous charges that no one believes! Your own peers are so offended by these charges that they will not even meet to try him! Please, my dear husband. Do not be harsh with Francis. He is our friend, and we have so few."

"We must make an example of this rogue!" thundered Maitland.

"Sir!" said the queen, angrily drawing herself up.

"You quite overstep yourself!" She turned to the king. "I should be very unhappy, sire, if ye punished our cousin severely. 'Tis midsummer, and if I know Francis he has but run off to go swimming."

She made it sound so unimportant. James put an arm about his pretty wife. "Let me think on it, lovey," he said soothingly, and bent to kiss her.

The queen turned and, walking slowly to her bed-chamber door, opened it. " 'Tis still early, Jamie. Dismiss Master Maitland, and come back to bed." Her blue eyes were innocent enough, but the look she gave him was very provocative, and the king felt a stirring in his loins.

Maitland was forced to retire for the moment. He was not one to give up easily. The queen had won this round by using her sex, a practice Maitland abhorred. He realized he needed something he could use against Hepburn which would anger the king and keep him angered long enough to allow for forfeiture proceedings.

Suddenly, memory pounced conveniently on the rumor about a woman who had ridden with Bothwell this spring. No one know who she was, but she was said to be very beautiful. Too, his spies had told him that when Bothwell had left for the border today, he had ridden with his bastard half-brother and a beautiful woman. Maitland didn't know whether knowledge of the lady would help him, but he felt he should have it. He sent for one of his most trustworthy men.

"Go to Hermitage Castle," ordered the chancellor, "and find out who Bothwell's woman is. I do not care how you get your information, but I must have it within a week."

Several days later the man returned and said to the anxious chancellor, "Lady Catriona Leslie, the Countess of Glenkirk."

"You are sure?" asked the amazed chancellor.

"I got it from her personal maid." The informant did not explain that he had lured the girl from the castle, tortured the name from her, and then cut her throat.

Maitland's memory leaped once again. The king's chamberboy had come into his pay, and he sent for the fellow. "What do you know of Catriona Leslie?"

Barra wrote his answer on the pad hanging from his waist. "She was the king's secret mistress, but she ran away from him. He still desires her." He tore the paper from the pad and handed it to the chancellor.

John Maitland read. Smiling, he handed Barra a small bag of gold. He was jubilant! Here was just the weapon he needed to destroy Francis Hepburn. But he had to be careful that his spies were absolutely correct.

Discreet inquiries over the period of a few days netted him the astounding information that Lady Bothwell had just been granted a divorce by the kirk. A further probe told him that the Countess of Glenkirk had applied for a divorce through her uncle, the Abbot of Glenkirk Abbey. The abbot was presenting her petition to the Scots prelate. Unable to contain his excitement, John Maitland hurried to Holyrood. By the time his coach had pulled into the courtyard, he had managed to calm himself somewhat. The king must not suspect that his chancellor knew his most intimate secret.

He waited almost the entire day until he was able to see the king alone. "I have," he said, "discovered an amusing sidelight to Francis Hepburn's life. I know the identity of the woman who's his latest mistress—the one who's been riding with him on raids."

James loved gossip. "Tell me, Maitland," he said impatiently. "Who is she?"

" 'Tis the most amazing thing, sire. Of all the noblewomen in Scotland I would have said this lady was the least likely candidate for Bothwell's bed. He plans to marry her, and Lady Bothwell has just been granted a divorce by the kirk. The lady I speak of is in the process of gaining her own freedom."

"Yes, Maitland, very interesting, but who is she?"

"Why, 'tis the Countess of Glenkirk, sire. Lady Catriona Leslie. That lovely creature they call the Virtuous Countess here at court."

For the briefest moment James Stewart thought his heart had stopped. "Who, Maitland? Who did ye say?"

"Lady Leslie, sire. Glenkirk's wife."

The king looked sick, so Maitland chose that moment to ask permission to withdraw. But as he went he heard the command. "Dinna leave the palace tonight." The chancellor departed, smiling to himself. Bothwell was as good as destroyed. Maitland hadn't missed the look of anguish in the king's face.

James paced his bedroom angrily. Francis Stewart-Hepburn was his nemesis and always had been. Four years older than the king, he had always been bigger, stronger, brighter. They were both handsome, but Francis was handsomer—almost godlike, with rugged good looks. James studied hard to acquire learning, but Francis sopped up knowledge like a sponge, easily and without strain. Women flocked to Bothwell. He was charming. James was quite uncomfortable with women, having been brought up in a male society where women were rarely included. In short, Francis was everything his cousin James longed to be.

Bothwell had gone too far when he had taken Cat Leslie from the king, and James would not forgive him that after all the rest. In bitter frustration, the king overlooked the circumstances under which Cat had fled him. All James chose to know at this point was that Cat had apparently offered Bothwell what she had refused the king. She had given Francis her heart.

He would stop the lovers. Cat would not get her divorce. James would instruct Chancellor Maitland to speak to the cardinal about it. He also intended declaring his popular cousin an outlaw. His estates and title would be forfeit. Cat could hardly remain with an outlaw.

James was angry with Catriona Leslie. He had honored this insignificant highland countess by making her a lady of his wife's bedchamber. She had disappointed him badly. She was no better than any of the other women at court who spread their legs for a man with such ease.

John Maitland came later on, as bidden, hoping he did not appear too eager. His face was a study in impassivity as the king ordered that Francis Stewart-Hepburn, fifth Earl of Bothwell, be put to the horn and his estates confiscated. The following morning a royal herald publicly announced the king's decision to the people of Edinburgh. He was pelted with garbage by the outraged citizens. They hated having their hero brought down.

The king was feeling put-upon. The queen was not speaking to him and she had locked the doors to her apartments. Lady Margaret Douglas had forced her way into his presence, insisting furiously that the crown had no right to confiscate anything other than Hermitage. She waved a paper which she claimed proved that Bothwell had signed over all of his estates except Hermitage to their eldest son, the earl's legitimate heir.

James turned on her. "While Francis was in my good graces, madame, his estates were his to do with as he pleased. Since he is no longer in my good graces his property is being confiscated by the crown."

"Ye cannot expect me to leave Crichton," snapped Margaret Douglas. "'Tis my home, and that of my children. Where are we to go?"

"Go to yer father, or go to the devil!" replied the

king. "I care not, Margaret, but stay out of my presence! Yer forbidden at court."

Margaret Douglas retired, defeated. She would be back, for she didn't intend seeing her eldest son robbed of his inheritance. But she needed time to marshal her forces.

By the following day, Francis Hepburn knew that the king had declared war on him. He did not know precisely why. Breaking out of his prison in Edinburgh Castle had probably not prompted this.

"He knows," said Cat with the certainty of a woman's intuition. "He knows we are lovers."

"Nonsense," returned Bothwell. "Even Jamie could not be that petty."

But she knew she was right, and when Lord Home arrived several days later his conversation with Francis confirmed her suspicions. Sandy Home caught her hand and raised it to his lips. "The most beautiful, *and* the costliest hand in Scotland," he whispered. He loosed her hand and turned to Bothwell. "I've been charged by the king to take ye," he chuckled. "However, if yer not of a mind to return to Edinburgh in the summer's heat, I'll understand, and I think I'll join ye here on the border."

"What's put Cousin Jamie in such a temper?" asked Bothwell.

"Maitland. He suggested forfeiture two weeks ago, but the queen defended ye, reminding the royal ingrate of yer loyalty and yer service to the crown." Home looked serious. "I believe all would hae been well, but I think the king has found out that Cat is here. When he charged me to come to Hermitage and make ye a prisoner of the crown, he kept harping on yer 'lustfulness' wi a 'certain lady' of the court. I dared not question him, Francis, but I am sure he meant Cat. How in hell could he have found out?"

"The girl who has been my maid since I came to Hermitage was found murdered in the woods near here," said Cat. "She had been cruelly tortured."

"Aye," added Bothwell. "The soles of her feet were burned black, and her throat was cut, poor lass. We pried this out of her hand. Do ye recognize it?" He dug into his pouch and held up a silver button.

Home took it and nodded. "One of Maitland's men. The badge on the button is the chancellor's. He probably sought knowledge of the woman wi ye. The bastard! He's found the weapon he sought to destroy ye."

"He'll nae destroy me, Sandy. But tell me, what of Margaret and the children?"

"With Angus."

"James made her leave Crichton? And she went? God's bones, I dinna believe it! Margaret always loved

Lord Home laughed. "She sought the king, Francis. Said only Hermitage belonged to ye, as ye had turned everything else over to yer eldest boy. James sent her and the children back to Angus."

Bothwell choked back his laughter. "Poor Margaret. Of course she must regain the estates for my heir. However, I am sure Angus will see to that. In fact, I imagine he's already anxious to get Margaret out of his house."

"And what of Hermitage, Francis?"

"If James wants Hermitage he must come himself and take it. There are two things I hold dear in this world," said Bothwell. "My home, and Catriona. I'll nae gie him either."

But Cat was frightened. "Let us leave Scotland, Francis," she begged him. "Jamie has taken everything ye own, and he will take me too if we do not flee him."

But he would not entertain the idea of running, even

when a messenger arrived from the Kiras with word
from the Abbot of Glenkirk. The cardinal had denied
Cat's petition for divorce. Charles Leslie, dissatisfied
with the answer, had personally gone to St. Andrew's
and explained the situation to the cardinal. It was then
that the cardinal explained to Charles Leslie that he
had been informed by Chancellor Maitland's confidential secretary that the king would be highly offended
if the divorce were approved. Considering the precarious situation the old kirk faced in Scotland today,
the cardinal would do nothing to jeopardize it further.
Unless James changed his mind, Cat Leslie could not
have her freedom. Nor could she marry Francis
Hepburn.

Again she begged him. "Take me away, Francis. In
France the church will nae have to answer to the
King of Scotland, and I can obtain my freedom."

"For a price, my darling."

"I am a very wealthy woman, Francis. I can bribe
any cleric living. Damnit! What is my money for if I
canna have what I want?"

Francis Hepburn laughed, and put an arm about Cat.
"My dearest, spoilt darling," he said tenderly. "Even
if I must leave Scotland to satisfy James, I would still
make my peace wi him before I go. And I must retain
Hermitage for the son ye will gie me one day."

"Oh, Bothwell, ye great fool! Jamie does nae intend to let us be together. Please take me away now!
I care not if we can ever wed if only we are together!"

But Francis thought they could manage. Francis
Hepburn was a man of honor. He did not really understand yet that the boy cousin he had done some of his
growing up with intended to be *the* King of Scotland
in *every* way. And he did not fully appreciate how
much his royal cousin desired Catriona Leslie. The

king wanted Cat back. And if he could not have her, then neither could Francis Hepburn.

During that summer of 1591, Bothwell rode the borders with his lovely mistress and Lord Home. They raided into England, but in general the peace between England and Scotland was kept. During that summer, James made his royal progress from Holyrood Palace in Edinburgh to Linlithgow, where his mother was born, to Stirling, to Falklands, and then across the Firth of Forth and back again to Edinburgh.

Chapter 29

✦§✦

THE Earl of Glenkirk stood nervously before the king. It was the first time Patrick had seen him since that terrible morning eight months prior. James looked up at Patrick Leslie.

"Why have ye pursued this divorce, Glenkirk? I informed the cardinal that it would be displeasing to me if ye and Cat were divorced."

"Sire, Cat wishes her freedom. I saw her in June, and she'll nae return to me. She's a different woman."

"Do ye know where she is, Cousin Patrick?"

"No, sire. She would nae tell me."

"I know where she is," said the king softly, leaning across his oak desk. "She ran from ye so she might be Bothwell's whore! And Cousin Francis is so besotted by her that he has divorced Angus' daughter in order to wed Cat. But . . . he'll nae wed her! She will nae get her divorce!"

Patrick Leslie was stunned. He could hardly believe what the king was saying. And then in a clear and blinding flash, he remembered her saying so many times, "Francis is my friend. Nothing more."

"I am," continued the king, "arranging to lure Bothwell into Leith in a few days' time. The chances are favorable that Cat will be with him. I want ye there to take her home. If she repents her folly she may return to us at court."

"Sire! Cat no longer wants or loves me."

The king looked coldly at the Earl of Glenkirk. "I dinna care whether she loves ye or not. I want ye to take her back. And I want ye to make sure she stays wi ye. Ye may leave me, cousin. I hae work to do."

Patrick Leslie returned to his townhouse. Making himself comfortable in the library with a cheerful fire and a decanter of whisky, he sat down to think. She had fled to Bothwell, yet he was sure that she was not Francis Hepburn's mistress when she left him. That had obviously happened later, and now Bothwell was in love with her—enough in love to have divorced Margaret Douglas. But unless the cardinal gave her a divorce, Cat could not wed anyone else. Patrick didn't know whether to be happy or sad. He was expected to go to Leith on the king's command and kidnap his wife. After that, Lord Bothwell would undoubtedly come north with his men to retrieve her.

"Damn these Stewarts!" he said out loud. He was caught between them, and all because of his beautiful wife. Oh Cat, he thought wistfully. Three men want ye, but only one can have ye, and 'tis nae the one ye want. He wondered why she had not fled with her lover when she learned that her divorce petition was denied. But then he remembered what he knew about Bothwell. He was an honest man, and that would surely lead to his downfall. The king had little of honor or honesty.

The following day Patrick was summoned by Maitland's confidential secretary, who told him that Bothwell was expected in Leith in two days. He always quartered himself at the Golden Anchor Tavern on the waterfront. Lady Leslie would be with him.

Two days later, on the 18th of October, the Earl of Glenkirk waited in a private room at the Golden Anchor Tavern for the Earl of Bothwell's arrival. He had told the landlord that he was Bothwell's cousin, and had

come to meet with him. Since the landlord believed the
border lord's visit a secret, he assumed that anyone who
knew of it must have been so informed by Bothwell
himself.

The Earl of Glenkirk waited alone. He had no intention of forcing his wife to return to him. He knew he
was deliberately disobeying the king, but he had his
pride. In the quiet of the misty dawn he heard suddenly
the arrival of a party of horsemen in the yard below.
There were footsteps on the stairs, and the door to the
private parlor flew open. "Good morning, Cousin Francis," he drawled. "Come in and join me for breakfast."

Francis Hepburn was surprised, but then a slow smile
crossed his face. "Cousin Patrick, a good morrow to
ye," he answered, and accepted the tankard of ale
handed him.

The two men sat facing one another.

"Is Cat wi ye?"

"Nay. I left her at Hermitage. Something didna smell
right about this meeting."

"Aye," returned Patrick Leslie. " 'Tis a trap, but
ye've time yet."

"What are ye doing here, Glenkirk?"

"Cousin Jamie sent me to reclaim my wife."

"I'll nae gie her back," said Bothwell softly, and his
blue eyes glittered dangerously.

The two men looked at one another for a moment,
then Patrick said quietly, "I still love her, Francis, but
I know I've lost her. For God's sake, man, take her
away and be happy before James destroys ye both!"

"I must make my peace wi the king, Patrick. I want
Cat for my wife, and I want Hermitage for our children."

"Take her away, Francis. Once ye gave me that same
advice, and I heeded ye not. Then when I found the
king wi his hands all over my wife I lost first my temper
and then Cat. Dinna make the same mistake I did."

"I would never do to Cat what ye did. I know what she went through. She relived it in her sleep for weeks. Christ, man! Why didn't ye just kill her?"

"If I had, cousin, ye would not have known the happiness ye know now," he replied angrily.

"*Touché*," said Bothwell. He stood up. "Gie Maitland my regrets, Patrick. Tell him a pressing engagement." Francis Hepburn swung a leg over the window sill and grinned. "I'll go the back way for safety's sake. Take my horse, Valentine, home wi ye. I know ye'll keep him safe." Then he was gone.

When Maitland and the king's soldiers arrived a short time afterwards they found the Earl of Glenkirk finishing up a large breakfast.

"Where is he?" demanded the chancellor.

"A pressing engagement called him away," said Patrick Leslie, a small smile playing at the corners of his mouth.

"Your wife?"

"She was not with him, Maitland. Yer information was incorrect. Bothwell knew it was a trap, and left her safe at Hermitage."

"Ye dinna seem to mind that your wife plays Bothwell's whore," said Maitland venomously.

Glenkirk was at his throat before the words had died in the chancellor's mouth. One big hand held the chancellor tightly at the neck, the other held a dirk to his plump belly.

"Ye are close to death, *Master* Maitland." The chancellor's eyes bugged, terrified. "Did yer mother never teach ye, *Master* Maitland, not to talk ill of yer betters? Whatever the problems between my wife and myself, they stem from the king, as ye well know, *Master* Maitland." Glenkirk stressed the chancellor's lack of a title, which he knew was a sore point with the man. "Dinna think," the earl continued, "I dinna know that ye seek to complicate those problems in yer desire to destroy

Lord Bothwell and his influence, *Master* Maitland.
Well, I dinna gie a damn for yer politics! My only in-
terest is in seeing Catriona kept safe." He gave the
chancellor a shake. "Yer a fine statesman I've no doubt,
Master Maitland, but ye know nothing of human nature.
Ye took Cousin Jamie's lust for my wife and used it to
fan the fires of his envy of Bothwell. Had ye kept silent,
Francis and Cat would hae been married and gone from
Scotland." Maitland's eyes widened in surprise. "Aye,"
said Glenkirk. "They were willing to accept exile. Now,
ye fool, ye hae cornered them, and Christ, man! How
Bothwell is going to fight James to keep her! How many
lives and how much money will be spent in this war
between the crowned and the uncrowned king?" He
loosed the chancellor and pushed him away.

Maitland rubbed his throat, then spoke. "Ye love her
still, my lord. I do not have to be a student of human
nature to see that. How can ye let her go? Don't ye
want her back?"

"Aye, I want her back, but she doesn't want me. And
that, *Master* Maitland, is my fault. She loves Francis
Hepburn, and if that makes her happy, then I want her
to have him." He smiled sadly at the chancellor. "Ye
dinna understand that kind of thing, do ye, *Master*
Maitland? Ah, well. I'll nae try to explain." The earl
picked up his cloak. "By the way, Bothwell's horse is
below. I'm taking it home wi me. Home to Glenkirk,
and my bairns. Ye'll gie my regrets to the king." And
he walked from the room, his footsteps echoing in the
stairwell as he descended.

Francis Hepburn rode with all haste back to Hermitage Castle and Catriona Leslie. He was torn. If he
could just get to his cousin, the king. If James would
only restore his lands to his eldest son! If only the king
would allow the cardinal to give Cat her divorce, he
would promise to take her and leave Scotland. If James

understood their love, surely he would cooperate. If! If! If! But first the chancellor must be gotten out of the way. His was the dangerous influence.

But the autumn was too beautiful for much worrying. The days were deliciously warm, and faintly hazed in purple. Bothwell rode a new stallion—a great dark-gray brute called Sian, which means "storm" in the Gaelic tongue. Cat and her lover rode alone, much as they had in the early spring. Sandy Home had gone to his own estates.

They enjoyed being alone together. The servants at Hermitage sensed this, and behaved with exquisite tact. In the cold clear evenings when the stars seemed brighter and nearer the earth than ever before, the lovers sat before the fire. Sometimes they were silent, sometimes they talked of what they would do when the king relented and allowed them to wed. Sometimes they sang together while he accompanied them on a lute. His voice was a deep baritone, hers a lilting soprano. The sounds of their happiness spread throughout the castle, causing the servants to smile indulgently. Never had they seen Francis Hepburn so calm, so happy. And why not? Lady Leslie was a sweet, gentle lady who loved their earl with all her heart.

Just before Christmas, Francis Hepburn gave to his beloved the best of all possible gifts. On a cold, bright mid-December afternoon a coach rumbled up the drive to Hermitage. As Catriona and the earl stood waiting, the coach lurched to a stop, the door opened, and four passengers jumped out.

Cat gasped, and then flew down the steps to meet her four oldest children, who were running up the steps towards her. Kneeling, she opened her arms and gathered them to her. "Oh, my bairns! My beautiful, beautiful, bairns!" She said it over and over again, and her face was wet with her tears. Standing, her arms still around

the four children, she looked to Bothwell. He knew he
had done the right thing.

He moved slowly down the steps. "Welcome to Hermitage," he said to the four young Leslies.

"Thank ye, my lord earl," the fourteen-year-old heir
to Glenkirk spoke for them all. "We are grateful for the
chance to see our mother again."

"The last time I saw ye, Jamie, ye called me Uncle
Francis. Will ye do so again? Or perhaps, as ye are
nearly a man, ye would prefer to call me just Francis."

The boy looked from the earl to his mother. He was
confused. "Is my mother yer mistress?" he finally burst
out.

"Jamie!"

"Nay, my darling, scold not the lad." He turned to
young James Leslie. "Yes, lad. Yer mother is my mistress. She would be my wife but for the king, who is
angry wi me and withholds permission for her divorce.
If she had the divorce, we would have wed."

"Do ye no longer love our father?" asked nine-year-
old Bess.

"I love Lord Bothwell, Bess. Your father and I will,
however, remain friendly. Come now, my bairns! 'Tis
cold out here. Let us go inside the hall."

They brought the children into a comfortable chamber with a good fire, and the servants served watered
wine and sweet cakes.

"Let me look at all of ye," she said happily. "Oh,
Jamie! How ye have grown! Ye were nae taller than I
when I saw ye last."

"I'll be going to the University at Aberdeen next
autumn," he answered her proudly. "I will leave our
cousin of Rothes in spring when Robert goes to be a
page."

"I am so proud of ye," she told him, and he forgot
his dignity long enough to hug her.

Her gaze lingered on her two younger sons, Colin, seven, and Robbie, six. Colin was already in service with the Earl of Rothes, and had begun to acquire the polish of a little courtier. His younger brother, still at Glenkirk, was yet a rough little highlander.

"Why did not Amanda and Morag come?" Cat asked.

"They are too young," answered Robbie with great superiority.

Bess shot him a quelling look that was so reminiscent of her grandmother, Meg, that Cat had to laugh. "Lord, my dear! How much like Meg ye look. Yer going to be quite lovely in a few years' time."

Bess blushed most becomingly, and said, "Grandmother Meg said she couldna bear Christmas wi all of us gone, and she knew ye would understand if she kept Manda and Morag."

"I do understand, lovey, and I am so glad to see ye four! How long can ye stay?"

"Colie and I must be back at Rothes' Edinburgh house no later than the week after Twelfth Night," said Jamie. "Bess and Robbie may stay all winter."

"Bothwell, ye wretch! Why did ye nae tell me? We must hire a tutor! Bess and Robbie canna miss a whole winter of lessons."

He laughed. "If I had told ye, 'twould not hae been a surprise. As to a tutor, I'll instruct the bairns myself this winter."

Francis Hepburn adored having Cat's children at Hermitage, and a whole new side of his character was revealed. He loved children, and he was good with them. After the initial discomfort over their parents' marital situation, the young Leslies of Glenkirk relaxed and enjoyed both Hermitage and the earl. How sad, thought Cat, that Margaret Douglas had estranged his own children from their father.

And in the dark of night when he lay deep within her

he cried out, "Oh, my sweetest love! Gie me sons and daughters like Glenkirk's! Loving bairns of our own to raise in this new century that is coming."

She wanted to. Oh God, how she longed to have his child in her belly! Had she thought the king would relent if she became pregnant she would have done so, but knowing James' viciousness too well, she waited. The king was now using her against Bothwell, but if she and the earl became parents, their child would be the king's most valuable pawn. She was careful not to give him that pawn. But her heart ached, for she wanted Francis Hepburn's child desperately.

Chapter 30

❦❧

ON Christmas day, as the Hermitage residents sat at dinner, two messengers arrived wearing the badge of the Duke of Lennox. Bothwell left the festive board and closeted himself with the men for close to an hour. When he returned, he said softly to Cat, "I must go to Edinburgh early in the morning. Dinna tell the bairns. I would nae spoil their day."

He finished his meal, and then called to the Leslie boys, "Come on, lads! I promised we'd go curling. Cat, love, please see to Lennox's men. Bess, will ye come and cheer us on to great victories?"

Cat saw to it that the duke's men were well fed and were given warm beds for the night, and that their horses were taken care of. Then, gathering up her cloak, she went to the little pond in the woods by the castle where the earl and her sons were playing at curls. Even little Bess had a broom, and was dashing wildly about the ice, her dark-brown curls flying, her cheeks rosy, her hazel eyes sparkling. Catriona Leslie didn't know who was enjoying the day more, Bothwell or the children. He was very handsome in his kilts, teamed with Bess against the three boys. Cat cheered them all on, her heart bursting with happiness. This was what she had wanted above all—her children, and Francis Hepburn. For this brief moment, she had it.

After they had seen the children safely to bed that night, they sat together in her bedchamber in a large

chair before the fire. For a long time they said nothing.
He absently stroked her lovely hair, and finally said,
"Lennox says that Maitland seeks to have James put a
price on my head. Maitland is spending Christmas at
Holyrood wi their majesties. The turd! He tries to climb
high, does Master Maitland. I must go to Edinburgh
tomorrow and settle this thing once and for all. If I can
see our royal cousin perhaps I can convince him to
change his stubborn mind."

"See him when the queen is also present, Francis.
He dare not let her guess the real reason why he refuses
us. She is young, and she is soft-hearted. She will plead
our cause because she likes us both. If ye can but get
the king's signature on the divorce petition, my Uncle
Charles says that a representative of the cardinal waits
in Edinburgh to finish the transaction. One moment of
weakness on Jamie's part, and we will be free to wed
quickly before he can change his mind!"

Bothwell chuckled. "Are ye sure ye Leslies are nae
cousins to the Medici? Yer great schemers." His hands
began to wander, and she sighed contentedly. "Will ye
be back in time for New Year's?" she asked. His mouth
found the soft curve between her shoulder and her neck,
and he kissed it. "I don't know, Cat. If I canna get here,
the children's gifts are in my wardrobe, and your gift—"
He stopped. "Nay. I'll not tell ye, for I want to gie ye
yer present myself." He turned her so she faced him,
kissed her, and then stood her up. "Let's go to bed,
my darling."

Pushing the little ribbon straps from her shoulders,
she allowed her nightgown to slide to the floor. "Will
ye be gone very long, Bothwell?" She slipped into the
featherbed.

Taking his own robe off, he joined her and pulled
her close to him. "I'm nae sure how long I'll be gone,"
he said thickly as his desire for her rose.

Tears sprang to her eyes, but he kissed them away. And after their lovemaking she wept stormily in his arms.

"What is it ye do to me, Francis? Why is it ye can touch me as no one ever has before?"

"Do ye want to weep and shout all at once?" he asked. "I do! I think it has something to do wi loving each other." He kissed her tenderly. "Damn, I dinna want to leave ye, even for a few days!"

But he did, riding out before the sun was even up. She stood alone in the window of her bedchamber in the cold December dark, clutching her shawl to her breasts, and watched him go. She could still feel the hardness of his mouth on hers.

While she watched him riding away she prayed that the king would relent. James could not be so stubborn as to believe she would leave Francis Hepburn under any circumstances. Perhaps James had grown weary of fighting.

On the evening of December 27, Francis Hepburn, Alexander Home, about forty border chiefs, and their followers slipped through the Duke of Lennox's stables and gained entrance to Holyrood Palace. Their first objective was John Maitland. But as they rounded the corner of a badly lit passage, they startled a pageboy, who cried out in fright.

Maitland, hearing the shout and the tramp of many feet, withdrew into his inner chamber. Lennox gave orders for the door to be broken, but the Earl of Bothwell, Lord Home, and Hercules, with most of their men, passed on, trying to gain entry to the royal apartments.

Maitland lowered one of his servants out of a window and gave him orders to toll the common bell. When it rang the citizens of Edinburgh came running from their houses and hurried towards the palace.

Lord Home pulled at Francis Hepburn's arm. "Come on, man! The game's up!"

But Bothwell was desperate. "No! I must get to Jamie. Damn, Sandy! I promised Cat!"

Hercules used his giant size to yank his brother around. "Listen, ye besotted fool! What will happen to her if I haul ye home on a slab? Come on now, man! We'll try again another time." He dragged the protesting earl down the passage.

Cat was so delighted to have him safely back that her disappointment was less than Bothwell had expected. Bothwell, however, was angry. "I wanted to start the New Year knowing we could set a wedding date," he complained.

"Dinna fret, my love. By this time next year 'twill surely all be settled," she soothed him. Pulling his head down, she kissed him passionately. "They canna separate us now," she whispered fiercely. "We belong to each other."

On New Year's Day the Earl of Bothwell handed out gifts to his staff, tenants, and retainers. In the afternoon he was able to be alone with Cat and the children. Though they did their best to hide it, the young Leslies were as excited by the prospect of gifts as children anywhere.

Jamie could hardly believe that the young red stallion prancing in the courtyard was really his. "He's a son of my Valentine," smiled the earl. "I call him Cupid."

For Cat's daughter, Bess, there was a beautiful cloak of burgundy velvet trimmed in soft pale gray rabbit fur with a little gold clasp studded in rubies. Colin Leslie, the budding courtier, received a round gold clan badge for wearing with his plaid. The griffin on it had sapphire eyes. Robert Leslie was given a puppy, born ten weeks earlier to Bothwell's favorite Skye terrier bitch.

The children were ecstatic. Bess put on her cloak, Colin pinned his badge to his shoulder, Robert found a lead for his puppy, and they all ran down to the courtyard to see Jamie try out his new horse. Bothwell and Cat watched indulgently for a few moments, and then turned away from the windows.

He wordlessly handed her a flat box which she opened eagerly. Cat gasped. On a bed of white satin lay a heavy gold chain which held a round gold pendant. Upon the pendant was a great lion rampant within a royal tressure debruised by a diamond-stubbed ribbon. The lion had emeralds for eyes, and diamonds studded his waving mane.

"Do ye mind that I mark ye wi my beast?" he asked her.

"I am proud to wear the Hepburn lion," she answered him.

Lifting it from its box, she handed it to him. "Fasten it on for me, my lord." When he had done so she preened before the pier glass, then walked over to the table and picked up the one remaining box. She handed it to him. In it was a large round emerald ring set in gold and into which his seal had been cut. "Emeralds are for constancy," she said in a low voice. "But wait, my lord. I hae one other thing for ye," and reaching into the purse that hung from her waist she drew out a plain gold band.

He laughed softly. Reaching into his own pouch he drew out a similar ring, which he gave to her. Her eyes closed, and two tears slipped out. "Damn, Bothwell! I did want to be wed to ye soon. Damn James Stewart! I hate him so!"

He held her close. "Poor love," he said. " 'Tis harder for ye than it is for me. I am sorry our raid failed. If James weren't so stinking stingy the passageway would

hae been lit better and that bloody boy would nae hae
cried out."

She began to laugh. The thought that the king's
cheeseparing ways were responsible for her misery was
ludicrous. Quickly picking up her thoughts, Francis
laughed with her. Neither of them, however, laughed for
very long.

Early on the morning of the 11th of January an exhausted messenger galloped into Hermitage. The king
had personally penned a proclamation offering a reward
to any man who would kill the Earl of Bothwell.

They were shocked, for they could not believe James
would do such a thing. Maitland had, according to the
messenger, frightened the king badly after the raid of
December 27, and had convinced James that his cousin
wished to kill him and rule in his place. After all, did
they not call Bothwell the uncrowned king? If the king
were prudent, he would kill Bothwell before Bothwell
killed him.

Francis Hepburn got on his horse and rode directly
to the capital. He wished to try to settle the matter with
his cousin, in person. He was forced to retreat to Hermitage when the king rode out after him with a large
troup of soldiers. James forced his horse into a bog in
pursuit of Bothwell and then nearly drowned. This
didn't help matters. Again there was talk of witchcraft.

The next three months saw a forced peace between
the king and his cousin, brought on by the advent of
severe winter weather. The roads were closed by heavy
snows throughout Scotland. Cat could not have been
more pleased. Though Jamie and Colin had returned to
Rothes, Bess and Robbie remained. Cat could pretend
during those precious months that they were a normal
family. Bess, her father's pet, was more reserved with
Francis than Cat would have wished, but Bothwell
understood, and treated the little girl with grave respect.

"We'll hae a wee lass of our own someday," he whispered softly to his mistress.

The young Robbie adored Francis Hepburn. The fourth of Cat's children, with two girls after him, he was truly a middle child. No one had ever had a great deal of time for Robbie, but that winter the great Earl of Bothwell found the time. In this six-and-a-half-year-old boy he found a quick, inquiring mind, and an ability to recall the smallest fact. Delighted, Bothwell taught him a great deal. Bess frequently joined them, particularly when they studied languages.

Bothwell and Catriona had been together a year now, and he could not believe that in twelve short months his life had changed so much for the better. Though he was involved in a life-and-death struggle with the king, Bothwell was sure that if he could see James and talk to him, he would be able to make him understand. When the warm weather came he would try again to get to the king.

In early April the roads opened again, and the earl and Cat escorted Bess and Robbie Leslie to Dundee, where Conall More-Leslie waited to return them to Glenkirk.

"Will ye never return to Glenkirk, mother?" asked Bess.

Cat put an arm around her eldest daughter. "Now, Bess, ye know that as soon as my divorce petition is granted I will marry wi Lord Bothwell, and live at Hermitage. Ye like Hermitage, don't ye?"

The girl nodded slowly, adding quickly, "But I love Glenkirk best of all! If ye marry Uncle Francis, who will be my father?"

Catriona Leslie saw once again how her divorce from Glenkirk would affect their children. Still, she thought, I hae been a good mother, and I will be a better one wed wi the man I love.

She bent and kissed the top of Bess's dark head. " 'Tis a silly question ye ask, Bess. Patrick Leslie is yer father. He always will be. Naught can change that. Francis will be yer stepfather."

"Will we live wi ye?"

"Aye, lovely."

"And who will live wi father?"

"Lord, Bess! Yer grandmother is at Glenkirk, and yer Uncle Adam and Aunt Fiona come often. Then too, yer father might find another wife someday."

"I think I would prefer to stay wi father," said Bess quietly. "He will be lonely wi'out bairns about him. Jamie and Colin are already gone, and Robbie goes in a short time. If ye take Manda and Morag from Glenkirk, father will hae no one. Unless I stay."

Cat gritted her teeth. Bess showed Leslie traits at the damnedest times. "Let us talk about it another time, lovey," she said.

Bess looked levelly at her mother and said, "As ye wish, madame," and Cat had the feeling she had lost the battle.

Conall met them on time, and was surly almost to the point of rudeness. She spoke sharply to him. "Dinna choose sides in a battle ye know naught about, Conall." He reddened. "How is Ellie?"

"Well enough. She misses ye, my lady."

"Tell her when this business is settled I would like her to come to Hermitage wi me. I miss her too."

"I'll tell her, my lady."

"Go carefully wi my bairns," she said to him. Turning slowly, she rode back to where Bothwell awaited her.

Conall had to admit that the border lord on his gray stallion, and Lady Leslie on her golden-bay gelding, made a handsome couple. He felt a kind of sadness as they raised their hands to the bairns in a gesture of farewell, and then turned and rode off.

Chapter 31

❧❧ ❧❧

WHEN the king learned that Bothwell was in the north, he left Edinburgh for Dundee. But by the time he arrived, the earl had already returned south to the borders with Cat. Francis Hepburn hoped that by remaining quiet and unassuming he could calm his nervous royal cousin. James, however, egged on by Maitland and constantly waylaid by either the Earl of Angus or his daughter—both lobbying for the return of Bothwell's possessions to the earl's heir—felt he was constantly assailed by Francis Hepburn.

When the parliament met on May 29, the king denounced the Earl of Bothwell, claiming he aspired to the throne and stating that he had no right to that throne. They might both be grandsons of James V, but Bothwell's line was the bastard one. Then the king proceeded to have his parliament ratify the sentence of forfeiture against his cousin.

Francis Hepburn was honestly astounded. He and Jamie had always rubbed each other, but he had tried hard to avoid an open confrontation with the king. That James could accuse him of wanting the throne was laughable. Of all the things he wanted in the world, the kingship of any land was the last on his list. However, he understood what his cousin was really up to. James was asking for support without doing so in plain words.

Had the nobility known that the king simply wanted

their support, they might have given it to him. But they saw John Maitland behind everything James did, and the nobility of Scotland hated Maitland. Consequently, they all but shouted their support of Francis Hepburn and their defiance of the king.

"He wants to destroy ye," said Cat. "Is there no kindness in him? All we ask is to wed and live in peace wi him."

"Maitland wants to make an example of me, Cat, and the fact that Jamie wants ye back in his bed doesna help matters."

"Would it help ye if I returned to him? I would sooner die than hae him touch me again, but if he would restore to ye yer possessions I would do it for ye, my love."

Roughly he pulled her to him. "I would strangle ye, lass, before I would ever let any man touch ye! I'll nae let ye go! Christ, my darling, the very thought of my royal cousin wi ye infuriates me!"

"But I dinna want to be responsible for hurting ye, Francis. Oh, my love! Take me away! Please take me away before it is too late!"

"Gie me a bit more time, my love. Let me try to make my peace wi Jamie."

Frightened, she clung to him, and like a cornered animal she felt a net closing about them. Then she quickly shook it off. He needed strength now, not a weak and weeping woman.

Word came that the king was at his palace of Falklands. Bothwell and his supporters rode forth, and Catriona Leslie rode with them. Between the hours of one and two a.m. on the morning of June 20, 1592, they surrounded Falklands. Unfortunately James had been warned in time by the watch, and he retired with the queen to a fortified tower. By seven a.m. the local country people were streaming to Falklands to see what

the matter was. Bothwell and his company were forced
to retire. They did so to the cheers of the locals, who
had recognized the border lord.

On July 2, a proclamation was issued for the raising
of a levy to pursue the Earl of Bothwell. The proclamation was pointedly ignored by one and all. James retired
to Dalkeith for the remainder of the summer. On August
1, the lairds of Logie and Burley smuggled Bothwell
into the palace in hopes of getting him into the king's
presence so he might publicly ask for royal pardon.

It had been decided that the queen's antechamber
would be the ideal place for the earl to catch the king.
James must pass through it on his way to his wife's
bedroom. Francis Hepburn knelt before his queen. He
took her extended hand, kissed it, and then turned it
over and kissed the palm.

"Rogue!" laughed the queen, snatching her hand
away. But her face was flushed and her heart beat
quicker.

Bothwell grinned up at her and rose to his feet.
"Thank ye, madame, for letting me wait for Jamie here.
I must make peace wi him. And too, he must allow the
cardinal to gie my lass her divorce so we may wed.
Catriona has always been a loyal servant of yer majesty,
and it hurts her too when Jamie punishes me."

"You love her very much, don't you, Francis?"

"Madame, I hae *never* known such happiness or such
peace since Cat came into my life. If only I were reconciled wi James. All we ask, yer majesty, is to live quietly
at Hermitage. We would even live abroad if it were the
king's pleasure. I ask only to retain Hermitage for any
bairns Cat will gie me. Our children must nae forget that
they are Scots, and loyal subjects of James Stewart—as
Cat and I are."

The queen was obviously touched by this speech. "I
will plead your case, cousin. James is not thinking

clearly at all. Master Maitland confuses him." She sat down and patted the space to her left. He sat next to her. "Beatrice," she said to Lady Ruthven. "Please watch for the king, and see we have plenty of warning." She looked to her other ladies. "The rest of you may make yourselves useful with your embroidery, or music. I wish to talk to the earl privately." The ladies of the queen's bedchamber settled themselves across the room from the windowseat where the queen and Bothwell sat conversing.

"Now, tell me, Cousin Francis, how did this great romance with the Countess of Glenkirk begin? I thought she truly loved her husband."

Carefully, he told her the story he had concocted when anticipating her question. "Cat and I became friends before yer majesty came to Scotland. Glenkirk and I are distant cousins. Did ye know his mother is a Stewart? I have always liked Cat. She is an educated woman, and I enjoyed being wi her. Never did anything improper occur between us in those early days. But as time went on, yer grace, I found that I was falling in love wi her. I fought my feelings, for I knew that she was no loose woman. Imagine my surprise to discover she was fighting the same feelings! Finally we could fight our emotions no longer. We love each other," he finished simply.

The queen's eyes were bright with unshed tears. "What of poor Glenkirk?"

"He loves her too, but is resigned to letting her go."

"Perhaps," said the queen, looking towards Christina Anders, "the earl might remarry. Mistress Anders' husband has recently expired from measles, and she is widowed again."

Bothwell did not think Patrick Leslie would marry Christina Anders, but he needed the queen's support, so he nodded affably and said, "Very possibly. But first he must be free, and the king will nae allow the Cardinal of St. Andrew's permission to sign the petition of divorce."

"I will help you, Francis," said the queen.

At this point Lady Ruthven returned white-faced. "Your grace. His majesty is in the corridor outside. He asks me to tell ye that he has learned the Earl of Bothwell is somewhere in the palace. He says he will punish *anyone* who tries to introduce the earl into his presence."

Francis Hepburn stood up. "Damn!" he said. And then turning to the queen he asked, "Is there another way I can leave?"

The queen led the way into her bedroom and, opening a small unobtrusive door, revealed a narrow staircase. "My tiring women use this. Follow it all the way to the bottom. It exits in the servant's courtyard."

He kissed her hand again in farewell. "Thank ye, madame, and God bless ye for yer help."

She smiled prettily at him. "I won't forget, Francis. Go with God."

The queen closed the door and returned to her antechamber. She picked up her embroidery. "Beatrice, go and ask the king if he intends standing in the corridor all night."

The queen's ladies giggled, and Anna bit her lip to keep from laughing as James entered her rooms with his guards. They rushed into her bedchamber, poking under the bed and behind the draperies with their pikes.

"Come, sire! What is the meaning of this?" demanded the queen.

"Bothwell is in the palace, Annie!"

The young queen drew herself up. "Well, sire! He is certainly not in my bedchamber. Or is this some new slander of Master Maitland's? First he alleges that the bonnie Earl of Moray is my lover . . . does he now say 'tis Bothwell?" She turned to her attendants. "Fling open the wardrobes, ladies, so the king may see we hide no earls!" She turned back to the king. "When ye have finished with this foolishness, please take your men and leave me. All this uproar has given me a terrible headache."

Disappointed, the king retired to his empty bed. Equally disappointed, Bothwell returned to Hermitage. He again set himself to living quietly, in hope of allaying the king's fears and calming his anger.

In October the king mounted a small expedition into the borders. Bothwell and Cat immediately left Hermitage for their secret and well-hidden hunting lodge. Hermitage Castle stood open to the king, who could not, under these circumstances, complain of his cousin's disobedience.

The king returned to Edinburgh only to be waylaid again by Lady Margaret Douglas. She had chosen to catch him publicly, in front of the gates of Edinburgh Castle, crying for mercy upon her and her children. In God's name she begged the return of Bothwell's property for her innocent children.

James was furious at having been placed in such an embarrassing position, and in public. He forbade the lady to enter his presence again. "I dinna know how Francis stood her as long as he did," said the king to his wife. "She doesna care for him—just his estates!"

This was the opening that Anna had been waiting for. "They were not happy, Jamie?" she inquired innocently.

" 'Twas a political thing. He's well rid of her."

"In that case, my love, why will ye not allow the cardinal to give Lady Leslie her divorce? Bothwell is deeply in love with her."

The king was startled. He had not been aware that his frivolous little queen knew of Bothwell's involvement with Catriona Leslie. He wondered nervously what else she knew, and decided to move cautiously. "Lady Leslie is nae a girl, Annie. She is the mother of six bairns. She is behaving like an infatuated maid, and must be brought to her senses."

"But Jamie! Glenkirk is willing to let her go, and now that my dearest Christina is widowed—oh, Jamie! 'Twould be so wonderful if Christina could be Glenkirk's wife. Then my little goddaughter, Anne Fitz-Leslie, could be brought up properly."

"My dear Annie, the Leslies hae been wed for fourteen years. I canna allow them to dissolve their marriage on a whim. 'Twould set a bad example for the court. There must be more morality in our court. If I allow the Leslies to divorce, then every man who becomes infatuated wi another woman will want to divorce his wife, and every man's mistress will expect her lover to wed wi her."

The queen thought that the king was making a great deal more of the matter than was warranted, and she felt that if he wished to reform the court he might do better by way of example than refuse a divorce for a couple who wished to marry. These people did not want to sin. However, she could argue no further with him at this time. She was disappointed, for she liked Francis and would have enjoyed helping him.

On New Year's Day, 1593, the Earl of Bothwell appealed to the kirk for aid, begging them not to despise him on account of the king's anger. He needed their help, but the kirk ignored him. The old Queen of England, however, did not. She saw to it that the border lord was financially comfortable. England offered money, and sanctuary if he should need it.

Elizabeth Tudor did not like James Stewart. He was her logical heir (though she had not named him officially yet) but she thought him a mealy-mouthed hypocrite. He was shifty, saying one thing and doing another.

She could not understand this sudden relentless pursuit of Francis Stewart-Hepburn. To the best of her knowledge, the Earl of Bothwell had always been loyal to the Scots crown.

Elizabeth chuckled. Bothwell had visited her court some years back. He had been young, but damn! He was a brilliant and elegant rogue even then. There was more to this than met the eye, yet her spies could come up with no explanation. So, because it pleased her to be perverse and to thwart James, and because she had always had a weakness for charming rogues, she lent her support to the border lord.

Again the winter closed in around them, and Cat was relieved. They kept Twelfth Night revels at Hermitage for the neighboring gentry. Though she was not Bothwell's wife, she was treated as such by the local lairds and their ladies. They had no patience with the king's unkindness towards their hero and his lady.

Cat had not seen her oldest children in almost a year. It was simply too dangerous for them to come now. She barely knew the two youngest ones, and sadly wondered if they remembered her at all.

Bothwell missed the children too. Catriona Leslie had the knack for making family life a warm and happy thing. Bothwell found it restful. And until they could marry, they dared not have a child of their own.

As the winter deepened Cat became increasingly eager to go to France, and finally he agreed that if, by the end of the year, he had not settled things with his cousin, they would leave Scotland.

Chapter 32

❧ ❦ ❧

WHEN James Stewart learned that his cousin the Queen of England was financing his cousin the Earl of Bothwell he sent word to Sir Robert Melville, his ambassador in England, to persuade Elizabeth to cease. Publicly exposed, she had no choice but to agree. Francis Hepburn was now in danger on both sides of the border. But worse was to come.

On July 21, 1593, sentence of forfeiture was again passed against Francis Stewart-Hepburn, the fifth Earl of Bothwell. But this time his arms were riven asunder at the Mercat cross in Edinburgh. Shocked, the Duke of Lennox and other noblemen determined to help Bothwell. If Maitland could turn the king against his own blood, what could happen to them?

Bothwell, accompanied only by his half-brother, rode for the capital. His borderers slipped into the city by twos and threes until Edinburgh had discreetly swelled with them. Catriona Leslie had been left behind at Hermitage.

"What will happen?" she had begged him.

"I dinna know. If I can get to James I must convince him to restore my lands, which I hae given to my heir. And I will force him, if necessary, to allow the cardinal to grant yer petition of divorce. Then, love, we'll be safe."

"And if ye canna reach him, Francis?"

"Then, my darling, we're for France. Let Angus fight the battle for his grandchildren."

She clung to him, her mouth inviting his kisses, her body soft and yielding. Accepting the invitation, he made passionate love to her, then slept for several hours, cradling her in his arms. When she awoke he was gone, and she was frightened.

Early on the morning of July 24, 1593, James Stewart awoke to the faint gray light of early dawn. The air felt damp, and he wondered if it were raining. He heard a faint noise, a chair scraping the floor. "Barra, laddie? Is it you?" he called. There was no answer. The king's heart began to pound violently against his ribs and his nightshirt became soaked in cold sweat. Ever so slowly, he turned and peered out of the bed curtains.

"Good morning, Jamie," drawled Francis Stewart-Hepburn.

The king screamed. Scrambling to the other side of the bed, he leaped out and quickly turned the handle of the queen's bedroom door. It would not give. James turned to face his antagonist, pressing his back to the queen's door as though he could press himself through it. For a moment the cousins stared at each other—the one disheveled and frightened in a damp silk nightshirt, the other calm and assured in his red plaid kilt, his sword drawn.

Slowly Bothwell closed the space between them. The king was shaking. Francis Hepburn's blue eyes narrowed. Catching his cousin's face between his thumb and his forefinger, he growled, "Lo, now, my fine bairn. Ye that hae said I sought yer life . . . look how I hold it in my hand!"

The king swayed as if he would faint.

"Christ, Jamie! I'm nae here to kill ye," said Bothwell impatiently. "Pull yerself together!"

James' eyes rolled in his head, and he looked wildly

at the earl. "Ye'll nae get my soul, Francis! Kill me if ye will, but ye'll nae get my soul!"

"Jesu!" exploded Bothwell. "What in God's name would I want wi yer soul, Jamie? I've but come to straighten this matter out between us. I dinna want yer life, yer soul, yer crown, or yer bloody kingdom, Jamie. I simply want my lands back for my heir and I want Cat Leslie for my wife. Gie me those things, and yer quit Bothwell forever if ye choose!"

"Maitland says ye want to kill me," said the king.

"Maitland is a puddock stool!" replied Bothwell.

The king laughed in spite of his fear. The border lord reached out and picked up the king's robe. "Put it on, Jamie. Ye look chilled." Drawing the king from the queen's door, he helped him into the warm garment. Then, pouring a dram of whisky, he made James drink. Color began to flow back into the king's face. Seeing this, Bothwell knelt before him and offered the hilt of his sword to his sovereign.

This simple act seemed to calm and even embarrass the king. "Oh get up, Francis, and put yer sword away."

The earl complied and, rising, threw some wood on the fire. With the king's permission, the two men sat facing one another.

"I suppose," said the king resignedly, "that my palace is full of yer men."

"Aye," grinned Bothwell ruefully. "And Lennox's men, and Angus' men, and Home's, and Colville's, and Logie's, and Burley's, and Huntley's. I'm nae a fool to come calling on ye, cousin, wi'out a few friends."

"They stand by ye as they hae never stood by me."

"Only because of Maitland, Jamie. Maitland wants to take away their rights. He is using me as a test, and they know that if I fall they are all in danger of falling. Their loyalty is to themselves."

"And where is yer loyalty, Francis?"

"Like theirs . . . first to myself and my own."

"Yer honest, Francis."

"I hae always been honest wi ye, Jamie, my bairn.
Now, 'tis time for ye to be honest wi me. I know ye'll
be fair about my lands. They rightfully belong to Margaret's boy."

"Not yer boy also, Francis?"

"I fathered him, Jamie, but he's never been mine.
None of them have. They're all Margaret's, and they're
Angus', but nae mine. That's why Cat is so important.
She is mine, and when we hae bairns, they'll be *ours*."

"No, Francis, they'll be bastards, for I'll nae gie my
permission for ye to wed wi Catriona Leslie."

For a few moments the room was very quiet, then
Bothwell said, "Why, Jamie?"

"Ye hae been honest wi me, cousin, so I will be
honest wi ye. If I canna hae Cat, then ye canna hae Cat."

"My God, James, do ye hate me so much? Ye've
taken everything I own, and riven my arms at Edinburgh
cross. I hae one thing left in this world. A wench. A
green-eyed wench that I love above all things. If I died
tomorrow she would nae come back to ye. What hae I
done to deserve this unkindness from ye? Is this how
ye repay my loyalty to ye?"

"She loves ye," said the king quietly. " 'Tis that I
canna forgie her for, Francis. I lay between her silken
thighs, but she gave me nothing of herself. I fucked her,
and her lovely body responded as I have never known
a woman to respond. But she gave me nothing for her
love, and since her no woman has been able to satisfy
me, including that sweet little featherhead I am wed to.
But to ye, cousin, Cat has shown her face of love. She
has defied convention, and both kirks of Scotland, to
be by yer side. She, who adored her bairns, has nae
seen them in several years for love of ye. I outlawed ye,
and took all from ye, yet she stayed wi ye. I can forgie

neither of ye yer love, Francis. I cannot command her to love me, but I can command her not to wed wi ye, and I can see she obeys that command."

"Christ, man! Hae ye no heart?"

"Love," said the king, "I dinna understand the word. No one has ever loved me, nor hae I ever loved anyone except Cat. At least I think that is the feeling I hae for her. I am nae certain, having had verra little experience with love."

"The queen loves ye, James, and I thought ye loved her."

"Annie doesna love me, Francis. Lord, man! We hae nothing in common, except perhaps we will soon. She is pregnant, and will deliver a child this winter. However, she does enjoy being queen."

The Earl of Bothwell looked carefully at his royal cousin. "In all the years we hae known each other, Jamie, I hae asked ye for little. Now, however—" and at this point Bothwell knelt on both knees before the king—"I beg ye, cousin! I beg ye to let me wed wi Cat. We will leave Scotland, and live quietly wherever ye say. In Christ's name, dinna take her from me!"

For the first time in all his life James had the advantage of his Cousin Francis. The border lord was at his mercy. In was too delicious, and the king could barely contain his excitement. Never had Francis exhibited a weakness of any sort, yet now he knelt and begged . . . and for a woman! A mere woman! No. Not a mere woman. An extraordinary woman. But Francis Hepburn was an extraordinary man, and they really did belong together. It was most unfortunate that he, James, did not choose to allow it. He looked down at his cousin. "Get up, Bothwell." The earl stood. "They call ye the uncrowned King of Scotland, Francis, and I know that Cat is yer chosen mate. Unfortunately it is a rule of royalty that kings and queens are nae ever happy in

love. I see no reason why ye and Cat should be. If ye
crawled from here to hell and back on yer hands and
knees I should not change my mind. I will see that yer
lands and yer honors are returned. They will remain
yers to do with as ye please as long as ye remain at
peace wi me. But on September first, I want Catriona
Leslie here in Edinburgh, to return to her husband."

"Go to hell, Jamie!" said Bothwell. "She'll nae return
to Patrick Leslie, and I'll nae let her."

"She will return to him, Francis, because if she does
not, I will have Maitland find a way that will allow me
to confiscate the lands and goods of not only the Leslies
of Glenkirk, but the Leslies of Sithean, and even of
Cat's own family, the Hays of Greyhaven. Ye know that
Cat will nae allow three branches of her family to be
destroyed! And our good Patrick will take her back for
the same reason. As for ye, my reckless cousin, if ye try
to defy me . . ." The king let it dangle, and Bothwell for
the first time in his life felt the bitter taste of defeat.
"There, Francis," said the king soothingly. "I hae given
ye plenty of time to say yer goodbyes. I could hae said
she must be back wi'in a week. Ye hae over a month."
He smiled in kindly fashion at his handsome cousin. "It
should add spice to yer relationship to see how many
times ye can fuck her in one month."

Bothwell clenched his fists. "I will call the others to
come in now. If I don't, I may give in to the urge to
commit regicide. Yer a bastard, James. Ye dinna know
what love is, and ye never will. 'Twill be a lonely life
for ye, cousin, and in yer old age—for we Stewarts are
inclined to longevity if we avoid wars—ye will have no
memories to warm ye in the dark nights. I am sorry for
ye, Jamie. Ye hae a mean spirit, and ye will always have
to live with yerself."

Before the discomfited king could reply his chamber
was filled with the great lords of the land. Seeing them
all massed together, James became nervous again. Both-

well offered to leave, but the others would not allow it until the king had agreed to publicly pass an act of condonation and remission in Bothwell's favor. The Earl of Angus was delighted. His grandchildren would be well taken care of, and Margaret could leave his house now.

Bothwell left for Lord Home's Edinburgh house. He was sick at heart. He knew there was no way for him to win this battle. Home offered his friend a bed, a bottle, and a sympathetic ear. There was nothing else he could do.

A short distance away at Glenkirk House, Patrick Leslie suffered a similar agony. He had just returned from Holyrood, where the king had told him privately that his wife would be returned to him on September 1. That she was being forced to return bothered James not at all, but it bothered Patrick Leslie. His wife, whom he still loved, was in love with another man. She had lived with this man for two and a half years while trying desperately to divorce Glenkirk. He had resigned himself to losing her because he did not believe he deserved her any longer. Patrick Leslie didn't know if his wife could take this forced reunion. He wasn't sure he could. He was tired, and he was a mass of conflicting emotions. He sat alone in his library, and as the afternoon progressed he drank a great deal of whisky. As evening drew in he fell asleep.

When at midevening he awoke it was to find the Earl of Bothwell sitting across from him. Glenkirk moved to rise. "Easy, Cousin Patrick," said Francis Hepburn softly. "I've only come to talk." Glenkirk, eyeing the elegant silver and mother-of-pearl pistol in Bothwell's hand, sat back carefully.

"I am riding back to Hermitage tonight," said the border lord. "I dinna know how I can tell Cat of the king's order, but first I must know that ye'll be kind to her."

"Christ, man! I love her too!"

They sat in silence for a few minutes. Then Bothwell spoke again. "It wasn't until ye and Jamie had at her, Patrick. Ye know that, don't ye? Even when the king forced her, she was faithful to ye in her heart."

"I know that now," said Patrick Leslie. "But tell me, Francis, why did she go to ye if there was nothing between ye?"

Bothwell smiled softly with remembrance. "We were friends, Patrick. I know that is a hard thing to understand, but when the first excitement of court wore off she found she was bored. She really was the Virtuous Countess. Sexual games were not for her. Neither was gossip. She's far too educated for a woman, and for our times. I understand that because I am also too educated for the times. God! How we talked! And how she listened! All the questions she asked! So, when she was hurt and frightened, she wanted to go where no one would find her. Since I was her only friend she came to me."

Again the silence, and then Patrick Leslie asked quietly, "When did she become yer mistress, Francis?"

"Not for a while," Bothwell answered in an equally quiet voice. He did not think that Patrick Leslie was entitled to detail. "It happened, cousin. It simply happened. Christ! What a coil." He leaned forward and spoke urgently. "Take her back to Glenkirk as quickly as ye can. She is nae going to be easy in this, but perhaps being wi her bairns will help."

The two men sat in silence for some time. Patrick rose quietly and added wood to the fire. Going to the cabinet, he took out another crystal glass and poured himself and Bothwell a good dram each of the potent whisky.

The pistol now lay in Hepburn's lap. Leaning forward once more, the whisky in his two hands, Francis said, "I love her, Patrick. I want ye to understand that. She wanted to go to France for her divorce, and I promised her we would if I failed to see Jamie this time. Now I wish to heaven I had not seen him! I return Cat to ye because I would nae have the destruction of yer family on my conscience. But if I ever hear that ye hae been cruel to her, I'll come. If it be from darkest hell, I'll come and take her back!"

It was with great shock that Patrick Leslie saw the naked pain in the deep-blue eyes of his cousin, the Earl of Bothwell. He, the husband, wanted to sympathize with his wife's lover. But he intuitively understood that if he so much as touched his cousin, the big man would lose control.

"Francis," said Glenkirk in a kindly voice. "I hae always loved her, from the time we were betrothed when she was a wee lass of four. I think she loved me because she was expected to love me, and she nae knew any others. I had known many women, and I appreciated the jewel that Mam had ordained would be mine. Had I not lost my temper two and a half years ago she would hae gone on loving me, but I did, and ye were wise enough to see her worth. Ye took what I so carelessly threw away. James has ordained that we be unhappy because he is unhappy. If he really loved Cat he would want her happy wi ye, as I do. Instead he forces her back on me. I swear to ye, man, that I will cherish her this time. She may never love me again, but this time I will keep her safe!"

Bothwell closed his eyes for a moment as if forcing back tears. When he spoke his voice was low and husky. "Ye must make love to her, Patrick. Dinna be polite wi her, and wait for her to recover her hurt. If ye do, ye'll never get her in yer bed again. We are so tied together, Cat and I—but ye can ease her pain if ye love her a bit. But, for pity's sake, man! Be gentle wi her. She is nae a castle wall to be breached. Treat her tenderly, and ye'll find she responds better." Glenkirk flushed, but

Bothwell did not notice, and stood up. "One more thing, Patrick. Before I leave Scotland I will want to see her."

"Leave?" said Glenkirk, puzzled. "Is Jamie going to banish ye?"

"Nay. He is too subtle for that, but we canna seem to live in the same country, the kingly bairn and I. Besides . . . he is not given to keeping his word. Before long he will start to haggle over the terms made today, and our good John Maitland will egg him on to new follies. James is determined to be king, Patrick. Make no mistake about that. The old way of life is done here in Scotland. Lennox, Angus, and the others use me to fight Jamie. Dinna think I don't know that. After the next round I will have to go, and I know it. 'Tis only a matter of time for me. But before I go I would bid my Cat a final farewell if she'll see me. Promise me ye'll forbid her not."

"God, Francis! Ye ask a lot of me!"

Bothwell's blue eyes became hard. "Hear me, Patrick Leslie. I could leave this room now, ride to Hermitage, tell Cat I couldna see Jamie, and be on a ship for France by week's end. By the time any news got to her she'd hae her divorce from the obliging French, be safely wed to me, and we'd hae a bairn started. Yer family would lose everything. Who is asking a lot of whom?"

Glenkirk cocked an eyebrow. "If, Francis, I actually thought ye'd do that I'd kill ye now," he said pleasantly. "However, like me, yer a man of honor. When ye go, Cat will see ye if she wishes." He stood, and held out his hand to his cousin.

Bothwell grasped it. For a moment their eyes locked. Then Francis Hepburn exited the room the same way he had entered it, through the casement windows. Patrick Leslie was inexplicably saddened.

Chapter 33

❦❦❦

BOTHWELL rode through the night and into the following morning, arriving at Hermitage towards midday. One look at his face told Cat the news was bad, but she asked nothing of him. Instead she led him to their apartments, pulled off his boots, and put him to bed. When Bothwell awoke that evening, she had a good supper ready for him. It wasn't until he had eaten that he spoke to her.

"The king has ordered yer return to Glenkirk by September first."

She whirled to face him, her eyes mirroring shock.

"If ye do not," he continued, "Jamie will reclaim the lands and goods of the Leslies of both Glenkirk and Sithean, as well as the Hays of Greyhaven."

"Let him!"

"Cat!"

"Let him, Bothwell! Wi'out ye I am a dead woman!"

He held her tightly in his arms. "Cat! Cat! Think, lass. Think! How many children hae ye?"

"Six."

"And among yer cousins, how many bairns are there now?"

"At least thirty," she said.

"And ye hae twenty cousins, and yer brothers, and yer parents' generation, and the More-Leslies. My God, Cat! Close to a hundred people! And then, my darling,

we have my children to consider too. All these innocent
people destroyed—the children and the old people. Nay,
love. Neither ye nor I could build a life on the wreckage
of both our families."

"Dinna send me away, Bothwell," she whispered
piteously. "I would sooner be dead."

"If we run, if we attempt to escape Jamie in any
manner, he will destroy our people. He was quite firm
wi me. He wants us punished, and he has found the most
exquiste torture to inflict upon us and on Patrick Leslie
as well. He still loves ye, Cat. Dinna be afraid to return
to him."

She looked up at him. "How can ye talk to me like
this, Francis?"

"Because I must! Christ, Cat! I canna bear it!" His
voice was breaking. "Yer my life, lass!"

They wept. The border lord and his love clung to
one another and wept until they could weep no more.
Then they stood together, holding onto each other until
Francis Hepburn swept her up in his arms and carried
Catriona Leslie to bed.

In the night she awoke to find him gone from their
bed. For a moment she was frightened until she saw him
standing by the windows looking out on the moonlit
landscape. He turned and she could see his face was wet
with tears. She pretended sleep, realizing it would only
add to his agony if he knew she had seen him. A dull
pain throbbed in her chest, and she stuffed her fist into
her mouth to stifle the cry that rose in her throat.

For the next few days neither Bothwell nor Cat could
bear to be out of each other's sight for more than a few
minutes. Knowing that only a month remained to them
was, as the king had anticipated, a terrible torment. It
was finally Cat who made the decision that was to ease
them through their last weeks.

"I want to go to the lodge," she told him. "I came to ye there. If I must leave ye, 'twill be from there."

He had already told her that the king had forbidden him to come within ten miles of Edinburgh, and he was expressly forbidden to accompany the Countess of Glenkirk from the borders. She would be escorted by Lord Home.

Bothwell sent his servants up into the Cheviot to clean, freshen, and stock the house. They would live as they had lived in the beginning—alone, to themselves. On the day they rode out from Hermitage together for the last time, they had three weeks left. They had not bidden the servants goodbye, for neither of them could have borne an emotional scene. Hercules would welcome Lord Home when he arrived to take charge of Cat, and would bring him to a meeting place.

It was late summer, and already the evenings were cool. They spent their days riding, walking, sitting silently on a hidden promontory that overlooked the border valleys, watching the eagles soar off into the west wind. Their nights were spent in a rapture of lovemaking such as neither of them had ever known, made bittersweet by the knowledge that they would soon be parted.

One morning she came downstairs to find him just entering the house. "Look, Cat," he said, holding up a fish. "I've caught a salmon, and I've found some late cress."

Cat burst into tears, remembering that on her first day in this house with him he had said almost the same words to her. As the realization came to Bothwell he swore, and then he swore again, for today was their last day. Managing to control herself at last, she looked at him through wet lashes. "And I suppose that smell from the kitchen is lamb broth?"

He nodded. She couldn't help but laugh, so doleful was his expression.

"Clean yer fish, Bothwell," she said lightly, "but I dinna want to eat it till late. What kind of a day is it?"

"Warm. I found a field full of Michaelmas daisies near the stream. "Let's go swimming!"

Her green eyes sparkled. "And will ye make love to me in the daisies afterwards?" she teased.

"Aye," he answered her slowly, his own blue eyes quietly serious.

She flung herself onto his chest, and clung to him. "Oh, Bothwell! Bothwell! I dinna think I can bear it!"

His arms tightened about her for a moment. "Go and get dressed, lass. I'll clean this fish, and get us some bread and cheese to take along today."

They rode slowly in the late-August sunshine. The valleys glowed below them in faintly purpled haze. They did swim in the icy waters of the stream, and afterwards he did make love to her. She kept laughing as fat bumblebees buzzed them while they lay amid the pungent flowers. Afterwards they ate the bread and cheese he had put into their saddlebags, drank dry white wine from a flask, and munched early apples. Too soon the sun began setting, and they rode home.

As they rode she asked quietly, "What time tomorrow are we to meet Lord Home?"

"Two hours past sunrise," he answered her, staring straight ahead. And then he heard her whisper, "So soon."

The sun had sunk in a blaze of hot orange behind them. As if to mock them, Venus glowed bright in the darkening sky above. The horses easily found their path back to Bothwell's lodge, and while the earl fed and watered the animals and bedded them down, Cat cooked their supper. They ate in silence until she said, "We had burgundy our first night."

"Aye. And ye got drunk."

"I want to get drunk tonight."

He came around the table and pulled her up to face him. "No, my darling. I want ye to remember everything that has happened between us—especially tonight."

She began to cry softly. "I hurt, Francis! My heart hurts so very much."

"I hurt also, my love, but I'll nae let Jamie Stewart know that he's killing me by taking away the one thing I hold dear. Our pain must be a private thing. But Catriona, my sweet, sweet love! I dinna want to forget a moment of our love, because I will need it to sustain me in the times to come."

"Ye'll be alone now, Francis. Who will look after ye?"

"Hercules will, my darling. Hardly a suitable replacement for the bonniest woman in Scotland, but . . ." He stopped, and gently wiped the tears from her cheeks. "Christ, Cat! Dinna weep, my precious love! I thank God Jamie is at least returning ye to Glenkirk. Patrick will look after ye."

"Aye," she said bitterly. "If he looks after me as well as he did before, 'twill be a short month afore I'm forced again to be the king's whore!"

"No, love! 'Twill nae happen! Patrick has promised me."

She stared at him. "Ye saw Patrick? When?"

"Last month when Jamie ordered me to return ye. I had to be sure he would care for ye properly. I had to know he wanted ye, for if he hadn't, I could nae have let ye go back. He loves ye very much, my darling. Even knowing ye belong to me, he still loves ye. Dinna be afraid to go back to Patrick Leslie."

She shivered. "He'll want to make love to me," she said in a low voice. "I'd as soon go into a convent than hae another man touch me."

Bothwell laughed softly. "Nay, Cat. Ye were made

for love. Wi'out it that lovely body would shrivel and die. Dinna be ashamed of it, and dinna deny it." Drawing her into the curve of his arm, he slid a hand into her silk shirt, and caressed the soft swell of her breasts. She murmured contentedly, her leaf-green eyes half-closed. He laughed again. "See, my darling?" he gently teased her, drawing his hand from her warmth.

"Beast!" she managed to say before his mouth took possession of hers. He was gentle, always so incredibly gentle with her. He kissed her with a melting tenderness while he quickly undressed her. Then, without losing her lips, he lifted her into his arms and carried her upstairs to their bedroom.

When he lay her on the bed she drew him down to her and slid her hands into his shirt, stroking his chest and broad back. She pushed the shirt off. Pulling him back to her, her soft bare breasts made contact with his smooth bare chest. He gasped with pleasure at the familiar contact, and felt the rising between his thighs. She loosed her grasp and whispered urgently, "Hurry, love!"

Quickly he tore off his remaining clothes and, mounting her, thrust deep into her throbbing warmth. His entry never failed to elicit a cry of pleasure from her. She strained to receive him, sobbing her frustration when he could go no further. He began a delicious torture, thrusting within her as deep as he could go, then pulling completely out of her until she begged him to stop, so painful had her own desire become. But he would not. He drove her to heights of passion she had not known existed, prolonging their painful pleasure, and when at last him own passion burst in a raging flood within her, she half-fainted from excitement.

Her head was whirling, her heart pounding, her ears filled with the sound of a ragged weeping that she gradually understood was her own. Bothwell gathered her into his arms and rocked her back and forth. His own senses were reeling. He had, in a terrible instant of clarity, realized that in a few hours he would send this woman out of his life, possibly forever.

Slowly their breathing returned to normal. She lay back against the pillows and drew him onto her breasts. "Why did ye wait until tonight to do that to me, Francis?" He said nothing and she continued. "It is so easy for ye men. Ye live by a strict code of honor that leaves no room for emotion. Tomorrow ye will turn me over to Sandy Home, who will turn me over to James Stewart, who will probably try to make love to me before turning me over to Patrick Leslie, who will make love to me because I am his wife, and it is his right. Ye will feel remorse at my loss. Sandy Home will regret the part he must play in this drama. Jamie will feel lust mixed wi a bit of guilt, but not enough to stop this terrible thing he is doing to us. And Patrick will feel apprehension at my return, which he will try to hide from me by being masterful.

"Where am I in all of this? I am alone again while ye all play at this game of honor. I am forced to submit my honor to a man I dinna love—all the while hungering for ye, Bothwell. Ye are *all* so honorable. So then why do I end up feeling like a whore? I would rather be dead, and even that is denied me."

"Dinna wish for death," he whispered huskily. "The only thing that keeps me sane in all of this is knowing that ye'll be alive and well wi Glenkirk." Sitting up, he looked at her, his blue eyes blazing angrily. "I care naught for honor, and if I thought we could build a life for ourselves from the wreckage of our families I would take ye away tonight! Could ye be happy knowing that we had destroyed Glenkirk, Sithean, and Greyhaven? Nay, love, I dinna believe ye could. At least my children have Angus and the Douglases. Yer Leslies hae been a law to themselves. Ye've taken an occasional outsider into yer group, but ye've been so busy preserving yer wealth together that ye hae no powerful ties."

"We needed none," she said. "Our wealth has been our power."

"It isna now, my darling, it is yer weakness. Now James Stewart uses yer wealth as a weapon against ye, and against me. I love ye, Cat. I love ye wi all my heart. I love ye as I hae never loved another woman, and when ye are gone from me my life will be an empty shell. I hae nothing left."

"Will we nae see each other again?"

"There will come a time—six months, a year or two from now—when I will have to leave Scotland. Before I go I will see ye . . . if ye still wish to see me. Patrick has promised me that."

She began to weep softly again, and he held her against him, stroking her long hair. There were no words left. Exhausted, they finally slept, waking several times before the dawn. He had to arise, but she caught him by the arm, and begged softly, "Once more, my rightful husband."

So with exquisite delicacy he made love to her, his mouth seeking the sweetness of her breasts, her belly, her thighs. Gently he entered her, bringing them quickly to a mutual satisfaction. Then, marveling, as he always did, he grew hard again within her. This time he took his time, enjoying her lovely body to its fullest, and again they dozed.

When she awoke for the second time he was already up, and a steaming tub stood before the fireplace. Without a word she arose and bathed. Downstairs he laid out a cold ham, oatcakes, and brown ale. She tried nibbling on an oatcake, but it tasted like ashes and she only managed to swallow it by gulping some of the bitter ale. She felt as cold as ice. Finally he said, "If we're to meet Sandy on time we must leave now." She looked up at

him, her lovely leaf-green eyes mirroring his pain.
Catching her to him, his mouth closed over hers, stifling
her cry. For a moment he lost himself in the sweetness
of her, and as Cat's lips parted beneath his and her
warm breath rushed into his mouth, he groaned.

Suddenly she tore herself away from him and, fleeing
outside, mounted her horse. For a moment he could not
move. Then he pulled himself together and joined her.

The day was gray and threatening. Here and there
the trees showed an early touch of color. They were to
meet outside the town of Teviothead at the St. Cuth-
bert's cross. They rode in silence. Though there was so
much she wanted to say to him, she could not speak.

Hercules, Lord Home, and his men were waiting.
Francis Hepburn shook hands with his friend. "Ye'll
look after her, Sandy? Dinna let her do anything
foolish." His voice was almost pleading, and Alexander
Home nodded wordlessly. Bothwell dismounted. He
lifted Cat off her horse. They stood for one long moment
looking at each other. Tenderly, he cupped her face in
his big hand.

"Ye'll take care of yerself?"

"Aye."

"And ye'll nae hold Glenkirk responsible for this?
He would have had ye happy, even at the cost of losing
ye."

"I know."

"And dinna let Jamie know he's won."

"Christ, no!" she exploded.

"I love ye, Catriona Mairi. Whatever happens, remember that. Remember."

The beloved leaf-green eyes burned into his. "I love
ye, Bothwell, and whatever happens I am always yers.
James can force me back to Glenkirk, but he can never
change the way I feel. I will never stop loving ye." She

pulled his head down, kissed him passionately, and then
quickly remounted her horse and kicked it into a canter.

Startled, Home looked at the Earl of Bothwell and
then signaled his men to ride off after her. For a moment
Francis Hepburn looked after them. Then suddenly his
big shoulders began to shake, and Hercules heard dry,
wracking sobs. He stood, helpless, not knowing what
to do. He had never known Francis to cry.

Unable to think of anything else, he threw an arm
around Bothwell's shoulder. "Come on, Francis! Let's
go home!"

Francis Hepburn turned to face his brother, and the
empty look in his eyes made Hercules recoil. "I hae no
home now, Hercules," said Bothwell. "She was my home
. . . and now she is gone."

Part IV

꧁ ꧂

Cat Leslie

Chapter 34

❧❧❧

A drizzle fell without letup, but Cat insisted on riding straight through to Edinburgh. She refused to spend the night at an inn, stopping twice instead so Home and his men could refresh and relieve themselves. She would take no food, but drank a cup of wine, which Lord Home instructed the innkeeper to lace with eggs and spices. Home's cousin, riding in their party, commented, "I hope ye get her to Edinburgh alive. Wi Bothwell behind ye and the king ahead of ye, I'd hate to be in yer boots, Sandy, if anything should happen to her."

"She'll get there," answered Lord Home grimly. "If only to hae the pleasure of spitting in the king's face. She's a brave lass, is Cat Leslie."

In the cold dark hours before dawn they reached Edinburgh. Lord Home insisted on stopping at this point. "Someone," he told Cat, "must go ahead to Holyrood House and inform the king yer here. He has insisted on seeing ye."

She did not argue, so Home sent his cousin, quietly instructing him to go first to Glenkirk House and inform the earl of his wife's arrival. Then he was to go to Holyrood and inform the king.

Home took Cat to his own townhouse, where his servants served them with a warm fire and a good break-

315

fast. "Ye must eat something, Cat luv," urged Home worriedly.

"Sandy, I canna eat, but get me some of that wine mixture. And I want a hot tub. I'm fair chilled, and 'twill nae do for me to appear before the king smelling of the road. Have one of yer men bring my saddlebags inside. I've a change of clothes." Her voice was calm, her request reasonable, but her eyes were fever-bright.

Having instructed his people, he put an arm about her and asked, "Are ye all right, Cat?"

"Dinna be kind to me, Sandy," she said softly. "If ye are, I'll break, and I canna break until I hae seen Cousin Jamie."

They set a hip bath before the fire and screened it off. The little maidservant took the cake of scented soap from her saddlebags and helped Cat bathe. When she came out from behind the screen, Home whistled low with both admiration and shock.

"God's bones, luv! Do ye mean to appear before James like that?"

She wore a low-necked gown of black velvet with long tight sleeves edged in cream-colored lace. Across her swelling breasts was draped a Hepburn plaid caught at the shoulder with a large gold pin, an emerald in its center. On her chest, above a marvelous display of breasts, rested the gold Hepburn lion pendant that Bothwell had given her. "Do ye think the king will object if I show my loyalties?" she asked.

"Ye know damn well he will! Ye can gain nothing by defying him, Cat!"

"I can lose nothing either, Sandy! He's already taken my life from me."

Lord Home shook his head. He couldn't reasonably argue with her. Instead he handed her the goblet of wine. "Drink it, luv. Yer going to need yer strength for the battle ahead."

An hour later he was relieved of his burden when the king's chamberboy escorted the Countess of Glenkirk into the king's private closet.

James Stewart wore a floorlength robe over his silk nightshirt. She curtsied and rose to face him. The hooded amber eyes swept over her, and then he said coldly, "I dinna care for yer gown, madame."

"I am in mourning, sire."

"For whom?"

"Myself," she replied equally coldly. "I died yesterday."

"Dinna defy me, madame! Ye should be severely punished for yer wanton behavior!"

She laughed harshly. "Instruct me, yer majesty. 'Tis quite permissible for me to be *yer* mistress, but 'tis not permissible for me to be Bothwell's mistress. Is that correct?"

"I loved ye," he said quietly.

"Ye lusted after me! Nothing grander than that," she shot back. "And even when that sweet girl became yer queen ye were nae content and wouldna behave decently. Ye had to once again force yer way into my bed, though ye knew it would cause trouble. I begged ye not to destroy my marriage to Patrick Leslie, and when he caught ye wi yer dirty hands all over me, ye made it all worse than it had to be. But Jamie, I forgie ye that because in forcing me to flee yer cruelty I fled to Francis Hepburn. And I fell in love. He's worth a hundred of ye, Jamie. And though ye've torn us apart, even death will nae stop our love because it is greater than even the damned royal Stewarts!" She turned from him.

He was stunned by her violence. "Cat . . ." He softly used her name for the first time. "Cat, love, dinna turn from me. I hae hungered so for ye all these months." He touched her shoulder and she shuddered.

"For pity's sake, Jamie, dinna touch me! Ye disgust me!"

His hand reached up and caressed the shining dark-gold hair she had bound loosely with a ribbon. "Yer lovely hair," he said. "Yer lovely soft hair. How I remember it tumbled on the pillows when I made love to ye. Or dropping like a shining curtain around us in bed. It is so beautiful. So very beautiful," he murmured softly.

She turned to him then, and as he watched, fascinated and unbelieving, she reached down to the gewgaws that hung from her waist and drew up a small pair of gold scissors. Before he could stop her she had cut through the thickly bound plait of hair just above the ribbon. "If ye like my hair so, Jamie, ye should hae it, for 'tis all ye'll ever get of Cat Leslie!" She flung the golden mass at him, her face blazing contempt.

The king drew back, horrified. It was at this point that the Earl of Glenkirk entered the room. For a moment James and Patrick stood side by side. Seeing them together, Cat's heart began to pound violently. It was Glenkirk who realized what was frightening her and, leaping the space betwen them, he caught her as she crumbled in a dead faint. Before she lost consciousness he heard her cry out piteously, "Francis! Help me!"

Cradling his wife in his arms, Patrick Leslie said quietly to the king, "I'll bid ye good day, Jamie. When Cat is fit to travel I am taking her home to Glenkirk. If ye try to stop me, I swear I'll return her to Bothwell myself, and the devil take the consequences!"

But James said nothing. He stared at the silken rope of hair in his hands. Patrick Leslie, following the king's chamberboy, carried his unconscious wife to his carriage and ordered the coachman to drive quickly back to Glenkirk House. Mrs. Kerr, clucking sympathetically, helped put Cat to bed.

Patrick was relieved to see that she was now merely in a deep sleep. That she was exhausted emotionally as well as physically he did not need to be told, though Lord Home had talked with him as they left the palace. The Earl of Glenkirk sat by his wife's bedside throughout the day, watching over her. He learned how deep her love for Francis Hepburn really was. Patrick Leslie felt a great sadness come over him as he listened to his wife talking in her sleep. He was not sure he could ever win her back, but he realized once more that he still loved her.

Towards late afternoon he saw signs that she would soon be awakening. Stepping into the upstairs hall, he called to Mrs. Kerr, instructing her to bring a tray with capon, bread and butter, and a small decanter of sweet white wine. When Cat opened her eyes she saw Patrick crossing the room with a tray in his hands.

"Good afternoon, sweetheart," he said gently. "How do ye feel?"

"How long have I been asleep?" she asked him.

"About ten hours." Putting the tray down on the bedside table he fluffed the goosedown pillows, and helped her to sit up. "Mrs. Kerr fixed ye this tray." He placed it on her lap.

"Take it away. I canna eat."

Patrick Leslie drew a chair up next to the bed and sat down. He held a capon wing under her nose. "Lord Home told me that ye did not eat during the whole trip from the borders. When did ye have yer last meal?"

"Two nights ago." She said it so softly that he barely heard her.

"Eat," he said quietly.

She raised her head up and looked at him. Her lovely eyes filled with tears that spilled down her cheeks in a torrent. He quickly put down the poultry wing and tenderly gathered her into his arms. He felt her stiffen, but chose to ignore it. "Cry!" he commanded. "Damnit, Catriona! Cry!" At this, the great sorrow that she had been forcing down welled up and spilled over. She wept until her eyes were red-rimmed and swollen, until she could weep no more. And all the while he held her protectively, crooning softly to her. When she was finally quiet he held her off from him a moment and, with a silken handkerchief, wiped her cheeks. But when he put the silk to her nose, she snatched it from him angrily. "I'm nae a child, Glenkirk!"

"No," he answered quietly, "yer not."

"Christ," she whispered at him fiercely, "how can ye want me back knowing that I love *him*? I will always love him!" She snatched the decanter up and poured herself some wine. The look she threw him was defiant, and pure Cat.

He laughed. "Dinna get drunk until ye've eaten something." He removed the decanter from the tray and put it on the bedside table. Going to the door, he called again to Mrs. Kerr to bring him a tray. It soon appeared, a distinct contrast to hers, containing raw oysters, several slices of ham, artichokes in oil, bread and butter, apples, a honeycomb, and a pitcher of red wine.

Warily she watched him wolf down his food while she forced herself to eat a slice of capon and some bread and butter. Knowing her sweet tooth, he laid a piece of honeycomb on her plate and was encouraged when she ate it. Then, having drunk up the little decanter of white wine, she took his pitcher of red and filled her goblet. He removed it from her hand.

"Ye'll be sick, Cat," he said, "and there is nothing more unpleasant than sleeping wi a drunken woman."

Her eyes widened. "Ye dinna mean to sleep in *this bed*? No! No! Ye canna be that cruel, Patrick. Gie me some time!"

It had come, and Patrick Leslie steeled himself for

what he must do. He was shocked to discover that Bothwell knew her a great deal better than he ever had. "Yer my wife, Cat," he said quietly. "Whether ye want to be or whether ye love me is nae longer important. By law ye belong to me, and though ye may not love me, I love ye very much. I hae been wi'out yer company now for over two years. I hae no intention of denying myself the pleasure of yer lovely body any longer."

While he spoke he carefully undressed himself. Now he walked over to the bed and, pulling back the coverlet, climbed in beside her. She tried to escape him by leaving the bed on the other side, but he caught her easily. Slowly and deliberately, he drew her fiercely struggling body to him. Forcing her back into the curve of his arm, he bent and captured her mouth. Her lips were cold and pressed tightly together. Gently he forced them open, plunging his tongue into her mouth while his free hand caressed the breasts he had skillfully freed from her bodice. She gasped as a wave of desire shot through her. Desperately she renewed her struggle. She did not want Patrick Leslie. She wanted Francis Hepburn, and she could hear his voice even now, mocking her. Just two nights ago he had said, "Ye were made for love. Ye canna deny that."

Her body was betraying her again, as it always had, by responding to lovemaking when she did not want it to. All the while her husband pleasured himself with her, her heart cried out to Bothwell. Glenkirk had never made love to her with such tenderness, and this calmed her somewhat. He moved rhythmically, finally crying out his relief. She found that, though his lovemaking had excited her body, she had not reached a climax emotionally. He realized it too. Withdrawing from her, he cradled her in his arms. "Go to sleep," he said gently. For some reason she felt safe, and obeyed.

They stayed in Edinburgh for several days, until he

was sure she could travel safely. Each night he made
love to her, as if to reaffirm his position. At last he took
her home to Glenkirk. They arrived a week after Bess
Leslie's eleventh birthday. Bess seemed to be the only
one not especially glad to see her mother.

Jamie, the Leslie heir, was now fifteen and on short
leave from the university. He stood as tall as his father,
and from the saucy looks the servant girls gave him, Cat
knew that her eldest son was already being instructed
in the arts of love. The thought disturbed her a little,
for she was only thirty-one. As she hugged him he
touched the unfamiliar short gold curls.

"What happened to yer hair, mother?"

"I gave it to the king," she answered.

"Jesu! Ye defied him?"

"Aye."

He saw the pain in her eyes, and saw as well that she
tried to hide it. Putting his arms about her he said softly,
"Dinna grieve, mother. We love ye too, and are very
glad to hae ye home again."

Colin and Robbie were home from Rothes. They
swarmed over her like young puppies. In great contrast,
Cat's two youngest daughters, Amanda, six, and Morag,
five, were quite shy with the beautiful, sad woman
whom Grandmother Meg said was their mother. Within
a few days, however, Cat had won the two little girls
over. Only Bess remained aloof.

"She is jealous of ye," said Meg with amusement.
"Soon she will be grown, and she's been feeling her own
femininity lately. Then ye come home—and lord, Catriona! Yer over thirty, and absolutely beautiful! 'Tis
very hard on poor Bess. She adores Patrick, and up until
now has had a great deal of his attention. Now he
spends most of his time wi ye."

The matter came to a head when it appeared that
Patrick's nightly efforts had borne fruit, and Cat began

to swell with another child. The unhappy Countess of
Glenkirk overheard her eldest daughter discussing the
matter with her oldest brother.

"I think it is disgusting," raged the girl, "at her age.
And especially after what she's done to our father by
whoring wi Lord Bothwell!"

There was the sound of a slap, and Bess shrieked,
"Ye hit me, Jamie. Ye hit me!"

"Aye," Jamie replied. "And, Mistress Jealousy, I'll
smack ye again if ye ever speak of mother like that.
We know naught of what happened between mother and
father, but I do know that mother loves Francis Hepburn. She has come back because she loves us too, and
would nae allow the king to destroy us."

"How do ye know that?" sneered Bess.

"Because John Leslie, the Rothes heir, is at University wi me, and he overheard his father telling his uncle
that Glenkirk only got his wife back because the king
threatened to destroy our whole family unless she left
Bothwell."

"Good for the king!" gloated Bess. "He is a godly
man."

Jamie laughed cruelly. "Yer a fool, little sister. Nay,
perhaps just a foolish little virgin. The king lusts after
mother, and when she refused him he forced her to leave
Bothwell by threatening us."

"Then why does she hae father's child if she doesna
love him?"

"To make peace between them, I would think, little
sister. She is a brave and bonnie lady, our mother, and
if ye are not civil to her in future I'll beat ye myself!"

Cat was amazed at how much her son knew and how
wise he was at his age. She could also see that she would
have to keep an eye on Bess. The child was growing
quickly, and understood enough half-truths to be confused. Cat knew that her daughter's angry opinions were

not her own, but were echoes of an adult voice. Suspecting the offender's identity, Cat took steps to remedy the situation.

When Cat had fled to Lord Bothwell, her faithful tiring woman had not known the reason for her mistress' behavior. Returned to Glenkirk, Ellen had taken care of Bess from the busy Sally and Lucy Kerr. As the months went by with no word from Cat, Ellen's confusion turned to anger. She unwisely expressed her anger to young and impressionable Bess. And now, with her lady's return, Ellen deserted Bess and resumed her duties with Cat, thus adding to poor Bess' bitterness.

Cat could see that Bess missed Ellen, and though Ellen had always been valuable to her, her over-solicitous attention had begun to get on Cat's nerves. Ellen seemed to think that Cat had done a terrible thing, and was fortunate that Patrick forgave her. Rather than scold her old servant, Cat took her aside and spoke to her confidentially. "Ellie, I am going to need yer help wi Bess. She is getting to the age where she needs an experienced hand to guide her. Ye looked after her while I was away. Would ye mind taking charge of her again? She is so fond of ye."

"I will do whatever ye wish, but who will take care of ye, my chick? Especially in yer condition."

"Ellie! Ye've become a foolish old woman. 'Tis not my first bairn. I canna replace ye, but I think yer niece, Susan, would do nicely."

"Aye," said Ellen thoughtfully, thinking of her plain and sensible niece. "Susan is nae a flibbertigibbety girl. She would do her job well, and I will guide her. But could she not be Mistress Bess' woman rather than me?"

"I think that Bess would be happier wi ye, Ellie, and ye were so good wi me at that age. However, I will leave the decision to ye."

Ellen decided—as Cat knew she would—that Bess would be a better mistress. It was easy to boss a young and unsure girl, and she no longer understood her lady Catriona. Feeling important once again, Ellen took charge of Bess and spoke well of Cat to her daughter.

Cat made certain to spend time with her three daughters. Amanda and Morag had lost their shyness of their mother, which gave Cat joy. Bess, though she remained wary, was friendlier than she had been, and even joined in games Cat played with the little ones.

Eight months after her return to Patrick Leslie, Cat Leslie went into labor. " 'Tis too soon," worried the earl to his mother. "I'm surprised she's lasted this long," observed Meg. "Dinna look so worried, my son. By nightfall there will be at least two more Leslies in this house. Cat is carrying twins, and multiple births always deliver early. I know because my mother's last children were twins. They run in our family."

The dowager countess was correct. Cat easily and quickly delivered a son and a daughter before the sun set on May 1 of 1594. The boy was baptized Ian, the girl Jane. Patrick was delighted that his wife had so thoughtfully named their children after his paternal grandparents. Cat cradled each child before she slept, and then quietly announced that she would not be nursing these children. Wet nurses were quickly found for the twins.

In mid-June Patrick Leslie was visited by Benjamin Kira, and the result was a journey to London. Thinking she would enjoy the trip, he asked Cat to go with him. She refused.

"I'll be gone from late summer till next spring, sweetheart. Please come wi me. We've been back together such a short time."

"No, Patrick. Ye promised *him* that before he left Scotland we might see each other. If I am in England

wi ye when he calls me, I will never see him again.
Dinna ask me to go away wi ye again."

He did not, though it pained him to admit that he
was saddened by her refusal. He had hoped the birth of
their twins would help her to forget the border lord.
On August 15, Patrick Leslie left Glenkirk bound for
London.

On September 15 the Countess of Glenkirk received
an invitation from George Gordon, the powerful Earl
of Huntley, to visit him and his wife at Huntley Castle.
Gossip had it that Bothwell was in the north. If he was,
then Cat knew he would be with the Gordons. On September 17 the Countess of Glenkirk left her castle for
Huntley.

Chapter 35

❧❧❧

THE truce between James Stewart and Francis Stewart-Hepburn had not worked out. Though the king had signed an agreement on August 14, 1593, to pardon his noble cousin and his equally noble supporters, and to restore all their estates, titles, and honors, he was soon tempted to go back on his word. On September 8, a convention of parliament was held at Stirling, and James attempted to modify the promises he had made in August. On September 22, the king forbade his cousin and his supporters to come within ten miles of him unless summoned by James himself. Should they disobey, the charge against them would be high treason. Maitland's power had not waned.

The royal gauntlet thrown down, it was picked up by Bothwell and armed friends. They assembled outside Linlithgow in early October while the king was in residence. On October 22, Bothwell was called before the high council to answer to the charge of high treason. Refusing to attend the proceedings, he was denounced.

All was quiet for several months, and then in the spring of 1594 James called twice for a levy of forces to bring his cousin to the king's justice. Suddenly Bothwell appeared with a powerful force outside of Leith. He had come, he said, to fight the Spaniards, whose imminent landing was rumored. His real purpose was to make a show of strength, in hope of bringing his royal cousin to terms.

James advanced towards Leith from Edinburgh while
Bothwell retreated in leisure towards Dalkeith, as
though he were not being pursued at all. James was
forced to go back to Edinburgh, having lost yet another
encounter with his cousin. The border lord then slipped
over the border into England, where he remained,
quietly, until Queen Elizabeth was forced to acknowledge his presence and eject him.

Francis Hepburn now had two choices. He could deliver himself up to James, or he could join with the
northern earls. Sensing that exile was near, he went
north so he could see Cat before leaving his homeland.
There was no one else left he cared to see. Hercules
had been caught and hanged in the previous bitter
February. Margaret Douglas and his children behaved
as if he did not exist. Only Cat Leslie remained. Would
she see him?

No one had told Cat so, but she knew intuitively that
he waited at Huntley for her. Gathering her daughters
about her, she told them she would be gone for a
while. "But I'll be back, my little loves," she promised,
"and then I'll nae leave ye again."

When Amanda and Morag had run off to play, Bess,
now twelve, asked quietly, "Is Lord Bothwell at Huntley, mother?"

Cat's first reaction was to tell her daughter it was
none of her business. But then she looked again at
Bess, who hovered between childhood and womanhood,
and thought better of it. The countess put an arm about
her eldest daughter. "Yes," she said. "I believe that
Lord Bothwell is at Huntley. Dinna be angry, Bess. Yer
father gave me his permission to see Francis. Someday
ye'll love a man. Perhaps then, Bess, ye'll understand
yer mother."

"I shall ne'er love any man but my true, wedded
lord, mother."

Cat laughed softly and squeezed her daughter
gently. "How wonderful to be *so* young, and *so* posi-
tive, my darling. I hope that in my absence ye will
help yer grandmother, and watch over yer sisters and
the twins."

Bess Leslie looked at her mother for a moment, and
then she clung to her. "Ye'll nae go away wi Lord
Bothwell? Ye will come home? Ye'll nae leave us
forever?"

"No, my child. I will be back." A lump rose in her
throat. "I will come back to ye, Bessie luv. Dinna fear."

Before Cat left Glenkirk, Margaret Leslie took her
daughter-in-law aside. "My son did a cruel and terrible
thing to ye, Catriona. Go—say your final goodbyes to
Francis Hepburn. Take whatever time ye need. But
when ye return to Glenkirk, ye must again be a good
wife to Patrick. He has been punished enough."

Now the beautiful Countess of Glenkirk rode
eagerly across the hills that separated her home from
Huntley. Ellen had wanted to come with her, saying
that her niece had not the experience to accompany her
mistress to a great house. Cat had cajoled her into
staying with Bess, saying the young girl needed Ellen
more than she did. The truth was that the countess did
not want her old servant intruding on her reunion with
Lord Bothwell. Susan was young and unsure enough
to be discreet.

At last the towers of Huntley Castle came into view,
and Cat's heart began pounding. Conall rode up beside
her. "I dinna suppose ye'll want us to stay," he said
disapprovingly.

"No," she answered him. "I dinna need Leslie protection in the house of the Gordons. My grandmother
was a Gordon."

" 'Twas nae the Gordons I was thinking ye needed
protection from, madame."

She smiled at him. "I dinna need any protection from my Lord Bothwell, Conall. Rather, he may need it from me."

Conall laughed despite himself. He had long ago given up hope of understanding his nobles. It only confused him to try.

They clattered into the courtyard of Huntley, where George Gordon and his lovely French wife, Henriette, awaited them. Having dismounted, Cat greeted them warmly, but her eyes were restlessly sweeping the courtyard. Lord Gordon laughed. "He got here about two hours ago, Cat, and insisted on having a bath. I doubt if he is ready to receive ye yet."

But suddenly she saw him at the top of the staircase. For a moment they gazed at one another, spellbound. Cat took a few steps forward, but then her legs refused to cooperate further, and began to give way beneath her. He was at her side in seconds, catching her up in his strong arms, his deep-blue eyes devouring her. Her arms went around his neck as he bent and found her mouth. Everything—the courtyard, the horses, the servants, the Gordons—melted away as they abandoned themselves to each other. Hungrily, eagerly, their lips demanded more and yet more.

It was Henriette Gordon who broke the spell by turning to her husband and saying, "But George! You did not tell me that Lady Leslie and Lord Bothwell knew each other. I have given them apartments at opposite ends of the castle."

Francis Hepburn broke away from Cat, and both of them burst into laughter. "Oh, George," teased the Countess of Glenkirk, "how could ye hae overlooked even such a small detail?"

Huntley looked rueful. Bothwell gently put Cat down on her feet. "Can ye stand now, my darling?" he asked.

"Aye, Francis. 'Tis all right now."

The border lord turned to his pretty hostess and, taking her plump little hand, smiled down at her. "Which of the two apartments is the larger, Riette?"

"Lady Leslie's. I thought—with a woman's clothes and things—she would need the large suite." The Countess of Huntley was flustered by the turn of events.

"Will ye then," said Lord Bothwell with grave courtesy, "please hae my things moved in with Lady Leslie's? We shall, after all, be needing only one bed." He turned to his host. "George, ye will excuse us now until the evening meal. My lady and I hae been parted for over a year. I know ye understand." Putting an arm about Cat's waist, he led her up the stairs and into the castle.

Henriette Gordon faced her amused husband with outrage. Laughing, he led her into their home, and when he had told her the tragic story of Bothwell and Cat, the pretty Countess of Huntley was on the verge of tears. "Oh, George! *Les pauvres!* James Stewart— *il est un cochon!*" she cried indignantly. And from that moment, she was their ally.

Bothwell waited patiently for an hour to be alone with Cat. There could be no privacy with servants traipsing in and out. Cat had ordered a hot bath to be set up for her by the fireplace. She was enchanted by the floral decorated porcelain tub. The hot water arrived, and Susan fussed until she found the hyacinth-scented bath oil. Francis Hepburn watched, amused, as the little maid shooed everyone out and tried to take him on as well. Laughing, he caught her by the waist and looked down at her. She blushed deep scarlet as his eyes boldly swept her. "Yer nae Ellen, are ye? Yer too young."

"No-no, sir," she replied shyly. "I am Susan, her niece. My aunt looks after young Mistress Bess now."

"Well, Susan," said Bothwell kindly, "yer to go to the servants hall and hae a good supper. And if any of the lads get rough wi ye, lass, yer to tell them they'll answer to me."

"But, sir! I must help my lady to bathe."

Gently but firmly, he propelled her out the door. "I will help yer lady to bathe, Susan. 'Twill nae be the first time. And dinna come back until yer sent for, lass." He locked the door behind her, then turned to find Cat helpless with laughter.

"Ah, Bothwell, ye rogue! She will talk about this the rest of her life!" chuckled the Countess of Glenkirk.

"Take yer bath, madame," he commanded.

"Unbutton me," she countered, turning her back to him.

His fingers fumbled down the long row of tiny silver buttons. She was amused by his trembling hands. She shrugged the velvet riding gown off and stepped out of it. Beneath it she wore a low-cut silk underblouse, beribboned busk, three silk petticoats, and lace stockings secured by garters. She unbuttoned the blouse and removed it, but it was he who unhooked the little busk. Naked to the waist, she gazed up at him, her eyes bright with desire.

"Bathe," he repeated, his voice thick.

Sliding the petticoats over her hips, she let them fall about her ankles. Stepping out of them, she kicked the white silk mound away from her. She was now completely naked except for the dark blue lace knit stockings and their pink garters. Groaning, he turned away. She smiled to herself and quickly rolled the stockings down and off her shapely legs. When he turned back she was comfortably settled in her tub.

He sat down next to her. "Ye could tempt a band of angels!"

"Ye must hae been very true to me, Bothwell, to be so quickly roused. I am flattered."

He looked at her somberly. "The truth's that I have lifted every skirt I could, to try to bank the fire ye left in my heart. I failed miserably, because I have never stopped loving ye, or needing ye. I dinna expect I ever shall."

"Oh, Francis," she cried. "I have ached for ye all these many months. I have never stopped loving ye either."

"Yet," he said, almost bitterly, "ye gave yer husband another child—nay, twins!"

She laughed, and the sound was silvery in the quiet of the room. "Oh, Bothwell, ye great fool! The bairns are yers! The bairns are yers!"

He was incredulous. "Ye canna be sure, Cat."

"But I can," she said. "I can. Oh, my sweet lord, did ye not think it strange when ye had already fathered so many bairns, and I was mother to six, that we had no child of our own?" He nodded, and she continued. "When Mam returned from the east she brought wi her a secret for controlling conception. All the women in our family know it. Until we were safely wed I could not let us have a child. When the king forbade my divorce I knew I dared not gie Jamie a weapon to use against us. Then he ordered us parted, and I realized I couldna leave ye wi'out something of ye to sustain me. I was over a month pregnant when I left ye, Francis! Glenkirk waited not a moment before claiming his rights, so he assumed the twins were his—especially when his mother said that twins ran in her family, and always came early."

"What did ye call them?"

"Ian and Jane."

"Ye named them after my parents?"

"Aye, but Patrick thinks they are named after his paternal grandparents."

"What are they like, my wee bairns? What are they like, Cat?"

The silvery laugh tinkled again. "Francis! They're but bairns! Five-month-old bairns." Seeing his crest-fallen look, she tried. "The lad is auburn-haired and blue-eyed. He is bright, I can tell, and very demanding. His sister is a blue-eyed reddish-blonde of very much the same temperament. The wet nurses and the nursery staff adore them, for they both hae great charm."

It was what he had wanted to hear, and his eyes misted. She felt a catch in her throat, and silently cursed once again their cousin the king. To keep from crying she said to him, "Hand me that cake of soap, my love," and proceeded to scrub herself down. When she had finished she stood and stepped out of the tub. Francis wrapped her in a towel and began to rub her dry. She stood quietly, luxuriating in the delicious sensation of his hands on her once again.

She could tell by his touch that he was near to losing that perfect control he prided himself on, and she wanted him as she had never wanted him before. Turning, she slid her slender arms about his neck. "Now, Francis," she said quietly. "Take me, now! I have waited over a year to be wi ye again, and 'tis nae time to be standoffish."

Pulling away from him, she walked slowly across the room and climbed into the big lace-trimmed, lavender-scented featherbed. Undressing, he asked, "Did Glenkirk nae make love to ye enough that yer so eager, my darling?"

"Glenkirk took every opportunity to use me, and though my body responds to him, I hae never since we last made love been able to find the heaven I find wi ye, Francis. Aye, my lord, I am eager for ye!" She held out her arms to him, and he waited no longer.

They cuddled together beneath the warmth of the coverlet. He had her cradled within one arm while the other caressed her soft breast and then wandered boldly to stroke her rounded belly, her firm, trembling thighs and the soft hidden places of her body. Her breath was coming in short gasps, but she suddenly squirmed free of him and pushed him back on the pillows.

Bending over him, her lips began a tantalizing descent down his long body. She was exciting him unbelievably, her petal-soft lips gentle, touching him here and then there, moving lower and lower until she reached his swollen manroot. Tenderly she took it in her hand and kissed the pink, throbbing head. Then, taking it into her warm mouth, she drew on it for just a moment. His whole body jerked, and he cried out as if in agony. Frightened, she released him. She looked into his face. "I only wanted to taste of ye, my love," she whispered.

He pulled her back under him, and looked passionately down at her. "What do I taste of?" he demanded thickly.

"S-salt," she answered him suddenly, feeling very shy.

He laughed softly. Quickly sliding down and between her slender legs, he slipped his hands beneath her round buttocks and lifted her up, so he might taste of her also. She cried out—half in joy, half in shame. She wanted him to take her this way even though she felt it was not quite right. "Sweet! Sweet!" she heard him murmur. "Christ, yer sweet, my love!"

She could feel herself slipping away into that golden world of sweet fulfillment that she had been unable to attain since last being with him. As the delicious ache began to spread through her lower belly, his hardness thrust into her, and she cried aloud her happiness.

Afterwards—almost immediately—they both fell into deep contented sleep, still joined, their bodies intertwined. When she awoke it was to find him awake too, and watching her. She smiled and touched his cheek gently. He caught her hand and tenderly kissed the palm and the inner wrist. Their eyes met, and she trembled, so great was the depth of his emotion. That two people could love as deeply as she and Bothwell loved terrified her.

Propping himself on one elbow, he ruffled her dark-gold curls. "What happened to yer lovely hair?" She told him the story of her meeting with the king, and he shook his head wonderingly. "Ye defied him for me? Christ! How that must hae hurt Jamie!" He put his arms about her. "Yer my wench, and have been from the start, haven't ye? My God, how am I going to survive wi'out ye? I have nae done well so far."

"I dinna want to think about it, Francis. Not today. Not now when we are together again."

"How long can ye stay wi me, my darling."

"As long as yer at Huntley. Glenkirk is in England until the spring."

"How damned convenient," murmured Bothwell. "However when he promised we might see each other again, I dinna think he meant ye should live wi me for any length of time." The border lord's eyes were brimming with amusement.

"I will do as I please, Bothwell! If I thought the Leslies could escape Jamie's wrath I would flee to France yi ye now! Both the king and my husband know that. Unfortunately I am bound to the Leslies. They hae all been at me since my return. My Uncle Patrick, the old Earl of Sithean, died two years ago, but his wife has nae stopped her whining that my shameless behavior endangers her precious Earl Charles, who is married to Glenkirk's sister, Janet. When I told my mother the truth of my estrangement from Patrick, she chided me for not making him understand the great honor done me by James Stewart. She, who was a

virgin till her wedding night, and who has *never* known
another man in her entire life but my father, chortled
about the 'honor' of being the king's mistress! They
make me sick! All of them! And yet—I am bound to
them, and I must sacrifice my happiness for their
safety. But, my love, my very life—I will nae sacrifice
this time wi ye. When ye leave Scotland, I shall never
see ye again. I know it! I feel it! We are surely doomed
to be separated, but I *will* hae this time wi ye!"

His arms tightened about her. "I know I hae never
done anything in this life to deserve love such as yers,
my sweet Catriona Mairi."

The clock on the mantel struck five, and she said,
"Good Lord! We're going to be late for dinner! What
will the Gordons think?" Reaching out, she yanked the
bellpull. Disengaging herself from his grasp, she stood
up.

He caught his breath at the perfection of her body.
Without her long hair the beautiful line of her back
was visible. He had made love to many women, but
none could hold a candle to her. He was not a man
to take pride in his ownership of a woman, but he was
very proud that she loved him.

Susan arrived and modestly set up a screen for her
mistress to dress behind. The Gordon valet assigned to
serve Lord Bothwell rushed to cover the earl's private
parts as he rose from the tumbled bed, but Susan's
flaming cheeks told him that he had been too late. Unable to resist, Bothwell winked at the little maidservant.
She almost swooned.

"Damnit, Francis! Stop teasing Susan! Ye've made
her all thumbs. No, child. The pendant!"

Bothwell had dressed in a kilt, and Cat's gaze swept
him. "Damn me, Francis," she said teasingly. "Ye've
the handsomest pair of legs I've ever seen in a kilt."

He grinned wickedly at her. "And ye, madame, hae

the handsomest pair of—" He was stopped by her
warning look, and he laughed and said, "Well, ye do,
my darling!"

She laughed helplessly. "Yer a most impossible man!
Take me down to supper."

They descended from their tower to the hall below,
where George and Henriette Gordon waited for them
alone. The Earl of Huntley had been sure that Bothwell and Cat would not welcome company, so there
was none.

George Gordon, called the Cock of the North, was
related to the king. Cat had met him at court. He had
wisely kept his wife from court. Henriette Gordon was
petite, with soft hair the color of a daffodil, and enormous golden-brown eyes. She was elegant, and educated, and had charming Gallic manners and a warm
heart. It did not take long for her to become friends
with Cat Leslie.

Knowing that Bothwell would be with them through
the winter, she had asked Cat to stay. Then she ascertained that though Cat's boys were no longer at home,
her daughters were, and she invited them to Huntley
for Christmas and Twelfth Night. When Cat demurred
because she did not want to leave Meg alone, Henriette
said she would invite the dowager as well.

The end result was that Bess, Amanda, and Morag
were coming for the holidays. But Meg had been
asked to Forbes Manor to stay with her youngest son,
Michael, and his wife, Isabelle. She did not often get
to see them, and she felt that this was the perfect opportunity. There was, she wrote, one complication. The
twins would have to go to Huntley. Meg did not want
them left alone at Glenkirk with the servants.

Bothwell was wild with excitement. "Our bairns!" he
said. "I shall get to see our bairns!"

"Ye canna admit to their paternity," she cautioned

him. "The world has never doubted that Patrick Leslie
is their father. I will allow no one—even ye—to endanger them."

It was a new side of her that he saw—this fierce and
protective mother. He put an arm about her. "Fate has
nae dealt kindly wi us, has it, Cat?"

"We're together now, Bothwell," she answered him.

The unspoken questions—"For how long?" "Until
when?"—lay between them, but neither Cat nor Francis
could ask those questions.

So while the autumn deepened about them, they accepted the Gordons' hospitality. It allowed them a
tranquil place to rest in their last months together. For
just a brief time they might forget the public contro-
versy that raged about Francis Stewart-Hepburn and
the private one that raged about them both. When the
future arrived they would face it courageously. But for
now, they basked in their good fortune.

Chapter 36

&ᵍᶠᵍ᷈&

GREEN and gold September gave way to a rainbow October. The trees about Huntley were clothed in their traditional brilliant colors. November was a gray-and-brown month, startling in contrast to the beauty of the previous month. The first snow fell late, on St. Thomas' Night, and the Leslie children arrived that day.

They had come, Bess riding a gentle brown mare, the other children and their attendants in carriages, escorted by Conall and fifty men-at-arms. Twelve-year-old Bess Leslie strove to appear grown-up. She wore an elegant riding habit of claret-colored velvet, a matching cloak trimmed in sable, and a small hat atop her dark, neatly braided hair. Cat had never seen her eldest daughter with her hair up.

"She is *très chic*," murmured Henriette.

"And very young yet," replied Cat with a catch in her throat.

"She does not approve of you," laughed Henriette behind her plump, beringed white hand. "The young—especially young virgins—are so terribly intolerant."

"Aye," smiled Cat in agreement. "I was at her age. Poor Bess! She likes Francis. She canna help it, but she loves her father, and feels it is disloyal to him to be polite to Bothwell. She canna understand why I no longer care for her father, and I dare not tell her the

340

truth, so I evade her questions, which only hurts and confuses her more."

"She would be more hurt, my friend, if she did know the truth. Come, Cat, do not fret. Let us go and meet your children."

Bess' serious young face lit up the moment she saw her mother. Forgetting dignity, she tumbled off her horse into Cat's arms. "Mama!" Cat hugged the girl to her. Then, releasing her, she admonished gently. "Bess, yer manners! Make yer curtsy to Lord and Lady Gordon, and Lord Bothwell." Blushing a rosy color, the girl turned and curtsied beautifully to the other adults.

Henriette Gordon kissed the girl on both cheeks and welcomed her warmly, and George Gordon murmured an appropriate welcome. But then Bothwell stepped forward and, taking the young girl's hand, raised it to his lips and kissed it. "I am delighted to see ye again, Lady Elizabeth," he said. His blue eyes twinkled at her. Damn him, thought Bess. I dinna want to like him—but I *do!*

And for the briefest moment, Bess caught a glimpse of the man that so fascinated her mother.

Amanda and Morag Leslie descended the carriage to make pretty curtsies to their host and hostess. Cat kissed each of her daughters in turn. At last the Kerr sisters exited the second coach, each clutching a twin.

"Ahhh," said the Countess of Glenkirk. "Look, everyone! My littlest bairns." She drew back the cover from Jane's bunting, revealing auburn curls peeping from a lace-edged bonnet, and dark lashes resting on pink cheeks. The baby slept. Ian, however, was wide awake. Cat was startled by the familiar expression in his dark-blue eyes.

"Art awake, lovely?" she crooned at the boy, and took him from Sally. "Now here's my wee laddie.

Madame et monsieurs. Je presente le seigneur Ian Leslie." She turned. "Here, Bothwell! Ye take him while I get my Jane from Lucy." She briskly handed him the child, scolding him, "Christ, Francis! He's nae wet! Dinna drop him!" Taking the baby girl from Lucy, she said, "Let's go indoors. 'Tis too raw out here for the bairns."

Francis Hepburn, looking nervous but pleased, followed her. He was admiring the clever way in which she had arranged for him to hold his son. Bothwell sat down by the fire in the Great Hall and held the child in a sitting position on his knee. "Hello, Ian, my small son," he said softly. The child looked back at him seriously and then, reaching a fat fist up to the bending man, grabbed a handful of hair, and yanked. "Owwwww!" roared the Earl of Bothwell, but a small chortle from the baby turned his outrage to mirth. "Yer a wee devil, lad," he chuckled, but Cat knew he was pleased with the boy.

"Best to gie Ian to his nanny now, Francis," she said quietly. He obeyed her. "What do ye think of his sister, my lord?" Bothwell looked at Jane, who was now awake, and smiled down at the baby girl. To his delight the child smiled shyly back. "She looks a bit like ye," he said. "Aye," replied Cat, "but she's got red hair. Meg says her coloring is Stewart, but the Leslies have red hair too."

For just a moment longer Bothwell gazed hungrily at the two children. In his secret heart he cursed James Stewart. His son and his daughter would grow up Leslies, never knowing him or their true heritage.

He wanted these children desperately. Sadly he watched as the Kerr sisters removed the twins to the Gordon nurseries.

Christmas Day dawned cold and gray. Bothwell, who had always moved back and forth between old and new kirk as politics dictated, attended mass with the Gordons' Catholic household. As he knelt with his mistress on the cold stone floor of the estate church he wondered again why there was this battle over the way to worship. Did God, if there was a God, really care?

Looking at Cat's face, he revised his thinking. Aye, there was a God. The only trouble was that God seemed to be on the king's side, though why God should approve of James was beyond him. It showed a great want of taste.

In Scotland, New Year's and Twelfth Night were the gayest celebrations of the winter season. On New Year's Eve there was to be a great celebration with a feast that had kept the cooks busy for three days. The 31st of December was bitterly cold, but clear. Cat and Francis had gone riding.

Returning late in the afternoon, they found the stableyard deserted. Everyone, from the lord to the lowest retainer, was out gathering wood for tonight's midnight bonfire. Neither Cat nor Bothwell was stranger to the art of horse care. They led their mounts into the stable, unaware that Bess watched from the loft above.

Several hours after her mother left that morning, Bess had decided that perhaps she would like to ride. After an hour, the cold having forced her back, she returned to find the grooms gone. Leading her mare into its stall, Bess unsaddled the animal, rubbed it down, and fed her. Then, curious, she climbed to the loft to see what she could see. From the loft of the Glenkirk stables you could—on a clear day—see all the way to the loch, and to the towers of Sithean.

From the loft of the Huntley stables she could see nothing but hills and more hills. Disappointed, she was about to climb down when she saw her mother and

Lord Bothwell enter the stables leading their horses.
Elizabeth Leslie could not have said why she remained
hidden in the Huntley's stable loft that day rather than
announcing her presence.

The adults below her talked quietly to each other
about ordinary things, of the celebration to come, and
of what they would be giving the children. Bess learned
that her mother and Bothwell would be presenting her
with a longed-for strand of pearls plus a bracelet, earrings, and matching brooch of pearls and diamonds. At
Twelfth Night she was to have a lynx cape, and a necklace and earrings of garnets.

"She grows so fast," sighed Cat. "We shall soon
have to arrange a suitable match for her. George and
Henriette have suggested that their second son, Andrew, might suit Bess."

"She's going to be a beautiful woman," agreed
Bothwell. "Keep her from court."

Cat nodded. "I will hae no problem there. Bess is
like her grandmothers. She prefers being a country
mouse. She will make the man she marries an admirable wife."

Bess preened silently in her hiding place, pleased
that her mother should have such faith in her. Then
Bothwell leaned over and said something Bess could
not hear. Her mother laughed and, grabbing a handful
of hay, tossed it at the earl. The chase was on, and the
two adults romped back and forth until they collapsed
laughing in a pile of hay in the empty stall directly
below Bess.

The young girl could not see what was going on
beneath her unless she peered over the edge. Lured by
assorted sounds, she carefully lay on her stomach and
looked down. Bess had only the vaguest idea of what
went on between a man and a woman. What she saw
below enlightened her somewhat.

Her mother lay on her back in the hay, the pale-violet velvet skirts of her riding habit turned up. Cat's long, shapely legs, sheathed in knitted purple lace stockings, were spread, and between them Lord Bothwell labored back and forth. Bess could see nothing of great note, for both Bothwell and her mother were kissing passionately while breathing roughly, and murmuring unintelligible things to each other. Then her mother cried out quite clearly, "Oh, Bothwell! I adore ye!" and all was quiet but for the sounds made by the horses.

So *that* was lovemaking! Strangely, she wasn't shocked. It was a curious matter, and it did clear up things she had overheard the maids speaking about when they thought she wasn't listening.

Lord Bothwell stood and adjusted his kilt, then pulled Cat's skirts back down. Bess saw her mother sit up, and was amazed at how lovely she was—all rose with her tawny, tousled hair. "Damn, Francis! That was nae wise. What if someone had come in?"

"They would have left rather quickly, I imagine," the great border lord laughed. "Besides, madame my love, I dinna hear ye complaining," he finished teasingly.

Cat laughed helplessly. "I have always wanted to be ravished in a haypile," she admitted, and he echoed her laughter.

But slowly, Cat sobered.

"I dinna think I can bear it, my love."

"Hush, my darling. Dinna think about it. Let us enjoy the time we have left."

"Let me come wi ye, Francis! Please let me come wi ye!"

"Cat!" His voice was patient, and very tender. "Sweeting, we hae been through this before. We canna be responsible for the destruction of all the Leslies.

Then too, my love, I am a poor man now. James has
everything I own. How would we live?"

"Surely Jamie has forgotten me now that Prince
Henry has been born. 'Tis said he fair dotes on the
bairn. Surely he would hae compassion on *our* children? As to our living—oh, Francis! I am a very
wealthy woman in my own right. Just a word to my
bankers, the Kiras, and my investments and gold can
be placed anywhere in the world!"

Bess was shocked to hear her mother talk of aban-
doning her family, especially when she had promised
to return to Glenkirk. She strained to hear what Bothwell would answer. She did not have long to wait.

"Never!" he spat. "Never would I allow a woman to
support me! As to James softening his stand, ye may
disabuse yerself of that notion, madame. James has not
altered his stand! At least my children are half Douglas,
and allied by blood to a great family which will protect them. But ye Leslies intermarry. Who will protect
them? Unless we obey Cousin Jamie he will destroy
them! Christ, my love! My sweet, sweet love! I hate
the thought of losing ye, but I cannot build a life wi ye
on the ruins of Glenkirk and all his family."

Bess could see her mother's face clearly now, and
the tragic look was almost too much for the girl to
bear. Cat stood very straight and, composing her face
into a mask of passivity, said, "I am sorry, my lord, for
adding to yer pain. What is it about ye lords of Bothwell that turn sensible women into irresponsible ones?
Mary Stewart lost both her kingdom and her only child
for love of yer Uncle James. And here am I ready to
sacrifice my entire family for ye."

He held her close. Her eyes closed, and she smelled
the damp leather of his jerkin. Sometimes, she thought
sadly, sometimes I wish I could just close my eyes, and

nae wake up. I dinna know how I bear life wi'out this man.

Then she realized that he would be even more alone than she would be. There would be no spouse, no family, no bairns for him. Penniless, he would roam the continent selling his sword to the highest bidder. Or being kept by women. There would always be women happy to take care of Francis. So why would he not let her do it?

As if reading her mind he said, "No. Not a penny-piece, my love. Never from ye, for I love ye. Wi the others it does nae matter."

She looked at him ruefully, in control of herself now. "Let us go in and get dressed for dinner, Francis."

"I will never stop loving ye, my darling," he said quietly. And turning from her, he strode from the stable.

"Oh, Christ!" Bess heard her mother swear softly. "Dear Christ, help me to be braver than I am. He needs me to be strong now." Then she followed Lord Bothwell from the stables.

Bess remained quietly in the loft, stunned by what she had heard. She had grown up in the last half-hour, and for some reason it hurt. It had not been the sight of her mother and Lord Bothwell coupled in close physical embrace that upset her, but rather the fact that their love brought them pain. Bess did not understand that, for she had always believed that love would be sweet. If it brought pain rather than pleasure, why did they pursue it?

Slowly she climbed down the loft ladder, then picked herself clean of telltale hay. She could not ask her mother for answers, but perhaps later on she could pursue this puzzle. For now, she had to hurry and change lest she be late for the celebration.

Chapter 37

❧

THE holidays had passed. Deepest winter had settled upon the land. The Leslie children had long since returned to Glenkirk. Though the king knew that Bothwell sheltered with the Gordons, he had not learned that the Countess of Glenkirk was with her lover. James sent the Earl of Huntley an arrogant letter offering him a full pardon if he would turn Bothwell over for execution. The great highland chief gave orders that the royal messenger be fed and allowed to rest the night. In the morning he had the man brought before him.

"I want the king, my cousin, to know that this message comes directly from me," he said quietly. "I do not believe that James would even hint that I violate the laws of hospitality. Therefore, I do not believe that this letter is from him." The Earl of Huntley quietly tore the parchment in two pieces and handed them to the royal messenger. "I return this to my lord the king in hopes that it will help him to trace the bold traitor who so blatantly uses the king's name for his own foul ends."

When Bothwell learned of Huntley's brave and clever ruse, he thanked him, but said, "I must go now. This is the end, and if James would really have me dead, there is no hope. Maitland thinks he has won," and Bothwell laughed harshly. "He actually believes that by breaking the back of the nobility he can substitute his own influence. But if he really thinks that, then he is a bigger fool than all the rest! Those stern men who molded the king did a better job than they realize. Jamie may be superstitious and a bit of a coward, but he will be the *only* king in this land, mark my words!"

"Wait at least until the spring," protested George Gordon. "And there is Cat. She is a brave lady, your Countess of Glenkirk, but this will break her heart."

Bothwell didn't need to be told that. They had been living in a fool's paradise, pretending they were normal people. She had been sleeping when he had left her to join Huntley, but he believed she would be awake now.

She was. Awake, and being sick into a basin. When she had finished he wiped her mouth with a damp towel and, holding her close, said, "I ought to beat yer backside black and blue for this."

She said nothing, so he continued. "My foolish, foolish love! Have ye gone mad? Ye canna foist this bairn on Glenkirk. Do ye think he will welcome ye back swelling wi our bastard?"

"The child is mine," she replied, looking fiercely at him.

"This child is *ours,* Cat. Yers and mine. With Patrick in England there can be no doubt. Christ! He's a proud man! He'll nae accept the bairn."

"He'll accept it," she said grimly. "He owes me that!"

"My God," said Bothwell in amazement. "Do ye mean to make him pay the rest of his life for one night's indiscretion? Hasn't he been punished enough?"

"No!" she spat angrily out at him. "In time, perhaps, I will forgie Patrick. But I will never forget. Never! That indiscretion, as you call it, has cost me every-thing—my happiness, my peace of mind. Where am

I in all this? Oh, God! It is so easy for ye men, with
yer pride and yer damned sacred code of ethics! I have
been destroyed by the three of ye. Patrick used me
like a common drab to soothe his injured pride. Yet
I am expected to be grateful that he took me back.
James dirtied me, and I will never be able to wash
away the stain he left on me. And ye, Francis?" She
rounded on him. "What was my first attraction for ye?
That Jamie wanted me? Is that why ye fell in love
wi me, my lord? To spite the king? Another victory
over the royal bairn?" She wanted to hurt this man
as they all had hurt her.

His big hand slashed out and slapped her before he
realized it. Her eyes filled with tears, but she made no
sound. Instead her fingers gingerly touched her cheek,
and felt the welts. Her head was ringing with the force
of his blow, but she could hear his voice raging.

"I love ye!" he shouted, and his fingers dug cruelly
into the soft flesh of her arms. "I hae from the beginning, but ye were the Virtuous Countess, and I respected that virtue. Ye see, my love, I only seduced
those women who wanted to be seduced. When Jamie
bragged he had forced ye into his bed, I was ashamed
for him, and I ached for the shame ye must be feeling.
Then Patrick and James hurt ye, so I grabbed at the
chance they so foolishly offered me. I love ye! Yer a
spoilt, stubborn bitch, but I love ye, Cat! It is hard
enough to leave ye behind, my darling, but to know
that I leave ye wi my child in yer belly—" He stopped.
Taking her chin between his thumb and forefinger he
tipped her face up to him. "Why, my darling? Why
did ye do this to us?"

"Because," she answered him softly, "because I
canna bear to lose ye entirely, my love. Do ye think
that because I am safe at Glenkirk 'twill be easier for
me? Christ, Bothwell! 'Twill be harder, never knowing

where ye are, or if yer safe, or if ye lack for anything.
When ye leave me this time I shall never see ye again
in this life. At least the child will gie me hope, Francis,
and 'twill be a constant reminder to me of our love.
Do ye understand that, my lord? Without the child I
should retreat into some twilight world to escape the
reality of what has happened to us. The child will help
me to maintain my sanity."

"When Glenkirk tells ye he will nae let ye keep the
bairn, send it to me. 'Twill nae be easy, but 'twould
be a comfort to hae our son wi me in my exile, and
the child shall nae suffer the stigma of bastardy. I will
legally acknowledge him so he may bear my name."

She laughed. " 'Twould be a damned inconvenience
to ye, my gallant lover, to tramp about Europe wi a
wee bairn. Besides, my lord, 'tis a lass I carry. I know.
I am always damnably ill in the beginning wi the
lasses!" Her eyes teared again for a moment. "Once
at Hermitage when Bess had been intolerably rude to
ye, ye promised me that one day we would hae a lass
of our own. Now we shall, and she shall be a comfort
to me in my loneliness."

"And I shall never see her," he said softly.

"Yes, ye will! Each year I shall send ye her miniature, and ye shall see how she grows."

" 'Tis small consolation, my dear, for a child I
shall never hold in my arms. 'Twas hard enough to
leave just ye behind, but now. . . ." He paused. "I
dinna mind overmuch about the twins, for Glenkirk
assumes them his, and they will grow up Leslies; but
this poor wee bairn. . . ." He put a big hand on her
belly. "Who will see that my little lass is nae hurt?"

"I will," she answered him softly. "No harm will
come to our daughter, Francis. I swear it!"

"If I were Patrick Leslie," said Bothwell quietly, "I
should probably kill ye."

"The Earl of Bothwell might kill his unfaithful wife, but the Earl of Glenkirk will not," she answered him with assurance. "Patrick is far too civilized."

"And I am not?" He cocked an amused eyebrow at her.

"Nay, Francis, yer not! If ye were more civilized ye'd nae be in the coil wi the king! But, oh, my love, dinna change, for I love ye as ye are!"

He laughed, but soon turned serious again. "Dinna press Glenkirk too hard, Cat. He loves ye, and he is pricked wi guilt for what he did, but he is a man, sweeting. 'Tis a large morsel yer asking him to swallow, and I fear he will not."

She nodded, and he had the oddest feeling that she would be deliberately reckless.

Pregnancy seemed to calm her, as the time for his departure drew near. For him, it was the opposite. It worried him tremendously to have to leave her behind. They fought over money again.

Wealthy in her own right, she was eager to put her money at Bothwell's disposal. But he was as proud as she was rich, and would take nothing from her.

"Fool!" she shouted at him. "Wi'out gold yer as helpless as a beetle on its back!"

"I will manage," he replied tersely.

"Bothwell! Bothwell! Listen to me, my love. France is nae Scotland, or England. Ye hae no real friends to shelter ye. Ye must hae money to live. Please let me help ye. The money is nae Patrick's. 'Tis mine! Left to *me*, by Mam. Invested by *me* over the years. Please take it! Let me instruct the Kiras to place my wealth at yer disposal in their Paris bank."

"No, my darling," he said quietly. But he was touched by her offer and her concern. "I told ye once that I could not accept so much as a pennypiece from ye, for I love ye. I would not have history say that

Francis Stewart-Hepburn loved the Countess of Glenkirk's money, rather than the countess herself."

"Alas, history never remembers women in love! My name shall die wi me." She looked up at him. "Dear God, Francis! *How will ye live?*"

"My sword will be fer hire. The French kings always have need of another good sword. 'Twill earn me a place to sleep, and a full stomach. Dinna fret, my love. I shall survive."

"I wonder," she mused, "whether a bed and a meal are enough for the master of Hermitage, Kelso, Coldingham, Liddesdale, and Crichton?"

"They will have to be until I can build a fuller life for myself. There are ways."

"Aye!" she hissed, suddenly furious at him. "Between some overblown duchess' legs, I'll wager!"

He laughed down at her. "Possibly, my darling. Yer love for me has blinded ye to the fact that I am a ruthless man."

"Take the money, Francis! Be safe, I beg of ye!"

"No, Catriona. No."

She knew she had lost. It was useless to argue further. Still, she vowed to instruct the Kiras to deliver to him whatever he needed if he should ask. And the King of France would have a large bribe to assure Bothwell's welcome—and his safety.

Meanwhile, in Edinburgh, the king sought to bribe a merchant friend of Bothwell's to betray the earl. Instead, Master Tennant arranged for a ship to aid the earl in his escape to France. It would await Bothwell off Rattray Head on April 18.

Though Bothwell argued against it, Cat rode with him. Her condition was fine. "I will nae lose this bairn," she assured him. And she had arranged with the Abbot of Deer Abbey to shelter them on the night before he would sail.

As they took their leave of the Gordons, Henriette whispered to her, "My maid, Nora, says that Glenkirk arrived home three days ago." Cat knew that Nora had been walking out with a Leslie man-at-arms since Christmas. "Say nothing," she whispered back. Henriette nodded.

They rode towards the coast with a troop of Gordon retainers to protect them, and reached the abbey by day's end. The abbot greeted them nervously, for he lived in terror that the king would learn he had sheltered the Earl of Bothwell. Still he owed his friend Abbot Charles Leslie a great favor, which he now repaid by sheltering for one night the Countess of Glenkirk and her infamous lover.

Settled in the abbey guest house, Cat told Bothwell, "I dinna want to sleep tonight. We hae the rest of our lives to sleep." He understood, and held her close so she would not see the tears in his own eyes.

Lately, he had seen her build a shield about her emotions. She would, he knew, make no scene. He loved her the more for it, for had she weakened for even a moment he could not have left her behind— just as he could not live with her knowing he had destroyed the Leslies. Francis Stewart-Hepburn was, whatever his enemies said about him, an honorable man. It would be his downfall.

They spent the night sprawled before the blazing fireplace, talking. And just once—in the early hours before the dawn—he made love to her. For the last time his hands roamed gently over her lovely body, bringing her passion to a delicate peak. For the last time she felt his hardness within her, and abandoned herself to the rapture he always brought her. And when it was over he bent and kissed her softly swelling belly.

They rode out from the abbey before dawn, reaching the coast as the light grew. Standing on the cliffs above

Rattray Head, they watched the bobbing ship, a black silhouette in the dark sea against the brightening sky. The signal had been given, and as they descended to the beach they could see a little boat making its way to the shore. The Gordon men-at-arms had positioned themselves discreetly about the beach.

Cat and Bothwell stood facing the sea. His arm was about her, yet she felt nothing. Then he turned her so she faced him, and gazed down at her. The small boat was almost to the shore. Pulling a sapphire ring with a gold lion on it from his finger, he gave it to her. "For my lass when she is old enough," he said.

She nodded wordlessly and put the ring in her pouch. He gently touched her cheek. "There will nae be anyone else, Cat. There never was anyone else. Ye know that, don't ye?"

"Y-yes, Francis." Her voice shook slightly.

"Dinna grieve, love. Ye'll be safe wi Glenkirk," he said. And then he drew her into his arms, and for the last time took possession of the mouth he loved so much. She melted against the hardness of him, her whole body protesting their fate. Neither of them had ever realized that a kiss could be so sweet. They clung to one another until an urgent voice pierced their awareness.

"My lord! My lord! We must hurry. 'Tis dawn, and the tide will soon be against us."

Reluctantly he pulled away, but his deep-blue eyes never left her leaf-green ones. "Farewell, my beloved," he said softly.

"Go safely, my dearest lord," she answered.

He turned and, hurrying across the sand, stepped into the little boat.

"*Francis!*"

He turned to find her running to the boat, and caught

her outstretched hands. "I love ye, Bothwell! There was never *anyone* else but ye. There never will be!"

He smiled gently at her. "I know, Catriona. I always knew. Now, my darling, gie me a smile. Let me see but once more the smile that enslaves me."

It was terribly difficult, but as the boat moved away and their hands were pulled apart, she smiled radiantly at him, and caught his last words coming over the hiss of the waves. "I will love ye forever, Catriona Mairi!"

She stood on the damp sand in the chill of the April morning watching the cockleshell skim across the waves to the ship. She saw him climb safely aboard, and watched as the anchor was hoisted. The sails filled quickly and the ship began to move slowly away. She stood looking after it until her eyes burned, and the ship was no longer even a speck in the distance. She was unaware of the waves lapping over her boots.

Suddenly she heard a familiar voice say quietly, "Come, madame! It is time for ye to go home."

She turned to face her husband, and his eyes were slivers of ice. Reaching out, he roughly pulled her cloak aside, and his gaze disdainfully raked her rounding belly. The force of his blow sent her to her knees. Arms clutched protectively about her body, she looked defiantly up at him.

"Hurt his bairn, and as God is my witness, I will go after him! Then ye may contend wi James Stewart by yerself!"

Pulling her roughly to her feet, he snarled at her, "I let ye whore wi yer lover, but I will nae claim his bastard! When ye've birthed it, it goes!"

"Then I go too, Patrick," she shouted back at him. "Had ye protected me from the king's attentions I should have remained yer good and faithful wife. But ye did not protect me, and I fell in love wi Francis. Now I must live the rest of my life alone, apart from my love. But I hae his bairn, and I will nae allow ye to take it from me! Ye must kill me first! If ye try to steal my child, I will take it and go after him!" Her voice was rising steadily. "I have been forced to sacrifice my happiness, and his own, for the damned Leslies! Now ye would try to take the one living memory I have of Francis? Christ! I hate ye! I hate ye!"

Angrily he caught her by the arm, and his fingers hurt her cruelly. "Control yerself, madame," he said softly through gritted teeth. "There is no need to inform the entire district of our differences. We will continue this discussion at Glenkirk."

She pulled away from him. "There is nothing to discuss, Patrick." She began climbing the path to the top of Rattray Head, where her horse waited patiently. It was then she realized that the Gordons had gone, and Leslies stood in their place. A sudden weariness overcame her, and she would have stumbled but for Patrick Leslie's strong hand beneath her arm.

"Keep moving, madame. 'Twould not do for Lord Bothwell's brave and bonnie whore to fall on her beautiful face now. We are riding straight through to Glenkirk."

"That's almost three days from here," she protested.

"Aye," he answered grimly.

"Ye'll nae kill me, or the bairn, Glenkirk! I've ridden the borders wi him."

He said nothing, but helped her to mount. She was exhausted physically and emotionally, and needed rest. But he would stop only briefly, to rest the horses and allow his men to relieve themselves. With each mile she grew whiter. At one point Conall spoke up. "God's mercy, sir! Yer going to kill her for sure. Let her rest!"

But before Patrick could answer she spoke up. "No! We go straight through to Glenkirk!"

He shot her an angry look. "I make those decisions,"
he said.

"Go to hell, Glenkirk," she replied evenly, and
spurred her horse ahead.

When they finally reached Glenkirk Castle she accepted his help dismounting, then walked alone to her
apartments, where she collapsed on the floor.

She never knew that it was Patrick alone who cared
for her in her delirium but he learned again from her
fevered ravings how terribly he, James, and even
Bothwell had hurt her. She relived it all, and sitting by
her side he was forced to share it all. For a time she
was back in the early days before their marriage, when
she had shyly given him her innocence and then angrily
fought him for her rights.

Far more shocking than he was prepared for was
the sudden and intimate knowledge of what the king
had done to her. Hearing her plead against performing
the perversions that James had forced her into sickened
him. And then he found himself reliving the rape
through her eyes. Weeping bitterly, she sat straight up
in their bed and, staring at him with sightless eyes,
held out her hands to him—begging him not to shame
her. He was devastated.

But the most painful experience of all for Patrick
Leslie that night was to hear once more of her love for
Bothwell. When she spoke of him, her face became a
totally different face from the one he had always loved.
It was a far more beautiful face—serene and mature.
That she and Bothwell adored each other was obvious,
and he who had loved her since she was a child ached
to learn that only Francis Stewart-Hepburn's love
could satisfy Cat.

He was touched to learn that she had tried to give
Bothwell her wealth, and equally touched to learn that
the great border lord had refused her. It was funny,

thought Glenkirk, but had they not loved the same woman, he and Bothwell might have been friends. One thing he did not learn, however, was the truth about the paternity of the twins. Even in her great illness she protected her children.

Several days later she came to her senses again, and with a frightened gesture, clutched her belly.

"Dinna fear," Glenkirk said harshly, "ye still hae yer bastard!" And he departed, leaving her in the care of her servants.

Cat was a tough creature, and she quickly regained her strength. Her color returned, and she grew sleek and plump with the passing weeks. She spent her time resting, and with her children. Only Bess was old enough to know that the child her mother carried was not her father's, and Bess wanted no more wars with her mother. She made her peace with Cat by asking to be the child's godmother, and Cat agreed, pleased. Bess had grown up.

Meg could say nothing to Cat, unwilling to choose sides between her stubborn son and her equally implacable daughter-in-law. They were both so proud. The dowager finally resolved her dilemma by going off to visit her youngest son and his wife for an indefinite stay.

The Earl of Glenkirk treated his wife with a cold courtesy. They were bound together by the church and by royal command. Cat responded in kind. It appeared an impossible situation.

In mid-August of 1595, the Countess of Glenkirk was delivered of her ninth child, a daughter. The following day she sat up in bed receiving her family. At her back were lace-edged pillows, and her tawny hair hung loose and shining about her shoulders. It was not until late afternoon that the Earl of Glenkirk visited his wife.

She had given up hope of his coming, and was alone
nursing her daughter. He stood in the doorway of her
bedroom watching her, and for a moment his eyes
softened. Then she looked up, and their eyes met. "May
I come in, Cat?"

She nodded. Drawing up a chair by her bedside, he
sat down and watched the child suck hungrily on the
plump breast. Shortly the baby fell asleep, and before
she could stop him, Glenkirk took the child from her.
He cradled the infant in the crook of his arm, and
looked down at it. It was pink-and-white, with a tiny
heart-shaped face and damp auburn curls. Thick, dark
eyelashes tipped in gold lay like half-moons on her
cheeks. He had seen enough infants in his time to know
that this one would be a great beauty.

"What will ye call her?" he asked.

"I had not thought on it yet," she answered.

"Since she is probably the last child we will ever
have, I should like to name her," he said.

Her eyes widened in surprise. "What would ye call
her?" she asked hesitantly.

"Frances," he said quietly. "Frances Leslie is to be
her name."

For the briefest moment she did not believe she had
heard him correctly, but his eyes were warm suddenly,
and he smiled at her. "I will nae ask yer forgiveness,
Cat, for what I did to ye cannot be erased, or forgotten.
But I dinna want James Stewart to destroy us and
our family as he destroyed Bothwell. I know ye'll
never love me again, but can we nae begin afresh, and
be friends? I have never stopped loving ye, sweetheart,
and I doubt I ever will."

She drew a deep breath, and felt her heart swell
until it ached. A hard lump rose in her throat and
tears burned her eyelids. Reaching out, she took his
free hand and pressed it to her cheek. Then she looked

up at him, and her eyes were like emeralds. "Bothwell was right," she said softly. "He said we would be safe wi ye."

Glenkirk lay the sleeping child in her cradle and then, returning to his wife's side, took both her hands in his. "I am a luckier man than he, sweetheart. I have been given a second chance." He smiled again at her, and she tremulously returned the smile.

She would make her peace with him for her daughter's sake, and because they would be safe with him. But no matter how long she lived she would not forget Francis Stewart-Hepburn, the great border lord, the uncrowned King of Scotland, and her beloved. He would always live fiercely in her secret heart.

BOOK II

Part V

❦

Flight to Love

Chapter 38

❧❦

CATRIONA Leslie sat quietly before her bedroom
fire watching the dancing flames and trying to
absorb the events of the past weeks. Her husband was
dead, or so everyone assumed. She could not, however,
imagine Patrick dead, nor did she feel he was. Still, she
sighed, the facts seemed indisputable.

Eighteen months ago Patrick had sailed from Leith
in a six-ship convoy aboard his flagship, the *Gallant
James*. They were bound for the New World on a fur-
buying expedition. It was a new venture in the Leslie
interests, and the Earl of Glenkirk had gone along to
be sure the new business would be successful.

In part Cat blamed herself for his departure. Though
they had made their peace after Frances Anne's birth,
and there was no enmity between them, neither was
there anything else. To all outward appearances the
Earl and Countess of Glenkirk were an ideal couple.
But Cat pined every waking moment for her exiled
lover, the Earl of Bothwell. She said nothing, but
Patrick Leslie knew, and continuously cursed himself
for the supreme act of stupidity that had cost him his
wife's love.

For close to a year now the earl had toyed with the
idea of mounting an expedition to the New World. Furs
had always been an important part of European
fashion, and the quality of skins beginning to trickle

in from the New World was quite superior. "Why,"
asked Patrick, "should our ships carry such valuable
cargo for others when we can buy the furs ourselves
and sell them in Europe ourselves?"

So it was decided that the first Leslie ships would
leave in early spring of 1596, followed three months
later by a second group, commanded by the earl's
brother, Adam Leslie. In the hope that his absence
would give her time to heal and perhaps begin thinking
of him in a more loving fashion, the Earl of Glenkirk
chose to lead the expedition himself. Cat had even gone
to Leith in the company of all their children to bid
him a safe journey.

"I will bring ye back enough beaver to make a whole
cloak," he promised gaily. "Dark fur shows yer beauty
to perfection." And he kissed her tenderly.

"Go safely, Patrick, and return soon," she answered
him.

"Ye'll be all right, Cat?"

She smiled up at him, and for a brief moment he
saw her as she had been before life had hurt her so
badly. "I'll be fine, Glenkirk!" And the leaf-green eyes
twinkled mischievously at him. "I am quite capable of
being on my own—if ye call being wi nine bairns being
alone!"

And they had parted. She had had no premonition
of disaster, no premonition that she would never see
him again. But six weeks ago, in mid-July of 1597, the
second convoy of Leslie ships had returned to Leith
heavy with a cargo of rich furs, and bringing also the
terrible news. Adam Leslie, not even waiting to oversee
the unloading, had spurred his horse cruelly to reach
Glenkirk with the announcement that Patrick Leslie
and his six ships had never reached their destination
in the New World.

The king had quickly learned of the tragedy, and

without consulting the Leslies, he declared young James Leslie the fifth Earl of Glenkirk. Cat was furious, though Glenkirk needed its lord. Once again James Stewart was interfering in her life. He had written to her this week that her mourning was not to exceed six months. She was to be back at court by spring.

His motive, couched in kindly rhetoric, made her laugh and swear alternately. The young earl was ordered to marry quickly to ensure the Glenkirk succession. Thank God, thought Cat to herself, that Patrick and I had the wit to betroth Jemmie to Isabelle Gordon two years ago—else King Jamie would interfere in that as well!

The king's letter continued. Since Patrick's mother, Meg, still lived, Glenkirk had the unusual distinction of having two dowager countesses. As the elder resided in the dower house, the younger must come to court so the young people might have their marital privacy, and so the older woman would not be disturbed.

Cat snorted. Ye dinna fool me, Jamie! Wi Patrick gone and Bothwell exiled, ye think to hae yer way wi me. Come to court and gie my son and his bride their privacy! Pah! Come to court and gie ye my body. You bastard! Ye say nothing of my other bairns. What would ye say if I arrived wi them all?

She was in a very difficult position and could not ask her young son for protection against the king.

But the young earl knew most of the reasons for his parents estrangement. Now, with the king seeking to entrap his mother again, Jemmie sought and found what he believed was a solution to free Cat without openly offending the king.

As he burst into her apartments she looked up, startled. "My God! Ye look so like Patrick," she said with a catch in her voice.

He knelt by her side, saying softly, "I hae the an-

swer to yer dilemma, mother! I know how we may
thwart the king wi'out bringing his wrath down on
the Leslies! 'Tis foolproof!"

She put a hand on his shoulder, and he saw the
sadness in her face. "Jemmie, my love, I thank ye, but
I am trapped, and I would nae shame yer father's
memory by destroying his family—our family. The
king wants me as his mistress and there is simply no
escape for me. I must obey him."

"Nay! Listen to me! The king is nae aware that I
know of his duplicity. What if after Bella and I and
Bess and Henry are married this winter, we all troup
to court, leaving ye here to complete yer mourning
period. We return to find ye gone. Only a note remains
. . . telling us ye've gone to visit our Leslie cousins
in France in hopes of overcoming yer depression."

"And," said Cat, excitedly catching his mood, "if as
soon as ye leave Edinburgh to return home, workmen
arrive at Glenkirk House to completely refurbish it,
the king will nae suspect that I dinna intend to return." She chuckled. "I will secretly transfer the deed
to Glenkirk House to Bella, and my lodge, A-Cuil, to
Bess. That way, when Jamie discovers that the bird has
flown, he canna confiscate them. Yer right, my son!
If ye play the loyal and loving subject then Jamie dare
not touch anything Leslie. His involvement has been
wi Bothwell, yer father, and me. If he believes ye
know nothing, he can nae punish you or our family.
His pride will nae permit it, for he is very anxious the
English hae a good report of him. The old queen has
never officially declared him her heir, and she might
name Arabella Stewart, his first cousin. But, Jamie. Ye
must publicly denounce my wicked behavior. Not
even Bella must know of our plot."

He grinned at her. "Aye, mother. Ye are indeed a
shameful hussy, but I'd hae ye no other way!" Then

he became more serious. "Ye'll need money. I'll ask the Kiras the best way of secretly handling funds for ye."

"Nay, Jemmie, but thank ye for the thought. There's nae been a need for ye to know, but I am a very wealthy woman in my own right. I will hae the Kiras begin to slowly transfer my funds to Europe."

"Where will ye go?" he asked her, knowing in his heart the answer she would give him.

She looked straight at him. "Why, Jemmie, I go to find Bothwell. If Francis will still hae me I will be the happiest woman alive."

"I dinna think ye need fear that Lord Bothwell doesna want ye. I understand he was recently expelled from France for killing a man in a duel. The unfortunate gentleman in question made an unkind remark regarding a lady of quality in Scotland who held Bothwell's devotion."

"And where is Francis now?" she asked evenly.

"Italy. He tried Spain, but the Spaniards are a bit too religious, and their court is quite stuffy. Ye'll find yer border lord in Naples. Go to him, mother, and be happy! Marry him as ye both always wanted. Glenkirk will ever be here for ye, but I dinna think you'll need it."

"Frances Anne?"

"Will remain here until yer safely established. I send her to ye then."

"Ian and Jane also," she said quietly.

James Leslie laughed softly. "I always suspected as much, though, thank God, father never did!"

She flushed under her eldest son's amused gaze. "Ye amaze me, Jemmie. How can ye be so tolerant?"

"I am tolerant because ye were always a good mother to us. I am tolerant because until the king forced ye into his bed ye were always a good and loving wife to my father. I am tolerant because the same hot blood that flows in your veins, mother, flows in mine. I have seen how other men look at ye, and as a page wi Lord Rothes' household I have overheard things. Whatever happened that lost my father yer love I blame on the king. I dinna suppose ye would tell me now, would ye?"

For a moment she was thoughtful, and then she spoke. "When yer father found the king wi me he was shocked and very, very hurt. The king might have saved Glenkirk's pride, but instead he cruelly praised my performance in his bed to your father. He took him into my antechamber and there they spent the next few hours drinking Glenkirk whisky, and talking. Afterwards, when they were both very drunk, they entered my bedroom, and . . ." She stopped for a minute, her face white with the memory. She resumed quietly, "Yer father and the king spent the rest of the night taking turns raping me. After several years I forgave yer father, Jemmie, but that night killed my love for him. I could understand, and, aye, even sympathize wi him, but for him to believe that I, who was ever faithful to him, had willingly betrayed him. . . ." She stopped, momentarily lost for words. "He was ever stubborn, was Patrick Leslie! I loved him once, Jemmie, but I always questioned our marriage. We were, I suppose, too alike.

"I fled after that night to the only friend I had— Lord Bothwell. I only meant to gain time, to have a little peace, to think. But Francis and I fell in love. The rest ye know.

"As for James Stewart, I despise him! He plays the good Christian king, the perfect husband, the ideal father. Alas, he is a hypocrite, and the greatest lecher I hae ever known!"

"I thought he was nae interested in women, but preferred men," said Jemmie.

"Nay. 'Tis a ruse he uses to hide his real desires."

"That father could treat ye so! He deserved to lose ye! If I had known, I would hae killed him myself!"

"Jemmie! Jemmie! Yer poor father suffered terribly for that one extravagant cruelty. He returned from Glenkirk eager to see me, and instead found his half-naked wife being fondled by the king. How would ye hae felt if it had been yer Bella? Nay! 'Tis James who is to blame! Yer father—may God assoil him—is gone. Francis is in the kingdom of Naples, and though I dare not communicate wi him, I will soon be going to him. The old life is almost over, and I will soon be on my way to Bothwell. For now, however, our thoughts must be on planning yer wedding to Isabelle Gordon."

"And yer plans, mother?"

"Will be taken care of, Jemmie. 'Tis best ye know nothing more lest ye innocently gie me away. When I am gone, and until I am out of disgrace wi the king, ye can secretly get in touch wi me through the Kiras." She kissed him on the cheek. "Despite my love for Bothwell," she said, "I would nae leave ye if I dinna think ye could handle yer title and the duties that go wi it. Learn a lesson from yer ancestors, Jemmie. Only the first Earl of Glenkirk lived to be a white-haired old man. Most of the others involved themselves wi the Stewarts and died young.

"If I had not been so insistent about going to court, perhaps none of this would hae happened. Yer father —and in fairness to his memory, Jemmie, I tell ye this—yer father warned me nae to get involved wi the Stewarts. I would nae listen, but *ye must!* Let yer Uncle Adam guide ye in business, and keep as much from court as ye possibly can."

"But what happens, mother, when the old queen in the south dies? What if our king goes to London?"

"He will, Jemmie. He impatiently waits for the day he may leave Scotland. Then yer Uncle Adam must go to London to represent our interests, but ye and Bella must remain here. Glenkirk must never be ruled by an absentee lord. 'Twould be its downfall. Teach yer sons a love of this land so it may never be wi'out a Leslie."

"Ye talk as if ye'll ne'er see Glenkirk again, mother."

"I won't, Jemmie. I dinna think James will ever forgie me the insult I will deliver him. Rest assured that should I ever set foot on English or Scottish soil while our royal cousin rules, I shall be quickly and quietly arrested, imprisoned, and aye, even killed. When I go, I am gone. I only pray that Francis still wants me."

James Leslie snorted. "He does! Of that I hae no doubt. God! How desperately he sought to keep ye! If ye had both been less honorable people . . . but then ye were not, and ye sacrificed yerselves for us Leslies. No more, mother! Though I will publicly condemn ye, ye go wi my blessing, and with my love."

The smile she gave him was radiant, and he was slightly taken aback. "Jesu, mother! If that is the way ye smile at all the men who please ye, I am surprised ye hae not been ravished at least a hundred times!"

She laughed happily. "A thousand, my impudent young lord! Now be off wi ye, Jemmie! I hae a wedding to plan." He turned to go. "Jemmie." He looked and she held his eyes while she rose in a gesture of respect. "I am most grateful to ye, my lord, most grateful. Ye'll make a fine earl. I am so verra sorry I canna be here to watch ye govern."

Young James Leslie bowed quickly to his mother and then was gone.

Chapter 39

❧§❧

JAMES Leslie's fiancée, Isabelle Gordon, was a younger daughter of George and Henriette Gordon, the Earl and Countess of Huntley. As Huntley House had been burned to the ground two years before by a group of fanatic dissenters, she was to be married at Glenkirk. Some said the Gordons had been singled out not because they were Roman Catholic—half of Scotland still was—but because they had openly sheltered the Earl of Bothwell several years ago.

Now, however, the king had given his blessing to the marriage, and was even coming to the wedding, which would be celebrated on December 20. The young couple would then keep the Christmas through Twelfth Night holidays there before going to Edinburgh for the winter season.

As soon as the wedding date was set, young Isabelle came to Glenkirk. Cat insisted, "She must learn how to run this castle if she is to be its chatelaine."

"But, madame," protested the future Countess of Glenkirk, who was pretty and sweet-natured though inclined to be lazy, "surely ye will always be here to help me."

"Nay, my dear Belle, I will nae be making Glenkirk my home. The king has suggested I return to court. I will be making my home in my townhouse in Edinburgh. Jemmie's grandmother, however, will be in the

dower house should ye need advice on running the
household. 'Tis really she ye should go to anyhow.
Meg knows Glenkirk better than any of us."

George Gordon looked across the cozy family hall
at Cat. "Bella, my dear," he said smoothly, "will ye
run to the nursery and see that old Nanny has settled
the littlest bairns for the night?"

"Yes, papa." Isabelle dutifully rose and did as she
was bid. Yet she wondered what they wanted to talk
about that she was not allowed to hear.

"Do ye need help, Cat?" asked Huntley when his
daughter had gone. "Dinna tell me that Jamie has dared
to pursue ye again."

"He has, George. I am allowed six months to mourn
Patrick, and then I must present myself at court for
the king's pleasure."

"The bastard!" swore Lord Gordon.

"Dinna fret, George. I will follow my heart."

The Earl of Huntley looked at the widowed Countess
of Glenkirk, and a slow smile spread over his face.
"Jesu! What a vixen ye are!" Then more seriously,
"He'll nae take his vengeance on Jemmie and Belle,
will he?"

"Nay, George. What reason could he offer in public
for attacking two innocent and loyal young subjects?
They know nothing of the matter."

"Is this why ye asked to have the wedding date set
now?"

"His majesty suggested it, George. He felt the Glenkirk succession should be protected as soon as possible."

Gordon chuckled. "More likely he felt ye should be
in his bed as soon as possible."

Cat laughed out loud. "Poor Jamie would be very
upset to know how transparent his motives are."

"Why shouldn't they be to us, Cat? Hell! The

Stewarts have fucked every noble family in Scotland. We're all cousins!"

Henriette Gordon leaned forward in her chair and asked softly, "What will ye do, Cat?"

"Dinna ask me questions I canna answer, Riette."

"But, Cat—"

"Hush yer pretty mouth, woman," said her husband.

So while she openly went about the business of preparing a lavish wedding for her eldest son, Cat Leslie secretly prepared for her escape to Italy. In this endeavor the Kiras, the Leslies' bankers and business associates for many years, willingly helped.

Over the next few months Cat's vast fortune would be transferred to the Kiras' Rome bank, by way of Paris. Though the King of France might have to cooperate with Scotland, the pope in Rome did not— especially when the matter involved a noble Catholic widow fighting to preserve her virtue against the chief Protestant heretic in Europe.

It was decided that Cat would sail down the North Sea, into the English Channel, and across into France. From there she would go overland to Italy, as the sea route was much too dangerous. The Mediterranean teemed with Turkish pirates. She would have her own coach, driver, footmen, and outriders. The only other person at Glenkirk aware of Cat's plans was Conall More-Leslie, Glenkirk's assistant captain-at-arms. Cat wanted only Glenkirk people in her entourage, and Conall was the man to arrange it.

"Well," he said dourly, "if it has to be marriage to Lord Bothwell or royal whoredom to Jamie Stewart, Bothwell is the lesser evil. I'll help ye, Mistress Cat, but gie me time to choose my men carefully. Catholics only. The Protestants would be too uncomfortable in Italy. Single, uninvolved men wi no one to come home to, so they'll stay wi us. No youngsters—too hotheaded.

But able men in their twenties or thirties. And I'll nae talk to any till just before we go. Less chance of the word getting to one of Jamie's spies. Who will ye take to serve ye?"

"Susan, mayhap one other."

He nodded, not surprised that she already had it all worked out. She was like her great-grandmother, Janet Leslie, and never did anything without carefully thinking it out. Too many people had underestimated her intelligence and resourcefulness.

He chuckled, and she asked, "Why do ye laugh?"

Blue eyes crinkling with mirth contrasted with his weathered face. He replied, "Because I would gie a year's pay to see the look on Jamie Stewart's face when he finds out ye've escaped him again!"

"Oh, Conall," she admonished him, her own laughter bubbling up, "hae ye no respect for the crown?"

"The crown, aye! But Cousin Jamie? 'Tis either a foolish man or an overly stubborn one who pursues a woman who so obviously doesna want him. Are these qualities that make a good king? I dinna think so."

"But in his kingly duties he is a good king, Conall. 'Tis in his personal life he falters. He has never really been comfortable wi his fellow man, though he would desperately like to be." She turned to the windows facing out across the hills. "Ah, Conall! All I ever wanted to do was live my life quietly at Glenkirk."

"Pah!" snapped the older man. "Dinna delude yerself. Ye've always been too restless. 'Twas nae Lord Patrick who yearned for court." Her stricken look stopped him. "Ah, lassie, dinna fret over it now! I'm a Leslie myself—albeit from the wrong side of the blanket—and I know 'tis the women in this family who hae always been the wild ones."

As the autumn deepened she took every opportunity to ride the Leslie lands, leaving the wedding plans in

Meg's competent hands. But Meg had always understood Cat far better than anyone else, and one day
the older dowager accompanied Cat on her ride.

" 'Tis much too lovely a day to be indoors," Meg
announced loudly, for the benefit of the stableboys.
"If I look out my window at those fields of Michaelmas
daisies once more, I shall go mad." She pulled herself
into the saddle and chuckled. "Lord! It must be two
years since I last rode. Come along, Cat!" And she
gently kicked the fat sides of her old brown mare.

Cat followed, wondering what had possessed Meg
to come riding with her. They rode in silence for at
least fifteen minutes, then Meg slowed her horse to a
walk and moved up next to her companion. Cat turned
to face her. "Well, Meg? What gets ye onto old
Brownie? And dinna rhapsodize to me over Michaelmas daisies!"

Meg Leslie laughed. "I thought that was a rather
nice touch, my dear, but ye are right of course.
Michaelmas daisies dinna interest me. Now tell me,
Cat, when do ye leave us?"

Cat was not startled, and answered quietly, "After
Bess and Henry's wedding."

"Ye go to Francis?"

"Aye."

"Is it safe for the family?"

"I believe so with all my heart, Meg. Since the king
doesna know that Jemmie knows the situation between
us, I dinna believe he will hold our young earl responsible for my defection. He will be angry, but Jemmie
will be angrier, and will vehemently castigate me for
the wretched manner in which I refused the wonderful
honor offered me."

Meg laughed again. "Then Jemmie knows yer
going."

"Knows? Why, bless me, Meg! He arranged it! I

was all ready to gie up, and yield myself to James. But Jemmie feels his very innocence in the matter will save us. He feels that this is the only chance I will have to escape, and he is right. What reason could James possibly give for an undue display of vengeance on our family now? We are at peace, and the Leslies of Glenkirk hae always been loyal to the crown. This is the one time I may flee wi'out endangering our clan."

"And if Francis has found a new love, my dear? He was always a man for the lasses, and never particularly constant."

"He was to me, Meg," replied Cat quietly.

"Aye," said the older woman. "He was . . . but he is gone from ye almost three years, Cat."

"He loves me yet, Meg, as I love him. I feel it."

"But," persisted Meg, "if he doesna, will ye return home?"

"Not as long as James pursues me, Meg. I simply cannot be the royal whore. I will settle in France if Bothwell doesna want me."

"He will, Cat," said Meg gently. "I simply wanted to be sure ye knew what ye were doing. There are many women in yer position who could be happy enough being the king's mistress."

"If I loved Jamie," said Cat, "I would be content. But I hae never been a woman who could lie wi a man she disliked, and I dinna care for the king. I will nae forgie him for what he did to poor Patrick. It was the act of a cruel man, and I detest deliberate cruelty!"

Then Meg said something that brought tears to Cat's lovely eyes. "Ye go wi my blessing, my dear. Strange as it may seem I know that Patrick would approve yer course. He never forgave himself, ye know."

"But I forgave him, Meg. I could no longer love him as I once did, but I did forgie him." She smiled. "Jemmie knows nothing more than that I go before spring. 'Tis better that way. Conall is coming wi me. Susan also, though I've said nought to her yet."

"What provision hae ye made for the children, Cat?"

"Colin and Robbie will remain wi the Earl of Rothes' household until they are each fourteen. Then they are to go to the University in Aberdeen as Jemmie did. Afterwards, their European tour, and then marriage. Jemmie and I hae just finished negotiating a marriage agreement wi my brother. Wi his only son dead, he is without an heir, and has four daughters to marry off. Colin will wed the eldest when he is twenty. As my brother's heir, he will be the next Master of Greyhaven. Robbie will wed wi the next daughter in the following year. I hae settled a good sum on Robbie, and bought him a fine house wi good lands near Greyhaven so he may always be quite independent of his older brother.

"Amanda I hae betrothed to Charles' heir. My daughter will be the next Countess of Sithean."

Meg raised her eyebrows. "I thought my daughter Janet aimed higher for her son."

Cat laughed. "Janet is not simply wed to a Leslie, she was born one. Her son may hae a title, but my daughter has an enormous dowry! And, by strange coincidence, Amanda is in possession of several hundred acres of pastureland needed by Sithean for their sheep.

"Little Morag will become Malcolm Gordon's wife. She's to hae a very large dowry, and a manor house of her own. Even younger Gordon sons come high!"

Meg's eyes sparkled. "Dear lord," she said breathlessly, "ye grow more like Mam as ye get older!" Then she became serious again. "The bairns? What of them? Ye canna leave yer little ones."

"Jemmie will send them to me when I am settled, Meg. 'Twould be dangerous for them to travel wi me, and they would slow me down. If the king sends his people after me, the bairns will make me vulnerable. 'Twill be only for a few months."

Meg nodded. "I suppose 'tis best." They rode in silence for a while longer. Then Meg spoke again. "Cat, I know I hae no right to ask, but Ian and Jane—"

"Are Bothwell's also. Aye, Meg. Even he did not know until just before he went into exile. When we first parted I thought I should never see him again, and I wanted his child. Patrick, however, no sooner had me back then he was bedding me, and he kept on bedding me until 'twas quite obvious I was wi child. He assumed the twins were his, and for all our sakes I said nought."

"Ye were right, my dear. But, poor Francis, having to leave Scotland knowing that he was leaving not only ye, but his bairns also. Ah, my Cat, ye both deserve yer happiness."

"Thank ye, Meg. Ye hae always been a good friend to me."

The older woman leaned from her saddle and, reaching out, gripped Cat's hand. "Yer more daughter to me than my own two. Be happy, Cat! Please be happy!"

Chapter 40

❧❧❧

JAMES Stewart smiled sweetly at his wife. "No, no, Annie! 'Tis unthinkable. Ye canna possibly go to Glenkirk for young James Leslie's wedding." He patted her distended belly fondly. "Nay. We must nae endanger the bairn."

"But it is so close to Christmas!" wailed the queen. "I do not want to be without ye then."

"I will be back to spend Christmas wi ye, Annie."

"Ye cannot unless ye leave immediately after the wedding, and that would be most rude!"

"Then I will nae be back," said the king irritably. "What difference does it make? I will be here for New Year's and Twelfth Night."

"But in Denmark we always celebrate Christmas *en famille!*"

James was becoming annoyed. "Ye are nae in Denmark, Annie! Yer Queen of Scotland!" he roared, and the queen began to cry.

Dear heaven, thought the king, I canna hae her guessing why I dinna want her wi me.

"There, there, m'dear," he said convincingly. "I canna offend the Leslies of Glenkirk. I must go to the young earl's wedding, especially since 'tis my cousin of Huntley's wench he weds. The Gordons gie me trouble enough, and I will nae gie them an excuse to start more trouble by not going to their daughter's

wedding. 'Tis winter, and the roads are bad. Be reasonable, sweetheart. Ye canna go junketing all over
Scotland in yer present condition."

"The child," sniffed the queen. "That's all the good
I am to ye, Jamie. A royal brood mare!"

"We can hae many bairns, Annie," said James, "but
where would I get another like ye?"

The queen's lovely sky blue eyes filled to overflowing. "Oh, Jamie," she said in a choked little voice.

The king put an arm about his wife. "Now let us
hear no more of this foolishness."

"Yes, Jamie," said the queen, sighing happily. But
he barely heard her, so intent was he on thoughts of
the lovely Cat Leslie, who would soon be his.

It was over four years since he had seen Cat, and
their last meeting had not been everything a man hopes
for from the woman he desires. But now, alone and
unprotected, the widowed Countess of Glenkirk should
prove more obedient to her royal master's wishes.

Awaiting his arrival, Cat knew what she might
expect. She realized that she could not escape James'
attentions even in her own house, and she steeled herself to be sweetly complacent so he might not suspect
that she intended fleeing. She must not even speak
openly with Jemmie.

With her son's marriage impending, Cat had removed her things from the apartments of the Earl and
Countess of Glenkirk. It had not been easy leaving
the rooms that had been hers all these years, but in a
few weeks they would rightfully belong to young Belle.
To camouflage her plans for escape, she went to the
expense of redoing an entire suite of rooms for herself
in the west-tower apartment, which had once belonged
to her great-grandmother, Janet, before that lady built
her own castle at Sithean. The tower had not been used
since, and Cat fancied she could feel the other woman's
presence.

"Well, Mam," she sighed aloud, "I am in another coil. Ye always warned us to stay clear of the Stewarts. My willfulness has cost us all, and now I must flee my home or submit to the king's lust. I wonder what ye would think of me if ye were here today."

She walked to the bedroom windows and gazed out across the Glenkirk hills to Sithean's loch, and to Greyhaven, her childhood home. Here she imagined her great-grandmother waiting for her lover, Colin Hay, the Master of Greyhaven. Well, if Mam could defy convention to be with her lover, thought Cat, then so can I!

She sighed. Ah, Bothwell! 'Tis almost three years since the terrible day I stood on Rattray Head and watched that damned ship take ye from me. And in all that time we hae nae dared to even correspond. I dinna doubt that there hae been many women in yer bed, but is there one who's love has made ye forget me? Dear God! Please! No!

And as she closed her eyes in an agony of doubt his face swam before her darkened eyelids. That dearly beloved rugged face. The deep sapphire eyes, the sensuous mouth, the marvelous auburn hair and elegant short tailored beard he always had.

As she leaned against the cold stone she imagined the velvet firmness of his broad shoulder, and his big hand gently stroking her long hair. Suddenly, for the first time in all these long months, Cat wept. She wept in great gulping sobs. She wept for Patrick Leslie, and the happy years they had had before James ruined their lives. She wept for their loss of innocence—both hers and Patrick's. But most of all she wept for the Earl of Bothwell, the man she loved, cruelly exiled and impoverished because of his cousin's jealousy. Francis —who so loved his castle, Hermitage, and his beloved borders—forced to wander Europe alone and friendless.

But soon, she vowed, soon she would seek him out across Europe, and when she found him. . . . She stopped. What if he had remarried? After all, even Francis might have to compromise his honor in order to live. *No!* He had not remarried. But they would marry when she found him, and then Jemmie would send their bairns to them, and they would live to a peaceful old age, far from the intrigues of the court.

But first, she must contend with Cousin Jamie. He would come crawling into her bed when he arrived for the wedding. Well, and she laughed through her tears, he would find her eager. She, who was so used to regular lovemaking, had not had a man since her husband went off those long months ago. She despised James, but her body craved a man's touch. For once it would be she who used him!

Seeking out her eldest son, she warned him, "Ye must nae let the king know that yer aware of his nocturnal visits to me while he's here."

The young earl was shocked. "Jesu, mother! Would he dare, under our very roof?"

She laughed at his outrage. "Dare? He is the king. Lord, Jemmie, James would dare almost anything with regard to his personal desires! If ye understand this, ye will understand him. Dinna be fooled by his show of piety and learning. He is outwardly pious because it keeps his Protestant kirk contented, and out of his private affairs. He is learned, yea, but he is also superstitious, cruel, and willful. Never trust him, no matter how fair he speaks to ye. Learn from my mistakes, Jemmie. Dinna involved yerself wi the king or the court."

"But what should be our attitude towards the Stewarts, mother?"

"Loyalty in times of danger to the crown or to the country. At all other times, maintain yer distance. When forced to be wi the king, show admiration and

affection. Be agreeable wi'out being a toady. Jamie
can be most charming, and his humor is quite droll.
He doesna mean to play the villain. Ye simply must nae
get too involved."

Jemmie nodded, but his brow was furrowed. "I wish
he were nae coming to the wedding. Do ye think the
queen will be wi him? At least her presence may help
to keep his lust in check."

"She will nae come, Jemmie. I hear she is breeding
again, and the king will use it as an excuse to keep
her in Edinburgh. Dinna fret, my son. If I am to escape
royal James, he must believe that I am ready to accept
his will. His visit here will reassure him completely.
The widow of Glenkirk will receive him hesitantly, but
sweetly. I shall worry about my position, and he will
offer comfort and encourage me to trust him completely. And once he has assuaged my fears, he will
leave feeling very self-satisfied and manly."

Jemmie Leslie looked at his mother in frank amazement. "Yer the most devious woman I've ever known,"
he chuckled. "I would nae like to hae ye for an
enemy, madame."

Cat laughed aloud. " 'Tis strange," she said, "but
yer father once said that same thing to me."

Five days before the wedding was to be celebrated,
James Stewart arrived at Glenkirk. He was greeted by
his distant cousins, the Leslies, and his closer cousins,
the Gordons. His amber eyes lingered a moment on the
black-garbed Countess of Glenkirk, and Cat flushed
uncomfortably under his gaze. It was her duty, and
Meg's, to escort the king to the suite of rooms set
aside for the occasional royal visitor.

James' glance swept the large rooms, each warm
with its own blazing fire. "Most attractive, dear Cousin
Margaret. Ye Leslies hae the knack of making a man
feel welcome. I hope all yer rooms are as pleasant."

"Oh, yes, James," replied Meg. "I may call ye James,

mayn't I? After all, I could be yer mother." Giving his arm a little squeeze, she smiled up into his face, her eyes twinkling in a kindly fashion, and Cat wondered if she were going mad. What on earth possessed Meg to simper so? "I am," continued the elder dowager, "supposed to make my home in the dower house, but I am here in the castle more often than not. I live in the south wing, where the sun can warm my old bones. The earl's suite is in the east wing, so that the morning sun—according to tradition—may wake him early, and send him about his duties."

Christ in his heaven, thought Cat, where is she getting such nonsense?

"The royal suite has always been here in the west wing so royal visitors will nae be wakened early, but find their rooms filled with warm afternoon sunlight after a morning's hunt," finished Meg triumphantly.

"What a charming and thoughtful custom," said the king. He turned to Cat, who had maintained her silence all this time. "Ye no longer reside in the earl's suite?"

"No, sire." Cat kept her eyes modestly lowered.

Meg chattered on. "Oh, no, James! We hae redone those rooms for little Belle. Cat's apartments are right here in the west wing—in the tower! She was her great-grandmother's favorite girlchild, and dearest Mam lived in the west tower. So, when Cat had to pick other rooms, she chose Mam's. Why, there is even a secret entrance from here to those rooms!"

"Meg! 'Tis a family secret," chided Cat softly.

"Ahhhh," breathed the king, "but I am family, sweet Cat. Tell me, Aunt Meg, what of this secret entrance?"

Meg giggled. "I am nae sure," she said, "but Cat would know. Come, dear one. I always remember Mam chuckling about that secret entrance where she used to let Colin Hay in when he came calling. I know ye know where it is, and it does have an exit into this very apartment, doesn't it?"

Cat hesitated, then spoke low. "Aye. It does."

The king tried to keep the impatience from his voice. It was obvious that the old woman liked him, and was slyly attempting to further his cause. "Come, Cat, dinna be coy wi me! What of this secret entrance? Is there one here?"

She walked across the bedchamber to the fireplace and pressed a rose carving on the left side of the mantel. A small door swung open. Taking a lighted candle from a wall sconce, Cat beckoned them to follow her. The flickering light wound up the cool, winding passage for two and a half flights. Then Cat stopped. Reaching up, she touched the molding around a door. The door sprang open. Walking through, they found themselves in what was obviously a woman's bedchamber.

"Gracious!" gasped Meg.

The king simply smiled.

"If ye followed the passage down," said Cat, "ye would exit at the bottom of the tower into a little courtyard."

"Fascinating," said James. "And now," he took the candle from Cat, "I shall see if I can find my way back alone."

"We will leave our door open, James, until yer safely back," said Meg. "Call out, my dear."

The king slipped through the door and began his descent. The flickering candle disappeared from view. At last they heard him call, "I am safe, Aunt Meg," and a door clicked closed.

Cat then closed up her end of the passage and, turning to her mother-in-law, exclaimed, "Jesu, madame! Ye surely missed yer calling. Ye should be selling maidenheads in the Highgate!"

Meg laughed. "Ye dinna think he suspects?"

"Nay. The only thing he suspects is that yer on his side. Bless ye, Meg! Now our Jemmie will surely be safe after I go. James will think all Leslies adore him!"

"And ye must indeed go, my dear. The way the king looks at ye, Cat. Dear heaven! It turns my blood cold! He would devour ye! Will ye be safe wi him here?"

"Aye, Meg. I am well used to handling Jamie. This time, however, I must play the shyly reluctant and very repentant mistress. 'Twill nae be easy, but the king must never guess that I merely bide my time." She went to the garderobe and drew out a deep-violet velvet gown. "I dinna think Patrick would mind if I came out of mourning for Jemmie's wedding." She turned. "Damn me, Meg! Where is he? I canna believe he is dead, and yet if his ship did not reach the New World, where is he? Am I a fool? Is it only that I feel guilty over his going?"

Meg nodded. "I hae had the same feeling. Surely I should feel something if my eldest child were dead. He is gone, and yet he is not. Still, ye go, Cat. Do ye feel he will ever return?"

"Not to me, Meg. I feel that Patrick has somehow passed from my life. If I did not feel that, I could nae go, even wi the threat of the king hanging over me."

"Get some rest, my dear," said Meg kindly. " 'Twill be a long evening, I fear." And she hugged Cat before she left.

Cat did not even bother to call her tiring woman. Instead she removed her dark gown, lay down upon her bed, and slept fitfully. When she awoke, Susan was busily filling the new porcelain hip bath. "Which scent, madame?"

"Lilac," said Cat, stretching lazily. "I am wearing the violet velvet gown, Susan. When ye've finished there, bring me my jewel case."

A few minutes later she sat sifting through her many necklaces, deciding what she would wear. A chain of gold filigree worked with chunky baroque pearls and large amethysts caught her eye. She held it against the violet of the dress and smiled. An hour later she was ready, bathed in lilac-scented water, gowned in the low-necked violet velvet, her generous breasts swelling provocatively above a single ruffle of creamy lace. Her honey-colored hair was parted in the center, drawn back over her ears, and twisted into a knot of curls at the back of her head. From the front it looked very severe. From the rear the tawny curls, caught with mauve and white silk flowers, were bewitchingly feminine.

In the great hall of Glenkirk that night there were over two hundred diners, including the Leslies of Glenkirk, headed by young James, the Leslies of Sithean with their earl, who was Cat's first cousin, Charles, and the Hays, with Cat's father as their chief. The immediate family totaled some ninety-five persons, not counting the More-Leslies, who were the family's bastard line. There were numerous Gordons, as George Gordon, Earl of Huntley, was the chief of his clan. And there were the king and his many retainers. In her entire life Cat had never seen the castle so full.

At the high table the king found himself between the bride-to-be and her mother. To his chagrin, Cat was seated on the other side of her son. The beautiful widow of Glenkirk did not lack for admirers. When at last the long meal ended, the dancing began. But Cat refused the eager gallants, pleading that she would dance at her son's wedding, but not before. She was, she gently reminded them, still in mourning.

She remained demurely seated on the dais, watching while the king danced first with Bella, then with Meg, and finally with Henriette. His duty done, James Stewart returned to the dais and sat next to Cat. A page put a goblet of chilled wine in his hand, and he sipped appreciatively. Finally he spoke. "How is it possible, madame, that yer more beautiful now than ye were four years ago? I am mad for ye, Cat! I long to be alone wi ye!"

"Yer majesty is most kind."

He made an impatient noise. "Why are ye so formal wi me, love? Ye hae nae said a warm word to me since I arrived."

"Yer majesty has me at a disadvantage," she said in a low voice. "We did nae part on the best of terms."

He laughed, softly triumphant. "We will resolve all that later, my love. Now, gie me a little smile." And reaching over, he tipped her face up to his.

She raised her leaf-green eyes to his amber ones and smiled shyly at him. The king could feel desire sweeping him. He wanted her, as he had always wanted her, but this time he intended gaining the upper hand immediately. She was a passionate little vixen, but once she accepted him as her master, he believed that she would be loyal.

Towards midnight Cat laughingly announced to their guests that those who wished to retire might, and those who did not might dance, drink, and play until dawn. Predictably, the older members of the gathering departed. The king, however, remained behind. It took time for Cat to bid her guests good night, but she was finally free to retire.

She allowed Susan to remove her gown, shoes, and jewelry and put them away. Thoughtfully she removed her silk underblouse and handed it to her tiring woman, who already had an armful of ruffled petticoats. Standing naked in her stockings and garters, she said, "Go to bed, Susan. 'Tis late, and I can finish myself. I will sleep late, so dinna disturb me till midmorning."

Susan curtsied and left the room. Cat sat down on

the bed. Removing her lace-edged garters, she rolled her stockings off. Brushing her thick hair, she recalled her last scene with James. After a time, exhausted by all the wedding preparations and by memories, she fell asleep. She awoke at the touch of a warm mouth against the nipple of her left breast. Startled, her eyes flew open and looked into a pair of very amused amber ones. Then suddenly the king's eyes grew serious, and he said, "Get up, Cat. We hae things to settle between us first."

Puzzled, she threw back the covers and stepped naked from the bed. His eyes grew warm at the sight of her, but he spoke coldly. "I am willing to forgie ye yer past misbehavior, madame. In the spring ye will return to court, and live openly wi me as my mistress. Ye will obey my slightest whim. I will brook no disobedience, Cat! Ye belong to me! Do ye understand?"

"Aye," she whispered. She was stunned by his new forcefulness.

"Then prostrate yerself as a slave would, and beg my pardon."

A wave of nausea shook her. "Jamie, please! Must ye shame me so? I know I must obey ye, but dinna make me do this."

"Cat, yer a proud woman. I cannot believe that ye truly mean to obey me unless ye will do what I hae commanded ye no matter how distasteful to ye. If ye mean to be obedient, then ye must begin wi this."

Though her appearance remained meek, inwardly she burned with rage. If she refused him, he would be distrustful of her. She knew she must yield to his demand in order to allay his fears. Swallowing hard, she knelt, leaning over until her head touched his slippered foot. "Forgie me, my lord king," she said softly.

For a terrifying moment he rested his foot on her slim neck. The merest pressure on his part would have broken it. Cat bit her lip until it bled in an effort to prevent an outward show of fear or anger. Ye'll pay for this, James Stewart, she thought! Dear God how I hope ye hurt when I leave ye! May it rankle and eat at ye the rest of yer life, and may ye ne'er find another woman who'll please ye as I do!

Then suddenly his foot was gone, and he was raising her up. The smile he gave her was sweet. "Forgie me, my love, but I had to be sure ye would yield to me this time wi'out a fight. There is no other woman in this world I would trouble so much for, but ye are worth it, Cat! Christ! Ye excite me!" He drew her into his arms and kissed her, quickly forcing her lips apart so his tongue could roam.

It took all of her self-control not to push him away. Instead she took refuge in tears of relief, lowering her head and sobbing into his shoulder. Pleased, convinced that he had mastered her for good now, James became generous. He lowered her onto the bed, took her face between his hands, and kissed her again. His fingers moved to the slender column of her throat, and then to her full breast. Crushing the softness of her in his hands, he bent and let his lips wander.

It was with an awful stunning clarity that Cat realized she felt nothing. Her body, which had always succumbed to the delicious intensity of lovemaking, was not responding. Frightened, she struggled weakly beneath him. James, mistaking the movement for passion, forced his knee between her thighs and thrust into her. So wrapped up in his own desire was he that he did not realize she was feeling nothing.

Sick with fear that he might comprehend her thoughts, Cat thrust her hips up to meet him, murmuring endearments into his ear. Apparently he noticed nothing, and when his passion broke in a wild storm about her, she held him in her arms and, closing her eyes, made soft, crooning noises.

Sated, he lay atop her breathing hard. "Christ!" he swore. "I hae never known a wench like ye, Cat! No woman has ever satisfied me as ye do!" He rolled off her, propped himself up on an elbow, and gazed down at her. "Was it good for ye, too, love? 'Tis been many months, I know, since ye've had a man." Playfully he nibbled at her breast. "Do I please ye, Cat?"

She turned away from him, unable to speak for a moment. Now she knew how the whores of the world probably felt. Silent tears rolled down her face. He turned her onto her back and gently brushed the tears from her cheeks.

"They call me a wise king," he said, "but wi the lasses I am a fool. 'Twas Patrick who last held ye in his arms and loved ye. I can see ye have nae accepted that he is dead." He gathered her into his arms. "I love ye, my lady of Glenkirk. I hae missed ye so very much, Cat. I was overeager to possess ye. Dinna weep, sweetheart. Patrick would be happy to know yer safe wi me."

She made a strangled sound that he interpreted as further sorrow, and he held her closer.

He gave her a little squeeze and, releasing her, rose from the bed and crossed the room. "I will leave ye now, sweetheart, for this day has exhausted ye. I can see that." Opening the secret passage, he stepped through, saying, "Sleep well, my beautiful love." The door closed behind him.

For once in his life, thought Cat, James has left at just the right moment. She lay flat on her back, hands beneath her head, staring at the velvet canopy over her bed. What was the matter with her? She had always considered her sensuality a curse of sorts, but now she wanted it back! Only once before had her body refused to respond, and that had been after the terrible time when Patrick and the king spent a night raping and sodomizing her. She had finally gotten over that.

What was wrong now? Was it James? Or was it her?
The king would be here at least another five nights, and
she had to do something.

What could she do? She was going to have to feign
passion and hope to God she could fool him. Cat
needed to talk with someone who would understand
the problem, and there was only one person who might
help her.

Though Adam Leslie rose early, his wife, Fiona, had
to be wakened by her tiring woman. "Susan says Mistress Cat would speak wi ye. Here! Get up, Mistress
Fiona! I've got yer robe for ye. Hurry!" called Flora.

Pushed and pulled into her gown, Fiona found herself led through a little-used back passage of the
castle to Cat's apartments in the west tower. She found
her beautiful cousin awaiting her impatiently.

"Leave us, Susan! I'll call when we need ye. If anyone asks, say I am still asleep."

As the girl closed the door behind her, Fiona helped
herself to a goblet of watered wine and said, "Ye
dinna look as if ye got any sleep at all."

"I didn't."

Fiona sprawled on the bed. "Let me guess," she
said. " 'Tis the king again. He still harbors a passion
for ye, I know. In the great hall last night he could
scarce take his eyes from ye. Ye'll nae escape him this
time, Cat. 'Tis plain to see he means to hae ye."

"He already has, Fiona," said Cat dryly, "and he
went away happy. There is only one problem. I felt
nothing. He is as good a lover as ever, and God knows
I needed it, and yet I could raise no passion. Last
night he was so hot to possess me that he did nae
notice. But what of tonight? My God, cousin! What
am I to do? Fiona, forgie me, but before ye wed wi
Adam ye had many lovers. Did ye feel passion wi all
of them, or did ye pretend wi some? I dinna know how
to pretend!"

"Nonsense," laughed Fiona. "Ye simply jog yer hips and roll yer head a bit. Then ye moan and breathe heavily. Most men are so intent on their own lust that they rarely notice whether a woman is really enjoying herself. Look, Cat, 'tis only a few nights. He will be gone after the wedding. Hold him tight, and tell him how marvelous he is, and that ye love what he does to ye. Ye know how, cousin."

"I think so, Fiona, but 'tis nae for a few nights. He has ordered me to court come spring."

"Hell, Cat! Why tell me that? Ye dinna intend going. Ye'll do what I would do if this were my dilemma. Ye'll run to Bothwell! And if ye don't, then yer the biggest fool I've ever known! Is it any wonder ye feel nothing for Jamie, having had Francis Hepburn between yer legs? Now, there's a man!"

Cat laughed delighted. "I'm glad we are friends, Fiona! Yer so deliciously sensible. Jesu, though, coz! I was so frightened last night! Jamie was randier than an old billy goat. And I felt nothing!"

Fiona's mouth twitched with amusement. "What did ye do?"

"I cried, and Jamie thought my tears were for Patrick. He soothed me by saying that Patrick would be relieved to know I was 'safe' wi him! Can ye believe the man?"

Fiona choked on her wine. " 'Tis a wonder Glenkirk's ghost didn't rise up and kick the king's royal ass!" Then she said, "Well, 'twas a good start. If Jamie detects any reluctance on yer part now, he will believe it stems from yer inability to accept Patrick's death."

Cat looked worried. "*Is* it Jamie, Fiona, or is something the matter wi me?"

" 'Tis Jamie," Fiona said without hesitation. "Ye've ne'er been a cold piece. Leslie women never are. Oh, ye and I may be the most obvious in our sensuality,

but dinna think that because they look so prim and
proper those milksop cousins of ours are cool. My
poor brother, Charles, is exhausted from all the demands of dear Janet, and I understand yer own brother
has been known to flee his eager Mary on occasion.
Why, I have it on the best authority that our brother-
in-law James must service Ailis daily else she flirts
wi the stableboys!"

Cat collapsed on the bed, helpless with laughter.
"Oh, Fiona!" she gasped. "How will I ever look Janet,
Mary, and Ailis in the eye again wi'out laughing? What
a wonderful bitch ye are, coz! And just how do ye
know all of this?"

Fiona raised an elegantly plucked eyebrow. "I hae
never been unfaithful to Adam, if that's what yer thinking," she said, and then her cheeks reddened with a
memory she shared with Cat. "Well . . . only once,"
she amended softly. "I am simply the kind of woman
men talk to, Cat."

For a moment the two women were silent, and then
Cat spoke again.

"Can I do it, Fiona?"

"If anyone can," Fiona replied, "ye can! Cousin
Jamie, in taking one kind of happiness from ye, has
unwittingly given ye another. Go after it, Cat Leslie!
Dinna let anyone stop ye this time!"

Chapter 41

ᦉ᪥ᦉ

GLENKIRK Castle filled to the bursting point as the wedding day drew near. The Earl of Huntley was a power to be reckoned with in Scotland, and the presence of the king put a special seal on the whole affair. The guests overflowed into the dower house, into the very eaves of the castle. Cat had even been forced to allow some ladies and their tiring women to sleep in her antechamber. Her body servants were doubling up in Susan's room in order to free two small rooms. Servants who had accompanied guests were sleeping in every available nook and cranny.

Fortunately the December weather was good, and the guests were able to spend their days out of doors, hunting with the king, who had a passion for it. Cat did not enjoy hunting and used the excuse of wedding preparations to avoid it. But Meg and the Gordons, along with the younger family members, rode daily with James. The king was delighted with the elder dowager of Glenkirk, whom he now addressed publicly as Aunt Meg. She rode knee to knee with him each day, rarely leaving his side. Young Jemmie also showed an admiration for James, which pleased the king greatly. He enjoyed this healthy, normal family. Once Cat's position in his life became public he intended including them in his own growing family.

To Cat's immense relief, the king was too busy during

the next two evenings to visit her. What she was not
aware of was that her son Jemmie had slipped a sleeping herb into the king's wine. James Stewart was scarcely
into his night shirt before he fell asleep.

On December 18, however, the king insisted that Cat
ride with him. As she detested the long riding skirts that
fashion decreed, she wore what she always wore when
riding—men's green trunk hose, high leather boots, a
leather jerkin, white silk shirt, wide belt, and a wide,
heavy Leslie plaid to wrap about her in case of very
cold weather. Tucked into her belt was a jeweled dagger,
and she wore soft leather gloves.

The men of the party were of one mind: Catriona
Leslie looked marvelous. Not only had she handsome
breasts that jutted out as impudently as a young girl's,
but she had a damned fine well-turned leg. The younger
women admired her daring. Among the older ones, there
were those who thought her costume shocking, and
those who were amused by the countess' apparent eccen-
tricity.

Though Cat detested the sport, she rode like a young
Diana. At the kill, it was Cat who leaped from her horse
and drove the dogs back with a small but fierce rawhide
whip. What no one knew was that she had learned to
handle the dogs in order to avoid seeing some beautiful
wild creature's throat cut. The dogs took all her concentration.

They had killed but two does and a stag when the
king ordered an end to the hunt. His amber eyes burned
with desire as he looked upon the Countess of Glenkirk.
The huntress had roused the king's passion, and to Cat's
embarrassment, he did nothing to hide it. The men now
eyed her boldly, and she knew they wondered if the
king would bed her. The women looked at her with
something akin to envy, for James Stewart had never
publicly sought any woman but his pretty young queen.
To be a king's mistress was considered an honor. Cat

was distressed. She wanted no public acknowledgment of the king's feelings towards her.

To break the tension she swung back into the saddle and, looking boldly about, declared in a loud voice, "Ten gold pieces there's nae a man here who can beat my Iolair back to the castle!" And pulling her horse about sharply, she kicked him into a gallop.

A dozen men—the king included—galloped after her. Adam Leslie turned to his wife, who was biting her lip with laughter. "She thinks to cool his ardor," said Fiona in a low voice to her husband, "but she only inflames him all the more."

Cat bent low over Iolaire's neck. The big golden-bay gelding moved with smooth strides, easily outdistancing his pursuers. "Go, my great, gold love," she crooned at him. "None can beat ye!" Suddenly she saw a dark, wicked-looking beast drawing up alongside her. It was the king's midnight-black stallion. James was a magnificent horseman, and he was determined to win. But Cat was not the type of woman to give him victory. He would have to take it if he could.

A dozen horses thundered down out of the forested hills onto a flat stretch of road that led to the castle. Wild highland yells rent the air, and it seemed that sparks flew from the flying hooves as they struck the frozen ground. On the castle battlements, Glenkirk's men-at-arms cheered their lady as the bay led and roared disapproval as the black gained. The men shouted as the bay pulled ahead again and galloped across the lowered drawbridge into Glenkirk's courtyard, followed just a second later by the king on his black, and a minute later by the rest of the party.

Cat leaped lightly from her saddle, tossing the reins to a stableboy. She rubbed the bay's muzzle and whispered something in its ear. Running up the steps, she turned.

"I'll be collecting the gold ye all owe me this evening,

gentlemen!" And she laughed at their expressions. "Ah,
Sandy," she teased Lord Home, "ye know Iolaire's
speed. Of all people why did ye take my wager?"

"That damn new gray of mine was supposed to be
so fast, Cat," muttered Lord Home irritably.

Laughter greeted his remark, and Cat called again,
"There's meat and wine in the great hall, gentlemen.
Eat hearty!" And she disappeared into the castle.

Laughing and talking, the noblemen dismounted and
trouped up the steps into the great hall. It wasn't until
they had poured themselves great goblets of sweet,
golden wine and were tearing off chunks of meat and
bread that they noticed the king was not among them.
Looking about him, one man observed, "Looks like
Jamie's not through riding for the day."

"Aye," murmured another softly but distinctly, "but
I'd surely rather mount and ride that honey-haired mare
than that wild black brute of his."

There was laughter, and then someone observed, "I
wager the mare is wilder than the stallion."

"But sweeter!" shot back another man.

Laughter rang as each of the noblemen tried to mask
his thoughts about the beautiful Countess of Glenkirk.

James Stewart mounted the stairs to Cat's apartments
two at a time and strode angrily into her bedroom.
Naked but for her silk shirt, she showed no surprise as
did the frightened face of her maid. "Go along, Susan
dear. I'll call ye when I need ye." The girl fled the room.

"Well, Jamie?" Her glance was haughty, and only the
jumping pulse in her throat revealed her nervousness.

"Vixen!" he snarled, his face dark with anger. "You
wanton vixen! Ye had the whole pack of them after ye
like dogs after a bitch! Ye belong to me, Cat! I'll hae
no other man imagining what 'twould be like to be between yer legs!"

He was in a high rage.

Lunging, he ripped away her silk shirt and shoved her back onto her bed. He was on her instantly, his knee forcing her thighs apart. Astounded, and equally angry, Cat fought back. She tried to claw him with her nails, but he caught her wrists with one hand and held them fast above her head. She twisted furiously beneath him, but James thrust his hardness into her unwilling and unready body. She cried out with pain and renewed her struggle. He lowered his head and cruelly bit her nipples. Cat screamed and struggled harder, but her resistance seemed to inflame him. He was gaining great pleasure from hurting her.

Frightened by the fury in his face, she changed her tactics. Her struggles ceased, and her hips began the sweet rhythm that maddened him so very much. His grip lessened. Freed, she caught his head in her hands and raised it to her lips. "Nay, hinny," she whispered huskily, arching to press her soft breasts against his damp chest. "Dinna hurt me, Jamie luv! Love me, my lord! Love me now!" And her ripe mouth found his, pressing demandingly against his lips until they opened and allowed her little tongue to dart like a flame in his mouth.

His cruelty turned to yearning and he hungrily sought to satisfy them both. "Witch," he murmured against the silken tangle of her golden hair. "I always said ye were a little witch! Ahhhhhh, my sweet love!" And then he lay quietly against her pounding heart.

Cat lay weak with relief. Her lack of ardor had once again escaped James' notice. Instead, he praised her sexual performance. "Christ, love! Ye leave me drained!" He placed a burning kiss on her breast where his teeth had marked her slightly. "I am sorry, Cat. I dinna mean to hurt ye, but ye made me so jealous, love. I couldna bear for them to look at ye so! Yer a mistress to be proud of, Cat. Ye drive men mad wi just looking at ye!

Come back to court wi me after the wedding! I canna wait any longer for ye, sweetheart."

Cat caught her breath. Here it was, the thing she had feared all along. Reaching up, she gently touched his face. "Nay, Jamie hinny. 'Tis but a bit over three months since ye declared Patrick dead. If ye do not care for my reputation, I do. After Jemmie's wedding there is Bess' to attend to, and then 'twill be but a little while till spring. 'Tis not so long, my lord. Will it nae be sweeter for the waiting, Jamie? Do not let the gossips say ye hold me in so little regard that ye will nae gie me time to mourn my lawful husband. Come spring no one can say I dishonored Glenkirk in my rush to gain yer favor and yer protection."

"Always prudent, always careful." His voice purred approval. "What a perfect mistress ye'll be, Cat! By this time next year I'll hae ye full to bursting wi my son, and what a son he'll be, our bairn! I'll wait, sweetheart! I'll wait!"

She smiled sweetly at him, thinking, I'd rot in hell before I'd bear yer bastard, James Stewart!

But she was truly safe now. When he left Glenkirk this time she would never see him again. Cat could feel almost kindly towards him now.

Again that night she escaped his attentions, and she managed to forestall him the following night as well, by pleading the wedding on the following day, for which she must be rested.

James Leslie's wedding to Isabelle Gordon was a triumph of good planning, good food, and good weather. The bride was radiantly lovely, the groom elegantly handsome. The wedding feast lasted a long time, with many courses and entertainments. At last, Cat, Bess, and Henriette took Isabelle from her new husband and, pursued by a group of rowdy young bucks, gained the safety of the earl's suite. The lovely wedding gown was removed and taken away by Belle's maid.

Quickly she was dressed in a pale shell-pink night-gown. Her face, hands, and neck were bathed in warm perfumed water, and her mother brushed her long, dark hair.

"Remember what I have told ye," said Henriette Gordon in a low voice.

Her daughter nodded.

"What did ye tell her?" asked Cat, amused.

"That she must defer to Jemmie in all things," replied Henriette simply.

"Nothing else?" Cat was incredulous. "Riette! How could ye?"

The little Countess of Huntley was close to tears. "Cat, I tried! Only yesterday she was my babe, and now suddenly she is fifteen and grown! I tried to tell her of what happens between a man and his wife in the marriage bed, but she looked so damned superior . . . it embarrassed me!"

"Get the Countess of Huntley some wine," Cat commanded a servant girl. "Bess, watch the door." She turned to Isabelle. "Well, my girl, do ye know of that which occurs between a man and a woman?"

"Nay, belle-mère," whispered the girl, her eyes lowered.

"Christ's bones," swore Cat. But before she could say another word, the door gave way and a group of men burst into the room pushing Jemmie ahead of them. While the caudle cup was passed about, Cat managed to get next to her son. Smelling of much wine, he bent to give her a kiss.

"Jemmie," she whispered urgently, "Belle is completely innocent. That ninny Henriette was too shy to talk wi her own daughter. Be extra-gentle wi the lass tonight. What happens the first time will color her whole attitude towards lovemaking."

He nodded quietly, his eyes becoming serious. "I understand, mother. I promise to be kind."

The toast drunk, the jests and good wishes shouted, the bridal chamber was emptied of all but the inhabitants for whom it was intended. In the crush of exiting the king found his way to Cat's side. "I must leave in the morning if I am to be home for Christmas. I shall be in yer bedchamber in an hour."

One last time, she thought. After this night I shall be forever free of ye, James Stewart.

But what was she to do tonight? Fiona's voice came back to her. "Love him, Cat. Ye know how." Returning to the great hall, she stayed long enough to drink another toast to the new Earl and Countess of Glenkirk and then, bidding the guests enjoy themselves, she departed.

Alone, for she had given Susan the night off, she filled a basin with water warmed in the fireplace kettle. Adding scented oil to it, she stripped her clothes off and cleansed her skin. Taking up a small bristle brush, she dipped it into a tiny crystal vial of salt and scrubbed her teeth. Lastly, she anointed her body with rare musk, touching the stopper between her breasts, at the base of her throat, and on the soft insides of her thighs. She was careful in her selection of a gown, for she wanted James to remember every detail of this night for the rest of his life. She hoped it would be a long, long life.

Her choice was an exquisite gossamer silk fashioned *à la grecque*. It was spring-green to match her eyes, and fastened only on the left shoulder, from which it fell straight to the floor in a rippling line of pleats. It shimmered as she walked, and her body gleamed temptingly through the thin silk. The garment was similar to one she had worn for the king several years ago. She was sure he would remember.

Brushing her hair vigorously with a brush dipped in musk, she secured it atop her head with several tortoiseshell pins and brushed the loose ends about her finger into damp curls. The king always enjoyed loosening her hair, and tonight she must capture his attention in every way so that when he finally left her, he would believe he had spent the most ecstatic night of his life.

Ready now, Cat rang for a maidservant to come lay the peat fire, then dismissed her for the night. Alone, she made herself as comfortable as possible on the oak settle by the fire, and waited. Her thoughts flew back to just a few short years before when she had been a cherished wife. Everything had been so simple.

The creak of the fireplace door alerted her, and she sprang up, forcing a smile of welcome. The king stepped into the room and, blowing out his candle, placed it on the mantel. His amber eyes swept her slim body in its translucent gown, resting for a moment on the fullness of her breasts.

Silently he crossed the room and without a word undid Cat's shoulder fastening. The gown slid to the floor with a hiss of silk. Drawing the tortoiseshell pins from her hair one by one, he dropped them on the thickly carpeted floor.

"Stand before the pier glass," he commanded her.

She obeyed him wordlessly, and was not surprised when he joined her a moment later. He had removed his creamy silk nightshirt and was as naked as she. She couldn't help thinking that he was a handsome man, with a firm, well-muscled body, and extremely large genitals. All the damned Stewarts were overendowed and oversexed, she thought sourly.

Putting a surprisingly hard arm about her, he drew her against him, and his head bent to place a burning kiss on her shoulder. Then he reached up and crushed her breasts passionately. Eyes closed, she shivered her revulsion and prayed he thought it was desire. She felt one hand caressing her belly, the long fingers moving lower to explore the warm wetness of her. Squirming from his grasp, she caught his hand and led him to the bed.

Her mouth curved in what she hoped was a seductive smile, and she spoke huskily, "Let me love ye, Jamie hinny." And pushing him back onto the bed, she knelt over him, her magnificent breasts hanging above him. The amber eyes were bright with lust. Half-sitting, James closed his mouth over the rosy nipple of one breast, but she laughingly pulled away from him, stopping his protest with a kiss.

Her lips covered his face with little kisses that were more like delicious little nibbles as they moved lower. Her soft kisses scorched his chest, moving down to his flat belly and lower until her mouth found his manhood. Taking it in her warm mouth, she nursed on it as a babe would its mother's breast.

The king groaned and shivered. "Christ! Christ! Ahhhhh, you witch!" and he moaned his pleasure over and over as his body arched to meet her mouth.

When he was hard and ready for her, she released his organ and mounted him. His half-closed eyes were glazed with passion as he reached up to fondle her breasts, and Cat rode him smoothly until he poured his foaming seed into her body. His arms tightened about her, and he rolled her over onto her back and looked down at her. "Once," he said thickly, "I told ye I would nae be ridden like a maid, but . . . oh, Cat! I dinna know, my love! I dinna know! When ye come to me in the springtime ye will do again what ye have done tonight. Yea, my huntress, ye'll fuck me sweetly, won't ye?"

She said nothing, but instead she stroked his long back, cupping his round buttocks in her warm hands and gently kneading them. He quickly grew hot for her again, and with an almost pained sob of pleasure thrust deep into her. Finally exhausted, the king fell into a deep, relaxed sleep. He lay on his stomach, his face turned away from her, one arm thrown carelessly across her. For a long time she lay quietly on her back. Then, convinced of the depth of his slumber, she gingerly removed the offending arm and slipped from the bed.

Wrapping a light wool robe about her, she crawled into the windowseat and gazed sightlessly out into the night. Hot tears poured silently down her cheeks, and her body shook with muffled sobs. Again she had felt nothing, and she had performed like a whore in the Highgate. But worst of all was the fact that James hadn't known. He had eagerly accepted all she gave with no knowledge of her feelings, or of the deception she played. Patrick Leslie would have known, and Francis too—but then, they had truly loved her. The king, for all his fine words, merely lusted for her. Though he might not know it, what he really wanted was a high-born whore to service the hot desires which his dull Danish queen could not.

As the shock eased, Cat began to feel a burning anger. James had used her as he would a common trull, and she hated him with a fierce fury. She had been forced to soil herself in a way she would never forget. But in doing so she had gained the revenge she had planned so long ago. The memory of this night would live with him forever. It would burn in his dreams like a flaming brand, and he would wake with aching loins.

Smiling cruelly, she rose from the windowseat. Shrugging off the robe, she climbed back into the bed, snuggling down beneath the goosedown coverlet. The king still slept, snoring gently now. Propped on one elbow, she gazed down on him, and her lips formed words he never heard. "Goodbye, Jamie! May ye rot in Hell before I ever see ye again!"

Chapter 42

❧ § ❧

THE wedding guests departed the following day, leaving the families of the bride and groom alone to celebrate the holidays. It was the first time in many years that the Leslies and the Hays had gathered under one roof for Christmas through Twelfth Night.

It was a bittersweet time for Cat. She knew it was unlikely she would ever be with them all again. She savored each day, and her bitterness against James Stewart increased as she realized even more fully what his lust would cost her.

When he had left that morning he had bowed low over her hand, turning it so he might kiss the palm and the inside of her wrist. "Sensuous witch," he murmured low. "Ye drive me wild! Until spring, my love. 'Twill be the longest winter of my life."

Longer than ye think, ye rutting bastard, she thought, smiling sweetly up at him. "Until we meet again, Jamie hinny," she said softly.

"Farewell, madame," he said loudly for all to hear. "Our thanks for your magnificent hospitality!"

And he was no sooner across the drawbridge than she ran to her bedroom in the west tower. She tore the sheets from the bed and stuffed them into the fireplace, where they burned with a fierce whoosh of smoke and flame.

Astounded, Susan asked, "Could we nae have washed them clean, my lady?"

"There isn't enough water in the world to cleanse those sheets, my girl! Take the pillows and the feather-bed to the linen room, and exchange them for fresh."

Cat picked up the exquisite nightgown she had worn and tossed it into the flames. Never again, she thought! Never again will I have to prostitute myself! Never!

"Get the hip bath from the garderobe," she commanded the two lads who brought in the day's supply of wood. "And then bring me enough hot water to fill it!"

She sat in the windowseat looking out over the tranquil black-and-white winter landscape. Behind her, two maids remade the bed with fresh linen. The tub was slowly filled with hot water, and then the room emptied but for her and Susan, who was pouring oil of wild-flowers into the steaming tub.

Cat rose and undressed. Naked, she surveyed herself in the pier glass. Her figure was still good although she was over thirty—her belly was still flat, her glorious breasts were firm, there wasn't an ounce of fat on her. She stepped into the tub and slid down into the hot water.

"Susan, bring the stool and sit near me," she said. "I would speak privately wi ye." The girl settled herself and looked trustingly into her mistress' face. "Tell me, child, do ye hae a special sweetheart?"

"Nay, madame. There are several lads who walk out wi me, but none I'd leg-shackle myself to for life."

"Do ye wish to marry, Susan?"

"I am nae looking, my lady. If the right man came along, perhaps. Me dad says I am like my great-grand-ma, with a wandering foot that 'twill get me into trouble one day."

Cat smiled. "Would ye like to travel?" she asked.

"Oh, aye, my lady!"

"Susan, what I say to ye now is a secret, and because ye are loyal to me I know ye will nae repeat it. The king seeks to make me his mistress, and though there are some who would think it an honor, I do not. After Bess' wedding I am leaving Scotland. I shall never be able to come home again, though ye may if ye wish. I want ye to come wi me."

"Do ye go to Lord Bothwell?" the girl asked bluntly. Cat nodded.

"Good! 'Tis where ye belong now. I'll go wi ye. Ye'll need more than one to wait on ye. Will ye take my little sister wi ye? She's fourteen. Her name is May, and she admires ye something fierce. I've been training her, so she's no greenhorn."

Cat smiled again. "Thank ye, Susan. Aye, we'll take young May, but yer nae to tell her until the very last minute. Should the king even suspect that I flee . . ."

Susan nodded wisely. The conversation finished, she rose to see to the warming of the towels. Cat took a soft brush and, standing, scrubbed herself down. Sliding back into the water, she said, "There, James Stewart! 'Tis the last of ye!"

"*Amen!*" said Susan, wrapping Cat in a fluffy towel as her mistress rose from the tub.

Cat laughed happily. "Why is it, Susan, that we get on so well, and ye've only been in my service a few years? Yer Aunt Ellen served me from the day I was born, and now gets on my nerves so!"

" 'Tis because she's been wi ye since ye were a babe, mistress. 'Tis nae easy to take someone seriously when ye've changed their nappies. She's better wi young Lady Bess. Besides, she's too old to change her attitudes and go gallivanting about the world."

"Aye, my prim little Bess suits Ellie. Lord, Susan! In less than two months Bess will be a bride!"

"Aye, she's well settled. But what of the others?"

" 'Tis taken care of, and we'll speak no more of it."

Susan took the hint. After helping her mistress to dress, she went about her other duties.

Christmas at Glenkirk was celebrated quietly with a beautiful midnight mass in the church of Glenkirk Abbey. Afterwards the family descended to the candlelit burial vault beneath the castle chapel and decorated it with greens. The rosary was said, led by Charles Leslie, the abbot. When the family departed, Cat remained behind, sitting on a small marble bench. In the flickering candlelight and deep silence she gained strength. Her eyes moved from tomb to tomb until it reached a large brass plaque that read: "PATRICK IAN JAMES LESLIE, FOURTH EARL OF GLENKIRK. BORN AUGUST 8, 1552. DIED AT SEA APRIL 1596. MOURNED BY HIS BELOVED WIFE, CATRIONA MAIRI, AND THEIR NINE CHILDREN. REST IN PEACE."

She felt the tears prick at her eyelids. "Oh, Patrick," she whispered, "they say ye are dead, and I dinna believe it, though it goes against all logic. But dead or alive, I know ye'll ne'er return here, Patrick. Jamie is after me again, and I must flee or else bring dishonor to Glenkirk. I am going to Bothwell, and I know ye would understand."

She stood up and moved to her great-grandmother's tomb. "Well, ye great schemer," she said softly, "even in death ye got yer way. I wed yer precious Patrick, and hae given Glenkirk a new generation. But now I will hae *my* way, Mam!" And a prickle went up her spine as she detected a faint silvery laugh. Or did she? She walked to the staircase. Turning to look back, she smiled. "Farewell, my bonnie ancestors!"

On New Year's Eve the weather was clear and cold, and the sky shone with bright stars and a nearly full moon. A huge feast was held that night, and the pipers circled the table so many times that Cat thought her head would burst with the noise. A few minutes before midnight the family ascended to the battlements of the castle and stood in the cold to watch great bonfires flaring among the surrounding hillsides. Scotland welcomed the new year, 1598.

A lone Glenkirk piper played the softly haunting "Leslie's Lament." As the pipes sounded in the deep winter stillness, the music was echoed by Sithean's piper across the hills.

Cat could not stop the silent tears that slipped down her cheek. Luckily, they went unnoticed by all except Jemmie, who put a comforting arm about his mother. Later as they walked towards the great hall she flashed him a quick smile and said, "I hope ye'll be as intuitive of yer wife's feelings as ye are of yer mother's."

His eyes twinkled. "Ahh, madame, I am. I certainly am!"

Her laughter was warm. "What a dear rogue ye are, Jemmie. Yer father was as proud of ye as I am. I know he would be relieved that Glenkirk is in such good hands now."

He gave her a grateful smile and, taking her aside, said, "I hae a wonderful New Year's gift for ye. Let me gie it to ye now." And he pulled her down the corridor to the earl's apartments. Sitting her down in a chair in the antechamber, he rushed into his bedroom. He returned a minute later with a flat red leather box.

For a moment she looked at the unopened box in her lap. Whatever was in it was of great value, she was certain. It was the first valuable thing he had ever given her. Another proof, she pondered sadly, that his father was gone. Shaking off the unhappy thought, she opened the box, and gasped. Nestled in black velvet lining was the most beautiful pendant Cat had ever seen. Circular, part of it was fashioned in a quarter-moon shape and the rest was a crisscross of openwork studded with tiny diamonds, and hung with tiny tinkling bells.

"Jemmie! Jemmie!" She lifted it out, admiring the exquisitely delicate chain.

" 'Tis a copy of one that Mam owned."

"I never saw Mam wear anything like this, and 'tis neither wi the Glenkirk or the Sithean jewels," remarked Cat.

"Yer right, mother. She left it behind when she returned from Istanbul. Father told me. In her apartments in the palace there was a wall of tile in the bedroom—by the fireplace, I believe. There was one tile with a thistle pattern. She had the wall behind it hollowed out, and lined in a fine wood. 'Twas there she kept her jewels safe. On the night she left, the pendant was overlooked in her haste. It had been lying towards the back. Mam told father that she always regretted the loss. The sultan had made it for her to celebrate the birth of their first son, Sultan Suleiman. 'Tis probably still there."

"But how did ye know what the pendant looked like if ye never saw it?"

"Mam described it in detail to father several times. He described it to me. He often said ye were like her—proud and willful, yet wise."

"Thank ye, Jemmie."

Suddenly he was a boy again. "I wanted ye to hae something to remember me by!" he said, his voice trembling ever so slightly as he fought to keep it under control.

"Why, my darling," she said catching his face between her hands, "I will nae forget ye! Yer my firstborn, and we share more than ye realize. When ye were but a wee little fish swimming about in my womb, I used to talk to ye. Ye were my strength."

He laughed. "What did ye speak on, mother?"

"All sorts of foolish things, Jemmie," and she paused a moment. "Ye'll nae be able to come for a few years, but once Jamie has forgotten me, ye and Belle can come to visit us."

He looked at her sadly and said softly, but very distinctly, "Damn James Stewart to a fiery hell!" And turning on his heel, he left the room.

Cat closed the jewel case with a click. "Ye echo my own sentiments, my son," she said, and followed him from the room.

The day following the Feast of Twelfth Night the young Earl and Countess of Glenkirk left for court, accompanied by the bride's parents. The rest of the guests dispersed in their various directions. In four and a half weeks Cat's daughter would wed, and then Cat would be free to go on her way.

There had always been a tension between mother and daughter because of Lord Bothwell. Not knowing her parents' problems, Bess, her father's favorite, had automatically taken his part. But Bess was now in love with her prospective husband. It was having a softening effect on the girl. Cat debated telling Bess that she would soon be leaving Scotland.

It was Bess, however, who spoke to her. A week before the wedding she came to her mother and said, "Once ye told me that when I fell in love I should understand how ye felt about Lord Bothwell. I returned ye a snide answer, mother. But now I understand . . . I truly do! Why do ye stay in Scotland? When the king was here at Christmas he looked at ye in a way that frightened me. Ye must find Uncle Francis, mother, and go to him. Only then will ye be safe!"

Cat hugged her daughter. "Thank ye, Bess. I will go now wi a lighter heart knowing ye really understand."

Bess' eyes widened and she opened her mouth to

speak, but Cat gently covered the girl's mouth with her hand. "Jemmie will speak of it wi ye one day, love."

"Yes, mother, I understand," said Bess, smiling at her.

What a pity, thought Cat, that we have become friends now that I must leave her.

The wedding of Bess Leslie and Henry Gordon was a quiet one compared to the previous wedding. Only the family attended. Jemmie and a sparkling Isabelle returned for the festivities, and two days later escorted the newlyweds back to Edinburgh for the winter season at court. Before they left, both Bess and Jemmie came to say a private farewell to their mother.

Jemmie was tall and looked so painfully like his father at that age that tears sprang up in Cat's eyes. Bess, so radiantly happy, was a dark-haired mixture of both her parents. "I want ye to know," said Cat softly, "that I love ye both well. How I shall miss ye!"

They both clung to her, and Bess began to weep. "Nay, hinny," scolded Cat, gently stroking her daughter's hair. "If the new bride is sad, the king may find me out. Be strong, my daughter, and help me win this battle that I fight wi Jamie. He *must not* suspect that any of ye knew."

Bess mastered herself. "The others?" she asked.

"I'll speak wi them, but nae the bairns. I know 'tis a great burden I put on ye, but please, Bess, and ye also, Jemmie, look after them for me. Later, when it is safe, ye may all come to visit wi me. But now I must travel quickly. Ye understand that?"

They nodded, and she kissed them each in turn. Leading them to the door, she saw them out. Later on that day she stood on the top step of the castle's main entrance, waving gaily and calling loudly for all ears to hear, "I will see ye in the spring, my dears! Gie my loving regards to his majesty!" She stayed there waving

until they were out of sight before retiring to her tower
to weep in private.

The following day would see her two younger sons,
fourteen-year-old Colin and twelve-and-a-half-year-old
Robert, on their way. Colin was going to the University
of Aberdeen, and Robert back to his duties as a page
with the Earl of Rothes' household. That night she drew
her four older children about her and told them that she
would be leaving Glenkirk, and why. She had worried
about disappearing from their lives without explanation
and had decided that telling them was worth the risk.
Her judgment was vindicated when her nine-year-old
daughter, Morag, said quietly, "I am glad ye go, mother.
I dinna like the king." Ten-year-old Amanda nodded in
agreement. "Aye. Dinna worry for us, mother. Besides,
ye've seen to our futures rather well. I shall enjoy being
Countess of Sithean."

Cat couldn't help but laugh. "Yer such a practical
little puss," she told her daughter.

"When?" asked Robbie.

"Soon."

Colin began to chuckle.

"What is so funny?" his mother asked him.

"I'm sorry I'm nae still wi Rothes," said the boy-man.
"I'd enjoy seeing Cousin James' face—the sanctimon-
ious lecher!"

"Thank God yer not wi Rothes!" said Cat. "Ye'd gie
me away for sure." But she laughed. "Conall said almost
the same thing," she told them, and the girls and Robbie
joined in the mirth.

The following morning the boys were gone, and for
the next few days Cat was dejected. She spent a good
deal of time in the nursery playing with her three babies.
Then one evening she appeared unexpected in her
mother-in-law's bedchamber. Meg understood instantly.
Wordlessly, she rose and hugged Cat to her.

"So soon?"

Cat nodded. " 'Tis dark of the moon, and there is no better time for me to go unnoticed. If I stay any longer I will nae be able to go, Meg. It tears at me even now!"

"Then God go wi ye, my daughter."

"Oh, Meg! Ye were always closer to me than my own mother. I shall miss ye so much! Try to explain to my parents, Meg."

"I will, my dear. Dinna think too harshly of yer mother. She has always lived in her own sensuous little world where the only other occupant was yer father. I will make her understand. And who knows—when yer safe, we may even come visiting!"

"My bairns . . . ye'll be sure to look after them, Meg?"

"Aye."

"And ye'll nae let them forget me until I can send for them?"

"Nay, love. Now go, Catriona! Go before ye make a foolish and emotional decision." Gently Meg kissed Cat's cheek and pushed her from her chambers.

For a moment Cat stood in the cold, dark corridor. I'll nae see this again, she thought, and the tears flowed down her cheeks. My God! If anyone sees me I'll be hard put to explain.

Fiercely she wiped the wetness from her cheeks and ran through the back passages of the castle to her own apartments. The servants—with the exceptions of Susan and her young sister, May—had all been sent to bed.

"Is everything done?" Cat asked Susan.

"Yes, my lady. Conall and his men hae seen to it. He said we were to leave as soon as ye returned." She hustled Cat into the bedchamber, where she had a steaming tub waiting. " 'Tis the last yer apt to get for a while."

Cat smiled weakly. "Did ye pack everything I told ye? And ye hae my jewel cases?"

"Aye to both questions. If the king's men come looking they'll find most of yer clothes still here awaiting yer return. Ah, what fun 'twill be to buy ye new clothes in France!"

The heaviness was beginning to lift from Cat's shoulders. "Ye and May shall have some new clothes too," she promised.

Within the hour she was dressed and ready. Then Susan, who stood behind her, unexpectedly fastened about Cat's neck the lion pendant given her by Lord Bothwell. "I thought ye should be reminded of what yer going to, my lady, nae what yer leaving."

Cat smiled, suddenly happy. "Susan, I didna think ye could understand the wrench this is for me. I thank ye, Susan, for helping me through a hard, hard time. Yer a good friend to me, and I willna forget it."

Catching up her fur-lined cloak, she walked to the fireplace and pressed the carving that opened the door to the secret passageway. "Be sure the door is shut tight behind ye, girls," she said, and taking a candle she stepped into the corridor.

Minutes later they exited at the foot of the west tower, where Conall waited with three horses. Cat swung herself onto Iolaire's back while Susan and May rode pillion. With Conall leading the way, they rode out from Glenkirk unseen by the watch. On a hill high above the castle they were joined by a party of men so large that Cat was taken aback.

"Christ!" she swore. "How many are there, Conall?"

"Fifty. I couldna hae ye chasing all over Europe wi just half a dozen men to protect ye. Ye can afford it." And raising his arm he signaled the start of their journey.

"*Wait!*" she commanded. Turning Iolaire, she looked

back down onto Glenkirk, looming dark against a darker sky. For a moment she hesitated, torn with one final doubt. Leave Glenkirk? Leave her bairns? Leave Scotland? Leave nearly all she held dear? And then she saw James' sensuous face before her, and she heard his voice, low and insinuating, saying, ". . . and ye will do to me what ye did this night . . ." Yanking her horse about, Cat shouted, "*Forward!*" and galloped away.

They would be sailing from Rattray Head, where Bothwell had left from so long ago. Since the *Gallant James* had disappeared with Patrick Leslie, the Leslie's new flagship, *New Venture*, would be taking Cat to France. Cat thought the name most appropriate.

They rode through the night, stopping twice to rest the horses. At dawn they made camp in the ruins of Huntley Castle. The ride in the cold night air had given Cat an enormous appetite, and she happily accepted a small rabbit broiled on a stick which was brought to her by one of the men. Susan supplied a loaf of bread, a cup, and a flask filled with sweet wine. Cat shared these offerings with her two servants and happily stuffed herself. Full at last, she wrapped herself in her heavy cloak and went to sleep by a small fire kindled in what was now a freestanding fireplace.

When she awoke it was midafternoon, and the camp was quiet. Susan and May were sleeping near her. She lay for a few minutes, drowsy and warm within the safety of her cloak, then slept again. When she woke in late afternoon the camp was abustle with the activities of cooking. Several lambs were turning over the cook fires, and on a large flat stone boasting a smaller fire beneath it rested a number of fresh-baked loaves. Well away from the heat stood several unopened casks of ale.

"Conall! To me!"

"Madame?"

"Where did all of this come from?"

"My lord of Huntley told his people to be on the lookout for ye and to see we were well fed and cared for while on Gordon lands."

Her face softened. "Why, bless George for that," she said. Then, "There's nae too much ale, is there? I dinna want the men too drunk to ride. We've a long night ahead of us, and we must reach Rattray before dawn."

"Just enough to keep them happy, my lady. There's a small cask of wine for ye too. Dinna forget to refill yer flask for tonight."

She nodded, and accepted the tin plate Susan handed her. It held thin, juicy slices of meat, early green cress, and hot bread dripping butter and honey. The cup was filled with rich malmsey, and put at her side on the ground. Again Cat stuffed herself. Afterwards, as the men ate, she stood and addressed them. "Conall has told ye of my journey. If any of ye have changed yer minds about going, now is the time to say so, and to return to Glenkirk. If ye go back, I only ask that ye remain silent as to my whereabouts." Silence greeted her words, and looking out at the Glenkirk men she felt quick tears prick her eyelids. Fighting to control herself, she said simply, "Thank ye. Thank ye all."

They were ahorse within the hour, and rode through most of the dark night. She could smell the sea long before they reached the coast, its salt tang growing stronger with every passing mile. They arrived at the rendezvous well before their deadline, and Conall signaled towards the sea with a lantern which he had managed somehow to stow in his bulging saddlebags. From the darkness came an answering light.

He drew forward a familiar-looking young man. "My son, Andrew," he announced gruffly.

Cat raised an eyebrow. "Dinna tell me, Conall. Ye

couldna find the time to wed wi his mother, but a Leslie always recognizes his own. Am I correct?"

"Aye, madame," he drawled, and she laughed. "Andrew and ten of the men will sail on the *New Venture* wi ye," he said. "I'll go wi the others and the horses on the *Anne la Reine* from Peterhead."

"Will ye be long behind us?" Cat asked nervously. "I dinna like landing in France wi so few men."

"We'll be ahead of ye. The *Anne la Reine* is lighter and a bit faster than the *New Venture*. Yer coach, horses, coachmen, and grooms left three days ago, and will be waiting for ye. Dinna fret, lass. I'll be waiting for ye."

She smiled warmly at him. "All right, Conall." Then she turned her smile on the young man. "Well, Andrew More-Leslie, not enough pretty girls to keep ye home at Glenkirk?"

"Too many, my lady—and an equal number of angry fathers."

Cat laughed. "Ye'll do, lad!"

They descended to the beach to meet the longboat. It slid up onto the sand and the sailors scrambled out to pull it safely onto the beach. For a moment Cat flew back in time, remembering when she had stood before on this wet and windy beach. It had been a bit less than three years ago, and she had ridden with the Earl of Bothwell to bid him goodbye as he began his exile. She had thought never to see him again. Now she stood on this very beach ready to begin her own self-imposed exile.

An officer detached himself from his men and bowed over her hand. "First Officer Malcolm More-Leslie at yer service, my lady. I am Hugh's son."

"Yer Susan and May's older brother?"

"Aye, madame."

"Is not the captain a More-Leslie?"

"Sandy. Alan's boy."

"Good God, Conall, I certainly sail well protected by the family!"

"*He* would have wanted it that way," Conall muttered fiercely.

Cat put out a hand and patted the older man's arm. "Ye wanted to go wi him, eh, Conall?"

"Aye! But he'd nae hae it. 'Stay home, Conall,' he said. 'Who else can I trust to look after her?' "

"Christ, man! Dinna tell me this now at the moment of my departure!"

"Madame, if I dinna think he'd approve of this road ye take, I'd nae be here. But I am, and while 'tis in my hands, I'll keep ye safe." And then he blushed beet-red as she stood on tiptoes and soundly kissed his cheek.

"God go wi ye, Conall," she said, and joined Susan and May, who were already in the boat. Without further ado the small boat was on its way through the darkness to the *New Venture*. Then she was being swung up and out over the water, and when she opened her eyes again she was on the deck being greeted by the captain.

"I've put ye and yer lasses in my own cabin, my lady. Ye'll be more comfortable there," he said.

"Thank ye, cousin," she said, bringing a flush of pleasure to his ruddy face. He'd heard about Cat Leslie, and what a fine woman she was. Her acknowledgment of their relationship—however tenuous that relationship was—pleased him. Too, it brought him extra stature in the eyes of his men. "Will ye take yer main meal wi me and my officers?" he asked.

"Gladly!"

The captain bowed. "I'll be about my business now, madame. Duncan will see ye safely to yer quarters."

The *New Venture* was a big, sleek caravel of some eighty tons. She carried a full dozen guns, and had been designed for speed and maneuverability, yet generous cargo space. Her crew's quarters were dry, warm, and comfortable, outstanding for the times. There was a separate cook's area incorporated into the seamen's quarters so the men might have warm food or ale when they finished their duties. The Leslies demanded absolute obedience and loyalty from their sailors, but they paid them well and cared for them properly. Consequently, Leslie employees were the best.

Duncan, the ship's boy, led Cat and her two serving women to a large cabin high in the stern of the ship. Through the leaded and paned bow windows Cat could see that the stars had faded and the sky was growing lighter. The cabin was comfortably furnished, with a good-sized bed and two trundles. There were Turkey carpets on the floor, and velvet hangings at the bow windows and the two smaller ports. Beautiful brass lamps lit the room, and on an oak table stood two decanters of wine—one red, one gold.

"Could ye eat, m'lady?" asked Duncan.

"Is there any fruit aboard, lad?"

"Apples, ma'am, and some Seville oranges."

"Bring both, and some hard cheese and bread."

"Ohh, my lady," said May plaintively, "I'm starving! I could eat a big bowl of porridge, I surely could! Wi honey and clotted cream!"

Cat laughed at the girl. "Not this morning, my lass. If ye would nae succumb to *mal de mer* ye will eat and drink sparingly this day."

Later, when the two young women lay sleeping, Cat sat in the velvet windowseat and watched the coast of Scotland slowly growing smaller. Above her she heard, "Set the course for Calais! East-southeast." And an echoing voice answered, "East-sou'east!"

The beautiful leaf-green eyes strained towards the fading coastline. A tear slid down her pale cheek, and then another, and another. She wept softly, bitterly, until the sadness began to lift and she had a sudden awareness of excitement growing within her. Behind her lay her old life, but ahead lay her very reason for life! Ahead was Francis Stewart-Hepburn! She could not be so ungrateful as to weep over what the gods had taken from her—not when they had given so much.

Chapter 43

❧❧❧

THE messenger sent by the king of Scotland to the younger dowager Countess of Glenkirk returned quickly to Edinburgh.

"What do ye mean she wasna there?" demanded the king in a tight little voice.

"She's gone to France, the auld dowager said, and proper upset she was too. Seems the young one just took off early one morning wi'out a word to anyone."

James sent for the Earl of Glenkirk, and his sister, Lady Elizabeth Gordon. "Do ye know where yer mother is?" he asked them.

"At Glenkirk, sire," said the earl without hesitation.

"She is nae at Glenkirk!" answered the king fiercely. "She is in France!"

For a moment both young faces registered surprise, then Bess said to Jemmie, "She went after all! Oh, I do hope 'twill cheer her!"

"What do ye mean, Lady Gordon?"

Bess smiled sweetly at the king and then said in the same warm, confidential tone she'd used with her brother, "Why, sire, she spoke of visiting our Leslie cousins in France. Ye see, 'tis been a terrible year for her. First our father dying. Then Jemmie marrying and coming wi Bella to court, and then my marrying and coming to court. Colin is away at the university and Robbie a page wi Rothes. Why sire—there's scarcely

427

anyone home but the bairns! She's been so lonely. She said she might go to France for a bit, but then she said nay." Bess smiled again, and shrugged elegant little shoulders. "I suppose she changed her mind again. We women are so unpredictable."

Amused, the king suppressed a smile, and then his mouth tightened in anger. "She was to come to court this spring."

"Oh, yes," said Bess brightly. " 'Twas the last thing she said to us when we left Glenkirk after my wedding—that she would see us at court in the spring, and to gie her loving regards to the king." She turned and stared accusingly at her brother. "Jemmie! I'll wager ye *forgot*, dolthead! How could ye?"

A small smile played at the corners of the king's mouth at the embarrassed look on the young earl's handsome face. They were such a charming family! "Thank ye, Lady Gordon. Ye may leave us. Jemmie, stay. I would speak further wi ye."

Bess curtsied prettily and left the room. James looked sharply at James Leslie. He saw nothing but open honesty and admiration. The king pursed his lips and said slowly, "Yer mother has displeased me, Glenkirk. In a sense she has deliberately disobeyed me." The young face looked genuinely distressed. "I commanded yer mother's presence at court this spring. In fact—" he paused a moment for effect—"I planned to make her my mistress, and she was well aware of it."

Surprise and incredulity registered on the young face. "Sire! This is a great honor ye do Glenkirk! Christ, sir! What can I say!" Then, "Damn me! Her behavior is intolerable! I always felt my father spoiled her. But I am sure she will return soon. She is simply willful, but I dinna believe disobedient."

The king looked pleased. There was no nonsense here. The lad was with him. She'd have no place to hide now. This was one Glenkirk he'd have no trouble with at all! The earl considered it an honor that James had singled out his mother—and rightly so! "I will send word to my good friend, King Henri, that yer mother is to be sent home."

Jemmie looked earnestly at the king. "I will write her also, sire. I am now the Lord of Glenkirk, and I honor my mother as much as she merits it, but she must understand that 'tis my word that is law at Glenkirk, not hers. She is, after all, but a woman, and therefore must be guided. Yer majesty has offered her yer protection. I will nae allow her to fling such graciousness away."

The king was pleased, but alone he brooded. Did she really intend returning? Or, as the little nagging doubt in the back of his mind suggested, had she fled him again? He had warned her once what he would do to her family if she refused him, but that was when her husband was alive. It would have been possible to trump up charges against Patrick. But the young earl was a different matter. Punishing him would be far too transparent, and would reap terrible consequences for the king.

The Leslies of Glenkirk were no longer a defenseless clan without powerful ties. The king's own cousin, George Gordon, the Earl of Huntley, was as troublesome in his way as Bothwell had been. He was not going to stand idly by and allow his daughter Isabelle's happiness to be destroyed, and James wanted no open clan rivalries left behind when he mounted the English throne. Then, too, there was the young Earl of Glenkirk himself. In the short time he had been at court he had made himself very popular, and he was openly admiring and supportive of the king. One could hardly accuse such a charming and loyal young man of perfidy. Besides, James genuinely liked the new Earl of Glenkirk.

The king slouched low in his chair, fingering the

diamond-and-black-pearl necklace he had sent to Cat with the messenger. He thought anxiously that she must come back. She must! He could not—nay, would not—spend a lifetime yearning for her. But what if she did not return? He groaned aloud. She must!

Chapter 44

ငာၵ

THE *New Venture* had made an easy passage from Rattray Head to Calais. The captain was heard to remark that in all his years of sailing he had never encountered such fair and constant winds in the North Sea, let alone the North Sea in late February. The *Anne la Reine* had arrived some twelve hours ahead of Cat's ship, and Conall and his men awaited their lady on the docks.

Because Conall deemed it safer, Cat and her two servants rode inside the coach on the four-day trip to Paris. Her entourage was extremely impressive. Two coachmen sat on the box, two footmen rode behind. Four grooms on horseback followed behind the coach, each leading yet another horse—Iolaire among them. Conall led fifteen men, while Andrew, with another fifteen, brought up the rear. On each side of the coach rode ten men.

Besides Cat and her servants, there was one other occupant of the coach, and when Cat had disembarked at Calais she had almost fainted at the sight of him. Conall had grasped her arm and said sharply, " 'Tis his bastard half-brother. He's been raised here."

And the young priest stepped forward and raised her hand to his lips. "I should not have startled ye so, madame. I have always been flattered to know that I look like Patrick. I did not realize how much until this moment."

"Aye, Father. Except that yer hair is blond and his was dark, yer his mirror image. Even the tone of yer voice!"

Learning of her visit—for Cat had sent a message ahead to her two uncles—the priest had come from Paris to meet her. His name was Niall Fitz-Leslie, and he had been the only bastard of the third Earl of Glenkirk. His mother had been the youngest daughter of the laird of Rae, and she had caught the earl's eye when Meg was pregnant with her last baby. The third earl had been unable to resist the ample and available charms of the laird's daughter. Nine months later Niall had been born.

Upon learning of his daughter's condition, the old laird had sent her off to his sister in Caithness. There she had remained until she died when her son was ten. The third Earl of Glenkirk had always seen to his bastard son's support, and when Niall was left motherless, his father had sent him to be raised by his brother, Donald, in France. Thus, Meg had never known of her beloved husband's one deviation. Formal recognition by his father had made Niall's acceptance into the church a certainty.

Donald Leslie of Glenkirk had been a third son, and it had been necessary for him to make his own fortune. With his cousin, David Leslie of Sithean—himself a fourth son—he had gone into military service as a mercenary. It was while serving France that the two cousins caught the fancies of two young heiresses who were also related.

Donald had wed himself to René de la Provence, and sired six children in rapid succession—five of them sons, so his father-in-law, the old Sieur de la Provence, had been made happy in his old age. Now that he was dead, Donald was the Sieur de la Provence.

David Leslie—brother to Cat's mother—had done

equally well by marrying Adèle de Peyrac, the only child of the elderly Sieur de Peyrac. He had sired four sons. The two Leslie cousins had, as part of their marriage contracts, agreed to add their wives' names to their own. Hence in France they were known as Donald Leslie de la Provence and David Leslie de Peyrac.

Cat had never met either of her uncles, as they had left Scotland before she was born.

"The entire family is quite excited by your visit, madame," Niall told her. "We realize, of course, that you are in mourning."

"No longer. Patrick would nae have liked it."

"I was saddened to learn of his death. I liked him."

"Ye knew him?"

Niall Fitz-Leslie smiled. "Yes. I knew him. When he was returning home to Scotland he stopped unexpectedly in Paris, and there was no time to remove me to another place. I will never forget the look on his face when he saw me. 'Twas a look of pure surprise. Then he laughed, and said, 'Little brother, I must obviously greet you so!' Before he left we had a long talk, and he told me of our father's death. He continued to pay for my support with our uncles, and after I became a priest he settled an amount on me with the Kiras. A man, he wrote me, is still a man even if he is a priest, and should always have his own money. He was a good man. I will pray for him."

"He was a good man," Cat replied. Then she looked at the young priest, and said, "Father, I should like you to hear my confession. Among other things it will answer all the questions I see in your eyes." She lowered the window of the coach and, hailing the nearest man, called, "Tell Conall I want to stop for a rest as soon as possible."

A few moments later the coach pulled into a sheltered clearing, and Susan and May exited to stretch their legs.

Kneeling on the padded floor of the luxurious vehicle, Cat put her two slim white hands into the large, tanned one of the priest. She remained this way for almost an hour while she spoke softly of the last few years of her life.

The priest's face remained impassive throughout her recital. When she stopped he said, "In the eyes of the church you have certainly sinned grievously, but you have paid a far greater penance than your sin demanded, my daughter. Your current flight puts your family here in some small jeopardy should King Henri be asked by King James to aid in your return. I think, however, that your king is gauche in pursuing you when you so obviously dislike him. Lord only knows Henri Quatre is a lover of great renown, but he has never, to my knowledge, forced a woman. James Stewart is obviously a barbarian. You will, of course, forestall any threat to your family here by staying only a short time?"

"I will, *mon père.* Only long enough to buy new clothes, as I left most of mine behind at Glenkirk."

The priest grinned. "An admirable excuse for a new wardrobe, *ma belle cousine.*"

She laughed. "I really do want to hurry, for I am most anxious to reach Lord Bothwell."

Niall Fitz-Leslie raised Cat up. "Sit back now, madame. Our business is over." He smiled at her. "Does Lord Bothwell know you are coming?"

"No. I dared not communicate with him before I left Glenkirk. I will arrange with our Paris bankers to send a message to Naples."

"I think he will be a very happy man," remarked the cleric. "When he was here at King Henri's court he seemed so . . . so . . ." The priest struggled for the right word. ". . . so incomplete! I realize that sounds strange, but something seemed to be missing in him and for him. Now I know what that something was."

Cat's face lit up, and Niall was staggered by the sudden flash of pure beauty. "*Mon Dieu, chérie!* You almost make me regret my vows of celibacy!" he said.

Her clear laughter rang within the coach. "You definitely have the Leslie charm, *mon père*. It is a good thing you have taken holy orders. There are already too many lusty Leslie men running about this earth!"

They continued their journey through Picardy into Isle de France, and up to Paris. Cat was enchanted with the city, and quite amazed to discover how unlike London, Edinburgh, or Aberdeen it was. She had assumed that all big cities were much alike. Paris was unlike any place she had ever seen. Now she understood why the current king had switched his allegiance from Protestantism to Catholicism in order to end religious wars in France, remarking that "Paris is well worth a Mass."

Cat would be staying with her Uncle David, whose house was thirty miles southeast of Paris, near the royal residence of Fontainbleau. When they reached the far side of the city, Niall instructed the coachmen as to the proper roads to travel, and rode on ahead so David Leslie de Peyrac might know of his niece's imminent arrival.

It was late afternoon when the coach and its escort drew into the courtyard of the Chateau Petit. Before Cat's grooms could jump down, two liveried footmen were at the coach door, opening it, lowering the steps, and helping Cat down. An elegant gentleman stepped forward. Had he not looked so like her mother, Cat would not have recognized him as her uncle. Smiling, he kissed her on both cheeks. "Catriona, welcome to France!" The Sieur de Peyrac drew forward a tall, dark-eyed woman. "Your Tante Adèle."

Cat curtsied.

"Welcome to Petit Chateau," smiled Adèle de Peyrac. "I am sorry your visit must be so short."

"Nonsense, *ma femme*! Catriona will stay as long as she likes!"

"It will not be long, uncle. I am bound for Naples, and I must reach there without delay. I stop only long enough to arrange for a new wardrobe in Paris, and to rest."

"You need not travel back to the city," said Adèle. "I have an excellent dressmaker who will come to the chateau. We will send for her tomorrow morning." And taking Cat's arm in a firm grip, she led her up the main staircase to an exquisitely decorated suite of rooms.

As the doors closed behind them, Cat pulled out of her aunt's grasp and, whirling about, said, "Very well, *tante*, let us talk!"

Adèle de Peyrac smiled. "Good. You are sensible. Tell me quickly now why have you come to France. I certainly hope you do not think you can make your home with us now that your son is married."

Cat was incredulous. The woman must be mad! "God's bones, madame! Why on earth would I want to live with you?"

"Do not be angry, my dear," replied Adèle. "We all know that a dowager countess has far less access to the gracious life as her son's mother than she had as her husband's wife. Perhaps you and your son's new wife do not get along, and it has been necessary for you to remove yourself? I do not imagine it is easy to be poor."

Cat resisted the strong urge to slap the smug face before her. "Madame," she said icily, "I do not know what gave you the erroneous idea that I am poor, but I beg to inform you that I am a very wealthy woman in my own right. I was when I married Glenkirk, and I still am. If I chose to I could live with my son and his bride, who is a sweet and loving girl. However, I prefer to remarry. I am on my way to Naples to do just that!"

"Remarry whom?"

"Lord Bothwell," said Cat evenly.

"*Mon Dieu*! He is a savage, and yet he is most charming, or so I have been told." With this pronouncement Adèle de Peyrac left the room.

Susan sniffed. "She doesna like us, does she, my lady?"

Cat laughed. "No Susan, she doesna like us."

"How long must we stay here, my lady?"

"Just a few weeks, Susan. 'Tis still winter, and I would wait a bit."

The following night Cat met her Uncle Donald and his wife, Renée, who was as warm with her Scots niece as Adèle was cold. "I wish you had stayed with us, *chère* Catherine. Adèle is not a particularly hospitable woman."

Cat patted the plump, dimpled hand. "It's all right, *ma chère tante*. I only stay a few weeks, and then I am gone."

Renée de la Provence leaned forward and whispered, "I must speak alone with you as quickly as possible. Make some excuse to go to your room."

A bit later, Cat discovered her Aunt Renée already awaiting her in Cat's room.

"Is it true, Catherine, that you are rich?"

Cat bit back her laughter, for the little woman looked so distressed. "Yes, *tante*, I am rich."

"Oh dear! Adèle thought at first that you were poor, and she could barely wait for you to come and be as quickly gone. Tonight, however, she told me that you were rich, and that she intended wedding you to her eldest son, Giles."

"Impossible!" Cat was angered and astounded. "I travel south to wed with Lord Bothwell. Besides, I thought all the de Peyracs were wed."

"Giles is a widower, and though he is my own nephew, I must tell you I do not like him. He was mar-

ried for five years to the daughter of my friend Marie
de Valmaison. Two years ago the girl committed suicide. Before she was wed to Giles she was the sweetest-
natured, brightest and sunniest girl imaginable! But
afterwards she became quiet . . . and frightened, always
looking to Giles for approval of every word she spoke.
It was as if she feared him."

"Do not fear for me, Tante Renée. I will wed no one
but Francis Hepburn."

"Nevertheless, child, beware Giles de Peyrac."

Back in the main hall of the chateau, Cat was introduced to her six de la Provence cousins—five charming
young men and their wives, and a delightful sixteen-
year-old girl named Marguerite, whom everyone called
MiMi. Then her Uncle David's sons and their wives
were presented to her. She quickly understood her
aunt's fear and dislike of Giles de Peyrac, although his
brothers were all pleasant enough.

The eldest de Peyrac son was tall and as austere as
his mother, with an almost Spanish look about him. His
hair was dark, and his black eyes held a peculiar gold
flame that flared when he was excited. He took her hand,
turning it over to kiss the inside of her palm and quickly
tickling it with his wet tongue. Cat snatched her hand
back, outraged. She was furious and repelled by his behavior, as well as disgusted by the strange eyes that
plunged deep into her décolletage and slowly swept upward to her face.

"We have much in common, *ma belle cousine*," said
Giles de Peyrac. "We are both left widowed in our
prime, and," he paused, "we are both experienced."

She ignored the remark, giving him a perfunctory
smile, and turned away to talk with MiMi. But when it
came time to sit down to the meal, she found him next
to her. To Cat's intense embarrassment, he made a great
fuss over her, choosing the choicest viands to put on her

plate, and insisting she drink from his cup. She could barely manage to be civil. Quickly turning to her other dinner partner, she discovered it was Niall Fitz-Leslie. His eyes were brimming with amusement, and she said quietly in Gaelic, "Do you not think my aunt is obvious in placing her odious son on one side of me, and a priest on the other?"

"The thought of her favorite child possessing your wealth is very tempting, Catriona." Then, "How did ye know I spoke Gaelic?"

"Ye told me ye spent several years in Caithness. What else would ye speak there?"

Annoyed at being ignored so pointedly, Giles de Peyrac asked, "What is that gibberish you speak? It has an ugly sound."

Cat gave him a cold look while Niall said, " 'Tis Gaelic we speak, cousin. Madame la comtesse speaks to me of my youth."

Cat managed to avoid her reptilian cousin the rest of the evening, and with the arrival the following day of the Parisian dressmaker she was prepared to forget him entirely. The woman had brought three assistants and an enormous collection of fabrics. One look at Cat, and she chortled, "Ah, madame la comtesse! What a pleasure it will be to dress you! *Mon Dieu!* What a tiny waist! What magnificent breasts! Such skin, eyes, hair! I can see that once you arrive at court it will not be long before our Evergreen Gallant has a new mistress. When I have finished with you, madame, there will be no one more ravishing!"

Cat laughed happily. "I regret I shall be a disappointment to you, Madame de Croix. I am not going to court, but to Italy to be married. You must make my clothes in the Italian fashion."

The little woman's face fell. "Where in Italy, madame la comtesse?"

"Naples."

"Ahhhh!" The smile reappeared. "Naples! The climate is temperate, and the nobility fashionable! We will use light velvets, cottons, linens, and silks of all weights. The necklines will be very, very low, the skirts fluid and flowing. You will be a vision!" She signaled to her assistants, who immediately began unrolling bolts of materials.

Cat gasped. Never had she seen such a marvelous display of fabric or colors. A soft lilac-colored silk caught her eye, and she pointed to it. "For my wedding gown," she said.

Madame de Croix smiled broadly. "*Oui*! But only for the overskirt. For the underskirt we use the same color in a light velvet, which we will embroider with gold thread and seed pearls. The sleeves will flow like water, and we will embroider their edges too. Very appropriate for Naples. Now, if you were to remain here and go to court, I should design the sleeves tight at the shoulder and wrist and full in the center, but—" she shrugged—" 'tis too stifling a fashion for a warm city. Now, madame la comtesse, let us get your measurements."

Clad only in her shift, Cat stood upon a stool while the dressmaker and her three assistants buzzed about her, chattering in their quick Parisian French. Suddenly Cat became aware of another person in the room, and looking up saw Giles de Peyrac leaning against the open bedroom door staring avidly at her. Ignoring him, she said to Susan in Gaelic, "Fetch Conall to remove that vermin!"

An uncomfortable few minutes passed, and then Conall was standing next to Giles de Peyrac. Speaking in soft, careful French, he said, "We can do this two ways, my lord. Either ye leave quietly, or on my lady's very explicit orders I will remove you."

Saying nothing, the Frenchman turned and departed, Conall following.

"How long," asked Cat, "would it take to make one dress for me? Could you do a dress in one day?"

"Using three girls, I could, madame la comtesse."

"Then send to Paris, Madame de Croix. I want two dozen of your best seamstresses, and I will pay their wages myself. Twelve are to work on my gowns and the others are to do everything else—the shifts, nightgarments, cloaks, embroidery, whatever!" At the woman's incredulous look, Cat smiled. "Send someone you trust to the banking house of Giscard Kira, and ask whether Madame la Comtesse de Glenkirk can afford such extravagance. You will find that I can. I wish to be gone from Chateau Petit within two weeks!"

Shuddering, Cat glanced at the now-empty doorway.

Chapter 45

❦

TWO days before Cat's departure, an unfamiliar horseman rode into Chateau Petit. Within the hour Cat was summoned to the library. David Leslie de Peyrac looked uncomfortable and a trifle nervous. Sprawling in a chair was an elegant gentleman who leaped to his feet as Cat entered the room.

"My niece, Madame la Comtesse de Glenkirk. Catriona, this is Monsieur le Marquis de la Victoire."

The elegant bowed low over her hand, kissing it reverently and holding it a moment too long. His blue eyes swept her admiringly, and he couldn't resist ogling her just a trifle, the waxed points of his moustache twitching slightly. "Madame, I am your devoted slave," he murmured with a violet-scented breath.

Cat's laughter rang clear, and her leaf-green eyes twinkled. "You overwhelm me with such attentions, monsieur le marquis," she protested prettily.

Delighted with this beautiful woman, who was obviously skilled in court repartee, the marquis spoke again. "Madame, it is my unbelievable good fortune to have been chosen by the king to escort you to Fontainebleau."

"Your king wishes to see me? There must be some mistake, monsieur le marquis. I am merely traveling through France on my way to Italy."

"You are the widow of Patrick Leslie?"

"Yes."

"Then there is no mistake, madame."

"I will need time to change, monsieur le marquis. And, of course, I must be properly chaperoned. I shall be accompanied by both my tiring women, my confessor, and my captain-at-arms and his men. And, of course, we shall travel in my coach."

"But, of course, madame! All the proprieties will be observed."

Another hour passed, and Cat found herself traveling the seven miles through the forest between Chateau Petit and Fontainebleau. On Niall's advice she had dressed herself in an elegantly seductive dark-green velvet dress that emphasized the color of her eyes and the whiteness of her skin. The neckline was cut very low to reveal the full swell of her breasts. Over it she had flung a hooded cloak fashioned of alternating bands of dark-green velvet and soft dark beaver. It closed at the neck with a large gold clasp set with an emerald.

Niall spoke quietly to her as they rode along. "Don't underestimate him, Catriona. Henri de Navarre is a shrewd man. Answer his questions candidly, but tell him only what you think he needs to know, no more. He enjoys women, especially women of spirit and intelligence. He has great charm."

"But what," she asked, "can he want with me?"

"I imagine James Stewart has discovered your absence, and has sent to his fellow king for aid in obtaining your return."

"I will *not* go back, Niall!"

"If that is why Henri wishes to see you, *ma belle*, then use *all* your charms to dissaude him. I know you can."

"*Mon père!*" Cat was shocked. "What is it you are telling me to do?"

"Whatever you must. Do you or do you not wish to be Lord Bothwell's wife?"

"I do! Dear God, I do!"

"Then do *whatever* you must do to achieve that goal."

A few minutes later they reached Fontainebleau, and the marquis was at the coach door to escort Cat to the French king. "Your women and your other people may wait here," he told her.

Niall slid easily from the coach to the courtyard. Looking directly at Robert de la Victoire, he said quietly, "I think I shall visit my old friend, Père Hugo, the king's confessor. I will be ready to return on your command, madame la comtesse."

Clutching her cloak about her, Cat followed the marquis through a maze of winding and dimly lit corridors until finally he stopped. Pointing to a paneled door, he directed, "Through there, madame." And turning around, he disappeared into the darkness. Cat gritted her teeth and, grasping the door handle, turned it and entered into a beautifully furnished small library.

At first glance the room appeared empty. Then a tall man stepped from a curtained alcove. "Come closer, madame la comtesse. I will not bite you."

She walked directly up to him and swept him a low curtsy. "Monseigneur, you are gracious to receive me."

A smile briefly touched the corner of his mouth. "Remove the cloak, madame. We will talk."

Cat unfastened the gold clasps. Laying the garment neatly on a chair, she turned back to the French king. He had a sensuous, handsome face, with deep-brown velvet eyes. They scrutinized her with frank approval. His gaze moved downward from her beautiful face to rest quite openly on her lovely breasts pushing above the neckline of her gown.

"*Magnifique*," he breathed. "I can well understand James Stewart's frantic desire to get you back, madame la comtesse."

Though she had been half-expecting it, the shock was almost too much for Cat. She swayed slightly. Instantly the French king was at her side, a strong arm about her waist. "I will not go back, monseigneur! Not unless it be in my coffin!"

Henri de Navarre was distressed. "Ahh, no, *chérie*, I cannot allow that to happen."

She swayed again, and the king scooped her up and swiftly carried her through the curtained alcove to a bed. His long slender fingers expertly loosed the laces of her bodice. Pouring a small amount of amber liquid into a goblet, he put an arm about her shoulders and forced her to drink.

Cat gasped, and coughed. "God's nightshirt! Whisky!"

The French king laughed. "An excellent restorative."

Suddenly aware of her dishabille, Cat struggled to relace herself, but another wave of dizziness overcame her, and she fell back. The king leaned over her, pinioning her gently between his arms. "Do not be afraid, *chérie*. I will not make you return to your king. It is all too obvious that he repels you, and I have never believed in forcing women. Sweet surrender in the battle between the sexes has far more charm than rape." The brown eyes caressed her warmly, and Cat felt herself blush under his very ardent gaze. His voice was soft. "Would you surrender to me, *chérie*?" he asked, and she barely had time to murmur, "Monseigneur," before his mouth closed warmly over hers.

Expecting to react as she had with James, Cat was startled to feel a tremor run through her body. The mouth on hers was tender, and expert. She felt herself relax. Her eyes closed, and she sighed deeply.

He laughed softly, and the slim fingers quickly undid her laces, baring her completely to the waist. His mouth moved down the slender column of her throat to the twin silken globes of her breasts. She couldn't stop him, though for a brief moment she tried to, struggling to escape the outrageously delicious feelings that were sweeping over her. This was wrong! She didn't even know him.

"*Non, non, chérie,*" he gently admonished her, pressing her back among the pillows. "You want this as much as I do."

And she realized with shock that he spoke the truth. She did not know him, yet she needed his very masculine body in order to reassure herself of her womanhood. James had made her feel like a whore. Henri of Navarre, a virtual stranger, was making her feel alive and feminine again.

His lips traced a pattern across her faintly trembling breasts, moving downward to her quivering navel. His large, soft hands caressed her with an expertise that left her breathless and half-fainting. She felt those hands beneath her full skirts, stroking her satiny thighs, and then moving to touch her more intimately. A throbbing, aching tightness began building within her. She cried out, "Monseigneur!" and felt him seeking her. Her breath was coming in short quick little gasps, and she sobbed gratefully as his hardness penetrated her.

He moved smoothly, delighting in her passionate response, lingering happily within her warmth, holding himself in perfect check as she sought and found her own heaven. Then, taking her one final time to the heights of ecstasy, he joined her in fulfillment. Cat, excited by this expert lover, first fainted and then drifted off into a relaxed sleep.

When she awoke several hours later he was quickly at her bedside with a glass of cool wine. Blushing furiously at the memory of what had passed between them, she accepted his offering with lowered eyes.

"Look at me, *chérie,*" he gently commanded her. His hand imperiously raised her heart-shaped face to his.

"I pity James, and I certainly envy my friend Lord Bothwell," he said.

Her leaf-green eyes widened, and she swallowed hard. "You—you know Francis?"

"Yes, *chérie*, I do. We spent many happy hours together before he so foolishly killed a de Guise in a duel. I have enough trouble with that family as it is, and I was forced to exile my friend."

"Then you know I journey to Naples to wed Francis?"

"Yes, *chérie*."

"And all along you intended to let me go my way?"

"Yes, *chérie*."

"Ohhhhhh!" Her eyes were wide with outrage. She struggled off the bed, desperately trying to lace herself up. "My God, monseigneur! How could you? How could you?"

Henri de Navarre could not help himself, and he began to laugh, catching at the angry little hand that pummeled his chest. "Because, you adorable creature, with a courtful of delicious and willing beauties, your François did nothing but sigh and moon over you! I simply could not believe such perfection existed. But now," and he smiled down at her, "I believe, *ma chérie*!" He tipped her face up to his. "You will not tell my good friend, François, that I took shameful advantage of you. Will you, *chérie*?"

Her lower lip began to tremble, and she struggled to retain her dignity. "You are an impossible man, monseigneur," she scolded him, beginning to laugh in spite of herself.

His fingers expertly laced her up. "Was it so terrible, what we did? I was under the distinct impression that you enjoyed yourself as much as I did."

Her eyes met his, and he heard her say, "I did, monseigneur, but for a reason you would not suspect."

"Tell me!"

"Last Christmas when my son wed Isabelle Gordon, James Stewart came to Glenkirk to spend his days hunting and his nights in my bed. When he touched me I felt nothing. I was forced to pretend an emotion I did not feel so as not to offend my royal cousin's pride. After several nights of it I became afraid that perhaps something was actually the matter with me."

"And today," chuckled Henri de Navarre, "you discovered that there is nothing the matter with you, *n'est-ce pas?*"

"Yes," she said softly.

"I am delighted to have had a part in reassuring you, madame la comtesse," he returned dryly.

She laughed mischievously. "Do not play the wounded one with me, monseigneur! 'Twas you who seduced me!"

Henri smiled down at her. "I will not deny, madame, that this has been a delightful interlude." His finger touched the tip of her nose, and he sighed. "But now you must return to your uncle's chateau, and prepare for your journey to Italy."

She caught up his hands and kissed them. "*Merci, merci,* monseigneur! *Mille mercis!*"

He again took her face in his two hands. "You love him very much, don't you, *chérie?*"

"Yes, monseigneur, I love him. It has been a long and very lonely three years. I have been as half a person without him."

"I have never felt like that about anyone," replied the French king.

"I do not believe many people do, monseigneur, and I do not understand why Francis and I were singled out to share such a love—but we do!"

Henri de Navarre gently traced a finger down her cheek. "How lovely you are, *chérie,* with all your innocent love shining out of those marvelous green eyes. Go safely to your beloved rogue, and tell him that I miss him. What an addition you both would have been to my court!" Picking up her cloak, he carefully draped it around her shoulders. Taking her hand, he led her to the door and opened it. "Here she is, *mon père*—safe and sound." He took her hand. Kissing it, he said, "Adieu, madame la comtesse."

The door to the study closed, and she was alone in the corridor with Niall Fitz-Leslie. The priest led her back to their coach in the courtyard. When they were safely on their way, he asked, "Well, madame, did you leave the lion's maw unscathed?"

Cat laughed. "Almost, *mon père*. Still, I like your king."

"Then you are free to go on to Lord Bothwell?"

"Yes, Niall. I am free."

The following day the two families gathered to bid Cat farewell. She retired as soon after the evening meal as was politely possible, for they planned an early start. Already the coach and a smaller secondary vehicle, brought to transport Cat's new wardrobe, had been packed and stood ready but for their horses. That very morning the Marquis de la Victoire had arrived with a certificate of safe passage from Henri de Navarre for Madame la Comtesse de Glenkirk. It would enable her to travel unmolested through France, and through various Italian territories as well.

In the deep of the night Cat woke suddenly, aware that she was not alone. Standing silently in the darkness at the foot of her bed was a man. She knew at once who it was. "What do you want, Giles?"

"How did you know it was me, Catherine?"

"Who else would dare to intrude on me, Giles?"

"Are you really leaving us in the morning?"

"Yes."

"Why?"

"Because," she said patiently, as if explaining to a child, "I travel to Naples to wed Lord Bothwell."

"He is not the man for you, Catherine! He is a cruel, crude Northerner. He killed my friend, Paul de Guise. You do not know what kind of a man he really is!"

" 'Tis you who do not know Lord Bothwell, Giles. I have known him for years. I love him, and I always have loved him."

For a moment Giles de Peyrac was silent, then she heard a sharp intake of breath. "You! Then *you* are the woman he mourned! You are the woman for whom he scorned and insulted Clarice de Guise!" Giles de Peyrac moved from the darkness into the half-light by Cat's bedside, and his voice was strained, vindictive. "We stripped him of almost everything he had in reparation before the king exiled him. When he left France he and that mangy servant of his had naught but the horses they rode and the clothes on their backs. Now you think to go to him, and make his life pleasant? My best friend is dead!" The strange gold light flickered in Giles de Peyrac's eyes. "I wonder, *ma belle cousine*, how your lover will receive you, knowing that I have used you like an animal? And he will know!"

"*Giles!*" She deliberately raised her voice, but he was so lost to reason that he did not notice. "*Giles! Leave my bedchamber at once!*" She heard a soft movement in her dressing room, and knew with relief that she had wakened her tiring women.

Giles de Peyrac reached out. Grasping the neckline of her nightgown, he ripped the sheer material away easily. Before she could stop him, he flung himself on her. Cat screamed, a scream cut off by his hand on her mouth. Cat twisted her body wildly, trying to escape the hands that pinched and hurt her. The black eyes glittered cruelly, the little gold flame flickering madly. "That's it," he whispered in an excited voice, "fight me! Fight me! I like it when women fight me!"

My God, Cat realized. He's mad! But I won't be raped again! Not again!

Suddenly Giles de Peyrac was lifted off her, his arms pinioned back by Andrew. "I warned you, lad," said Conall quietly, and then he plunged his dirk directly into his prisoner's heart. Giles de Peyrac's odd eyes widened in surprise and then went blank as he crumpled to the floor. Amazed, Cat watched as Niall stepped from the darkness. Having administered last rites, he commanded, "Dump him outside the walls by the servants' gate. It will look like footpads." Andrew and Conall picked up the body silently and carried it from the room.

Gasping, Cat began to weep with relief, vaguely aware that she was being gathered against a broad chest. Niall Fitz-Leslie held her easily, his hand stroking the tawny hair. Suddenly be became aware of the soft bare breasts pressing against his chest. His heart began to beat wildly, and for a brief moment he closed his eyes, enjoying the sensation. Then, gathering his weakening self-control, he said quietly, "Giles de Peyrac was a depraved monster who virtually killed his own wife. I want you to forget this ever happened. Are you all right now?"

Still clinging to him, she turned her tear-streaked face up to him, and he groaned, "Christ, Catriona! Don't look at me like that! I am a priest, but I am a man also, *ma belle*!"

"Then let me go, Niall. I can feel you trembling against me. Go away before we are foolish!"

Reluctantly he released her, and she drew the sheets up over her nakedness. Though celibacy was a vow often broken among the priesthood, he himself had never before been tempted. He had had his share of wenches before admitting to his vocation, and had never regretted leaving carnality behind. But now?

As if reading his thoughts, she said quietly, "Honest doubt makes for a stronger faith, *mon père*. Thank you

for rescuing me, but I would rest now. 'Twill soon be
dawn, and whatever happens I must be on my way
today."

He nodded dumbly.

"Will you hear my confession before I go? I think it
would be best to keep this in the family."

Finding his voice, he said, "Yes. Come to the chapel
at dawn. I will be waiting." And he slowly walked from
the room.

Susan came to see that she was all right. Cat smiled
wanly and patted her arm. "I am fine. Thank ye for
getting Conall. I knew if I raised my voice ye'd hear
me."

Susan flushed. " 'Twas nae me, my lady. 'Twas May.
She sleeps light."

"Thank God for it! Now go back to bed, child. 'Twill
soon be morning."

Cat dozed in the darkness until her inner sense told
her that dawn was near. Waking, she dressed herself
quietly and made her way to the chapel, where Niall
waited. The young priest was composed again, but had
a haggard look about him. Kneeling, Cat placed her
hands in his and began her confession. He listened
quietly as she recited a list of small indiscretions, and
the slightly larger sin of her few hours with Henri de
Navarre. The penance he gave her was light, and his
hand shook slightly as he absolved her, touching her
bowed head. She looked up at him, then, green eyes
twinkling, and said, "And for your sins, *mon père*, three
Aves and three Paters."

Niall Fitz-Leslie choked back his laughter. "Catriona,
you are impossibly irreverent, and I thank you. I have
made a great to-do over nothing, haven't I?"

"Yes, *mon père*, you have. There is a world of difference between the thought and the deed."

"*Merci, ma fille.*"

She kissed the hand extended to her, rose, and allowed him to escort her from the chapel. Lowering his voice, he spoke in Gaelic. "The body has not been found yet. If you leave quickly you should be gone before it is."

"We are ready now."

"Have you eaten?"

"No. We will do so on the road."

When they entered the courtyard of the chateau they found David Leslie de Peyrac awaiting them. "Adèle bid me say her adieu if you left. She seemed to feel you might stay, though I know not why." He kissed her soundly on both cheeks. "Before you go, niece, will you satisfy my personal curiosity? From whom do you run?"

"From James Stewart," she answered him frankly.

"And King Henri knows, yet gives you safe passage?"

"Yes, uncle."

The Sieur de Peyrac chuckled. "Go with God, niece, and if you should ever need my help you have but to ask. Though with your powerful friends, I doubt you'll need *me*."

"Sometimes family is best, uncle. Thank you," she replied and kissed him. He handed her into the coach and she leaned from the window and said, "Adieu, *mon père et mon beau-frère* Niall. Thank you for everything."

Niall Fitz-Leslie kissed the slim hand extended him. "Adieu, *ma belle*. Be happy."

"I shall! Conall, forward!"

And the Countess of Glenkirk's entourage rumbled out of the courtyard of Chateau Petit, and onto the main road which led through the Forest of Fontainebleau and south to the Mediterranean coast. As soon as they were clear of the castle, the coach pulled into a clearing and Cat descended, a bundle under her arm, and disappeared into the thick undergrowth.

Several minutes later she reappeared dressed for riding in her hose and leather jerkin, her hair tucked beneath a tam. She tossed her clothes to Susan and May within the coach as Conall rode up leading Iolaire. Swinging easily into the saddle, she stretched. Clamping her knees against the horse's sides, she kicked him forward.

"I'm free, Conall," she laughed. "At last I am free! To Naples! To Bothwell! I am free!"

Part VI

❧❧❧

My Lord Bothwell

Chapter 46

❧

DOWN the plump backside of France they rode through towns and villages that eventually began to blur and hold a sameness. Nemours . . . Briare . . . Nevers . . . Lyons . . . Vienne . . . Avignon . . . Marseilles. And now Cat got her first glimpse of a southern sea, so different from the cold north. It dappled aqua here, green there, turquoise to the left, purple to the right, and clear to its sandy or coral bottom.

They remained several days in Marseilles, and Cat delighted in the city and its waterfront markets with fruits and fish and spices. There were French, Spanish, Turkish, Russian, Moorish, English, Venetian, Genoese, Sicilian, and even black sailors! Seeing the ships lining the quaysides she wished that she could sail out into the Golfe du Lion through the Ligurian Sea, past Corsica and Sardinia, and into the Tyrrhenian Sea to Naples. But Cat knew well that beyond the safety of Marseilles' harbor, Turkish corsairs lurked waiting to pounce upon any poorly guarded ship.

Before they left Marseilles, the messenger sent to Naples by Giscard Kira joined them to report that, though he had delivered the message to the villa where Lord Bothwell was staying, he had not seen Bothwell. The earl had been away. Cat became anxious to resume her journey. Giles de Peyrac had said that Francis had been stripped of everything but his clothes and his horse.

If Francis was living comfortably, he must have a wealthy protector. It could, of course, be a male friend, but Cat would have wagered her entire new wardrobe that it was a woman.

It was. Angela Maria di LiCosa was a contessa by both her marriage to Alfredo, Conte di LiCosa, and her birth as the daughter of Scipio, Conte di Cicala. Her mother, Maria Teresa, had been born a Muslim in the Ottoman Empire. At fourteen, Maria Teresa had been captured in a raid by Christian knights, and her captor, Scipio di Cicala, had not hesitated in ravishing her. But he had fallen deeply in love with his slavegirl and she, finding herself pregnant, did the intelligent thing. She converted to Christianity and married her lover in time to legitimatize their eldest son. Their youngest child was Angela. She grew to be as beautiful as the angels for whom she was named, and as wicked as the devil she worshipped. Her parents—especially her gentle mother—despaired of her, and as soon as she was old enough, they married her to Alfredo di LiCosa, twenty years Angela's senior.

She came to her husband a virgin, but soon tired of his lovemaking. After giving him two sons, she began taking lovers. Alfredo di LiCosa was a sophisticated man, and as long as his wife was discreet, he turned a blind eyes to her infidelities. After all, he had his diversions too. Besides, she was absolutely insatiable, and he was no longer a boy. Even when Angela brought her lovers into his house he did not mind, provided there was a good covering excuse for their being there. Proprieties must always be observed.

Francis Stewart-Hepburn had come into the house of Alfredo di LiCosa innocently enough. From France he had gone to Spain, but feeling the hot breath of the Inquisition on his neck he had left for Naples with his manservant, Angus. He brought with him an introduction from a friend of the Spanish king to the Conte di LiCosa, who was happy to shelter him. That Lord Bothwell should become the contessa's lover was inevitable. Francis appreciated beautiful women, and Angela di LiCosa was indeed a beautiful woman.

Willow-slim, she had exquisite, high, cone-shaped breasts, and a waist a man could span with his hands. Her skin was milk-white with no touch of color, even in the cheeks. Her eyes were like a night sky—deep and fathomless—with beautiful winged brows riding high above them. Her long, straight hair was blue-black, and hung nearly to her ankles.

She was a charming woman when she chose to be, and she generally chose to be charming with men. Other women she merely tolerated, or ignored. She was not particularly well educated, though she could write and read a little. She had been raised to be an ornament, and she was successful in that.

In the Earl of Bothwell, Angela di LiCosa recognized a man of wit, charm, education, and great sexual appetite. And Bothwell, always desperately seeking to blur the memory of his only love, was willing to be Angela's lover as long as it amused him.

He was no saint, and he had to live. Cat had offered him her entire fortune before he left Scotland, but he had refused to take even a pennypiece from her. She had raged angrily at his foolish pride, knowing that money could mean safety to him. From those for whom he cared only in passing, Francis would accept money. It was his way.

The thought of him in another woman's arms sent Cat spurring out of Marseilles. They raced through Toulon following the coastal road to Monaco, where she spent but one night in an ordinary inn, refusing the prince's invitation to rest a few days at his palace. The party moved on into the state of Genoa, and through

Tuscany to Rome. Conall forced her to stop in Rome and rest a few days. "Christ, woman," he roared. "Yer killing my men wi this pace! The earl knows yer coming. He'll be rid of his doxy before ye get there!"

She was exhausted, with deep purple shadows beneath her eyes. She slept for two days, but on her third evening in Rome she told Conall, "We leave in the morning. I want to make Naples in three days."

"I sent the coaches ahead wi half the men this morning," he told her. "Susan and May are wi 'em."

"I wondered where my women had got to, and thought that perhaps some of these dark-eyed young men had lured them away."

Conall sniffed. "Not likely. They're my brother's own girls, and I'd nae like to answer to Hugh if harm befell them."

" 'Tis a pity ye dinna think so piously when yer happily fucking wi another man's daughter, Conall," she answered him, a mischievous light dancing in her eyes.

He glowered at her. "Do ye think ye can get yerself up and ready to leave by dawn?" he demanded.

"Aye," she drawled back. "And will ye be sleeping alone also, Conall?"

He burst out laughing. "Gie over, lass! Ye've a wicked tongue in yer pretty head for sure! I'll be up. See that ye are!"

The following morning saw Cat and her men on the road to Naples. By their second evening they had caught up with the lumbering, laden coach and baggage wagon. They were nearer to Naples than they had anticipated. The following day, Cat rode until they were within a few miles of the city, stopping then at a small inn to bathe and change clothes.

The innkeeper's wife clucked with disapproval at the dusty, long-legged woman who strode into her inn and up the stairs to the best bedroom. But a tub of hot water and almost two hours later the innkeeper's wife smiled broadly her approval at the exquisitely gowned and coifed woman descending the stairs.

Cat and her women reentered the coach, which proceeded into the city and to the house of Signor Pietro Kira. It was midafternoon, and the banker was away on business. His eldest son escorted the countess to her newly purchased home near the village of Amalfi, south of Naples. It was, the young Kira explained, fully furnished and staffed according to instructions received from Benjamin Kira in Edinburgh.

Cat gasped at the view through the coach windows. The road they traveled was precariously high above the sea, which glittered in at least three shades of blue beneath them. Finally they turned into a small tree-lined side road, through gates with a bronze plaque reading "Villa del Pesce d'Oro." Within minutes an exquisite house came into view. It was unlike anything Cat had lived in before. The roof was of red tiles, the villa itself a pale, creamy yellow. The white gravel driveway swung around in a circle and up to the house. In the center of the circle was a velvety green lawn bordered with flower beds already filled to overflowing with multicolored blooms. In the middle of the lawn was a round fountain with a laughing cupid riding a golden fish. All the area about the house was planted with flowers of every description.

"Ohhhh, my lady," breathed young May. " 'Tis the most beautiful thing I've ever seen!"

"For once the child doesna blather nonsense," agreed Susan. "At home the snowdrops will be but daring to poke their little heads up, and here 'tis already June!"

Cat smiled at them both, thinking that this was a house for lovers. And if he was not already waiting, Bothwell would soon be here. The coach stopped, and

her grooms let down the steps as the house servants
emerged from the villa. Young Signor Kira introduced
them. There was the major-domo, Paolo, and his wife,
Maria, the housekeeper-cook. There were two kitchen
maids, two housemaids, and half a dozen gardeners.

"Lord Bothwell," she asked Paolo, "has he arrived
yet?"

"No one has come, Madonna."

Cat turned to Signor Kira. "Your messenger said he
delivered my note to Lord Bothwell's villa. Where is his
villa?"

"Quite near, signora contessa."

She turned to Paolo again. "Have one of the gardeners show my captain the way."

"Sì, Madonna!"

"Conall, go!"

The highlander swung back into his saddle. " 'Tis
shameful how anxious ye are," he grumbled.

"Dinna fret," she shot back at him. "I'm sure that
currant-eyed wench ye've been ogling will wait," and
she laughed at the rude noise he made as he rode off.
She turned to the young Kira. "You are my guest tonight, signor. It is too late for you to ride back to the
city alone."

They entered the villa. Cat was very pleased. The
main floor boasted a square foyer with a center staircase and three salons, a library, a family dining room,
a formal dining room, and three kitchens. Maria spoke
as they ascended to the second floor. "It is a very small
house, I fear, Madonna. There are only six bedcham-
bers. However, the third floor is spacious, and I have
given your women a nice room just above you." She
waddled down the hallway to a pair of carved doors
with lion-head decorations and exquisite gold-and-
porcelain handles. Flinging open the doors she announced, "Ecco, Madonna! Your bedchamber."

Cat walked into a spacious, airy room with two long double windows that opened onto small iron balconies over the rear gardens. The room looked out to the sea. There was a large high bed hung with sheer, sea-green silk draperies, and a matching coverlet. The furniture was a warm, well-polished walnut and the walls were cream-colored with gilt designs near the upper part and on the ceiling. Heavy silk draperies—also sea-green— hung on either side of the two windows. Between the windows, sheer creamy silk curtains blew in the soft breeze. On the cool tile floors were thick sheepskin rugs. Across from the windows and to the left of the bed was a large fireplace with a carved marble mantelpiece. The only other furniture in the room was a large armoire, a table, and some chairs.

On the wall opposite the bed and to the right there was a door. Maria opened it with a flourish. "Your bath, signora contessa," she said.

Cat's eyes widened. The walls and floor of the room were a marvellous blue tile, and in the center of the floor was a large sunken marble tub, shaped like a shell, with golden fish ornaments at one end.

"Look, Madonna," said Maria excitedly. She leaned over and twisted one of the three golden fishes on the edge of the tub. Water flowed into the tub. "And when you wish to empty it," she chortled, pulling the center fish up, "see! Is it not marvelous? The last owner of this house was a Turkish merchant. They bathe far more than is healthy, but no matter!"

"How is the water made hot?" asked Cat.

"It is stored in a porcelain barrel which always has a low flame burning beneath it."

"Look, Susan, May! Isn't it wonderful? No more lugging barrels of water! You can draw me a bath right now! Lord Bothwell will soon be here!"

And while Cat swam about her scented tub, Conall

followed the young gardener several miles across the
hills to another great villa, well hidden within the trees.
Here the gardener stopped and pointed.

"Well, come on," said the Scotsman.

"No, signor capitano. I go no further. If *she* knows
that I came to help take her man away, she will curse
me!"

"Who?" Conall was puzzled.

"The witch!"

"What witch?"

"The Contessa di LiCosa. It is her house. The Lord
Bothwell is her lover."

Conall thought for a moment. Well . . . the man had
to live. And yet, he had not been at the villa to greet
the woman he professed to love. Conall had assumed
that they would meet somewhere on the road between
Rome and Naples. Then he remembered what the messenger had told them. He had not delivered the message
directly into Lord Bothwell's hand because the earl had
not been at the villa. Was it possible that the earl had
never received the message? Yes! It most certainly was!
A typical woman's trick!

"Wait here for me," he told the nervous gardener and
started his horse up the road. He rode unchallenged.
When he reached the house he found it ablaze with
lights. Dismounting, he banged on the door. It was
opened a few moments later by an imperious-looking
major-domo. "I wish to see Lord Bothwell."

"I am sorry. He cannot be disturbed. Who shall I say
called?"

"I am Captain More-Leslie, man," said Conall, pushing the officious servant aside, "and I intend disturbing
his lordship right now! *A Bothwell! To me! A Bothwell!
A Bothwell!*"

From the upper story of the house Conall heard the
slamming of a door, and Francis Stewart-Hepburn appeared, leaping lightly down the stairs, sword drawn.

Walking to Conall, he peered closely at him. "Conall? Conall More-Leslie?"

"Aye, my lord."

A smile lit the earl's face, and he grasped Conall's hand with his free one. "Christ, man! 'Tis good to see ye! What are ye doing here?"

"Ye didna receive the message delivered here for you several weeks ago?"

"No. Are ye sure yer messenger came here?"

"Aye, my lord, he came. He was told ye were away, but that the message would be delivered to ye on yer return."

"I havena left here in months, Conall." Suddenly the earl's face went white. "Cat? Is she all right?"

Conall sighed with relief. "Aye, my lord, she is fine, but she grows very impatient for yer company. She awaits yer lordship at the Villa del Pesce d'Oro."

"*What?*"

"Aye, sir! She is waiting now. If ye've nothing of value here, let us get yer man Angus and go!"

Francis Stewart-Hepburn smiled slowly at Conall More-Leslie. "I've nought of value here, man. Angus! To me!"

Then suddenly, at the top of the stairs, there appeared one of the most beautiful women Conall had ever seen. She glided down the stairs like a cat and purred in a deep voice, "*Caro?* Where do you go? Our guests will soon be arriving."

"Why was I not given the message delivered here several weeks ago?"

"What message, *caro?*" But her dark eyes flashed angrily at Conall.

Bothwell saw her and laughed. "You are a very bad liar, Angela *mia*. I warned you that one day I would turn to you and say goodbye. This is that day."

"Now? With guests coming? Could you not wait until tomorrow? Who will be my host?"

"You might ask your husband, Angela."

"Francisco!" She held out her beautiful hands in a pleading fashion. "I love you!"

He laughed again. "Angela *mia*, you are a marvelous actress. There is only one thing in this world that would take me from your side, and she is waiting for me now. Adieu, *cara mia*!"

Within minutes they were on the road back to the Villa del Pesce d'Oro, and they never heard the shrieks of outrage made by the beautiful Contessa di LiCosa.

"What is Cat doing here?" shouted Lord Bothwell over the wind and the pounding of the horses' hooves.

"She will tell ye herself, my lord," Conall shouted back.

The sun was sinking into the western sea when they reached the villa. She waited in the doorway, and he slid from the saddle before his horse had even stopped. Everything was suddenly very quiet as they stood stock still looking at each other. The servants were frozen silent, not daring to move, so charged was the very air about them.

"Cat." His voice caressed her, and she swayed. "Cat, my precious love, how come ye here?"

"I am a widow, Francis. Patrick is dead."

"God assoil him." They moved towards each other. "Angus! Fetch a priest!" commanded Lord Bothwell. And then he caught her to him, and slowly enfolding her in his arms, he found her eagerly waiting mouth. He drank in the sweetness of her, murmuring softly against her lips.

Surrendering herself completely to the storm tearing at her, she clung to him. She could hardly stand. She could hear her heart pounding within her own ears. Finally she managed to gasp, "Why a priest?"

His strong arm supporting her, he looked down into her upturned face. "Because, my darling, I intend marrying ye now! Tonight! Before kings, or families, or anyone can come between us ever again!"

"Oh, Francis," she whispered, "I hae missed ye so damned much!" And she began to cry.

"Dinna weep, my darling. Yer safe wi me now, and this time no one will separate us! Now, love, tell me—why did Jamie relent, and let ye come to me?"

"He didn't, Francis. I ran. Jemmie is now the Glenkirk, and he felt 'twas the only chance I would have. What was between James Stewart, Patrick, and us had nothing to do wi Jemmie. He didna think that Jamie would try and revenge himself on the Leslies now." She drew him into the house.

"Does our royal cousin know where ye are?"

"He was told that I went to France to recover from my widow's depression, but I imagine he's very angry at me, for I was ordered to return to court this spring. He even sent to King Henri and demanded his aid in arranging my return. Henri of Navarre sends his regards to ye."

"Ye met him?"

"Aye. He was most kind. He told me how very much he regretted having to send ye away."

"Henri was always kind to women," chuckled Bothwell. "Young or old. Fair or ugly. He has unbelievable charm, and the ladies love it!"

But before he could pursue the conversation further, Cat led him into one of the salons overlooking the sea. Whirling about, she demanded, "And who is the owner of the villa in which ye hae be staying?"

"The Conte di LiCosa," said Bothwell smoothly.

"Is it his wife or his daughter ye've been sleeping with these long nights, my lord?"

Francis' deep-blue eyes twinkled. "Jealous, my darling?" he teased.

"If she ever looks at ye again I will tear her heart out!"

He laughed happily. "Beware, my darling. The Contessa de LiCosa is reputed to be a witch."

"Is she?" Cat was not impressed.

He chuckled. "She likes the peasants and the other uneducated masses to think so, and she really is quite talented in herbal medicine. She enjoys the small power her reputation gives her. She's half-Turkish, as her mother was born in Morea and captured by Angela's father years ago. She has two brothers, the older of whom, in an odd quirk of fate, was himself captured by Turks twenty years ago. Just as his mother once converted to Christianity, he became a Muslim. He is now one of the sultan's generals."

"Is she very beautiful?" asked Cat.

"Yes," replied Bothwell honestly, "but the peasants call her l'Angela del Diavolo—the Devil's Angel." He moved to take her in his arms. "Cat, my love, I dinna want to talk of Angela. My God, I canna believe 'tis ye! Do ye know how many times I have dreamed of such a reunion, knowing it was impossible? Do ye know how I have longed for ye, sure that I would never hold ye in my arms again in this life? I have lain alone more nights than not aching for ye!" Gently he traced his finger down a tear streak. "Our bairns?"

"Well," she whispered in a choked little voice. "Safe at Glenkirk wi Meg. Jemmie will send them to us when 'tis safe. A few months at most, and then we shall be a family at last."

His arms tightened about her, and his mouth brushed against hers. "I should like to be a bridegroom before I am a father, my darling."

She laughed softly. "Perhaps ye should have thought about that before ye sired three children on me, my lord."

" 'Tis siring the fourth one I'm looking forward to, my pet!"

The door to the salon opened on them, and a grinning Conall entered accompanied by Angus and a black-robed cleric. "So, Francisco! 'Tis you who summon me in such unruly fashion!"

"Bishop Pasquale! When did you get back from Rome?"

"This afternoon, and a good thing I did. These two wildmen came roaring into the church demanding a priest. They frightened my priests half to death! What is your great need of a priest, Bothwell? You don't look to me as if you're dying."

The earl drew Cat forward. "My lord bishop, may I present to you Caterina Maria Leslie, the Countess of Glenkirk. We wish to be married."

"No, Bothwell. There have been no banns read."

"Waive them, my friend!"

The bishop smiled. "Why should I, Francisco? My child," he said, directing his gaze on Cat, "how well do you know this man?"

"He is the father of my three youngest children, my lord bishop," answered Cat. "We would have been wed six years ago had our king not threatened the Cardinal of St. Andrew's with persecution of the church if he dissolved my marriage. Now I am a widow, and though King James seeks to make me his mistress, I fled my land to wed with Lord Bothwell. Please, my lord bishop, waive the banns. I have been traveling almost two months, and have come over a thousand miles. My lord and I have been separated three long years. Marry us tonight!"

"How long have you been widowed, my daughter?" asked the bishop.

"My first husband sailed for the new world two years ago this month. His ship never reached its destination."

The bishop looked at the two people standing before him. They were certainly not impetuous children, but adults obviously in love. That in itself was unusual in marriage between people of rank. Then, too, the bishop liked Lord Bothwell, and believed that the sooner he was safe from Angela di LiCosa, the better. That the beauteous woman before him could separate Bothwell permanently from Angela he had no doubt.

"Very well, Francisco and Caterina. I will marry you tonight. Be at the Church of Santa Maria del Mare in Amalfi within the hour."

"There is a consecrated chapel here in this villa, my lord bishop," said Cat softly.

"Very well, my daughter. Here it shall be. When?"

"Give me but time to change my clothing." She turned to Bothwell and spoke in Scots English. "When I wed wi Patrick 'twas in a dressing gown, and I was already in labor wi Jemmie. All this winter I hae done nothing but prepare brides for their weddings. So, beloved, for you and for me, I shall take time to be a bride."

He took her by the shoulders and kissed her forehead. "Go along, my love. I shall see the bishop is comfortable."

Bishop Pasquale settled himself comfortably and sipped appreciatively at the goblet of sweet pale-golden wine that Lord Bothwell handed him. "I have always believed that you were born under a lucky star, Francisco, else your head would long ago have parted company from your shoulders. Your betrothed is a lovely creature. So the Scots king covets her?"

"Aye. He hides his lust from public view, but what he did to her—I shall not distress you with unsavory details. But before James Stewart forced her into his bed by threatening her family she was a good and faithful wife. She was called the Virtuous Countess, and that in itself was what first attracted him."

"And when did you become involved with her, Francisco?"

"I knew her at court, but not until she was forced to flee from both the king and her husband—who was shocked and hurt to discover her dilemma—did we become intimate. We were friends, and she had nowhere else to go. What happened between us . . . simply happened. I have never known such happiness as I have with her. Nor have I ever known such agony as without her."

The bishop nodded. "My son," he said, "do you know how fortunate you are? I know kings who would give anything for what you have. Cherish it! Cherish this woman who makes you so happy! God has blessed you both greatly."

At the end of the hour Cat reentered the salon with her two tiring women, and found only Conall awaiting her. He was dressed—to her amazement—in his Leslie kilt, and full highland regalia.

"Where did ye find that, man?"

He looked shocked. "Ye dinna think I'd travel wi'out my kilt, lassie? If I'd died on the journey, what would ye hae buried me in, pray? However, 'tis in the capacity of yer father that I act now. Being yer nearest relative here, I shall lead ye to yer betrothed." Offering her his arm, he swept her from the room and to the chapel. Behind them Susan and May, each in her finest, followed.

The chapel of the villa had been in existence longer than the house. It was small, and of Romanesque design. Used as a mosque by the villa's former owner, it had been rededicated to the Christian faith on the orders of Benjamin Kira, the Jewish banker who knew and admired his client's quiet devotion to the Roman faith in a Scotland turned Protestant. When he had been informed that the house purchased for the Countess of Glenkirk had an ancient chapel, Kira ordered it refur-

bished at his own expense. This was his gift to the
extraordinary woman he had admired since her girl-
hood, and whom he would very likely never see again.

The chapel was simply furnished with a white marble
altar topped by two magnificent heavy gold candlesticks
studded with diamonds, rubies, emeralds, and amethysts. There was a matching carved gold crucifix. The
small windows were newly redone in precious stained
glass, and the vigil lamps were of heavy ruby glass
hand-blown in Murano, set into holders of filigreed gold
and silver. The entire chapel glowed softly in the light
of at least fifty beeswax tapers.

As Conall led her down the chapel aisle to the altar,
Cat saw her six houseservants and all of her Glenkirk
men standing witness to the ceremony. No one would
be able to question the legitimacy of this marriage. As
her eyes swept past them she saw Bothwell waiting for
her. He, like Conall, was attired in full dress kilt. Suddenly clearly aware of what was happening, she smiled
happily at him.

He smiled back at her, his eyes shining approval of
her gown. The sleeveless lilac silk overdress glowed
softly in the candlelight, and the slightly darker underskirt with its gold and pearl embroidery shimmered. The
sleeves of the underdress were of lilac gauze, and her
rounded arms gleamed seductively through them. Her
honey-colored hair was parted in the center and caught
up over her ears in a mass of ringlets that spilled down
over the back of her neck and shoulders. She wore a
misty mauve veil topped by a small crown of sweet-
smelling night-blooming white flowers.

Conall solemnly led Cat up to Lord Bothwell and
placed her slim hanad firmly into his. "Treat her well,
man," growled Conall huskily, "or ye'll answer first to
me before the young earl has a go at ye!"

"She is my life," returned Bothwell quietly, meeting
Conall's look evenly.

As the ceremony got underway, their joy was so great that neither quite believed it was happening. They went through the ceremony in a haze, hearing the bishop's words vaguely and responding automatically. And then it was over. They were wed! For a moment they stood staring at each other. Then they began to smile at one another, and they could not stop. Finally the bishop stepped down and put an arm about them. "It is true, my children. You are wed. Do I dare hope there is a bit of wine left with which we may toast this happy occasion?"

Cat blushed, which the bishop found charming in a woman over thirty. Bothwell laughed happily and, pulling himself together, put an arm about his wife and led the way back to the main part of the villa, where Maria and Paolo had rushed ahead to bring up several bottles of wine from the cellars. A few of the Glenkirk men had brought their bagpipes with them, and they began to serenade the newlyweds. Cat gazed at them intently. There was one wedding gift that only her men could give her husband.

Standing before them during a lull in their playing, she spoke quietly. "My mother was born a Leslie of Sithean, and I was wed for eighteen years to the Glenkirk. Tonight ye hae been witnesses to my second marriage to the Earl of Bothwell. We are both exiled from Scotland, exiled by our king, who threatened the Leslies with destruction unless I became his mistress. What ye hae just witnessed in the chapel of this villa is my answer to King James. Ye hae protected me loyally, and brought me safely to my dear husband. Now ye must decide what yer futures will be. Ye may return to your homes at Glenkirk, and ye'll hae my blessing. Or ye may pledge yerselves to the Earl of Bothwell. The choice is yers."

Conall stood. "The men who came wi ye came because there is nothing to keep them at Glenkirk. We are

happy to pledge ourselves to Lord Bothwell . . . but on
one condition. Should the Leslies or our homeland ever
need us, we will go." He directed his gaze to Bothwell.
"We know that ye would go under those circumstances
if ye could, sir."

Francis nodded. "I would," he said. Turning to his
wife, he said simply, "Thank ye, love."

She smiled back at him. "I will retire now, my lord,"
she answered him softly.

She hurried up the stairs to the master bedchamber,
followed by her women. Silently, the three women removed Cat's gown and petticoats. While Susan hung the
gown within the armoire and May brought Cat a basin
of warm, scented water, Cat rolled her stockings off.
Naked, she took the cloth handed her and washed herself. Pulling the pins from her hair, she fiercely brushed
her tawny mass until it gleamed in the candlelight.
Susan slipped a simple long, loose gown of palest lilac
over her, and then the two servants withdrew.

"Lord," whispered young May in a shocked voice,
"my lady Cat is overeager for her husband."

"Nay, silly puss," chided her older and wiser sister.
"She but wanted time alone before he comes."

"What on earth for?" asked May.

"Ye'd need to be more of a woman to understand
that, pet."

Puzzled, May shook her head.

Cat stood on one of the bedchamber balconies overlooking the moonlit garden. She welcomed the soft night
air on her skin, and smelled the sweetness of the night
blooms. Her mind was whirling. This morning she had
wakened a widow, but now she was a bride awaiting her
husband in their nuptial chamber. Everything had happened so quickly. For a moment she was frightened.
Then she heard his voice.

"Cat."

She turned and saw him standing across the room,

gazing longingly at her. He held out his arms, and suddenly she was shy. She hesitated. Instantly comprehending her mood, he moved quietly across the room and gently enfolded her in his arms. His hand slowly caressed her silken hair, and a tremor ran through her. " 'Tis been a long, long time, my darling," he said.

"I feel so foolish," she whispered into his shoulder. "I am behaving like a virgin faced with a stranger instead of a grown woman faced with her beloved and wonderfully familiar husband."

"Nay, my darling. I love yer shyness. Ye hae always had a charming innocence about ye that I love. If ye dinna want to make love we will not. I know ye are tired after yer long journey."

"Francis! Kiss me!" And she raised her head up.

For a moment he gazed lovingly at the face turned expectantly to him. His slender fingers explored it, gently touching her cheeks, her closed eyelids, her nose, her mouth, her stubborn little chin. Then he bent, his arms circling her waist, pressing her against him. His mouth tenderly touched hers. He had always made love to her with incredible gentleness, and that had not changed. Yet she felt that tonight there lurked beneath the surface of that calm a fierceness that he was fighting to hold in check.

Deep within her a flame of passion flickered, and she shuddered. The mouth on hers suddenly became more demanding, and her arms slid up and around his neck. His hands caressed her long back, and she moaned softly, her body beginning to tremble weakly against his. Slowly he moved across the room until he felt the bed against the back of his legs. They fell to the bed. Turning quickly, he reversed their positions so that she was beneath him. Smiling down at her, he undid the row of tiny ribbons holding her gown together. She caught his hands, and their eyes met.

"Francis, I love ye! Dear heaven, how I love ye!"

"And I love ye, my beautiful, precious wife!" His head dipped low, and his mouth found her breast. She gave a soft cry, and he reassured her. "Only if ye want it, sweetheart."

"But I do, Francis! How can I make ye understand how much I want ye? For three years—since that last night we made love in the guest house of Deer Abbey —I have dreamed of being in yer arms again . . . though I dinna believe it could happen. I have hungered for the feel of ye, the taste of ye! Other men have possessed me. My poor Patrick, who sought so desperately to regain that which he had lost. Our cousin, James, who thought he could command my love and who used me like a common whore. I sheathed my body in a protective coating so they should nae destroy me. Tonight for the first time in three years I feel completely alive, Francis, and if ye dinna make love to me now, I shall die!"

"I hae always said," he answered, smiling that slow smile she loved so, "that ye were the only woman who could keep up wi me. For three years I hae tried to forget ye between the legs of any woman who smiled my way. I dinna have to forget any longer, my sweet Cat. But I warn ye, my darling, my hunger is fierce this night!"

The leaf-green eyes regarded him levelly. "Do your worst, my lord!" she challenged, and pulling his head down, she kissed him slowly, tauntingly, daring him on.

He felt a stab of desire pierce him, and forcing her lips apart he ravaged her mouth tenderly. His tongue flickered across her taut breasts, teasing the nipples into hard little points. It moved on, sliding between the warm valley of her breasts and down to her navel. She cried out as a burning began and spread through her loins. Sated momentarily with her sweetness, he easily straddled her, lowering his head so his mouth might close over a pink and tempting nipple. She moaned beneath him, struggling to shift him into a closer proximity, her rounded hips thrusting upwards hungrily.

"Please, Francis," she begged him. "Please, now!"

He wanted to prolong the delight, but as hungry as she was for him, his own desire was even greater. His hand caressed the heart-shaped face. "All right, love," he murmured into her ear, and thrust deep within her, gaining an almost equal pleasure from both his possession of her and the long shuddering sigh that tore through her.

She was whole again for the first time in three years! Lost in that lovely silvery-gold world between consciousness and unconsciousness, she murmured contentedly as his hardness sent wave after wave of pleasure pouring over her. And it didn't stop even when the hardness broke, flooding her with his seed. He pulled her into his arms and kissed her tenderly.

She said nothing, her beautiful eyes saying it for her, and he smiled happily. "Sweet Cat," he whispered. "My beloved adversary, my dearest love. 'Tis all right now, my darling. 'Tis all right. We hae come home at last."

Chapter 47

❧ ❦ ❧

THE little Church of Santa Maria del Mare was the fashionable house of worship for the noble and wealthy who lived near Amalfi. On the fourth Sunday in April of the year 1598, the Earl and Countess of Bothwell attended midday mass. As they walked together afterwards from the church, Cat saw an exquisitely dressed and very beautiful woman standing just ahead. Instinct and Francis' slight pressure on her arm told her that this was her husband's cast-off mistress.

Before he could speak, the familiar deep voice called, "So, Francisco! This is your new whore!"

The silence in the church piazza was instantaneous as heads turned to view the coming battle.

Cat froze. Bothwell's eyes were blue ice, but his voice was steady and honied as he turned to Alfredo, Conte di LiCosa, and said, "Fredo, may I present *my wife*, Caterina Maria, the Contessa di Bothwell. Bishop Pasquale married us five nights ago."

"And a more beauteous and radiant bride I have never seen," injected the bishop, confirming the earl's announcement.

The Conte di LiCosa bowed over Cat's extended hand. "Contessa, the pleasure is all mine, I assure you." His dark eyes twinkled.

The corners of Cat's mouth turned up for a moment,

478

and she murmured a polite response. Then her leaf-green eyes slowly and coolly raked Angela di LiCosa, who stood looking furiously back at her with blazing black eyes. Finally Cat turned away. Looking up at her husband, she drawled clearly, "Really, darling, she's hardly up to your usual standard."

Angela di LiCosa stepped angrily forward, her hand raised threateningly. Cat, not flinching, grasped the hand in her own. "Do it, madame, and you will spend the rest of your life minus a hand," she hissed. "And while we have this moment together, my dear, let me warn you to forget Francis. He will not come back to you." She dropped the other woman's hand.

Angela rubbed her wrist. "Then why do you warn me?"

"Because I can see you are that foolish type of woman who will persist because her pride is damaged. Remember that he left your house at the mere mention of my name. We were wed that same night. Do not embarrass us, or your family. There is more binding Francis and me than you can imagine."

Cat turned her back on the other woman. Taking her husband's arm, she moved away to accept the congratulations and good wishes of the neighboring nobility, all of whom were delighted to see the Contessa di LiCosa get her comeuppance.

Alfredo di LiCosa chuckled. "Well, my dear, I had never thought I should live to see the day when you were bested."

"Be quiet, you snake!" she snarled furiously at him. "I will kill her! No! That would be too easy. I will make her suffer! I will do it slowly. Painfully! She will wish she were dead!"

The Conte di LiCosa, smiling at his friends and neighbors, hustled his angry wife into their coach. "You will do nothing, Angela! Do you understand me? Nothing!

Your reputation already has the Inquisition looking in your direction."

"Let them look," she spat back at him. "They can prove nothing!"

"The Inquisition does not *have* to prove anything! Just a hint of suspicion is enough. Face the truth, my darling. Francisco amused himself with you as you amused yourself with him. It is obvious that the man is deeply in love with his wife. Let it be! I do not want Lord Bothwell for an enemy, and if I must choose between him or you, it will be him! He, at least, is trustworthy."

But Angela di LiCosa could not forget the beautiful Cat. The Contessa di Bothwell had to be at least several years older than she was, and yet she did not look it. Nor did she use the heavy cosmetics of the day. Her skin was flawless, with its own lively natural coloring. Her body was young and firm. Angela imagined that beautiful face and body scarred, ruined. Would Francisco love her then? The answer sounded resoundingly in her head. Yes, he would!

Angela had seen how Bothwell had looked at his wife. He had never looked at Angela that way. Angela had never admitted the painful fact to herself before, and the reality outraged her: Francisco had never looked deeply at her at all.

During the next few weeks, Angela di LiCosa's desire for vengeance grew. It seemed that every noble family in the area had to give a party for the newlyweds, and she and Alfredo were always invited. Refusal was unthinkable. The Countess of Bothwell quickly became a popular figure among the men and the women. She was lauded for her beauty, her charm, her wit. Lord Bothwell—always the rover—barely left his wife's side, and the looks of adoration that passed between them became legend.

It was this very devotion that gave Angela her idea for the perfect revenge. In these past weeks she had learned that Lord Bothwell and his bride had been in love for years, but had been separated for varied reasons until only recently. Together at last, they were gloriously happy. Angela di LiCosa decided to separate them—permanently. She had thought of having one of them assassinated—preferably Cat. But the finger of suspicion would have pointed directly at her, so she discarded that idea. Too, the pain of separation would be greater if they both lived. If the beautiful Countess of Bothwell were forced to submit to another man's attentions and if her husband knew it and were powerless to rescue her, the anguish would be unbearable.

She believed her plan to be foolproof. No one was likely to consider her responsible. Angela's oldest brother had been captured by the Turks at the age of eighteen. When he had gone off to sea, determined to fight the Ottoman corsairs who were constantly raiding their coast, his Turkish mother had told him, "If you are captured, loudly proclaim your nobility. Tell them that you are the son of Ferhad Bey's daughter, Fatima of Morea, who was captured twenty years ago. Submit to Islam as I have to Christianity and your fortune will be made!"

He had been captured, for to pursue the Turk in the Mediterranean was foolhardy. But he remembered his mother's words and followed her advice. He was saved from the marble quarries and entered in the Princes' School. Over the years he rose swiftly through the ranks until he had become one of the empire's most skilled generals. Called Cicalazade Pasha, and trusted by his captors, he might have escaped back to his homeland.

But he chose not to go home. The best he could hope for in Italy was to succeed to his father's title, conte, and inherit a moldering castle that grew more expensive to maintain as each year passed. He would be married off to the best dowry available and expected to father several sons. If he were lucky he would be able to afford one elegant mistress. If not, he would have to make do with the local peasant women.

As Cicalazade Pasha he owned a magnificent palace on the Bosporus, well staffed by an army of slaves. He was married to a granddaughter of Suleiman the Magnificent, and he had recently been appointed a grand vizier to Sultan Mohammed, his wife's cousin. He maintained a large harem which catered to his sophisticated and varied sexual tastes. Cica Pasha's hobby was beautiful women. All through the civilized world, his slave merchants were on the lookout for beautiful, exotic women to satisfy his appetite. Beauty and personality attracted him. Virginity mattered not. His harem was stocked with rare beauties, and fabled throughout the East.

Angela di LiCosa gave credit where credit was due. The Countess of Bothwell was an unusually beautiful woman, and Angela was quite sure that her rapacious brother would welcome the exquisite addition to his bed. There would be no problem in transporting her victim either, for a Turkish fleet lurked off the coast. Angela knew one of its captains.

He was called Khair-ad-Din after the famed admiral of the time of Suleiman the Magnificent. One of his duties was to carry messages between Cicalazade Pasha and his Italian family. Angela could get in touch with him easily. She would learn how soon he planned to sail home.

Several days later a peasant woman sat drinking wine with a sailor in a Neapolitan waterfront café. "You tell Khair-ad-Din that I don't care how dangerous he thinks it is! I must meet with him personally. There is a small, crescent-shaped beach two miles to the southeast of

Amalfi. I will be there tomorrow night an hour after sunset. The signal will be two lanterns burning on the beach." The woman got up and hobbled out. The sailor finished his mug. Cursing softly under his breath, he slapped some coins down on the table and left the café.

The following night a boat rowed by six sweating black slaves slid onto the sand of that beach. An enormous man dressed in bright-red pantaloons and a red-and-black-striped shirt, his large waist wrapped with a gold cloth sash from which protruded both a jeweled dagger and a scimitar, heaved himself out and walked up onto the beach. He had small feet for such a large man, and they wore elegant gold leather boots with red tassels.

A heavily masked and cloaked woman stepped from the shadows. "I am the Contessa di LiCosa," she said.

"Take off the mask so I may see with whom I speak," said Khair-ad-Din gruffly, and when she did he nodded. "You look nothing like your brother. Well, little girl, what can I do for you?"

"I want you to take a gift to my brother."

"You got me off my ship to tell me you want me to carry some damned trinket to my lord Cicalazade? Women! Pah!"

"This is a very special gift, captain. It is a woman for my brother's harem. She is a prize beyond compare, a noblewoman of beauty, breeding, and charm. Bring her safely to my brother. I will reward you in gold, and I am sure you will gain great favor with my brother."

"Who is this woman, contessa?"

"Her identity is not your concern, but her villa is on the other side of this point. You probably know the house well, for it once belonged to Abdul Mehmet, the merchant. In a few days this woman's husband will be called away. If you attack the house at dawn in his absence you will meet no resistance. There are only six houseservants, five of whom are women. I assume she also has a body servant. I don't care what happens to the servants, but treat this woman gently. I want her delivered safely to my brother."

Khair-ad-Din looked sharply at Angela di LiCosa. "Why do you do this, signora la contessa? It is not like you to seek slaves for your brother. Is this a plot between you and the woman's husband, to rid him of her?"

Angela's face reflected hate so virulent that Khair-ad-Din stepped back in surprise. "I hate them both," she hissed. " 'Tis my vengeance on them. He will die a thousand times knowing that she is a slave, and that he is powerless to do anything about it!"

"What if the woman dies?"

"Not her," laughed the Contessa di LiCosa cruelly. "She will survive, hoping to return to her beloved Francisco . . . but that will never happen!"

Khair-ad-Din considered a moment. Even if the woman were a gift from Cicalazade Pasha's sister, he too would gain a certain measure of favor by conveying her safely to her new master. "How will I know when it is safe to kidnap the woman?"

"Watch the skies off this beach in the hours before and after midnight for the next few nights. A red rocket will be the signal that you may attack the following dawn." She held out a bag to him. "A small token of my gratitude, captain."

Feeling the weight of the bag, he smiled broadly. "Signora la contessa, it is a pleasure to do business with you. Is there any other message you wish to send your brother?"

She handed him a sealed packet and, without another word, turned and disappeared back into the shadows. Khair-ad-Din made a small grimace and, turning, walked back down the beach to his boat. She was a cruel one, was the Contessa di LiCosa. He wondered what her poor victim had done.

As his boat bobbed back over the waves to his ship, he thought that perhaps he should clear out the cabin next to his. It was a decent size and could be made comfortable for a woman and her servant. He had decided that he would instruct his men to bring along the lady's woman to serve her. It had been his experience in dealing with women captives that those who had a friend did better than those who were all alone. If this poor woman did not reach the grand vizier in good condition, then he would be blamed.

Safely back aboard his ship, he called his officers together and told them of the planned raid on the Villa del Pesce d'Oro. "Other than the noblewoman and her servant, take no captives. We're not a stinking slave carrier. Treat them gently, or by Allah, I'll castrate the lot of you! *No rape*. The woman is for Cicalazade's pleasure and his pleasure only."

"What about the servantgirl?" asked the first officer.

"Well . . . perhaps when we're safely under sail. But waste no time at the villa."

"You can't expect the men to pass up a group of young girls, captain. They rarely get ashore on this type of duty."

"All right, all right," chuckled Khair-ad-Din indulgently. "Let the men who go with you have the servant girls, but bring me the lady and her personal servant *untouched*."

"About two dozen men should do it," said the first officer. "Now all we need do is sit and wait for the next few days."

Chapter 48

❧§❧

C AT sat crosslegged in the center of a very tumbled bed watching her husband dress. She was naked and rosy from their recent lovemaking, and her pretty mouth pouted. "Why can't I come wi ye, Francis?"

"Because, my beautiful bride," he smiled at her, " 'tis nae a social call I am making. The Duke of Avellino wants us to clean out the bandits that have recently been infesting his district."

"I've gone on border raids wi ye," she protested.

"Aye," he smiled again, his eyes misting at the memory. "Ye were the most fetching borderer I ever knew wi yer sweet bouncing breasts, and yer long legs in their green hose. Damn, Cat! I miss it, and I miss our Hermitage, but this is Italy, my darling. If ye rode wi me I would nae be taken seriously as a mercenary, and despite the fact ye are a rich woman, I feel better earning my living wi our men. We should nae be gone more than two weeks. Why don't ye write to Jemmie, and see if he can arrange to send the children? I think 'tis time our bairns met their father."

She smiled teasingly at him. "Will ye miss me, Bothwell?" And she stood up, stretched, and slunk provocatively across the room.

He gently smacked her pretty bottom. "Dinna wiggle yerself at me, wench! 'Tis hard enough to have to leave ye after less than two months." He bent his head and found her eager mouth. "Oh, Cat! Sweet Cat!" he mur-mured between hungry kisses. Then, "Damn! Ye've done it again! I never knew a woman who could rouse me so!"

She laughed low and wriggled out of his grasp. "Go play at war, my randy lord!"

He looked at her ruefully. "Put some clothes on, nymph, and bid me and our men a proper goodbye."

She arrived in the foyer of the villa in time to hear Conall say, "I still think we should leave some men here to guard the villa."

"Guard us from what?" demanded Cat. "My God, I never knew such a peaceful place!"

"I don't know," said Bothwell thoughtfully. "Conall could be right. There are always pirates lurking off the coast."

"There is nothing of value here to attract pirates. Dinna be foolish. Ye need every man ye've got."

The two men looked at each other and shrugged. Cat was right. They joined their men, who were mounted and waiting. Conall climbed into his saddle and moved to the front of the group, but Bothwell stood for a mo-ment facing his wife, his elegant hands on her shoulders. "I wish ye could come wi me, my darling," he said, "but it should nae take us long to wipe out the nest of mangy beggars that disturbs Avellino's peace. Thank ye for gieing me yer Glenkirk men for my own. Christ! To be useful again!" He crushed her to him. "I love ye, Catriona Stewart-Hepburn!" And he kissed her pas-sionately, his mouth bruising hers with a sweetness that sent desire racing through her. Her lips were petal-soft, and warm beneath his. He began to wish the Duke of Avellino's bandits safe in hell.

"Are ye for Avellino, or are ye for bed, my lord earl?" demanded Conall's scathing voice.

Bothwell reluctantly moved away from his wife. "If

that man were nae the best captain in Christendom I
would cheerfully strangle him," he said through gritted
teeth as he mounted his own stallion.

Cat laughed softly. Putting a hand on her husband's
leg, she smiled up at him. "I love ye, Francis. Come
home safe to me." She turned to Conall. "Take care of
him. Always be at his back."

"Aye! Aye!" said the captain impatiently.

Then they were off down the driveway, the dust swirl-
ing around and behind them. She stood before the villa
until they had all disappeared. Then, running inside, she
called to Paolo.

"Sì, signora la contessa?"

"What engagements do we have planned for the
week?"

"Only a dinner party on Saturday evening at the
Conte di LiCosa's villa."

She sighed with relief. "Cancel it, Paolo. With Lord
Bothwell away, I have the perfect excuse to avoid that
wretched woman."

Paolo smiled. He liked the Contessa di LiCosa no
more than his mistress did. She was an evil woman.
The following day he did as his mistress had ordered,
and sent word to the di LiCosa villa that the Countess
of Bothwell could not attend the fête, due to her husband's absence.

Angela di LiCosa laughed happily. The timing was
unbelievable, and her own alibi was now unchallenge-
able. It would be so easy to slip away from her party
to signal Khair-ad-Din. Better yet, she could send her
servant to make the signal. A roomful of people would
attest to her constant presence! And as the Villa del
Pesce d'Oro's gardeners would not be at work on Sunday, the pirates' raid would go unnoticed for a full day.
By that time the Countess of Bothwell would be well on

her way to Cicalazade's harem. Angela's laughter rever-
berated wildly through the house. Hearing it, the servants crossed themselves, and murmured among themselves. "When l'Angela del Diavolo laughs, beware!"

And that evening at her fête the Contessa di LiCosa
was more charming, more delightful than ever before.
The party was such a success that it did not end until
close to dawn, when the last of the guests stumbled,
happily drunk, to their beds.

Across the misty hills at the Villa del Pesce d'Oro a
scream tore through the clear dawn. Cat sat straight up
in bed, wide awake, listening. Hearing another shriek
and the sound of running feet, she leaped from her bed
and ran to the window. The sight before her momentarily froze her with terror.

The garden was swarming with men in baggy pantaloons, and it did not take more than a second to realize
that they were under attack by Turkish pirates. Maria,
the cook, and her two little kitchen maids lay upon the
ground being raped, surrounded by men who were
waiting their turns. The two housemaids were fleeing
from some four or five men across the garden. Paolo
lay in the kitchen garden near a basket of freshly cut
herbs, his head bashed to a bloody pulp.

"Christ hae mercy," whispered Susan's voice next to
her, and then Cat heard little May weeping with fright.
"Get into the linen chest, you two," she commanded
them. "They'll nae touch me. I'll be ransomed. Hurry!"

Susan was already opening the chest. Quickly pulling
out an armful of sheets, she helped May to snuggle
down. "Stay there until yer absolutely sure they're gone,
lass. Then go quickly to Carlo the gardener's home, and
remain hidden till his lordship returns!"

"But Susan," protested the girl, "ye must hide wi
me!"

"I must stay by my lady Cat, lassie." Susan gently covered her younger sister with the linens and closed the chest firmly down.

Cat looked at her tiring woman. "They'll rape ye, Susan. I will nae be able to stop them."

Susan looked levelly back at her mistress. "I'm nae a virgin, my lady, but May is, and it would surely kill her. Besides, ye'll need me."

There was no more time for talk. The bedroom door splintered under a strong shoulder and burst open, revealing close to a dozen men. Unable to control their terror, the two women screamed, clinging to each other in fright. A huge figure of a man came through the door. He examined them briefly, then said to Cat in guttural Italian, "What is your name, little girl?"

"I am the Contessa di Bothwell," said Cat, amazed to find that she still had a voice.

"And the other?"

"My tiring woman, Susan," she answered him, beginning to shake.

"Don't be frightened, little girl," said the giant. "I am Captain Khair-ad-Din of Sultan Mohammed's imperial navy. I have orders to transport you to the harem of our grand vizier, Cicalazade Pasha. Neither I nor my men will harm you."

Cat's eyes grew wide with a mixture of fury and fear. "No!" she shouted. It was too much. Three years separation from Francis! A wild flight from Scotland, and James Stewart. Then, at last—happiness. Now it was to be snatched away from her! "Nooooo!" she screamed. "No! Noooooo!" And as the giant stepped forward to reach for her, she paled and collapsed onto the rugs.

Khair-ad-Din nodded to one of his men, who picked Cat up carefully and started out the doorway with her. Susan needed no encouragement to follow, but her own heart almost stopped when one of the men asked the captain in Italian, "Shall we fire the house?" Khair-ad-Din snorted. "And let the entire district know we're here?" he snapped. "No, fool!"

As they crossed the garden Susan was glad that Cat had fainted. The women servants lay naked, their throats cut, their limbs twisted grotesquely. Three of the maids had the bloody stain of their lost virginity on their bruised thighs, and Susan silently thanked God that May had not had to suffer this cruelty. That her turn was coming she had no doubt. She was afraid, for she had lied to Cat, and was as virgin as the day she was born.

As they helped her into the little boat that would take them to the great ship anchored off their beach, the men's hands were all over her. They laughed as she angrily slapped them away. They spoke their ribald comments in Italian so she would understand them. Susan gritted her teeth and reminded herself that she was Susan More-Leslie of Glenkirk, and not to be terrorized by a bunch of ragtag foreigners.

Her fears lessened somewhat when she and Cat were put into a comfortable cabin. The sailor who had carried Cat lay her carefully upon the bunk and left the room. The lock turned in the door. Looking around, Susan found a pitcher of water, a silver ewer, and a soft linen cloth. Susan poured some of the water into the basin, wrung the cloth out in it, and lay the compress upon her mistress' head. She rubbed the slender wrists, peering worriedly into Cat's still, white face.

The door behind her opened, and Khair-ad-Din entered the cabin. "How is the little girl?" he asked kindly.

"Still unconscious, and no thanks to you!" snapped Susan. "You frightened her half to death telling her she was being put in a harem. Whatever the ransom for us, Lord Bothwell will pay it."

"There is no ransom. I have orders to convey this

woman to the harem of our grand vizier, Cicalazade Pasha. She is a gift to him from his sister."

Susan looked puzzled. "His sister? Who is this sister, and what right has she to give my mistress to her brother? My mistress is a freeborn noblewoman, and a cousin to the King of Scotland!"

"The vizier's sister is the Contessa di LiCosa," said Khair-ad-Din.

Susan was astounded. "That bitch? By God, I'll kill her myself when I get my hands on her, the jealous whore!"

A great rumble of laughter burst from Khair-ad-Din. "My very thoughts on the woman, little girl. But tell me, why does she hate your lady so?"

"Because," said Susan angrily, "the Contessa di LiCosa covets my lady's husband, and he will have nothing to do with the witch."

The captain nodded. Sensing sympathy, Susan said quickly, "Oh, please sir! My lord and lady are rich beyond measure. Return us, and they will reward ye a hundred times more than ye ask!"

"I wish I could, little girl, for I do not like being part of a woman's war. But alas, I cannot. The man to whom I take your mistress stands high in the sultan's favor. If he learned that I had disobeyed his sister—and he would —I should be flayed alive! I am truly sorry, little girl. You and your beautiful mistress must accept your fates. It will not be so bad. Cicalazade Pasha is good to his women."

Susan was desperate. She could hear the creak of the ship as it prepared to get under way. "Oh sir, you do not understand. My lady and her husband are but newly married after many years of separation. She will surely die without him. And when he finds her gone he will tear the earth apart to get her back."

"That is not my problem, little girl. I must get you

safely to Istanbul. Your mistress will not die, for I can see she is of stronger stuff than that. Look at her now. She is no longer unconscious, but merely sleeps."

Susan knelt at Cat's side and saw that the captain spoke the truth. Cat's breathing was regular and even, and the color was back in her cheeks. "Thank God," breathed Susan. Khair-ad-Din left the cabin, locking it behind him.

Susan sat by the sleeping woman all day. Cat did not awaken, and Susan knew it was because she was still in shock. That evening Khair-ad-Din returned to the cabin, and his large hand fell on Susan's shoulder. "Now, little girl, the time has come for you to entertain my officers."

Susan stood up, her face white with fright. "Please," she pleaded with Khair-ad-Din.

"I might have let you be taken by my crew in the same way as those girls at the villa were taken," he said quietly. "But because you are her servant I saved you for my officers. They will not hurt you, little girl. There are only three of them." Opening the cabin door leading to the officer's common room, he gently but firmly, pushed her through and closed the door behind her.

Susan stood frozen, praying that if she didn't move the men would not notice her. The three sat across the room around a low table, drinking coffee and talking. Then one looked up and called, "Why here's the wench! Come here, girl!" She shrank back against the door, her heart hammering wildly as the man stood up and came towards her. He was tall and swarthy, with dark hair and eyes, even white teeth, and a well-barbered black beard. He pulled her away from the door and into the light. Susan cried out, and the man's eyes softened. "Don't be shy, girl. We want to be friends—don't we, lads?" The two other men grinned at Susan, and she shivered.

"My name is Hussein, and I am Khair-ad-Din's first

officer. The fellow with the bushy beard is Abdul, the second officer, and the beardless youth is Ibrahim, our navigator. Here, you two savages," he berated his companions, "give the wench some coffee. She looks cold and frightened."

Sitting back on the cushions, he pulled Susan down onto his lap. Ripping the front of her nightgown to the hem, he began fondling her breasts. Hussein laughed indulgently when she screamed. "Come on, little girl, don't be foolish. You know why you're here. Whether you cooperate or not the results will be the same. You're going to be fucked. It won't be so bad. You could be one of those poor creatures back at the villa who serviced the crew. *We* won't hurt you. We just want a bit of loving."

The tears spilled down her cheeks. "Please," she sobbed, "oh, please don't. I am so afraid. I—I—I've never—"

"By Allah," said Hussein, "I think we've got us a virgin!" He tipped her face up to his. "Are you a virgin, little girl?" Wordlessly she nodded. "Get the dice, Ibrahim," commanded the first officer. "We always dice to see who has the first taste when we have a virgin," he explained matter-of-factly to Susan. "Stand still, girl."

She obeyed, terrified. He towered above her for a moment, and then bent and tore the rest of her garment from her, the thin material of her nightgown shredding as she fought to hold onto it. He laughed at her efforts and patted her bottom. Outraged, she rallied and slapped at him, then gasped with shock as he squeezed one of her breasts. "There she is, gentlemen, and as pretty a piece as I've seen in a long time. Clean . . . sweet as honey with breasts like summer melons!"

For a moment the three men gazed hungrily at the girl. Then Abdul growled, "Come on! Make your toss! I'm so hard already you could break it off!" Smiling,

Hussein handed the dice to the young navigator. "Go on, Ibrahim. You first." Ibrahim's toss netted him a three, and he laughed good-naturedly. "I always end up last." Abdul snatched up the dice, and chuckled as an eight showed. He eyed the naked girl, licking his lips in open anticipation. "You'll have to go some to beat that, Hussein," he gloated, but the first officer coolly took up the dice and, after rolling them around in his palm for a moment, suddenly threw them across the table. "Allah curse you," muttered Abdul as nine came up. Hussein laughed. Ibrahim, snatching up the dice, said to the angry second officer, "Come on, Abdul . . . we might as well continue dicing while lucky Hussein has his turn with the girl."

Pushing Susan down onto the cushions, Hussein straddled his terrified prize. Hungrily he kissed her, his tongue thrusting into her mouth, darting about like wildfire, rousing emotions in the unwilling virgin that she had never known she could feel. His hands seemed everywhere, feeling eagerly, touching gently, squeezing cruelly. Then his hand was between her legs, seeking to ascertain the truth of virginity—he grunted satisfaction to find her intact. Struggling wildly, she tried to fight him off, and he laughed.

"I like spirit, wench, but you'll not win!" She felt his manhood hard and seeking against her thighs, and she tried to turn her body away. To her shame the other two men were kneeling at her side, encouraging Hussein and offering advice.

"Is the little virgin too much woman for you, Hussein?" mocked Abdul. "Get off her, man. I'll show you how to put it in right!"

"Can we hold her down for you?" teased Ibrahim. "I'll take the fight out of her when it's my turn."

"She'll have no fight left after a real man's had her, boy," bragged Abdul.

At that point Susan felt a burning pain spread through her loins, and she screamed with it. But as Hussein moved quickly back and forth within her, the pain lessened and her screams died to a wailing moan. To her everlasting shame she could not control her own hips, and they moved in time with Hussein's. The man atop her suddenly convulsed and collapsed on her. He was quickly pulled off. Above her, the bushy, bearded Abdul loosened his baggy pantaloons and fell on her. She tried to buck him off, but he slapped her cruelly, and her teeth cut her lower lip, drawing blood. He was in her quickly but, to the amusement of his companion, was as quickly drained of his passion.

The boy was immediately in his place, groaning and straining above her. Unable to bear any more, Susan fainted. But when she had regained consciousness, she found that her ordeal was not over. She was forced to submit to each of them again.

Finally, they let her sleep. But again in the morning she was forced to service each of them. By this time, however, her shame had eased, and she demanded they bring her water for washing the dried blood and semen from her thighs. Laughing and patting various parts of her anatomy, they brought her a small wooden tub and a rough towel, and somewhere Hussein found a sliver of soap, which he offered her, grinning.

Clean and wrapped in a towel, she demanded of him, "And what am I to wear, you who were so quick to tear my only garment?"

"There's a trunk in your cabin. You'll find suitable garments in it for both you and your mistress." Then he patted her cheek. "You're a good little wench," he said kindly. "I hope we didn't hurt you too greatly last night."

"No," she whispered, blushing furiously. And fleeing back to the cabin next door, she allowed herself the luxury of a few tears. She found the trunk and, opening it, saw that it contained all manner of indecent-looking garments. She lifted out sheer silk pantaloons, gauze blouses, brocaded boleros, see-through little veils, and soft kid slippers.

"Are ye all right?" The question made her jump, and she turned to see Cat sitting up in the bunk.

"Aye, my lady."

"Were ye raped?"

Susan's head drooped, and she sank down beside her mistress. "Aye," she whispered.

"Why did ye lie to me, lass? Ye were a virgin, weren't ye?"

Susan nodded, then said simply, "I couldn't leave ye alone, my lady. I thought ye'd need me. It wasn't too terrible. Just the officers, and there were only three of them—one just a boy."

Cat put a protective arm about her servant. "Oh, Susan! I am so sorry, my dear. I would nae have had this happen to ye for all the world. I was no help to ye at all, fainting like a green girl! What has happened? Where are we? And who are they?"

"Everyone at the villa is dead except May. Once they had us they did not search further, thank God. They are Turkish corsairs, and have orders to convey us to Istanbul. Ye are to be a gift to the grand vizier, Cicalazade Pasha—from his sister, the Contessa di LiCosa."

"What?" Cat's face was incredulous. " 'Tis absurd! She canna do such a thing!" Then, "My God! She has! I hope Francis strangles her! If her brother is anything like Angela . . ."

"Khair-ad-Din tells me that the vizier is very important. There will be no ransom. And no escape."

Cat closed her eyes for a moment, then said, "We must not panic. Yesterday I gave in to fear, but I will not allow it to conquer me again. I must survive to

revenge myself on Angela di LiCosa. I must survive to
return to Francis. Dinna be afraid, my faithful Susan."
The leaf-green eyes twinkled for a moment. "Ye did tell
me ye wanted to travel, did ye not, lass? What stories
ye'll have to tell yer grandchildren!"

Susan couldn't help but laugh, and Cat was relieved.
The young woman was indeed made of strong fiber.
Well, why not? She was a Leslie!

"Get dressed, my girl, and pick something out for me
too. My God, the garments are thin enough, aren't they?
Oh, Susan—one thing. Confide in no one but me. Trust
no one but me. Together we shall outwit the Turk. And
I, for one, shall enjoy it!"

Happy to see that she had cheered Susan, Cat wondered silently to herself if there would ever come a time
again when her life was quiet and orderly. Then, forcing
herself to the humor in her predicament, she laughed
and said, "Oh, well, I should probably be very bored
with an orderly existence!"

Part VII

❧ ❧

The Vizier

Chapter 49

E VEN the fates seemed to be conspiring to whisk
her quickly to her destination. The ship sped down
the Tyrrhenian Sea through the Straits of Messina, and
into the Mediterranean towards Crete, where they
stopped to take on water and fresh food. A small shiver
ruffled Cat's outward calm as she gazed at the shoreline and realized that she was following in her great-
grandmother's footsteps.

For the first time the fairy story of Janet Leslie's life
became real to her great-granddaughter, and Cat was
afraid. She wondered if the thirteen-year-old Janet had
been afraid. At least I won't be exhibited naked on the
slave block, she thought with relief. If you please the
grand vizier you won't, a small nagging voice whispered
in her head. But what if he does not like you? How can
you possibly compete with young girls? You are over
thirty!

"Why do you frown so, little girl?" inquired Khair-
ad-Din, who had taken to playing chess with her in the
evenings. "Are you finally ready to admit that I am a
better chess player than a mere woman?"

Forced from her nightmare, Cat laughed. "No, you
old sea trout! I am not!" Then her lovely face became
serious again.

"Tell me," he said. "Share your troubles with me, and
perhaps I can ease them."

"I am afraid, Khair-ad-Din. I am no nubile virgin to be offered to the grand vizier. I am a grown woman with children. I have been married twice. What can I possibly offer Cicalazade Pasha? He will laugh at his sister's gift, and sell me in some slave market."

The fat man sitting opposite her looked back at her with sympathy. "Little girl," he said patiently, "have you looked in a mirror lately? There is not a man alive who, given his choice between you and some poor virgin, would choose the virgin. And neither would Cicalazade Pasha. His harem is quite famous. The vizier prefers beauty, charm, and wit to innocence. Let the sultan amuse himself with a weekly procession of virgins—not so with my lord Cicalazade. And another thing, my beauty. If my lord Cicalazade desires to sell you off, I will buy you myself!" And his laughter rumbled throughout the cabin. "I have as much chance of that as I do of being pope," he wheezed, chuckling happily.

The ship sailed on into the Aegean Sea, skirting the small Greek islands. When the ship slipped through the Dardanelles and into the Sea of Marmara, Cat felt a wrench of real loss, knowing that she now had truly left her world.

Already the Turkish clothing she wore felt familiar and comfortable, and she could not help but wonder what Cicalazade Pasha was like. Perhaps when she explained the situation to him he would accept a ransom for her, and allow her and Susan to return home. His reputation belied that of a man so desperate for a woman that he would hold one against her will. Cat comforted herself with that thought. He sounded almost civilized.

They reached Istanbul in late afternoon when the sun was spreading its light across the Golden Horn, giving the newcomers an understanding of the famed waterway's name. Khair-ad-Din sent a messenger immediately to the palace of the grand vizier, and within an hour a closed litter and a troup of armed guards appeared at the ship to take them away.

"It is unlikely I will ever see you again, little girl," said Khair-ad-Din to Cat. "May Allah guide you—even if you are a better chess player than I am."

The tears sprang to her eyes. Impulsively, she kissed his cheek. He patted her shoulder and led her onto the deck, where he turned her and Susan over to a black eunuch.

"I suppose, captain," said the eunuch pettishly to Khair-ad-Din, "that they do not understand Turkish. Which of the barbaric Western tongues must I use?"

Cat stamped her foot angrily and, speaking in flawless Turkish, berated the eunuch. "Toad! Uncircumcised spawn of pig's offal! How dare you speak to me in such a fashion? In my land I am a great lady. I will not be shown disrespect by such as you!"

The eunuch almost fainted, and Khair-ad-Din bit back his laughter. "The noble lady speaks the truth, Osman. Though she be here against her will, she is a special gift from Cicalazade's sister. She and her servant are to be treated gently."

Osman eyed Cat warily. Here was trouble. His judgment of women slaves was always infallible, and this one would be trouble. "How is it, noble lady, that you speak our tongue? Does your servant also?"

"I learned many languages as a child," replied Cat, "and yours was one of them. My servant is just learning, but has a good ear."

The eunuch nodded. "It is always easier when they understand you," he observed to Khair-ad-Din as if Cat wasn't there. "Very well, noble lady," he said, turning back to her, "if you and your woman will follow me to the litter." He looked at them. "Are your veils tight? Ah, yes, I can see that they are."

And before she could say another word, she and Susan were hustled off the ship. She barely had time to turn and raise her hand in a gesture of farewell to Khair-ad-Din. The curtains were pulled tightly shut, and she felt a little jolt as the slaves raised the litter and trotted off. She and Susan looked at each other in wonder. Where were they going? They would have given anything to peek through the hangings, but when they ventured a peep out, Osman squeaked with outrage.

The litter moved at an even pace through the noise, breeze, and sea smell of the waterfront to the noise, heat, and human smells of the city, and then to the cooler, quieter area near the Yeni Serai of the sultan. Here along the shores of the Bosporus near the imperial palace was located the smaller palace of the grand vizier. Safe within its courtyard the litter stopped, and was set down, and the curtains opened.

"Please to step out, noble lady," said Osman, and they climbed from the litter. "Your servant will be taken to your quarters, noble lady. You are to come with me to Hammid, the grand eunuch." And Susan found herself being led off by a black slavewoman.

Cat followed Osman into the palace through what seemed a maze of corridors, and finally through a large, carved door into a square room. Sitting on a pile of cushions was a short but enormous coal-black man, dressed in red and blue silk robes. Upon his head was a cloth-of-silver turban with a large center ruby.

"Make obeisance to the grand eunuch," hissed Osman frantically, falling to his knees and bowing low.

"Insect," she whispered fiercely at him. "I am a king's cousin. I kneel to no one but God and my lord."

Rich laughter rumbled forth from the great mountain of flesh. "Well said, woman! My lord Cicalazade likes spirit—provided it is tempered with wisdom." The voice was high, and seemed strange in so large a man. "Osman, wait outside." And as Osman left, the head eunuch turned to Cat. "I am Hammid, master of the vizier's household. What is your name, my beauty?"

Drawing herself up proudly, she said, "I am the Lady Catriona Stewart-Hepburn, the Countess of Bothwell. I am a cousin to his majesty King James of Scotland, who will, on the death of Queen Elizabeth, also be King of England. I am here against my will, having been kidnapped with my servant from my home by your master's sister. She covets my husband, and he refused her. She thinks to revenge herself on us by sending me here. If you will but send word to my husband, Lord Bothwell, he will pay your master double whatever ransom he wishes. There will be a rich reward for you also."

"The vizier is not in the habit of collecting ransoms, woman. You were not sent here for that purpose, as you are well aware. If the vizier's sister wished to extort monies from you she would have done so. She wished you removed from your husband, and saw a chance to do her brother a good turn at the same time." He watched her from beneath hooded lids to see the effect his words would have on her. This was his way of judging her worth. He would have been very disappointed had she not showed spirit.

"I am a married woman," said Cat. "I will not submit to your master. I would sooner be dead!"

The eunuch's laughter again rumbled across the room. "Nonsense," he said. "You are life itself! Do not make idle threats. I have dealt too long with your sex to know when they are serious about suicide." He saw the glint of tears in her eyes, but she shed not a one, and he was pleased that she showed courage in this difficult situation. "Do not be afraid, woman. You are not to be delivered shrieking to my master. You will need a few days of rest to recover from your ordeal,

and to observe our ways. Come closer now so I may
see you better."

She slowly moved forward until she was standing
directly in front of him.

"Disrobe for me, woman."

"No!" She looked startled at his request, even
mutinous.

Hammid sighed. "I do not wish to embarrass you,
woman, but if you do not obey me I shall simply call
in Osman, and he will do it for me."

For a moment she stood rigid with anger, determined
to make it difficult for him. Then, realizing the futility
of her situation she shrugged and slowly pulled the veil
from her face and then from her head. Next she removed the satin brocade bolero. Her fingers trembled
as she undid the tiny pearl buttons on the gauze blouse
and took it off. Lastly she kicked the kid slippers from
her feet, and stepped from the silk pantaloons.

"Put your hands up behind your head, woman," and
when she obeyed him he murmured, "Superb" at her
beautiful rounded breasts with their dark-rose nipples.
"Loosen your hair, and turn for me." The tawny, honey-
colored hair tumbled almost to her waist. He smiled.
"When my master sees you, woman, he will be lost.
You are a delight to the eye. Now dress yourself again,
and Osman will take you to your quarters, where your
body servant waits. Are you hungry?" She nodded. "I
will give orders that you be served a supper immediately. Afterwards you will have a bath, a massage,
and a good night's sleep. You will be a new woman. In
three days' time I will take you into the city myself, for
there is something I wish you to see."

He clapped his hands, and Osman reappeared to lead
her out. Hammid sat motionless for a moment after
they left, and then said, "Well, master, I think your

sister has unknowingly done you a great kindness. What do you think of the woman?"

A tall man stepped from behind a carved screen behind the grand eunuch. "She is magnificent! Allah, Hammid, I am eager to have her! Already my loins burn to have her beneath me, helpless and half-fainting with my love!"

"Gently, my lord. She will be yours, I promise you, but first I must win her over and gain her trust. This is a prize worth waiting for, my lord."

"But will she yield, my friend? I see a stubborn streak in her that will be hard to break."

Hammid smiled. "She will yield, my lord. Did you note the lushness of her body? It is the body of a woman used to almost daily lovemaking. It has been several weeks since she was captured, and Kapitan Khair-ad-Din assures me that she was untouched during the voyage. Though her mind will not admit to it, her body already grows eager for a man's touch. We will make her world one of sensuous delights until her sexual hunger far outweighs her desire to withstand us. A week, two at the most, my lord Cica, and she will be yours!"

Cicalazade Pasha's white teeth flashed in a smile. "What shall we call her?"

"Incili," replied Hammid.

"Incili—the Pearl—yes! I like it, Hammid!"

And while they continued to talk, Cat followed Osman again through the maze of corridors, realizing suddenly that they had crossed some invisible line and were in the harem section of the palace. There were women everywhere, women of all races and colors, women of privilege and servants. Cat was able to hear some of their comments, but managed to keep her face impassive.

"Allah! What a beauty!"

"I wonder if the brain matches the face?"

"They seldom do, Feriyke."

"Lateefa Sultan will certainly have her royal nose put out of joint by this one."

"Isn't that too bad."

Then there was laughter, and then she was being led into a pleasant, airy room, and Susan was there. Mistress and tiring woman fell happily into each other's arms.

"I was so worried," said Susan. "Can we be ransomed?"

"No," said Cat. "We will have to think of something else. However, I am safe from the vizier for the present."

Osman, unable to understand them, demanded, "What language is it you speak, woman? Speak Turkish, or if your slavegirl is not facile enough to converse with you, speak French or Italian so I may understand you."

Cat laughed at him. "We speak Gaelic, the tongue of our ancestors, but if it discomfits you we will speak Turkish."

Osman looked uncomfortable. "The slaves will bring you supper, noble lady. Afterwards the grand eunuch has given orders that you be taken to the baths. I will return in the morning to see you."

They were brought a large bowl of lamb chunks in a sauce of onions and peppers, two small loaves of hot, flat bread, a dish of yogurt, half a dozen ripe peaches, and a little bowl of sugared almonds. A decanter of lemon sherbet was provided for drink. The slavegirl who served them brought two bowls and two goblets, but there were no implements for eating. When Cat asked why, she was told that new captives were never given anything that might aid them in suicide. They would have to use their fingers, and the flat bread which had been provided. They ate ravenously, as they had not eaten since midmorning, and were surprised to discover how good it all was.

When they had finished, the slavegirl brought them a bowl of perfumed water and towels. Then an old slavewoman arrived to escort them to the harem baths. Susan was expected to fend for herself, but Cat was put into the capable hands of the bath mistress, who first saw that she was thoroughly washed, including her hair. Next a pale-pink paste was carefully smeared over the haired areas of her body, and when it was wiped away a half-hour later, she was completely denuded of body hair. While she waited for the pink paste to do its work, her fingernails and toenails were carefully pared. It would have been unthinkable for her lord and master to be scratched. She was exposed to a steam room, and then to a more temperate bath where she was stretched out on a marble bench and massaged. Cat was so relaxed and weak by this time that she could barely walk back to their quarters, where she immediately fell into a deep, peaceful sleep.

The next three days were spent quietly, with Osman coming each morning to escort them, heavily veiled, on their walk through the vizier's gardens. Each afternoon she was escorted to the baths, where she was bathed and massaged with oils and creams until her skin began to be extremely sensitive to the touch of nearly anything. In the evening she was allowed to watch certain of the harem entertainments, usually dancing. Cat was at first astounded and then intrigued by the open sexual suggestions made by the dancer's movements.

As boredom began to set in on the fourth day, Osman arrived with the information that she must put on her outdoor clothing and veil and follow him. "Your slavegirl will remain here."

"It's all right," Cat told a protesting Susan.

She was led to a large litter and, once inside, was

surprised to find herself sitting opposite Hammid.
"Good morning," he said cheerfully. "I see these three
days of rest and relaxation have done you good. I did
not think it possible that you could be lovelier, but
you are."

"I was beginning to get bored. I am not used to in-
activity. Is this all your women *do*? Sit around waiting
to be summoned to their master's bed? How awful!"
She stopped a moment to catch her breath and then
asked, "Where are we going?"

"To the slave market. You are a woman of great
determination. I will show you what will happen if you
oppose my master. His bedchamber must be like a
beautiful garden—peaceful, fragrant, and a delight to
the senses. If you do not yield to him, but fight him
instead, he will order you sold off. If this happens, you
and your servant will undoubtedly be separated, and it
is very possible that your exquisite fairness will attract
a slave broker from the Arabian Peninsula, or the Afri-
can interior. I do not think you would enjoy being
stripped naked and inspected by prospective buyers.
I do not think you would enjoy being sold to a jungle
chief. If you yield to my master, however, your safety
and comfort are assured. The choice is yours."

The look she gave him was a candid one. "Why do
you torture me, Hammid? You know that I must yield
to your master."

He nodded. "You are an intelligent woman, my
beauty, but if you yield only your body to my lord Cica,
he will know and be offended. You must yield all—your
mind and your body!"

"I cannot! And you cannot expect me to, Hammid!"

"You must!"

They rode in silence until finally the slaves stopped
and the litter was lowered to the ground. The grand

eunuch climbed out and, offering her a hand, helped her out. "There are many slave markets in this city," he said, "but this one deals only in beautiful women."

Cat looked about her, and saw women of varied ages, sizes, shapes, and colors. On the raised platform a beautiful girl was now being auctioned. She was completely nude, and the prospective buyers were not shy about poking and squeezing the girl. Her face revealed shame and fright. Cat shivered. Finally the girl was purchased by a man with a fierce mustache. Cat was forced to stand quietly watching for almost an hour. Then Hammid got involved in the bidding on an exquisite golden-blond Circassian girl of about thirteen. When he had secured her purchase Cat heard him tell the slave merchant, "Send the maiden to the Yeni Serai with the Vizier Cicalazade Pasha's compliments." Then he and Cat returned to their litter.

As they rode Cat said quietly, "I will try, Hammid, but I promise you nothing. It will not be easy for me."

He smiled. "Good! I have not misjudged your character. Do not be afraid, my beauty. I will give you time to accept your status. You will be happy, I promise you. The vizier is a magnificent lover and he will pleasure you as no man ever has. He is like a young bull—hot and inexhaustible."

Cat lowered her head as a flush swept her cheeks. It had been weeks now since she had last lain with Francis, and she was frankly edgy, but she would have died rather than allow Hammid to know this. The eunuch knew her thought and smiled. "I have decided upon your Turkish name," he told her. "You will answer to the name of Incili. It means Beautiful Pearl, and you are that indeed. We will call your servant Mara."

The next few days were quiet ones. Though she was permitted to mingle with the other women of the harem, she felt no particular urge to make friends. She was frankly curious about Lateefa Sultan, the vizier's wife, but she never saw her.

When she had been in the harem for over two weeks, she returned from the baths one afternoon to find the grand eunuch, Hammid, waiting for her.

"I am going to present you to the vizier tonight," he said.

Stricken, she implored him, "So soon?"

"The time is propitious," he told her. "Come now, Incili, you are no virgin, but a woman of experience. Does your lovely body not ache for a man's touch? Do you not crave a man's hardness deep within you? How long now has it been since you last lay swooning in a lover's arms?"

"Stop," she whispered. "Oh, please stop!"

"I have left special clothing for you. I will come for you at eight."

At eight she stood shivering in the hot summer night, waiting for Hammid. Her garments were the sheerest of pale-pink-mauve silk gauze. The pantaloons were embroidered at the ankles with a band of gold-and-silver thread, and a matching band rode her hips below her navel. A tiny sleeveless open bolero, its edges embroidered in seed pearls, barely covered her breasts. She was, of course, veiled. A second, longer veil had been placed over the first.

Hammid arrived with a small litter and walked alongside it as it was carried towards the vizier's bedchamber. "I will go in with you tonight. Do not be afraid, Incili. My lord Cica will be kind." Then they were there. His hand was at her elbow as he guided her through the door.

"I have brought the woman, Incili, as my lord commanded," the eunuch said to a tall man in the shadows. Hammid then removed the head veil, the face veil, and the bolero. As her breasts were exposed, Cat heard a soft intake of breath from the man. The eunuch's hands were swiftly drawing the pantaloons down and off. She was completely naked.

"Thank you, Hammid. You may go now."

As the door closed behind her she stood frozen, frightened, wondering what to expect. Then the man stepped from the shadows, and Cat saw before her the handsomest man she had ever seen in her entire life.

He was tall, and ruggedly tan, but where his white pantaloons rode low on his slim hips she could see his skin was as fair as hers. His hair was dark, wavy, and cropped short with just a touch of silver at the temples. His eyes were, to her surprise, a light gray-blue. He was nothing at all like his sister, Angela. His facial features were those of a classic Greek statue, with high cheekbones, straight nose, well-spaced eyes, and a full, sensuous mouth. He wore a beautifully clipped and tailored dark mustache.

He held out his hand, his eyes locking hers. Automatically she placed her slender hand in his. His touch was like fire. "I have never possessed anything as exquisite as you, Incili." The voice was warm velvet.

"You do not possess me yet, my lord Cicalazade," she answered him coolly.

The white, even teeth flashed in a quick smile, and he laughed. "It is but a matter of time, Incili, is it not?" Bending, he picked up the larger of the two veils and, twisting it into a rope, put it about her waist and drew her towards him. As her breasts touched his bare chest she began to tremble, instinct warning her that this was not a man easily led. One hand firmly lifted her chin, bringing her face up so he might look down at her. He smiled. "Green eyes," he said softly. "They are beautiful, Incili, but then you know that, don't you?"

Her heart was hammering wildly, and she could not

speak. She was furious with herself. What was the
matter with her? She tried to turn away, but his head
dipped quickly, and his mouth closed over hers. Un-
reasonable panic gripped her, and she struggled to
escape him, but he simply held her closer, gently forcing
her lips apart to allow his tongue entry.

She tore her head away from him, her eyes wide,
gasping great gulps of air to clear her mind. Her hands
flew up, palms against his hairy chest, trying to hold
him off. He laughed low and, catching her hands in his,
forced them behind her back so that once again their
bodies were intimately pressing against each other.
Again he took deliberate possession of her mouth, and
when his tongue darted deep within her mouth, lightly
touching, hungrily stroking, she felt deep within her the
banked fires flicker into flame. Slowly she ceased her
resistance, and began instead to respond to the warm
pressure of his mouth.

Feeling her yield, he brought one hand around to
delicately caress a round breast. "Incili . . ." His voice
was low, edged with passion. "You rouse me as no
woman ever has," and he was leading her through an
alcove to a large bed upon a dais. Falling backwards
onto the bed, he gently drew her down to him. He held
her just slightly above him so that her breasts hung like
ripe fruits. Lifting his head to them, he licked the
nipples, sending shock waves of desire racing through
her. Turning her over onto her back, his dark head
dipped, and his mouth closed hungrily over a breast,
nursing on it eagerly, sending streaks of hot delight
through her. His lips began a tortuous exploration of her
beautiful body, searing her. And then he saw her tiny
mole—that outrageously enticing little mark of Venus
—perched high atop the cleft of her womanhood. His
hand reached down to loosen his pantaloons. Squirming against her, he worked them down and off, returning

his attention to the fascinating little mole that beckoned him onward.

His eyes widened with delight, and a little smile touched his lips. The mole was an invitation impossible to ignore. He bent and kissed it, pleased with the tremor that shook her. Now he was almost level with her again, and taking her hand, he guided it to touch him, groaning when her hand closed over him.

He gazed down for a moment at the beautiful woman beneath him. For the first time in his life he believed he had a woman whose sexual appetite matched his own. Her hand released him, and he swung over her, his hands gently spreading her thighs. He knelt between her legs now, and she raised her eyes to him, gasping at the great blue-veined ivory shaft that sprang from the black mat between his legs. Grasping her buttocks, he drew her slowly towards him and impaled her on his swollen manhood.

For a surprised moment he almost lost his control, for she was not only warm and moist but almost as tight as a virgin. Feeling her squeezing him, he groaned with delight. Regaining control of himself, he began to move smoothly within her. Then he slowly lowered her to the bed, straddling her more comfortably. Her body was covered in a fine damp mist, and her head thrashed wildly on the pillow. His big hands caressed her gently, and his voice sought to sooth her. Suddenly the leaf-green eyes opened and looked into his gray-blue ones. She began to weep softly.

"No, Incili. No, my exquisite one," he said tenderly. "I see the shadow of another man in your beautiful eyes. I would vanquish that man, for you will never see him again. You are mine for eternity!" he exulted. "Yield yourself completely to me, my beloved!"

"I cannot," she sobbed. "I cannot!"

The teasing hands caressed her again, and his lips

pressed little kisses on her face and throat. "I will make you forget him," the deep voice promised. And again he began the sweet rhythm of passion, losing himself in her warmth and sweetness. When he had brought them to a tumultuous climax he held the weeping woman against his broad chest until, exhausted, she sobbed herself to sleep.

She slept like a child, relaxed and curled into a little ball. Smiling, he rose from the tumbled bed and, moving to a low table, poured himself a goblet of fresh orange sherbet. Sprawling on some cushions, he thoughtfully sipped and watched his beautiful sleeping slave. Hammid had been right, she was worth special handling. But Allah! She was a challenge! He had but to command, and the women of his harem strove to please him. Even his proud princess of a wife was eager that he be happy.

With Incili, however, the positions were reversed. It was he who was striving to win her over. He would continue to do so until he possessed her body and her soul. Never had he known such ecstasy as tonight's. He shivered, thinking what she would be like when she finally yielded herself to him completely.

Chapter 50

❧ ❧ ❧

CAT awoke, surprised to find herself back in her own bed. Sitting up, she asked Susan, "How did I get back here?"

"*He* brought you. Lord Cicalazade himself! He said you looked so peaceful he did not want to disturb you. I was so frightened when he walked through the door carrying you, but he was very kind, not at all the monster I thought he would be. I like him."

"He is not a cruel man," Cat said dully. Then her voice began to quiver. "But I cannot reconcile myself to this life, Susan. I want my Francis! I want to go home! I want to be free!" And she began to cry.

When she had wept for some minutes without stopping, Susan sent a slave for the eunuch Osman, who hurried in, demanding, "What is it, Mara?"

"It is my lady, sir. She will not stop crying! I have done everything!"

Osman bent over Cat. "Why do you weep, Incili? Does something pain you?"

Cat ignored him. In frustration, Osman sent for Hammid. The grand eunuch arrived and quietly dismissed Susan and Osman from the room. Then he sat down by Cat's bed and waited. The hysterical weeping continued for some minutes, then began to abate slowly until finally it stopped entirely. She sat up, her face wet and swollen. Wordlessly he handed her a large red silk

517

handkerchief. After mopping her face, she noisily blew her nose.

"Very well, Incili, tell me what troubles you," he said.

"Everything!" she burst out. "I want to be free! I cannot bear being cooped up like this! In my country women are free to roam their own lands. Here I am confined to the harem and a daily walk in a walled garden. I hate it! I hate it!"

Hammid nodded understandingly. This was not an uncommon problem with new captives, and he was willing to make great concessions to see that this woman was content. For years he had sought for a woman who could balance Lateefa Sultan's influence over his master. The Ottoman princess was beautiful and clever. She had dutifully borne her husband three sons and twin daughters, but her sex drive was low. Consequently she did not mind that her husband kept a large harem to satisfy his great appetite. But Hammid worried that his master might fall under the influence of the wrong woman. The wrong woman could turn Hammid's carefully tended household into a battleground of warring factions. The wrong woman could even affect national policy as long as Cicalazade Pasha was a vizier to Sultan Mohammed.

In Incili he had found exactly what he sought to counterbalance his royal mistress. He had quickly ascertained that she was not only intelligent, but ethical. She was a beauty with a wisdom seldom found in women. Most important of all, he had seen that her sexual appetite could be as great as his master's. Hammid even believed that Lateefa Sultan and Incili could be friends, and with these two women he hoped to aid Cicalazade in becoming a great vizier. For Hammid was an ambitious man, and to be master of a great man's household was a goal worth his reaching for.

"I will gain permission for you to walk in Lateefa

Sultan's garden. It is not walled, but open to sea and sky. I will also suggest to our master that he take you cruising in his caique. Would you like that?" She nodded. "And later," he continued, "when you are more settled, I will allow you trips to the bazaars of the city."

"Oh, yes, please, Hammid!"

"Good! Now, are the hysterics gone?"

"Yes."

He smiled in a kindly fashion. "I am pleased, Incili. Lord Cica spoke to me this morning of his delight with you. You have pleasured him as no woman ever has. You are to go to him again tonight."

Cat's mind raced. She thought to herself, If I must endure this for the present, I will make it as pleasant for myself and for Susan as possible.

She looked at the grand eunuch. "I have no clothing. The lowliest maiden in this harem has more to wear than I! Am I to be parceled out little gauze garments each night? If I am to please my lord Cica then I must be allowed to choose my own wardrobe. It has been my experience, Hammid, that it takes more than skill in a man's bed to hold him. Or perhaps you really do not care if Cica Pasha grows quickly bored with me."

Hammid was delighted. She might not be completely ready to yield herself, but this typically feminine interest in clothing was extremely encouraging. "I will send for the women bazaar vendors so you may choose whatever you like. If you see materials you also fancy, buy them! I will have our seamstresses fashion garments for you. You may also purchase jewelry, cosmetics, and perfumes." He was feeling very generous. "When you have made your choices, Osman will see that the women are paid."

The bazaar vendors brought an enormous variety of things for Cat to look at. Cat treated herself generously, buying several dozen gauze blouses in whites and colors,

pantaloons with matching jackets and long caftans in
lime green, mauve, lilac, turquoise, pale blue, and blos-
som pink. She found several bolts of fabric that pleased
her, a deep-blue silk embroidered with tiny silver stars,
a heavy red satin, a pale-green brocade shot with gold
threads, and two gauzes—one of gold, the other of
silver.

From the cosmetic vendor she bought only a little
kohl, refusing the white mercury paste, the henna, and
the red paste used to color lips.

The perfume vendor fared better, leaving three crystal flasks with Cat. One held musk, one a fragrance of
wild spring flowers, and the third a foresty thing of
green fern and moss with just a hint of ambergris.

Now came women with trays of jewelry, and Cat
bought carefully—a dozen little gold bangles and a
dozen of silver. Delicate gold chains, some plain, some
studded with amethyst, garnet, topaz, aquamarine, or
peridot caught her fancy. She bought several ropes of
beads, both pink and white coral, turquoise and jade.
She bought ropes of pearls strung on thin gold wires,
and earrings to go with everything else she had already
bought.

When Osman protested her extravagance, she rounded
on him. "Go to the grand eunuch, insect! If he says no,
then I will obey." Osman sighed and paid the happy
vendors.

She ate lightly and then spent two luxurious hours
in the harem baths being pampered, for word had already reached the bath mistress of Cat's favor with the
master. Back in her room, she slept to be awakened in
early evening, when she again ate lightly of fresh yogurt
and fruit.

Studying the garments she had purchased, she decided upon the lime green. The ankles of the silk pantaloons had bands of a slightly deeper green, em-

broidered in gold-thread flowers. With it she wore a
sheer, long-sleeved gauze silk blouse striped in the two
greens, and topped it with a short, sleeveless lime-green
silk jacket with its sides and bottom banded in heavy
gold embroidery and seed pearls. The bolero was
fringed in tiny pearls. Below her hips was tied a gold-
and-green striped silk sash. Her kid slippers were
studded with pearl flowers. Over her long, dark-gold
hair she wore a long diaphanous green silk veil. About
her neck she had fastened a rope of jade and a rope of
pearls. Gold bangles jingled on her arms, and gold-and-
jade earrings bobbed from her ears.

Hammid's fat face split into a wide grin when he saw
her. "Magnificent, Incili!" he exclaimed. "You have
taste, and a flair for style." He escorted her as far as the
door to the vizier's bedchamber. There he left her, saying, "I wish you joy this night."

She walked into the room calmly to find him waiting.
She saw the approval in his gray-blue eyes, and he teasingly said, "I hear you have been spending my money."
Reaching out, he pulled the veils from her face and
head.

"You imply you find favor with me, my lord," she
said coolly, "yet until today the lowliest female in your
harem had more than I. I am neither a greedy nor an
acquisitive woman, but I must have clothes."

"With or without them you are the loveliest of
women, Incili," and she saw the quick desire flickering
in his eyes.

Seeing a chess set on the low table, she quickly asked,
"Will you play with me my lord Cica?"

He was amused. "Do you play?" he asked.

"Very well, or so both my husbands told me," she
answered with a poise she was far from feeling.

His hand indicated the pillows opposite the ivory
chess pieces, while he himself sat opposite the black

onyx ones. Then suddenly a wicked light came into his eyes, and he said, "Wait!" She looked questioningly at him. "Remove your jacket, and your blouse, Incili. If you would forestall the inevitable, I shall at least have the delightful pleasure of your breasts." She flushed, and he was pleased. She was angry but she was forced to obey him. She was a wonderful, wild thing, and he was very much enjoying their battle. Eventually, of course, he would tame her completely. The thought of her begging his favors excited him greatly and, like a great beast, his manhood awoke and stretched itself.

She played with a serious concentration that he admired, and because he could not take his eyes from her beautiful breasts, he found himself in danger of losing to her. She deliberately thrust her breasts forward and moved in such a way that they bobbed provocatively. In order to even the odds again, he moved around the table to sit next to her. Casually putting an arm about her, he fondled a soft breast, enjoying her disconcerted gasp and the sudden hardening of a rosy nipple. His head dropped, and he kissed her silken shoulder while moving his king piece into an apparently vulnerable position. Flustered and unthinking Cat quickly moved her queen piece, and was horrified to hear the vizier chuckle. "Check, my distracting beauty, and—" he pushed her back into the pillows—"mate!"

Before she had realized what was happening he was atop her, laughing down at her. His hands stroked the tight, quivering globes beneath his touch. "Do not be angry with me, my sweet Incili. You are too delicious to resist, and I do not want to play games with you, I want to make love to you."

"I am not one of your soft harem beauties, quick to spread her legs for the master," she spat at him. "I will not yield. It will be rape!"

He laughed again, and his eyes twinkled. "All right," he said, "then it will be rape, which could be very titillating." And she felt his hands on her hips untying the striped sash and inching her silk pantaloons off.

"No," she shrieked. "No!" Struggling angrily against him, she tried to claw at him, and he laughed. He was stronger by far, and Cat began to tire. Successfully stripping her, the vizier slid his own pantaloons off while still straddling her. Now he lay his warm naked body the length of her naked body, enjoying the satiny feel of her. He made to kiss her, but she furiously turned away from him. Chuckling, he caught her head between his hands and his mouth swooped down on hers.

Gently he ran his tongue along her little white teeth, and though she tried to deny him, the fires of her own desire were fast rising. Her lips parted with a despairing little moan, and as his tongue darted into the fragrant cavity of her mouth, she shivered beneath him. His lips moved to tenderly kiss her eyelids and then her cheeks, wet with silent tears. He stopped, and raising himself on one elbow he asked quietly, "Why can you not give yourself to me completely? Your body longs for mine, yet you deny me a full victory."

"I—I—I do not love you, my lord Cicalazade. I love my husband. In my land a woman who yields her body to a man she does not love is considered the lowest of creatures."

"But I love you. No, Incili, don't look incredulous. I speak the truth. Were I only interested in your lovely body I should not care about your feelings. But I do care. Unless I have all of you, my love, I have none of you, and that is intolerable to me." The intensity of his voice was frightening. "You will never see your husband again. You belong to me now, but I will be patient, for I want you to love me." And the sensuous mouth was again closing hungrily over hers, demanding, searing.

Unable to stop herself, Cat clung to this passionate man and felt his hands stroking her trembling body. His lips were on her breasts, his tongue tracing tantalizing patterns, torturing the nipples into hard, hurting little peaks. The teasing tongue moved across her shrinking belly, sinking lower and lower, seeking access to her sweetness.

His tongue was like soft fire burning into her writhing body, thrusting deeper and deeper until she was mindless with the waves of pleasure sweeping over her. Then he was in her, hard and hurting, making her cry out in rapture, begging him—to her shame—not to stop.

Never in all of his life had he wanted so desperately to prolong his own passion. She consumed him with a flame of lust unequal to anything he had ever experienced as he strove to bring her to complete fulfillment. He didn't want to stop, but then his foaming seed was pouring fiercely into her, and she cried out her joy.

But afterwards she wept again in his arms, sobbing against the dark mat of his broad chest. He held her tightly while one hand caressed her tawny head, soothing her. For a brief moment he understood her anguish, for he knew that if he ever lost her his own world would be meaningless. He, Cicalazade Pasha, grand vizier to Sultan Mohammed III, caught in the silken web of his beautiful, unwilling slavewoman. What irony!

The weeping had stopped and he slept, cradling her against him. Awaking in the dark of night, he sensed that she was not sleeping. "Hammid tells me," he said softly, "that you are feeling confined. Would you like to go with me tomorrow night? It is the night of the full moon, and I own a small island down the Bosporus. On it is a little kiosk with a roof that opens to the sky. Tomorrow night I will take you there, and make love to you beneath the moonlit heavens."

He felt her tremble next to him and, turning, pulled her into his arms. His lips were tender, and so was his body now as he gently took her again, delighting in her little moan of surrender. This time she did not weep afterwards, but for a few moments cuddled sweetly against him.

It was fortunate that on the following day he had no state business to attend to, for he could not keep his mind on anything but Incili. He spent part of the morning conferring with his household master about the arrangements for the evening. Late in the morning he went to see his wife.

Lateefa Sultan was a great-granddaughter of Selim I. Her grandmother had been a half-sister to Suleiman the Magnificent. She was a beautiful woman who had inherited the magnificent coloring of her great-grandmother, Firousi Kadin, and the gentle disposition of her grandmother, Guzel Sultan. Her long hair was silvery blond, and her eyes a turquoise blue. She had been married to Cicalazade Pasha as a girl, and their children were now grown and gone. She lived a quiet life surrounded by every comfort, secure in the friendship of her husband. One night weekly, each Friday, he visited her bed—but it was usually to sleep, for she did not particularly care for lovemaking. Since his vast harem satisfied that part of his nature and since she had dutifully borne his children, he respected her sensibilities. They were old and good friends, the vizier and his wife.

On this bright morning he sat with her in a small kiosk overlooking the water. He looked slightly haggard and was, she thought, beginning to show his age.

"In all the years we have been together I have never asked for a favor," he said.

She smiled. "It must be a large favor you ask, since you remind me that you have never before requested one."

"As an Ottoman princess you have never had to fear the advent of another wife, for I can have no wife but you—unless, of course, you give me your permission to take another. Until now I have never wanted to take another wife."

"It is the new slave, Incili," said Lateefa calmly. "Is it not enough that you possess her body?"

"No," he replied quietly. "I want more, and I do not believe she will yield it to me until she is my wife."

"Has she said so?"

"She is ignorant of our ways. I do not think it has occurred to her that I would want her as a wife. You would like her though, Lateefa."

"So Hammid assures me," she answered him dryly. Then, looking closely at him, she said, "I am not sure that I believe my own eyes, but they tell me you are in love. Can it be that after all these years the great Cicalazade Pasha is actually in love with a mere woman? Have you finally succumbed to that tender passion?"

"Do not mock me, Lateefa." His voice was hard.

"Oh, my dearest Cica, I do not! Believe me I do not! It's just that you have always prided yourself on the careful noninvolvement of your emotions. Now, however, I see a different man. Very well, my lord. Hammid tells me I will not have to play the forgotten Gulbehar to your beloved's Kurhem, so I will give you my permission to take Incili as your second wife. When will the happy event take place?"

"Later today, before I take her to the Island of a Thousand Flowers."

"So soon, my lord?"

"I would erase the past to which she clings so tenaciously. Once she is my wife she will begin to settle down." He knelt and, taking Lateefa's hands in his, kissed them tenderly. "Thank you, my gentle dove. You have always been the most understanding of women."

Lateefa, watching him stride back across the garden, felt a wave of pity sweep over her. She had not met the woman they called Incili and yet she felt that her husband, in seeking to possess this woman, sought the moon. It was a desire he could never fulfill.

Chapter 51

❧

"YOU are to become a Muslim, Incili," said Hammid quietly.

Cat's green eyes widened. "Never!" she answered.

"Do not be foolish, my beauty," chided the eunuch. "It is but a formality. Six times a day you must kneel towards Mecca and pray. Who is to know what is in your heart but God?"

Cat thought a moment. His words made sense, and undoubtedly her great-grandmother had thought the same way, for she could not have been a sultan's favorite wife and an avowed Christian too. Besides, survival and escape were all that mattered. "Very well," she told Hammid. "I will do what you ask."

Early in the afternoon she was given a special bath of purification and brought to a women's mosque near the vizier's palace, where she automatically answered the questions put to her by the elderly muezzin. By late afternoon she was officially a convert to Mohammed.

She was not, however, aware of the fact that as soon as she returned to Cicalazade's palace the vizier signed papers making her his second wife. According to Muslim law, neither her knowledge nor her consent were necessary. Only the permission of her legal guardian was required. Hammid, who accepted a large sum of gold as her bridal gift, was that guardian.

When evening came, Cat waited impatiently for the

litter that would carry her to the vizier's caique. Her
small excursion of the afternoon had whetted her appetite for freedom, and she had even managed to reconcile
herself to the fact that, for the present, Cicalazade Pasha
owned her. She had decided to cease her resistance to
him. Her objective was to return to her husband in Italy,
and in order to do this she must be able to speak with
the Kira family in Constantinople. She could only gain
that privilege if she were trusted, and she would only
be trusted if she appeared to have accepted her fate.

Not even her loyal Susan must suspect her thoughts.
It was a secret she would keep to herself until her plans
were completed. She started guiltily at the sound of
Hammid's voice.

"You look so serious, Incili. What is it you think of,
my beauty? Profound thoughts are not good for a
woman."

She laughed. "You have indeed caught me, Hammid,
but I think you would approve the direction of my
thoughts. I have been thinking that you are right. I will
not say that it is easy for me, but I have decided to try
to accept my fate. After all, 'tis not so terrible a fate.
Perhaps in time I shall be able to love my lord Cicalazade. Do you think it will happen, Hammid? The vizier
does appear to harbor some small affection for me."

Hammid could scarcely control his delight and excitement. She could not have made her decision at a
better time. "I can," he said carefully, "if you will allow
me, ease some of your anxiety. Will you trust me?"

"I will try," she answered him, "but what is it you
would do?"

"It is an ancient form of relaxation and suggestion
called hypnosis. I will place you in a trance, and suggest
certain things to you. When you awaken you will be
more at ease with your situation. Do not fear this, however, for if you do not wish to obey my suggestions,

the hypnosis will not work. Your own strong will is your best protection."

"I trust you, Hammid," she said. "Proceed."

The eunuch took a gold chain with a small diamond tear from about his neck. "Watch the tear, Incili." He swung it slowly before her eyes. "Is it not beautiful with its rainbow colors?" The voice was soothing and kindly. Cat felt a delicious warmth wash over her. "You must concentrate on the tear, my child, and soon you will begin to relax." The pendant swung slowly, and Cat felt her body growing languorous, her eyes heavier and heavier as they slowly closed.

"Are you asleep, Incili?"

"Yes, Hammid."

The eunuch took a pin from his robe and, lifting her foot, jabbed it quickly into her tender sole. She neither pulled away nor cried out, and he was satisfied that she was really in a hypnotic state. "Are you ready to submit to Cicalazade Pasha as your lord and master?"

"Yes, Hammid. I will try hard to please him."

"I am happy with you, Incili, and I want you to be happy. You have only to follow the dictates of your body, my beauty. Let your lovely body overrule your quick intellect. Lord Cicalazade loves you deeply. You have affected him as no woman ever has. Will you not give him the satisfaction of knowing that he has pleasured you?"

For a moment she was silent, as if struggling with her emotions, then her soft voice said, "Yes, Hammid, I will yield myself to my lord Cica."

The eunuch smiled, satisfied. "Thank you, my dear. I am content that you will both be very happy. One other thing, however. You must not mention to the vizier that we have had this conversation."

"I will not."

"Very well, Incili. On the count of three you will

awaken refreshed, and ready to spend a night pleasing your lord, One . . . two . . . three."

Cat's eyes opened. "Fascinating," she said. "I slept, yet I heard you clearly, and I feel ever so much more at ease, Hammid. Thank you."

The eunuch smiled again. "Are you ready to join the vizier now?"

"Yes."

"And again tonight I compliment you on your costume."

Cat smiled. She enjoyed wearing the luxurious clothing of a priveleged woman, and she took great pains with her appearance. Tonight she wore pale-pink silk shot with silver threads. Her gauze blouse was rose, her jacket edged in silver and bits of blue lapis. Her hip sash and slippers bore alternating stripes of silver and turquoise. She wore silver baubles on her arms and large drop earrings of carved turquoise.

Susan had done Cat's hair in a new fashion. Drawn back and up, the honey-colored mass was woven into one large braid with turquoise ribbons and a string of tiny seed pearls. Across the beautiful face, Hammid fastened a veil of rose gauze.

She settled herself comfortably in the litter, almost bouncing with excitement in anticipation of her outing. The bearers moved quickly through the harem corridors, out across the gardens, and down to the private marble quay where the vizier's caique awaited.

It was a graceful vessel, completely gilded, with a red lacquer design along the sides. The oars were alternately pale-blue enamel and silver, and the slaves who pulled those oars were all coal-black. Those who pulled on the silver oars wore blue satin pantaloons sashed in silver. Those who pulled on the pale-blue oars were garbed in blue-sashed silver cloth pantaloons. The awning of the vessel was stripped in red, gold, blue, and silver, and held up by four gilded posts carved around with flowers and leaves. The silk curtains were scarlet and gold gauze, and the deck was polished rosewood. Beneath the awning was an enormous assortment of multicolored pillows, where Cicalazade Pasha awaited.

Hammid carefully handed her from the litter into the caique. Reclining comfortably on her side, she raised her eyes to him and said in a low, sultry voice, "Good evening, my lord."

A smile lit his face. "Good evening, Incili." Turning to the oarmaster, he nodded. The caique began to pull slowly away from the quay, moving directly into the Bosporus in the direction of the Black Sea. The sun had not yet set, and she could see the summer-green hills tumbling into the water. Behind them the sky was a riot of pinks, golds, mauves, corals, and deep purple against blue.

Cat breathed deeply and the vizier laughed. "Do not tell me that the air outside my garden smells better, beloved."

" 'Tis the smell of freedom, my lord."

His eyes were troubled, and then he said quietly, "Do not chafe so, my beautiful captive dove. Today I have changed your humble status. My wife, Lateefa Sultan, is an Ottoman princess, and I may not have other wives except with her permission."

"I thought Muslim men were allowed four wives."

"All except those wed to imperial princesses. This afternoon, however, with Lateefa's permission, I took you as my second wife." Her eyes widened. Pleased, he continued, "You are, I know, wondering how this can be. Under Muslim law neither your knowledge nor your permission was necessary. You are no longer a slave, my precious one. Are you not happy?" His face radiated pleasure as he looked expectantly at her.

The blood was pounding angrily in her ears. It took

tremendous effort but she quickly caught hold of her
emotions. Speaking so softly that he was forced to bend
to hear her, she said, "You do me an incredible honor,
my lord." She was unable to say any more for fear of
betraying herself.

It was enough. He drew her into his arms, kissing
the mouth that opened easily beneath his. He covered
the upturned face with kisses, moving to the slim pillar
of her throat and down to her breasts. Eagerly he pulled
the rose gauze blouse open, tearing it in his haste.
Hungrily he sucked at her nipples, each in turn, and
then, laying his head against her heart, he sighed contentedly, sure that he had won her over completely.

"Tonight we begin anew, my precious Incili." His
deep voice vibrated with emotion. "The past is dead,
my beautiful bride. Only the present and the future will
concern us. Look! The full moon is rising, and above it,
Venus, the planet of the Goddess of Love! Soon we
will be at the Island of a Thousand Flowers, and there
in the Starlight Kiosk we will spend a night of rapture."
Raising his head from her breasts, he gazed at her, little
gold lights dancing in his gray-blue eyes.

She was speechless. Drawing his head back down to
her breasts so he could not see her face, she suppressed
the urge to scream. Furious, she wondered how her
great-grandmother had managed to live so many years
in a Muslim world. So neither her permission nor even
her knowledge had been necessary for marriage to take
place! Now she knew why Hammid had insisted on her
quick conversion to Islam.

He had pretended to be her friend, lulling her into a
false sense of security in order to aid his master. She
would never trust him again. But she would play the
game—her way, this time—and Hammid would not
know it. For the time being she would be the adoring
second wife of the vizier. She would not allow outrage

to betray her. She would make them all think she had been pacified and tamed.

The caique was approaching the island quay, and Cat could smell flowers. "My lord Cica," she said softly, "we near our destination. I would rearrange my blouse lest the slaves see what they should not."

Sighing, he raised his head. "I could stay like this forever, beloved."

"We will soon be in our bridal chamber, my lord, and then you may resume your dozing," she teased playfully.

"Neither of us will rest this night, my wife." His voice thickened with passion, and she shivered.

The caique bumped the quay, and the vizier leaped from the vessel to tie it fast. "We will not need you until morning," he told the oarmaster. "See the rowers are made comfortable, but do not unchain them. The temptation to escape would be too great." Reaching down, he took her hand and drew her out of the boat. "I regret we must walk, my love, but I did not wish on this night of nights to be burdened with slaves."

"My lord Cica forgets that I am no pampered Eastern beauty. In my country women not only walk but ride horses too. Lead on, my lord, I follow."

They ascended the island, climbing up a flight of stairs cut into the side of the cliff, and it seemed to Cat that the island was no more than a tall rock. However, when they had reached the top, she was surprised to find herself in a beautiful, carefully tended garden in the center of which was a marble kiosk. The moonlight was so bright now that she could easily see and identify many of the flowers. There were damask roses, Gold of Ophir roses, sultan's balsam, bougainvillea, lilies, sweet night-blooming nicotiana, and moonflowers. There were trees heavy with ripening peaches and pears, and cypress, pine, and other ornamental trees were set among the small bubbling fountains.

"It's exquisite," she said honestly. "Never have I seen such a beautiful garden."

"I laid it out myself," he told her proudly. She had not discerned this side of his nature. "Like my master, the sultan, I have learned a trade. He took her hand and led her down the white gravel path towards the kiosk, set in the center of an oval reflecting pool.

The kiosk, rectangular, was of cream-colored marble, with a small pillared porch. Crossing a narrow lattice-work bridge, they entered the kiosk through an open wooden door studded in brass nails. Cat was stunned by the room.

Directly across from her, a wall of leaded windows looked beyond the pool, across the garden, to the moonlit sea beyond. Beneath her feet was an enormous Medallion rug woven in red, green, gold, and varying blues. On the wall to her right a silk hanging depicted a Persian garden. On the wall to her left was a door, and next to it was another silk carpet, this one showing a pair of lovers seated in their garden. In one corner of the room was a low round brass table surrounded by pillows. Gold and silver lamps burning scented oil hung from the painted and beamed ceiling.

But the major piece of furniture in the room was an enormous square bed set upon a carpeted dais in the very center of the room. It had neither a head nor a foot. Nor were there any hangings. It was simply a square platform with silken sheets and a down coverlet. On the dais near it were several small low tables of ebony, inlaid with bits of colored mosaic or iridescent mother-of-pearl. Upon the tables were carafes of golden liquid and bowls of fruit, olives, and sugared almonds.

Coming silently up behind her, he put an arm around her, one hand cupping her breast while his thumb rubbed the nipple. "Do you like it, beloved?"

"It is all unbelievably beautiful," she answered sincerely.

"Look above the bed," he said, and she glanced up to see the ceiling roll back to reveal a glass dome, giving a magnificent view of the night sky.

She gasped. "I have never seen anything like that! How it is done?"

"By a process far too complicated for your sweet little head to comprehend, my dove," he answered, spinning her about and kissing the tip of her nose.

Cat's temper rose, but she quickly swallowed it and tipped her face up to him, inviting him to kiss her again. He brushed his mouth lightly against hers and then said, "Let us to bed, my beloved."

"May I valet you, my lord?" She moved behind him to remove the sleeveless red-and-gold brocade robe. Beneath it he wore a silk shirt embroidered in gold and silver thread, blue pantaloons trimmed with silver, a jeweled blue sash, and red leather boots. She helped him with each item of his wardrobe, unable to keep her hands from straying to the broad hairy chest. None of her lovers had been particularly hirsute, and she was fascinated by his hairiness.

Naked, he sprawled on the bed. "Disrobe for me now," he commanded her, "and do it with grace."

The leaf-green eyes looked intently at him, and he felt a tingle go through his limp member. Then her fingers gently peeled back the sleeveless jacket until she was able to shrug it off. Her fingers moved to the rose gauze blouse, loosened it, and then stopped. Instead, she removed her sash. A delightful smile lit his features as she kicked her little kid slippers off. Then, turning her back to him, she slid the blouse off. She could hear his breath becoming faster, and ragged. Loosening the drawstring on her silk pantaloons, she let them slip slowly to the rug and, stepping away from them, she turned quickly to face him.

He smiled again. "The carafe with the gold liquid, Incili. Pour us each a goblet."

She caught the scent of rich wine. Puzzled, she looked to him. "I thought liquor was forbidden the Muslim."

"The sultan drinks," he answered, "and the mufti has ruled that when a sultan takes to drink it is permissible for all to do the same, and for poets to celebrate it. In general I hold with the Koran. I neither drink nor allow it in my household. But this night, beloved, is our wedding night. We will toast each other in the sweet wines of Cyprus." He raised his goblet and said, "To you Incili, my wife. Though you be second in my house, you are first in my heart." Looking directly at her, he drained his goblet.

Cat knew she was expected to reply in kind. Raising her own goblet, she spoke softly. "To you, my lord Cica. As long as it pleases Allah that I be your wife, I will endeavor to please you." And she drank her goblet empty.

"It is not necessary for you to call me 'my lord' in the privacy of our bedchamber, beloved. You will call me Cica, or husband. Yes! Call me husband! I have yet to hear you say it to me. Say it, Incili! Say husband!"

Silently Cat prayed, "*Forgie me, Bothwell,*" and then, looking at Cicalazade Pasha, she said, "Husband."

His eyes burned into hers, and she felt heat sweeping over her body. He smiled at her. "You can feel the heat, can you not? Do not be afraid. Hammid has put something into the wine that will enable us to prolong our pleasure. We will go on and on this night." She shivered, terrified at the meaning behind his words. Then he stood, commanding her to kneel before him. She obeyed him, and her heart hammered wildly when he said, "Taste of me, my sweet, as I will soon taste of you."

Before her his manhood lay limp, nesting within the wiry black hair. "Obey me!" His voice demanded sharply. With trembling hand she lifted the drooping member and kissed its tip. Knowing she had no other choice, she placed it in her warm mouth, and sucked. "Allah! Allah!" he groaned with delight. After a few minutes he reached down and pulled her up. They fell onto the bed, Cat on her back. His mouth found hers, and as his kiss deepened in passion, Cat felt the burning heat pouring through her body. His touch was inflaming her and she was losing control. She suddenly wanted him desperately, and she wiggled beneath him moaning her pleasure at the long skillful fingers that teased her desire, begging him to increase his efforts, allowing him complete and unchecked freedom with her body. Hammid's posthypnotic suggestion that she obey the dictates of her body and the powerful aphrodisiac was combining to drive her to a frenzy.

As he looked down at her she whispered, "You are like a bull, my husband! A mighty black bull!"

The gray-blue eyes glittered, and he answered, "And you, beloved, are the bull's mate—a sweet little golden heifer. Quickly, my pet. Onto your hands and knees, and I shall love you as the bull does the heifer." And he turned her onto her stomach, pushing her knees up. Swiftly he mounted her, sighing happily at the warm, wet welcome of her, his hands fondling the breasts that hung, quivering. She gasped with pleasure as he rode, crying her rapture at the waves of delight washing over her. It didn't stop. He was utterly inexhaustible as he drove deeper and deeper into her, again and again, until she finally fainted.

When she regained consciousness he had turned her onto her back and was bending anxiously over her. She reached up a slim hand, touching his cheek gently, and said, " 'Tis all right, Cica." And then she felt him spreading her thighs to push himself into her again. Above her the moon passed slowly over the glass dome, leaving the black sky to fade with the dawn.

Chapter 52

❦

F RANCIS Stewart-Hepburn reached Avellino to find
that the bandits who had been plaguing the district
had disappeared as suddenly as they had come. Their
recent presence was distressingly evident in the burned-
out farms, fresh graves, and frightened women and
children.

For several days Bothwell and his men poked about.
Discovering nothing, they returned to the Villa del Pesce
d'Oro and found an empty house. There were six new
graves in the garden.

Fortunately for the earl's sanity, the head gardener
had been waiting for his master to return. Nodding to
the graves, Carlo said, "Paolo, Maria, and the maids.
The little May is with me. Signora la contessa and Susan
were carried off. Come, my lord. The girl can tell you.
She was there but escaped somehow. I know not how,
for she has not spoken much since she fled to us almost
three weeks ago. I think, however, that she will speak
to you."

At the sight of them, May flung herself into Conall's
arms weeping. "Ohhhh, Uncle Conall, 'twas terrible!
The pirates carried off my mistress and Susan!"

Conall grasped the girl hard by her shoulders. "Pull
yourself together, lassie, and tell us exactly what happened. Think carefully, May, and leave nothing out."

Gulping her sobs back, the girl rallied. "Susan and

I were sleeping on the trundle in my lady's room while ye were away. It was Sunday dawn, and we awoke to a terrible screaming. When we ran to the windows and looked out, the garden was full of Turkish pirates! Paolo was already dead. They bashed his head in while he was cutting the herbs for the breakfast eggs. Maria and the girls had their throats cut . . . after the pirates were finished with them. They were r-r-r—" But she couldn't get the word out, and Bothwell put a gentle hand over her mouth.

"Don't lassie. We can imagine what happened. Tell us how you escaped. Tell us of my wife and your sister," and he withdrew his hand.

Two large tears ran down the girl's cheeks, but she began again. "My lady bid my sister and me hide in the linen chest, but Susan would not. She told my lady it dinna matter what happened to her, since she was nae a virgin. 'Twas a lie she told, my lord, for Susan is as virgin as I am!" And unable to help herself, May began to cry again.

They let her weep for a few minutes, and then Bothwell said quietly, "Go on, lass. What happened next?"

"They hid me in the chest, and bid me not move until 'twas absolutely quiet, and I was sure the pirates had gone. Then I was to go to Carlo's and remain until ye returned. No sooner was the lid down than I heard the bedchamber door being smashed in, and then I heard the pirates entering. They dinna hurt my lady or Susan, but they took them away."

"Did they say anything you could understand, Susan?" asked Conall.

The girl thought a moment, then her features cleared. "Aye! The captain was very polite to my lady. He said his name was . . . it sounded like 'Karoteen.' He also said he had orders to take my lady to the grand vizier, Cica-something Pasha."

"Santa Maria!" gasped Carlo. He did not understand the girl's story, because she spoke in her own language, but he understood the names she spoke.

"Khair-ad-Din, my lord," he said excitedly. "Kapitan Khair-ad-Din—the namesake, and some say the grandson, of the great Kapitan Pasha of Suleiman the Magnificent! He is in the personal service of Cicalazade Pasha, the grand vizier of the Ottoman Empire."

"But what would some damned Turk want with my wife?"

Carlo looked uncomfortable. Bearers of bad tidings were never liked. Still, his lord must know. "Cicalazade Pasha is only half-Turkish. His father is the Conte di Cicala, my lord. He is also the older brother of the Contessa de LiCosa."

"I will personally kill the bitch," said Bothwell in a deadly voice.

"Not if I reach her first," said Conall quietly.

Simultaneously they turned, mounted their horses, and rode to the Conte di LiCosa's home.

As quiet as the grounds at the Villa del Pesce d'Oro had been, those at the Villa del Mare were quieter. At first Bothwell feared it deserted. But when they reached the house a servant ran out to take their horses, and another escorted them to Alfredo di LiCosa.

"I want Angela," said Bothwell with no preamble.

"You are too late, my friend. The Inquisition has her. She will burn tomorrow in the main market square of Naples."

"Have you seen her? Can she still talk? Do you know what she did? She has sent my wife into slavery in her brother's harem! I must talk with her before she dies!"

"So that was it," sighed Alfredo di LiCosa. "Her servant, Barto, was caught signaling the Turkish pirates. He implicated her, and then accused her of witchcraft, claiming that she held his soul in bondage so he was forced to do her bidding. Naturally the Inquisition heard and came for her immediately. They have been waiting for something like this, for Angela has made no secret of her contempt for the church. It was as if she'd gone mad! She laughed at them, and made no attempt to save herself. I don't think she really believed it. They didn't even bother to torture her, they simply condemned her to the stake. And she truly doesn't care."

"Where is she being kept, Alfredo?"

"In Naples at the Inquisition prison. I will go with you, Francisco, and we will get Bishop Pasquale too. He can get us the necessary permissions."

Bothwell nodded. "Tell me, Fredo, is there anything Angela is afraid of? Anything at all? I must have a lever to force her to talk with me."

"Snakes," answered the Conte di LiCosa. "Angela is terrified of snakes."

Bothwell looked to Conall and nodded. "Go back to the gardener, man."

Conall returned the nod. "Aye! I'll get them, and I'll meet you at the cross of San Genaro on the Naples road."

With his captain-at-arms gone, Bothwell turned again to the conte. "I am sorry, Fredo. I would not add to your pain. I know you love Angela. I want my wife back. If I must move heaven and hell to get her, I will!"

"You'll never see her again, Francisco. If Angela sent Caterina to Cicalazade Pasha, your wife is gone. If you could even get as far as Istanbul she would already be either dishonored or dead. Face your loss, and accept it as I am accepting mine."

"Never! Do you think I care if she's forced by another man as long as I can have her back? Do not tell me that I cannot get her back, for I can, and I will!"

The Conte di LiCosa shook his head sadly, but as he had promised, he accompanied Bothwell on his journey.

First they saw Bishop Pasquale who, hearing the story, changed from his clerical robes into his riding clothes and led the way to the Naples road.

Conall was already waiting by the San Genaro cross, a small covered reed basket attached to his saddle. It was close to evening by the time they reached the city. Had the bishop not been with them Bothwell was sure they would never have been admitted to the grim black stone fortress. All the windows were barred, and smoking pitch torches lit the entrance.

Riding authoritatively up to the entrance, the bishop demanded immediate entry and speech with the prison governor. They were quickly admitted. Conall gingerly removed the basket from the pommel horn of his saddle and followed the guard into the prison. They were immediately assaulted by the odor of rotting food, of unwashed bodies, of feces and urine. A low wailing assailed their ears.

"Jesu," whispered Conall to Bothwell, "we've gone to hell!"

The earl shot him a warning look, and they were led up a twisting flight of stairs to the governor's apartment. There they were greeted by Bishop Guido Massini, the prison governor, who said to Bothwell, "I have heard of you, my lord. There was some discussion in your country regarding witchcraft . . . and you are a heretic, I believe."

"No, Guido," said Bishop Pasquale quietly. "Lord Bothwell, having seen the error of his ways, has returned to Holy Church. He is married to a most virtuous and devout woman. They both attend mass regularly and are extremely generous to both the church and the poor."

"I am relieved to hear it," answered the bishop, a deceptively merry-looking little man whose smiling features were belied by his icy black eyes. "What may I do for you, my lord?"

"The prisoner Angela di LiCosa, Guido. We wish to see her. She is responsible for the abduction of Lord Bothwell's wife by Turkish pirates. Before she dies tomorrow we must learn from her what instructions she gave the pirates."

Bishop Massini was most irritated. "Is there no end to that woman's infamy? Yes, of course you may see her. However, even if she will tell you, there is little hope of your getting your wife back from the infidels."

But the bishop's face softened with Bothwell's look. "But I must! I must!" he said.

"I will write the pass for you."

"For my captain-at-arms also, and we must see her alone."

The bishop looked first at Bothwell's distraught face, and then at Conall's grim one. "What is in the basket?" he asked the captain. Then, raising a fat white hand, he hurriedly said, "No. I really don't want to know." Pulling out a prewritten parchment, he scrawled the name of Angela di LiCosa in one place and his own at the bottom. Holding out the parchment to Bothwell, he said, "Come back and have a goblet of wine with me when you have your information." He turned to the other two men. "Remain here if you do not wish to accompany them."

Francis looked to Alfredo di LiCosa, who shook his head. "No. I have said my goodbyes. I do not wish to see her ever again."

Bothwell and Conall followed the guard up a flight of stairs. "She is lodged quite decently, thanks to her husband," the guard remarked conversationally. "Most of the witches are below with the water rats."

"We are to see her alone," replied Bothwell coldly. "You are to remain outside the cell. And no matter what you hear, you will remain there unless my captain or I call you."

"Makes no difference to me," came the reply. The guard stopped before a door, found the right key, and opened the door.

They stepped through into the cell and heard the door close behind them. Angela di LiCosa stood, her back to them, gazing out through the barred window. "If you're another priest, go away," she said.

She whirled about. "Francisco, *caro!* So there is a God." But the welcome in her eyes died in Bothwell's icy gaze.

"I have come," said the earl coldly, "because I hope that even you will want to clear your conscience before you die. Regarding the matter of my wife, what exactly did you arrange?"

Her black eyes widened, and she burst into hysterical laughter. Outside the closed door the guard shuddered at the sound. Angela wiped the damp from her eyes with a ragged sleeve. "Really, Francisco! You are simply incredible! Yes, I arranged for your wife's disposal, but she must truly have God on her side, for that idiot servant of mine was caught. So . . . tomorrow I die. Alas, if I cannot have you then neither can she." She laughed again, a bit ruefully this time. "You will have neither of us, Francisco, and that isn't at all what I had planned!"

"Once more, Angela. What exactly did you do with her?"

The woman regarded him with some amusement and shook her head. Francis reached out and, wrapping the soft blue-black hair around his hand, cruelly yanked her to him. "I have no time to waste, Angela. Where is she?"

The black eyes glittered viciously, but she said nothing. Using his other hand, Bothwell ripped the prison smock from the woman's body and brutally shoved her onto the straw mattress of the cell cot. Before she realized what had happened, her arms and legs were bound to the cot posts in a spread-eagled position.

"What are you doing?" she shrieked. "I will call the guard!"

"He will not answer, Angela. I have the prison governor's permission to obtain my information in *any* way necessary. Now, what instructions did you give your Turkish friends regarding my wife?"

She regarded him coldly for a second and then, raising her head, spat full in his face. Bothwell nodded to his captain. Conall opened the woven basket. Looking into it thoughtfully, he chose a short, plump green snake. He handed it to Bothwell, who wrapped the reptile about his hand and caressed the weaving, darting head. Sliding it off his hand, he placed it on the straw mattress between Angela's open legs.

The Contessa di LiCosa shrieked wildly. "Francisco! For the love of God! Take it away! Take it away!"

"What exactly did you do with my wife?"

She strained against her bonds, her black eyes dark mirrors of terror, but still she would not answer him. He could see the pounding of her heart in her chest. The snake uncurled itself and began to move slowly towards her. She screamed again, a long wailing moan of animal fear.

"It goes for the warmth and moistness of you, Angela. Soon it will seek the darkness of your womb, where so many have been before it. And when it is safely up inside you wriggling around, I shall take another from the basket, and another, and another . . . until your belly is a nest of snakes. Can you feel them inside you already, Angela? Does it feel good, my dear?" The cruel eyes bore pitilessly down at her. For the briefest moment, amazement at his cruelty overcame her fear. But then the fear returned tenfold, slamming into her so fiercely that for a moment she couldn't draw a breath.

Finally she was able to gasp, "I sent her to my brother! Take that reptile away! I will tell you all! Only take it away!"

Casually Bothwell lifted the snake from the mattress and dropped it back into its container. "Talk then, you bitch, or I'll shove the entire basket up you!"

"I sent your precious bride to my brother, Cicalazade Pasha, the sultan's grand vizier. He is quite a connoisseur of beautiful women, and his prowess is legendary. She is not there yet, Francisco, but she will be soon. Then Cica's head eunuch will have her bathed and perfumed, and he will lead her to my brother, where she will be stripped naked for his inspection. When he has seen her—for I admit that she is beautiful—he will pleasure himself on her body."

"You bitch," snarled Bothwell.

Angela di LiCosa laughed. "You will never see her again! She is lost to you! Soon she will lie beneath my brother, moaning her desire." She lowered her voice to an intimate level. "They say he is a bull, and he will teach her to please him. You will have nothing but a memory, and the knowledge that another man is fucking her!" Angela's voice now became silky soft, and caressing. "Think of it, Francisco. Her tawny hair spread upon the pillows, her firm white legs eagerly open to receive her master's swollen manhood. She will beg for his favors! Living in a harem of a hundred other beauties, she will compete for his attentions as eagerly as any of them!"

The savagery of her words ripped into him, and Bothwell rose from the edge of the cot, his face a mask of pain and anguish. Crossing the cell, he pulled the door open and exited. Slowly Conall moved to stand beside the condemned woman. For a moment he stood staring silently down at her. Angela was frightened, for this man did not regard her nakedness with desire. This one showed no emotion whatsoever. "You are a wicked woman," he said quietly, "but do not think that you have won. We will bring her safely back to us. I have not watched over her since she was a child to see her end this way."

Bending, he took his knife and cut through the contessa's bonds. And before she realized what he was doing, he lifted the basket of green snakes and dumped them in her lap.

As he left the cell he smiled wolfishly, hearing the shrieks behind. "Lock it up again," he commanded the guard. "It's not to be opened again until morning."

Conall More-Leslie was not surprised, the following day, to hear that the Devil had come for the soul of Angela di LiCosa during the night, leaving her body and half a dozen green garden snakes as a memento of his visit. The crowd gathered to see a live Angela executed was disappointed. The body was tied to the waiting stake and burned to ashes, giving the cheering crowd a small satisfaction.

Chapter 53

❧§§❧

CONALL More-Leslie allowed the Earl of Bothwell exactly twenty-four hours to wallow in his grief. Then he dragged Francis to a bathhouse in the Turkish quarter of Naples, where two burly bath attendants scrubbed the drunken man down. Next he was put into a hot steam room until every pore was open and running freely. Then he was sloshed with scented tepid water and allowed to sleep on a marble bath bench in a slightly less volcanic steamroom. Awakened after an hour with a cup of boiling Turkish coffee, he vomited up most of the wine he had imbibed and was then taken into another tepidarium to be shaved and bathed again. Lastly he was dressed in his own fresh, clean clothes, which Conall had brought with them. His old clothes were burned. Finally he was bowed back out into the street, where his captain waited.

Bothwell was so weakened that he could barely mount his horse, and he cursed Conall roundly. Conall simply said, "I've found a tavern several streets over owned by an Englishman who knows how to cook beef decently," and led the way to La Rosa Anglo. A table in a private room awaited them. The landlord, himself from the north of England, served them slices of hot half-raw roast beef dripping its bloody juices onto great slabs of Yorkshire pudding. The table held a pottery bowl of artichokes in oil and vinegar, a tub of sweet butter, and a hot round loaf of crusty bread. The flagons were filled to the brim with foaming brown ale, at the sight of which Bothwell's eyebrows shot up.

The tavern keeper grinned toothily. "Aye, me lord! October ale it is! I makes it and casks it meself each year. 'Tis no easy task in this place!"

Bothwell sat down. He didn't feel particularly hungry, but suddenly the scent of the beef began to work its magic on him and he reached for the salt. Half an hour later he pushed back his chair and said, "Thank you, Conall."

The captain nodded. "I've taken the liberty," he said, "of asking Master Kira to see you. He'll be waiting for us now, my lord."

"Can he help?"

"Possibly, my lord. The Kiras' main banking branch and their family head are both located in Istanbul."

Bothwell rose and paid the landlord. The man gaped at the generous coin in his hand. "Thank ye, sir," he babbled. "Anytime we can serve the border lord, we're proud to do so!"

But Bothwell had already mounted and was riding towards the Jewish section of the city, and Pietro Kira's house. Conall smiled, pleased that he had roused the earl from self-pity. They reached the Kira dwelling and were quickly ushered into the best salon. Servants hurried in with wine and biscuits.

Then came Pietro Kira, elegant in a long, fur-trimmed black gown, a large gold chain and pendant hanging about his neck and shoulders. He grasped Lord Bothwell's hand, saying, "I am so sorry to receive you under these circumstances, my lord. Let us sit down. You will tell me everything that you know."

The earl repeated what he had learned from young May, and from Angela di LiCosa. "Yes," nodded the banker, "we knew all of that, but it is good to have it confirmed. We have already sent a message to the head of the family in Istanbul. Do not be afraid for your wife, my lord. She has friends about her, and when the time is right we will contact her. She is a brave and resourceful lady."

"I would go to Istanbul as soon as possible, Signor Kira."

"Indeed you would, my lord, but you must not. At least not yet. Not until we have ascertained that the countess has arrived, is safe, and has been contacted by our people. For you to show up in the sultan's capital demanding your wife's return would be absolutely fatal to you and possibly also to your wife.

"Sultan Mohammed is a strange man given to alternating moods of great kindness and unbelievable cruelty. He is deeply fond of his vizier. If Cicalazade Pasha is taken with your beautiful wife and you arrive to demand her back, you could find yourself quickly dead, my lord. Let us move slowly and carefully. The countess is quite safe. It would not serve Cicalazade Pasha's purpose to hurt her."

"But how will I get her back, Pietro Kira? How?"

"When we know what we must regarding your wife's position, then we can plan, my lord. It may be possible to ransom her. More likely, we will have to abduct her. In the meantime, please return to your home and wait to hear from me. And, my lord, I think you should know that your wife's monies are at your complete disposal. Prior to her arrival here in Naples she arranged with the House of Kira that you and your children should inherit her wealth should anything befall her."

Bothwell looked pained. "I cannot touch a pennypiece of her money," he said.

Conall said quietly, "Ye'll need gold for the running of the household, my lord. Why not simply have all the bills sent to Signor Kira? He will keep a strict accounting. I know ye would ne'er take her wealth for yourself. But lord, man, yer her husband, and she'd nae thank me if I let ye starve to death afore she comes home!"

Bothwell nodded sadly, absently. "Whatever ye think is right, Conall. I leave it to ye."

Conall turned again to the banker. "Your messengers are swifter than ours, sir. Will you see that the young Earl of Glenkirk is informed that my lady's children are to remain safely with him until further notice? She had sent a message asking that they be sent out to her, but now, of course, 'tis impossible."

"We will see to it, captain," said Pietro Kira, already thinking about the message he would be sending to his uncle in the Ottoman capital.

Istanbul was the home of the Kira family. Once a small merchant family of Jews, they had, thanks to their matriarch Esther Kira, risen to become one of the most powerful banking houses in all of Europe and Asia.

Esther Kira had been born in 1490. At six, she and her small brother, Joseph, were orphaned and taken into the house of their father's oldest brother. At twelve, Esther was peddling hard-to-obtain merchandise to the harem ladies of the rich. At sixteen, she was allowed entry to the imperial harem, and at twenty, her family's fortune was made when she met Cyra Hafise, mother of Suleiman the Magnificent. When Sultan Suleiman ascended the throne in 1520, Esther Kira and her family were forever exempted from the paying of taxes for services rendered the crown. No one, including Esther's family, ever knew what those services were, but it would have been unthinkable to question the imperial word.

Considered of value now by her uncle, Esther was married off to his younger son. When her only brother-in-law died childless, it was Esther's sons who inherited the now-great banking house. That was only just, since it was Esther's efforts that had brought the Kiras their stunning success.

Just as Esther had been a favorite of Suleiman's mother, she became the favorite of Suleiman's favorite wife, Khurrem Kadin, and of Selim II's favorite, Nur-U-Banu, and of Murad III's favorite, Safiye. Safiye was the mother of the present sultan. Esther Kira was now in her hundred and eighth year, showed no signs of slowing down, and enjoyed nothing more than a good intrigue. The times, she often complained, were not nearly as exciting as they had once been.

The current head of the House of Kira was Esther's fifty-three-year-old grandson, Eli, eldest son of her eldest son, Solomon, who had recently died in his mid-eighties. Eli Kira was confused as to what Cousin Pietro expected of him. He had, after all, never even slightly circumvented the law, let alone contemplated breaking it entirely by stealing a woman from someone else's harem. Obedient, however, to the lesson drummed into him since childhood, he immediately consulted with his grandmother.

The once lustrous dark hair was now snow-white, but the currant-black eyes had lost none of their sparkle. Had Cat's great-grandmother Cyra Hafise still been alive, she would easily have recognized her old friend. "I will," she told her worried grandson, "pay a call upon Lateefa Sultan. If this woman is indeed in the harem of Cicalazade Pasha, the princess will know." She chuckled richly. "And if this woman is anything like my lady Cyra . . ." She stopped, and the chuckle became a cackle of laughter. "Aiiiiii! May Yahweh have mercy on the poor vizier!" This information did nothing to reassure Eli Kira of the wisdom of his course, but he was a man of scrupulous honor, and his family's success was due to this woman's family. Therefore he owed her, and he would pay the debt.

Lateefa Sultan was delighted to see Esther Kira. "It has been much too long," she said, settling the old woman comfortably, and directing the slavewomen to bring sweet sherbets and the sticky paste candy that she remembered Esther loved.

"I am old beyond time, my child," said Esther Kira, "and it is not often I go to see friends. My strength is not as it once was."

Lateefa Sultan cocked her head to one side. "You know that I am delighted you are here," she said, "yet I do not fool myself that you have expended your precious strength on a mere social call."

The old woman nodded. "A new woman has recently been introduced into your husband's harem."

"There are many new women, Esther. They come weekly."

"Do not play word games with me, my child. I was old before you were born. You know the one of whom I speak."

"Incili," said Lateefa quietly. "I am quite sure you mean Incili."

"What do you know of this woman, my princess?"

"Very little, Esther. She was sent to my lord by his sister. He is besotted with her." Here Lateefa paused a moment. "It is not common knowledge yet, Esther, but Cicalazade Pasha has—with my permission, of course—taken Incili as his second wife."

Esther Kira sucked in her breath sharply. "Then it must be she whom I seek. Will you introduce me to her, Lateefa Sultan?"

"Who is she, Esther? How do you know of her?"

As they were alone, Esther decided to take the princess into her confidence. She would need her aid. "She was born a noblewoman in her own land," said the old lady. "Her first husband was a great lord of their country, her second a greater lord. She is beloved by her own king, who wanted her for his mistress. She is admired by the French king, who would have been delighted had she remained at his court. And more, Lateefa Sultan. What I would tell you now must remain a secret even from the Lord Cicalazade. Do you agree to it?" The princess nodded. "Your husband's second wife is a great-granddaughter of Cyra Hafise herself. Eighty years ago I smuggled the youngest of Cyra Hafise's and Selim I's sons, Prince Karim, out of the Eski Serai. I put him aboard a ship bound for Scotland. He was accompanied by my brother, Joseph.

"The little prince was six years old, and the last of Selim's sons other than his full older brother, Suleiman. Cyra Hafise was afraid that the child would be a rallying point for malcontents when her husband died and Suleiman ascended the throne. She did not want him killed. Though Suleiman loved his little brother, he would eventually have had to dispose of the boy if his own reign was to stay trouble-free.

"An epidemic of plague struck the city that summer, and Cyra Hafise and I arranged that it appear the little prince had the disease. She took him into isolation. After several days I smuggled the dead body of a child the same size as Prince Karim to her, and I took the living child out the same way. The long-decayed bones resting in the grave of Prince Karim are those of a poor, nameless boy.

"And that, my child, is why the Kiras were exempted from paying taxes when Sultan Suleiman became our ruler. Neither he, nor his father, nor anyone else in this land knew that Prince Karim lived. And in Cyra Hafise's homeland of Scotland, only my brother, Joseph, a priest, and Cyra Hafise's brother and father knew the child's true parentage."

Lateefa's eyes were wide in amazement, and old Esther Kira laughed. "There is more, my child! That was just the beginning of the intrigue. If you were to open the coffin of the great Cyra Hafise herself, you would find naught but stones! Twice Suleiman's favorite wife, Khurrem—may Allah curse her memory—tried to poison my dear lady. My lady Cyra knew but two ways to stop her. Either she had to go, or Khurrem had to go. Cyra Hafise's one weakness was that she loved her son too well. She feigned her own death, and returned to her homeland. Before she did so, however, she told Sultan Suleiman that he must be on his guard against Khurrem in the future. He wept and made a great protest at her secret going, but he heeded her not. Khurrem was later responsible for the deaths of Suleiman's two best sons—Prince Mustafa and Prince Bajazet. This left the misfit Selim II to inherit the Ottoman Empire.

"Do you know the day when Cyra Hafise actually died? On the very same day that Sultan Suleiman did! And Incili is a great-granddaughter of Cyra Hafise and Sultan Selim, and a granddaughter of Prince Karim, as you are a great-granddaughter of Firousi Kadin and Sultan Selim, and a granddaughter of Guzel Sultan." The old woman cackled and nodded her head. "Lateefa Sultan and Incili share more than a husband!"

"Does she know of her imperial ancestry, Esther?"

"I do not know that, my princess, but I would imagine she knows at least some of it."

"Then why has she not spoken?"

"Possibly because she was not sure how to use the information. She has probably not yet decided how to escape from here."

"Escape? Good heavens, Esther! Why would she want to escape from here? My lord is madly in love with her, and she has every luxury money can buy."

"She does not have her freedom, my child. In her land women are free to roam as they please. As for luxury, she is a fabulously wealthy woman in her own

right. But most important of all . . . when she was stolen
away she was a bride of two months, wed to a man she
has loved deeply for many years. He reciprocates her
feelings, and it has been all my nephew in Naples can·
do to keep him from coming with a rescue force to retrieve her. You must help me to aid her in escaping,
Lateefa Sultan."

"I would never deliberately do anything to harm my
lord Cica. He loves Incili as he has never loved anyone
—even me. I do not want him hurt."

"Listen to me, my child. If Incili is one-tenth the
woman her great-grandmother was, she will try to escape. She will die trying rather than be separated forever
from her true husband. Will that not hurt your lord
Cica more? He is a proud man, and if he is openly
scorned by this woman, it will hurt him more. Until now
you have held the place of honor in your husband's
heart and household. But if Incili remains, he will soon
put her above you. Your royal family will be publicly
shamed, which means the sultan will become involved.
Who knows what he will do?"

Lateefa Sultan looked wretchedly uncomfortable for
a moment. Then she clapped her hands and a slave
entered. "Go to the lady Incili, and tell her that Lateefa
Sultan has an old friend visiting whom she would like
to present to her."

When the slave had left the room, Lateefa turned to
Esther Kira. "I have met her only once, but she is
charming. I know that Cica will not accept a ransom
for her. I have never seen him this way about any
woman. He bitterly resents any time spent away from
her."

"And how do you think she feels?" asked the old
woman.

"In public she is quite reserved, but obedient. How
she behaves in the privacy of her bedchamber I do not

know. She has made no effort to make friends with anyone, and will be served only by her own servant, who came with her. The other women of the harem are fearfully jealous of her. She is extravagantly beautiful, Esther. She even makes me a little jealous."

Esther Kira smiled a little smile of remembrance. "Her great-grandmother," she said, "was the most beautiful creature I have ever seen. Her hair was the most fantastic red-gold, and her eyes were green-gold! Sultan Selim worshipped her and, strangely, his other three wives loved her too. Ahhh, my child! Those were the good days! Sultan Selim's four kadins were unselfish women, devoted to the preservation of the dynasty and the empire. Not like those creatures living in the Yeni Serai today who scheme for themselves alone.

"It began, you know, with that wicked Khurrem, and continues right down to the sultan's own mother, Safiye, who today fights with not only her son's favorite, but her grandson's as well! The sultans were once strong, and great warriors even as your own husband, Cicalazade Pasha. It is wicked wives and mothers who have ruined them!" the old woman finished passionately.

As her words died, the door to the apartment opened and a woman entered. She nodded pleasantly to the princess, saying, "Good afternoon, Lateefa Sultan. I have come at your request, and I thank you for including me in your party." Then the green eyes settled on Esther Kira, widened for a moment, and then grew puzzled. The visitor said softly, "But it cannot be."

"But it is!" the old woman chortled triumphantly. "I am one hundred and eight years old, great-granddaughter of Cyra Hafise. She must have described me very well if you recognize me."

"You are really Esther Kira?"

"Yes, child, I am. And Lateefa Sultan is your cousin, for she is the great-granddaughter of my lady Cyra's dearest friend, Firousi Kadin, who was your mutual great-grandfather's second wife. Come, my daughters, you must be friends—as they were."

The two younger woman looked at each other for a moment, and then Lateefa held out her hands to Cat. "Come, Incili. If I am to help you we should be friends, and trust one another."

Cat took the two hands in her own. "I have been very frightened," she said. "Now I no longer need be, knowing that I have friends. Thank you, Lateefa, and you also, Esther Kira."

"Ah, child," said Esther Kira, "how much like my lady Cyra you are when you smile. But otherwise, I should not know you."

"They say I look like my great-grandmother's mother," she replied.

The three women sat down around a low table, and the old lady leaned forward. "Your husband, my dear, is still safe in Naples, though restraining him and your captain-at-arms has not been easy. If you will please write and reassure him I will see that the letter is safely delivered. We have yet to come up with a plan for your escape. But, be patient. We will."

"My tiring woman was captured with me, Esther, and she must return with me. I cannot leave her behind."

Esther Kira shrugged philosophically. "One is impossible, two is only slightly more impossible."

Suddenly the doors flew open and Cicalazade Pasha strode into their midst. Lateefa and Cat rose quickly and bowed prettily. "Esther Kira!" boomed the vizier. "They told me you had ventured out, old friend. What brings you to my house?"

"I came to see the new beauty who has won your crusty heart, my lord. And Lateefa Sultan tells me the rumors in the city are true. You have taken a second wife. I have spent a pleasant time this afternoon being cosseted by your wives and having a good gossip."

The vizier beamed and put a possessive arm about each of the two young women. "The sultan himself would envy me my luck, eh, Esther? Is my Lateefa not sweet?" The princess gazed adoringly at her husband, who glanced fondly but briefly at her before turning hungry eyes on Cat. "And is my Incili not a rare and perfect jewel?"

Esther Kira saw the steel in the smile Cat turned on Cicalazade Pasha, and the tenseness of her body. This woman is a survivor, she thought to herself. We will get her safely to her husband.

She signaled to a slave, who helped her to her feet. "I must go, my dears. It has been a lovely visit." She turned to the vizier. "You will let your wives come to visit with me, will you not, my lord?"

"Of course, Esther, of course! In fact, I believe my Incili would enjoy being able to visit in the city. She chafes at confinement, don't you, my dove?"

"A bit, my lord Cica," came the soft-spoken reply.

"Then I will tell Hammid you both have my permission to shop and visit in the city whenever you want—provided, of course, that you go in a closed litter, and are chaperoned." Though he spoke to them both he saw only Cat. "Come, Incili," he said, "I desire your presence." He looked again at Esther. "You honor my house, my friend. Thank you for coming. Lateefa will arrange a proper escort for you. Come, Incili!" And he and Cat were gone.

Alone, Lateefa said softly, "You see how he is, Esther? He is wild for her. He will spend the rest of this afternoon, the evening, and the entire night in her company. Only a summons from the sultan will move him from her side."

"She does not love him, my princess. She endures the

situation so that she may survive and escape. She is
made of the same steel as Cyra Hafise. I see determination in her eyes, and the same firm set of the mouth
as my dear lady had."

Lateefa sighed. "She is so very beautiful. It is no
wonder Cica loves her."

"Beauty, pash!" snorted the old woman. "Beauty is a
flower that fades quickly, my child. If the vizier loves
her only for her beauty then he is a fool. Like her great-
grandmother, Incili is a many-faceted woman. Besides,
you are the image of Firousi Kadin, my dear, and she
was considered as lovely as Cyra Hafise. Now, child,
I really must go. Help me to my litter."

And leaning on Lateefa Sultan, Esther Kira made her
way out of the courtyard.

Chapter 54

❧❦❧

WITHIN the privacy of her bedchamber or his, the grand vizier insisted that his second wife be completely naked. Her tawny gold hair was pulled back and braided in one large braid, the hair mixed with jeweled ribbons. She was permitted to wear her thin gold and silver bracelets and anklets. She was expected to serve him unquestioningly in all his desires. She did so, quietly aware that this was the key to her survival. Outwardly sweet and calm, Cat raged inwardly at every humiliation. This sudden thrusting of her person into an age where women counted less than horses was a terrible shock.

When Cicalazade Pasha desired Incili, all the other slaves were instantly dismissed from his presence. He particularly enjoyed having her serve him in his bath. There she was expected to join him in the warm water, gently bathing his entire body with sweet soaps. Afterwards they rubbed one another's bodies with scented oils. These sessions generally ended as one might expect.

Cat, far from flattered, could not help but feel denigrated by the vizier's unquenchable desire. The fact of his keeping her nude was offensive, as well as a blatant invitation to his lust. He was insatiable, often taking her three and four times in a single night. Only her indomitable spirit and her passionate desire to escape kept Cat unbroken.

Most important to Cat was her friendship with Lateefa Sultan. The knowledge that they were cousins
descended from Selim I and that their great-grand-
mothers had been the best of friends invited their own
friendship. Lateefa told Cat stories she had heard from
her grandmother, Guzel, stories of Guzel's childhood.
Then the wives and children of Prince Selim lived above
the shores of the Black Sea in a palace known as the
Moonlight Serai. There was a feeling of love to these
stories. Respect for Cyra Hafise was also evident in
them.

"I wish I had known her," said Lateefa. "Grandmother Guzel and her sister, my Aunt Hale, always
spoke of her with such love. She treated them as she
treated her own daughter, Nilufer Sultan."

"I knew her," said Cat. "She died when I was a child
of four, but I remember a beautiful and imperious old
lady whose many grandchildren, grandnieces and
grandnephews always deferred to her. In the great hall
of Glenkirk Castle there is a large portrait of her,
painted just before she came to Turkey. It was always
difficult for me to reconcile the painting of that beautiful, proud young girl with the imperious, elegant old
woman."

Lateefa's eyes sparkled mischievously, and she leaned
forward and whispered conspiratorially, "Our religion
forbids the painting of the human form but Firousi
Kadin was an artist of some talent. She painted many
little portraits of the family, and when she died she
passed them on to her daughter, my grandmother Guzel,
who passed them on to me. Come—I will show you!"
She clapped her hands and said to the slave who answered her summons, "Fetch the red lacquer chest at
the bottom of the large brassbound cedar chest."

When the small chest was carefully placed in her lap,
Lateefa opened it reverently. The box was divided into

several trays. Lateefa gently lifted a piece of velvet from the top tray, revealing six oval miniatures. There were two men and four women. Cat recognized her own great-grandmother and her best friend, Firousi Kadin, whose great-granddaughter Lateefa was her image.

The princess smiled. "Beautiful, weren't they? The Chinese is Zuleika Kadin, Selim I's third wife. The tempestous-looking girl with the amber-gold eyes is Sarina Kadin, his fourth wife. The younger of the men is Sultan Suleiman, Cyra's eldest son. The older man is Sultan Selim I."

Cat stared at these people and at their offspring, whose miniatures were hidden in the subsequent trays. She was particularly enchanted with the chubby-cheeked toddler whom she learned was Prince Karim—her grandfather, Charles Leslie, the first Earl of Sithean! Born and raised a Scot, Cat had never even considered this small part of her heritage, yet there was no denying that her maternal grandfather had been born an Ottoman prince even if he had lived most of his life as a Scot. She had just as much right to the title "Sultan" after her name as Lateefa had, though no one would ever know that fact.

"It is so strange," said Cat, "for me to realize that some of these people are also *my* ancestors."

"Knowing it, dearest Incili, can you not be happy with us?"

Cat sighed patiently. Her cousin was such a child. "Lateefa," she said quietly, "I am no child as Cyra was when she came to this land. Behind me are my second husband, for whom I defied my own king, and my nine children. I cannot simply dismiss these people from my heart. I do not love Cica. I love my true husband, Lord Bothwell.

"You, who do love the vizier, and have been his wife for so many years, should want only the best for him.

Help me to escape, my cousin! Help me to return to
my own lord! How would *you* feel if you were stolen
from Cica, and forced to be wife to another? Do you
know that the vizier always keeps me naked in his
presence? That I am allowed to wear only ribbons and
baubles?"

Lateefa flushed a delicate rose. Her voice was a whisper. "I did not know, Incili. He has ever been the
sensualist. 'Tis why I never minded when he gathered
a large harem. The others sated his appetite, so that
after our children were born I was relatively free of
his demands. I do not enjoy such things. Do you?"

"Only with my true lord, and then very much. Each
time I must pretend to submit to our lord Cica it pains
me. I feel less a real woman, more a doll, a thing."

Lateefa nodded, and then confided to Cat, "Once
several years ago, Cica and my cousin, Sultan Mohammed, had a contest to see how many virgins they could
take within the period of one day. Mohammed won,
deflowering twenty-four helpless girls. Cica, however,
was but one behind him, so they decided the real winner
would be he who had impregnated the most girls. The
sultan won with sixteen ripe maidens. Only nine of
Cica's girls bore children.

"Lateefa, please!" Cat protested. "Let us visit Esther
Kira tomorrow. I must plan my escape or I shall go
mad. And see if our friend Hammid can find some
tempting young charmers to divert Cica from my bed—
even if only occasionally!"

The princess nodded sympathetically, and on the
following day the vizier's two wives honored the Kira
house with a visit. There Cat was able to write a brief
note to Francis, assuring him of her safety, her love for
him, and her desire to be speedily reunited with him.
She saw the note dispatched, and then, turning to
Esther, she asked, "Have you come up with a plan for
my escape yet, Esther Kira?"

"Possibly, but your husband will have to come to Istanbul to aid us in our plan." She looked to Lateefa. "Go into the garden, my child. When Cicalazade Pasha asks you if you know how Incili escaped, I should prefer you to answer honestly that you do not know."

The princess nodded her agreement and gratitude, and left them alone. "I would," the old woman continued, "have your husband come to us traveling the same route you will return by. If it is familiar to him it will be easier later. Your pursuers will not expect you to travel overland. So you will do just that, at least partway.

"You will leave by small boat, and go down the Sea of Marmara through the Dardanelles into the Aegean Sea. Once there you will cross to the island of Lemnos, and from there to Thessaly. You will enter the Peneus River at its mouth, and travel upstream to its source in the mountains. When you can go no farther on the Peneus you will continue on foot across the hills to the Aous River, where a second boat will await you. You will then sail it all the way downstream into the Adriatic Sea, and cross over to Italy. Both these rivers run through sparsely populated areas, and except for two small towns on the Peneus you should encounter no one. There is always danger of recapture, however, for you travel exclusively within the boundaries of the Ottoman Empire until you land in Italy. If you are caught it will mean death."

"Better death with Bothwell than life with Cicalazade Pasha," said Cat fiercely. "When, Esther Kira? When?"

The old woman shook her head. "I never expected to meet another like Cyra Hafise. What do they feed you in that wild land of your birth, Incili, that makes its women so determined?"

Cat smiled slowly, the smile lighting her face with savage joy. "They feed us *freedom*, Esther Kira. Large doses of pure freedom, self-reliance, and independence!

Now . . . when? When will I be able to shake the dust of this land from my slippers?"

"Patience, child! First we must smuggle your husband and his man into Constantinople. Then we must keep them hidden here, and wait for the right moment. When it arrives you must come at once, bringing nothing but your servant. What you need we will supply."

"You will tell me when he is safely here, Esther?"

"No, my child, I will not. If you knew you could not play the part of the vizier's loving second wife. I will contact you when it is time to make good your escape."

Cat felt the tears prick at her eyelids, and she swallowed back the lump in her throat. "You are right," she admitted. "I would not endanger him." Then a thought struck her. "Esther, where did my great-grandmother live when her son became sultan?"

"In the Eski Serai, the old palace. But it is in disrepair, and damaged by fire. No one has lived there since the time of Selim II. Why do you ask?"

"Are the rooms in which my great-grandmother lived still there?"

"Yes, child. The rooms were sealed by order of her son at the time of her 'official' death. Twenty-four years ago there was a terrible fire in the Eski Serai, but her apartments were in the Forest Court, separated from the rest of the harem, and the fire never reached there."

"I would go there, Esther Kira! In the rush of her secret departure, Cyra Hafise left something behind that was very precious to her. I know where it is, and I want it!"

The old lady's eyes sparkled. "I will take you there myself, child. I have not seen the Eski Serai since the great fire, and I have not been in Cyra Hafise's apartments in over fifty years. Once more before I die I would revisit my youth. Go into the garden and fetch Lateefa Sultan. We will never get away from the overvigilant Osman without her. Do you mind if she comes with us?"

"Not as long as she will agree that, should I find what I seek, it is mine."

"She will agree."

When Lateefa Sultan heard of what Cat and old Esther Kira planned she clapped her hands enthusiastically. "I have never been in the Eski Serai," she told them. "My grandmother lived outside it after her marriage, and my father was born in Guzel's house, not the palace."

"Who was your mother?" asked Cat.

"My mother was Aisha Sultan, the daughter of Cyra Hafise's only daughter, Nilufer, sister to your grandfather."

"Then we are doubly related," said Cat, surprised. "Why did you not tell me? What I seek could rightfully belong to you as a great-grandchild of Cyra Hafise."

"No, my cousin. Whatever you seek, you have the stronger claim, since you descend through the male line while I descend from the female. The right is yours, and besides—" the lovely turquoise eyes twinkled—"I somehow think Cyra would want you to have whatever it is. You are surely more like her than I am. Now let us go and fend off the diligent Osman so our visit may be a private one."

In the courtyard of the house, Esther Kira settled herself comfortably in her own large litter while the bearers stood ready. In the second litter Cat sat listening while Lateefa ordered their chaperon to remain behind.

"Master Kira is supplying us with a dozen guards," she told the eunuch. "Esther Kira and I would show Incili where my great-grandmother lived. There is no need for you to go. Stay and continue your visit with your friend, Ali."

Torn between duty and the very pleasant time he was having with the Kira family's head eunuch, Osman hesitated. As he did so, Cat slid from the litter, her leaf-green eyes narrowing dangerously above her gossamer veil.

"Insect!" she hissed at him. "How dare you disobey my lady Lateefa Sultan? If you do not return inside the house this instant I shall tell my lord Cica of your insolence towards his first wife. He will have you beaten to death for your rudeness!" And turning her back on him she smiled wickedly at Lateefa, who was struggling to hold back her laughter. The frightened eunuch turned ashen and then fled into the house.

As the two women settled themselves into the litter, Lateefa chuckled softly. "You may have been born a Scot, my Western cousin, but there is Ottoman in you. And it shows!"

"When the enemy hesitates, Lateefa, never give him a chance to regroup either his thoughts or his forces. 'Tis an old highland battle tactic."

The two litters were swiftly carried through the noisy streets until, as the noise began to fade, Cat could feel the bearers straining uphill. Finally they stopped. Leaning over, Lateefa drew the curtains aside. Stepping out, she offered a hand to Cat, who quickly joined her cousin.

Before them stood the fire-racked ruins of the once-great palace which had long ago crowned one of Constantinople's seven hills. Below them, sparkling in all its late-afternoon glory, was the Golden Horn. They saw the city itself and, off in the distance, both the Yeni Serai and the blue Bosporus. For a moment the three women stood transfixed, then Esther Kira said, "Come, my children, and I will show you the Forest Court where the great Cyra Hafise once lived." She signaled to two of the guards to follow them. "They can hear, but are mute," she said with a crafty smile. "They can say nothing of what they see or hear."

They followed the old woman around the crumbling walls of the Eski Serai until they came to a small iron gate overgrown with weeds. Here Esther stopped and said to their escort, "Cut the growth just enough so that we may pass, but not enough to cause notice in anyone else passing by."

"What if the gate is locked?" asked Lateefa.

"It should be, my dear, but I was entrusted with a key which will—after all these years—probably still work." So saying, she stepped forward and carefully tried the cobwebbed lock. After a moment of jiggling the cranky lock turned with a creeking noise. The rusted hinges protesting, the gate slowly opened. "Remain here," Esther commanded their mutes, and then she walked slowly into what had once been the garden of Cyra Hafise. The area was waist-high in ferns, weeds, and autumn flowers. They overran the once neat boundaries of their original beds and the mossy brick walks. The garden had been carefully tended until the fire of 1574. But now the hedges—untrimmed these last twenty-four years—stood like high green walls along the gravel paths. To the amazement of the three women, the fountains were still operable, and filled with not only water lilies gone wild, but enormous goldfish as well.

"Where does the water come from?" asked Cat.

"It is pumped underground from one of the old Byzantine or Roman aqueducts. This was originally an imperial palace when Mohammed the Conqueror took the city from the Byzantines. Ah, there is the Forest Court of Cyra Hafise."

Cat shivered suddenly. Never in her wildest dreams had she expected to be in Istanbul, let alone in the very palace from which her great-grandmother—that imperious old woman—had secretly ruled an empire. This was one of the places where Cyra had been young, beautiful, and very much loved by a great sultan. Cat had never before thought of Cyra in this way, the memory of the old woman being too strong. Awestruck, she followed Lateefa as Esther Kira opened a door into the building and stepped through into a dust-covered, cobweb-laden room.

All was still. Cat shivered again, feeling about her the ghosts of the past. Beside her Esther Kira stood lost in memory.

As Cat's eyes grew accustomed to the gloom, they sought and quickly found the tile fireplace wall. Walking over to it, she carefully looked for the thistle tile mentioned by her son. Finding it, she gently pressed the tile, and it fell into her hand. Without a moment's hesitation she reached into the opening, smiling as her fingers found and curled about a hard object in a soft, rotting velvet bag. Drawing it forth, she opened the bag, drew the pendant out, and triumphantly held it high. "Do your old eyes recognize this, Esther Kira?" And she danced over to the old woman, holding the pendant out to her.

Esther Kira nodded and smiled with remembrance. "The pendant made by Selim I himself to celebrate the birth of his first child, Sultan Suleiman! Look on the back. Here is his tugra. Why did she not take it with her, Incili? She prized it above all her jewels."

"In the rush of departure, young Ruth missed it. They did not even realize it was not among her things until they reached Scotland. My eldest son gave me a copy of the pendant this New Year's. Since I am here, I thought I should like to retrieve the original. I would like you to keep it for me, Esther, or better yet send it to the Kira bank in Rome for me. When I escape I should not like to be encumbered with such a valuable jewel."

"You are wise to trust me with it, Incili. If it were found among your things it would be difficult to explain. I will wager that the vizier does not give you enough pin money to account for such an expensive toy!"

"Let me see it," asked Lateefa softly. And she reverently took it from the old woman's gnarled hands. "It is beautiful! How much he loved her. He placed her above all women. How wonderful to be loved like that! So few of us ever are." Sighing, she handed the pendant back to Esther Kira, who returned it to its bag and placed the bag in a pocket somewhere within her voluminous robes.

For a few minutes longer the women wandered about the imperial apartments of the long-dead Sultan Valide, Cyra Hafise. Cat could not shake the feeling that she was intruding. Replacing the thistle tile, she regretted that she had not thought to ask Susan along. Susan's grandmother, Ruth, had spent her early years in this very palace.

Finally Esther led them back out through the garden again to their litters. As they returned to the Kira house, both Cat and Lateefa were strangely silent. In the courtyard of the house they hugged the old lady and thanked her profusely for the tour as Osman stood fussily by, wanting to hurry them but not daring to do so. Returning to the vizier's palace, they talked softly of the secrets they shared, bound even more closely by the afternoon.

Cicalazade Pasha awaited them impatiently. His eyes were narrow, his expression sulky, and they should have been warned. But both Lateefa and Cat were happy, exhilarated by their outing.

"Where have you been?" he demanded. "I returned from the Yeni Serai to find my house deserted."

"We have been visiting Esther Kira, my lord," said Lateefa merrily. "She took us to the old Eski Serai, and we showed Incili where the great Cyra Hafise once lived. It was a delightful afternoon, and we thank you for giving us your permission to go."

"I have spent the afternoon devoid of companionship," complained the vizier.

"My lord Cica," teased Lateefa, smiling winningly up

at him, "you have the most famous harem in the empire
—next to my cousin, the sultan. I cannot believe that
you were bored other than by choice."

Without warning the vizier's hand shot out and
slapped Lateefa's face. Astounded, she gasped, her eyes
filling with tears. Shocked, for he had never been known
to beat his wife, the slaves stood impassive, scarcely
breathing. But Cat flew at the vizier, furiously beating
on his chest. "Don't you dare touch her!" she raged at
him. "She did nought to you! You are unkind and
unfair!"

Truly frightened now, Lateefa tried to pull Cat away.
"No! No! Incili, you must beg my lord Cica's pardon,"
and she attempted to draw Cat down to her knees.

Cat turned from the vizier and gently touched Lateefa's cheek. A handprint showed white against the
red. "Never! He had no right to slap you."

"He has every right," said Lateefa, desperately trying
to stem the anger she saw burning in Cicalazade's gray-
blue eyes. "He is our lord and master. We are nothing
but that which he makes us, Incili."

"You can't really believe that?" pleaded Cat.

Turning, Lateefa knelt before the vizier, her head
touching the toe of his outstretched boot. "Forgive me
my insolence, my lord, and forgive her also. She is still
new to our ways, and I know she meant no harm!"

Cicalazade Pasha put a gentle hand on Lateefa's
head. "I will forgive her for your sake, my dear. But
she must still be punished, lest others in my house think
I am a weak master." He nodded curtly to two eunuchs,
who grasped Cat by the arms. "Take her to the whipping
post and prepare her for punishment," he commanded.

"Oh, my lord," sobbed Lateefa, raising a tear-stained
face to him, "please do not whip Incili. She is my
friend!"

The vizier again nodded to a eunuch. "Take the lady Lateefa to her apartments," he said quietly. Afraid, Lateefa obeyed him.

The eunuchs dragged Cat into the center of the courtyard, where, after removing her jacket, they chained her between two posts. Her gauze blouse was ripped away entirely, baring not only her long, lovely back, but her full breasts. Slowly the vizier walked across the courtyard and stood silent beside her for what seemed an eternity. Then, cruelly grasping her tawny hair, he pulled her head back and said in a soft voice, "The punishment will be mild this time, Incili, but *never* defy me again— publicly or otherwise. I adore you, my jewel, but I will not be shamed. That is why I will personally mete out this chastisement. If you will beg my pardon I will cease. Otherwise you will receive the full twenty lashes." He bent his head and kissed her fiercely, laughing softly.

She bit him on the lower lip, drawing blood.

"Little bitch."

He loosed her head and she heard him walk back across the courtyard, where Osman waited with the whip. "Fool!" The vizier swore at a eunuch. "Ply the lash. I don't want her skin marked like a crocodile's!"

The suspense was terrible, and Cat felt her heart pounding with a mixture of fright and anger. The whip cracked several times as the vizier tested it, and her stomach heaved uneasily. Then she heard a sharp hiss, and the first blow touched her back. Her teeth bit into her own lip now, also drawing blood. The third blow drew a soft moan from her, the fifth a small cry. On the eighth she could bear no more. She screamed, unable to bear the cruel pain. For he was not being gentle. Her back was afire, and the pain grew worse with each blow, yet she would not beg his pardon. Finally, unable to endure any more, she fainted. But Osman was quickly there, waving a burnt feather beneath her nose, dragging her back to the terrible reality of consciousness.

"Miserable woman," he chortled, "you will not escape your punishment!"

Forcing her eyes open, she glared at him with an icy green stare. She heard Hammid's voice saying, "You are a fool to antagonize her, Osman. The lady Incili is not out of favor, nor is she likely to be. She is only disobedient." Then the chief eunuch's face came into view. "Yield to him, my daughter."

The whip bit into her burning back. "Never!" she managed to gasp as the blackness rose up to claim her again.

The eunuch shook his head, then called out, "She craves your pardon, my lord." The look on his face dared Osman to challenge his word.

"Release her," commanded Cicalazade Pasha, "and see that her back is tended to at once. I shall expect her in my bed later this evening."

They carried her to her apartments, where both Lateefa and a white-faced Susan waited. Carefully the slavewoman removed the rest of Cat's clothing, and she was placed stomach down on her bed. Her back was a mass of angry red welts, and Susan began to weep.

"How could he? How could he? No one has ever treated my lady thus! No one!"

"Do not weep, girl," said Lateefa kindly. "It looks worse than it really is. See. The lash was plied, and the skin is not broken. There will be no scars, and in a few days both the pain and the welts will be gone." Then she carefully bathed the injured back herself with cool water, and gently rubbed a pale-green cream into the welts. "It's a special salve," she told Susan, "and it will take some of the pain from the welts. Now sit by your mistress until I return."

Lateefa hurried through the corridors of the palace

to her husband's apartments. "I would beg leave to speak with you alone," she said humbly. Dismissing the slaves, he motioned for her to sit by him. "I myself have cared for Incili's injuries, my lord, but she will be un-available to you for at least two or three days. She is yet unconscious, and running a slight fever. You pun-ished her cruelly, Cica. Had the lash not been plied you could have killed her."

"She will be all right?" he asked anxiously, and La-teefa's heart contracted at the worry in his voice. Esther Kira is right, she thought. "I did not mean to hurt her," the vizier continued, "but she was so defiant! She would not beg my pardon until eleven lashes had been meted out."

"What did you expect, Cica?" asked Lateefa quietly. "This is no peasant girl you've taken for your second wife. This is a proud European noblewoman. She is used to speaking her mind. I am trying to teach her our ways, but it will take time. You must be patient with her."

"You like her," he said. "I am glad! I am glad that you have become friends."

"Yes, we are friends, Cica. Now, please, my lord, give her a few days to heal both her back and her spirit. She will not forgive you easily. This time I am afraid you will have to amuse yourself with your harem. You have ignored them shamefully since Incili came, and there is an outright rebellion there, my lord. Hammid can tell you."

"Very well," he acquiesced sulkily. "I give her three days. At the end of that time I expect her back in my bed, docile and obedient to my will."

Lateefa bit back the smile that threatened to burst forth. "It will be as you wish, my lord husband," she answered him quietly, and she left him to return to Cat's bedchamber.

"How is she?" she asked Susan.

"Still unconscious. A bit restless too, my lady."

"Go to your bed, Mara. Your mistress received this punishment in defense of me. It is only right that I sit with her tonight. Bring me my embroidery before you retire."

During the first few hours, Lateefa Sultan sat quietly, plying her needle. Twice she trimmed the wicks of the lamps and refilled them with scented oil. Once she rubbed the green salve into Cat's back again. Her eyes grew tired and blurred with the ache of watching the colored threads on the snow-white linen. She admired the beautiful lines of her cousin's back and buttocks, wondering if she really enjoyed a man's lovemaking as she said, or if she hated it as Lateefa did.

Within the harem there were those women who loved each other, Lateefa knew. This sort of thing was forbidden, but the eunuchs had a tendency to turn a blind eye to it, as a happy woman caused less trouble than an unhappy one. Lateefa was above the women of the harem by birth and by rank. None of them would dare approach her, and she had never approached any of them. She wondered whether a woman lover would be as rough as Cicalazade was.

Cat moaned, still unconscious, and turned over, calling, "Francis! Francis!"

Lateefa was stunned by the beauty of her cousin's breasts and torso. They were flawless and creamy. Bending over, Lateefa said softly, "Hush, Incili. It's all right now, my dear."

But Cat called again. "Francis! Francis! Oh, yes, my love! Yes!"

Lateefa could not understand the words, for they were not Turkish, but she could see from the look on her cousin's face what it was she dreamed about. It was the face of a woman being made love to by a man she adored. Cat thrashed slightly. Fearful that she would injure herself, Lateefa reached out to quiet her. Her hand brushed the unconscious woman's breast. Instantly the nipple sprang erect, and Cat moaned. Unable to help herself, Lateefa reached out and caressed the soft globe of rounded flesh, feeling a thrill as the beautiful woman on the bed strained to her touch.

Trembling, the princess rose from her chair and divested herself of her robes. She lay down on the bed next to Cat, her shaking hands caressing the naked body of her unconscious cousin, careful to avoid the sore back. Cat writhed beneath the touch. Lateefa bent her head, eagerly licking Cat's nipples. Cat moaned again, and Lateefa turned over on her stomach, her fingers teasing at her own womanhood, her hips moving against the action of her own hand until she collapsed with a great sigh of relief onto the mattress.

For a few minutes she lay there, flushed, her breath ragged. Then she rose from the bed, dressed, and picked up her embroidery. She sat back down in her chair, stunned by what she had done.

In the beginning of their marriage Cica had often made her caress him, and she had hated it. She had not hated touching Cat. Cat's skin was smooth and lovely. She dozed, to be awakened later by Susan's gentle touch.

"Let me watch now, my lady," said the girl softly. Nodding her silent thanks, Lateefa Sultan gratefully departed for her own bed, and for the shy, pretty new slavegirl she had recently acquired, who would be waiting up for her. The girl was lonely and frightened, Lateefa knew. Several times her hands had touched her mistress intimately. Blushing prettily with confusion, the girl had begged her pardon. Lateefa had thought nothing of it. Now, however, she knew that the girl would respond to her favor and her kindness, should she decide to proffer them. Cicalazade Pasha might take ten women to his bed every night. His wife Lateefa Sultan no longer intended being lonely.

Chapter 55

❧❦❧

THREE nights later, her back sufficiently healed, Cat was back in Cicalazade's bed. Her return was a sulky and defiant one, but the vizier was bored with the succession of compliant beauties who had recently shared his bed and chose to be amused rather than angry. It was this very show of independence that made her interesting to him.

Though Cat came to understand his position, she could not forgive him.

The Christian New Year of 1599 began, and Cat, standing alone on Lateefa's terrace overlooking the sea, found herself straining to hear the sound of the Glenkirk bagpipe. A single tear slid down her cheek, and she wondered if Francis were with the Kiras yet.

The winter deepened, and the vizier's passion for her did not abate. She no longer fought against him, having accepted that she must endure her fate until she could change it. With the new year she instinctively knew that Bothwell was near. Soon she would escape! The early spring came, and with it arrived problems along the Hungarian-Austrian border of the empire. The sultan would send Cicalazade Pasha to the border.

Mohammed III was a big man with fair skin, deep brown eyes, and black hair, beard, and mustache. He could be kinder than most and crueler than any man alive. Upon his ascension four years earlier he had or-

dered the execution of his nineteen brothers, the oldest
of whom was eleven, and he had drowned the seven of
his father's concubines who had had the misfortune to
be pregnant.

His sexual appetite was legendary. His beautiful
Venetian mother, Safiye, had encouraged his every desire in an effort to remain in control of him.

The sultan had one admirable trait. He was loyal to
those who were loyal to him, and treated the men who
served him with great kindness and generosity. Noting
the crestfallen expression on his vizier's face, he asked,
"What is it that stems your enthusiasm, Cica? A year
ago you would have been eager for an assignment like
this one."

The vizier sighed. "You will think me a fool, my
padishah, but last year I took a second wife, and I am
saddened at the thought of being away from her."

The sultan's eyes glittered. "I had heard that she is
an exquisite creature. Is it true then?"

Cicalazade Pasha sighed again. "She consumes me
with her beauty!"

"Take her with you, then. There is nothing unusual
about a woman on campaign with her master."

"Thank you, my lord, but no," said the vizier, genuine regret in his voice. "If I took Incili with me, I
should not attend to my lord's best interests."

The sultan chuckled. "I am grateful that you put our
interests above your lust. But tell me, Cica, do you dare
to leave Lateefa and your new wife together? They will
undoubtedly tear each other and your house apart in
your absence."

"Nay, sire! 'Tis amazing, but they are like sisters. In
fact, several months ago I was obliged to chastise Lateefa, and Incili flew at me like a vixen in an effort to
defend her friend. I beat her for her insolence, of
course."

The sultan nodded sympathetically. "You were wise, my friend. Women are good only for one thing. They must ever be taught who is master." Then he clapped his vizier on the shoulder. "Cheer up, my friend! You'll only be gone a few months, and think how eager your Incili will be for your return."

The two men laughed companionably, and then the sultan said, "If Lateefa and Incili are friends, Cica, why not have them both in the same bed with you? Taking two women at once is delicious." He lowered his voice so that only Cicalazade would hear him. The vizier's eyes narrowed, then grew wide, and he replied, "I will try that when I get home, my lord. It sounds most diverting."

The sultan's eyes were dreamy. "It is, my friend. It is very diverting." Then he grew businesslike again. "I will have Yakub Bey see to the readiness of your troops. He is to be your second-in-command. Take your wife Incili to your island for a few days, but be ready to leave a week from now. Allah go with you."

Cicalazade Pasha rode back through the late morning to his palace. "Have Incili transported to the Island of a Thousand Flowers within the next few hours," he commanded Hammid. "I want the island well stocked with fruits, nuts, coffee, sherbets, eggs, and sweets. One hot meal daily is to be delivered in the early evening. I will allow only two servants on the island to serve us. Send Incili's woman, Mara, and a young eunuch."

Towards midafternoon Cat found herself being rowed down the Bosporus in the vizier's caique. Susan sat opposite her, wide-eyed, and a young eunuch sat in the front of the boat.

"Why," asked Susan, "are we being hurried to the island?"

"Because the vizier is being sent to quell a disturbance and will not be back for several months." She lowered her voice and spoke in Scots English. "Just a little while more, Susan, and I shall be free of him for the next few months." She did not tell her serving woman that she had received a message from Esther Kira that very afternoon, shoved into her hand by a jewelry vendor visiting the vizier's harem.

The message had read, "Make an excuse to stay on the island when it is time for the vizier to leave."

She had later burned the paper in a brazier, amazed that the Kiras already knew the vizier's plans when she herself had only just learned of them.

Unused to the East, she could not know that gossip was important in keeping up with current events. At the same time the vizier had been with the sultan, Esther Kira had been with the sultan's mother. After the vizier had left the palace, the sultan had joined his mother and her elderly friend for coffee. He related with some amusement how loath was his good friend Cica to leave his new bride. They had all enjoyed a good laugh at the vizier's expense. Esther Kira had returned home to inform Francis Stewart-Hepburn that he would, in a few days' time, be reunited with his wife.

The plan was really quite simple. They would wait until the vizier and his army were several days' march from the city, and then Lord Bothwell and Conall would take the island, killing the slaves. It would be several days more before the vizier's household discovered the absence of Incili and Mara. By that time they would all be on the Aegean.

Of all this, Cat knew nothing. When they arrived on the island, Cat delighted in showing Susan the gardens. They were alone but for a white eunuch, Feisal, the caique having returned to the vizier's palace. Cat showed the two servants the two tiny cubicles where they were to remain once the master arrived. They were expected to be useful but as invisible as possible.

No sooner had the vizier arrived than he commanded Cat to remove her garments. She protested. "I spend a fortune on clothes and jewels to please you, my lord Cica, and you rarely allow me to wear them."

"Wear them for your friends. I love you as Allah fashioned you."

Pouting, she obeyed him, slowly and teasingly removing each article of clothing as his eyes glittered hungrily. Susan then served them a hot supper. Cat noted that the meal was filled with foods and spices considered conducive to lovemaking. She shuddered imperceptibly, knowing that the next three days would be exhausting.

When the dishes had been cleared away, the vizier told Susan, "You may sleep, Mara. But tell Feisal to remain on call in his chamber."

"Yes, master," replied Susan as she left the room.

Now he turned his gaze on Cat. "Come here, Incili," and she moved around the low table next to him. Drawing her across his lap, he sighed with contentment as his hands began caressing her.

"Look at me," he commanded, and she raised her green eyes to meet his gray-blue ones. It was as she had feared. The pupils of his eyes were dilated, and tiny gold flames danced within them. He had obviously consumed a quantity of aphrodisiacs, and would be utterly insatiable. She trembled, and he laughed as if he knew her thoughts.

His deep voice was low and intimate. "We do not have to hurry, my love. Indeed, we will not," and his free hand slid between her legs to caress her. She felt her strength ebbing as the familiar languorous feelings began to wash over her. At first his touch was delicate, but it soon became an irritation. She tried to squirm away from him but he held her fast.

Cat began to experience a warmth where he touched her, and a moan escaped her. She could not believe it, but she was fast losing control of herself, sliding away into a rainbow world where exquisite sensation followed exquisite sensation until she was gasping with a passion she was unable to stop. It occurred to her vaguely that he had fed her the same aphrodisiacs he had taken.

Frightened, she cried out and tried to sit up, but he gently lifted her from his lap and placed her carefully on the colored cushions, her fair-skinned body in startling contrast against the deep, rich colors of the velvets and satins. Looming over her, he looked like a colossus as he stripped his wide trousers off. Her heart beat wildly at the sight of his long, smooth, well-muscled legs. He knelt and, pushing her legs up, found with his mouth the place where his fingers had lately been. Soon satisfied that he had rendered her mindless, he drew her legs back down. Pulling himself up, he drove into her. She sobbed with relief.

He thrust cruelly back and forth, deliberately hurting her, yet the pain he inflicted was a part of the wildly sensual experience and she relished it. He caught a nipple in his teeth and bit down sharply on it. She screamed and tried to twist away, but then his hot tongue licked furiously at the injured nipple, soothing away the hurt.

She began to shiver violently and, unable to control it, she panicked. Desperately she sought to escape the man responsible for what was happening to her. But now, his passion mounting uncontrollably, he was unreachable. She fought him. She was being violently assaulted, buffeted by a stronger sexual force than she had ever known, and she simply couldn't handle it. Then suddenly it was over, and she was falling, falling away into the sweet peaceful darkness of unconsciousness.

A gentle stroking of her body was her first awareness of returning consciousness. Cat lay quietly with her eyes closed. Her whole being rebelled at this sensuous man who called her "wife," yet treated her solely as an object for his pleasure.

"Open your eyes, Incili."

She obeyed, keeping her lashes modestly lowered lest he see the terrible mixture of fear and repulsion she felt.

"It is time for you to bathe me, Incili."

"Yes, my lord Cica," she answered. Rising from the bed, she walked across the room to the bath. She was amazed that her legs could hold up. At her call the eunuch came and the bath was made ready. Her slim fingers decanted the bottles holding the both oils. She sniffed each, finally choosing an attar of roses. Pouring it into the tub, she dismissed the eunuch and called to the vizier, "Your bath is ready, my lord."

Naked, Cicalazade Pasha came into the bath, where Cat waited to serve him. He stood quietly while she laved his body with warm water. Now her hands were gently rubbing a soft soap over his broad chest and back. Kneeling, she soaped his legs, and his genitals quivered. She quickly caught up a boar's-bristle brush and scrubbed him down, sluicing him once more with warm, fresh water.

"There, my lord," she said briskly, "you may now soak in your tub."

The voice that answered her was amused. "Thank you, my love. Wash quickly, and join me," and he submerged himself in the large square green-tiled pool.

Slowly she soaped herself, putting off the moment when she must join him in the bath. He watched her from beneath hooded eyelids, knowing almost precisely what she was thinking and thoroughly enjoying her discomfort. He kept her nude and forced her to these menial duties in an attempt to tame her. Too, her helplessness gave him a delicious feeling of power. The pleasure he gained from this constant battle between them was far better than the easy conquest of a dozen other beautiful women.

Finally, unable to delay any longer, she was forced to enter the heavily scented tub. He immediately reached out and drew her against him, her soft breasts straining against his chest, the tender nipples irritated by the dark furry mat of his chest. His mouth closed over hers for the first time that evening, his probing tongue almost gagging her. He drew her arms around his neck. Then his hands slid beneath the water to cup her buttocks and, pressing her against the back of the tile tub wall, he raised her up and impaled her on his hardness. She gasped her surprise, but the sound was muffled by his lips. Pressing fierce little thrusts into her, he released his passion, and then held her more tenderly, for she was half-fainting.

Chuckling happily at his sense of dominance, he vaulted quickly from the water and, reaching down, drew her out. Weakened by the warm water and the vizier's lovemaking, but still obedient to her duties, she picked up a warmed towel from the top of the tile stove and wrapped it about him. Taking a second towel, she sat him down and dried him, careful to rub the dampness from between his toes. Stretching him out face down on a marble bath bench, she massaged his muscled body with body cream smelling of roses. As her hands skillfully kneaded the firm body, he rumbled contentment like a large, sleek cat.

Finally he called, "Enough," and rose up to reveal a once again engorged organ. Laughing at the look on her face, he said, "The night has just begun, Incili, and I have yet to get enough of you. I must somehow cool the fires you create in my loins if we are to be parted for several months."

She was shaking. Holding out her hands, she pleaded

with him, "Please, my lord husband, no more! Not just yet!"

It was if she had not spoken. Catching her hands, he forced her facedown onto the same marble bench and, straddling her, he parted her thighs and entered her gently from behind. His hands raised her a little so he could fondle her breasts. He crushed the warm flesh in his big hands, reveling in its softness, pinching the nipples so that she cried out.

In that moment Cat's tolerance of Cicalazade Pasha vanished. He was using her like an animal, without any thought for her at all. Only the knowledge that she would soon be free of him kept her from shrieking her fury. As it was, her temples had begun to throb.

Grunting with pleasure, he finally loosed her and rose up, exclaiming, "I have labored hard so far this evening, and I am thirsty. Fetch me a sherbet, my dove!"

She stood for a moment on trembling legs, then left the bath and crossed the bedchamber to the table where the sherbet decanters stood. Mixing his favorites together, she looked carefully to see where he was, and found him sprawled on the bed looking up through the glass dome at the night sky. With a thumbnail she carefully flicked open the top of her turquoise ring and dropped a pinch of white powder into his cup. Esther Kira had given her the sleeping potion, but she had never dared use it before. Tonight, however, she could take no more, and she knew that the aphrodisiacs he had consumed would confuse him anyway.

She smilingly crossed the room and presented him with the cup. He drank it down thirstily and, carelessly flinging the cup to the floor, pulled her onto the bed. "You are so beautiful," he said. "How you please me, ncili! You please me greatly. Did you know that, my jewel? I treasure you above all my women. Never has a mere female delighted me so much."

She pressed her face into his shoulder so he might not see it. "It makes me happy that I pleasure you, my lord husband," she lied smoothly.

He groped for her breasts, fumbling at her, his movements beginning to become clumsy. Then suddenly she heard him snore lightly. She eased herself out of his grasp and lay apart from him, waiting to see whether he missed her. He was sound asleep, drugged by the white powder she had slipped into his sherbet. In the morning she would add a different powder to his coffee, one which would counteract the effect of the aphrodisiacs and render him almost desireless. That should keep her safe for at least part of the day.

Rising from the rumpled bed, she returned to the bath. Filling and refilling the silver ewer, she laved herself over and over, washing away all evidence of the past hour. The bath was the one aspect of Turkish life she truly enjoyed. Dry again, she slipped a sheer nightgarment over her head. When he awoke he would object and demand its removal. But for now she would have some protection from the cool night air.

Laying herself at the farthest edge of the bed, she wrapped herself in a light wool blanket and immediately fell asleep.

When she awoke the sun was already rising. Cicalazade Pasha lay sprawled on his back snoring mightily, much as she had left him last night. She stretched and, unrolling herself from the blanket, got up. The air was chilly, so she lifted from her trunk a soft white wool caftan and slid it over her nightgown. She slipped her feet into a pair of wool-lined slippers and, checking again to be sure the vizier was asleep, she ran out into the garden.

The wet grass glistened diamondlike in the early sunlight, and the beds of tulips and narcissus were just beginning to open and perfume the air. A faint silvery haze hung just above the dark sea, and the surrounding hillsides were bright-green with spring growth. For a few minutes she was free again, and she reveled in it. If she could get through the next two days and could convince Cica to let her remain on the island, the Kiras would liberate her. Obviously it would be easier to free her from the island than from Cicalazade's palace. She was sorry she had not been able to say goodbye to Lateefa. When she was safe again she would send her kindly cousin a message through the Kiras. . . .

Suddenly a smile lit Cat's face. She had just thought how she could convince the vizier to leave her on the island for a few days. She would use his masculine pride against him to gain her own ends. It would serve the bastard right!

It bothered Cicalazade that she had not become pregnant. He knew she had borne nine living children and he had sired Lateefa's children and forty on the harem women besides. He longed for a child of her body and, not knowing of the potion she took to prevent conception, could not understand why she had not swelled with his fruit.

She would tell him she believed she was pregnant. Pleading the strange fancies of a breeding woman, she would beg to remain a few extra days on the island. Should he refuse her she would weep and pout to gain her way. He would expect it, as he had no view of women other than as soft, foolish creatures.

A little breeze had sprung up, and Cat shivered in anticipation. She always enjoyed mapping battle strategy. Laughing to herself, she wondered which side of her ancestry was asserting itself—the Scots or the Turkish?

Chapter 56

❧❦❧

"**N**O!" said the vizier firmly. "I will not allow it, Incili."

She burst into tears. "You do not love me," she sobbed. "You have stolen me from my husband and used me like an animal! You care nothing for me! Would that the child and I were dead!"

"Child?" His mouth fell open. "What child?"

She raised a teary face to him. "I am not completely sure, my lord, for it is a trifle too early to be entirely sure, but there is a strong possibility that I am with child."

A look of incredulous delight passed over his face, and she nearly allowed herself a twinge of guilt. "A child," he breathed. "Then, my dove, there can be no question of your remaining here. I will not endanger my son."

She forced a fresh torrent of tears from her eyes. "I cannot bear to be penned within the harem right now, my lord husband! It is so pleasant and peaceful here." She lowered her voice so that he was forced to bend down in order to hear her. It also allowed him a wonderful view of her swelling breasts. The seductive scent that issued from the valley between those glorious hills was deliciously overpowering to the vizier.

"We have spent so many joyous hours here, my husband. It is the one place I do not have to share with

589

anyone, even my dear Lateefa." She caught at his arm
and pressed it meaningfully. "We have yet another wonderful day ahead of us and—" her lashes fanned down
over her pink cheeks—"another wonderful night. Let
me remain here dreaming but a few days after you leave
me. I need a few more days to be completely sure. It
would make me so happy. Don't you want me to be
happy, my husband?" And her green eyes filled with
tears that threatened to overflow while her soft mouth
pouted.

He was tolerantly amused by the obviousness of her
approach. She was so typically, predictably feminine,
and it delighted him. The look she cast up at him bespoke a night of incredible pleasures should he consent
to her wishes, and he could honestly see no harm in
allowing her to have her way in this. She was no girl
swelling with her first child. She was a successful and a
proven breeder. He knew that pregnant women had
strange whims which should be indulged whenever possible. She would be perfectly safe on his island with her
female servant for companionship. But he intended
sending back Osman and half a dozen others so there
would be protection—not that anyone would dare to
intrude on his island.

He tried to look stern and thoughtful, and she knew
she had won. "Very well," he said. "I will allow you to
remain for a week, but Osman will come to guard you."

"Of course, my lord," she answered him demurely.
He pulled her across his lap into his arms. "Do I not get
a reward, my dove?" She pulled his head down and
kissed him deeply and convincingly, beginning another
session of sensuality.

In the morning he left the island in his caique and
was rowed back down the Bosporus to his palace in the
city, where he made arrangements for Cat's stay on the
island.

She stood on the stone quay waving him goodbye, but no sooner was he out of hearing than she whirled about with joy, shouting in her own language, "Goodbye, my lord vizier! Farewell forever!"

Susan was astounded at Cat's behavior. "My lady, are you all right?"

"Better than I have been in almost a year, my girl," laughed Cat. "Now that he is gone I dare tell ye. My beloved Francis is near, and yer Uncle Conall too! I dinna know when, but we'll be rescued in a few days at the most!"

"Thank God," breathed Susan fervently.

" 'Twill nae be easy," Cat warned her. "We hae a long and dangerous journey ahead of us. But I should rather die wi Bothwell than spend my days a pampered wife of Cicalazade Pasha!"

"Then yer nae wi bairn? He said ye were, and that I should take extra care of ye."

"God's bones, no! I'd nae bear that lustful devil's bairn! 'Twas but an excuse so we might remain here. 'Tis easier to escape from here than from the vizier's palace. Now, keep yer wits about ye, girl. Osman and a few others will be arriving later today to aid Feisel in 'protecting' me. Ye must nae gie them *any* reason to be suspicious of us."

"Will my lord kill the eunuchs here?"

"Of course. We'll need all the time we can get for a head start before they discover us gone."

"Good! I hate Osman, and I want him dead!"

Cat looked at Susan with amazement. "Why? What has he done to you?"

They had climbed back up to the top of the island. They sat down on a marble bench by the edge of a small goldfish pond.

"Ye know that eunuchs dinna function as normal men," said Susan, "but there are several ways of gelding a male. Some have the rod and sac cut away. These are usually small children. Boys who are older are gelded by simply cutting the sac away so they may not reproduce. Though they are not supposed to, they can function with the aid of special drugs. They cannot have children, of course. Osman is one of these. If a girl takes a eunuch's fancy . . ." She stopped. "Well, they have several ways of satisfying themselves."

"And Osman singled ye out?" said Cat furiously. "He dared? Why did ye nae tell me, girl? I would hae put an instant stop to it!"

"I thought ye had enough to contend wi, my lady," said Susan simply.

Cat put an arm about her servant and hugged her. "Ah, Susan! When we are safely out of this I swear ye'll nae lack for anything ever again. As yer great-grandmam and yer grandmother were loyal to my ancestress, so hae ye been faithful to me. I will nae forget it."

"We are family, my lady, though ye be the mistress and I the tiring woman. A Leslie dinna forget his own."

"Aye, Susan, a Leslie dinna forget," replied Cat.

And as the two women sat quietly watching the fantail goldfish cavorting in the small blue-tiled pool, Bothwell impatiently paced a room in the Kiras' Instanbul house. His wife had been kidnapped amost a year ago, in the early summer of 1598. In mid-September of the same year, Lord Bothwell and Conall More-Leslie had begun a dangerous journey sailing a small fishing boat from Brindisi across the Adriatic Sea to Elyria, and the mouth of the Aous River.

They had entered the river by night and sailed up it for many days until they could go no farther. They had then left the boat, after dragging it ashore and well back into a hidden cave. As they hiked across the mountain forest the weather remained mild, and they encountered no snow. Reaching the headwaters of the Peneus River in Thessaly, they found, following Pietro Kira's directions, another well-stocked boat. Waiting with the boat was a young man who introduced himself as Asher Kira, the son of Eli.

Asher Kira was to escort them safely to the Kira house in Istanbul, and he would teach them the rudiments of Jewish domestic life. Bothwell and Conall were to be introduced into the household as a distant cousin and his servant, come to study the business methods of the main branch of the Kira bank. This would deflect curiosity and allow the two men freedom to move about the city.

Bothwell had grown a fine bushy auburn red beard for disguise, and dressed in the baggy pants, widesleeved blouse, turban, and embroidered sash and vest of the country, he was the very essence of the Turkish citizen. Conall with his black beard was even more impressive.

Asher Kira had piloted them successfully and they had arrived in Istanbul in mid-December of 1598. The trip had taken them exactly three months.

It was now April of 1599, and Bothwell had been waiting several months now for a chance to rescue his wife. Late one afternoon a servant entered the room where he was working on accounts and told him that Esther Kira would speak with him in her garden. When he entered the old woman's presence she motioned him to the bench next to her. Though she looked as if a puff of wind could blow her away, her voice was strong and her gaze unwavering.

"How do you get on, my friend?" she asked him.

"Well, madame, but I grow more anxious daily to complete my mission."

"I spent this morning at the palace. The vizier will be leaving the city for the Hungarian province in a few days. I would say that you will be able to retrieve your property several days after he's gone."

"Is she all right?"

"Yes. But it has not been easy for her, and the next few days will be the hardest. She knows the time is near, and she must use all her wiles to convince him to leave her on his island. That is the safest place for the rescue. I have thought and thought, and there is simply no way to take her from the vizier's palace without raising an immediate hue and cry which would bring almost certain recapture, with all its ensuing difficulties. The island is the only place we may take her from and still have time for getting away." She stopped for a moment. "My lord," she spoke gently to him, "my lord, there's something you must know. You were told that the vizier prizes Incili above all women. You were not told that after he obtained his royal wife's permission, he made Incili his second wife."

Bothwell swore a ripe oath under his breath, and Esther smiled briefly before continuing. "So, my lord, you will not simply be retrieving *your* wife, you will also be stealing *his*!"

Francis began to laugh. "What is it about the wench that all men who love her want to make her their wife?" he chuckled. "My poor cousin no sooner took his royal Danish bride for dynastic purposes than he was trying to force Cat to accept the position of *maitress en titre*. Her first husband, Patrick Leslie, had to chase her over half of Scotland for almost a year before he could get her to the altar. And I, may God help me, ended up an exile without lands or country for—among other alleged sins—trying to make her my wife. Now you tell me that Cicalazade Pasha asked permission of his royal Ottomon wife to take *my* wife for *his* own?"

The old woman's cackling laughter joined Bothwell's deep chuckle. Stopping, she wiped her damp eyes and said, "We will go over our plans in a few days."

Part VIII

❧❦❧

The Escape

Chapter 57

❧ ♥ ❧

SHE struggled up through the blackness, fighting the smothered feeling that overwhelmed her, clawing at the hard hand clamped over her mouth. Full consciousness returned as the voice in her ear became wonderfully familiar.

"Shhh, love! 'Tis me. 'Tis Francis!"

Her eyes flew open and then widened at the sight of the bearded man bending over her. The hand was taken away. Catching her breath, she laughingly sobbed, "Damn me, Bothwell, ye look like the sultan himself!" Then the tears spilled out of her and she flung herself at him, weeping soundlessly.

Holding her closely, he smoothed the head beneath his hand and said in a gentle, teasing voice, "Can I not go off to earn us a living, madame, without yer getting captured by pirates? Ye've led me a fine chase to be sure!" Her shoulders shook all the harder. "Sweetheart, 'tis all right," he soothed. "I am here to take ye home. Dinna weep, lass. Ye've been so brave. Esther Kira has told me how brave ye've been."

She squirmed out of his grasp and turned a stricken face up to him. "Do ye love me, Bothwell?"

For a moment he looked stunned, and then he mused, "Now, let me think a bit. I've crossed three seas and come through two straits. I must now turn about and go back the same way, dragging two women wi me. It will be a bloody miracle if we get to Italy alive! Perhaps I did it for the adventure of it? Christ, madame, what do ye think?"

"I am used, Bothwell. I am terribly used. I hae been the vizier's favorite. Do ye still want me back?"

He began to laugh, then became serious again. "My ever honest Cat. Do ye think I dinna know what yer life has been? Angela di LiCosa made it very plain what kind of a man her brother was. If all I wanted was a body in my bed, Cat, I might—though not easily, I'll admit—have substituted another woman for ye." He wound her tawny hair about his hand and pulled her to him. His mouth gently brushed hers, and his warm sapphire-blue eyes smiled down at her. "But then, my dearest love, who would have sworn at me in Gaelic, or helped me to raise our bairns, or talked wi me of Scotland on the long winter nights in the years to come?"

She caught her lip in her teeth, and her eyelids closed in a futile attempt to hold back the hot tears that poured again down her cheeks.

"Aye, Cat, I love ye," he said. "Now let us stop this foolishness. In less than two hours the sun will be rising. 'Tis best if we're quickly gone from here."

The guards?" she asked.

"Conall and I dispatched them."

"There were six. Did ye kill them all?"

"Aye."

"The bodies?"

"Where they died."

"No! The vultures will get them, and the birds will be seen by the peasants. Someone is bound to get curious and investigate. The supplies for my week's stay came yesterday. No one will come here for at least a week unless something is amiss. Weigh the bodies with stones and sink them into the sea. Then there will be no carrion for the birds, and therefore no curiosity."

He shook his head admiringly. "Madame, ye constantly surprise me," he said, and handed her a bundle from the floor. "Yer traveling clothes. Get dressed while I get Conall and attend to the other business. Susan is waiting in the boat. Go down to the landing when yer ready, and dinna be fearful of the young man there. 'Tis Esther's great-grandson, Asher. He goes with us partway."

" 'Tis nae the *young* men who frighten me, Bothwell."

Standing up, he grinned rakishly at her. "Yer a fetching sight, madame, with yer pretty tits pointing at me like that. Would that we had some time. This bed looks comfortable."

"Never here," she answered him vehemently. "I've spent too many unhappy hours here! I'd sooner be tumbled under a hedgerow!"

"Once we are safely away from here, madame, I will see if I can accommodate ye," he chuckled, and ducked a well-aimed pillow. Laughing, he ran from the kiosk.

Cat sprang from the bed. I am alive again, she thought triumphantly. Once more I have survived!

And she laughed aloud as she undid the bundle he had given her. She found women's underclothes, but the dark-blue pantaloons, white shirt, vest, sash, boots, and turban of a young man. Dressing quickly, she pinned her hair tightly and covered it with a bandanna before placing the little turban on her head. Pulling on the boots, she stood up and wrapped the sash about her waist. Catching a glimpse of herself in a mirror, she unwrapped the sash, removed her shirt, and bound her full breasts with a linen cloth. Then she dressed again, adding the embroidered vest over her shirt. Another look in the mirror brought a smile to her face. No one looking at the young man would suspect him of being the vizier's beautiful second wife!

She looked about the room a final time, but there was nothing she wanted to take with her. From her conversations with Esther Kira, Cat knew that whatever she needed for the long journey would be provided by the Kira family. She would take none of the jewelry given her by the vizier. On her right hand she wore the heart-shaped ruby that had been given her by Patrick Leslie, and the turquoise ring Esther Kira had given her to hold potions. On her left hand was the great emerald wedding band Francis had given her. She needed nothing else. She didn't even turn back for a last look as she went through the kiosk door.

She walked swiftly through the lovely gardens. It gave her a savage pleasure to think that the man who had used her body as he might have used a dumb animal would no longer enjoy his beautiful island. That would be her small revenge on Cicalazade Pasha. He would always associate the island with her, and he would quickly hate his pleasure palace with its hundred memories.

Suddenly she stumbled over a body in the center of the neat gravel path. It was Osman. She felt no regret. Stepping over it, she continued on her way, carefully descending to the quay where the boat waited.

Exactly one week later the vizier's caique arrived to take his wife back to the palace. There was no one waiting on the quay, and after several minutes the oarmaster climbed the stone steps to the island's top. He found both the gardens and the kiosk empty. He called out for Osman, but his voice died in the clear morning air. It was frighteningly obvious that the island was deserted. Running back down the steps to the caique, the oarmaster shouted, "Back to the palace!"

The caique made a tight turn and glided back down

the Bosporus the way it had come. The oarmaster did not even wait for his boat to dock, but leaped to the landing and ran at top speed to find Hammid.

Finding him with the lady Lateefa Sultan, the oarmaster flung himself to his knees and cried, "Disaster, Hammid! There is no one living or dead on the Island of a Thousand Flowers. It is deserted. I searched myself."

Lateefa Sultan watched as Hammid turned ashen. Momentarily her loyalties were torn between the eunuch who had been with her almost her entire life and the beautiful woman who was her cousin. She was genuinely sorry about Hammid's position, but she was relieved that Incili was gone. The immediate problem was Hammid. Cica Pasha was going to hold him responsible for Incili's loss, and his anger would be fierce.

"I will go to the island myself," said the eunuch. "You must be mistaken. There has to be someone there!"

"There is no one, I tell you," repeated the oarmaster. "I even called out. The island is deserted."

"Change the rowers," commanded the eunuch. "I am going."

Several hours later he returned and sought Lateefa Sultan. "The island is indeed empty. There are no signs of violence. No blood. No bodies. Nothing. It is as if they never existed. What am I to tell the master, my princess? He adores Incili. She was to bear his child. What can I say to him? He will kill me." This last was said with a sad finality, and Lateefa felt so sorry for the eunuch that she was almost tempted to tell him the truth—almost, but not quite.

"Tell him the truth, Hammid. You obeyed his orders. You sent Osman and four others to the island as my lord Cica instructed. You sent supplies for seven days, and at the end of that time you sent the caique. There

has been no report of trouble. Why should you suspect
that anything was amiss? Is it your fault the island was
deserted?"

"I must go back to the island tomorrow," said Hammid grimly. "There has to be something that will tell
me what happened! I will find it!"

"Do what you think is best," answered Lateefa
Sultan.

The following day Hammid returned to the Island of
a Thousand Flowers. Knowing he would spend a restless night otherwise, he had gulped a strong sedative
so he might sleep and be clearheaded for his task.

Slowly he ascended to the garden, eyes on the ground,
carefully studying the gravel paths. There had been no
rain to wash away any evidence such as blood for seven
days. The Starlight Kiosk was silent. He opened the
doors and stood for a moment observing the room. The
huge bed was rumpled and unmade, the faint imprint of
her head still on the pillow. He walked closer and saw
that her sleeping garment lay where she had thrown it.
Nothing else in the room was out of place. Her clothes
and jewels were neatly stored in her chest. Nothing was
missing.

There were no signs of force. Eight people were missing, and he had absolutely no idea where they were or
how they had gone. But he was going to do his best to
find out. It was all well and good for Lateefa to say
that he must tell the truth to the vizier, but what truth?
My lord vizier, your second wife has mysteriously disappeared and we know not how. Cicalazade Pasha was
not going to accept that.

Outside again in the garden, he gazed out over the
Bosporus. The sunlight dappled the blue waters, and
then, suddenly, he saw it. Six dark patches were contrasted against the aquamarine of the sea. Hurrying as
quickly as his bulk would allow, he returned to the quay

and spoke in low tones with the oarmaster. The caique was rowed out a bit into the stream and one of the rowers, stripped of his clothes, dove deep into the Bosporus. He surfaced moments later and was pulled aboard.

"What is down there?" demanded Hammid.

The rower shivered. "Bodies, lord. Six bodies, all with their throats cut."

Hammid nodded. "Return to the palace," he said, sinking wearily to the cushions. Now he knew, or thought he knew, what had happened to Incili. The eunuchs had been taken by surprise and murdered. Incili had been carried off. But, remembering the neatness of the kiosk, he revised his theory.

Incili had escaped. But who had helped her? She was in a strange land, cloistered from the world, yet she had managed to find aid and escape. As he searched his mind he kept returning to one constant: Esther Kira. The venerable *grande dame* of the House of Kira was the only person from outside the palace who had known Incili. Yet why would the old woman risk her family to aid a captive?

He commanded the oarmaster to row him to the Yeni Serai. There he spoke with his friend and mentor the Aga Kislar. The aga agreed that the situation was a delicate one, but he disliked the friendship between his mistress, the Sultan Valide Safiye, and Esther Kira. The old woman was a virtual institution with the valides, having been an intimate to four of them. She seemed indestructible, but if she was involved in this scandal then this was his chance to be rid of her.

The aga gained the sultan's ear, telling him only what he felt he should know. "Cicalazade Pasha's second wife appears to have been stolen from the vizier's island," the aga said. "We believe that we know some of the people involved, but we need your permission to proceed further. Will you sign this order?"

Recalling the conversation with his vizier of just two weeks ago, Mohammed III gave the aga his permission, and affixed his tugra seal to the order giving Hammid and the aga *carte blanche* to pursue their investigations. Soon a troop of janizaries was dispatched to the Kira house in the Jewish ghetto. The two black eunuchs followed them in litters.

Eli Kira greeted the two men and led them into a salon, where they were served coffee, honey, and almond-paste cakes, and sticky red and green candies. The banker knew there was something wrong when these two men came calling with a troop of the sultan's elite.

He waited a discreet time, indulging in small talk. Then, looking to the aga, he asked, "Well, my lord aga, why do you come to my home so heavily guarded? Is something amiss? Is there some unrest within the city that I have not heard about?"

"The wife of Cicalazade Pasha was stolen off his island retreat, Eli Kira. What do you know of it?"

The banker's face remained impassive. Not a muscle twitched, nor did any expression ruffle his features. There is no way they can know anything, Eli Kira silently reminded himself. His dark eyes now widened in surprise. "Lateefa Sultan stolen?" he exclaimed, hoping his look was incredulous enough.

A faint smile touched the aga's lips. Hammid's suspicions were correct. The Kiras knew something. "Not Lateefa Sultan," he said patiently, "but the vizier's new second wife, the lady Incili."

"Why should I know anything of this?" asked the banker haughtily. "I did not even know the lady."

"Perhaps you do not," conceded the aga, "but I will wager your grandmother does. The lady Incili was a stranger to this land. The only person from the outside she ever had contact with was Esther Kira, and the lady needed outside aid to escape."

"I thought you said she was stolen," said Eli Kira. "Is it not possible that she bribed the eunuchs to aid her? Why do you assume that because my grandmother casually knew this woman she has masterminded a plot? Where is your proof? You are insulting, my lord aga! I shall personally complain to the sultan about your actions!"

Slowly the aga drew from the sleeve of his robe a rolled parchment, which he handed to the banker. "If you will but take the time to glance at this, you will find that it is an order from the sultan giving me permission to take whatever action is necessary in this investigation. The sultan does not want his friend and valuable servant, Cicalazade Pasha, to be unhappy. And believe me, Eli Kira, the vizier will be very unhappy when he finds his favorite wife gone."

Eli Kira looked steadily and directly at the Aga Kislar, and then he turned his gaze on the vizier's grand eunuch. "I know nothing of this affair," he said firmly, "and if you have no tangible proof other than your outrageous suspicions, I must ask you to leave my house."

"No, Eli Kira. I intend questioning other members of your family. At this very moment, on my orders, my janizaries are entering your women's quarters."

"How dare you!" shouted the banker, his face going purple with outrage and anger. And he ran from the room towards the other end of the house, followed at a surprisingly swift pace by the two eunuchs.

They could already hear the shrieks of surprise and terror coming from the Kira harem, and the scene that greeted them was quite satisfying to the aga. He had wanted to instill just this type of fear in the Kira women. Now, as his reptilian gaze swept the room, he knew what tack to take.

Maryam Kira was white-faced and obviously very

much frightened. She stood protectively clutching her
two younger daughters, Rebecca and Sarah. Her eldest
daughter, Debra, stood next to her mother, equally pale.
Old Esther Kira was seated in a large chair looking frail
but as fierce as a hawk. The room was full of brawny
young janizaries, and several of the servant girls had
obviously been molested.

Angry, red-faced, and fast becoming frightened, Eli
Kira blustered at the aga. "This is the final offense,
Ali Ziya! I shall send a messenger immediately to the
sultan! You accuse us of some plot, but you offer no
proof! You invade the privacy of my home with your
soldiers, molest my servants, frighten my women! Show
me some proof or get out!"

"Be silent! All of you!" All eyes turned to the old
woman in the chair. "What is the problem, Ali Ziya?
The Sultan Valide Safiye will not be pleased if I tell her
of this unpleasantness."

The Aga Kislar looked to the old woman. Here was
the real power behind the Kiras, this tiny, apparently
delicate old woman with her all-knowing black-currant
eyes. She stared unblinkingly at him, and he shivered.
He smiled at her. "What have you done with Cicalazade
Pasha's wife, Incili, Esther Kira?"

"What has happened to her, Ali Ziya?"

"I do not know, but I think you do."

"Nonsense! I know not of what you speak."

The aga smiled again, and decided to play his bluff.
"Is this all of your family, Eli Kira?" he asked.

"No. There are my sons."

"Fetch them," came the command.

The banker nodded curtly to a servant girl, and
several minutes later she returned with four of the boys.

"Is this all?"

"There is Asher, and our cousin John," said Debra
innocently.

The aga pounced. "Where is your son, Asher, and who is this cousin?"

"They have gone off on business for the bank, and will not return for some time."

"Where? And who's this John Kira?"

"I sent them to Damascus, and our cousin comes from northern Europe."

"From Cousin Benjamin in Scotland," spoke Debra again.

Eli Kira shot his daughter a fierce look. "Be silent, Debra. You are not to speak unless spoken to. Your manners are too forward for a maiden."

"Ali Ziya!" All eyes turned to Hammid. "Ali Ziya!" The high voice was excited. "The woman Incili came from Scotland! I remember her telling me that when we first received her."

The aga's eyes narrowed. Here was his connection. He swung about and looked at Eli Kira and his sons. "Those two!" He pointed at the two youngest Kira boys. "What are their ages?"

"Thirteen and sixteen," came the reply.

"A good age," came the reply, and then the next words fell like hammer blows. "I will honor your house, Eli Kira. I will accept these two fine young men into the corps of janizaries."

"*No!*" shrieked Maryam Kira.

The banker's voice was firm, but his heart was beating very fast. "You cannot do that, Ali Ziya. I pay the head tax. My sons are exempt."

"This is an honor I do you, Eli Kira. Your sons enter an elite military unit dedicated to the sultan himself. You cannot refuse my generosity without offending my master. And . . . I will do your loyal family even further honor." His eyes swung over to where young Debra stood. "I am taking your eldest daughter for my master's harem. Never have I seen such beautiful eyes. Their violet color is quite unique. I am sure that, with the proper training, she will enchant him."

"*No!*" Eli Kira was shouting now. "The girl is betrothed! She is to be wed in two days!"

"You are wrong, my friend," the aga smiled. "In three nights I will present her to the sultan, and she will enter his bed as his new plaything. Perhaps she will captivate him. If not, she will live out her life in the Palace of Forgotten Women."

Maryam Kira flung herself at the aga's feet. "What is it you seek?" she begged. "I will help you if I can. But do not take my children, I pray you!"

"Maryam!" Eli pulled his groveling wife up.

"Eli! Eli!" She turned a frightened, tear-ravaged face to him. "What have you done? What is so important that you would sacrifice David and Lev? What is so important that you would condemn Debra to a life of loneliness and shame? If you know anything, tell him! In Yahweh's name tell him, I beg you!"

Eli Kira looked desperately towards his grandmother. Years of training now conflicted violently with his paternal feelings. He simply did not know what to do.

Esther Kira sighed. "Clear the room of all but Ali Ziya, Hammid, and my grandson, who ought to be told what this terror is all about. Do not touch any of my great-grandchildren, or you will learn nothing!"

"Take your men and wait in the courtyard. Touch no one and nothing," the aga commanded.

Slowly the room cleared until only the old woman, Eli Kira, and the two eunuchs remained. "Sit! Sit!" commanded Esther Kira. "This is a complicated story." And she settled herself comfortably. They looked expectantly at her. "Do any of you know when I was born?" she asked, and then cackled. "I was born on April first in the Christian year 1490. I am one hundred and nine years old! Now, of what I am about to tell you, my poor bemused grandson knows nothing. Since, however, *my*"—she stressed the word—"actions have brought difficulties to him, I think he should hear this."

Eli Kira kept his face impassive. There was absolutely nothing that he did not know of his family's business, but he understood what his grandmother was doing. By removing the blame from him, she was trying to save the family. It was a prime example of the first lesson she had ever taught him—survival at any cost. He felt a sudden burst of tenderness and affection for the lady who had built his family's fortune. He wished he might take her in his arms and hug her. Instead he sat quietly, a slightly expectant look on his face.

Good, thought Esther Kira, he understood my tactic. Then she continued. "Your suspicions are correct, Ali Ziya. I did help the woman you call Incili to return to her own people. So would you have, had you known who she was."

"She was a European noblewoman," came Hammid's voice.

"She was a descendant of Cyra Hafise," came back the reply.

"How can that be, old woman?" demanded Ali Ziya. "Cyra Hafise left only her son, Sultan Suleiman, and a daughter who was wed to Ibrahim Pasha. Of the imperial grandchildren, the princes Mustafa and Bajazet were murdered. Prince Janhagir died, Prince Selim became Sultan Selim II, and Princess Mihrmah was wed to Rustem Pasha. The children of Ibrahim Pasha and Princess Nilufer never left this land. Your vast age has finally addled your wits, Esther Kira."

"You are a third my age, Ali Ziya, and my wits are still sharper than yours," came the quick reply. "I was for many years a close friend and confidant of Cyra Hafise. I knew all about her, and her family. She had a brother, the Earl of Glenkirk. Incili is descended from him, and so was her first husband—also an Earl of Glenkirk. Her oldest son is the current earl. Because of the kind intervention of Cyra Hafise, the Kira family has managed the great fortune of the Leslies of Glenkirk for many years.

"I doubt that Incili ever heard of Cyra Hafise, but I almost fainted the first time I saw her. She is the mirror image of my long-dead friend, as Lateefa Sultan is of her ancestress, Firousi Kadin. To see them standing together took me back eighty-five years, and I thought for a moment that I had died and my two friends were coming to greet me."

She paused for a moment to gauge the effect this tale was having on her audience. In her grandson's eyes she caught a hint of admiration. The two eunuchs sat spellbound, and she chuckled within herself. Eunuchs were such children. She continued.

"After I had spoken awhile with the lady Incili and drawn her out a bit, I knew for certain who she was. With the aid of Lateefa Sultan, I attempted to get her to accept this as her life. But you yourself know, Hammid, how restless she was. Then her second husband and his servant arrived to rescue her. I introduced them into the house as John Kira, a cousin, and his servant. I secretly instructed him in the way of Jewish life so that during the time he was here no one would suspect his real identity and mission.

"I had no choice but to help him. He is a favorite cousin of the Scots king, who is the old English queen's heir. The Scots king is very fond of his cousin, and is bound to complain to the English queen, who will write to her friend the Sultan Valide Safiye, who will speak to her son, the sultan.

"The whole thing would have become a public scandal. The sultan's best friend and vizier, holding against her will in carnal bondage the *cousin* of Scotland's *king*? You know how these Christians are about sexual morals. How do you think the sultan would have felt caught in such a tangle?

"The woman, Incili, should never have been sent to Cicalazade Pasha. It was a vicious trick on the part of the vizier's sister, who is a jealous and cruel woman of bad repute." She turned accusingly to the grand eunuch. "You knew that, Hammid. Incili told you who she was, and begged you to have her ransomed. She could have made you a rich man. Instead, you used her to sate the never-satisfied appetite of your master in the hopes of furthering your own ambitions. Do you realize the embarrassment you could have caused the sultan and his government?"

Neatly she had shifted the blame from her own frail shoulders onto his fat ones. Eli Kira was open-mouthed in admiration. Ali Ziya was thoughtful.

"Incili is long gone," said Esther Kira. "Once again I have loyally served the House of Osman. When Cicalazade Pasha returns from his campaign, tell him that the lady Incili miscarried and died. She was not, by the way, really with child. It was a ruse she used to remain on the island so that her husband might rescue her. The eunuchs are dead and cannot talk. Your rowers can be sold off and replaced, and the oarmaster disposed of some way. No one else knows that Incili is gone. They will believe whatever you tell them."

"The sultan knows," said Ali Ziya.

"Tell him that the woman died, and that the eunuchs lied and hid themselves for fear of being blamed. Then tell him that everyone involved has been punished. It is not important to him, and he will forget."

Ali Ziya nodded. "You are right, Esther Kira. You know the imperial Ottoman well."

"I should," replied the old lady. "I have been dealing with them successfully for almost a hundred years."

The eunuchs stood up, as did Eli Kira. "I apologize, Eli Kira, for this invasion of your home. It did appear as if a crime had been committed in which your family was involved. I hope you will not find it necessary to complain to the sultan."

"No," said the banker quickly. "I understand it was just a terrible misunderstanding. You simply did your duty."

The Aga Kislar looked at Esther Kira. "You are a remarkable old woman," he said dryly. Turning, he left the room, followed by Hammid and Eli Kira.

Alone in the main courtyard of the house, the aga turned to Hammid. "Do as she suggested. If there is ever any question, I will back you up."

"Do you believe her, Ali?"

"Yes—and no," came the reply. The aga climbed into his litter, giving the signal for his departure. Returning to the Yeni Serai, Ali Ziya decided one thing. Esther Kira's influence with the imperial family must be discredited, and without a doubt she must die. Even in her old age she was far too astute, and very dangerous. Then too, she was a living link with a time when the Ottoman sultans were strong men who ruled alone, without the advice of women or eunuchs. Ali Ziya did not want to see that time return.

Chapter 58

❧❦❧

T HE coast of Thessaly stood dark in the early morning. Purple mountains speared the sunrise sky,
snowcapped Olympus and Ossa towering above all. Between these two giants of the Pindus range spread the
fertile plain of Thessaly, split by the Peneus River,
which flowed into the Aegean Sea.

In that short time between the ebb and the flood
tides, when the dark-green waters of the river mixed
lazily with the turquoise waters of the sea, a small boat
moved from the Aegean into the Peneus.

They had been anchored off this particular piece of
coast all night waiting for the calm to get them safely
into the river and the floodtide that followed to sweep
them up it. To the passing casual shoreline observer the
boat contained four men and a woman. Obviously it
was a family boat, a coastal trading vessel, heading upstream to Larissa to sell its cargo.

Within the boat the occupants heaved a collective
sigh of relief. Another stage of their journey was over,
and thus far it had been unbelievably simple. From the
moment they had cast off from the Island of a Thousand
Flowers, the skies had remained benevolent and the seas
cooperative. They had sped down the Sea of Marmara
past the island of the same name where imperial Ottoman slaves quarried marble for the sultan's export trade.
Onward through the Dardanelles, and across the Aegean,

Cat could not remember them seeing more than two
other boats. They had stopped only once, at the island
of Lemnos, to take on fresh water.

After all the blue and gold of the sea, the river was
a startling change. Cat was stunned by the rugged
beauty surrounding her. Seated in the bow of the boat,
her dark cloak wrapped about her, she did not know
which way to look next. To her right, the precipices
descended like the gods themselves from Mount Olympus and fell steeply to the river. Mount Ossa rose the
highest on her left, rising fifteen hundred feet straight
up from the floor of the valley.

The valley was lush, and there were beautiful horses
grazing in the grassy meadows.

"Are they wild?" asked Cat, for she saw neither
houses nor people.

"Nay," Bothwell answered her. "They are specially
raised, and have been since earliest times. Now the
Turks own the ranches, but we're not apt to see any
people until we reach Larissa. The Turks are on the
ranches, and in the cities, and this river passes through
only two towns."

The river began to narrow into a gorge. "The Vale
of Tempe," he said, as their boat slipped into a close,
greenlit world. "Legend says that Poseidon, the Greek
god of the sea, created it so he might have a beautiful
bower in which to woo a daughter of the river god."

Cat looked up at him, her green eyes reflecting the
light of the vale. "How beautiful! Did he win her love?"

"I dinna know, but 'tis a most romantic place for
lovers. The vale is also connected to the sun god,
Apollo. A maiden named Daphne fled here to escape
his lecherous advances. Daphne was dedicated to
Apollo's twin sister, the virgin moon goddess, Diana.
Apollo was determined to have Daphne, and he cor-

nered her here. She cried out to Diana to save her from shame, and the goddess obliged her handmaiden by turning the girl into a flowering laurel bush. Since then the Vale of Tempe is sacred to Apollo, and in ancient times the laurel for the victor's wreaths at the Pythian Games was gathered here."

"Had you been Apollo and I Daphne, I would never have fled ye, Francis."

He smiled at her, and she smiled back. The trip across the sea had turned her creamy skin a rich golden color, and her eyes appeared even greener than usual. Her rich honey-colored hair had been, in the Aegean, free of its bandanna and turban; and the sun had bleached it a pale gold. She was very lovely, and it had been months now since they had last made love. Unfortunately this was not the time, though the place would have been perfect. Ahead were the ruins of the Temple of Apollo, set high above the river within a grove of tall, ancient oaks. He would have enjoyed making love to her in that romantic setting.

Francis sighed, and catching her looking at him, grinned guiltily. She laughed softly. "I regret it also, Bothwell," she said, reading his thoughts.

"Yer a witch," he chuckled.

"Nay. Just yer other half, Francis," and she caught his big hand and pressed it to her lips.

"Will we get home safely, Bothwell?" she pleaded.

"We will get home safely, Cat. I promise you."

The Vale of Tempe behind them, the plain of Thessaly spread itself out again in the glory of early summer, and before the sun had reached its zenith, the walls of ancient Larissa came into view. Cat bound up her beautiful hair again, and Susan hid her pretty face behind the voluminous folds of a black feridji, leaving only her eyes visible.

After paying the dockage fee to the Turkish port-master they were directed to a pier near the waterfront market. They tied up without incident.

"Saul Kira's house is near enough to walk," said Asher. "He is a widower, his children grown and gone. Only his widowed sister is in the house to care for him. We should be safe for the moment." And he led them across the crowded market, alive with mooing, baaing, clucking, and quacking livestock. The noise made by the animals and haggling merchants was ferocious, and Cat sighed gratefully when they had crossed the market square.

They entered the small courtyard to a yellow brick house. Saul Kira greeted them warmly, putting Cat and Susan into the custody of his sister, Abigail. Abigail bas Kira looked at Cat suspiciously, wondering whether this really was a young man. Cat drew off her headgear so that her long hair tumbled down her back. The old woman nodded, satisfied. "What can I get you?" she asked them.

"A bath," breathed Cat and Susan together, and then they laughed at their singlemindedness.

An hour later they were bathed, their hair washed free of sea salt. Abigail bas Kira had given them each clean clothing, and Cat's bandanna and turban were washed and dried. The Jews never wore them, so there were none in the house.

While Susan helped to lay the table, Cat joined the men. Bothwell put an arm about his wife. "Good news . . . and some bad," he said.

"The good?" she asked.

"We are not pursued. They felt they could not pick up the trail, and so they decided to tell your 'lord and master' that you had died miscarrying. We will have to continue to move cautiously, however, as I do not want us to run into any Ottoman officials asking embarrassing questions, or slavers with sharp eyes."

She sighed. "Thank God they dinna pursue us. But what is the bad news, my love."

"Esther Kira is dead."

"Oh, Francis! But then, she was a very old lady—well over a hundred. Well, God assoil her soul. I know she had a great one."

"Aye," he nodded. He was grateful that she assumed age was the cause of Esther's death. It had not been. There had been a sudden fluctuation in the valuation of the Turkish currency. Rumors flew through the city, and the people had deliberately been aroused against the bankers. Old Esther Kira, returning from the palace, where she had been visiting with the sultan's mother, was dragged from her litter and stoned. The following day the value of currency had miraculously returned to normal. By that time, Esther Kira was dead.

The sultan and his mother were lavish in their grief, but no one was ever brought before the kadi for this obvious murder.

The Kiras, however, plainly understood the nature of the warning visited upon them by the death of their matriarch. Asher Kira was told to go on to Italy with his charges, and settle in Rome with his uncle. The main branch of the Kira bank then returned to business as usual, but less conspicuously now, and without royal favor.

There was no need for Cat to know these things. Lord Bothwell did not want to burden his wife with guilt or grief. The worst of their journey lay ahead of them, and she would need all her courage and strength for that. There was no time for weeping. He did ask her if she wanted to communicate with Lateefa Sultan, but Cat decided to wait until they were safely in Italy. Then she would send her Ottoman cousin a special gift—a replica of Cyra Hafise's pendant—along with a letter.

There was no need to tarry in Larissa. The following

day they bid farewell to Saul and Abigail and headed
upstream to Tricca. As they left, Saul Kira released a
pigeon who would fly to Istanbul as a signal that Eli
Kira's oldest son had gotten as far as Larissa in safety.

They reached Tricca in two days. Still keeping to the
guise of coastal traders they sold their small cargo of
Brusa silks to a delighted broker who rarely saw such
fine quality. They then loaded their boat with just a
small quantity of trade goods for barter. It was unlikely
that anyone would inspect the boat and discover that
most of its cargo was stones.

They departed Tricca the day after their arrival and
slowly began to make their way upstream. As they left
the town behind, the river grew wilder and rockier, with
little patches of whitewater rapids. Bothwell and Asher
took turns at the helm of the little boat while, from the
bow, Cat and Susan alternated in keeping watch of the
river ahead. Conall clung to his precarious perch high
up on the mast, peering ahead for dangerous waters.

They could not travel at night now. For safety's sake
they remained in the middle of the stream, using their
sea anchor, and there was always a watch posted. As
the countryside became wilder, less inhabited by farmers
and herdsmen, it grew thick with bandits.

Finally they could go no further on the Peneus. They
were near the source of its headwaters, and the stream
became narrow, shallow, and very rocky. They would
now have a two-day trek through the forest in order to
reach the Aous River in Illyria, and then a short march
to reach the spot where Bothwell and Conall had hidden
their boat.

The little boat that had carried them in safety from
the heart of the Ottomon Empire was sunk without a
trace. Bothwell continued to take no chances.

They were in a vast forest, and it amazed Cat that
Francis and Conall were able to find their way. The

Earl of Bothwell enlightened his wife by explaining that when they had come through the forest on their way to Istanbul, he had cut small, deep notches into various trees along their route. After nearly a year, the marks were still there.

The woodland with its oak, elm, pine, and birch trees was similar to those found in Scotland. So was the wildlife. They saw deer, bear, wolves, and wild boar as well as fowl and birds of all kinds, most familiar.

They each carried only a small amount of food. There was a pouch of finely ground grain which, when mixed with water, could be boiled and eaten as a cereal, or boiled and then roasted on hot stones to make a cake. A second pouch contained dried figs, raisins, and peaches. Asher had a small brick wrapped in red and silver foil made up of dark, dried leaves which he called "te." Added to boiling water, it made a refreshing amber drink which they found sustaining.

They were all armed. Susan had a dagger. Cat and Asher had both dagger and scimitar. Conall and Bothwell carried, in addition to those weapons, English longbows and arrows.

The first day they walked many miles before making camp. Conall managed to shoot two ducks. Susan and Cat plucked and cleaned them, and stuffed them with dandelion greens and some dried fruit. Bothwell, never able to resist fishing a good mountain brook, managed to catch three trout. It was a satisfying meal.

The following morning they carefully watered the fire down and buried it. They began to walk again. They reached the headwaters of the Aous River by midday, and another hour's march along the waterside brought them to an overgrown but still serviceable road. Stopping for a time to eat some fruit and drink some water, Cat asked about the road.

"Roman," answered Bothwell. "Illyria was a favorite

province of the empire. There are two legends regarding its name. The Romans say the name is derived from Illyricus, the son of the Cyclops Polythemus and the sea nymph Galatea. The Greeks, however, claim that Illyricus was the son of Cadmus and Harmonia."

"Why was the province favored, Francis?"

"Because the Illyrians are born fighters—tough, hardy, natural soldiers. The Romans recruited heavily among them. In the third century after Christ the first wave of barbarians hit the empire, and Illyria became the last bulwark of the Roman and Western cultures. Most of the outstanding emperors of that period were Illyrian, elected right on the field of battle by their soldiers. Now, of course, 'tis just a part of the sultan's vast empire, but there are fewer Turks here because the population of this country turned Muslim when first conquered rather than lose control of their lands. The sultan has firm control of the cities and the lowlands, but here in the mountains the tribes are left to enjoy their ancient autonomy. They pay a high tribute for it. . . . We'll have to move with caution here. I dinna want to attract any attention."

She looked levelly at him. "Are we in danger?"

"Let us just say I dinna want to run into any bandits. I would say we're safe as long as we keep moving, and as long as it's dark. Fearing pagan taboos, they do not attack at night."

It was midafternoon of the following day when they reached the cave where Bothwell and Conall had hidden their boat. It was still there, the cave entrance well covered and quite undisturbed. They might have dragged the boat to the river then, but Bothwell thought the women looked weary.

"We'll stop and camp here the night," he ordered. "Come morning we'll be fresh, and on our way at first light. Asher, help the women set up camp while Conall and I go hunting for our meal."

They decided to camp within the cave. There would be less chance of their fire being spotted, of wild animals, or of being caught in a sudden rain. Susan cut reeds from the riverbank and bound them to make torches for the cave. With Asher Kira's help she gathered firewood. Asher then left them to try his hand at fishing, and Cat gave her young tiring woman leave to bathe while she finished up within the cave. The lessons she had learned riding the Scots borders with Bothwell served her well now. She built a fire, lay out the cooking gear, and took a jug to the river.

Directly below the cave lay a small crescent-shaped sandy beach which bordered a shallow pool within the river made by an almost circular formation of rocks. Susan bathed in the pool and Cat promised to join her shortly.

Returning to the cave, she placed the jug on a rock ledge so that no one would trip over it, then looked about to see if she had forgotten anything. The fire burned hot in a carefully dug pit. On opposite sides of the fire the iron spit holders were imbedded firmly in the ground, the spit, a wooden spoon, and an iron pot nearby. When the men returned, the women would be ready for them.

Satisfied that she had done her part, Cat was ready to go swimming. Suddenly she heard a high scream of terror from Susan. Without thinking, she ran out of the cave and leaped down the small incline to the beach below. Too late, she realized her mistake. She was weaponless except for a dagger, having left her scimitar in the cave. There was a man on the beach and two more in the water, chasing after Susan, who swam frantically this way and that, trying to escape. The man on the beach turned to face Cat. Drawing her dagger, she crouched to meet him.

"The mermaid has a boy companion with her," he called in Turkish to his companions. Cat realized now that they were Ottoman soldiers, and not Illyrian bandits as she had first assumed.

Deepening her voice, Cat shouted, "Leave my sister be! We are loyal citizens of the sultan—may Allah grant him long life! Is this how the sultan's soldiers behave? Attacking helpless travelers?" Her voice rang with scorn.

They looked surprised, and for a moment Cat thought they might leave them in peace. Then one of the men waded from the water and made straight for her. Cat gasped, for the man stood close to seven feet tall. It took all her courage not to break and run. When he was quite close she called out, "Stop! Come no further or I'll slit your belly wide open!"

The giant stopped, eyeing her with some amusement. "I think, my young fighting cock, that you are really in no position to give orders. But my curiosity is aroused. You're not Illyrian, so why are you here?"

"We're from Tricca," answered Cat, "on our way to visit our grandmother, whose second husband is Illyrian. We came up the Peneus with a friend, a river trader. We have been walking for two days now, and our grandmother's house is but a few hours from here. My sister wanted to bathe before going on."

The giant smiled slowly, and a knowing fear clutched Cat. "I am Omar," he said. "A captain with the Illyrian regulars. We have been here in the mountains collecting the sultan's tribute from the local tribes. With Illyrians we must maintain good manners, lest we cause the sultan difficulties. Their women are forbidden contact with us, and we do not molest them. It has been weeks now since my men have enjoyed female companionship. Your sister is very pretty." He turned to his men. "Get the river nymph," he commanded sharply. Then he turned to Cat. "Pretty young men also make good sport," he laughed, jumping forward.

Cat's knife bit into his arm. Omar cursed roundly but

kept coming. Several more times she bloodied him, but
he kept forcing her backward until she found herself
against the embankment below the cave. For a moment
they stood still, facing each other. Her heart was beating
wildly, and she was panting with fright and exhaustion.
She could hear Susan screaming, and she trembled.

She leaped at him but he turned quickly, grunting
with surprise as the knife buried itself deep in the
muscle of his shoulder. With his good arm he hit her
a fierce blow on the side of the head, and she fell to
the ground. Her turban and bandanna fell away onto
the ground.

There was a moment of silence while the captain removed the knife from his shoulder and dabbed the
wound. Then he glanced back at the half-conscious
woman at his feet. He shouted his delight. "By Allah!
Another woman! A fighting wildcat, but a female!"

Reaching down, he pulled Cat up by the arm and,
catching her face between his thumb and forefinger,
looked hard at her. "By Allah!" he muttered almost to
himself. "You're a beauty! A real little prize."

Numb, she stood quietly as he quickly and expertly
stripped her naked. "Allah bless me! My fortune is
made," the captain chortled as he ran his hands over
her shrinking body. She shivered as feeling began to
come back to her. "Easy, my beauty," he said quietly.
"You need have no fear of me, and I'll protect you
from my men. You're worth more to me as you are
than bloodied by them. They'll sate their lust on the
other."

She saw with horror that Susan had been dragged
from the water and now lay on her back, held by one
man while the other prepared to rape her. Her servant's
plight roused pity in Cat, pity for the girl who had
known only rape and depravity from men, never any
tenderness or love. At least I have had that, thought Cat.

"Come!" The voice startled her from her reflections.

The giant pulled her a little way down the beach and, sitting, drew her down into his lap. She braced herself for the struggle to come. His laughter rumbled as he saw her face contort with fear. "Don't be frightened, my beauty. I'm not going to force you, though Allah knows you would tempt a holy man. Alas, I have not functioned as a man since a fever took me several months back. Still," and he chuckled again, "I know other ways to make a girl happy. When my men sleep tonight perhaps we'll try some, eh?"

Cat shuddered. "What are you going to do with me?" she asked.

"Why—sell you, woman! Allah! Have you never looked in a mirror? You will bring me a fortune, though whether I can get a better price for you in the open market or from Fatima the procuress I will not know until we reach Apollonia."

Helplessness swept over Cat. Oh, God, she wailed silently! Not again. Then she caught herself. The captain and his two men were not aware that the helpless women they had captured travelled with three men. If she could only keep them here until the others returned, she and Susan had a chance. But once the two soldiers finished amusing themselves with Susan, their captain would want to be on his way. There was only one way to keep him here, and though she shrank from it, she knew she must detain them.

The captain was fondling her breasts. He might be temporarily impotent, but the thought was strong. So much the better. Saying a prayer for the men's quick arrival, Cat made her voice softly innocent and said hesitantly, "I have been a widow two years now, captain, and my husband was a very simple man. What . . . what . . ." She stopped. Lowering her eyes as if in confused embarrassment, she giggled nervously. "What did you mean when you said there are 'other ways' to make a girl happy?" she finished in a breathless rush.

Captain Omar's piglike little eyes narrowed and then began to glitter with anticipatory delight. "A widow for two years? A pretty girl like yourself, and no suitors to play with?"

"I was in mourning, and then my father became ill and my sister and I nursed him until he died. There was no time for suitors," she finished modestly.

"Surely your husband was a lusty man, and showed you many a fine bed trick?"

"Oh, no, captain! My husband was many years my senior. He was a wealthy man when I married him, and father got a very good bride price for me. When my poor husband died, however, he had lost his wealth through poor investments. Had my dear father not taken me back, I should have been destitute."

"You're no virgin still, are you?"

Cat knew she dare not lie. "Oh, no, captain! My husband did his duty by me once weekly."

"Once weekly? Once weekly!" roared the giant. "Allah, woman! If you had been my wife I'd have fucked you three times nightly and double on the sabbath!" He chuckled. "So you were wed to a graybeard who could barely do it, and here you are a lusty, hot young widow, innocent of all the nice things a man can do for a woman to make her feel good. Tell me, my pretty one—would you like me to do some of those things to you now?"

Cat hid her face in the giant's shoulder. Taking coyness for assent, the captain chuckled again, the deep rumbling sound of a pleased tomcat, and ran a thick finger along the line of her tightly closed legs. Cat closed her eyes and concentrated on not screaming.

In the woods, downstream of the river, Asher Kira had heard Susan shrieking. Quickly, but cautiously, he had hurried to investigate. Shocked by the scene before him, the gentle young banker soiled himself. In his youthful fantasies he had imagined the taking of a reluc-

tant woman, but the unpleasant reality of rape terrified
him. Gasping for breath, he fought to control his anger
and disgust. Reason prevailed. He could scarcely fight
off three men alone. Melting back into the thick cover
of the undergrowth, Asher Kira set off for Lord Bothwell.

It took him over half an hour, for he moved carefully,
marking his trail so he might find his way back easily.
He found Conall first, and poured out his story. The
Scots captain paled. Grasping the younger man by the
arm, Conall pulled him along to the earl. Bothwell's face
darkened with rage, and he might have gone crashing
back through the underbrush had it not been for the
restraining influence of his companions.

"Ye'll nae stop the deviltry now, my lord," said
Conall grimly. "What we want is to get them back
alive."

Francis did not think that he could bear it. His beautiful, brave Cat was being hurt again! Could the fates
not leave them in peace? And he knew in a fury that
nearly overcame him, he was going to kill her tormenter
himself.

It was almost night as they grimly made their way
back to the campsite. Silently observing the beach from
the little bluff above it, they saw that the three soldiers
had made a fire and were seated about it. Susan was not
to be seen, but Cat—still naked—was clasped in the
captain's big lap. As they crept closer they could hear
the men arguing.

"I don't see why you won't let us have her, captain,"
said one of the soldiers. "Because you can't do it yourself any more, you deny Mustafa and me."

"You have the other girl, Issa."

"She's unconscious now, captain," whined the soldier. "It's no fun fucking a woman who doesn't move.
Let us have a go on Goldenhair. Come on, now. You've
never been one to hoard the goods all to yourself."

"You're a pair of fools! This woman is a *real* beauty! If I don't let you two damage her we'll get a fine price for her in Apollonia. *Then* you can buy all the women you want. This one you leave alone!"

"We saw what you were doing to her before, captain," said Issa. "Let us do at least that. Aw, hell! She's got such wonderful big tits. I want a feel. Come on, captain! Let us have a little feel."

Captain Omar stood up, dumping Cat, and roared, "No! No! And again, no! You'll bruise the devil out of her. I know you two. You're animals! Fuck the other, and think about how much money this one will bring us when we sell her." Then he plumped himself down again, yanking Cat back into the comparative safety of his massive lap.

Watching from his hidden vantage, Bothwell thanked God she hadn't been raped. Susan, poor lass, had taken the brunt of the brutality. The earl vowed he would do his best to care for her. If they got out of this alive, Susan would never again lack for anything.

Slipping back into the forest, he signaled silently to Conall and Asher to follow him. They reached a small clearing, and Bothwell said quietly, "I think we're well advised to wait until they sleep. We'll each take one of them, but the captain is mine." The two nodded. The earl asked Asher, "Do ye think ye can kill a man, lad?"

Asher Kira nodded. "Yes, my lord, I can. After what I saw them doing to Susan, I can kill one of the men who did it."

The earl smiled grimly, and the three men settled down to wait.

The moonless night grew darker, and gradually the noise from the soldiers died until only snoring broke the stillness. Carefully now they crept up again to the perimeter of the camp. The fire burned low. The three men were all there. The man who should have been on guard slept as noisily as his companions. Bothwell shook his head in wonder. These Turks—alleged to be the world's finest military—were poor soldiers. Instead of sleeping in close formation about the fire, they were scattered—easy prey for man or animal.

The earl nodded to Conall and Asher. Shadowlike the three men stepped from the darkness into the faint glow of the firelight. Methodically they went about their task. A hard hand was clasped quickly about a mouth to stifle the cry while the throat was cut from ear to ear. The two soldiers died swiftly. Captain Omar was left.

A bloodcurdling Scots war cry ripped through the night. The Turkish captain scrambled to his feet, terrified. A quick glance about him told him his companions were dead. Slowly, he turned to face his adversaries. There were three of them—a beardless youth not worth bothering with, and two hardened veterans. Omar was no coward, but he did not like the odds.

"I am Captain Omar of the sultan's Illyrian regulars," he said. "Who are you?"

The tallest of the men stepped forward. "My name matters not, spawn of pig's offal! You will not live long enough to repeat it!"

The insult was enormous, yet the captain was puzzled. "Do I know you, my lord? What is your quarrel with me?" He shifted his weight slightly.

"Do not move, captain," said the tall man. "My young friend has a pistol pointed directly at you. It is primed and ready. If his finger should slip . . ." He paused and smiled. "Have you ever seen a man die of a bullet wound, captain? A large hole blown clean through his middle? The guts oozing out onto the ground like a string of sausages? Move one step, and you will experience that most exquisite agony."

The giant Turk swallowed hard and glanced over at the boy he had regarded so lightly. Asher Kira glared coldly back. His slender hand was wrapped lightly about a large, evil-looking weapon. He seemed quite familiar with it, even comfortable. Captain Omar stood very still.

Bothwell turned to Conall. "Susan?"

"Alive, my lord," came the choked reply. The weatherworn face, wet with tears, implored him.

"Christ, mon, what sort of human does this to a young girl?" And he tenderly cradled the battered body of his niece in his arms.

"Cat!" The earl's voice called.

She came slowly from behind the captain, still naked. Removing his heavy cloak, Bothwell wrapped her in it. "Asher will take you and Susan to the boat as soon as he and Conall have launched it."

"And you?"

"The captain and I have unfinished business."

"I will stay till it is finished," she stated.

A slow smile crinkled the corners of his eyes. "You were never one to run from danger, were you, my love? Very well then. It would be easier if you had some clothes on, madame. Are there any extra among us?"

Nodding, she said, "I will not be long, Francis," and climbed back up to the cave. Taking Susan's extra undergarments, pants from Asher, and a shirt from Conall, she was able to put together a decent wardrobe. Her own sash and boots were salvageable.

While she dressed, the others pressed Captain Omar's strength into service. They dragged the boat from its hiding place and anchored it in the river, just off the beach. Asher Kira waited in it with the injured Susan. Having regained consciousness, she alternated between relief and tears. Conall built up the fire to light the area while the two combatants stripped off shirts and boots.

"Understand me, Turk," said Bothwell. "If I do not kill you, which I intend doing, my captain will do it. But because I believe every condemned man has the right to know why he dies I will tell you now that the

lady you intended selling into bondage is my wife. The
girl your men brutalized is my captain's niece."

Captain Omar let the words slide over him, looking
his challenger over. Bothwell was almost as tall as he,
but weighed a good deal less. Omar felt confidence
swelling through him. He would quickly crush the
infidel dog. As for his bandy-legged companion, he
presented no threat at all. But it would be wise to dispose of him quickly. Whirling, he turned on the surprised Conall and felled him with a great blow to the
head. The Scotsman slid silently to the sand as Cat
screamed his name.

Now Captain Omar turned to Bothwell. The two men
circled each other, each assessing the other's strength.
Their knives flashed in the firelight. Suddenly terrified,
Cat knelt by the unconscious Conall, watching and
praying.

There was a sudden glint of steel and a reddening
wound. Then there was another, and another. The two
men fought on, past taunts now, an occasional grunt
punctuating the silence. Neither seemed to weary, and
the firelight dappled their sweat-soaked bodies. Suddenly the Turk flung aside his knife and leaped at Bothwell, enveloping him in a great bear hug. Bothwell was
caught as surely as a rabbit in a snare. He could not
struggle, and his knife dropped from his hand. The
giant seemed to be squeezing the very life from him.

"Cat!" He managed to gasp. "To the boat, lass!
Run!"

He felt a rib crack and struggled harder against both
his massive enemy and fast-rising unconsciousness. He
knew that if the blackness claimed him he was a dead
man. The ignominy of the situation struck at his native
pride.

That he, Francis Stewart-Hepburn, should die at the
hands of a mindless Turk! Through the roaring in his

ears he thought he heard his wife's voice, and it gave him courage. If he died, she was doomed to a living hell.

Scrambling across the sand, Cat picked up first the Turk's knife and then Bothwell's. Legs shaking, she plunged both knives repeatedly into the mountain of flesh that was the Turk, but she could not seem to find a vital spot. Her blows were no more effective than a gnat's bite. But, like the insect, she became a great irritant. Dropping his half-conscious victim, Omar turned on her.

"Woman!" he shouted, and she jumped backwards. He reached for the knives and, disarming her, slapped her several light blows. Terrified for Bothwell, and feeling more helpless than she had ever felt, Cat dropped to her knees. The Turk turned back to the earl. Suddenly a roar tore the stillness. Spinning about, Captain Omar clutched at his middle, a look of pure surprise on his face. He removed his hands slowly to look, then clamped them quickly back over the hole in his belly as a length of pink gut rolled out. But he was not able to contain the blood that poured forth.

Sickened, Cat scrambled away from him, but he kept coming towards her, his lips moving, mouthing words she could not hear. The pink intestines were uncontainable now, spilling between his clutching fingers, blood spurting over her. Beyond him stood Asher Kira, the smoking pistol in his hands. Nearby both Bothwell and Conall lay unmoving on the damp sand.

Horrified, she slowly scanned the scene of carnage in which she had played a leading role. Suddenly Captain Omar crumbled dead at her feet. Terror filling her eyes, she screamed, "Oh, God! No more! No more! No more!"

Part IX

⋙⋘

The Healing

Chapter 59

❦❧

IN the cool green hills overlooking Rome there nestled a beautiful villa, commanding a view of the sea many miles beyond. A park surrounded the house, but the gates leading to it were always closed unless someone was entering or leaving. It was called simply Villa Mia, and had been built a hundred years before for a mistress of the Borgia pope, Alexander VI. The park was filled with greenery, deer, birds, and little lakes.

The house was now owned by the foreigner Lord Stuarti. The local people knew little else about him. The new lord had a large force of men-at-arms, but only their captain was ever seen entering the house. The servants were all women, imported from Rome. Tradesmen were stopped at the back door. No one from the surrounding area had ever been inside the villa.

There was a rumor that Lord Stuarti had a wife, but she was never seen, and it was known that he occasionally visited the widowed innkeeper, Giovanna Russo.

When the other women of the village attempted to elicit information from Giovanna, she would say nothing other than "He is a good man with much pain. Do not ask again for I will tell you nothing." This was strange, for Giovanna was a warm-hearted woman who was known to enjoy a good gossip. Eventually, however, the villagers accepted the mysterious Lord Stuarti and no longer paid any particular attention to the Villa Mia.

Francis Stewart-Hepburn had never intended to return to Naples. The Villa del Pesce d'Oro would have held too many frightening ghosts. So, the new villa had already been purchased, and was waiting when he and Cat returned. Bothwell thanked God he had a home to bring her to, and that it was isolated.

She had been near death for many weeks after the terrible ordeal, and he was convinced that only his own willpower, his desperate desire that she stay alive, had kept her alive.

Cat had drifted in and out of consciousness throughout the homeward journey running a low, steady fever. She would eat nothing, pushing food away angrily in her only show of emotion. It was all he could do to get liquids into her. He had kept her alive in spite of herself, getting her safely to Italy.

Strangely, it was Cat's plight which made Susan refrain from self-pity. Susan had suffered terribly, but hardly to the extent that her mistress had. The young woman blamed herself for Cat's plight.

" 'Tis my fault she is so hurt," she said, tears threatening. "But I will help to get her well, my lord! I swear I will," she vowed. Bothwell was grateful, and glad for her company.

When they reached the Villa Mia, young May was waiting. The two sisters embraced. May, grateful to both her older sister and her mistress for saving her in the attack on Villa del Pesce d'Oro, eagerly aided Susan in her efforts to bring Cat back to sanity.

The Countess of Bothwell had not spoken a word since the night of her rescue, and her beautiful eyes remained void of all expression. Sometimes the earl felt her staring at him, but when he turned, it was to be met with the all-too-familiar blank look. Still he loved her as never before and, desperate, tried to carry on as if all were normal.

He did not share her bed, sleeping instead in a room adjoining hers. At night the door between the rooms remained open so that he would hear her if she called. Though her face expressed nothing and she was mute, she seemed to understand all that was said to her. She communicated by looks and signs.

Other than her husband, Conall, and young Asher Kira, no men were ever allowed into her presence. The proximity of a strange male was apt to set her to weeping and moaning.

They had arrived in midsummer, and now as the Roman autumn progressed she began to venture out of the villa into the gardens for long walks. She was always accompanied by either Susan or May, and the gardeners were warned to remove themselves the moment she appeared. The mistress, they were told, had been very ill, and strangers upset her.

Now the gossip in the village began anew, and the talk was all about the Madonna Stuarti. Though the gardeners removed themselves from Cat's sight, no one had said they might not look upon her from the cover of the bushes. In the tavern of Giovanna Russo they raved about Cat's pale-gold hair (for her hair had never regained its tawny shade), they sang praises to her leaf-green eyes, they rhapsodized over her beautiful, unlined face and her young girl's figure.

Giovanna Russo filled their tankards with the region's best, slapped away roving hands, and listened. She had often wondered about her lover's wife, for he never spoke of her. Yet she was sure that the sadness afflicting him stemmed from a tragedy which had befallen his wife. He came to Giovanna for release only, but she was satisfied. He was the best lover she had ever had—strong, tender, and considerate.

One day, Giovanna managed to slip into the villa

gardens. She needed to see her rival. Having seen her, Giovanna Russo was deeply torn.

If the beautiful lady became well again, Giovanna would lose her lover. Yet she loved Bothwell in her own fashion, and she wanted him to be happy. A kind woman, she began lighting candles for Cat in the village church.

One beautiful afternoon, Bothwell waved both his wife's attendants away and, tucking Cat's thin hand through his arm, walked with her out into the sunlit gardens. "Susan tells me yer taking more nourishment," he said. "It shows. That and the air have made yer cheeks rosy again."

She said nothing, but there was the faintest shadow of a smile on her lips. They continued to walk in silence, and then, suddenly, he caught her by the shoulders and looked down into her face. "Cat! For God's sake, my darling! Speak to me!" He had recently seen the blank look receding from her eyes. "I love ye, hinny! More now than ever before. Dinna shut me out, Cat! Dinna go away from me again!"

"How can ye love me, Francis?" Her voice was low, so low that he was not sure she was speaking. But he had seen her lips move.

"Why shouldn't I love ye, sweetheart?"

Her voice dripped scorn. "God, Bothwell, hae ye no pride? I am dirtied! I am used filth, and I shall never be clean again!"

"You are unclean only if ye believe it, Cat. Men have used yer body cruelly, I'll nae deny it." His fingers dug into the soft flesh of her upper arms, and his eyes bore into hers. "But no man ever really possessed ye, my darling. Not ever! Yer soul was always yer own!"

"Be satisfied with yer plump innkeeper, Francis," she said wearily. "If any man touches me ever again, I shall die."

He was surprised by neither her attitude nor her knowledge of Giovanna. "Very well, my love, I shall not attempt to make love to ye. But there will come a night when ye will change yer mind. I will wait, Cat. But in the meantime, please dinna stop talking to me. If God wills that I have naught but the sound of yer voice for the rest of my days, I shall be satisfied."

For a moment her old smile flashed. "Hypocrite!" she said. But her eyes were twinkling.

From that afternoon on she began to improve. Without telling her, he had written to her son, the Earl of Glenkirk, requesting that their children be sent to them. The children would be arriving by Christmas. Bothwell pursued her, seeking her love and her trust once again. Each morning now he breakfasted with her in her bedroom after they had attended mass together in their chapel. Afterwards he left her, sometimes reappearing for lunch. He was always with her in the evenings.

He personally planned each evening, though she did not know this. With exquisite taste he chose the menu, the wines, the flowers that graced their table. He delighted in giving her little gifts, a small wood box inlaid with mother-of-pearl, a pale-green silk nightgown, a cage of brightly colored, singing finches. She accepted each offering quietly: the box with a smile, the nightgown with a blush, the birds with a little cry of pleasure.

Often now he caught her looking at him from beneath her thick lashes, and in the night—for he limited his visits to Giovanna and never went to her after dark—he heard her moving restlessly about her chamber. He did not approach her, for her wounds were still too grievously deep to allow her a physical life. He knew that a woman as deeply sensuous as Cat would eventually recover, and want love once more. He waited.

On December 21, the Feast of St. Thomas, a coach rumbled down the white graveled drive of the Villa Mia.

As it drew up to the front of the house, Bothwell hurried his wife outside to greet their guests.

"How could ye," she raged at him. "I dinna want to see anyone!" But he chuckled. "Wait, hinny! 'Tis a happy surprise."

Suddenly her heart began to beat wildly, with certainty. "Oh, Francis." She trembled. "Is it our bairns?"

His arm tightened about her shoulders. "Aye," he smiled. " 'Tis our bairns."

The coach stopped, and the footmen leaped to open its door. And then a boy appeared in the doorway of the coach, and it was Bothwell's turn to tremble. The child who stood there was his mirror image.

"Ian!" She pulled from her husband's protective grasp, and caught the boy in an embrace that he endured for only a moment. "Mother!" And he buried his small, suddenly vulnerable face in her soft neck. Then, demanding to be put down, he looked up at Bothwell. His sapphire-blue eyes were steady as he said, "My half-brother, the Earl of Glenkirk, has explained the situation, sir. He has given us the option to use either the Leslie name or yours. I think, father," and Bothwell trembled again, "I think we would prefer to acknowledge ye as our sire, since ye hae been so kind as to acknowledge us."

The Earl of Bothwell swallowed hard, and then grinned down at his small son. Unable to contain himself, he grabbed the boy up with a whoop and hugged him hard. The grin that came back at him nearly shattered his heart. And it was with great amusement that he heard the boy whisper conspiratorially, "Please, father, put me down or my sisters will feel slighted. They are used to being spoiled by the men."

Bothwell complied and turned back to his wife, who knelt and embraced the two little girls. The larger of the two was Cat all over again, with tawny hair and leaf-green eyes. But the tinier of the two was a mixture of both her parents, with her father's auburn hair and her mother's green eyes. At a whisper from their mother, they turned to greet him, and the little piping voices that called him "papa" swelled his heart to bursting.

In the next few days she came back to life, and he knew that it was the children who had driven away the remaining ghosts for her. Now the air rang with the sound of children's voices. To Bothwell's amazement, he reveled in parenthood.

This Christmas was their first all together. They attended a mass of thanksgiving in the villa's chapel, and then Cat and her daughters distributed alms and gifts to the poor of the village. The village women were awed by the slender beautiful woman with the pale-gold hair and green eyes who spoke their language so well. They were equally enchanted by Cat's daughters, who had decided they preferred the Italian versions of their names and were now called la donna Gianetta and la donna Francesca.

Their baskets empty, the earl's party stopped at the inn, where the ladies of the Villa Mia were offered seasonal refreshments. And while the children munched Christmas sweets and cuddled a litter of kittens they had found in the innyard, their mother coolly accepted a goblet of wine from the innkeeper, Giovanna Russo.

Innkeeper and Contessa studied one another for a moment. Then the innkeeper said in a voice audible only to Cat, "If I were lucky enough to be married to Francisco Stuarti, I should not continue to deny him my bed, signora la contessa."

"You know nothing about it, innkeeper," hissed Cat.

"I know that every time he lies with me he pretends 'tis you," came the retort.

Cat was stricken, suddenly close to tears. "I cannot,"

she whispered. "You do not know what has been done to me."

Intuitive comprehension rose in Giovanna. "*Dio mio*," she gasped. "So—being a rich noblewoman is no protection *either*!" And impulsively she caught Cat's hands and looked into her face. "It has happened to me also, signora. In the last damned war a troop of French soldiers . . ." She stopped and spat. "They used the inn as their headquarters. They were here almost a week, and in all that time I don't think I was allowed off my back more than a few hours daily, to cook for them, of course. They killed my husband because he objected. After they had gone I did not think I could ever stand to be touched by a man again."

"And yet you are my husband's mistress."

"The right man came along. He was *simpatico*, and I wanted him," smiled Giovanna. "Is not my lord Francisco *simpatico* to you? And in your heart . . . do you not want him?"

The beautiful tear-filled eyes gave Giovanna the answer she sought. "I will pray for you, my lady," she said quietly. And turning, Giovanna walked away from Cat, knowing that she had lost her kind Francisco forever.

Chapter 60

❧§ℰ❧

CAT had known she was not the first woman in the world to suffer at the hands of men. But there had been no room in her heart for anything besides her own hurt. Now she realized how many others had suffered. And she saw that she had been blaming Francis for many of her misfortunes.

Deep down, she felt that if he had not been involved with Angela di LiCosa, the kidnapping would not have happened. Yet it had, and no amount of wishing was going to change it. If she allowed it to kill their love, then Angela's evil spirit would triumph.

She struggled with herself for several days. For weeks she had been restless, waking nightly to walk ceaselessly about her room. She loved him, yet she did not know if she could bear to have his hands on her. She was frightened, too, that she had been drained of all sexual feeling.

She knew she must make the first move. Being sensitive to her feelings, Francis would not. Too, if she were in control of the situation she might draw back at any time without hurting him.

On the 31st day of December, Bothwell rode into Rome on business. He promised to return by nightfall so they might celebrate the New Year together. For several hours after he left she debated with herself, hesitated and then decided. She did not deny to herself that

she was afraid, but she could also not deny that she
wanted him again.

While the maids made up her large bed with fresh
lavender-scented linens, and the cook prepared a fat
capon for a midnight feast, Cat spent the afternoon with
her children. They remembered her well, and this confused her until she heard them relating among themselves incidents about her that they were in no position
to recall.

"How do ye know these things?" she asked them.

"Why, Bess told us, mother," they replied. Cat sent
her eldest daughter a mental prayer of thanks. Without
Bess, it seemed, her little ones would have forgotten her.

This last afternoon of the old year she oversaw their
baths, and when they sat about their supper table she
sat with them. The meal over, she surprised them with a
silver paper box of Pinoccati, a diamond-shaped red-
and-brown sugar candy. Their nursemaid, Lucy Kerr,
smiled as Cat told the children the wild wonderful
stories of their homeland.

Finally she heard their prayers and tucked them into
bed, kissing them tenderly, reveling in their happiness.
Bidding good night, she hurried to her own room, where
Susan and May were readying a bath for her.

"What will ye wear, my lady?" asked May.

"Put out the green nightgown that my lord gave me,"
she said.

Susan's eyebrow was raised just slightly as she reached
for the bath scents. "Wildflowers," she heard her mistress say. "The ones we brought from Scotland, in the
silver flacon." So, thought the tiring woman happily,
she is finally going to try her wings again. Susan smiled
to herself, and hoped that her lady's return to the world
of sensual delights would be as pleasant as her own had
been. Susan was in love for the first time in her life. The
cause of her happiness was one of the men-at-arms who

had accompanied them from Scotland. Robert Fitz-Gordon had taught Susan that love could be sweet. They were to be wed soon after the New Year.

Cat snuggled herself deep into the sweet water of the porcelain tub. Her pale hair had been carefully secured atop her head with tortoiseshell pins. The warmth of the water and of the nearby fire combined to make her drowsy and very relaxed. The two servants bustled about her, putting away her clothes.

She heard his footsteps in the doorway, and her eyes flew open. He stood for a brief moment gazing longingly at her, and then caught himself. "I beg your pardon, my darling. I dinna know ye were bathing."

"Francis!" Damn! She had not meant her voice to sound so desperate. He turned back to her. "I would have ye stay, and tell me of your day, my lord." Her heart contracted painfully at the hope she saw leap into his eyes. "Susan, May . . . ye may leave us. See that cook will have supper ready when we ring. Ye may have the rest of the evening to yerselves."

They curtsied and left quickly. "Come sit by me, Francis. How is Asher Kira?"

Seating himself, he spoke at some length of the business that had taken him to the city. He tried to keep his eyes on her face, but they kept straying to her soft breasts, but barely concealed by the water. He swallowed hard and forced his eyes upward again. She lowered her lashes, but he had caught a quick glimpse of the laughter in her eyes.

"Cat!" His voice was suddenly sharp, and she looked up at him. "I am no saint. I simply cannot continue to sit here and not touch you. Ye hae always had that effect on me—as ye know."

He rose, and she cried, "No, Francis! Dinna go from me." His eyes caught hers and held them in a puzzled gaze. Then he heard her say softly, "Do ye remember the first time I came to ye, Francis?"

"Aye," he answered, his eyes never leaving hers. "Ye rode two days to get to me, and ye were grievously hurt."

"I am once more grievously hurt, my lord," and her voice crackled, "but I would be yer wife again."

For a moment the room was silent, then he asked quietly, "Do you trust me, Cat?" She nodded. "Then stand up, my love."

She rose from her tub, the scented water cascading down her. He took the hard cake of soap from its little silver dish and, lathering his hands, began to soap her. She trembled under his touch, but stood quietly while his hands moved down her shoulders, back, and buttocks. Reaching for the sponge, he rinsed her off, the soapy water running down between her unsteady legs. "Turn around."

She faced him, her eyes lowered. His hands now soaped her breasts, and he smiled faintly as the rosy nipples hardened. He moved on to her belly, which quivered beneath his fingers and lower, the soap sliding across her skin as one finger touched the tiny mole. She cried out softly, shuddering, catching at his hands with her own hands. For a long moment she held him in restraint, and then her hands loosed his and fell quietly to her sides. Wordlessly he continued to wash her, moving on to the satiny skin of her inner thighs. Again the sopping sponge rinsed her free of the suds.

He lifted her out of the tub and set her gently on the rug before the fire. Several large Turkish towels hung warming on the oaken rack. Removing one, he dried her carefully. Tilting her small, heart-shaped face to his, he smiled down on her. "There, my darling, that was nae so terrible, was it?"

"No." Her voice was barely a whisper.

Tenderly he put his arms about her and stood silently for a few moments while her shining head rested against his broad chest. Then he loosed her, saying, "I stink of horses, my pet. 'Tis your turn to wash me." And before she could protest he had pulled off his clothes and was climbing into her tub. He tried to settle himself for a soak. Looking at the great masculine animal attempting to lounge against her white porcelain tub with its dainty gold border and floral decor, his knees sticking out above the water, Cat giggled.

"And what," he asked in an aggrieved voice, "is so funny, madame?"

The giggles became a silvery peal of laughter. She laughed until the tears came to her eyes. Unaware of the cause of her amusement, but very relieved to hear her laughter after these many months, Bothwell laughed too. Finally controlling herself, she managed to gasp, "Francis! Ye look so silly in my little tub amid the little, pale flowers."

For a moment he looked disgruntled, then he gave her a wry grin. "I probably do, sweetheart," he agreed. "I miss the great oak tub we had at Hermitage."

For a moment they were silent, remembering the blissful days they had spent at his great border house before the king had exiled him from Scotland. Then Bothwell rose from the tub and said quietly, "Wash me as ye used to, Cat."

Shyly, she took the soap, losing it momentarily in the water, retrieving it, and then touching his back with shaking hands. As her fingers moved lightly over his skin she felt the familiarity of him return, and as she grew bolder, her hands became surer. He felt the lukewarm water sluicing down his back, and he turned to face her. Faintly amused, he watched as she scrubbed his chest, his flat belly, and then bravely moved lower to soap his genitals.

As he responded to her touch she gasped softly, color flooded her cheeks, and her eyes flew upward. He stood perfectly still, barely breathing. Regaining her courage, she rinsed him off. Stepping from the tub, he took his towel, dried himself, and asked, "Are ye brave enough to proceed, Cat?"

She nodded. Going to their bed, she dropped her towel and slid between the sheets, holding them open for him. He slipped beneath the sweet silk and drew her into his arms. She was as stiff and as unyielding as an oak staff. He held her gently, and when several minutes had passed she began to relax.

"I am so afraid, Francis," she whispered.

"I know, my darling," he answered, "but ye must remember that I hae never hurt ye, and I will not now."

"But ye want me."

"Aye, sweetheart, I want ye."

"Yet ye will not force me. Why?"

"Because I do love ye, Cat. Because I know that ye hae been cruelly used. Ye hae every right to your fear, but I swear to ye, love, I will not hurt ye."

Suddenly he felt her body shaking, and tipping her face up he saw that it was wet with tears. "Cat!" The word was an anguished plea. Then she felt his mouth closing over hers, and before she could think she found her body melted against his.

As the warmth of his love penetrated her, she felt her fears sliding away. Memories fell away as his lips kissed her. There were only the two of them now. All else was unimportant. Tenderly he ran his tongue along her lips, and felt them open, her warm breath rushing into his mouth. Gently he explored her, as though for the very first time, feeling her quivering against him.

"Look at me, Cat! Open your eyes, my darling. I am Francis, no one else, and I love ye!"

Shyly her dark-gold lashes lifted off her cheeks, and

she looked at him. His eyes never left hers as his hands caressed her back, his long, slim fingers gently kneading away the tension. He drew her into the crook of his arm and cupped one breast in his hand. And all the while, he held her eyes with his own.

She shivered. She could feel her heart hammering wildly against her chest as if it wished to escape. A fire was pouring into her loins, and the wave of desire that slammed into her shook her terribly. That she could feel this way after all that had happened! With a fierce exultation she realized that she wanted him! She wanted him!

Gently he pushed her onto her back and, half straddling her, his lips ran riot across her body, closing over a pink nipple, moving lower, teasing her flesh with tiny kisses.

She arched to meet his mouth, catching at his head with trembling hands. He groaned, a sobbing sound, completely lost in the moment as she writhed under his hands and mouth. And then he heard, through his own pounding desire, the voice of his beloved pleading with him to take her, take her now.

Kneeling, he spread her thighs, and his voice was thick. "Look at me, Cat! I want you to look at me when I enter you! I want you to know 'tis me, not an awful nightmare memory!"

A tremor tore through her, but she raised her eyes to his and whispered again, "Take me, Bothwell! Take me now!" and without further hesitation he thrust himself into her while looking deep into her shining eyes.

She whirled through space, free and whole again, exulting in their love. And then suddenly she felt herself falling, falling through endless time. Through the dimness she heard him anxiously calling her name. Voicing a little protest, she opened her eyes to find him smiling happily down at her, her eyes warm and loving.

"Why, my darling," he said gently, "how far away ye were."

She flushed rosy, and he laughed softly. " 'Twould hae been a crime against nature if ye had continued being fearful of love, my darling." He touched her cheek with his finger. She caught his hand and held it against her face.

Then he heard her voice low and level. "I love ye, Francis, but if ye love me, I beg of ye, my lord, never leave me again, for each time ye leave me some catastrophe befalls me. If I am not being kidnapped, or chased by the Scots king, I am being bedded by Henri Quatre. Aye, Bothwell, ye may well look astonished. Yer charming royal friend ordered me to Fontainebleau, terrified me into believing that he was returning me to Jamie, and then seduced me."

Standing up, Cat walked across the room and picked up the gossamer silk nightgown Bothwell had given her. Sliding it over her head, she let it slither down her body. Its neckline plunged to her navel, the gown clinging to her like a second skin. She whirled about, and heard him swear, "Jesu!" as his blue eyes raked her from head to toe.

"Always," she went on, "just when I think I am safe, something happens. I must be safe from now on, Francis. I must.

"I am a very rich woman, Bothwell, and ye are a very proud man. We cannot live wi'out my money, but we *can* live wi'out yer excessive pride. It has cost us several years of togetherness, and it has almost cost us our lives and our bairns. I'll hae no more of it! If ye canna reconcile yerself to my fortune, then I might as well return to Scotland and beg Jamie's forgieness. As the king's mistress I will at least be safe—and hear me, Francis Stewart-Hepburn! I'll nae be chased, seduced, or raped ever again! I won't!"

Now it was his turn to rise from the bed. He walked across the room and, picking up a towel, wrapped it about his loins. The light from the fire dappled his broad back, and his face was grave. She could hear her heart thumping wildly, and she wondered what possessed her to issue such an ultimatum. What had she done? How would he respond?

He stood quietly on the window balcony of their bedroom. Coming up behind him, she slipped her arms about him, pressing her silken-clad body against him, her cheek against his hard shoulder. "Am I not worth it, Francis?" she whispered huskily. "Is it so hard for ye to accept that what was mine is now also yours? Would ye not be willing to share a fortune wi me? Are ye nae tired? I am, Francis. I am weary of being abused. I love ye, and would be wi ye."

She could feel his heart beating evenly beneath her hands, and he said softly, "We will nae be able to go home again, Cat."

"I know, Francis, and I shall miss Scotland, but for me home is where ye are. I have learned that in the years we have been separated."

"I suppose we could get used to the quiet life."

"Aye, Francis, we could."

He turned then so they faced each other. His hands rested lightly on her waist, hers on his shoulders. "Would ye really leave me, Cat?"

Tipping her head back, she looked lovingly up at him, her beautiful green eyes diamond-bright with tears. "Why, damn me, Bothwell! I could nae ever leave ye. I love ye! I hae always loved ye! And may God ha mercy on me, for I will always love ye!"

He sighed deeply with relief, and she laughed happily. "Why Francis, did ye doubt me?"

"My dear wife, from the moment we first met I could

nae be sure what ye'd do, or what would happen next. It has always been one of yer greatest charms."

Suddenly they heard bells all around them. From the village, from the villages in the valley below them, from the many churches in the city of Rome across the hills. The bells were tolling out 1599, the end of the sixteenth century. They joyfully rang in the new year, 1600, and a new century.

As Francis Stewart-Hepburn bent to kiss his wife, a jubilant thought ran through his mind. Together they had beaten them! He and his Cat had survived all the pain and the cruelty the world could inflict on them. Now, what could they not do in this wonderful new century?

"Happy New Year, my darling," he said, and then he found her mouth once more, sweeping her away into that special world that belonged to them alone, and where no man would ever again intrude.

Epilogue

❧ ❦

Spring 1601

IN the spring of the year 1601, James Leslie, the fifth Earl of Glenkirk, was informed by his sergeant-at-arms that a tall masked gentleman was asking to enter his private presence. The earl agreed to the audience, saying, "I hae no enemies." It was true. The current Glenkirk kept from court, supported the king only when support was necessary, and spent most of his time running his vast estates and several thriving businesses, and indulging his two small sons while waiting for his pregnant wife to produce the third.

Offering his mysterious guest a whisky, he said, "Will ye remove yer mask, sir?"

"Aye," came a familiar voice, and the fifth Earl of Glenkirk found himself looking at the fourth Earl of Glenkirk. "Well, Jemmie, ye might say yer glad to see me," said Patrick Leslie wryly.

"Father!" The young man's face was a study in shock. "My God, father! Ye were dead! They said yer ship never reached its destination."

"Explanations in a minute, Jemmie, but first tell me of yer mother, and of mine."

Oh, lord, thought Jemmie. Bad news in both quarters for him. He sighed and began. "Grandmother Meg died this past winter. 'Twas an easy death, for she was nae ill. She simply went to sleep one night, and did nae wake again."

"Damn!" said Patrick Leslie softly. "If I'd only come a little sooner." Then he demanded, "And yer mother? What of my wife?"

James Leslie hesitated again. Then, as there was

nothing for it but to tell the truth, he answered, "Mother is gone, father."

"Gone?" He stopped suddenly, then said, "Ah, yes, of course. The king would nae wait long before claiming her, would he? Is she at court? Is she happy?"

"She is in Italy, father. She is Lord Bothwell's wife. They share exile together."

"The treacherous bitch! How long did she wait before endangering the family and running off to her lover?"

"Dinna ever speak of her in that tone to me again," Patrick heard his son snarl, and looking closely at the young man he was surprised. "She was devastated when Uncle Adam brought word that yer ship was lost. She held herself completely responsible for yer 'death,' and would probably have remained here at Glenkirk mourning ye the rest of her life, but for the king. Yer right— the moment he heard ye were lost, he declared ye legally dead, and me the fifth earl. I was ordered to wed immediately in order to preserve the Glenkirk succession. Mother was told she had till spring to mourn. Then she was expected to return to court—and the king's bed.

"She would hae done it, too, but for me. The king did not know that I knew of what had gone on between him, ye, Lord Bothwell, and mother. Therefore, I could also not be expected to know of his threats against us. I supported him loudly and publicly, appearing to push mother at him. When he came to my wedding he spent his days hunting deer and his nights in mother's bed.

"I can assure ye I seemed most angry and highly offended when she fled her royal master. I even went so far as to write a letter to her, demanding that she return. I took the chance that James would nae revenge himself on me, as I was supposed to be ignorant of the whole drama. And I won, father! *I won!*"

"Jesu, Jemmie!" There was admiration in Patrick Leslie's voice. "Yer a cool one!"

"I planned every detail of mother's escape myself," said Jemmie proudly. "Susan and her younger sister went with her. So did Conall, and about fifty young Glenkirk men who were looking for adventure."

"Is she happy, Jemmie?"

James Leslie's eyes softened for a moment. Looking at his father, he thought: You fool—to have lost her! "Aye," he answered simply. "She is very happy."

Patrick Leslie sighed. "I should hae let her go wi Francis when he was exiled, but the king was determined that if he could nae have her, then neither could his great rival, Bothwell. It almost broke her heart, and I know but for the bairn she carried she would hae died." For a moment he was quiet, lost in his memories, and then he asked, "My bairns?"

James smiled. "Mother made provisions for us all before she left. I wed Bella Gordon, as ye had both arranged. Bess was wed to Bella's brother, Henry. I hae two lads, and Bess a lad and a lass. My uncle of Grey-haven's son died, and mother arranged wi her brother that Colin wed wi his eldest girl, and become the next Master of Greyhaven. Robbie will be wed wi the youngest Greyhaven girl at the same time. Mother settled an income and a manor on him so he would be independent. Amanda's to be the next Countess of Sithean. She'll be married in December. And wee Morag goes to Huntley's youngest son, Malcolm, wi a fine big dowry including her own house."

Patrick nodded. "She did well by the older bairns, Jemmie. What of the little ones?"

"When it was safe, and James Stewart had decided to forget, I sent them to their parents."

For a moment Patrick Leslie was silent. Then he said, "Are ye telling me that Ian and Jane were nae my bairns? That Bothwell fathered them as well?"

"Aye. So mother told me. I'd hae kept them and

raised them as Leslies even so, but once she and Lord
Bothwell were settled they wanted their children."
Jemmie gazed into Patrick's saddened face. "Ye lost her
long ago, father. I canna find it in my heart to condemn
her. 'Twas ye who threw away her love. Ye canna
complain now, father."

The fourth earl was silent for a moment. "Ye know
it all, don't ye? The whole story."

"Aye, though when she told me she spent half her
time defending ye, and yer actions." The two men sat
quietly for a few minutes. Then James Leslie spoke
again. "Ye've been gone five years, father. Did ye really
expect to return and find nothing changed? Where were
ye that ye could not come back to us sooner, and how
did ye finally get here?"

Patrick Leslie held out his glass. "More whisky, lad.
'Tis the one thing we dinna have in the New World that
I miss." And when his son had refilled the glass, Patrick
sipped it appreciatively, then spoke.

"The *Gallant James* put out from Leith on March
twenty-seventh, 1596. We cruised quickly down the
North Sea, through the English Channel, and out into
the Atlantic. For the next few weeks we sailed west-
northwest under clear skies, fresh winds, and in smooth
seas. Then suddenly, from nowhere, a storm struck us.
I hae seen some wicked storms in my lifetime, Jemmie,
but nothing like that! Somehow—though only God
knows how—we kept the vessel righted. At one point
a wave the color of green ice and the size of a small
mountain bore down on us out of the raging sea. I
managed to grab hold of a rope that was wound about
one of the masts, but half the crew on deck were washed
overboard with that killer wave.

"When the storm finally abated we had been blown
far off our course, though until several days later I
didna know how far. The ship, or what was left of her,

was badly crippled. We might have died out there had we not been taken in tow by a Spanish vessel.

"At first they thought we were English, and were all for destroying the heretics. Fortunately my Spanish is pure Castilian. Let that be a lesson to ye, Jemmie. If ye keep yer languages up ye'll ne'er be at a loss in a tight spot!

"I explained to the captain of our rescue ship that we were not English, but Scots, and we were nae Protestants, but Catholics. I believe I even mentioned Uncle Charles, the abbot, and my Uncle Francis, who is now the pope's secretary. Captain Velasquez was quite impressed and, seeing the medals about our necks, believed us."

"But where were ye, father?"

"The storm had blown us south, Jemmie, to a tip of the continent, a place the Spanish call Florida. We were taken to a small town called St. Augustine, and for many months we were kept there.

"I have since learned that they quickly ascertained my true identity by sending to their ambassador in Edinburgh. Cousin Jamie, however, sent return word to the Spanish governor in St. Augustine that, though I should not be harmed, I was to be detained for as long as possible. I think he hoped to bind Cat to him so completely that when I did return we would both be forced to accept the king's will." Patrick Leslie sighed. "The little bastard!" Then he continued.

"Though we were prisoners we were royally treated. I had a small house of my own, and the few crew that survived wi me were all decently cared for. Eventually, as they saw my restlessness, I was allowed to ride out wi my captors.

"Lord, Jemmie! What a country that New World is! The land goes on forever, and the variety of it is incredible. Mountains! Deserts and great forests filled with trees. It's a rich land, my son."

"Is that why ye didna come back sooner, father?"

"What?"

"Five years, father. Ye've been gone five years!"

Patrick Leslie looked slightly bemused. "The time went so quickly," he said softly. "Ah. Jemmie! What a wonderful country it is! Ye should see it!"

"Perhaps I shall," said the younger earl, "and yet ye came home, father. Ye came home to Glenkirk. What are we to do now?"

"I dinna intend remaining here, my son. I hae tasted real freedom in that vast and rich New World. I dinna plan to remain in this poor, old one. There a man can carve an empire for himself, and must toady to nae king. In the fresh new world there are no kings!

"I came back to see my mother, and to see Cat. Now I find that Meg is dead and yer mother is long gone."

"Considering the circumstances between ye when ye left," said James Leslie, "did ye really expect mother to be waiting? If only ye had seen the king wi her. He could scarce wait to show his royal ownership of her. Did ye think I could stand by and let her be held up to shame like that? There are some who think it an honor to be a king's mistress, but we Leslies do not! I could nae protect her, and I knew that she had nae ever stopped loving Francis Hepburn. She deserved any happiness she could get wi him.

"How can I write her now, and say that ye are alive, and that the marriage she contracted in good faith three years ago is a bigamous one? That once again she must be torn from Bothwell? I canna do that to her! I canna!"

"Then don't, Jemmie. The king declared me dead four years ago. Therefore yer mother's marriage to me was legally dissolved. I came back because I love ye all. And I owed it to Cat to come back. If her feelings about me had changed, she might have wanted to return wi me to the New World. I had that in mind when I returned.

"Now, however, my conscious is clear. She is safe and happy. Glenkirk is certainly in good hands wi ye for its lord, and already there are heirs in the nursery. I would see my family, though, Jemmie. Just the bairns, and Adam and Fiona. I cannot cut myself off entirely from Glenkirk. Dinna fear, though, for no Leslie will gie me away.

"Besides, if yer to do business wi me, 'tis better that there's no secrecy. When I return there is a great deal to do setting up a link between us."

"What do ye go back to, father?"

Patrick Leslie smiled. "I stopped at Benjamin Kira's house in Edinburgh before coming to Glenkirk. I brought wi me furs, silver, gold, and jewels of various kinds. I can continue to supply ye wi these items, and Benjamin assures me that he can find the market for them. I am a wealthy man again, but this time in my own right. I'll need naught from Glenkirk, Jemmie."

The younger earl was slightly, though guiltily, relieved. Knowing his thoughts, Patrick Leslie laughed. Then James asked, "But will ye nae be lonely, father?"

"I will miss ye, and my bairns, and certainly my grandsons, who I'm soon to meet. However," and he grinned the rakish grin that Jemmie remembered so well, "there waits anxiously for me in St. Augustine a Señorita Consuela Maria Luisa O'Brien. She is eighteen"—and here James Leslie swallowed hard, for his father's lady was but a year younger than his sister, Bess—"with pale golden skin, blue-black hair, a good Irish temper inherited from her father, and eyes the color of a southern sea. They are so limpid, and inviting, Jemmie, that a man could drown in them!

"As your mother has remarried, I see no reason why

I should not do so also. Luisa's mother was the daughter of a Spanish grandee, and her Irish father is my business partner. He will be damned glad to hae me for a son-in-law. Luisa knows of my marriage to Cat, and promised she would wait for my return." Patrick chuckled. "The little wildcat said she would rather be my mistress than another man's wife. Her father would hae beat her black and blue had I not declared myself then and there."

The young earl laughed and looked at his father admiringly. "Mother always said ye were never at a loss for the lasses," he said.

For a brief moment Patrick Leslie's face was shadowed in sadness. He said seriously, "Only wi her was I ever at a loss, Jemmie. We had good times, Cat and I, and we had six fine bairns. But I must say honestly that she was hesitant from the very first about being my wife. I sometimes think that, left to herself, she might never hae wed wi me.

"Ah, well, 'tis a new century we live in, Jemmie, and though he'll never know it, James did us a great favor in separating us." He raised his half-filled glass. "I gie ye Catriona, the Countess of Bothwell! God keep her safe and happy, for she deserves it!"

Slowly James Leslie raised his own glass and, looking with love and pride at his father, exclaimed, "The beautiful Countess of Bothwell! God bless her!"

The WONDER of WOODIWISS

continues with the publication of
her newest novel in paperback—

FOREVER IN YOUR EMBRACE

☐ #77246-9
$6.50 U.S. ($7.50 Canada)

THE FLAME AND THE FLOWER

☐ #00525-5
$6.50 U.S. ($8.50 Canada)

ASHES IN THE WIND

☐ #76984-0
$6.50 U.S. ($8.50 Canada)

THE WOLF AND THE DOVE

☐ #00778-9
$6.99 U.S. ($8.99 Canada)

A ROSE IN WINTER

☐ #84400-1
$6.50 U.S. ($8.50 Canada)

SHANNA

☐ #38588-0
$6.99 U.S. ($8.99 Canada)

COME LOVE A STRANGER

☐ #89936-1
$6.99 U.S. ($8.99 Canada)

SO WORTHY MY LOVE

☐ #76148-3
$6.50 U.S. ($8.50 Canada)